THE HORIZON LIES BELOW

Additional copies may be ordered from the publisher for educational, business, promotional or premium use.
For information, contact ALIVE Book Publishing at:
alivebookpublishing.com

Cover art by Dimitri Morake
Book design by Alex P. Johnson

ISBN 13
978-1-63132-262-4
Library of Congress Control Number: 2025915472

Library of Congress Cataloging-in-Publication Data
is available upon request.

First Edition

Published in the United States of America by ALIVE Book Publishing
an imprint of Advanced Publishing LLC
3200 A Danville Blvd., Suite 204, Alamo, California 94507
alivebookpublishing.com

PRINTED IN THE UNITED STATES OF AMERICA

10 9 8 7 6 5 4 3 2 1

THE HORIZON LIES BELOW

BRIAN REISS

Alive Book Publishing

To Dimitri Morake,
my closest friend and most trusted confidant.
You were seated beside me
when this story appeared in my mind
and you've been an ear for me
every step of the way.

CONTENTS

Chap

Ch   t
  a   e r
            1 .
        p   . .
          t   .

C   .   1
          e
  h   .   .
                                        e

  a   ag
                r   p

                        .
                            .   7
    p   ..
                              .
    t   .
            2

                        .   e
    e
                    .
                            g   6

                .   a

                        p
                    .
        r   . .   4
                    .

                            4
            3

                    .   e

ACKNOWLEDGEMENTS

This book became a much bigger project than I originally thought it would be. In the early stages I'd even suspected it might only become a short story. The current result required a great deal more time and effort than I'd ever anticipated. Of course, not all the effort belongs to me, and those that contributed should be made known.

Deepest thanks to Alive Book Publishing for being so patient with me while I wrote, edited, rewrote, rewrote again, and generally floundered through the creation of this.

To all my friends and family that listened through my word-vomit style of describing ideas over the years I grew this project, I appreciate your patience. Thank you in particular to my mom and dad who were the first to believe in and support me in my writing endeavors.

Thank you to my copy editor and one of my oldest friends, Josie Koznarek, for going above and beyond in every conceivable way. My mistakes would be horrendously distracting without you. Owl look forward to working with you in the future!

Thank you to my Aunt B. and Uncle Al who opened their home to me many times to stay and to work. It was in your neighborhood that most of this book was written.

Finally, thank you to Dimitri Morake, my closest friend, confidant, and collaborator. You were my first reader, editor, brainstorming buddy, and audience. You've contributed more than your art to this story and there is no one I trust so much with my works as you.

*"Exposing a young child
to the realities of love and death
is far less dangerous
than exposing them to the lie
of the happy ending."*

—Caitlin Doughty

CHAPTER 1

igh on cliffs above a canopy's mist, a girl, almost a young woman, scaled the rocky slopes, a cut on her hand seeping blood into dusty handholds as she climbed. The air was crisp, the sun high, and the dreams of night hours behind her. The girl's name was Eowen, and though she was thirteen years old, she was shorter and skinnier than most girls her age and so gave the impression of one younger. She was not a terribly good climber and, wearing her yellow wrap and sandals, was not well equipped for it, either. Even the small pack she wore had become a great burden. She persisted though, and as midday wheeled towards a vibrant sunset, Eowen mounted the final landing of her climb. Huffing, she rested on the thick, smooth stone for only a moment before taking the final few steps up to the peak. The climb had taken all her strength, but now Eowen stood high above the lands that bordered the Vast Jungle ahead and the great savannah behind.

Eowen allowed herself this victory and this rest, exalting in the feeling of her sweat getting wicked away by cool winds. She turned to look over the cliff at where she'd started her journey, a village nested around one of the massive, bleached-white trees her people dubbed bone trees. The trees were not only named for their appearance, but also for the sacred herons that built their nests atop them from the bones of other creatures. The giant, leafless baobabs grew across the lower savannah and jungle, their pale trunks and barren branches twisting toward the sky. Eowen's people always built their villages beneath them, offering the bones of their dead to the sacred birds as a communal burial rite. Turning towards the Vast Jungle again, she could see for many miles where the other villages of her people were, centered around each distant, ghostly bastion. With a finger extended, she traced her path forward, choosing ways through the jungle that plainly avoided where they towered over the canopy.

Further north, where her finger-tracing ended, Eowen's gaze fell upon the hazy shapes of massive mountains that dwarfed the one she stood upon. Her accomplishment, the day's climb, seemed to shrivel up when faced with such a daunting barrier. Eowen grimaced, chewed her tongue, and curled her hands into fists, which stung as her fingers dug into her cut. She wiped at the dust to get a better look.

It's more of a deep scratch than anything, she thought. Sitting down, she pulled out a waterskin, washed it out, then dug a little wooden box from her pack, undoing its tooth and twine clasp to access the ointment inside. Before more blood could ooze, she applied the ointment to her cut and wrapped it with a strip of white cloth. Eowen was accustomed to treating such wounds; her skin, from arms to ribs, from back to legs, were covered in scars and scabbed-over scrapes. She didn't avoid looking at them. Most were the results of a lifetime of clumsiness, accidental self-inflictions that she felt she deserved. The rest were not accidents, nor self-inflicted, but she knew she deserved them even more.

Eowen tied the cloth off with her teeth and sighed, a weariness settling in. She held up a bandaged hand toward her home village, which was situated under a savannah bone tree even further from the jungle one she'd started from. The first leg of her journey, a morning hike through familiar territory, had felt much longer and more accomplished at the time.

Being able to look down on her path made the distance Eowen traveled seem disappointingly small, yet mysteriously vast. She didn't want a difficult journey. In fact, each step she had to take felt impossibly daunting when realistically considered. Eowen did, however, wish for trials and tribulations to face where overcoming them was a foregone conclusion. She didn't want to face the mundane difficulties that were inevitable; she wanted to be like the heroes in stories, where grave dangers were merely the prelude to fantastic deeds.

In her daydreams, Eowen had already ranged through the landscape before her, scaled the Elder Mountains, parlayed with the furtive mountain folk, and reached new peoples and places on the other side. The setting sun warped the growing shadows below her into impossible creatures, hidden temples, and terrain far less amiable than her own two feet had ever touched, her mind pushing her spirit through experiences both familiar and strange.

She snapped back to herself again as the sun dove for shelter over the western canopies. These were only dreams—reality was ahead of her.

Turning to the right, the plane of her rocky mountain cliff angled gently into the Vast Jungle's canopy, which swayed like an ocean in the winds that rolled off the distant Elder Mountains. The ancient peaks, like the very teeth of the world, were partially obscured behind dense, motionless clouds, where sleepy thunder drummed in those billowing heights. There were always clouds around the peaks of the Elder Mountains, and Eowen could believe that those storms had been perched there since the dawn of time. The last rays of the setting sun threaded through the Vast Jungle, staining the sky above pink and orange and red. Even the Elder mountains were painted with the colors of the dying day. Such a sight was only possible from Eowen's current vantage. Nowhere else in her people's lands was high enough.

Facing such a view, Eowen felt like destiny had been literally laid out before her in a bewitching tapestry. She found herself craving more adventure, no matter how deadly it may be. She took a swig from her waterskin, stamped her foot in joy, raised a fist, and screeched with an adolescent crack to her voice, which she gleefully leaned into.

"I have crested Mount Joramu!" she shouted, stamping again for emphasis. "The Vast Jungle is next!"

As if in answer, a chill wind cut into the girl, sending shivers up her spine and goosebumps across her limbs. She swiftly squatted and wrapped her scarf around her shoulders.

"The E-elder M-mountains are after that," she stammered, shaking off some of the gooseflesh. Eowen jammed her bandaged hand into her pack, rifling through it before pulling out some flat, hard bread.

"After that," she shivered, "find the pass... called... What did he call the pass?" she muttered, growing nervous in the face of her shortcomings.

"Well, I'll find the pass. It's just north of here, through the mountains," she assured herself, though in her life thus far, north had meant little more than towards the Elder Mountains.

Her bread rested in her lap as she gazed at the massive stretch of jungle before her. Eowen peeked into her pack and did a quick calculation of how many days her food would last. *Maybe a week if supplemented with foraging,* she assessed in her mind. She did the same for her medical equipment, now taking into consideration how injury-prone she was. The merchant she'd questioned a few weeks ago had made the route seem so simple—just cross the Elder Mountains, go through the pass she couldn't remember the name of, and she'd arrive on the other side. Then it was just the simple matter of finding her long-lost cousin and bringing him back home.

"Simple," Eowen said, shivering again. She could still go back, ditch her pack, and pretend she'd gotten lost on her way home; it wouldn't be the first time. She certainly couldn't blame her departure on the news brought by that traveling merchant. After Tavo had disappeared, no one in her tribe believed he was still alive. He had to be, though. The description the merchant had given her matched him perfectly. A young man of the correct age from the jungle and savannah tribes who was a brilliant warrior, scholar, and linguist. Hair straighter than most of her people's, eyebrows thin, skin the same dark brown as hers. It had to be him, her people never left their lands.

Except for Tavo, she thought, a quality of stagnant reverence and stale loss to her internal voice. *And when I bring him home, everything will go back to how it was before he left.* Eowen was certain of this. Her life was all wrong, had been all wrong for the last three years.

The sun touched down fully behind the western canopy, and again a bitter wind from snow-covered caps cut across the Vast Jungle into her bones. Eowen was suddenly very aware of her clothing: sandals, a sort of robe made up of a thin top-wrapping, a side-slit skirt, and her insubstantial scarf. She looked down along her cliff and spotted a small cave below. More of a slight overhang than a cave, but it was conveniently angled against the wind. She scaled down to take shelter in it for the night, protected from the winds, though not the chill in her mind. If she was found wandering far from home, she'd be dragged back and beaten.

I can always give up tomorrow, she thought as she laid out her supplies for the night. There was no real rush to face her new failures when the old ones were still fresh. *After failing another apprenticeship, I'll be punished either way.*

The girl bundled into her sleeping blanket, cradling her bandaged hand. After the day's climb she had no trouble drifting off, though in fact she'd never had any trouble falling asleep. For her, there was no escape from the waking world so perfect as unconscious oblivion. Eowen, whose mind dreamt even while awake, belonged in her dreams more than anywhere. How strange it was then that, despite how vivid the dreams of her waking hours were, she could never seem to recall the ones she had while asleep. While no details remained, Eowen always awoke with impressions of vastness, and of sweet sorrows, and of purpose. Perhaps losing her dreams upon waking was for the best; although she enjoyed the feeling they left her with, it always seemed as if her dreams were too big for her.

****

[Listen, for you cannot hear me yet.]

****

Chapter 2

The next day Eowen was up and on her way before dawn, her fears from the previous night discarded with her dreams. She set off down the mountain slope, and within minutes found edible fruit and a clean stream to fill her water-skin, all without incurring any new injuries.

She watched for the gargantuan bone-trees, retracing her route in her head. Eowen knew to avoid getting too close to them and the many scattered villages of her tribe that gathered at their bases. Deception was another skill she lacked, and she couldn't come up with any believable excuse that would explain why she was so far from home. Eowen had been sent to nearly every one of her tribe's villages, only to be sent home as a failure. Because of this, attempting to pass through them would absolutely get her recognized. Her path would have to wind wildly through untamed stretches of the Vast Jungle to avoid being spotted. It would make what could have been a two to three day stroll into a trek through the brush of a week or more, but it was effectively her only option. Eowen hoisted her pack and set off into the unknown, hoping for smooth travels in her head but craving fantastical dangers in her heart.

Her expectations fell short and maintained that position throughout the day. Despite being in an undomesticated part of the jungle, everything Eowen came across was still aggravatingly familiar. She glared at the plants she foraged for her meals while glancing hopefully at the poisonous, thorny, and stinky flora she knew well enough to avoid. All such obstacles were avoided effortlessly, the result of traveling alone to one village after another since childhood. Later, as she scavenged some bits from the forest floor, she spotted the snakelike form of a cotel gliding above her in the canopy, their colorful feathers standing out amidst the green. Long before one of them could swoop down on her with the kind of venom that could kill ten men, she scared it off with a rattle made of empty nut-shells tied to a stick. It was extremely effective, and terribly boring. Meanwhile, highly poisonous newts skittered across the roots in front of her. Eowen was barely cognizant of her actions as she skewered one of the newts with a stick she plucked in passing. Moments later she used its bright body to ward away a great, scaled monitor-bear with seven limbs, likely having lost one in a fight for territory. No creature native to the Vast Jungle would risk a meal with the threat of the poison newt. It was a trick her cousin Tavo had taught her, and with a small encyclopedia of other survival tactics he'd passed on, she moved forward with little difficulty. She sighed, impatient to be in alien lands with threats that she couldn't even imagine, let alone prepare for.

Eowen made more progress than anticipated, passing the third great bone-tree just after dark and finding a mossy hollow to share with a few critters for the night. There were seven bone-trees with villages between her and the mountains; Eowen had originally predicted she would pass one per day.

"After how easy today was, it will probably take closer to three, maybe four days to reach the mountains," she said to herself.

The greatest risk would be near the fifth bone tree. To the

east of it lay one of her tribe's larger and far more social settlements, which regularly sent envoys to bring back news from other villages, their sister tribes to the far west, and occasionally the Elder Mountains when travelers were scarce.

Eowen could not remember hearing of anyone making it through the deadly mountain range without the guidance of the ranger, her people's most valued tracker, hunter, and religious leader. Tavo had been apprenticed to become the next one, which was the primary reason she suspected he might still be alive. This observation, that only the best of the best could get through the mountains, should have given her pause, but confidence from her progress thus far numbed any whisper of warning. Listening to the sounds of the night creatures, Eowen soon fell asleep in the soft moss of her hollow.

****

[Listen, for you cannot hear me yet.]

****

The sun skated around the Elder Mountains as the air chilled Eowen's shoulders. It was the end of her fourth day; she'd already passed the seventh bone tree, and her travels had gone without incident. No one from the villages had spotted her, and none of the jungle's dangers had posed a real threat.

Eowen spent the final hours of that day gathering as many resources as she could; thick leaves that she thought could protect her against the cold of the mountains, as much food as she could carry, water, and medicinal plants. Above her she could see snow in the distance, blinding white as it reflected the sun, that would eventually melt into frigid streams and chill rain by the time it reached the jungle. She'd heard that snow was frozen water but had never seen it up close, let alone touched it.

It must be like clouds but heavy, so that it sits on things instead of floating through the sky. Eowen grinned at the thought, fidgeting with anticipation that she'd soon find out. She sat in the cozy nest of leaves she'd made in a shallow cave on the side of a hill, sipped her water, and ate some berries. She'd turn the flesh of a heavier, more starchy fruit she'd collected into a dough and bake it on a stone over a fire later. For now, she enjoyed the light, sweet fare. From her vantage, Eowen could appreciate her last view of the Vast Jungle and the sunset behind it, the now-distant top of Joramu Mountain a blotch of pink color and black contrast above the intense green of the lower canopy. She stretched and yawned, comfortably tired after her days of hiking. Eowen leaned back and began drifting off to sleep. She felt she deserved a nap and maybe even a full day's rest before braving the mountains.

Her respite was interrupted by something strange in the distance, a slight vibration below, a shudder in the air. Eowen sat up, looking and feeling around for the source of the disturbance. It didn't feel like a large creature approaching, nor a storm. The disturbance intensified. There was no doubt now that the earth was moving and the air shifting on strange winds. The ground rumbled, but it was unlike any earthquake or gathering storm she'd felt before.

Eowen scanned the Vast Jungle from the closest trees to

where it met the horizon. She could not tell what, but something was different. She rubbed her eyes, and when she opened them she bolted upright, looking harder. Something was very wrong. She felt it in her bones. She looked further left and right, trying to catch what bothered her, but the movement of it was fast and twitchy, hidden among the swaying canopy. For a very rare moment, the wind across the Vast Jungle died down completely, and the leaves stilled. In the wind's absence, other things were still moving amidst the swaying canopy. A chill went up Eowen's spine. Her eyes watered. She blinked, and then she saw.

The things amidst the canopy were twitching and jerking ever so slightly. Barely discernible in the fading light, they seemed like huge, starry tree trunks with gnarled, witch-hand branches that were reaching and contracting as though to grasp at something. The wind picked up again as Eowen backed up into her shelter and pulled her blanket tighter around herself. The things' twitching grew more erratic as they began to twist and rise up from the ground.

Eowen bit her blanket in pure terror as the things emerged fully from the jungle trees and shook aside the canopy, sending soil and flora flying, lunging upward as though seeking something to grasp. In seconds they had become huge pillars in the sky, their horrible spider-like digits scrabbling for purchase. The sky suddenly became very dark, though it should have been another half-hour from full night. All above Eowen was rendered nearly ink-black and devoid of stars, the things distantly sparkling against it. Eowen couldn't move as the things continued to rise, dirt cascading from their bases, until they halted abruptly. There were several pillars only a few kilometers from her position, but in the distance she could see dense vertical lines cleaving the sky above the other side of Joramu Mountain as well. Eowen's hands flew to her mouth and she stifled a panicked sob; whatever was happening in front of her was happening much further away as well, possibly everywhere.

Eowen shook helplessly, her still-injured hand reaching toward her family. She looked up to find that the sky had adopted a strange texture, like cloth or skin. The things, which now towered immeasurably high, reached with their twisted fingers, gaining fistfuls of celestial fabric. Then, as soon as the first one had a good grip, they raced back toward the earth, bringing the sky with them. The muted heavens were wrested from their firmament and pulled downward by the great pillars, like a tent being collapsed from the inside. The sky fell, and Eowen watched it swallow the world.

First the Elder Mountain peaks above her were enveloped, their snow-caps swallowed into the wave of it, then the middle of the mountains, then their bases. Below it all, Eowen was frozen and mute as the inexorable heavens rapidly descended. The girl, cowering in her cave, couldn't even utter a cry as the falling sky swept away the hills, the canopy, the villages, and finally her as well.

****

[Listen, for you cannot hear me yet]

LOVE WAS BORN WHEN THE WORLD COULD NO LONGER BEAR TO BE WITHOUT THEM.

****

Eowen was alone, everything was dark, and she wasn't breathing. She blacked out.

****

[Listen, for you cannot hear me yet]

THEY WERE BORN ON A MOUNTAIN NORTH OF HERE, WEST OF THERE, TEN PACES FORWARD, THREE LOOKS BACK.

****

Eowen re-emerged from unconsciousness but could not find air, and the darkness grew. She writhed in desperation, found nothing to breathe, and slipped away again.

****

[Listen, for you cannot hear me yet]

THE MOUNTAIN, CALLED AH'OM, WAS NAMED FOR THE SOUND OF BREATHING, THE SOUND THAT BREATH MADE AFTER IT CAME IN THEN WAS LET OUT. BECAUSE WHEN SHE WAS BORN THE MOUNTAIN'S PARENTS FELT, FOR THE FIRST TIME, LIKE THEY COULD BREATHE A FULL BREATH.

****

Eowen never remembered her dreams; the vastness left vibrant but vague smears on her psyche that grew dark and incomprehensible as she moved toward waking. So as Eowen drifted back towards the shores of consciousness, it at first seemed that, as usual, her dreams had left her waking self with nothing. Yet this time was different, and from Eowen's oceanic subconsciousness, something had followed her back, something simple and necessary: air.

Eowen's eyes snapped open to the blinding darkness around her. She could breathe again, she wasn't dying. As she awoke fully, the air faded, and she dropped back into unconsciousness. It was only for a moment this time, as the very need for air, and the certainty that she should be breathing it, caused a rush of oxygen to bloom around her.

Eowen woke again, sucking at it desperately. Her eyes rolled behind their lids and her head hurt, but her lungs were working, she had air, and she would not die.

As her breathing stabilized, Eowen curled from prone to fetal and noticed she was naked. She wrapped her arms around herself, expecting to be cold, and then suddenly she was. Her mind struggled as she emerged from the fog of fear and unconsciousness.

What happened? Where's the jungle and... did this happen to anyone else? She glanced at the black void around her, but it offered no answers.

As her thoughts drifted away from her people to ponder the dark place she was now in, the smell of more familiar places bloomed around her. The perfumes of a thousand fruits and flowers mixed with a cornucopia of animal stink, all of it heavy, humid, and earthy in the air. As these sensations intruded, her attention turned back to the jungle and her people.

Out the corner of her eye, sprouts of flora, fresh earth and humming insects that had somehow emerged snapped out of existence. The moment she had given the new smells any attention, it all stopped, leaving only the echoes of sensation and a patch of dirt beneath her. In their place, the scent of her neighbor's cooking and the sounds of her mother threshing something filtered in, but just as with the jungle-like sensations, these disappeared upon examination as well.

"Hello, is anyone there?" Eowen felt herself call out, but her voice seemed to stop at her lips, eaten up by the nothing around her.

She sat up, too confused and afraid to think clearly, but one certainty did emerge: Eowen hated being naked, possibly more than almost dying. Her skin crawled, and she was prepared to ignore every other problem till she'd solved that one. The discomfort raced from her mind into her skin, which was all goosebumps now, and from there to her deep psyche.

She examined her surroundings and saw that, aside from the small mound of earth she was now curled up on, everything around her was black. Each direction was completely empty save for down, which, when she peeked over the edge of her dirt island, revealed itself to be a distant, faint starfield. Stricken by vertigo, Eowen scrambled back to the center of her mound and hugged herself, desperate for comfort and clothing.

As her desire to wear something, anything, grew in the back of her psyche, the light of the distant starfield below her began to glow a little brighter. She leaned forward as the darkness around her seemed to press in on her hands. In a way, the darkness clinging to her hands felt like it could be cloth, like it should be but wasn't yet.

Eowen chose not to question what was happening, and

instead completely followed her instincts. The girl dipped her enshadowed hands toward the welcoming light of the stars, which glowed brighter as she approached. Something happened when the light touched the darkness, something in the recesses of her mind and in reality before her. The implication of clothing became more than that; it became something she could believe in, something she could know was real. In a moment that felt removed from time, the darkness and light in Eowen's hands sifted through each other to deposit something where before there was nothing. It felt like cloth, the objects smelled like her home village in the savannah, and they looked like her yellow skirt, top wrapping, and scarf.

Eowen hugged them close, breathed them in with tears in her eyes, then tripped over her gangly limbs in a mad rush to wear them. She was smiling in triumph, her eyes wide and wild, and was on the verge of laughing when the air became short again. Her lungs grasped at nothing, her mind flashed with panic, and the ground below brightened. Darkness rushed in to crash with the light, and suddenly there was a misting of perfectly clean air all around her. Eowen nodded at no one and nothing in particular, maybe at the air itself, and took a seat.

"That's better... I think," she muttered, now able to hear herself.

Eowen took a slow turn, trying to get her bearings, and was still rewarded with absolutely nothing. All around her the darkness persisted, and below her was her dirt mound and the distant starfield. From what she could tell, the world no longer appeared to be present at all. She scraped idly at the earth she was sitting on and found it only went down a few centimeters before it exposed the starfield below.

Eowen's heart hammered. She reached out to prod the starfield, and her hand met a surface of sorts. It didn't feel hot, nor was it cold, nor soft, nor hard. The surface didn't feel like anything to her at all. But it was solid enough that her hand could go flat against it, and when she stood up and stepped off her dirt island, her feet were level. It didn't seem to present any resistance when she pressed against it though, so she tried knocking on it increasingly hard. Still she felt nothing; her hand would simply stop on the perfectly flat surface of the starfield. This fact annoyed her to no end. She spent a moment jabbing and probing at the ground in various ways without satisfaction.

"This makes no sense!" Eowen huffed. She glared at the starfield, but couldn't be aggravated for long. She took deep breaths and tried to think rationally and critically. There wasn't much for her to puzzle out though; all she could figure out was that the world had somehow become what it was now and that she didn't understand how things worked.

"Alright, so air and clothing appeared when I needed them. Sort of."

She frowned. The statement didn't ring true to her.

"No, I didn't need clothing at all. I'd wanted clothing. So wanting things can make them appear?" Eowen dismissed that theory, as she very much wanted to be home but that clearly wasn't happening. She hadn't wanted dirt beneath her either, nor the small sprouts of flora in it, nor the bugs she was now aware of crawling around her.

"Maybe it's not want, but need? Or thinking of needing something? Air didn't exactly come when I'd needed it though, and I almost died because of that. I also didn't think about needing dirt or the smells of cooking or the sound of threshing. And even so, it all just drifted in and away. Hmm."

Eowen was stuck on that train of thought till her stomach growled. Her near-death experiences had drained a lot of energy, and all the food she'd packed and foraged for was now long gone.

Then it hit her.

"Everything is gone," she whispered. She spun around, looking desperately for any sign of anything other than the endless darkness, and its implication finally dawned on her. Eowen's knees gave out. It was heavy, far heavier than she could carry, and she felt in her spirit that the world was gone—all of it, every plant, animal, cloud, even the people.

Does that mean I'm all alone? This new terror settled quickly in her heart, making itself at home in the young girl. *Are my parents and the tribe gone too?*

Tears welled in her eyes, which were rudely accompanied by her stomach gurgling again. She groaned, a long, irritated sound that changed into hysterical sobs before finally lowering into a primal growl of abject frustration. She coughed as the air thinned again, and before she could even acknowledge the loss with her conscious mind, a sort of command rang through her subconscious that was akin to calling a dog to heel. A puff of air enveloped her and settled into a gentle atmosphere.

Eowen dropped her head into her hands, rubbing at her eyes furiously to get rid of her tears. Crying over anything was unacceptable in her home; it was followed by a switch to the back and a question: 'Is what you're crying about worse than this?' Tears did escape though, and breathing was hard, but her sobs remained as silent tremors through her body. She hid her face, for even as alone as she was, she was still too self conscious to risk being seen like this.

After some time she spoke again. "I just want something to eat," she muttered into her hands, and almost instantly memories of home crashed over her, a tidal wave of smells, sounds, and images that churned with longing. She curled up to shake with sobs and fight back tears, her mind conjuring memories of home so vivid and powerful that at times she believed she was really there. But whenever she opened her eyes, only the void met her. Her own mind, in its depths believing her current reality could be a dream and that her imaginings could be real, generated the familiar senses of home. A horrible joke the universe seemed to be playing sank claws of despair into her over and over. Eowen could not make sense of it yet; she could only suffer at the hands of her own mind as it dangled her heart's desire all around her, only to make it disappear when she would open her eyes and reach for it.

She couldn't measure time in any consistent way without a sun or moon to go by, but many hours passed Eowen by in her lonely prison of wanting until, eventually, she exhausted herself. It felt like very little time at all passed without a world to anchor her, and she drifted through her dreams and daydreams aimlessly, fully surrendering to the escape they offered. The hours turned into most of a day; the day passed into two as she dozed without dreaming. Her limbs ached from being prone so long, so she stood and walked around till terror and loneliness took hold. Hunger sapped her energy, tears pushed out her salt and dehydrated her, and a dull acceptance of her circumstances bled through her mind. Two days passed into three, pangs of hunger became constant pain, and it became all too easy to give up. Her energy seeped from her, her mind began to shut down, and Eowen, after four days of maddening solitude and deprivation, began to fall into a deep and unshakable sleep, a sleep-like death in which she could peacefully die.

Eowen would have died during this torturous interim, but the subconscious workings of her mind supplied water and food directly to her body—not much, but just enough to barely hold onto survival. She was not aware of this, just as she was not fully aware of the passage of time, nor the feeling of her life slipping away.

But slip it did, away into the cruel dark and quiet until even the sounds and smells of home began to seep away, leaving her with nothing to hold onto. This time, she did not even dream in a way that would be forgotten upon waking at all. It seemed death was the sleep she was headed towards.

****

[Eowen.]

****

Her name rang out as a command in her spirit, denying her the right to die. She bolted upright, gasping for air as the atmosphere disappeared again. Adrenaline rushed through her, igniting the last vestiges of life in her that raged against her circumstances. In the deep recesses of her mind and heart, something clicked.

Air bloomed up around her, even greater than before, a thrillingly oxygenated atmosphere full of tastes and smells. Her thoughts were still sluggish such that she found herself disoriented, but she was still hungry, still thirsty, and now refused to let death take her.

She straightened and took deep breaths of her

manufactured air, trying one last time to produce what she would need to stave off death. She wanted food, yet she knew that wanting something wouldn't make it happen, nor would needing it make it appear. Even thinking about the thing wouldn't work, as she was currently thinking a lot about melon bread dripping with honey and yet none appeared before her. Eowen observed herself carefully as she let these feelings and thoughts wash over her, producing no effect. She loosened her grasp on the imaginings and desires, letting them flow away into the recesses of her mind.

As she'd hoped, the world responded with the shadows and light that gathered around her. The convergence took shape, and within seconds it more closely resembled a hot loaf of melon bread sandwiching a steamed sweet leaf, dripping with honeycomb. The food emerged a few centimeters away, and the delicious smell bowled her over.

Eowen didn't question it and slammed the food into her face, slopping crumbs and spit everywhere as she munched and drooled over the treat. She choked for a moment, craving water to wash it down, though she knew there was none here. She knew that to be true, just as she knew there wasn't melon bread with honey comb in this place.

So then, what am I eating?

"At least I can feed myself," she muttered. A new instinct was rapidly forming within her, one guided by faith and acceptance rather than sense, a new framework for what was sensible.

Eowen cupped her hands against the ground, miming the action of scooping water up from a clean mountain stream while daydreaming about the Elder Mountain waters that fed the Vast Jungle. She didn't believe anything would happen, not really, but she knew that something could, and somehow knowing seemed more important than believing. Eowen had never believed the sky of her old world was blue; it was just something she had known to be true, and she had accepted it as such. So Eowen wasn't trying to believe that cool mountain water was flowing into her hands, but know it was and accept that it was. Yet the creation stubbornly refused to emerge. Something was blocking her.

She considered what had happened with the bread and her clothes. Her thoughts moved more smoothly now; the food had charged her with a sense of vitality and purpose. She leaned back, closed her eyes, and settled her hands in her lap. It wasn't enough just to accept an idea. Eowen had to accept it as a thing deeper than ideas, accept it from a place in her subconscious. The girl gently guided her wandering daydreams towards the reality that a cool mountain stream was flowing past her. The daydream became real, overtaking her current reality, torturing her with its absence as the memories of home had. This time, even as tears welled in her eyes, she did not let it become only suffering, only longing, only a dream. She simply accepted that a mountain stream was flowing past her. She let go of effort and let herself know it was real, and then it was.

A molding of shadow and light took place all around her, and when she opened her eyes, frigid water gurgled past. Eowen's eyes lit up as she dunked her arms into the chill, cupped her hands, and sucked in handfuls. She smiled like a fool and laughed till she cried all over again, this time tears of relief and wonder. She took another bite of her melon bread, knocked the tears away, and scooped water with her other hand, slapping it into her mouth with relish.

Eowen looked around, habitually taking stock of her surroundings, and was surprised to see that the stream of water, which flowed past her little dirt island, disappeared after a few meters, ceasing to exist rather than pooling. Experimentally, she passed her hand through the stream to where it faded out of reality an arm's reach away. In the water, her hand was still wet, still cold, but at the end of the stream, it was just gone, uncaptured by anything, as though it only existed by as much as she'd seen in her daydreams. Eowen cocked her head to the side and her brows furrowed.

"It... does only exist as much as I'd wanted it to, or... imagined... No, felt it should."

Eowen continued taking stock of her surroundings, noting that the dirt island had subtly increased in size. More foliage had sprung up, and everything around her had become more like a typical place in the Vast Jungle. Sounds, smells, and even the way the air felt on her skin were reminiscent of home. She turned toward the origin of the stream that flowed behind her and gasped.

A mountain was planted there like some great vulture perched overhead, dark and looming. From it the stream rolled down, fed by what she imagined snowmelt to be. It wasn't a full size mountain, only a few meters tall, but to Eowen it looked and felt real. The shining, snow-covered peak was only a few meters away, so she climbed up and found herself centimeters away from snow for the first time in her life. With a trembling hand, she reached out to touch it, and her hand passed through it like fog, or a cloud, just like she'd imagined. She grinned, twisting her hand over, feeling how it passed right through the snow, picking up moisture. The snow felt denser than fog or mist, pressed on her slightly from all angles, and was just as cold as the stream it flowed into.

"I knew it!" she murmured triumphantly. "Like a cloud

but heavier." She cupped it and pushed, watching it waft and roll till it broke apart into heavy, thick drips of water that she shook off into the stream.

She climbed down from her perch on the mini-mountain and stood again at the edge of her little island, looking out at the vast void before her, up and down only differentiated by the gentle glow of the stars beneath her. She finished her meal, washed it down with a scoop of water, and considered her next course of action. This proved to be difficult as, despite there being nothing in Eowen's way, she had no idea what to actually do next. The extent of her solitude was, once again, impossible to ignore, and without air, food, clothing, or water to worry about, Eowen had nothing to distract her from that condition.

Without knowing any way to deal with such intense isolation, she curled up on her little dirt island in the fetal position and squeezed her eyes tight. When tears threatened to leak out, she clenched her whole body up, trying to suck them back in, afraid that if she let anything out another flood would follow. Sometime later, blissful exhaustion took over, sinking deep into her bones, and after just a few minutes of fighting with her emotions, both body and mind gave out. Her last thought, more of a feeling, was one of gratitude that even in such a place as this, she could still retreat behind the black velvet curtains of sleep, and that the world, no matter how terrible, could always be dreamt away.

****

[Listen, for you cannot hear me yet]

LOVE LIVED ON AH'OM AND SPOKE WITH THE SUN, BUT NOT AS MUCH AS THE MOON, THOUGH THE MOON MADE TEA FROM SPRING WATER AND BONES SOME NIGHTS, WHICH THEY SHARED UNDER STARLESS SKIES.

****

She awoke once, groggily, to the familiar scents and sounds from her savannah home that her dreaming mind had conjured into existence. In her exhausted state she didn't even question her surroundings. She stepped away from her island to relieve herself, then curled back up on her little bed of soft dirt and immediately passed out again.

****

[Listen, for you cannot hear me yet]

THE MOON MADE LOVE BREAD FROM THE BARK ON THE TREES (WHICH WOULDN'T GROW BACK) AND THE THINGS BEHIND IN THE DARK.

****

Eowen bolted upright from her sleep, terrified by shadowy, indistinct shapes all around her that shifted in the resemblance of familiar things. They evoked human movement, trees swaying in the wind, grass waves from the savannah, and small animals skittering about. Above her she felt the shapes of massive things silently drifting with glacial power and certainty. The impressions faded as Eowen rubbed away the fog of sleep. Still, much seemed present at her peripheries, as if just out of reach.

She splashed the stream-water on her face and scooped at the shadows and starlight to pull more bread into reality. Eowen faced the darkness beyond her little patch of land and sighed in resignation. She had to decide what to do. Two options emerged within her, fighting for a foothold in her psyche, the first being that she could stay where she was. She had food and water after all. Eowen drummed her fingers on her knee.

"It's not that I have food and water, but I can... make it." Her shoulders were stiff and her expression strained. Knowing how things really worked was unanswerable, but she took solace in that, at least for now, surviving was not in question.

I could probably stay here, in this one spot, forever if I needed to.

She scanned the empty darkness all around her again and grimaced.

No, I'll go crazy like that.

Thus, the second option was really the only option available to her; leaving to explore the empty expanse.

"There must be other people. What happened with the sky and the trees didn't just happen to me, it happened to the whole world."

Eowen squeezed her hands together, terrified not by the prospect of finding something out in the empty expanse, but of finding nothing at all. As she considered her options, illusory phantoms of sensory input continued to play at her periphery. Always just out of sight, barely heard, faintly smelt, the occasional impressions of touch or taste that disappeared as soon as she attempted to identify them with any clarity. She idled on imaginings of what might be out there, in the dark with only faint stars below.

What kind of creature is native to such a place? The exploration of an empty expanse was not what she had expected to contend with when she left to—

"Tavo!"

Eowen stood and strided out in no particular direction, then turned the opposite way, aimless until it became frantic pacing. She'd left home, abandoned her entire life just on the chance her cousin was still alive and that she could bring him back. She hadn't managed to find him before the sky was brought down, hadn't even gotten close, but somehow it felt as though she'd lost him again.

A tangible sort of despair set in where there hadn't quite been a place for it before. The loss of her entire world; all its people, plants, animals, geography, clothing, food; was horrifying for sure, but till just then it had felt strangely impersonal and removed. The loss of Tavo, or rather the loss of a chance to find him, wasn't the same, as it represented a loss of purpose and motivation. Eowen had trudged through years of failed apprenticeships, been punished for being the disappointment that she was with grim acceptance, and settled into what she believed was her lot in life. It had been easy enough to accept because none of it had been her choice, it had all just been the way things were. Her quest for Tavo had been different though. It had been hers, and when the sky had fallen, among everything else, it had robbed her of the first real ambition she'd ever had.

Eowen's heart beat out a panicked rhythm, her blood

rushing hard enough that she could feel a pulse in her teeth. Despair and indignant rage fed on each other in an unfamiliar and sickening combination, bringing Eowen to her knees. Her mind buzzed with a mad rush of emotion, disrupting rational thought. Around her, the shadows and light writhed violently and, without purpose, were unable to become anything. The effect ranged out all around her, escalating into a cyclone of possibility that smeared potential shapes into formlessness. It was light and shadow, wind and earthquake, churning the environment around her into violence.

Eowen closed her eyes and covered her ears but it was no use. Her every sense was exposed to the very manifestation of her panic, its externalization feeding the internal and elevating both. She curled fetal, wailing below the din, and rocked herself to no avail as the madness raged on, fueled by something greater than herself. It might have continued, escalating into an unstoppable storm of chaotic un-creation forever, if she'd remained there all alone.

"Calm down, girl!"

It was a voice she didn't know in a language she did not recognize, but she was too far gone to notice it. In the state she was in, Eowen assumed it to be more of her madness until an old, wrinkled hand seized her wrist.

The thirteen-year-old screamed and backpedaled like a crab, slipping and kicking. Strange creatures crawled toward her in the shadows, their limbs and bodies writhing in no natural way.

"Get away from me!"

She kicked one and felt skin and hair, something like a hand reached for her and grazed her leg. Eowen screamed again and leaped up as the forms twisted and grew into larger and far more frightening shapes with teeth and claws. Her atmosphere billowed around her, mimicking her panic, and shadow and light welled up as if awaiting her command.

When the light from below grew bright enough, it revealed what the horrors creeping toward her in the dark really were. The terrible shadows melted away, seemingly with reluctance, to expose a group of humans. In the new light they and Eowen froze, staring at each other.

These people had deep golden brown skin, lighter than hers, and thin, black, straight hair hung down like willow tresses. Their eyes were lighter than her people's and less round, and their eyebrows were narrow and long where her people's were thick and bushy. They were naked, desperately crawling with their faces inches from the ground, looking weak, sick, and close to death. But Eowen had seen people like this before and the recognition banished her fears, as she had been expecting to encounter them before the sky had been brought down.

"Mountain folk," she whispered.

"Girl down! Air!" She didn't understand the language as one of them, an elderly man, gestured for her to get her face down where theirs were, nearly pressed against the ground and starfield below. She realized that their strange movements had been the way their elbows and legs had been bent up so they could crawl with their faces pressed to the starfield below. Eowen knelt, confused, and took in their group. There were five in total; an older man, a boy younger than her, two girls around her age, and one very little girl riding the old man the way a baby monkey might cling to their mother's back. They were panting, the small effort of chasing her debilitating for their sunken bodies.

"Oh no, you poor people," she whispered, moving closer.

They hadn't figured out that they could bring the air up to themselves; they hadn't discovered food, water, or clothing as she had. "Oh gods, people!"

Eowen knelt and scooted toward them, tears easily flowing from her at the pure joy of not being alone. She grasped for the closest one, the older man, and held his head in her arms. Her airfield ballooned out, and the strangers gasped as one as the sudden atmosphere provided them with more air than they'd had in days. They stared at her in wonder as she scooped water into their mouths with her hands from her spring.

The older man appeared to have been the weakest of them, in all likelihood expending the most energy to keep his small band alive, so Eowen tended to him first. It was enough for him to muster the energy to help the little ones, who lacked the strength to even sit up. She wanted to ask them about their experience in the new world, if they'd seen the sky brought down as she had, who they were, if they'd encountered other people, if they'd seen her people, how much they knew about how things worked here. Eowen couldn't ask though; no words were getting past her hiccupy sobs as she and the five survivors held each other and wept. Their feeble grip made her horribly aware of how close they'd come to death.

Questions and greetings were set aside while Eowen cared for them, bathing them in her stream. The two girls around her age pitched in immediately, and it was strangely nostalgic caring for the older man and the two young children with the girls, for it reminded Eowen of the duties she did with girls of her village. She idly wondered if perhaps that small commonality was the same across the world, and it made her feel more at home in a way, if only for that moment.

After bathing them, Eowen set about making food. "Um, I've only done this once so we'll see how it goes. I'm sorry if I fail."

She bowed to them apologetically but they regarded her with an unflinching awe, hanging on her every word despite not knowing her language. Rather than making her nervous, their attention gave her a feeling similar to confidence, but not quite the same. They expected something great from her, as if whatever she would do next was guaranteed. It was a rare thing, but for the first in a very long time someone was looking at Eowen without assuming she'd fail at whatever she was doing. In fact, they were not only expecting her to succeed, they were assuming she could. It made Eowen feel as if she had a duty to protect them. Naked and helpless, just as she'd been, they had crawled through the dark until they'd found a clothed girl surrounded by water and a small jungle island. All they knew of her was that she could do things in this world that they could not. With their desperate and hopeful eyes upon her, Eowen set herself to saving them.

She closed her eyes and entered a meditative state, allowing her thoughts to drift through her until they stopped having any real sense to them. The unending darkness felt more real this way, more full of strange potential, neither pressing in nor feeling totally empty. There was tension in the space around her, loose form within the shadows which light would set free. Eowen felt like her mind was calm, really truly tranquil for the first time since arriving in this new reality. Not empty, but smooth like a beach after gentle waves. She felt the glow of purpose and knew, with a certainty quite foreign to her, what she intended to do and to make. Somewhere out in those waters beyond the smooth beach was a place in her subconscious where intent and dream could meet. Reaching it felt like sending a bit of wood out into an ocean; there was no way to guarantee it would reach the spot you wanted it to once you let go. You only had the guidance you gave it to start with, your ability to read the waves, and the hope that it would arrive at the right destination.

In the depths of her mind, Eowen set herself adrift in just the right way, reading the currents, feeling the timing, and accepting that wherever she ended up, even if it wasn't where she was trying to go, things would still be alright. To Eowen, this subconscious journey was peaceful and enlightening.

But to the mountain folk, it was like being at the edge of a cliff as great storm-winds heralded the approach of forces no mortal can oppose. Auras of possibility and intent surrounded them as that interplay of dark and light danced around Eowen. They too possessed auras of potential creation, but theirs was much smaller, weaker, and less formed than hers. As she dipped into that realm of her subconscious where her creations had come from, her aura flowed out and dwarfed them all. The mountain folk were frozen, overcome by the presence that left room enough for them to exist but not to think or feel.

The moment came. Eowen reached through her waters, grasped something, and pulled it back into reality. She emerged from her meditation, bringing with her a simple wooden bowl filled with stew, the kind fed to the sick in her home village. It didn't come alone though; alongside her creation flowed out wind and rain, fire and earth. Music like that from her tribe burst forth alongside animal screeches and cracking thunder. The world smelled of cut fruits, wet wool, burning feces, hair-oils, and dusty grasslands. Eowen's small, dirt island expanded to a small and chaotic oasis of jungle with the stream running through, settling into itself as the smells and sounds faded. The mountain folk were astounded, terrified, confused, but awe was the umbrella feeling under which all their emotions sat.

The old man and his small group turned this way and that to behold all the creation until the old man's eyes landed on the simple bowl of food. Above the girl, a great form loomed in shadow that never quite moved into reality, but watching the scene from behind Eowen. The mountain folk saw it, but in their exhausted and starved state it did not register as any stranger than everything else.

When Eowen returned to herself, the form behind her dissipated and her eyes refocused to see the old man feeding the younger children, salting the stew with his tears and offering her thanks and praise. Eowen created more of the simple food for them, taking over feeding the weak mountain folk children so that the old man could finally rest. Each creation of food afterward became far less dramatic such that by the fifth bowl there were almost no unintended creations that followed. It seemed to her that navigating back to the same place in her subconscious where particular creations could be made was easier with practice.

Once fed, the mountain folk huddled together, muttering to themselves and occasionally expressing their thanks to Eowen as best they could. They were still naked, afraid, but no longer at risk of dying, and Eowen was no longer alone. The little ones were fading into sleep and the older girls were not far behind.

"Thank you girl," the older man said, struggling through Eowen's language as his eyes drooped. Eowen wiped more tears from her eyes, which had continued sprouting and would not soon stop.

"No, th-thank you." She was no longer alone, but more than that was the new hope in her. If these people were alive and in this new world, then surely her people were as well.

The mountain folk passed out in a pile, but despite how exhausted Eowen was her mind was too active to let her sleep. While the mountain folk rested she set about preparing a feast for them, carefully pulling foods into creation that she hadn't tried before. Raw meat, fresh fruits, fish, and a sweet, tough treat made from the bark of a tree that grew in the Vast Jungle. Eowen wondered for a moment how she would make a fire to cook the meat without flint and paced for a few steps before the obvious occurred to her.

"Oh, of course," she whispered. "I can probably create fire." She crouched to do so and was about to delve into her subconscious when the even more obvious occurred to her.

"Oh. I can just make meat already cooked."

The ability to skip such fundamental steps felt somehow transgressive to her, even after all she'd seen and done, but Eowen reasoned it had to be possible. It was the work of a moment; cooked fish, smoked beef, and roast bird were all ready when the mountain folk awoke again. After thanks, the old man portioned everything out into small rations despite the ravenous look in his companions eyes. The old man smiled sweetly and pantomimed at Eowen to communicate.

"Thank you, much food, we eat little now," he said in her language.

"Of course, take your time." Eowen was smiling, a desperate one she couldn't help that made her cheeks ache. She found herself reaching out to hold their hands and touch their faces. The mountain folk responded in kind, thanking her over and again, first in their language, then in hers as the older man taught them how to say it.

Finally, as they ate, Eowen set to making them clothes. She produced bolts of cloth to cover their nakedness, and with each new creation the group froze and stared at her with a mix of expressions that all centered around wonder. One of the mountain girls around Eowen's age even dropped some half-eaten fruit as her mouth was agape. She made to scoop the partially eaten slop off the ground to eat when Eowen stopped her and manifested some more, fresh and ripe, directly into the girl's hand. Even their desperate hunger took pause with Eowen's increasingly casual displays of creation, and they muttered questions to themselves in their own language.

"Is she of this strange place? We found her with clothes and air, and she was not starving," the older girl said as she wrapped herself in the clothes Eowen made.

"How is that happening?" the young boy asked.

"Did a god give her this power?" the youngest girl asked.

"She might be one," the oldest girl said.

"Or is a witch!" the second oldest girl responded.

"Enough!" The older man gave a hard look to his charges. "We live now only on her charity, and the tears she shed for us were those which only a living mortal would make. I will learn what I can from her, but we will not speak poorly of her, and certainly not behind her back in a language she does not know. If you have questions for her then ask, and I will try to translate. We owe her our lives, children."

The old man wilted from the effort of his speech, leaning into the supportive hands of Eowen. He met her eyes and smiled, his intense gratitude and awe disarming. He gently grasped her arms, motioning for her to help him stand. Once he was up he clasped his hands in front of him and bowed to her, swaying a bit, but otherwise keeping his posture.

In Eowen's language he said: "You, ah, our debt, our life. Thank you girl." He gestured to the children. "Questions. Good people, young, questions." He switched to his own language. "Thank her formally." The children all stood and bowed to Eowen as the old man had. Eowen flushed and gestured for them to sit.

"Please, we... We're all in this together, aren't we? We have to help each other." The old man didn't fully understand her, but nodded all the same. "Really, I should be thanking all of you. I-I thought I was alone. I thought everyone was gone! I didn't think I'd ever see my family again, but they might be alive!"

One of the girls Eowen's age reached for her hand and gave it a squeeze. Eowen choked out a laugh and a sob, hardly believing it wasn't one of her daydreams. Exhaustion very suddenly took her, all the excitement of this meeting draining out as relief fully took its place. Eowen swayed; she'd been awake for almost sixteen hours caring for the mountain folk, manifesting food and clothes for them.

One of the older girls caught her and laid her down gently. In a moment she was silent, then sobbing, then completely unconscious. Her breathing was soft and even. The older man gave an approving nod and gestured for his charges to move behind the small mountain from which the stream flowed. The boy curled up next to him, laying his head on the old man's lap.

"Give her space and privacy. She won't want us hanging over her like vultures when she wakes up."

"What is she, Yawin?" the boy asked as he yawned and stretched out next to the others.

"Just a girl, Ne." Yawin stroked the boy's hair. "Be nice to her; she saved our lives. That's all we need to know about her, isn't it?" Yawin looked down at the boy for an answer, but he was already fast asleep.

"Just a normal girl," he repeated to himself, but the food in his stomach, the water on his lips, and the very air in his lungs made him wonder if it was true.

The girl that had laid Eowen down did not move away immediately, but instead knelt over Eowen. The mountain girl stared down at her sleeping savor, amazed that the miraculous things that had just happened were all the work of a person.

"Hale, get over here. Leave her be!" Yawin said. Hale shook her head, her eyes clear.

"Of course, Yawin." The mountain folk left her alone, and Eowen dreamt.

****

[Listen, for you cannot hear me yet]

NO ANIMALS LIVED ON AH'OM, BUT THERE WERE PLANTS. IT NEVER RAINED ON AH'OM, BUT THERE WAS SILENT LIGHTNING.

****

Eowen woke up well rested and more excited to be awake than she had been in years. She stretched, splashed some cold water in her face, and set about refilling the bowls with fresh food. Manifesting these basic needs was becoming easy for her, almost mundane.

The mountain folk were still sleeping on the other side of the small mountain and Eowen resolved not to wake them yet. Her mouth moved silently during her work and, very slowly, she brought the things into reality. Food emerged around her and as she created her mouth moved silently to the shapes of words that she gave no sound to. She was becoming more familiar with the process, the feel of being upon a great shore, of delving into a great ocean of possibility, and guiding herself towards her goal amidst all the chaos. Making food was easy, and maintaining the atmosphere around her had become as automatic as breathing it.

One of the girls around her age, the oldest one, stirred. Eowen watched as she rubbed her eyes and stretched. The girl noticed the food, then noticed Eowen was awake, made the same gesture of thanks as before, and readjusted the unfamiliar clothes she wore.

"Oh, here, let me help." Eowen reached out and set the wrapping that went over the shoulder, over the chest, and around the waist just right. The girl smiled, the simple interaction anchoring them in comfortable familiarity despite their alien surroundings. They ate together and the girl brightened significantly, already looking much healthier than hours before. She put her hand to her chest and said some words Eowen did not know, but emphasized one word several times:

"Genia," the girl said. Eowen took the cue and pointed to the girl's chest.

"Geneea. Your name is Geneea then?"

"Geh-nee-ah," Genia corrected.

"Geh-nee-ah. Genia?" The girl nodded and pointed to Eowen's chest. "Oh, my name is Eowen. Eh-oh-wen."

The girl repeated her name "Eiuwen?"

"Close, Eh-oh-wen."

"Eh. Oh. Wen." Eowen nodded and Genia smiled. "Eowen."

"Yes!" Eowen reached out to hold Genia's hands. "It is good to meet you, Genia."

Genia responded in kind, her smile bright and friendly, her eyes gentle and kind. She pointed in turn to the other members of their party, putting names to their sleeping faces. The older man was named Yawin, the little boy Ne, the other girl around their age Hale, and the youngest one, a little girl no older than eight, was Zerinley.

Eowen was practicing their names and pointing to them with Genia's coaching when Yawin stirred. He greeted the girls and took a shy drink from the stream. The others awoke soon after, and Genia had the pleasure of introducing them all to Eowen by name. They greeted each other in the ways of their people; bows from the mountain folk with one arm in front and one behind with both hands open and standing a half step back from Eowen. They laughed and chatted together about the absurdity they were in, Yawin translating as best he could. They shared what little they understood about what had happened over their meal and exclaimed at the absurdity of it. The two younger children splashed in Eowen's stream, the older girls chastised them, but splashed back, and Yawin smiled in a way that made his whole face crinkle up. It wasn't that any of them were any less afraid or confused, but to have such small, simple vestiges of the old world available to them as food, water, clothes, and the jungle around them, set their minds at ease for the first time since arriving. No one was about to ruin the moment with fears and questions; there would be time for that later. For now, it was time to celebrate the incredible fact that they were alive.

After some time, when the group had been properly fed and given ample time to enjoy the luxury of an atmosphere, Eowen set about making them better clothing, since what she'd initially produced for some of them were little more than blankets. Again, shadow and light came together in a way that seemed to carve Eowen's creations out of the nothing around them into reality. The clothes were much more comfortable and wearable, fitting their owners quite well. They seemed to have been printed with colors and patterns from her home village.

While the mountain folk marveled at her creations, Eowen took pride in being able to create that which she'd never succeeded at crafting in the old world. Weaving had been one of her many apprenticeships, and it was empowering to produce that which she'd always been able to envision in her mind but had never been able to make with her hands. Eowen looked at her plain, yellow wrappings and resolved to make something more interesting for herself afterward.

She drew forth simple wrappings with patterned hems, embroidery, and color. The five mountain folk were munching on a melon as they watched Eowen create, trying to study her technique. After the third outfit, Eowen found the inconsistent light bothersome. The way it would rise up from below during creation and fade away afterward into the faint starfield made it hard to tell how her creations were coming out. Without any conscious effort or intent, Eowen gestured toward the starfield below and a light, like a tiny sun, emerged as though scooped from the void. It floated up to sit just above her head.

The mountain folk were stunned into silence, but it took a moment for Eowen to even notice the small light now floating above her. The youngest of the mountain folk exclaimed and pointed. Eowen looked up and hiccuped in surprise, the light bobbing with her head. She swatted at it as though it were an insect, and she extinguished the small light, blinking in the sudden dark. Once Eowen had digested her surprise, she manifested a new light, brighter and steadier, floating higher above her than the last. The mountain folk were wrapt, watching to see what she'd do next. Eowen cleared her throat, and felt herself blushing, more embarrassed about the attention than anything.

"I'm sorry," she muttered. "I'll finish making you all clothes in a moment." She fumbled with the last two outfits, awkwardly grasping at indistinct folds of light and shadow which refused to transition into reality. The old man named Yawin reached out and grasped Eowen's hand, disrupting her creation, which faded away into nothing.

"You stop, please. We are helped. See? It is enough," he said, choosing his words carefully.

Eowen was caught between the unfamiliarity of Yawin's supportiveness and the refusal to accept failure that was ingrained into her in the years after Tavo's disappearance. She took a deep breath, nodded, and stepped back. A moment passed silently, then her eyes opened, clouded over. She whispered to herself words she did not know, and into being the last two outfits emerged. Eowen came back to herself, looked over the clothes, and nodded approvingly.

"Now it's enough."

"How do you do all this!" the young boy, Ne, asked in his language. Eowen was startled, but managed to smile genuinely. She clasped her hands and leaned in toward him, glancing to Yawin for help.

"What did you say... Ne?"

"Yawin, Yawin!" Ne was pulling on the older man's clothes.

"Ask her how she made the food and clothes and water, and she has a light floating above her too, maybe she knows where we are or what happened! She made the air too right?" Yawin patted his arm and calmed him down in their own language before attempting to communicate with Eowen.

"You... Make all." He gestured at the things around them.

"Oh! I didn't do all this!" Eowen gestured at the entire world around them. Yawin made a 'settle down' motion and tried again.

"Maaake." He drew it out and gestured definitively at the food and water. He breathed loudly and picked at his clothes.

"Oh, yes, I suppose I did do those things." Eowen glowed with a shy sort of pride, a neighbor to embarrassment.

"How?" he asked.

"Oh..." Eowen looked down and pressed her hands together, trying to think of how to explain. She stared hard at the starfield and hunched over, trying to recall exactly how she'd done these things. Any clarity on the subject was escaping her. Her brow furrowed and a hard frown bent her lips. The children were muttering to themselves. Genia pulled at Yawin to ask him what he and Eowen had said. When he explained, the children exploded with questions, and Yawin had to hush them down, insisting upon patience.

"No need, no need," Yawin said, trying to tell Eowen that he didn't need an answer, though he desperately wanted one. Eowen, however, had transitioned from frustration to a distant and detached look. It seemed to Yawin that she wasn't seeing anything around her at all, that she was looking beyond them to something else, something intractable. The distant star field below grew brighter. Eowen's body slouched into a more relaxed position. The question rang in her mind:

How have I been doing all this? How exactly does it really work?

The light below grew almost too bright to bear, and the mountain folk shielded their eyes. Just when it would have become completely blinding, shadows that were filled with illusory shape, scent, and sound, met the light in a collision. Like waves on rocks they broke and sprayed their power about, and something began to emerge from the meeting.

The mountain folk backpedaled, watching in awe as a white, skeletal, tree emerged between them, not growing so much as unfolding, becoming real in such a way as to fill the space with itself. It was just a small thing, able to fit within Eowen's encircled arms. Its bark was flat and white, its branches thick and many. It was a bone-tree, like those in her old home. It did not become as massive as the ones near Eowen's village and throughout the Vast Jungle, but its familiar presence was rendered into stark contrast with the empty, alien world.

Eowen refocused and scanned the tree before her, then stood and walked around to the other side where the mountain folk had scuttled away to. Ne and Hale both ran up to Eowen insisting with words she couldn't understand that what she'd done was amazing and to do it again. Genia looked excited too, but it was overshadowed by uncertainty, while the little girl, Zerinley, seemed to be simply enjoying all the excitement around her and wanted someone's attention. Yawin stepped between the children to get Eowen's attention and again asked her how she had done it as best he could.

"Yawin, ummm..." She pointed to her head, "Thinking? Thoughts?"

Yawin confirmed he knew the word, but looked more confused.

"Yes, ah, head? Miin-ed?" he said, then muttered a bit in his language.

"Yes, the mind. MM-II-N-D. Mind?"

"Yes, min-ed."

"Yes!" Eowen pointed at him. Then she gestured around her head vaguely, making swirling motions that she was sure made her look extremely foolish. It didn't help that the little children, Ne and Zerinley, were giggling at her. Eowen blushed, stuttered, and tripped over several more explanations, none of which seemed to reasonably breach the language barrier. The little ones were still distractingly excited, which made her thoughts even more garbled. Yawin settled them down and insisted everyone take a seat, though Hale and Ne were still bouncing.

Eowen gestured ineffectually for a moment, leaned against her new tree, and realized there were other things that had accompanied the creation of the tree. The scent of earth and mountain air, a sound like the wind, and what seemed to be a vague buzzing or chittering of small creatures. There were no animals to be seen though, and even the lighting around the tree had a different quality to it as it cast a gentle shadow from no visible source of light. Eowen's sphere of light above her head was too low to be casting the shadow that the tree did. It seemed that some of the random sensory inputs had accompanied the tree into the world, like stowaways on its ride through the void. Eowen focused back on Yawin and did her best.

"Thinking, thoughts," she repeated, accompanying her motions. Yawin nodded, but his arms were crossed and his eyebrows furrowed. He responded with what Eowen could only assume were those words in his language and gestured for her to continue.

"Mind...make?" He stumbled over the words and repeated his words for thinking and thoughts. "Yes?" He looked to her for confirmation.

Eowen nodded, but made a gesture to indicate: 'sorta.'

"Mind, make?" Yawin tried again, pointing at the tree, but Eowen shook her head and Yawin's face fell.

"Mind," Eowen established again, pointing at her head. Yawin gestured for her to continue. "Thoughts," she said with significant inflection and again Yawin confirmed he was following her. Then, Eowen made an X with her arms and shook her head vigorously. "No mind, not thoughts, no thinking at all."

Yawin was looking annoyed now, and the children were chattering again. He was asking himself questions, and the children were asking him more as well, though he gave no answers. He crossed his arms in frustration and Eowen flushed, annoyed she couldn't explain what happened inside her when she created things.

Why was making these things easier than describing how I did it, even with a language barrier? It should not be this hard to explain!

The children were getting loud and Yawin wasn't doing a very good job of quieting them down, so Eowen clapped her hands and shouted: "Hey!"

Instantly, they all stopped to listen. Eowen pointed at their eyes.

"You all, watch me." She pointed at her own eyes. "Watch me, watch my eyes. Don't watch what I make, watch my eee-y-ees. Understand?" Yawin filled them in on what words Eowen had said that he knew, and they seemed to follow.

Eowen gestured to her eyes again, insisting that they watch her closely. Then she set to creating, though it was much harder to perform under such pressure. Eowen still didn't fully understand how the creation of things worked, but what she did know was that in this small group, she was the only authority on the subject. She rolled her shoulders, took deep breaths, and left the present moment to drift into daydreams, letting their currents unbind her dreaming mind and set her adrift on that ocean of the subconscious once more. This time, she did not merely float out into the currents, she sailed out, catching the winds and waves of her deepest mind like a galleon at full mast.

To the five mountain folk, all they saw was Eowen's body going slack, and a very strange expression that might loosely be considered a smile curving her lips like a brushstroke. They saw her eyes glaze over, and Eowen moved her hand mechanically to the starfield below where light was gathering again. Shadows seemed to reach over her shoulders to meet the starlight. She held her hands out like a bowl, and as the light and shadow passed into them, a small mass of water appeared in her cupped hands. The astonishment of the mountain folk grew as each of them realized the water was not slipping between her fingers, nor spilling over the bowl of her hands. In fact, it had the appearance of a tiny ocean, with tiny white-capped waves crashing into her fingers and a gallant ship swaying on the crests. Unrelated sensory inputs followed the creation, things like the smell of citrus, dust in the eyes, the feel of a bug on the skin, and bark peeling off a tree.

Eowen came back to the present, refocused, and her face lit up. She looked at each of the mountain folk in turn, pausing at Yawin.

"No thoughts," she said emphatically.

"No thinking," he said in his own language.

"Um... Dreams. Dream?" Eowen said to him, hoping he understood the new word.

"Dream?" Yawin repeated. He put his hands together and

laid his head on them cocked to the side, and took a couple snore-like breaths. "Sleep dream?"

Eowen bobbed her head excitedly. Yawin tried to explain as best he could to the children while Eowen grinned, considering this moment a triumph as she sipped at the ocean in her hands. She immediately spat it out into Genia's face, who groaned and wiped at the water while Ne laughed at her. Eowen cringed and shrugged apologetically, still holding her little ocean.

"Sorry! Bleh! I didn't know it would be salty!"

They spent hours after her demonstration struggling to establish better communication, but it was mentally exhausting and the strangeness of their circumstances was a perpetual burden on their minds. Eowen soon found herself drifting off along with the children under Yawin's care. The mountain folk gathered into a pile near Eowen, and they were soon asleep. Eowen's floating light winked out and they were surrounded entirely by darkness once more.

****

[Listen, for you cannot hear me yet]

LOVE'S CLOSEST CONFIDANT WAS THE CAVE AT THE BOTTOM OF THE MOUNTAIN, WHO TOLD LOVE ALL ABOUT THE MOUNTAIN'S MOTHER AND FATHER, WHO WERE PEOPLE, LIKE LOVE, WHO BREATHED THE WAY PEOPLE DO, ATE THE WAY PEOPLE ATE, SANG THE WAY PEOPLE SANG, AND LOVED THE WAY PEOPLE LOVED.

****

Eowen awoke first, and though there was no such thing as day and night in the new world, it had been a week's worth of time since she'd arrived and two days since the mountain folk had found her. They had recovered well and were full of health and energy. Eowen was proud of the good she'd done for them, but a new problem had been festering in her, one she could no longer avoid.

"What do we do next?" she mouthed silently, though of course she knew the answer; they had to go and look for more people. They had to leave and find out if there were answers to the question of what had happened to their world and what they should do moving forward.

Surely there are many people that can navigate this world better than I. My mother and Priestess Mein can tell me what to do.

The mountain folk stirred and greeted each other in a combination of languages. Eowen thought she should try to make something special to eat this time, something to show her appreciation. She created the food, and over a meal of sweetened tea and fermented bean-loaf with a spicy fish paste, a favorite among Eowen's people that mountain folk politely consumed, she brought up the topic of leaving their little encampment.

She cleared her throat to get their attention and the five mountain folk immediately locked onto her, some of them mid-chew. Eowen was still quite unused to being the center of such attention and took a sip of water to give her a moment to collect herself. There was a certain unnerving reverence in the way they waited on her every action and word, and while it could be endearing from the younger children, the looks

Yawin gave her, hungry for guidance, felt heavy. She cleared her throat again.

"Family." She pointed at the mountain folk. "Umm, tribe? Village? Family?" She gestured generally over them again. Yawin nodded in understanding.

"Yes, family." He pointed to Ne and Genia. "Tribe." He circled them all with his finger.

Good, he knows these words, that'll make this easier.

Yawin's face fell and he covered his eyes. Eowen was confused until his shoulders started shaking up and down. He was sobbing, silently and without visible tears. Genia huddled in close and muttered soothingly to Yawin while stroking his back. Hale could not contain herself and began to openly weep. The little ones moved in to hug her but were the least emotional. They stared, stone-faced, at the stars below, their youth in heartbreaking contrast with whatever memories were playing out in their minds. Yawin wiped his eyes, thanked Genia, and hugged them all close. Eowen wanted to ask what had happened but couldn't interrupt such a moment, so she averted her eyes and placed her hands in her lap respectfully. Genia whispered back and forth with Yawin, glancing at Eowen, until he'd mustered the resolve to try and explain.

"Eowen, tribe... dead." He covered his mouth with a hand and sobbed. "No air," he said imploringly, his eyes begging Eowen to understand. Eowen nodded, a terrible cold spreading up through her. Yawin counted on his fingers for her to see till he'd passed over both hands many times. "Dead, number dead." He had counted out more than sixty from their village, and the cold feeling in Eowen spread further through her.

Of course, they'd barely been able to make air when they found me, if the others in their tribe couldn't at all...

Eowen remembered how she herself had almost died upon arriving in the new world and felt that she should have known what had happened. She suppressed all thoughts of her own people's fate before she ended up in the weeping pile with them.

Just because their people ended up like that doesn't mean mine did.

It was hollow reasoning, but without evidence to the contrary she held onto it. Eowen gave them a moment and used it to collect herself. Yawin waved off the children and shook his shoulders.

"Please, talk more." At his insistence Eowen gave a small bow.

"My tribe." She put her hand to her chest. Then pretended to shade her eyes and scan the nonexistent horizon. "Find?"

"Ah, find is search?" he asked, and Eowen confirmed he'd used the right word.

"I need to search for them, will you come with me?" Eowen spoke slowly, accompanying her words with charades. Yawin and the rest seemed to understand, but he explained to the children in their language just to make sure.

"We are going to join Eowen in the search for her tribe. We owe this to her for saving our lives, understood?" His charges agreed, though there was no enthusiasm, for they knew what Eowen was likely to discover. Yawin gave Eowen a nod and offered his hand to shake. "Yes, we search with you."

Eowen made all the preparations, creating packs with three days worth of food, medical supplies, sleeping blankets, and some basic tools. Eowen scanned the world around her in a circle. She had long since lost track of what direction she might have been facing when the world had ended. There were no indicators whatsoever of which direction had once been north or south, or if such directions even held meaning in this new world. She asked Yawin which direction he had come from and he pointed away from Eowen's little mountain stream.

"Alright then, we go the opposite way."

They had all the supplies they'd need, but as Eowen stood at the edge of her little dirt island she found it impossible to take that first step out over the stars and into the black expanse ahead. She tried, her foot hovering, but a shaking overtook her limbs and the cold fear she'd suppressed clawed at her lungs till she became lightheaded. When, again, she tried to take that first step and failed, Genia took her hand and whispered something Eowen did not understand. Eowen was not tall, but Genia was even shorter, all round and stocky. Genia was seventeen, though she did look younger, and in subtle ways she'd been the emotional rock of her small party. Something in her eyes, a steady and persistent kindness, an iron-clad resolve to love, had kept her fellow mountain folk from despair. Now she shared this with Eowen, whispering the way she'd whispered to Yawin, Hale, Zerinley, and Ne in their first desperate days in the new world.

No language barrier got in the way of her supportive words, and before she knew it, Eowen had taken her first, second, and third steps. Genia nodded her approval, and let go of Eowen's hand, stepping back to see where the young woman from the jungle and savannah tribes would take them. Eowen checked her trajectory one more time, took a deep breath, and with entirely false confidence strode off into the dark expanse, followed by the mountain folk and the faint slivers of starlight that filtered up from below. Travel was relatively easy since there was no terrain to contend with, though the packs Eowen had made were not at all comfortable and the straps chafed terribly.

"I'm sorry everyone, I'll make new ones with softer straps," Eowen said as she rubbed away the redness on her shoulder. They took a break while she sat down to do that. She prepared to enter her dreaming state but it was taking longer than usual, a stray thought itching at the edges of her mind. Eowen's eyes widened and she smacked her forehead.

"Oh I'm so stupid!" The mountain folk froze, concerned, but Eowen was grinning and laughing. "We don't need these!" She flung her pack away and it landed without a sound, spilling out all the contents. The mountain folk were confused until Eowen casually created all the contents of their packs, gesturing to her work emphatically. "I can just make everything on the go!" It clicked and the mountain folk followed suit, tossing their packs aside.

"She can make all this, no need to bring anything, we could even go naked!" Hale said.

"We are not going naked!" Zerinley shouted.

Eowen smiled shyly and continued leading the way. The mountain children expressed boredom after some time and Yawin suggested some games. Eowen watched them chatter and gesture, following rules she didn't know. After an hour of it she asked Yawin to explain, and the old man made it clear that they were playing. Thereafter began a cultural exchange of sorts between the children. As they walked, Genia and Hale taught her hand games that were played in the mountains with complex rhythm rules. These games were meant to be played at great distances in the mountains with players situated across ravines and between distant peaks. Eowen taught them skipping games that were popular in the flats of the savannah, which Ne and Zerinley took to right away since they'd not yet learned to keep up with the fast rhythms of the mountain folk games. Yawin joined in with the rhythm games while Eowen played with the little ones, laughing as he thrashed the girls at double speed.

"I play long, long time," he explained to Eowen with a toothy grin as Genia lamented her sixth loss in a row. Hours upon hours passed and eventually they grew tired of games, walking in silence for long stretches. They broke it up with bits of conversation, keeping Yawin busy translating questions.

"Why do your clothes look like that?" Ne asked.

"My mother made me clothes like these. I suppose I created them like this out of habit." Eowen said.

"Where are you from exactly?" Zerinely said.

"My family are all from the tribes of the jungle and savannah, but the tribe I was born into is mostly on the savannah side of the border."

"Does everyone south of the mountains have skin as dark as yours? Because we've met travelers from the other side of the mountains that look like you do, but kinda different, and also people from the north with very light skin, like a ghost!" Hale said.

"I, um, I don't know. I've never been past the mountains or very far south...Truth be told I don't know what people look like anywhere else. "

"Does everyone have brown eyes where you're from?"

"Yes."

"Who taught you your games?"

"My cousins. My parents don't like to play games. Who taught you yours?"

"Everybody knows games!" Ne had asked that question and Yawin clarified.

"All mountain people play, game teach talk, ah, far away?"

"Oh, so it allows you to communicate over long distances?" Eowen asked.

"Yes, loud sky also," Yawin explained, making whooshing sounds and waving his arms around to indicate a loud storm. "Very cold, we wear heavy clothing."

Eowen hadn't properly considered how different the weather would be up in the mountains. She'd known it was colder, but had assumed that it would just resemble the temperature of the savannah at night. She paused, bringing their little caravan to a stop, remembering that she'd been planning to climb the great Elder Mountains in clothes designed for the ever-hot jungle and savannah.

"Wow, I guess it's a good thing I never made it into the mountains. I might have died," she muttered to herself.

Hale asked Yawin what Eowen had said, but he only shrugged as he hadn't caught it. Ne insisted Yawin teach him some of Eowen's language as he was getting tired of having to wait for translations, and the others expressed an interest in learning bits as well. Yawin explained this to Eowen and she hesitantly agreed if Yawin acted as an intermediary whenever possible.

"I've never been responsible for teaching anything to anyone where I'm from, so, uh, please be patient with me," which was true; she'd never made it far enough in an apprenticeship to even consider teaching a trade to someone else. "Please teach me your language as well."

At their first rest, Eowen began running through all the vocabulary for basic conversation with Yawin, mostly to clarify what he already knew. Yawin already had a very good grasp of Eowen's language since, as she found out, he had been a part of several trade caravans in his youth. Largely what he needed was a refresher since it had been almost a decade since he'd spent time with a member of Eowen's tribe, and her regional dialect was slightly different than what he was familiar with. Within the hour Yawin was speaking with more confidence, though he still needed to go slow and think through the translations.

"Eowen, I am fifty and three years. When I was age twenty to thirty... Um, when we, my caravan, traded with jungle people. The I, ah..." Yawin paused, and muttered in his own language. He put his hands together and looked to Eowen. "Um, love, together, make children... Hmm, wife?"

"Your wife? Is marriage the word? To get married?" Eowen asked.

"Yes! I marriage my wife—or I married my wife. We moved to live deeper in mountains... then moved back to edge near jungle when my father and mother were sick. They die, many years ago, and—" Yawin's voice caught in his throat "—When... this happened..." Yawin gestured around, not having the words in Eowen's language to describe how the world had come to its end. His eyes were misting, but he blinked it away and walked a few steps ahead so that he would be properly out of sight of the children. "... is when my wife die."

"I'm so sorry," Eowen said to the old man, but Yawin only waved his hand dismissively and pressed on. His feelings had been tamped down, the pain of losing his wife obviously there, but set aside for his responsibility to look after the children.

Eowen glanced over them, very suddenly aware of the extent of their tragedy. It wasn't just random members of their tribe who had died; it was their parents, brothers, sisters, cousins, and friends. They likely died right before their eyes, suffocating as Eowen had in her first moments in the new world. Tears welled up and she put a hand to Yawin's shoulder, avoiding looking at them as well.

"Oh gods, Yawin, did they see, I mean, did their families die in front of them?" she whispered.

"Yes, they did," Yawin whispered back. "I do not think Zerinley understands, and Ne thinks he is being strong for her because she is littler than him. I don't know what Hale and Genia think, ah, feel. Mountain women do not mourn with men, they will not show me, they mourn in secret."

Eowen kept her hand over her mouth to stifle any sounds, but nodded to confirm she understood. Her imagination turned to her own tribe, her own family. The tears stopped, the ice began to spread from Eowen's stomach, up through her heart, down the winding paths in her veins, and into the tips of her fingers. She could feel the cold slither up her throat, and in a way, the numbness and detachment of the cold felt safe. The icy feeling never reached the top of her head, though; a soft little hand grabbed hers, shattering the spell. Ne yawned as he rubbed his eyes with a pudgy little fist and squeezed Eowen's hand.

"Sleep?" he said in Eowen's language, one of the words he'd picked up. Eowen squeezed Ne's hand back. She couldn't let herself despair, not when there might still be hope that her loved ones lived, not while the mountain folk still relied on her.

"You're right Ne, we have been walking for a long time. Yawin, do you think we should sleep now?" Yawin took a long moment to translate his response, muttering silently to himself.

"A caravan travel behind most slow dog," he said.

"A common saying?" Eowen asked.

"Of course, let us look for a rest place." They looked around. "I think any place is as good as any other."

Eowen created bedrolls, food, and water as before, but this time, Eowen made wood and flint to light a fire and they gathered around the cozy setting, feeling more at home with the familiar light source than with any of the other comforts Eowen had provided. As usual, Eowen's manifestations brought with them unintended effects like bits of foliage, smells, lighting effects, and sounds. These came from the recesses of her mind purely out of association, but she was learning to suppress them and keep her creations focused. The mountain children had largely gotten used to it and chatted away to themselves, occasionally prompting Yawin to translate for them as they attempted to include Eowen, but for the most part she and Yawin spoke between themselves. Ne and Zerinley were already falling fast asleep, and the older girls soon followed suit while Yawin kept Eowen up with light conversation.

Once it was just the two of them, he broached the topic of his tribe's fate. It was much the way Eowen expected; naked and alone, they'd suffocated, unable to make their own air. The children and Yawin had thought it all a bad dream as they'd fallen in and out of unconsciousness, but eventually they'd become capable enough at making their own air to stay awake, and it was then that they all witnessed the truth. Twisted bodies, eyes bulging, rigor mortis had preserved their suffering. Yawin had found the four children by their crying, and they had crawled away from the dead for days before they came across Eowen.

He spared no details. He wanted Eowen to understand the tragedy, to prepare her for what she might face if they found her family. Neither Yawin nor Eowen wept as the story was told. They were stony faced and grim. It didn't matter that Yawin was Eowen's senior by decades, that she was a girl, or that she was of a different people; they had both become protectors and providers. The weight of that shared responsibility inspired an austere camaraderie in them, and in the quiet they looked over the mountain children. Though Hale and Genia were older than Eowen at fifteen and seventeen, all five of the mountain folk had become dependent upon her. Yawin cleared his throat.

"Children need a strong person in me," he whispered. "I do not let the children be sad. I know that if we stop, we die. They need to not think about death, so I force we all to crawl." His face twisted with guilt and his hands balled into fists. "I was cruel. I did not let sleep, I did not let rest. I shout, push, anything except stop and die. I hurt them."

Eowen placed a hand on his shoulder. "You had to, Yawin. They're alive and safe now. They understand that."

"Maybe they understand. Maybe no. But we are alive. Because luck, or..." he gestured vaguely, not knowing the word for fate in Eowen's language, "...but most because of you, Eowen. I believe you will save many."

Eowen turned away, letting the shadow cast from the fire hide her face. She didn't want this responsibility. Despite her abilities, she did not feel herself to be the leader Yawin was. He had saved the children, no matter what he said. He'd been the one to look for an answer amidst the void, while Eowen had stayed on her tiny dirt island, safe and well-fed. At that moment, Eowen didn't feel like she'd really saved anyone, and certainly didn't feel like she could be a savior for anyone else.

"I think I need my sleep now, Yawin."

The old man smiled, pulled Eowen in for a hug, then laid down next to the pile of children with an arm stretched out protectively over them.

"You sleep well, Eowen. We have debt with you, for all time," he said, his voice already drowsily fading off into light snores.

Eowen felt a weight settle in. It made her heart ache and her stomach turn.

This must be a fraction of what Yawin has been feeling. This is nothing. I have to do better.

She silently stood and walked away from them, feeling claustrophobic despite being surrounded by nothing. At ten paces away from the camp, Eowen heard one of the girls gasp. She spun around to see Hale, who was the furthest from Eowen stir in her sleep, seeming to have trouble breathing. Eowen moved back in a panic, and Hale's breathing evened out.

"Oh, I suppose that's as far as my air goes."

Faced with this clear radius to her power, Eowen was struck by a feeling of insignificance, like all she had done and learned to do in this place of dreams was actually very small. Despite the clothes, food, and air, the vast void around her dwarfed her accomplishments, begging to be filled with creation.

She returned to the group, sat with her back to the fire, but did not sleep for some time. Her mind moved through the concerns for which there was currently no answer, until something occurred to her that she could take some comfort in.

"Maybe I can teach them how to create things the way I do. If I can do that, they won't have to rely on me, they can fill this place with me. We could save people together, teach them, and it could keep going like that. Until the whole world is saved."

Eowen yawned, the warmth of the fire and the long walk sinking into her. She snuggled drowsily into the folds of her bedroll. As she drifted into dreams, gentle manifestations pushed pleasant breezes and faint lullabies over her, smoothing out the wrinkles in her forehead. In sleep, the shadows around her danced with a vitality that her waking mind suppressed, but rarely did the starlight below rise to deliver form to the darkness.

****

[Listen, for you cannot hear me yet]

LOVE ONCE ASKED THE CAVE WHAT THEY WERE, AND THE CAVE SAID: YOU ARE NEED, YOU ARE THAT WHICH WAS NEEDED, BY THE NEEDFUL THAT THERE IS AND WAS, BY THAT WHICH COULD NOT BE WITHOUT YOU.

****

When the mountain folk awoke Eowen made them more food and water, but all the while she was thinking about how she could teach them. She again cleared her throat for their attention.

"Yawin, I think I should teach you all how to... do what I do." He seemed confused so Eowen gestured at the food. "This." His eyes lit up.

"Oh! You think we can?"

"I don't see why not. You were able to create your own air." She didn't mention that they could only do so with their faces pressed to the ground. "I could hardly make my own air at first, and I learned how to do all this." She also didn't mention that virtually all of her knowledge of creation had been accidents rather than things she'd learned. "If you practice, then I'm sure that soon you'll all be able to do what I do."

Yawin explained things to the children, who were immediately excited to learn. It was a slow process, but between the walking and learning the languages and the art of creation, the small party passed the time. Time was hard to track in the new world without day or night. The only way Eowen and the mountain folk could do so were by the changes they experienced in their bodies: hunger, thirst, exhaustion.

Yawin requested a tough white cloth, like canvas, then wood and fire to make a charcoal writing implement. Eowen created the canvas as requested, but instead of fire and wood simply created a charcoal writing tool. When Eowen handed over the materials Yawin's eyes went wide and his head cocked to the side.

"Oh... Yes, thank you." Skipping such steps to the creation of something caused a bit of mental whiplash akin to culture shock.

Yawin used the charcoal and canvas to tick each meal and time they slept, insisting that they all at least sleep at the same time as each other to keep it reasonably consistent, and do so after at least two meals. He also scheduled their lessons with the charcoal, insisting that consistency was the main ingredient of success. Eowen began learning their language as well, and with little else to do everyone took to their studies with relish. It was not only an excellent distraction, but there was a great sense of relief in learning to do what Eowen could do, as it made her feel less alien and the mountain folk feel more independent.

Over the hours of travel they learned the basics; clothes, food, water, air. More often than not the mountain folk's clothes came out lumpy and strange. Clumps of woven or knitted material manifested with colors and patterns all twisted about, but they were somewhat better at producing animal skins. After plenty of successes, and strange failures, they managed to alter their outfits to be more culturally familiar, with thick wooly pieces made from mountainous animal skins and fleeces. It wasn't that they needed warm clothing, but it was comforting to be in familiar garb.

As the mountain folk began making their own air, Eowen noted that it smelled of stone, and was a bit cooler than her own. The air around her was always warm, either humid or dry and dusty, and smelled of the jungle and savannah. She tried to explain that even without realizing it, they were all making small, subconscious adjustments to the world around them. Yawin didn't seem to understand, but tried to translate what he could.

The little ones took to it the most quickly, followed by Genia, but Hale and Yawin had a great deal of trouble. Yawin was always a source of patience and strength to the children and smiled off his staggered progress with humility. He urged Eowen to continue the lessons for his young charges, and they continued exchanging each other's language.

Soon, most of the mountain folk were making foods unfamiliar to Eowen and water that tasted differently than the water she created. Hers tasted full of plants and animals, like the jungle, while theirs was cold and tasted like minerals. Eowen smiled as she sipped, thinking of the great snowy peaks she'd been approaching and how the water there didn't run through rivers filled with life, but instead melted from snow and ran through barren troughs of stone. They introduced her to berries that were tiny, red, and bitter, but edible enough, which they enjoyed like it was a great treat. Eowen found the berries terrible and resolved to introduce them to the huge, sweet, and juicy fruits of the jungle.

Despite their progress, the mountain folk's creations always seemed lacking compared to Eowen's. Sometimes the berries seemed perfect on one side, but insubstantial and ghostlike on the other. Their water felt wet to the mouth and hands, but sometimes didn't quench one's thirst and seemed to lack weight in the stomach when swallowed. The mountain folk were too excited by their progress to notice, so Eowen continued to encourage them. After many hours of walking, they made a similar camp as before and slept.

****

[Listen, for you cannot hear me yet]

YOU ARE A RESULT.

****

The mountain folk's manifestations made great progress after their next waking, and eventually the group could even spread out as each person learned to produce their own atmospheres. Eowen was especially glad for this, as she was feeling stifled with them constantly huddling around her to survive. It was impossible to perfectly track time, but after what Yawin estimated to be about three days of walking, little Zerinley exclaimed and pointed. The others followed Zerinley, who ran to pick something up. When the rest of the party arrived, they found the little girl holding a strap that resembled leather.

They investigated further, and found that scattered around was evidence of a simple campsite. There were scraps of food, cloth, some ashes, water, plant-matter, and other unidentifiable items. The items seemed to be indisputable evidence that other people besides themselves had been there, and that those people were on the move as well. They cheered and jumped around, for the prospect of finding people, society, and answers was worth more than anything to them. The endless void and the quiet stars below seemed to stretch out forever, but they knew they'd find people out there somewhere.

Everyone was ecstatic and congratulated little Zerinley, but Eowen was silent as she spotted something among the discarded bits of creation. Underneath a poorly made piece of clothing was a shard of ivory no bigger than her thumb. It had been carved with a dull, crumbly stone she found next to it, so the resulting sculpture was rough at best. Even so, Eowen recognized an insignia bearing a resemblance to the giant baobab trees with a person standing beneath it.

"They were here," she breathed. *But which way did they go?*

Eowen rallied the group, explaining what she'd found as best she could in a combination of their language and hers, relying on Yawin to fill in the gaps. She insisted they try to track the direction her tribe had gone. The little children, Ne and Zerinley, took to it immediately like it was a game, and found discarded items heading in about the same direction that their little party had already been going. After a proper search around the campsite, the direction of travel seemed clear. Eowen was eager to go chasing after her people, but Yawin curbed her fervor.

"Look, we have already stopped to eat three times today." He gestured to his cloth with the charcoal marks on it. "I know how much this means to you, but we must be ready. If we search while tired, we will miss clues."

Behind him, Zerinley yawned, prompting Ne to, and before long it spread to Eowen through the entire group.

"Fine, you're right," conceded Eowen. The light she kept floating above her at all times bobbed when she nodded. "Let's make camp here."

They bedded down and Eowen dismissed the little light that floated above her.

****

[Listen, for you cannot hear me yet]

THERE ARE MANY THINGS LIKE YOU, THERE WILL BE MANY AFTER YOU, YOU ARE NOT ALONE, REMEMBER THAT TO BE LIKE IS NOT TO BE, AND SO TO FEEL ALONE IS NOT TO BE ALONE, AND TO LIVE IS THE BE BREATH IN OTHERS' LUNGS

****

"Good morning Eowen," Genia said in Eowen's language.

"Morning... There's no such thing as morning," Eowen muttered.

"What was that?" Genia asked.

"Nothing, good morning Genia," Eowen said in the mountain folk's language.

The rest awoke and they shared in a meal made by Genia that resembled the dried meat of a goat-like mountain creature. Eowen found it too salty, but the mountain folk chewed and sucked on it with relish.

They began their search again, and it only took a few kilometers before Eowen spotted their next bit of evidence. It was another campsite with more scraps around it, things that resembled clothes and tools, but they were so poorly made that they simply faded into nothing upon use, barely holding onto existence. Eowen gazed out at the vast expanse, worry eating away at her stomach as she imagined how her people were suffering without being able to create the way she could. The mountain folk were debating what direction they should go next when something caught Eowen's eye. She wasn't sure what it was, but there was something in the distance that she could only identify as different from the empty blackness around them.

Eowen looked down at the bright starfield beneath her, which faded outside of her aura of creation, and visualized where the flat surface they stood upon would extend to in the distance. That's when she realized that what she was looking at was another starfield softly lit up as if people were standing above it, just as the starfield was lit up beneath her and the mountain folk.

"I see someone!" she shouted to her party.

Ne immediately ran past her and she chased after him.

But as they approached the underlit group, Eowen thought that the forms in the distance might not be people at all. They were creatures for sure, shuffling along, huddled together, and covered with shifty black hides that might have been covered in fur, feathers, or shedding reptilian skin for all Eowen knew.

As they drew closer the creatures became clearer, which did nothing to reassure Eowen, for the things looked strange and unknown to her. Their faces were gray and unnaturally smooth, like stretched leather, and trunks emerged where mouths should have been which hung down to the stars below while gaping black holes took the place of eyes.

Ne had already slowed down and Eowen pulled him behind her, putting a hand out to halt the rest of her group as they arrived. They were about ten meters from the creatures, which had all turned to look at them. There were no less than thirty of them, a shifting crowd of unknown creatures. Eowen heard voices like bubbles from a tar pit, then very human hands emerged to point at her. The forms shuffled toward Eowen's group as Zerinley screamed.

Yawin took a stance next to Eowen while her mind rushed with panic. She'd never been responsible for anyone before, but she had become the mountain folk's guardian, and a dangerous part of herself that she hadn't known existed stirred. The ocean of her subconscious roiled as the threat of violence blanketed the world around her. The shadows around her cracked and jumped, eager to become whatever would destroy the monstrous things approaching.

"Stay back!" Yawin ordered in his language, which produced some confused shuffling from the beings, but did not stop them. Several at the forefront of the group approached with their hands, unnervingly human-like, raised up as if to grab them.

"Ioowun, izd aout ouu?" One of the things seemed to speak, but the sounds it made were garbled and leathery. Eowen's mind scrambled, realizing she may have to make some kind of attack. She didn't know what it would be, but the shadows around her implied fire, flood, and lightning.

The creature closest to her grasped its own face, seeming intent upon ripping it off. Eowen's heart rammed against her chest, her jaw was clenched, and power crackled around her. Many could have died there, such was her panic and such were the unknown depths of her power. But when that creature removed what had seemed to be its face, it was not a gaping maw or exposed innards, but someone familiar.

"Daddy?"

The danger evaporated. Eowen's father stood before her with tears in his eyes. His cheeks were puffed as though he were holding his breath, and he looked desperately joyful. They stared, taking each other in for a moment until her father gasped and pulled the mask Eowen had thought to be a face back over his head, heaving as he took breaths. Eowen bounded forward and tackled him to the ground.

"Eoowon!" His voice was less muffled up close.

"Dad, take this off!" She pulled at the mask, taking him by surprise.

"No! Eowen, I nee—d it to... breathe." His words trailed off, but here was her father—short and skinny like her, sweet and lined around the eyes with a lifetime of smiles. He was thinner, scruffier, and his lips were more chapped than normal, but he was alive and in her arms. Wide-eyed by being able to breathe, her father hesitated, then hugged his daughter while she planted kisses on his scruffy cheek.

"I love you! I missed you! I can't believe I found you!" Eowen hugged him tight till someone tapped on his shoulder.

"Di, can you breathe?"

"Yes, there's air! Take off your mask, everyone, take off your masks!" The one who'd asked took off her mask first, revealing an ancient woman with a pinched and severe face.

"Air! How is this possible?" the old woman said.

"Mein!" Eowen wrapped her arms around the old woman, their village priestess, who held the girl in frail arms.

"Where have you been, Eowen? How did you find us? Everyone! Everyone, take off your masks, there is air here."

Gradually the group did as Mein said, and Eowen could see that the dark mass of creatures was, in fact, members of her tribe, some from her own village but most from others. There was a murmuring among the crowd with an overwhelming amount of attention paid to Eowen. She couldn't begin to listen to what everyone was saying and asking, opting instead to bury her face in Mein's chest to be held and comforted. The people crowded in and Mein let go of Eowen to placate them. She sat Eowen down, seemed to notice the mountain folk for the first time, and glared at them. Eowen followed Mein's gaze after wiping some tears from her eyes.

"Oh, these are some friends of mine. I met them along the way and they helped me. Yawin, please come here, meet my father and Mein, she is the priestess of our village." Eowen placed her hands together as if in prayer and made gestures of ceremony, reverence and deference towards Mein. Yawin seemed to understand and made a small bow to Mein, clasping his hands as Eowen had done.

"Everyone sit, we'll rest here for now, get to food and water," Mein commanded the group, which was almost entirely unmasked now. "And you girl," she said, poking Eowen in the chest, "are going to tell me everything."

"Oh... Mein, there's a lot to tell," Eowen trailed off in thought, but her father put an arm around her shoulders and sat her down.

"Eowen, my little one." His tears fell openly, and Eowen leaned gratefully into her father while Mein conferred with Yawin in the mountain folk's language. Eowen tried to organize her chaotic thoughts and find the right questions to ask or information to offer. It was difficult though; her people whispered and glanced suspiciously at her, setting her on edge. She was also having trouble coming to grips with reality, since the people of her tribe felt more real than the mountain folk. It wasn't that the mountain folk had seemed fake to Eowen, it was that they were unfamiliar people who, for all she knew, had sprung into existence in this new world. Her father, Mein, and the rest of her tribe, on the other hand, were such irrefutable artifacts of the world before that their sudden presence in the new world felt terribly wrong and disorienting.

Eowen looked them over with nervous, shaking eyes full of tears that blurred the details, melding the mass of them, all in rough black rags, into a monstrous form. Mein was patient with Eowen and allowed Yawin to tell the story of their journey together, only occasionally interrupted by one of the mountain children. Mein interrupted him only to ask about things like their clothes and food and water, which prompted Yawin to gesture at Eowen. Mein would stare at Eowen with a hardness bordering on anger when he did, then insisted he continue.

Eowen avoided eye contact, and found herself instead staring at the starfield beneath her people. They were attempting to draw water and food from it, and having a great deal of difficulty. Several of them were clasping their hands as if in prayer, while others sat in front of those praying with their hands cupped, catching tiny drifts of water that burbled up.

Eowen moved to the water makers. "It's alright, I can do it," she said, and all eyes were suddenly on her.

The stars flared up gently, their faint light setting a spotlight upon Eowen that was brighter for her than for anyone else. All around them the material darkness writhed and knitted into the implication of shape. Her creation began and the mountain folk watched calmly, accustomed to it, while her people backed up. A collection of every human expression was present from abject terror to joyous wonder. Eowen's father watched on in disbelief, and Mein glared. From the darkness and the stars, a great stone basin, large enough for a grown man to bathe in, was brushed into existence as if by a giant calligrapher as the basin filled with crystal clear water and splashed about in waves of abundance.

Everyone had a different reaction as Eowen casually achieved what her tribe had been struggling to do since their first moments in the new world. They scuttled away as the basin spawned beneath their feet and forced them back amidst gasps.

Eowen returned to her senses and smiled victoriously, looking around for acknowledgment, yet she was only met with mutters and stares. Her smile fell and she averted her eyes.

"Oh, right, you must be hungry as well. I'm sorry." She fell out of reality and into her dreaming, where she forced great bay leaves to appear leaden with meats, breads, fruits, and porridge. When she'd done that she looked around shyly to see her people's reactions, which were still mixed, confused, nervous. And then she spotted Mein, who whispered something to Yawin as she glared openly.

"I-I'm sorry, I can do better!"

"No, Eowen." Her father reached out to her but she was already gone, deep in her dreaming amidst an unkind ocean of subconscious currents and winds. Her manifestations flowed out as beneath their feet spread a carpet of earth, grass, and ferns. The basin expanded into a pool, then a pond. People yelped as shoots weeded up between their toes and inflated into full trees that bore the marks of old growth.

"I can do better!"

Atmosphere, dense and textured with scents and sounds burst out of her in a shockwave that pushed the crowd back. Jungle and savannah folk shouted, Mein advanced on Eowen, her father tried to reach her, but she was deep in her dreaming. All the tension and power that had gathered when Eowen had believed she was under threat had not disappeared; it had hung around, waiting in the borders of her influence to become something. Things emerged into reality, creatures burst into life, fully grown, skittering, flapping, bounding, sick and severely disoriented at their sudden summoning. Eowen was deep in her dreaming, deeper than she'd ever gone, and no longer knew the way back.

****

[Listen, for you cannot hear me yet]

LOVE HAD MORE QUESTIONS THOUGH, QUESTIONS THAT THE SUN, MOON, CAVE, AND ALL

OF CREATION UPON THEIR HOME DID NOT HAVE THE ANSWERS TO, QUESTIONS OF BEYONDS THAT THEY COULD NEVER REACH.

****

The intense flow of creation might have remained only a very strange display at worst and an amazing one at best if, among the animals she created, Eowen had not accidentally generated the most dangerous one in the Vast Jungle. Within the shadows of the expanding foliage, a growl-hiss could be heard. A huge, confused monitor-bear appeared from the interplay of shadow and light. Eowen's people screamed, children were swept into arms, but Eowen herself was in a trance as the beast crashed through the foliage, even more terrified at its sudden birthing than the people around it.

"Eowen!" her father shouted, trying to reach his daughter as a palm seemed to fold out of thin air and threw him back.

"What is she doing?" Mein shouted at Yawin.

"I don't know! I've never seen this before. I do not think she is doing it on purpose!"

The monitor-bear thrashed, aware only of the maddening sounds that overloaded its new senses. Everyone ran, but one of its great paws connected with a woman, sending her flying into a tree.

"Stop her, now!" Mein screamed.

Eowen's father finally got around the palm and tried to tackle his daughter, but she was rooted in space, her power making her body stone-like in its incessant flow.

"Eowen, my little one, please come back to me!" Eowen blinked, the flow of creation abated slightly. The monitor-bear saw an opening in the chaotic foliage and skitter-galloped out into the void. "My Eowen, come back to me, you must stop!"

"Father?" Eowen's voice seemed to come from everywhere as the rush of her creations slowed more.

"Yes, my darling, come back."

Inside Eowen's mind she was drowning. The roiling storms of her subconscious had ripped her from the ship of her mind as wave upon wave of the chaos crushed her into the depths of herself. She might have been lost if anyone else had been the one attempting to call her back, but her father was not anyone. He was the source of love in her life, the gentle salve to all her hurts, and it was his voice in her ears.

"Father, I-I'm in a storm." Her eyes cleared some and she looked at him, still lost but looking to be found.

"I know my little Eowen, I know, but it's not real. We are, I am, come back to us."

Her father's voice was a lifeline, and she clung to it desperately. Soon, she could feel his arms, see his face, and the Storm within her faded away. The chaotic rush of her dreaming stopped, and Eowen slumped into his arms.

"I wanted to help," she whispered, barely conscious.

"I know, I know my sweet girl," her father crooned, his face a mask of love and suffering. Beyond the border of her atmosphere, which had expanded massively, the monitor-bear writhed in agony, snapping its jaws about. It died without air, just as so many people had upon entering the new world, unable to save themselves. The myriad of other creatures Eowen'd created had also fled from the sudden patch of newly minted jungle, seeking out the comforting darkness beyond, and dying there. Amidst her people, who cried in fear, pain, or both, was a brand new oasis of jungle, surrounded by a ring of dead animals. Her mind hazy, Eowen surveyed the scene before she passed out.

******

[Listen, for you cannot hear me yet]

**SO THE CAVE SOUGHT OUT ONE THEY KNEW WHO MIGHT ANSWER THOSE QUESTIONS,
ONE OLDER, STRONGER, AND MORE FAR-SEEING THAN POWERS SUCH AS CREATION COULD ACCOUNT FOR.**

******

Eowen awoke. "Daddy?"

"Yes my girl."

"It's really you." Eowen reached out for his hand, but he flinched back.

"I... I'm sorry. Did I do something wrong?" Her voice shook. It was dark where they were and she could not see his face.

His mouth opened and closed while his eyes darted everywhere but at his daughter. They were in a small shelter made from sticks and massive leaves, foraged from the jungle Eowen had made.

"Father, please talk to me." His uncertainty settled and he took his daughter's hand.

"Yes, I'm really here, and so are you."

"I missed you Dad, I really thought I'd never see you

again. I believed it, but I had to try and find you!" Her voice cracked.

"You did very good to find us my little one... Eowen, we need to talk about something." He measured his words out, trying to effect a calming and neutral tone. "You remember what you did when you found us, don't you?"

"I think so... I saw you and Mein, I took your mask off, and then..." Eowen's brows furrowed as she tried to remember. "People were trying to make water but couldn't, so I made water and food."

"Yes, that's right."

"It was good, right? I did it right, didn't I?"

"Y-you did..."

"Oh, thank goodness, that's good."

"But, Eowen."

"Yes?"

"You did more than just that." His tone was strained with fear.

"Oh." Gooseflesh ran up her arms. "What did I do?"

"Well, all this." Di gestured the other direction at the patch of jungle, but it was too dark to see very clearly.

"I don't see—one moment." Eowen sat up and created a floating light, much larger than any she'd made in the past. "Oh. Oh!"

The massive patch of jungle was rendered starkly in all its floral colors, textured by deep shadows from which members of Eowen's tribe had been watching them. In the sudden presence of the light they skittered away out of sight. She and her father were camped a few meters from the edge of the biome.

"So... I did all that?"

"Yes, I think. And more." Di pointed away from the

jungle, out towards the void beyond where Eowen's light revealed the ring of dead creatures. Birds, rodents, reptiles, and more had fled into the void upon their creation only to die an airless death.

"I made those?" Eowen got up to run toward the creatures but her father stopped her.

"Yes, you did, but there is something important we need to talk about right now."

"Father, I made all this!"

"Yes, I know, Eowen—"

"I made things that are alive!" Eowen didn't know how exactly she felt about it, all she knew was that it felt significant beyond anything she'd considered before—

"You hurt someone!"

Eowen could count on one hand the number of times her father had raised his voice at her. It was more than enough to get her full attention.

"What?" Her voice shook and her hands felt clammy.

"Sit down." She obeyed. "When you did all that—" he gestured uncertainly at the jungle, "—you pushed people back. They were hit by things, the trees and roots. People are bruised and have cuts."

"T-that's... but it's also good? There's air in there and water?"

"Yes, but—"

"So even though I didn't do it perfectly I still did good?"

"You made a monitor-bear!"

Eowen started, her eyes went wide and she whipped around to look at the ring of dead creatures again. There it was, about a dozen meters away, the massive slumped corpse of the monitor-bear.

"I really did, didn't I?"

"It almost killed someone."

"What?" It was too much. Eowen was on the verge of panic, her breaths coming and going too fast.

"Shh, shh, calm down my little one, breathe slowly. They are... healing."

"They a-are?"

"Yes."

"Who was it?"

"Amuul, from past the southern river. Eowen, I need you to listen to me very carefully now."

"Ok. Ok." Her breath was coming fast and nervous. "I'm listening. Everything's going to be alright, isn't it?"

Di didn't answer the question, but the gap of silence he left seemed to. Eowen waited, hoping he'd do what he always did, say something comforting, hug her, tell her it'd be alright, and assure her that next time would be different. When he finally broke the silence, he did none of those things.

"Eowen, Priestess Mein has questions for you. I'm going to go get her and you're going to answer whatever she asks truthfully. You're going to do this, my girl."

"Dad?"

"You will answer her with honesty, understood? No matter what she asks. I convinced her to let you rest."

"I don't understand!" Eowen was on the verge of tears, but her father grasped her by the shoulders and shook her, and the look in his eyes terrified her. It was wilder, more desperate, and more pained than anything she'd ever seen from him.

"She is considering exile! You disappeared, we were left to die and scrape life from this," he swung an arm to encompass everything, "and you returned well fed, clothed, and with outsiders!" Her father spat the word. "And when you returned you almost killed us all, I-I... I don't know what to do!"

Eowen had retreated into a ball, frightened. Her father had never had an outburst like that.

"I'm sorry, I don't know anything, I don't know what happened!"

"I can't hear this. Priestess Mein will come, you'll tell her everything, you understand? She'll know what to do, she's wise and fair. You must tell the truth though. Do you understand?"

"But I don't know anything!"

"Don't lie to me!"

Everything in Eowen stopped, her thoughts the roil of her emotions. She felt that her heart might have stopped, too. Di had never spoken to her this way, not once in her life, but now his eyes blazed in the light above her, all fear and pain. Eowen nodded, her lips pressed tightly together. Di sighed.

"I'm going to bring Mein." He turned his back on his daughter and shuffled off into the trees, trailing scraps of the black rags all her people now wore. Eowen rested her head in her hands and resisted the urge to daydream where unkind reality and unknown fantasies could exchange values. She could not know what sort of thing might emerge if she allowed her mind to run wild. She didn't trust herself to create anything that wasn't simple and familiar, things like air, food, water, clothes. Eowen got an idea, the image of her tribe's horrible rags in her mind. She could earn their trust with something as simple as that, just clothing.

"I can do that..." She drew up an image of her mother and father's clothes from the world before. Di wore green with yellow zig-zags, embroidered with the patterns of Usowu, their patron deity of the arts. Her mother, Monda, had worn purple with no patterns, the simple garb for those acknowledged to have a talent for guiding others to their destined paths. Monda had earned the distinguished purple after she'd taken in Tavo, for it was after adopting him that he'd displayed talents befitting the next ranger. It was her greatest shame that Tavo had abandoned his people, though Monda had refused to give up her color. Eowen had never fully grasped the social and political implications of her mother achieving such a status, only to be under threat of it being taken away. All Eowen knew was that each year that passed without Eowen making something of herself further threatened all that her mother had achieved. After years of failures Eowen had come to the conclusion that she could never properly serve her people or honor her mother, till she learned that Tavo was still alive. It was the only hope she'd had. But now in this new world where she could create that which others could not, she felt a new opportunity on the rise.

If I can keep from doing something like that again... She glanced at the jungle and the ring of dead creatures.

Eowen's hands shook as she attempted to capture the mindset necessary to make clothing for her mother and father. The images of what they should look and feel like drifted off into the depths of her mind, and the girl followed after them.

I want to make you proud, Mom. Maybe I can redeem you, and myself, in this world.

The shadows about her thickened into the shapes, as though the clothes were hanging out to dry, and the lights were almost like hands. Gently, carefully, fearfully, Eowen put a mental harness on her intent, an almost painful vice upon her mind as she delved into the act of creation. The result was a pinprick-like focus that was nearly guaranteed to create manifestations without any random or unintended side effects at all, but the strain it put on her felt wrong. Her mind ached to daydream, its natural currents of unbidden thought pulling her in every direction. The shadows and light of implicit possibility danced frantically around her, desperate to become more than she was allowing, yet her control did not falter. While possibilities strained against the walls of her discipline, begging to become, the clothing emerged, folded gently in front of her in two perfect piles. Eowen gradually, carefully, returned to herself, denying her other dreamings the right to follow into reality. She couldn't know how successful she'd been until she was back in her conscious mind, but to Eowen it felt successful, it felt like—

Mein slapped Eowen across the face, her hand bursting through the separation between reality and implication and destroying all of Eowen's careful control. "You stupid, foolish girl!"

The piled shadows around Eowen suddenly emerged into creation as a shockwave of wind, music, ferns, leather, a lizard, and a myriad of other creations welled up around her as if from a spring. Eowen reeled, so disoriented that her vision blurred, her control and intent faded to wisps of thought and then to nothing. "What's going on?"

"You did it again! Thank the gods I stopped you, look at the chaos you've sown!" Mein was shaking Eowen, she grasped the girl by the back of the neck and forced her to look at the creations around her. More dirt, more jungle, bits of what might have been a house, her frightened father, and a curious lizard, regarded her, waiting to see what happened next.

"I-I was just trying to, um—" Eowen couldn't quite remember what she'd been doing, she was too bewildered from being shaken out of the state of mind for her creations so roughly.

"You could have killed us, you stupid girl! If I had not stepped in there is no telling what might have happened."

"No! I—" Eowen closed her mouth and she looked down, burning in shame. Her attempt to help before had almost killed someone and injured several others. Her eyes fell on the clothes and Eowen looked at her father, pleading with her eyes while on the verge of tears. She lifted the folded outfits toward her father. "I was just trying to make clothes for you and mom."

Mein backed up as if struck, her eyes wide. The entire world seemed to shift with the priestess as she directed her anger on Di. "You haven't told her?" Di knelt down in front of Eowen as the girl looked between the old priestess and her father, seeking answers.

"Told me... what?" Eowen whimpered. Her father would not meet her eyes but he touched the neatly folded outfits, so much finer than any they could have made in the previous world. Yet they were undeniably, even perfectly, made for him and his wife. He lifted the purple outfit and twisted it in his shaking hands. "See, they're like yours and Mom's old ones. I made them for you."

Di began to cry. Eowen reached out to touch his shoulder and the rags he wore broke apart in her hand.

"Dad, put them on, your clothes are falling apart. See, this one's for you and those are for mom."

Di embraced his daughter, shaking silently with sobs. Eowen looked to Mein for answers over his shoulder. The old priestess glared at Di, but after a moment her expression softened and she faced Eowen.

"We'll talk later, girl." The priestess turned to leave revealing Yawin, who'd been standing some meters away watching the events unfold, his expression a twisted mixture of empathy, anguish and uncertainty. "I'll be waiting, Di. You will present her to me as soon as you're done." Di choked on a sob in response, he squeezed Eowen tighter.

"Done with what? Mein, Yawin?" The old mountain man opened his mouth to speak, but Mein cut him off with a gesture. "Daddy?"

Her father pulled back and tried to speak between sobs. "E-eowen, my girl, y-your mother..."

"Oh!" Eowen's eyes shot wide open. She knew many had died, she knew that upon finding her people most would probably be dead, but somehow the idea that her family would be among them hadn't seemed possible. Upon finding her father alive, she'd just assumed. For Eowen, associating her mother with the dead was too difficult a gap to bridge without evidence. Her mother was less of a person to her as a construct, a part of the world, more consistent than the sun and moon, more unshakable than the earth beneath her. Eowen couldn't properly feel that her mother would die, because that would mean she didn't exist anymore, and that was as impossible as the sky falling. Di was saying something to her, but none of it registered.

"Oh?" Eowen muttered, her mind still struggling with this new reality. Memories of the sky as it fell played out at the forefront of her mind. The clouds getting wiped away, the mountains being swallowed up, the trees disappearing behind the curtain of some great magic trick, but still no image of her dead mother.

Di pulled his daughter to a standing position and held her arm as he guided her out past the patch of jungle. They walked till they passed through a large camp filled with discarded things. Some of her people still milled about with the terrifying masks on, more comfortable with getting their air from the starfield below through the trunks than by the oasis's atmosphere. The hollow eyes followed Eowen and her father, her yellow outfit like a beacon in the black expanse. A hundred paces or so past the camp, Eowen could see the bodies, lined up and laid out in rigor mortis rows. Some lay neatly, arranged before the stiffness of death could freeze them into the shapes of agony that their last moments had been. Others were not. There were hundreds, and as they passed through new additions were being brought in, the grim work shared by all across the new world.

She knew they'd reached her when her father stopped, stiffened, and looked away. There she was, Monda of the jungle and savannah tribes, wife of Di, mother to Eowen and adopted mother to her nephew Tavo, deceased. Eowen left her father where he was, a few paces away, and knelt beside the body of her mother. She took in the wrinkles of Mondas face, and even in death, Eowen felt she was being looked upon with discontent. Her father had tried to arrange her features peacefully, but Monda had not been a woman of peace, and a lifetime of glaring had left her with such an expression.

Eowen set the folded, purple clothes on her mother's naked chest. Di felt it was his responsibility to tell Eowen what had happened, how he'd been next to her mother when the sky had come down and had passed out, barely able to make air for himself. She knew though; everyone knew what had happened after the fall. Di had awoken to find his wife dead. He'd screamed, wept, bargained and cursed. He hadn't been the only one. It was a shared rite of passage, the price of survival that all had paid for making it into the new world. Save for those like Eowen, who had been alone. But now it was her turn.

Di mustered his courage, looked upon his wife, and choked down a sob. He knelt beside Eowen and took her hand. "She was worried about you," he whispered, but Eowen felt it was a lie.

"I know," she said.

"She hoped you would come back."

That made Eowen's jaw clench. "I know."

"She loved you."

Eowen didn't respond to that.

Did she love me? Did she really? Her mother had cared for her, raised her, tried to find something useful that Eowen could do with her life, but Eowen wasn't sure her mother had ever loved her. Her mother had been powerful, intractable. To Eowen, she'd been like the mountains or the sea or the earth itself, but the sea didn't love, the mountains didn't hope, and the earth didn't miss you. They were just there, fixtures, or at least they had been.

"You... you can cry," Di said, uncomfortable with his daughter's stoicism. He didn't know quite how to respond to this stony silence emanating from her, and the cold way she was analyzing his wife's corpse, which he could barely stand to look upon, unnerved him. "Eowen... You can—"

"I know," she cut him off, and turned to embrace him so he wouldn't see her face. Something felt stuck in her chest, some painfully twisted lump of emotions too tightly tangled to be understood. Her father didn't understand, Eowen didn't understand, all she knew was that there were clear feelings of grief she was supposed to be going through but could not. Her father was waiting for something from her, and she didn't want to lie to him. "I... already cried a lot. I assumed the worst might have happened."

It wasn't totally a lie, but it certainly wasn't truthful. Her thoughts were all of her mother, but none of them charitable.

I guess I'm actually a lot like you, mom. I've never seen you cry, and see? No tears.

Her father still seemed to be waiting for something from her, so she tried to say something, anything.

"I was so relieved to find you, Dad!" That at least was true. She hugged him tighter and pushed down her tangled knot of pained emotion. "I was so scared, but we'll be ok now, won't we?"

"Of course we will my girl," Di lied. "Of course we will." They returned to their little campsite, and Eowen was allowed to sleep once more before Mein would see her.

****

[Listen, for you cannot hear me yet]

THAT ONE THEY SOUGHT WAS ME, A GIANT.

****

"Be up, Eowen." The priestess's voice cut into Eowen's dreams.

"Hmm? Oh. Hello priestess Mein."

"Quiet, girl. You're coming with me, now." Despite her

age, Mein was much stronger than she looked, and she hauled the Eowen to her feet by one arm.

"Priestess, my father—"

"Shh!" Mein pulled Eowen till they were out of earshot. "I allowed you to rest and see your mother. This was a privilege, girl, but now we must address what to do with you." She looked Eowen up and down, seeming to appraise her like a tree that might fall on a house. "What to do with you indeed." Mein marched off again with Eowen in tow. Eowen panicked. She didn't want to be alone with Mein, and she dragged her feet.

"Priestess Mein, wait, what about my father? Shouldn't he come with us?" Mein glared at the girl in the withering way that had inspired her predecessor to take her in as an apprentice in the first place.

"Don't worry, girl. I'll make sure your father knows his daughter hasn't abandoned him a second time."

This cowed Eowen. She flushed, shamed, and followed along dutifully with her eyes on Mein's ankles. They circled the oasis in the opposite direction of the makeshift cemetery. Eowen glanced at the oasis and noticed that its diameter seemed larger than before.

"Um. Priestess Mein."

"What?"

"Is the oasis... larger?"

"Yes."

"Oh. I didn't know that would happen," Eowen trailed off, gazing at her creation in wonder.

Mein scanned the trees as though looking for something lurking within it. The old woman kept her expression in check, but her spirit felt weak, stretched thin. Mein didn't know what to do with the girl. She didn't know what the rules in this new place were or what might indicate danger. The only thing as mysterious as why the world had become what it was now was why Eowen, a girl there'd been little reason to pay attention to, could now do the things she did. Some of her people were watching from the trees, and Mein knew they were desperate for her guidance. For their sakes, she would not allow herself to seem uncertain about anything. She would be strong, harsh if need be, but she would be a fixed point for her people to revolve around. Thus far the priestess had managed this, till Eowen had shown up. Mein glanced at the girl but Eowen didn't notice, still staring at the oasis, analyzing it.

They arrived at Mein's personal camp, and waiting for them was Yawin. Seeing the old man, Eowen broke into a smile and ran forward.

"Yawin!" He opened his arms to receive her but Mein's voice cut in.

"Ahem!" Eowen stopped just short of Yawin and turned. "Eowen," Mein said, glancing at Yawin, then at the oasis. "I believe it would be best not to show such favoritism to outsiders when your position with your own people is still... undecided." The word outsiders wasn't so much spat as chewed and dropped. Yawin looked unsettled and angry for a moment, but took a calming breath and bowed respectfully.

"Oh, of course," Eowen responded, glancing between them. She made a gesture of respect to Mein, then bowed to Yawin, waited for the two of them to sit, then took a seat next to Mein. The old priestess straightened her back, cleared her throat, and with a small hand gesture and a shift of body language erected an atmosphere of ceremony around them. It didn't matter that they lacked the holy sites of the old world or the traditional vestments of their religion. Mein carried authority in her bones.

"Eowen, daughter of Di and... Monda, now deceased. Our people face an unprecedented emergency. Many lives have been lost and none have been spared from tragedy. We who are left have managed to learn the ways of this new world and survive. We will continue to do so no matter what. It has been hard and it will continue to be, but we shall join our efforts and prevail through this trial."

Mein's words enveloped the space, and her casual exclusion of the rest of the world from the conversation came out so naturally that even Yawin forgot his people existed for a moment. Her suggestion that understanding how to progress through the unknowns of the world was merely a 'trial' inspired a confidence, despite there being no clear direction forward.

"In this new world, there is nothing more important than securing the safety and wellbeing of what few of our people remain." Eowen and Yawin found themselves nodding. "Aside from that, there is also nothing of greater importance than ensuring we are safe from any potential... threats."

Eowen and Yawin had been so caught up in Mein's flow that it took them a moment to notice the way Mein leveled her gaze at Eowen. When she did realize, Eowen's eyebrows shot up, and she raised her hands placatingly to stammer out a defense for herself.

"P-priestess Mein, I, uh—" Mein cut her off with a withering look. Yawin tried to step in to defend Eowen.

"Most honorable priestess—"

"You, outsider, and your charges are tolerated only for returning one of our own to us. Your presence at this meeting is only because your fate is now tied to hers, and your input is not welcomed!"

Mein closed her eyes and pressed her forehead to her clasped hands, trying to settle her temper. She had to maintain control. She could not let the outsiders or Eowen get any foothold or there was no telling what might happen. She didn't know if Eowen's wild creations and the danger they posed were localized only to the girl, or if others might develop similar traits, or if it was somehow all the mountain folk's fault. In a way it didn't matter to her; ensuring no possible threat could grow in her community was her top priority. Mein opened her eyes and upon looking at Eowen her expression softened, just a bit. The girl was shaking and seemed on the verge of crying.

Inside Eowen's mind was a world of fears and worry. She, of course, barely understood why or how the things that happened around her did, and her father's fear that Mein might exile her had grown to a certainty that she would. She balled her clothes up into her fists and twisted them about, feeling more helpless and weak than ever in her life. Being under Mein's harsh attention even rivaled the terror of her near-death experience upon entering the new world.

Mein composed herself, reminded herself that nothing was decided yet, and reached out to hold Eowen's hands. The girl met the priestess's eyes and the desperation in them melted Mein's coldness for just a moment.

"Girl... Eowen, my dear. I know you meant well, you are a sweet child. Sweet, and foolish." Eowen smiled and nodded, tears in her eyes, drinking up whatever encouragement she could get. Yawin watched on, disturbed but unsure of what to do, for he could not tell if how Mein was acting was cruelly manipulative and demeaning or merely a cultural quirk he was unfamiliar with. "If only you knew how to act on your own, but you need guidance don't you?"

"Yes, priestess!"

"Yes indeed, my girl. Follow my lead, do as I say, and we may yet find a place for you in this new world without risking calamity." She pulled Eowen in for a hug and kissed her head.

Yawin averted his eyes. It pained him to see the young girl spoken to in such a way only to accept it. Cultural gap or not, Eowen had saved him and the children. She'd done miraculous things. Whatever threat she represented, he was convinced it was lesser than the value she held, both in her abilities and the kindness with which she used them. When Mein released Eowen from her embrace the girl was smiling weakly, crying openly, though her eyes still darted around in fear.

"Thank you Mein. Then your decision is to let me stay?"

"That decision is not yet made, and it cannot be made only by me. We are gathering our people from the other villages. There are... so few of us now that we cannot live apart. We must band together to survive. Worry not, no one has ever been banished without a formal tribunal, and your fate will not be decided until such a time either. We will assemble a council first" Mein looked away in thought and her expression fell. "From whoever's still alive," she whispered. "For now, stay with your father, do no more creation, and speak to no one, am I understood?"

"Yes, Priestess Mein." Eowen hung on the old woman's words as though they were keeping her from drowning. Then Mein drew her posture up formally, regathering her ceremonial air.

"I must ask you an important question. Why were you not with your parents when the sky was brought down?"

Eowen sucked in a breath that she held onto. *I can't tell her I was looking for Tavo, that would be the worst thing I could say!* Eowen hadn't fully considered how foolish the quest for her cousin would have seemed until that moment. She was terrible at lying, but she thought that maybe there was a way to tell part of the truth.

"I was... returning from the village to the northwest of ours, the river-cross village with the big bridge."

"Yes, I know it, why were you returning from there?"

"It was because of my apprenticeship there." Eowen looked down to hide the blush of shame in her cheeks. "I'd been sent by my..." Eowen swallowed down the lump in her throat. "Mother. To, um, apprentice under the bridge-maker there, Elloui."

"Yes, I remember that now. You said you were returning from it?" Mein was eyeing Eowen carefully.

"Yes, priestess."

"It did not go well then." Mein's statement was flat as can be, no question within it at all. "And you got lost on the way back?"

"Yes, priestess."

"So far lost that you ran into the mountain folk?" Mein frowned in a skeptical way.

"I, uh, do you recall that the year before I was released from my apprenticeship to cartographer Doro from the east of our village?"

Mein's expression dipped into aching nostalgia. "Yes, I remember that. You'd no sense of direction at all, no hand for detail."

"That's right. And also, as you said, the mountain folk

returned me to our people. They were the ones that found me, not the other way around." Eowen kept her head low to show shame, but was secretly relieved Mein hadn't pressed her further. If it was known that she'd tried to run away, even if her intentions for doing so had been good, it would absolutely condemn her.

"You understand why I had to ask this, don't you girl? You survived this catastrophe on your own before these outsiders found you." Mein gestured her acknowledgement at Yawin. "But your mother perished. You could have been there, you could have saved her if you'd been there. Isn't that right?" Eowen burned with shame, her lips shook.

"P-priestess, I-I, even if I had been there, I don't know if—"

"Honorable Priestess!" Yawin's voice cut in. Mein's look said for him to shut up, but he met her gaze levelly. "Eowen saved our lives with food and water. When we find—found her she did not breathe. Only a little. We, Eowen and us, saved each other. Do you understand?"

Mein looked between Yawin and Eowen, who seemed to be having trouble breathing at that very moment, and nodded. "Thank you for your clarification, Yawin, I believe I have a good understanding of what happened. But you'll not speak out of turn again in my presence, understood?"

Yawin nodded as Mein turned away, content for now that he'd been able to defend the girl.

"Eowen," Mein said. "Our people need guidance more than anything else, and they need me to guide them. So I'll not repeat myself again. You need only obey and all will be well." Mein dismissed them both with a gesture, and that was the end of it.

Yawin made his way back to his people while Eowen shuffled off back to her father in the opposite direction.

Yawin's desire to protect the girl was in a tug of war with his reluctance to interfere with a culture that wasn't his. He owed a life-debt, though how he could repay it was uncertain. He looked back many times, but Eowen did not. She kept her eyes down and her hands clasped.

When they'd gone far enough, Mein sighed, finally out of sight and earshot, and allowed her posture to slump. She'd never been so exhausted in her life, but her worries were still far from over. As she watched the retreating form of Eowen the shadows seemed to twist around the girl as though they were alive, large and lurking, watching and waiting. The lights below her shined bright, eager to reach up. Mein shivered. She felt this new world was too eager to respond to Eowen, and from what she'd seen the girl had no control over what might emerge. She shook her head, and for perhaps the first time in her life truly did not know what to do.

Eowen described Mein's decision to her father and he sighed with relief. "You see my girl? She is fair and just. We must only wait until a council is gathered, and by then you will have proven that you are no longer... that there will be no harm in remaining among us. You must simply do as she says."

"Yes, of course, Father... only, she didn't actually say what I should do."

Yawin frowned. "What do you mean? Did she not give you any instruction at all?"

"Well, she said to remain with you—"

"Of course, very sensible."

"to not do any more creation—"

Eowen's father nodded at this gravely.

"and to, um, not speak to anyone?" Her voice trailed off. Mein's orders felt less sensible coming from her own mouth, but her father's expression said that what he'd heard was sage advice. "But... then how... if I don't go anywhere—"

"Yes?"

"do anything or talk to anyone, how am I supposed to prove my worth to stay?" Di shook his head and put his hands on Eowen's shoulders.

"My child, that is how you prove your worth. You shall show that you can... not make things worse." Di tried to smile kindly at his daughter but it was painfully forced.

"But Dad, I can do so much good! I-I helped the mountain folk—"

"Keep your voice down!" Di looked around nervously, but the other members of their tribe were still keeping their distance, likely on Mein's orders. "Listen to me very closely my child; you must not speak of the mountain folk anymore. You have done enough harm to your reputation by bringing them here."

Eowen opened her mouth to ask what her father meant when the pieces fit together in her mind. She had only been thinking how she had helped the mountain folk, and how it was evidence that she could help her people, but to the rest of the tribe that very aid was evidence that she couldn't be trusted. Yawin and his people were tolerated for bringing Eowen back, and by that story they had objectively done a service to the people of the jungle and savannah. However, the narrative of Eowen bringing the mountain folk, outsiders, to her tribe had the exact opposite connotation. To those secluded from the world behind mountains and ocean, the outside world was filled with people that were dangerous and corrupt. In truth, outsiders were barely considered human by her tribe, regarded almost as other species. It had never occurred to Eowen until that moment that, in her language, the word for outsider could be literally translated as 'not-human.' Inviting outsiders into their midst wasn't just unacceptable; she had practically betrayed her people by doing so.

Amidst all these realizations was an overarching one that tied the rest together in Eowen's mind. Mein, by ordering her to avoid the mountain folk, was protecting her. The narrative that the mountain folk had saved her was a good one, but the narrative that she had saved them, not-humans, over her own people, would forever destroy their perception of her. It didn't help that she had accidentally hurt her people with her creations upon returning. Eowen understood now; to have any chance at a life with her people again, she had to do as Mein ordered.

"I'm glad you understand my child," Di said, gently putting a hand to his daughter's face.

"I do. I'm sorry, Father."

"It is alright my child, we are together and we are alive." Di's voice cracked at that word. "We must be thankful for what we have."

There was little to do in the new world, and Eowen slept often to pass the time, for what better way was there to stay out of trouble than to not even be awake.

****

[Listen, for you cannot hear me yet]

VERY FAR AWAY, ONE MIGHT SAY AS FAR AS FAR CAN BE, I WAS CALLED UPON BY NAME AS I DRIFTED BETWEEN THE GRAVEYARD OF UNFINISHED TOWERS.

****

Eowen was whispering something upon waking in a voice that reached far and wide.

"What was that?" Di was on edge. Everything his daughter said and did made him nervous. Eowen rubbed the sleep from her eyes and tried to recall what she'd just said, but the words faded along with her dreams.

"I don't remember..." Eowen opened her eyes and saw how her father was looking at her, which is to say he wasn't. Where he did look was at the space around her as though a crowd were standing behind Eowen expectantly. Eowen turned around but there was nothing there, just the flow of shadow and light that accompanied her. The strange aura of potential around Eowen was calm, latent.

What does he think I'm going to do? Eowen thought, but it occurred to her that even she didn't know for sure. She was pleased to see that her father was wearing the clothes she'd made for him, which brightened her mood. "Here Dad, let me make us something to eat."

"No!" Di grasped his daughter by the shoulders. "No, don't do anything! Do you not remember what Mein said?" Eowen was frozen in shock but recovered when her father brought up Mein.

"Right, she said no creation. How will we eat though?"

"Someone will bring us food, a few of us have learned to make things like y—" Her father cleared his throat. "To make things we need."

Eowen sat back, disappointed, as an awkward silence grew between them. Soon enough, a young woman did arrive with food, but it was nowhere near as good of fare as what Eowen could make. Bread that either fell apart or was too hard, a bowl of stale water, and something hard to identify that resembled dried meat. Di thanked the woman, who seemed to look everywhere but at Eowen. The woman left with a bow. The meal was bland, unsatisfying, and seemed barely enough to live off of. Eowen knew she could have done so much better, but she had to resist the temptation.

"I suppose that's just the way things are now," she muttered.

"Yes, but we're together and we're alive. That's all that matters, right?" Di smiled at his daughter and Eowen forced a smile back.

"Right."

After eating, Di went to visit his wife's body, but Eowen stayed behind. He returned and slept for many hours, and while he slept Eowen watched her people in the distance. They scurried about, felling the trees of her ever-expanding oasis and setting up huts like that of the old world. Eowen began pacing. Time was hard to track without night and day, so people slept when tired, ate when hungry, and worked either to exhaustion or without motivation at all. Eowen could see Mein at times as she tried to supervise everything, organize everyone. The hunters and other elders of the old world were delegating as well.

After a day and a half's worth of time she arrived at Eowen and Di's small camp along with several men bearing building materials.

"Priestess Mein, welcome," Di greeted her, elbowing his daughter to do the same.

"Yes, welcome honorable priestess."

Mein waved away the greeting and pulled Eowen aside while her father helped the men erect a hut for them to live in. The old priestess and the girl stood awkwardly next to each other, pretending to watch the operations with great interest. Mein did so very successfully, a long career of interpreting divine knowledge serving her with the ability to seem authoritative in any context by expression alone. Eowen's professional life, on the other hand, had consisted of rarely knowing what was going on at all, and her expression said as much. Yet also in her eye was a faraway look as daydreams of how she could create such huts without cutting down trees, without tools, played out. In the theater of her mind, huts of the old world became archaic as structures of grandness and immensity hitherto unknown seemed possible. The day and a half without creating anything was making her itch to do so. She closed her eyes, and when she opened them again they were clouded over with dreaming, and the power of potential creation which had gathered around her began to move in active shadow and light.

"Girl!" Mein's sharp voice cut into her wandering subconscious.

"Yes!" Eowen responded a little too loud, drawing the attention of the workers. She turned away in embarrassment but Mein took her hand, patting it comfortingly.

"I've kept an eye on you from a distance, my girl. You've been doing as instructed. That's good. You're doing well."

Eowen shrugged. "I'm just staying at camp... Sleeping... I haven't talked to anyone except my dad."

And hardly to him at all.

"Exactly, keep it up." Mein smiled, nodded her approval. "Just keep that... drifting off in check, yeah?" Mein whispered.

"Of course Priestess," Eowen whispered back.

The men finished the hut within an hour, breaking for food brought from the oasis. Mein and Eowen ate together, and Eowen noted how all the food was of a similar faded quality except the fruit, which was delicious.

"I didn't know anyone had figured out how to make fruit like this, it's wonderful!" Eowen said, and continued eating. It took her a moment to notice that the workers had gone quiet and were staring at their own half-eaten fruits. Some were looking at the oasis, and Eowen followed their gaze.

Oh, this fruit is from the trees I created.

"A thankfully harmless thing," Mein interjected. "We'll soon have our own method of reproducing these." She took a big bite of melon, and the workers looked relieved and followed suit.

Eowen felt for the first time more than thankfulness that Mein was giving her a chance, but respect for the weight of her responsibility. Everyone was looking to her for answers and assurances, and she was doing her best to provide that all the time. In the midst of such unprecedented chaos and tragedy, the old priestess had kept her people alive, together, and purposeful so as not to fall into despair. Eowen gave the old woman a small nod, and Mein responded with a shrug. With this alone Eowen felt that things were improving for her. She couldn't help a small smile that she hid with a sip from her water bowl.

The workers left, and aside from meal deliveries, the next two days worth of time passed without any visitors to Eowen and her father's hut. Di tried to fill the time with his daughter by talking about the past, but there were precious few memories to revisit that didn't involve tears, for they all included Eowen's mother. Eventually, Di moved into a pattern of visiting his wife's body, sleeping, eating, and repeating.

Eowen, in secret, created his old carving tools to the best of her ability and left them for him to find upon waking while she was pretending to be asleep. Di picked them up gingerly, then gripped them till his knuckles stuck out rigidly. He left the hut, to where Eowen did not know, and came back with wood from the oasis to carve. He did not thank her for them or acknowledge that she had made them at all. When Eowen asked how he liked the tools, her father only put them down and silently walked away. They never spoke on the matter again, and from then on Di never let his daughter see him carving. His hands itched for the peace his craft brought, but he couldn't let Eowen feel it was alright for her to be creating things, else Mein would find out and she'd surely be banished.

Eowen was feeling ever more restless though, and to be unable to even escape into daydreams for fear of what she might create, the tension in her dreaming aura of shadows and light grew. By the third day after the construction of their hut, Eowen had had enough of waiting around with nothing to do.

****

[Listen, for you cannot hear me yet]

IT IS UNUSUAL TO HEAR MY NAME CALLED, FOR I HAVE A GREAT NAME THAT MEANS YAWNING AND FIRE THAT IS ONLY RED AND HAIR TIPS THAT CAN FEEL AND THE SHIFT OF A FOOT UPON SAND UPON

STONE AND PERFECT FINGERNAILS AND BELLS THAT CANNOT BREAK AND A FEELING FOR WHICH THERE ARE NO WORDS TO DESCRIBE, BUT IT IS SIMILAR TO THE FEELING OF SINGING SO BEAUTIFULLY THAT YOUR HEARTLESS FATHER, FOR WHOM YOU HAVE NO LOVE, WEEPS AND IS NEVER HEARTLESS AGAIN.

****

"I'll see you later, Eowen," Di said as he left the hut to visit his wife. Eowen sat up and watched him go from the window of their hut. They'd made camp almost fifty meters from the oasis originally, but now it was almost at their hut. Soon they'd be inside the patch of jungle, and presumably it would keep spreading after that.

I wonder if it will keep going forever and make the whole world a jungle.

Eowen sat back down in her hut and prepared for when her father would return. She had not created anything intentionally since the tools and the prospect of it made her nervous, mostly because her fate was certain if Mein found out, but—

I can't just stay cooped up in here!

She dipped cleanly into her subconscious and gathered the shadows and light. She created as fast as she could without drawing attention, and as quickly as they'd come the swirling shadows and light were gone, leaving behind a black cloak, a few leaves, and the sound of birdsong. Eowen brushed the leaves under her bedroll and lifted the cloak up, turning it this way and that. She was having some trouble looking at it because the material had a strangely slippery quality to it that seemed to push one's gaze away. She smiled and nodded approvingly, then slipped it on to test out.

Her excursion into the oasis was a brief one, only a half an hour at most. Her father was usually gone visiting her mother's body for two to three hours, but she didn't want to risk anything. Eowen crept along through the jungle, keeping to the shadows and darker trees as much as possible. Soon she heard some of the people of her tribe and tip-toed closer. It was a small flock of children playing in the trees, climbing and swinging from branch to branch just as they had in the old world. They were smiling, laughing, and wearing clothes that, while not as fine as Eowen's, were better than the black rags they'd had before. Tears sprang into Eowen's eyes as she saw her people still capable of joy. She even recognized some of them from her village, a little girl named Funkei that had been inseparable from her older sister.

Eowen stepped forward and crouched under a great fern. The children whooped and squealed, but one of them slipped on a smooth branch, falling to the jungle floor. It was little Funkei, who'd thankfully landed on soft leaves, but the wind was knocked out of her and she began to cry for someone named Amme. Eowen remembered that Funkei had a big sister but couldn't remember her name. Eowen wanted to move in and comfort the girl, but she kept still. An older girl, probably around sixteen, swung down from a branch and landed next to Funkei.

"You all go ahead, I've got her!" the older girl said to her friends. She picked up Funkei who was now on the verge of wailing.

"I w-want Amme!"

"Shhh, shhh. I know you do, I know. Come, let's see your back. See, you're alright aren't you? Just a little fall."

"I s-still want Amme."

"I know, I know." The older girl hugged Funkei, cooing to her. "Shhh, shhh, you're alright, you're ok. I'll be your big sister from now on. Shhh, I'm here, I'm your big sister." Eowen's tears dried up, a cold, clawed grip seized her heart, and memories of the many bodies of her tribe all laid out flashed through her mind. There'd been plenty of children among them.

Eowen felt she'd already seen too much of a private moment and made to leave but stepped directly onto a twig which snapped. The girls looked up.

"Who's there?" the older girl asked. Eowen dipped her head down so the hood hung over her face and held still. The older girl let go of Funkei to move towards Eowen. Eowen Held her breath and pressed herself flat against the tree behind her. "Hello?" the older girl called and Funkei came up behind her.

"Is someone there, Keit?" Funkei asked. The older girl, Keit, took another step forward and Eowen's heart jumped into her throat. There was no way Keit wouldn't see her, no matter how good her cloak was, she was too close. Keit scanned the jungle, looked right at Eowen, but her gaze passed by.

"I don't think so. Come on kid, let's catch up with the others, unless you're afraid to fall out of another tree?" Keit took on a playful tone and Funkei giggled before running off through the trees. Keit left without a backwards glance and Eowen let out the breath she'd been holding. She fingered her cloak, looking at it closely.

"I guess it is that good!"

She hurried home hours before her father returned and planned her next moves. He hardly noticed the barely contained excitement she was buzzing with as they ate in silence. When Di fell asleep, Eowen donned her cloak again and crept off through and around the oasis. She didn't try to make a decoy in her bedroll as that would be far more suspicious upon finding than saying she'd lost track of time on a stroll. She passed by the ring of dead animals, then continued to where she'd heard the mountain folk were camped, staying to the edge of the oasis so that she could duck in or out of it to best avoid people.

It seemed that a pattern had emerged where new arrivals saw the oasis as a familiar wonder and accepted it immediately. Eventually they'd hear of its origins and meet those that had been hurt by it. Many would move out and away from it after that, but some stayed in, usually those with children. Easy access to air, food, and water managed to trump most other fears when children were involved. As a result it was usually older, more easily frightened people Eowen saw wandering around camps and huts beyond the treeline, and young families within.

She passed within sight-range of many, but none remarked on her. Her heart beat out an excited tattoo everytime she passed by, but it appeared that her cloak's hiding trait was working. Her people were in various stages of desperation, but those who'd arrived at the oasis more recently were looking progressively healthier. Dark circles and red eyes were common, but then few could sleep well. Those without the common nightmare that the apocalypse had inflicted were few and far between.

Within an hour Eowen had found the camp of the mountain folk, far out beyond two other camps of her people that seemed to consist of hunters and warriors. Eowen had idly wondered at one point why the mountain folk had not come to visit her, even against Mein's wishes, but had assumed there was a good reason, and was relieved and disturbed to have such suspicions confirmed. She slipped past the camps, which curved to almost surround the mountain folk's camp, and made for their dwelling.

Unlike the huts her people made from tree-trunks and a type of river clay from the jungle that air-dried into a robust material, the mountain folk had set up a massive tent covered in animal skins. Eowen could hear voices as she approached what appeared to be a door flap. She pulled it aside with care, peeking in, and what she saw blossomed joy in her. The mountain folk were sitting in a circle holding hands and singing a song with the shape of a lullaby. A thicker atmosphere of creation than any Eowen had felt from another was present with shadowy implications orbiting gently around them, waiting for the light that grew from the center of their circle. Eowen watched with wonder as the mountain folk performed a group manifestation using their lullaby as a medium to focus their collective subconscious. When the shadows and light finally converged, it was like a gentle current of water pushing the grime off a coin till it shone bright and new.

Eowen looked eager to see what it was they'd created, but found herself crestfallen when it turned out to be nothing more than a brooch made of bone with some kind of metal accentuating it. It certainly looked nice, but not terribly impressive by how skilled at creation the mountain folk should have become if they'd been practicing. Zerinley opened her eyes first and lunged for the brooch.

"How is it?" Genia asked in the mountain folk's language.

"Hmm. Not quite right, the bone part here wasn't so big. Closer than the others." When Zerinley said that, Eowen noticed a bowl beyond them filled with other similar brooches.

"Let's try again!" Ne was bouncing with excitement, as creating suited him well.

Eowen smiled, happy to see the mountain folk were well and sidled over to them. Their tent was massive and they'd filled it with other creations from home; clothes, games, weapons, tools, toys, and art. She was trying to pick her way carefully over to them so she could undo her cloak with a dramatic swish and have an exciting reunion. Instead she tripped on some toys, collided with a ceremonial looking mask which crunched under her weight. The mountain folk whipped around to look at where Eowen had fallen, but none of them focused on her.

"Yawin, what was that?" Zerinley put her hand in the old man's and glanced around fearfully.

"I don't know," Yawin said, putting Ne and Zerinley behind him. "Hale!" He nodded at a spear nearby and Hale flipped it into her hands with a flick of her foot. The armed girl advanced on the spot where Eowen had fallen.

"Ow! Oh, I'm sorry, was this important?" Eowen's disembodied voice set Hale on edge and the young woman thrust the spear towards it, nearly reaching Eowen.

"Who goes there?" Hale said in her own language.

"Hale, calm down, it's just me!" Eowen shouted. Fortunately, Genia spoke up before Hale could thrust the spear again.

"That's Eowen's voice!"

"Eowen? Are you here?" Zerinley practically shrieked. Yawin shushed her, glancing at the doorway.

"Keep quiet, if she is here it's probably without permission," the old man said.

"That's true," Eowen said.

"What if it's a trick?" Hale adjusted the grip on her spear.

"Put that away!" Genia marched up and pushed the speartip down, almost burying it in Eowen's leg.

"Hey, watch it!" Eowen scuttled back.

"Hard to watch it when we can't see you. Where are you?" Genia asked.

"Oh right, let me just take this off." Eowen reached for her cloak, but realized that it had fallen off her when she'd fallen and was in a pile somewhere amidst the clutter. "Wait, why can't you see me?"

"Why would we know?" That was Ne.

"No, you don't understand, I made this cloak to conceal me and make it harder to see me so I could sneak over, but it fell off already. You should be able to see me."

Eowen's voice trailed off as she looked more closely at the space around her. It was hard to tell but there was a sort of layer to the air, a thin veneer of her dreaming aura that was persisting around her despite her not calling upon it. She couldn't so much actually see it as sense, just barely, that it was there. It was a barrier of sorts, but it was also part of her, like a freckle or a mole.

"Wait, there's something here..." Eowen reached out to where the barrier was in front of her and it moved out to keep with her hand. She pulled her hand back and refocused on it with her eyes closed. She knew it was there, and it was hers, she only needed to...

The barrier silently popped open like a bubble, presenting Eowen to the mountain folk, and her presence was immediately followed with gasps and cheers. The children ran to hug her. The older girls let them get there first then followed suit, and Yawin stood back shushing them while grinning ear-to-ear. The children showered her with questions in a mix of their language and a broken version of hers, only quieting down when Yawin pulled them all in for a big hug.

"Alright, alright," the old man said between laughs. "Quiet kids, we don't want to attract attention." He gave Eowen a curious look.

"How did she do that?" Hale asked, which Yawin translated.

"Well," Eowen began, "I think it happened when I was trying to make this cloak." She picked it up and demonstrated how it did indeed make her harder to see, though not totally invisible. "The cloak worked, but I must have unconsciously made the barrier around me," Eowen trailed off. "I was tired of how they looked at me," she whispered.

Yawin sat Eowen down indicating that the others should as well. "It is good to see you, Eowen. I am worried because you move here in secret. Your priestess did not make a decision yet?"

"No, Priestess Mein is still gathering her council. Then she'll decide what to do about... me, about us."

Yawin was in deep thought, but the others were too excited for a serious conversation. They ran around the tent, showing Eowen all the things they'd created and having Yawin explain what they were. She noticed the brooch they'd made had been dropped in the bowl with the others. She resolved to ask about it later and they fell to chattering and playing as they had while traveling together. Around an hour passed when Eowen noticed Yawin marking down a tick on his time-keeping paper.

"Oh! I've been here too long. Everyone, I've missed you

but I have to go. I'll visit again, I promise!" Eowen gave them all quick hugs except for Zerinley, who refused to let go so fast. Then Eowen faced the tent-flap that served as a door, set her feet, balled her hands into fists, and moved her mind into her ocean of subconscious possibility. Eowen knew she'd done what she'd meant to by the feel of the barrier around her, but the mountain folk indicated as much by their reactions. Yawin gasped and Ne said something in his language excitedly. She was fully invisible again.

"I'll be back the next time my dad goes to sleep," Eowen whispered. She waved at them and waited for a response, till she realized that of course they wouldn't wave back, and slipped out.

She found her way home with ease, went undetected, and lay in her bedroll awake for hours before her father ever stirred, and even then only to relieve himself.

"It's harmless, I won't hurt anyone and Mein won't know. Once it's decided that I can stay I can create things freely. It'll all work out," she told herself as she drifted to sleep.

****

[Listen, for you cannot hear me yet]

I WAS GENTLE AS I MOVED, AND SO ONLY WORLDS, GODS, AND TIME WERE CRUSHED BENEATH MY FEET. SO SOFT WAS MY TREAD THAT ONLY THE STARS SHOOK AND ONLY THE DARK CRACKED BETWEEN THEM.

****

From then on, Eowen visited the mountain folk everytime her father lay down to sleep. He was rarely awake and his rests were becoming longer and longer, which made it easier to visit, but it disturbed Eowen. She tried not to bring her problems to the mountain folk though, seeking to enjoy her time with them as an escape from her worries. Over the next two weeks they did little else besides practice each other's language, play games, tell stories from the old world, and create things. They switched off which language they would use each visit, and soon enough the mountain folk and Eowen became conversationally fluent with each other's tongue.

Eowen also remarked on their group creation method. Yawin explained that the children's song and the shared effort helped them to create things that were very particular or beyond the ability of any individual. Eowen commented on the bowl of brooches and Zerinley answered.

"We want special stuff from before the fall. My mom wore one like these, but not exactly like them." Zerinley frowned at the bowl. "It's easy to make, but hard to make right."

Eowen was invited to try creating with them, just something simple, a bowl of water. She sat in the circle with them and held hands. They did not sing the lullaby from before but picked a song Ne had taught Eowen. It started out fine; they sang holding hands, and the shadows around them grew and moved with potential. The light below shone up to reach them, eager to create. It seemed as though it would all go smoothly, but the balance could not be kept. The aura that surrounded the mountain folk mixed together cleanly, intent aligning with intuition, but Eowen's did not.

Eowen's aura of potential was denser, grander, and wilder than they'd accounted for, and attempting to join theirs with hers was like trying to shake hands with an avalanche. Eowen's selfhood poured over them, flooding their dreaming auras with her own, and her subconscious hijacked their intent. A bowl of water was created, but so was a whirlwind of unintended other results further empowered by the mountain folk. Shadow and light curled down into the center of the space between them and manifested a bowl with edges that never settled. The water rippled with weight that such a small amount shouldn't have had. Outwards from the bowl danced forms that grew to encompass the group, things that might have become but were ripped apart into pure potential too quickly. The cyclone spread, grasping with almost-hands at the layers of the tent, lifting the many objects and flinging them around, seeming almost to be alive. Eowen's power arced out and fused them together, keeping the event intact, wind and heat and a deep rumbling noise shaking through them.

They were helpless in the flow of creation till Genia broke it. The mountain girl managed to drag her mind from the currents of power streaming out of Eowen, ripping her hand out of Eowen and Yawin's and escaping from the circle. Without the connection, Eowen's grasp of the moment collapsed, as did the manifestations. There were some leftovers; random objects, but no new oasis, no animals to run off confused and die. The mountain folk were panting, glancing around at each other, confused. The silence between them stretched until they heard the voices of Eowen's tribe approaching. Eowen scuttled back and made herself unseen.

"What's going on here?" A tall warrior, too young to be in a named position yet but intimidating enough with the spear he carried, entered with his weapon pointed at Yawin.

"Nothing," said Yawin, his hands raised placatingly. "The children were just playing."

"It didn't sound like playing, it sounded like," the young warrior searched for the words, "like nothing I've heard before!"

"It's alright young man, there is nothing going on here except children playing." Yawin gestured around the room, which looked like a tornado had passed through it. He searched for Eowen and was relieved to not find her. The young guard seemed unsure of what to do exactly, but he'd been put in a position of authority and he figured that exerting it might be the right course of action.

"You don't talk back to me like that! If I say something... else... was going on here then it was! And you're going to tell me what, now!" The guard jabbed the air with his spear, so Yawin clasped his hands and tried to look as harmless as possible. To the guard's left Hale took a small step toward a stone ax leaning against the tent wall. There was a look in her eyes that said if Yawin were hurt, she'd put the ax through the one that did it.

Eowen watched all this, unseen, and knew she had to do something. She crept forward, got right next to the guard, and before he could say another word or take another step, put her foot solidly in front of his.

The young warrior fell on his face and tumbled into a fur cloak which tangled up his spear. "Ah! What did you do?"

The young children laughed, Genia sighed in relief, Hale took the opportunity to pick up the ax, and Yawin moved in to help him up.

"Here my friend." Yawin offered his hand. The guard disengaged from the cloak and glared at Yawin's hand.

"Get away from me, mountain outsider!"

"Take his hand." Everyone stopped moving when the deep, commanding voice rang through the tent, and all eyes went to the entrance. Sekani, Ranger of Eowen's tribe and their most trusted leader of the hunt, war, and the gods that work through those mediums, stood before them. He was not the tallest man in her tribe, below average even, but he had a presence about him that gave the impression he was a big brother to all. His smile was always a little different for everyone, as if he felt a special joy just when meeting them. He was terrifyingly capable as a hunter, and in the trees or pursuing quarry he could outdo most animals, let alone people. Eowen hadn't seen him in person since the days of Tavo's apprenticeship under him.

Two of the other warriors were holding open the tent flap as Sekani took in the scene inside. He scanned the place, pausing on Hale with the ax in hand. Sekani held a weapon himself, a sort of short machete made of stone with a leather handle. He shook his head, just slightly, and set his weapon down outside the tent. Hale hesitated, then lowered her ax, but she did not let it go. Sekani seemed satisfied and turned his attention back to the young guard on the ground. "I think you've scared them enough, Boullu."

"But Ranger, they—"

"They are our guests, they returned one of our own. That we must relegate them to this tent is a dishonor to how we would normally show such thanks." Eowen's people wouldn't normally show much thanks at all to outsiders, even those that had done right by them, but the way Sekani spoke implied a much more accepting culture than that. "Now take..." Sekani squinted at Yawin. "Yawin, correct?"

"Yes." Yawin smiled at him.

"Take Yawin's hand. He is offering to help you up after you intruded and broke their possessions." The young warrior, Boullu, set his mouth in a thin line but took Yawin's hand. "There, now what happened?" Boullu tried to answer but Sekani cut him off with a gesture that indicated Yawin should answer.

"The children were playing. I'm sorry for the noise we caused," Yawin said, exuding respect.

"That's not what happened!" Boullu whined. "Something strange was going on in here, they were doing something!" Sekani's smile disappeared and with a single look Boullu was silent.

"How would you know, Boullu? They are outsiders, their songs and games and..." Sekani scanned the room again, "...customs may be strange, but they have been harmless and respectful. Now come, and leave them be." Boullu looked like he wanted to argue, but Sekani had spoken, and he left with his head down, somehow looking much smaller than Sekani despite being almost a head and a half taller. "Mountain folk, Yawin, I'm sorry for the disturbance. I want you to know that I respect you for your devotion to staying for the sake of our Eowen after returning her. You have been peaceful and worthy neighbors." He eyed Hale again, and the young woman finally put down her ax. "We promise to... resolve her fate soon so you may return to your own people. Goodbye now."

With that, the Ranger stepped out and his two warriors let the tent flap fall back in place. Eowen had forgotten, after being sent to other villages so many times, how powerful of a personality Sekani had. He and Mein had made a potent combination since the day Sekani had been made Ranger, and they guided their people well.

"Well, that was interesting," Genia said.

"Eowen, where are you?" Yawin whispered. Eowen was awash with shame and refused to let her barrier down. She crept toward the entrance but knocked something over. Hale lunged for her and managed to find an arm.

"Eowen, do not go, it was accident, you did no harm. We... did not know that would happen," Genia said. Eowen tugged, but Hale's grip was strong.

"Eowen is leaving?" Ne asked.

"No!" said Hale

"Yes," Yawin cut in. "Let her go, Hale. But Eowen, promise you will return."

Tears were gathering in Eowen's eyes. She'd only wanted to see her new friends, to be with people she hadn't caused problems for, but she felt that even with the mountain folk she'd nearly ruined everything.

A fight could have started, people could have died, and they didn't even know it was me here!

"You are welcome with us Eowen, and we will stay until your fate is decided but I know your people will welcome you. There are very good people, like that Sekani man," Yawin said. Hale let go, and Eowen didn't run.

"Ok. I'll be back." Then she was gone.

****

[Listen, for you cannot hear me yet]

NONE BUT A FEW FELL.

****

For a few days worth of time, Eowen did not visit the

mountain folk. It was three weeks since she'd returned and almost all her people had been brought together. Mein's council was only one short, a new person needing to be elected. The dead stretched out where they'd been set down, and none could mourn properly without the bone trees or bone herons to perform their funeral rites with. The people Mein deemed appropriate learned the art of creation, and the need for food and water became a bygone problem, though none of their creations were as substantial, varied, or generally successful as Eowen's or the mountain folk's. Eowen spent the three days away from the mountain folk sneaking among her people invisibly. She developed a method for silence around her and became, for all intents and purposes, undetectable.

Mein didn't come to visit her except to announce that she'd soon hold the tribunal, but the old priestess seemed unfocused and exhausted. Eowen assumed she was the cause of Mein's exhaustion and stress, so she followed the old woman as she went about her business. Eowen was humbled to learn that Mein's life did not constantly revolve around the question of what to do with Eowen. The old priestess was pulled in every direction. Everyone wanted her approval and direction all the time. People were afraid of the oasis expanding, afraid of the void beyond, wanted her to oversee them every time they made food, clothes, water, anything. Parents came to her when their children wanted to play in the forest, when they wanted to play outside the forest. Huts had to be approved, works of art acknowledged, tasks allocated, duties and roles bestowed. Mein tried to delegate, but more often than not the delegates she chose would come to her for confirmation before deciding on the things she had appointed them to decide on, effectively making the same amount of work for her either way. Everyone was too unsure to trust themselves, with Sekani seeming to be the only one confident in his own authority. The one thing Mein could not bring herself to brush off or delegate were the requests to pray over the dead, a task that was endless. Eowen left with a new respect for the burden on Mein, and a new guilt for what she added to it. She knew that so many of those burdens could be relieved with her ability to create, and yet she could not be trusted to do so.

Eowen followed others, listening to them, watching their lives, and was both relieved and disappointed at how small a part she played in them. Everyone was only trying to get by, to find some way to live with purpose in this new reality, and most of all to reconcile their losses. Many visited the dead and wept or spoke for hours, but Eowen also saw people create, play, sing, dance, and pursue crafts. It was heartening, but there seemed to be fewer people pursuing activities than there should have been.

Have some of the tribe gone off to establish a new village elsewhere? Eowen's wondered, and her question was answered when one day she followed someone back to their hut. She hadn't been so curious or bold as to watch people in their private residence, but had become attached to watching a woman she didn't recognize. There was something about the sadness the woman carried and the way she still managed to keep active that Eowen wanted to learn from. The woman visited friends, checked the integrity of the hut's roofs, prayed over her son's body, and returned home to sleep. Before the woman could bed down though, she had to take care of her mother.

"Come mother, up, up," the woman cooed. The old woman stared vacantly around, hardly recognizing her surroundings. She'd been in the hut all day and she'd soiled herself. The old woman's daughter dutifully cleaned her, fed her, and lay down to sleep next to her.

Eowen left feeling sick, but couldn't help looking into other homes, a morbid curiosity seizing her. Almost every hut had at least one person that never left it, too disturbed and dissociated to do so. They moaned, they rocked back and forth while fetal, they cried out as if in pain at the sight of someone, they clutched at little tokens, and they slept. Some were very hard to wake, and those worried Eowen the most. All across the settlement of the jungle and savannah tribes were broken people being cared for as much as the caregivers could manage. Only about one fourth of the population were still alive, but a smaller number were really living.

Eventually, she returned home to her father to see him still asleep. She'd been out long enough that he should have woken. Eowen's hands shook and she grabbed him by the shoulders.

"Dad. Dad! Wake up!"

Di stirred, huffing as he emerged from his quiet and calming dreams into his quiet and disturbing reality.

"Huh! What? What is it?" His daughter's eyes jumped over him, wide with panic, as though looking for a wound that would be fatal if not treated. "I'm awake girl, did you need something?" Eowen shook her head, her lungs slowing their activity.

"I just... wanted to..." She trailed off and sat back. Di rubbed his eyes. He'd been asleep for eleven hours, but it seemed no amount would be enough.

"Come here girl." He leaned forward to hug his daughter, and after a breath she hugged him back.

"I don't want you to... I want you to be ok," Eowen whispered. Di suppressed a yawn. He wanted to be present for his daughter, to talk through her worries and tell her how she didn't need them, but he was too tired. Sleep was calling him again.

"I am ok, I've got you my girl. You're all I need. Now, leave me be." He released her to stretch and yawn. "I just need a little more sleep."

Eowen let him lay down, but she couldn't look away from the way his bones stuck out or how sunken his eyes were. She stayed for some moments next to her father, letting him get the sleep he'd requested. She hoped he'd wake up soon so they could play or talk or do something, anything together. He did not wake though, and hours pressed in, burdening the hut with Eowen's dreaming. Her dark mood infected the aura around her, making it a heavy, choking thing. She might not have noticed how it clutched at her father if the young women who delivered them food hadn't arrived. The young woman had to fight through the aura, wheezing and leaning heavily on the doorframe. Eowen perked up at her arrival, coming out of her spiraling thoughts.

"Greetings Di and... Eowen." The woman slid down to her knees, sweating, her arms struggling to lift her basket of food.

"Thank you." Eowen rose to receive the basket. "Are you alright?"

"I think so, it's just hard to breathe for some reason." Eowen frowned because there was plenty of air for herself. She looked back at her father and saw how he sweated as well, how his breaths struggled. "Here, take the basket please. I have to go!" The woman thrust the basket forward and ran off, tripping over her feet until she was several meters away where she, very suddenly, stood up straight. It was as though she'd passed through some border where it was much heavier and there was less air.

A border... Eowen thought. *What's the border though?*

Eowen looked at her father struggling like the woman had been and realized what her aura of dreaming was doing. She established her barriers of sight and sound and slipped away to find the mountain folk. Watching her father through the entrance to their hut, Eowen could see his breathing become easier once she was far enough away. She flushed with guilt and hurried off. The further she got from him, the more relaxed she became, and her dreaming aura relinquished its oppressive weight.

Yawin and the children were asleep in their tent but as Eowen entered Zerinley awoke. The little girl rubbed her eyes and yawned, then looked around the tent.

"Eowen?" Eowen undid her barriers and appeared near her.

"How'd you know I was here?" Eowen asked and Zerinley considered the question.

"I do not know." The little girl yawned loudly which woke up Yawin and Genia.

"Oh, welcome," Yawin said. Genia just greeted her with a little wave, then curled back up. Hale and Ne both snored on. "I'll wake up the others," Yawin said.

"No, don't." Eowen whispered. "I'm not here to do anything in particular. I just wanted some company." She watched for the heavy breathing and discomfort that her father and the woman who'd delivered food had displayed, but the mountain folk seemed fine.

Of course, I can be myself with them. They're not afraid of what I might do, and I'm not afraid of them. Or of hurting them.

"Can I sleep here for a bit, with all of you?" Before Yawin could answer, Zerinley had pulled her blanket over and curled up against Eowen. The old man smiled at Zerinley fondly and gestured in a way that said: 'She's fine with it so I am too.'

"Won't your father notice you're gone though?" Yawin asked. Eowen's expression darkened. She looked away from Yawin and curled up around Zerinley.

"No. I don't think he will."

****

[Listen, for you cannot hear me yet]

WHAT DID THE LITTLE ONES FEAR NEAR ME, THE VERY LITTLE ONES BENEATH MY STEP, BRUSHED PAST MY SHOULDERS, SWEPT TO THE SPHERES BY MY HANDS?

****

Yawin shook Eowen awake, which also woke Zerinley up.

"What is it Dad?" Eowen cleared her eyes and looked away, embarrassed. "I'm sorry, Yawin, I didn't mean to say that."

He waved away her apology and put a finger to his lips.

"Are we being secret?" Zerinley asked, mirroring his gesture.

"Go back to sleep, Zerinley.

"But I'm not tired anymore."

"I need to speak with Eowen in private."

"You do?" Eowen glanced at the others nervously.

"Yes." The old man's expression was grave, his brow set and his lips a hard line, though his eyes were gentle. Zerinley pouted, but didn't argue when Eowen and Yawin stood up. "Put up your barrier please. You must not be seen," Yawin said. Eowen did as instructed and followed him out of the tent. Yawin waved to a guard that was awake, set to watch the darkness beyond the settlement. Yawin sat down with his legs crossed and Eowen followed suit.

"Eowen," he whispered, "can you extend your silence to both of us?"

Eowen hadn't considered if that was possible till he'd suggested it. She folded her hands in her lap and reached out her consciousness to the barrier of silence. It was a part of her, as much as her arm, and though she'd never thought to do anything with it like extending it, she found that moving and molding it was as natural and easy as opening and closing her hand. It was like controlling an invisible third limb that happened to be in the shape of a bubble. She pushed it out and the barrier enveloped them such that it allowed outside sound in but didn't let their own sound out of it. They could still hear Hale snoring inside.

"Can you hear me now?" Eowen asked.

"Yes, can anyone else hear us?"

"No."

"Interesting, how can you tell? I can still hear the kids inside." Eowen shrugged.

"I can feel what the barrier does. In the same way I can make it, I somehow know what it is doing, and how to change it." Eowen smiled shyly, but she was still invisible to Yawin and he waited silently for more of an explanation. "I... don't know exactly how it does it. It's like everything else we create. Our dreams, when we believe them, just become things. My thoughts and dreams are always moving around."

Eowen paused here, and for the first time put to words

what she'd been experiencing for another to understand. "The part of my mind that creates is like the sea. It's got waves and currents and winds, and it moves all on its own. It's vast and mysterious, but full of possibilities. I don't control it, I can only find my way to the places where things are and try to... heh, fish them up?"

Yawin considered this for some time, scratching his chin. He'd been slightly scruffy when Eowen had first met him, hair growing out from having been clean shaven. Now he had a beard and mustache that were filling out.

"You make things that never were. I have been wondering how you found the way to imagine, or know of things that have never existed before the fall." Yawin gestured where he thought Eowen was, as she was still invisible to him. "This silence and not-seeing wall are like magic. You have done something that is not a part of nature. How?"

Eowen thought about this. "I suppose you're right, walls of sound and sight like this didn't exist in the old world. But isn't it all like magic no matter what you make?" Yawin raised an eyebrow. Eowen sailed her dreaming mind effortlessly to a familiar part of her subconscious so that a loaf of bread emerged in front of Yawin. "That was just as magical as my barriers that block sound and sight, wasn't it? The plants for this bread weren't grown, the flour and water weren't combined into dough, no fire was lit to bake it. It just became what I knew it to be." Eowen altered her barrier of sight so Yawin could see her, causing him to gasp and look at the guards. "Don't worry, just like the sound, only you can see me." She tore a piece off the loaf and chewed it slowly. It tasted and was textured exactly as if it were a real loaf. It slid down her throat the same way, and it sat in her stomach just as bread should have. Eowen knew her body would digest it and later she'd have to let it out the same way as normal bread. Yet, it wasn't real, it was made of dreams. Yawin took a piece for himself and smiled as he chewed it.

"I think I understand. Or rather, I am understanding how to do things, or how the doing of them work. Though why it all does is still a mystery. Do you know how it feels for me to create things?" Eowen shook her head. "I feel as though I am trying to start a fire with my bow string wound around the stick." Yawin mimed out the action with one hand acting as if holding the bow perpendicular to the ground and one above it as though he were holding the stone that kept the stick the bowstring was wrapped around still. He moved the bow-hand side to side. "It is like I'm drawing out the flame, but then as the sparks fly I must somehow catch them as well, all while keeping the bow going. It has been difficult to learn this. It is like learning to have two new hands I never knew existed. They are clumsy, like a baby."

Yawin's expression went blank as he too went into dreaming, and from the aura of potential creation around him Eowen could almost feel the bow, the stick, and the sparks in the depths of his mind. Shadows and light gathered and from Yawin's cupped hand a voice whispered out a song in the language of the mountain folk. He created a singing voice from nowhere for them to listen to. Eowen caught enough words to understand that it was a song about a woman at market, bargaining for a better price. It was a cute song, a silly little one, the kind where the words hardly mattered because the tune was easy and catchy enough.

The song faded and Yawin's expression took on a wistful quality as he gazed out over the expanse beyond. His mind was far away and Eowen wanted to know where it had gone. She did not ask though, for he also looked terribly sad in the way of those who cannot cry, for they have cried too much already, and Eowen did not feel strong enough to help him carry his feelings.

"So what exactly was it that we needed to talk about secretly?" she said.

"Your father," Yawin said without breaking his expression. Eowen swallowed, nervous.

"What about him?"

"You're worried about him."

"Yes. I'm worried about many. My people aren't dying anymore, they have food and water, but some, like my father, lay all day and speak to no one. I don't know what to do. I feel as if there is a way to help them but I cannot do anything without creation, and Priestess Mein forbids me to." A silence fell between them as Yawin thought it over. Eventually he retreated into the tent and returned with his parchment and charcoal, the system by which he'd been tracking time.

"This has helped me some. We have all lost loved ones, and in this world it can seem as though time is not passing and that we shall be trapped in this moment of loss and death forever. When my parents died I felt that way even with a changing world around me. I kept myself sane by watching the sun and moon go by, and each day was different in the sky, even if the world below seemed to stay in that moment. This parchment and charcoal has served a similar purpose here. It lets me know each moment is real and different." He looked over Eowen sympathetically, and in his heart ached. "I do not know what your father or the rest of your people need, but I know you can find it. Your priestess is wise and just, I am sure, but does she understand this place any better than we do? No, how can she? She cannot always be right, Eowen. Perhaps you need to show her that."

Eowen frowned. "So you're saying I should create something, against Priestess Mein's orders?" Yawin shrugged.

"I do not know what the answer is, if it is creation or some other thing you could do. I only feel that we all must accept the world as it is now, and learn to live in it. I believe you are already doing so, and we are trying to. Perhaps... your people and this priestess of yours are not ready yet, but eventually they must be. No matter what happens, we will stay for you." The two of them lapsed into a silence where they twiddled their thumbs and avoided each others' eyes.

Maybe I could go against orders. Perhaps that's the right thing to do. Who knows what is right or wrong here? Does Mein really know?

Eowen only knew that in her was the ever-building urge to do something, and each waiting moment without direction was torture. Something Yawin had said bothered her, his promise that they would stay and wait to see what became of her fate with her people. They had been waiting for weeks, sacrificing the time they could have spent looking for and helping their own people because of Eowen's uncertain fate. All at once she felt a hot flash of corrosive feelings. There was rage at Mein for keeping the mountain folk waiting. Even if it was to assemble some council, Eowen felt ashamed that the reason Mein even needed to assemble some council was because of her. She still felt guilty that she had been so incompetent as to cause harm the moment she'd found her people again. Eowen stood up.

"Thank you Yawin, I have something I need to do." Before he could say goodbye she was gone, invisible and silent. She drifted past her people, the camp of guards, the small settlements, the huts at the ever-growing oasis's edge.

Eowen's mind was like a steel trap locked onto the idea of something that would show the worth of her abilities, that would be good and bring her people hope. The oasis had provided life and familiarity to her people, and even if she had hurt people unintentionally, she had to believe that the creation had proven its worth by them. Eowen resolved to do something grand again, like the oasis, but this time she would get it right. Eowen approached her and her father's hut as somewhere in the back of her mind she heard a voice like her mother's greet her as though returning from another failed apprenticeship: *Back again in failure? What a useless girl I am burdened with!*

Eowen stepped around back and undid her barriers. Her hands shook but she forced herself to go in. Di was awake, twisting a piece of clothing in his hands.

"Greetings Father."

Di looked up through crusted eyes, and his whole face hung down as though it were melting wax. "Where have you been?" His feeble voice was strained with exhaustion and worry. Eowen's heart jumped into her throat.

"I... I was visiting Mother." The lie tasted bitter.

"Oh, were you?" Di's voice trembled. "I was there a little while ago, I did not see you."

"I, um, took the long way." Eowen's stomach turned, her tongue felt like it was in acid.

Such a useless girl, you make nothing of yourself!

"Oh, that's good then. I thought... it doesn't matter." Di put down the cloth and rolled over to sleep again. Eowen saw that it was the outfit she'd made for her mother.

At least we had Tavo, now we are left only with you.

Her mother's voice warped and twisted in her mind, becoming crueler than it had ever been, all mocking and jeers.

The shadows, which danced about and hung over her father, seemed to become some distorted effigy of her mother with a toothy smile that split its way past her ears and eyes full of cruel joy. Eowen faced it, hate and shame so evenly coalesced in her that they became an unnameable emotion more terrible than the sum of its parts. Eowen opened her mouth to speak but had to swallow back bile first. "Father, I've a gift for you."

Di stirred. "What, my child?"

"I see how often you sleep. I know that time is hard to keep here without the sun and moon." Di blinked at her and tried to focus.

"I suppose," he said, but his eyes and voice were milky and thin. He could not focus. "I feel less like a person the longer I am here without... Without what we once had." He looked at the clothes Eowen had made for her mother. Eowen didn't notice, for she had her eyes on the distorted form hanging over her father. Together the two stared at the specters of who they had lost, fully engrossed in their own fantasy of what she had once been and fully incapable of imagining, let alone reconciling, how the other felt. Eowen felt the flow of her subconscious all around her as the sea of possibility whipped up waves and winds, but she knew how to navigate them.

"Close your eyes Dad, I have a gift for you." Eowen's voice carried a power that rang like a bell past hearing and into the heart. It wasn't a commanding toll but it was an unignorable one, and Di, so weak, exhausted, and sad, did what she asked.

"Alright my gir—Eowen." Di put his hands over his eyes. "Why must I close them, what sort of gift is this?" He sounded nervous.

"Don't worry, I want to give you something from the old

world." Hearing this, Di relaxed some while Eowen reached up, gathering her dreaming in force. It was much more than was needed for her creation, but it wouldn't stop growing. The specter of her mother mocked her and fed on the energy that Eowen gathered to oppose it. It was a stalemate until Eowen closed her own eyes to avoid the madness in the ones before her.

A dense haze of potential manifested around her, bloating the atmosphere with power. Eowen clung to her consciousness as the currents and waves of her subconscious mind grew dangerous. She looked up dreamily into the empty darkness above, which steadily became less empty as her aura of shadows and creation gathered, folded, knitted. Light arced up from below till, with a splash upon the fabric of unreality and a ripple of creation, a sun bloomed into being. It was casting light that didn't so much banish the darkness of the surrounding void as paint it into more familiar shades of the old world.

Eowen could feel her work like it was a part of herself, and she could feel that this creation wasn't done, for the atmosphere around her was still saturated with potential. Eowen's plan had been a tiny sun in her and her father's home that would transition into a moon on a cycle similar to that of the old world. Eowen had arrived at this, but the storm within her subconscious battered at her control. The border between her dreaming mind and the reality around her broke down. Her hands shook, her eyes rolled back, and a cracked breath rolled out of her like an injured animal at the end of its flight.

Di heard it, removed his hands, saw the sun, and lunged for his daughter in a panic. "Eowen, no!"

His touch snapped her control and Eowen's ship of

consciousness broke upon the waves in her mind. Di was blasted back, their hut ripped asunder as water, fire, bird, stone, mountain, insect, cloth, hoof, branch, wine, and all manner of creation from grimy dust to the burning stuff of stars arced in violent, graceful, and terrible turns. Creation, destruction, reformation, transformation raged out into an adagio horde of notions with Eowen at the center. Di scrambled back as a rampage of possibility built of all the tension of the moment and of the days Eowen had spent repressing herself emerged. Amidst the chaos Eowen fell into the cold depths of her subconscious mind, and she perceived no more.

The sun swelled and rose, ballooning into a massive form above the ruined hut, and the Storm followed with winds that ripped through the oasis and rains that pelted the world around, blooming into all manner of chaos and creation. Eowen's people cowered from the onslaught, and the guards near the mountain folk rushed to the site with weapons ready and faces uncertain. The mountain folk turned to Yawin for guidance, and he took Ne and little Zerinley's hands.

"Genia, you're the best of us at creation. Eowen needs you. Hale, get her safely to Eowen's side." Hale kicked her ax into her hands as Genia hugged herself.

"M-me?" Genia said and glanced from Yawin to Hale to the children. "I'm not—"

"We don't have the luxury to hesitate, Hale, take her!"

"Yes sir!" Hale had continued her warrior's training as best she could in the new world and her limbs were like steel. She linked arms with Genia and all but dragged the taller girl towards the chaos.

"Wait, no, what do I do?" Genia called to Yawin, but he turned away with the children.

"Yawin, that's Eowen, isn't it?" Ne said, putting on a brave face.

"Yes, come, we're going to meet up with the girls, but we must go around this way." He pulled them along as Ne fought tears while Zerinley glanced between them and the Storm of Eowen's creation.

From the porch of her hut, Priestess Mein watched as the fragile security of her people crumbled beneath the light of a new sun. Cries, gasps, and exclamations erupted from the oasis as her people beheld the creation. The emergence of the sun's light bore down on the new world, casting it into unambiguous reality. Mouths were left agape and hands dropped what was in them as minds failed to comprehend the wonder of such power beyond their reckoning. A guard stationed by her home approached, looking as uncertain and terrified as Mein felt, though not a hint of the old priestess's inner turmoil showed through. Mein exuded confidence and certainty, she had to, for among all her people she knew she was the only one who could.

"Take me there, Kuffe," she said to her guard.

"Yes, priestess," Kuffe sighed, relieved to have a clear direction and to be serving someone who seemed confident. With an arm around the old woman, made his way forward.

Above the wreck of Di and Eowen's home, the sun hung as though cradled by a great invisible hand. Eowen's power swayed it to and fro as though uncertain of where to put it. She was still unaware of all else around her, a mere conduit for the work moving through her, a wonder of proportions once attributed to gods and distant creators. The mountain girls, Mein, the warriors, and those of Eowen's people who desperately wanted to know what was happening, approached. They saw the creations flowing out, the sun, and within it all Eowen sat, legs crossed, gazing up blindly. Her mind perceived her creation, and she could feel that if she were to only follow this flow of power, her wish would come true, no matter what it was or would become.

****

[Listen, for you cannot hear me yet]

WHAT DOES A FLEA FEEL IN A THUNDERSTORM, OR DUST IN A VOLCANO, OR A MORTAL GIRL WHEN THE SKY FALLS DOWN AND SWALLOWS UP EVERYTHING BUT DREAMS?

****

Something was there, a thing with an enormous presence that looked at her, then through her, as though she were a tunnel. Some power was trying to enter her from some outside place, but just before it did, another power intervened, one that felt like the even vaster presence she sometimes felt in her dreams. Eowen's heart swelled to an ache and with it the torrent abandoned her, fading out from whence it came into darkness and starlight. The Storm of creation faded, Eowen's subconscious aura of shifting shadows and promised potential evened to a normal level, and the girl fell back into herself. She awoke from the dream, the torrent about her dispersed, but the sun remained. It hung above the oasis, a true wonder.

All eyes stared into it save four pairs: Eowen's searched

the starfield below as she tried to recall the dream she'd had within that moment of great creation, the voice that had spoken of her, the presence that had tried to move through her. Hale was beside Eowen, watching the hunters of Eowen's tribe with her ax at the ready. The only hunter not staring at the sun was their ranger, Sekani. He held his spear lightly and smiled casually at Hale, but sweat ran down his brow and the hand he hid behind his back shook. The last one was Mein herself. The sun pulled at her attention like a magnet but she stubbornly refused to acknowledge it. Her eyes darted over the whole of the situation, taking everything in. Her mind churned through decades of procedure, tradition, ceremony, none of which would serve the present circumstances.

"Astounding," Genia whispered, trying to grasp where in the flow of the subconscious such an unprecedented wonder could be dredged up from. Sekani approached and faced off with Hale, the two warriors standing just outside the distance of engagement. One step forward by either would put their weapons in striking range.

"Hale, was it?" Sekani called. "No need for violence. Uhh," he adjusted to a broken version of the mountain folk's language and held his spear more loosely, "no hit, no, uh, battle. Yes?"

"That depends on you!" Hale thrust her ax at him, speaking in Eowen's language. Her shout shook those present from their astonishment and back into the tension of the moment. The hunters that had accompanied Sekani leveled their spears, Genia stood in front of Eowen as though to protect her, Hale's breath increased in speed as her heart drummed out the call for battle. Eowen's mind still reeled, she felt dizzy and sick as she tried to grapple with the enormity of her creation, the implications of her dream, and the present danger. She stumbled into Genia's arms and was sick at her feet.

"Genia, get her out of here! I think they mean to kill her!" Hale said in her language.

"Enough!" Priestess Mein's commanding shot through the standoff. "You all behave like chattering monkeys. Spears down you fools, it is one girl before you, Sekani is enough. Skeh!" Mein hissed out an order that scattered the hunters from their formation.

"You and you," Mein pointed to two of the hunters. "Come here." She whispered in their ears and sent them off, then she gave Sekani a glance and he gestured for the rest of the hunters to disperse, taking the others of Eowen's tribe with them back to the trees of the oasis. Hundreds of eyes still watched from a distance, but Mein was satisfied. Sekani put his spear down and held his hands out placatingly to Hale, but the mountain warrior kept her ax at the ready.

"Hale," Eowen croaked, "please put it down. You can't take him, with or without a weapon." Hale glanced at Eowen, uncertain, but the look in Eowen's eyes convinced her. Eowen had seen Sekani best three warriors larger than himself at once. He was ranger to all the villages of her tribe for a reason, he could easily kill Hale with his bare hands. Mein took a deep breath through her nose and shambled forward to address Eowen and the mountain folk.

"This was you." Mein's voice was cold and low. It carried like a chill through the bones and those listening shivered.

"Mein, please listen, I think I've discovered something important, I'm just trying to remember—"

"Haask!" Mein hissed Eowen into silence and glared down the mountain girls so there'd be no rebuttal. The old priestess turned slowly, taking in everything around them, and in doing so drew the attention of all present to what her eyes fell on. Eowen and her father's hut lay around them in fragments. Most of Eowen's Storm of creation had dispersed without fully taking form, or had fed into the sun. Some of it had remained to litter the starfield far and wide. Half-made things, half-real vestiges of the dreaming mind. It was the same as always, Eowen's creations always brought the unintended with it, objects, plants, animals, smells, sounds. In the silence of the moment a strange twinkling music could be heard, grafted to the very space they occupied with no evidence that it would fade or disperse. Mein's silence and demeanor leveled these things as a prosecutor laying charges at Eowen's feet.

She finished her rotation to find Yawin, Ne, and Zerinley standing behind her. The old man glared at Mein and she matched it. Some unspoken exchange occurred, a communication of values and wisdom acquired not by culture but by time. The moment broke when Eowen spoke up.

"Where's my father?"

Mein's attention turned to Eowen and through all her exhaustion, age, and internal turmoil the spirit of the priestess of the jungle and savannah people rose up to cast judgment upon the girl.

"How did Di and Monda produced a child such as this?" The words like a lash across Eowen's back, she whimpered at her mother's name. "You have changed, girl." Mein's words were hot irons, her voice was the hiss as she pressed them in. "You've always been a useless burden upon your honorable parents, but at least you were a good and obedient child. Obedience was all that was required of you, respect and adherence to our ways, but you have changed, and it was not when the sky fell and our world became... this. It was when you left us. You abandoned our people, you became someone else. You are an outsider, girl, you've brought harm and threatened my people for the last time. Go now or be driven off like a wild beast, rid us of you, join your kind. You are not welcome."

"Honorable priestess," Yawin stepped forward to defend Eowen. "surely you cannot—"

"You're no longer welcome, Yawin of the mountain outsiders. Nor are your charges. We tolerated your presence for returning one of our own until such a time as we could determine if she still was one of our own. That probation has expired."

Eowen reached for Mein's hand. "Priestess Mein, please, I can—"

"Ah! Even now you would speak up against your elders. I should not be surprised, we are not your people are we?" Eowen wept in Genia's arms, unable to stand, Yawin and Hale had moved around her protectively.

"Please, my father, is he hurt?" Eowen choked out between sobs. No one responded after her question but the mountain folk and Sekani scanned the wreckage of Eowen's hut. Mein softened, just a bit.

"Eowen... Your father lives." The old priestess pulled herself together and cleared her throat. Her next words had to be harsh, to resound powerfully with the command of her status and the faith her people had placed with her.

"You are hereby banished, outsider girl. You are no longer welcome among the people. Begone."

Her ultimatum lacked the power she'd meant to put in it. It only sounded flat and sad. Eowen covered her weeping face with her hands, then blinked out of all perception.

Mein kept her expression carefully neutral while her breath caught in her throat. Sekani gasped. The mountain folk turned to Yawin, who glared at the old priestess and led his people off into the darkness.

"We'll find Eowen and meet at our old camp," Yawin said to his charges. "We'll have to split up."

"No, I know where she is." Genia was looking out towards the direction of the cemetery, squinting.

"Where?" Ne ran ahead looking to and fro.

"Somewhere over there. I can still feel her but she's getting far away." Genia started in the direction. "I'll find her, let's meet at the last camp we made before we found Eowen's people." Yawin nodded and shepherded the children away. Hale followed after Genia though.

"Hale, this way!" Yawin called.

"I'm going to keep Genia safe."

"No, they need to be kept safe more than I." Genia waved Hale off. "Besides, I don't think you can help here." Hale seemed torn but followed with Yawin. The old man held both of the little children's hands, shushing them as they questioned what was happening, where they were going next, and what they were going to do. Mein watched them leave and sighed with relief, leaning heavily on Sekani.

"What do we do next, priestess?"

"What indeed?" Mein muttered under her breath. She glanced up at the sun, a movement only of her eyes that was a fraction of a second. That fraction sealed the final vestige of hope that life could ever resemble what it had once been. It was like a great story of old, full of magic and powers from before the time of the gods. Mein shook her head. Those stories were only ever supposed to be stories, yet above her very head the sun was already transitioning into a moon.

Mein gestured for one of the onlookers to help her, a young woman, and she leaned on her as they made their way back to their hut. "Check on everyone, Sekani, make sure there are no others injured. I'll call upon you when I have more orders." The ranger hurried off to do her bidding, relieved to have a goal with a purpose.

Mein, for all of her faults, was one to practice what she preached. When they arrived Mein dismissed the woman and shambled into the doorway. Quiet, tortured sobs could be heard from without and the young woman that had lead Mein to her hut stuck around, curious. She leaned in to listen through the doorway.

"It is done. You may leave."

The young woman backpedaled as the two hunters Mein had sent away earlier emerged. Their expressions were the hung frowns and hard eyes of those who have hard and unpleasant jobs but know they do them well. They glared the young woman away from the hut and took seats in the oasis, where they could watch the hut but not hear within.

"About time we were rid of her. She's been a plague on us all, especially him," said the younger of the hunters. The older one scratched his neck and stared at the sun.

"I don't know if we are rid of her. Not sure we'll ever be."

Within the hut, Di wept on a mat on the floor. His arms were already becoming mottled with dark bruises from the hunters restraining him. Mein hobbled over to him and took a seat. She put a hand on the man's back, pressing him to rise and face her.

"I could not let you interfere, Di. You would protect your daughter even in opposition to all laws and decisions by your elders. This is right and just. It is as it should be. You have acted in accordance with the best nature of your spirit, and I can only take pride in your faithfulness to your daughter. Still, just as I could never sway you from this, nor can you sway me from my decision."

Di stared woodenly back but nodded. They sat in silence for some time, waiting for the other to say something that would feel right, or for the right thing to occur to them. Nothing came to them though, so Mein gestured a dismissal. "It is done, Di. That is all I can say. Leave now. Find me when you are ready."

Di stood, blind to the world, and stumbled out, bumping the door-frame on his way out. Finally alone behind closed doors, Mein collapsed.

"Oh, oh! Mondai of the earth beneath from which all life does grow, tell me... Ernu of the sea, wisest who ever moves and acts, what changes must we make... Shalaiyt, the winds that know every word spoken, guide mine breath to...to...TO!"

The prayers broke on her tongue, for her religion had been of the old world and meant nothing without the world around her. The words which had once invoked guidance from the gods had lasted generations. They were words she'd once known to be more real than her own hands, more sweet than honey, and more filling than porridge. Now they were like rancid flesh on her tongue. She could not choke them down. Witnessed only by darkness and silence, the old priestess felt the solid mantle of her vocation, which she'd worn proudly upon her spirit since the days of her apprenticeship, peel off like shed skin. The displacement of this weight brought no relief though, it had been like a stopper to a bottle filled with smoke, and with the stopper gone Mein's identity drifted out.

"I am alone!" she whimpered between sobs. The darkness

played around her as her subconscious trolled for dreams that her faith had tamped down, the starlight below glowed patiently, awaiting its moment to cast implication into reality.

Eowen ran with no direction in mind while a sort of compass within her took over. Within moments she was deep in the field of the dead, body after body merely covered with blankets. There were no mourners here this time so she let her barriers down. Eowen paced through the rows and columns looking left and right through her tear-blurred eyes, casting about for something familiar, something comforting, something she could rely on. The girl had no direction in mind, no intention behind her movements, but in moments she had arrived at a familiar place where a familiar face awaited her. The compass in her heart stopped pulling. She wiped away her tears and saw who she now stood next to. Eowen's sobs caught in her throat and her tears, which had flown so easily so often, now stubbornly refused to fall.

"Hello, Mother," Eowen's voice cracked.

Ah, I see, Eowen thought. *At least this is familiar.*

"I always come back to you after my failures don't I? I never really know how much of a disappointment I am until you tell me. I thought I could avoid that when I ran away, but here I am after all."

The knot in Eowen's chest twisted and she bent over in pain. "I thought I'd been doing well. I arrived here all by myself. Except I brought the mountain folk with me. I found you all though... Everyone that was left. But I wouldn't have had to if I hadn't left in the first place. You'd probably still be alive, Daddy might not be in the state he's in." Goosebumps ran up her arms, over her shoulders, and found their way to the small of her back. She dropped to a crouch and hugged herself, trying to breath as the twisted knot in her chest made it impossible. "It's ok, you don't have to be alive, you don't have to say anything. I know what you'd say."

Eowen managed to force a haggard breath. The shadows and light about her twisted and played, responding to her emotions, but there were no dreams for them to imprint upon. Her mind was locked in the present reality.

"I thought we were different, since you never cried for me ever. Well look at me. No crying! Not for you." Eowen convulsed as if to vomit but nothing came out. "I thought we were different because of how I failed you and Daddy over and over. You never failed at anything, but we're really more alike than I thought, aren't we? Because, for instance, I've always been as disappointed in myself as you were with me!" Eowen cried out between choked coughs as her body twisted into a painful knot. She raggedly pushed out and sucked in one breath after another, but it was torture. The shadows and light around her roiled, their potential stretching for kilometers, threatening calamity, yet becoming nothing. Eowen's heart twisted in upon itself, breaking at her spirit and crushing any emerging dream. She lay fetal, staring at her mother's unmoving face, wishing it would move and speak, because no matter how much Eowen ruined things or disappointed or failed all she had to do was return home, take her mothers shouts and lashes, then wait to be sent away once again.

"Is that all I need to do? Shout how I'm a failure, hit myself?" Eowen beat her fist against her leg but hardly felt it. Her mother had thick, tree-branch arms while Eowen's were reeds. She scooted closer, putting her face within centimeters of her mother's. "I'm a failure! I'm a weak pathetic useless burden!" She opened her mouth and screamed wordlessly into her mother's face until she ran out of breath, her eyes skittering about wildly. "I-I...I can't even do that right!"

"Be quiet!" Genia marched up, tears streaming and glaring at Eowen.

"Genia? How'd you find me?" Eowen backed up on her hands as Genia bore down on her. The mountain girl ran up, slid on her knees and crashed into Eowen, awkwardly tackling her into a hug. "What are you doing?"

"You listen to me Eowen! Your people might not want you, and you might not be good at controlling your creations, and your mother might have been an awful person," Eowen had not known how bad Genia was at comforting people until that moment, "but you saved our lives!" Eowen's heart fell further.

"You don't owe me anything." She tried to push Genia away but instead was hugged tighter. "Genia, you're—"

"No, you are wrong! We owe you everything. We owe you our lives, and you could have asked anything of us. We would have followed you anywhere, done anything for you, died for you." She thought for a moment. "Maybe not all of us, but Hale would have died for you, she would die for less. You could have made us serve you for life, but instead you became our friend. We traveled together and ate food together and played games together. We learned how this world works together." Genia's rambling bounced between their languages as she abandoned any words she couldn't immediately translate.

"Genia, please—"

"Do you even know what the rest of us think of you?" Genia shook herself and Eowen. "Hale likes you! That's not saying much, she likes people easily, but she also dislikes people for nothing. And Yawin thinks of you as his own kid the way he thinks of us, and I..." Genia trailed off. "You and Hale and Zerinly are like sisters to me. It was just Ne and I until I found the others and you. Eowen, I—"

"Stop, please!" Eowen squirmed out of Genia's embrace.

"I don't want to lose you!" Genia finished, struggling with tears. "So please, I know they don't want you anymore," she flung her hand back towards the oasis, "but we do. Won't you come with us?"

Eowen's head ached. She didn't know what to do or where to go. Every direction was meaningless except the one that led to her people, yet that was now the one place she was forbidden.

"You're going home then?" Eowen asked. Genia wiped away her tears, cleared her throat and created some water to wipe her face with.

"We don't have a home. Right? No one does, not anymore." She stood up, fixed her posture, straightened her clothes, and held out a hand for Eowen. "We've just got each other. And we're all in this together, aren't we?"

Eowen knew that Genia was wrong, no matter how close they felt to her or what debt they owed her. She'd never be one of them. She knew that one could only belong to the people they were born into, and if they renounced you it meant you were forever without a people. But her heart yearned for belonging, had yearned for it all the years of her life that she'd failed to find a niche within her own tribe. Now she'd never have that, not with the mountain folk nor her own. She would forever be alone. But still Genia was holding out a hand for her, and somewhere the rest of the mountain folk were waiting. It wouldn't be like truly belonging. At best they would appreciate her, and in truth they would tolerate her for saving the lives of a few of their kins-folk, just as

Eowen's people had tolerated the mountain folk for the same narrative.

But maybe it will be as close to belonging as I'll ever get. Besides, where else am I supposed to go?

It took only a moment for these thoughts and feelings to pass through Eowen's mind before she reached out to take Genia's hand. The girl from the mountains smiled at Eowen, radiating love and relief, but Eowen could not return the expression.

"Come, sister," Genia said. "I'll take care of you from now on." Genia pulled her along. Eowen looked back one last time to see her mother's face fading in the dark and distance, and was relieved for one thing.

At least she's not alive to see what's become of me.

****

[Listen, for you cannot hear me yet]

WHO CAN KNOW?
CERTAINLY NOT A GIANT SUCH AS I.

****

Yawin ticked his time-keeping sheet with his charcoal stick, recounted the lines, reviewed his memories, and accepted that he'd tracked the time as best he could. By his count, it had been a week since Eowen's exile, eight since the world ended. Hale glanced over his shoulder and went through her mental map of time much faster than Yawin, shrugged, and nodded approvingly. Zerinley pulled the sheet down and counted the ticks out loud but got bored after the numbers got into the double digits. Ne was practicing with Genia as she attempted to teach him some of the wonders that Eowen had managed to teach her; how to make creations that float and change according to your will, how to make oneself invisible, and how to make little orbs of light. The little boy didn't have the knack for it, but he seemed to enjoy failing only to try again. His creations would almost converge, or be held for a moment, then flicker out like a match pinched between two fingers. He'd lick his lips and pretend to pop the joints in his hands like Hale would before practicing with her weapons, then continue.

Eowen stood some ways away, her toes a hair's breadth from the little island of dirt that she'd lived on during her first week in the new world. To arrive back at Eowen's first encampment, they had carefully and slowly traced their way back from camp to camp. As it turned out, wandering aimlessly into the unknown till you discovered something was a much faster process than trying to retrace one's steps through the void. Yawin rolled up the sheet and swayed with Zerinley on his lap.

"Tell me the story about the queen of gold," Zerinley said, tugging on Yawin's sleeve.

"He's told that story a hundred times, pick a different one." Hale flicked Zerinley's ear.

"Ow! No he hasn't!"

"How would you know? You can't count past ten."

"I can!"

"Prove it!"

Yawin took the opportunity to walk away after Zerinley jumped up from his lap to argue.

"Onetwothreefourfivesixseven—" she paused to gasp, "—

eightnineteneleventwelve—" She continued into the thirties and by then Hale had begun to encourage her, clapping along with her counting. Genia's concentration broke and the water she'd been floating fell back to her hand.

"They could keep it down," she muttered, shaking off droplets.

"They're just nervous," Yawin said as he passed by. "We all are."

Genia flicked a glance in the direction they'd come from before finding Eowen. Somewhere, out in the dark beyond their sight, was the very spot they'd been when the world had ended, along with all the dead mountain folk they'd been surrounded by that had not survived. Ne was watching his big sister, whose hands began to shake the longer she stared into the distance. He scooted closer and patted her leg.

"Show me again?" Ne said.

Yawin stood next to Eowen and they kept to a companionable silence, both lost in thought for a long moment till Eowen broke the silence.

"It feels like it's been so long since I was back here, where it all began for me," she said in the mountain folk's language. They had spoken it exclusively since Eowen's exile to better prepare her to live with the rest of the mountain folk.

"Hmm." Yawin's hand automatically reached for his counting sheet. "It's been fifty-eight days." Eowen looked at him with an eyebrow up. "Approximately," he amended.

"Over eight weeks then?"

"Yes. It feels like much longer, doesn't it?" Eowen returned her gaze to the little dirt island with the creek running alongside it. It was perfectly undisturbed, her old footprints, scraps of food, even the air around it felt like it hadn't moved since they'd left.

"Much longer," she answered. "I'm going to turn in."

Eowen walked away and, before Yawin could think of something to say to her, something kind, or encouraging, or wise, a swipe of shadow and light painted a tent into reality around her. He returned to settle down the children and tell a story, though he was running out of ones he hadn't repeated several times. They listened closely, hoping to be distracted from the tragedy they'd be facing next. No one succeeded in this. Ne snuggled into his sister, crying silently while she resisted the urge. Yawin prepared himself to see his wife's face by imagining it. Hale and Zerinley held hands and resisted such thoughts as best they could.

****

[Listen, for you cannot hear me yet]

I HEARD A VOICE, A VERY SMALL ONE THAT BELONGED TO ONE MUCH YOUNGER AND MUCH SMALLER THAN I.

****

Something buffeted against Eowen's aura of dreaming and potential that did not give way to its density and currents. The change was as sudden and bracing as ice down one's back. It changed the world, filled it with interplay and distortion. She sat up and dismissed her tent into non-existence with a thought.

"Something is coming!" she shouted, and Hale responded

first by rolling over Zerinley and picking up her ax in one fluid motion.

"What? Where?" Hale looked about into the darkness beyond the faint light of the starfield below them. The rest were up, Genia and Eowen floated lights above them, Ne made one as well but it stayed in his hands, Yawin picked up Zerinley and pulled Eowen, who took Ne's hand, behind Hale.

"What's happening?" Zerinley squealed from Yawin's arms.

"Eowen said something is coming," Hale said and traced the dark beyond with her weapon. Everyone held their breath, listening and straining to see into the dark, looking aimlessly save for Eowen who was fixated on a particular direction.

"Eowen," Yawin shook her hand. "What are you sensing?"

"You can't feel that?" She met her companions eyes incredulously. "It's right out there!" Eowen pointed in the direction of the feeling. It was like a buzzing, or a rushing, like the sound and feel of river rapids washing over her.

"You're doing a prank, aren't you?" Ne looked suspicious, and poked Eowen's leg.

"No! I wouldn't joke about whatever this is." Eowen was annoyed on the verge of being worried that she was crazy, when Genia yelped and backed up into her brother.

"I just felt it too!" Like dominoes, the rest of the mountain folk sensed the approaching entity at the edge of their dreaming auras as whatever it was crashed into theirs as well.

"See?" Eowen twisted her robe in her hand.

"It feels like you," Zerinley said, squirming from Yawin's arms. Eowen looked at the little girl like she was crazy.

"What are you talking about?"

"No, she's right." Yawin put the little girl down but kept hold of her hand. "Not exactly like you, but the amount of force behind it is similar."

"What do you mean? I've never felt like this." Eowen backed up a bit.

"Well," Hale said, taking a step forward. "You've never been around yourself."

The presence drew closer, the force of its aura enveloping the space so that the atmosphere seemed made only of its presence. Eowen's aura of power met it and an interplay began, like two anvil clouds slamming together and dropping their combined stores of rain. An ebb and flow of distorted dreams and shadowy potential equalized into a massive vortex of possibility. The party had several lights floating above them but their radius didn't reach very far. A figure, not much taller than Eowen, stepped into their lights.

"Finally, I found you!"

It was a boy, around Eowen's age, darker skinned, less curly haired, and speaking a dialect of her language. His aura of dreaming was flowing out and filling a massive area, similar to Eowen's, and the closer they stood the more their power warped the implicit reality into strange currents.

"You, you're... like me?" Eowen took a step back, feeling the forces of their combined auras play about her with even just that small movement.

"Oh wow, this is new!" The boy swayed, staggered, and caught himself, grinning as the experience washed over him. Then, he closed his eyes and took one deep breath that lasted longer than should have been possible. His inhale seemed to pull at all the space around them, drawing in not just air but the shadows and light as well. The dreaming potential that had been on the precipice of becoming a Storm of chaotic creation abated, gathered into his lungs, and while he held his breath time seemed to halt. The boy smiled to himself and exhaled into his hands. He lost track of the creation for a moment and the power responded with a fluctuation that burst out like a sudden breeze, but the boy regained his composure and finished. As simple as can be, the gathered power coalesced, solidified, lost its potential and became a pile of sand in his palm. "Thought I'd lose my grip for a moment there."

The boy tipped his hand and the sand trickled onto the ground, ordinary by all accounts yet miraculous for that very reason. He brushed the rest off on the side of his shirt. Both his and Eowen's dreaming aura's, previously saturated with chaotic force, had diluted into a calm and mirrored sea of their subconscious. The boy waved his hand and smiled at them, like an old friend passing by, completely at ease.

A little hand poking his leg got his attention. "I'm Zerinley, what's your name?" Zerinley said in her own language. Yawin did a double take, glancing at his side where he'd thought Zerinley had been standing.

"Hey, get back here!" he called, but she and the boy were already shaking hands and exchanging greetings.

"Hello little one," the boy said in his language. "My name is Hani. What's yours?"

"I told you my name." Zerinley switched to Eowen's language.

"Oh! You speak like a savannah person."

"So do you, but it sounds weird." They shook hands, which Zerinley took very seriously. "Are you one of Eowen's people?"

"Oh, that must be your name," the boy named Hani said, smiling at Eowen.

"Hey! You scared us, so you talk to me!" Zerinley poked his leg again.

"My apologies." Hani's eyes practically twinkled with joyful amusement at the little girl's brazenness. He stepped back and performed a hand motion that Eowen found vaguely familiar. Zerinley frowned at the hand motion, puzzled until Genia stepped up from behind and put her hands on Zerinley's shoulders.

"You know mountain folk's hand-speech?" Genia said, which made Zerinley brighten up.

"He does! You're bad at it though," Zerinley said.

"Well," Hani flashed his smile at Genia then Zerinley again, "you'll have to teach me, I only know that greeting."

Zerinley nodded seriously. With the tension broken, Yawin let out a breath he hadn't known he was holding. He stepped forward and put a hand over Hale's, who was still gripping her weapon.

"I think it'll be alright," he whispered. Hale nodded, and set her ax down. Yawin created a bonfire and gestured for everyone to sit around it. They followed his directions and Yawin took the seat next to Hani. "Greetings. My name is Yawin. I have been the guardian of these children since the fall. That is Genia, Hale, Ne, and Zerinley. Eowen was our savior though. We managed to find her in, I assume, much the same way you did."

Hani nodded enthusiastically. "By her presence." He leaned forward to better look at her. "You're incredible by the way! I've been following the feel of your power since I left home. You made that whole jungle and the sun above it, didn't you?" Eowen shifted uncomfortably and didn't answer except to look away.

"I think we'd all like to know why you've been following us." Yawin brought Hani's attention back to him.

"Well, I wasn't exactly tracking you in particular. You just happened to be going in a similar direction as I was, and I thought you might have some news. Have any of you heard of a man named Captain Asobrab?"

Everyone shook their heads.

"I see." For the first time Hani's sparkling enthusiasm faded a touch, but with a clap of his hands he rallied. "Yawin, you wouldn't happen to know which way the Britchen people are? I'm looking for those from Port Disoke."

Eowen turned to Genia, who leaned in and whispered to her. "The people on the other side of the mountains, they call themselves the Britchen. Port Disoke is their capital city... or it was before the fall."

Yawin rummaged for his time-keeping sheet and unrolled it. He flipped it over and began drawing a crude map of dots and lines.

"I believe we can assume that proximity to one another in the old world determined proximity upon arriving in this one," Yawin said.

"That's what I found while traveling here." Hani leaned in to look at Yawin's map.

"This dot here is meant to represent where we found ourselves, and this is where Eowen was when she first arrived and we found her."

"I see."

"And this is the oasis her people now reside in."

Hani narrowed his eyes and scratched his chin. "That's..." He looked at Eowen. "So based on that, you arrived here." He glanced between Eowen and the little dirt island. "Huh, I knew you'd created the island, it's suffused with your presence.

I thought it was a recent thing though." He looked at her, plainly curious as to why she'd arrived here, gone back to where her people were, and then returned back to here. Eowen didn't like the way Hani's eyes pieced together parts of her story from such limited information and she stubbornly avoided meeting them. Fortunately, Yawin drew his attention back to the map.

"These dots represent some primary settlements of my people, one near the center of the mountains, one at the furthest edge that bordered the land of the Britchen people. Here is where Port Disoke would have once been, if the proximity rule does hold true."

"I think it does based on all the people I've passed by thus far. Though without landmarks, stars, or anything, it's hard to figure out where people are. I mostly follow the feeling they leave behind." He grinned at Eowen again. "Fortunately some people are like us and are more noticeable than others!"

Eowen met his expression with a searching look. He'd been reminding her of someone, but she couldn't place who. The similarity was tugging at her gut and making her shoulders feel heavy. His aura of dreaming, though depleted of power at the moment, was still massive. He was the type that filled a space with his presence. Zerinley had taken an immediate liking to him and was explaining more mountain folk hand-speech as Yawin added more details to his map, running them by Hani for confirmation.

Eowen turned to Genia. "I'm going back to sleep." The mention of sleep made Ne yawn.

"That's a good idea." Genia rose with Eowen and pulled Ne along. "Come Ne, come sister. Excuse us Hani, we're going back to sleep."

"Oh, I'm sorry, I didn't know I'd interrupted your sleeping time. Zerinley, how do you do 'goodnight' with hand-speech?" The little girl lifted her hands, but paused, thought about it, then made a gesture. Yawin caught her attention and did the correct one, which she repeated for Hani again. "So smart! You're excellent at this!" Hani mussed Zerinley's hair and the little girl giggled.

"Yes, off to sleep," Yawin said with a wave. "You too Zerinley, Hale."

Zerinley pouted and Hale backed her up. "If it's all the same to you, we'll stay up a bit longer." Hale had her ax laying across her legs and she held it meaningfully.

"You don't trust easily, do you?" Hani sounded amused, his eyes gently mocking.

"No, she doesn't!" Zerinley matched his expression and faced Hale with it. The warrior girl huffed, but leaned back with her hands behind her head and legs crossed.

"I'm here if you need me Yawin," she said.

Eowen laid down and prepared to create the tent around her once more, but Genia interrupted.

"Eowen, would you like to sleep next to us instead of alone?" Eowen avoided Genia's eyes, shook her head, and covered herself with a tent, barriers, and a suffusing darkness that pressed in like deep water. Genia sighed and settled down with the other mountain children. Ne had produced a lean-to tent that would block out the firelight Yawin and Hani were using. "Well done, little brother." Ne resisted the praise by stubbornly crossing his arms and setting his mouth in a thin line.

"This is nothing." He tried to sound grown-up. Genia kissed his head and pulled him in for a hug. "Hey!"

"What a cute little brother I've got!"

"Get off!" Ne squirmed out of her grasp but she managed to pull him in again.

"Settle down, little Ne." Genia stifled a yawn. "We need our rest." The two curled up, and gradually their breathing began to take on that matched rhythm of sleep that two people achieve by true trust, comfort and proximity. Ne wasn't quite asleep though, and his thoughts were of the next waking and what it would bring.

"Hey, Genia." He poked his sister awake.

"Hmm, what? Need to pee?"

"We're going to see Mom and Dad tomorrow," he whispered, and Genia fully woke up. She didn't answer right away, or even for a long moment after. Yawin and Hani's quiet voices sprinkled the atmosphere with the sweetly nostalgic sound of background conversations; sound carried in the mountains and whispered conversations went far. The mountain folk's time with Eowen hadn't been an escape from the nightmare of their dead loved ones, but it had been a reprieve. The next time they awoke, the reprieve would be over.

"Yes, we are."

"Will we hold a funeral?" Genia looked at her little brother, surprised. His eyes were wet with tears and he looked afraid, but he had also set his brows in the way an eleven-year-old might when trying to look tough. Genia hugged him closer and gave him another kiss on the head.

When did my little brother get so grown up? she wondered. *If he can try to be brave, then so can I.*

"Yes we will. They'd be so proud of you, Ne."

"You too," Ne whispered.

From her tent Eowen listened, not as cut off from the world outside as she seemed. A barrier around her tent acted like the reverse of the one that removed sound, making it easier to hear those at a distance. Ne, Genia, and Zerinley were fast asleep in minutes. Hale refused to sleep, but otherwise didn't stir except to get water as Yawin and Hani spoke for hours. She learned that the boy was, indeed, from the islands to the south of the jungle and savannah tribes. That he had shown an immediate adaptation to the new world and had managed to save almost his entire island. He had set up food, air, and infrastructure for the other islands that his people lived on as well. Eowen noted that he never clearly said why he'd left home, but it seemed that it had something to do with Captain Asobrab. Eowen couldn't help but wonder if he had been exiled too. She could not imagine that someone would choose to leave their people willingly and risk the world beyond, especially considering what it had become.

Still, something about him is familiar, Eowen thought, running what little she knew about him through her mind. Nothing stuck though. Her mind twisted everything back to her own exile and everything in her life felt, as though it somehow fit into the box of that experience. She let some tears form as memories of Mein, twisted to seem crueler and more imposing than in reality, made the pain of the moment fresh. She felt sick when she thought of her father and the extent at which she had betrayed and disappointed him. Then her mother's face, not dead but glowering, daring her to try an excuse. Eventually, she did sleep, but it took time and her dreams were troubled.

****

[Listen, for you cannot hear me yet]

I BENT DOWN, PUSHING ASIDE DESTINIES, SKIES, AND HEAVENS AS ONE DOES CURTAINS, TO INSPECT A VERY SMALL PLACE AS ONE DOES THE LAST DEW ON A BLADE OF GRASS.

****

Yawin approached Eowen's tent with bags under his eyes. Before he could touch it Eowen dismissed it from existence. "Oh, good morning."

"I'm fine with Hani traveling with us," Eowen said.

"You heard us?"

Eowen nodded.

"Alright then. I suppose I'll ask the others." The old man straightened up and stretched, groaning as his joints protested their use. Then he shuffled over to Genia and Ne. "Ne, Genia, wake up." He shook them gently. Genia had to rub her eyes for quite a while but Ne sat up right away.

"What's for breakfast?" Ne asked.

"My thoughts exactly!" Hani called from the remains of their campfire. Zerinley woke up from where she'd been sleeping next to Hale and everyone gathered at the campfire. With ease, Hani created food for everyone, wooden bowls full of some delicious smelling mix of rice, vegetables, fish, and the flesh of some land creature. His creations came out effortlessly, quickly, and accurately, shadow and light spinning out the meal as easily as one snaps their fingers. Eowen felt a little pang of jealousy. It was unpleasant and unfamiliar, and she couldn't help but hate Hani just a bit.

"Here, you eat it with these." In another breath everyone had a stack of leaves in their hands to scoop the food with. "It's rock pig, rice, moonfish, and... some vegetables. I don't know which but it should taste great!"

"Rock pig? How can a pig be made of rocks?" Zerinley eyed the dish skeptically.

"By eating rocks," Hani said through a mouthful.

"He's lying," Ne said to Zerinley and rolled his eyes.

"I'm actually not. The pig eats soft volcanic stone and digests the minerals in it. Making it taste fantastic. Go on try." Hale and Yawin were already eating, the old man thanked Hani politely and Hale shrugged nonchalantly. Everyone joined in and Hale had seconds. After their meal, Yawin cleared his throat for attention.

"Hani, would you please give us privacy? I must discuss something with the children."

"Of course, I'll be over there." Hani pointed to the never-ending stream Eowen had made in her first arrival. Yawin waited till he was out of earshot then turned to Eowen.

"Eowen, would you place a sound barrier around us?"

"I can do it!" Ne raised his hand.

"I'm sure you can," Yawin said to him and smiled patiently. "But Hani is quite... capable. I would like to be certain of our privacy." Ne seemed a little put out but accepted Yawin's logic. Eowen took a deep breath and drifted into her dreaming, establishing a barrier around all of them.

"It's ready," she said.

"Thank you. Children, we will likely find our people when we leave this site. Hani wishes to travel with us so that he may more easily reach his destination. He seemed harmless enough so I allowed him to stay with us tonight, but we do not know if he has other intentions than stated.

The world is strange and we do not know who or what may be a threat. In this new world, one's capability in creation and the number of people who can create effectively may determine the power of a place. It is not something I have wanted to think about, not with all the death there has already been, but we must be prepared. I would not openly lead a stranger to our people before consulting all of you." He smiled then. "Together, I am sure we can judge his character."

"I like him!" Zerinley beamed and rocked on her seat.

"Of course you like him," Ne said, purely argumentative. "He played with you, that's all you need to like someone." Zerinley was the picture of an offended toddler, she stamped her foot and pouted with her lip out.

"No!" Before Ne could respond Genia cut in to chastise her brother.

"Why are you being like that with her, you liked Hani too."

Ne blushed. "Well, yes, but I just wanted to point out that Zerinley was being stupid."

"I'm not stupid!"

"I didn't say you're stupid, I said you were being stupid."

"Shut it!" Hale struck a stone she'd created with her ax, making a clang with a similar effect to a gavel. "Make a vote, then you two are done."

"But—"

"Vote!" Ne sulked and Zerinley seemed to consider it a victory.

"He's coming!" Zerinley said, then looked at Ne.

"Fine, he doesn't seem bad."

"I trust you Yawin," Genia said.

"Me too," Hale responded. Yawin nodded thoughtfully,

then turned to Eowen. It took her a moment to notice that everyone was staring at her.

"Me?"

"Yes, what's your vote?"

Thoughts spun through Eowen's head quickly, the emotional weight of them falling onto the scales in her heart. She hadn't expected to be considered important enough to cast a vote, she'd assumed they'd just used her for the barrier. After all, it was their people they were traveling towards. *I don't have the right to weigh in on this. I'm not one of them.*

The jealousy she'd felt towards Hani was still lingering. Then there was the fact that Hani seemed to have just as much potential for creation as her, but didn't seem to struggle with control at all. Even the barrier she'd just established had come with some minor unintended creations. Plants had sprung up at the border of it, little wisps of heat, scent, and taste had curled off of it. Minor things, insignificant enough for most of her creations that one wouldn't usually notice, but each tiny random effect was a reminder of the accidental damage she was capable of. The mountain folk insisted she had earned a place with them, and she could feel a glow of loving joy and belonging from them, though she couldn't bring herself to completely believe in it. Now, however, she felt she had reason to doubt the sincerity of the mountain folk's affection. Hani's presence as a completely new person that the mountain folk appeared to immediately trust made her wonder if they were only keeping her around for the convenience of her abilities and would replace her as soon as she proved too much of a hazard. She dismissed that as unlikely, though the emotional weight of it still fell on the scales. On the other hand, Hani claimed to be looking for someone, which would mean he wouldn't stay with them either way.

What finally did tip the scales was the strange familiarity of him. Eowen wanted to know who he felt so similar to. It echoed in her spirit of some old loss and recent motivation. Without being entirely aware of it, Eowen's hand had risen in an affirming gesture as her considerations had flown through her mind.

"It's settled then," Yawin said. "Hani comes with us." Eowen returned from the realm of her deep thoughts and noticed for herself that her hand was up.

"Oh, yes. I'm fine with that."

* * *

Hani was in high spirits, but seemed unsurprised at their decision. Over some tea created by Ne, Yawin explained the proceedings. He told Hani how he did not know what the rest of the mountain folk had been up to since their absence. He explained the state he and the children's settlement had been in when they'd found Eowen. Finally, he gave a very brief summary of their timeline since finding Eowen, omitting any details about how the jungle and savannah people had treated them. He did not say a thing about why Eowen was with them now, and though Hani's curiosity saturated his dreaming aura to the point of being obnoxiously obvious, he did not ask. Zerinley was quickly becoming more attached to him; he clearly had a way with children.

Eowen glanced at the little island that had been her anchor of sanity in those first days when the world ended. She didn't want to cry anymore or feel homesick and heartsick, but the little dirt island smelled like the savannah, the creek sounded like the jungle. Once she walked past it, she would be the furthest she'd ever been from her people. Though there was no clear border or boundary, when Eowen stood at the far end of her first camp she felt like one does chest deep in the sea, where one more step will put you over unknown depths.

She took the step forward and something in the world did change, some force unraveling from her like the sail of a ship cut free. Her dreaming aura spooled out behind her in a massive arc, going even beyond her perception. It was a creation, occurring unbidden and without her control, and the group could feel it, watching the light and shadow spread out, only to seemingly become nothing. Then, the creation snapped with some kind of elastic quality, and a barrier established itself as an enormous dome that covered the entire zone of Eowen's people, from her little island a few feet away, to the jungle with its sun-moon floating overhead. The barrier had no visual quality and could only be felt with one's dreaming aura. It did not have any obvious traits, and without feeling it one wouldn't know it was there, save for the random detritus of creation that always accompanied what Eowen made littering the border of the barrier.

"What was that?" Genia asked.

"I don't know," Eowen answered seriously. She took a step backward and the world turned. She became immediately disoriented and fell. Ne rushed over to pick her up.

"Are you ok?"

"Yes, I'm ok. I'm fine, just a bit dizzy is all." Eowen allowed the little boy to help her up. He took her hand and leaned back, leveraging all his weight. "I think it's supposed to keep people out."

"You don't know?" Hale stepped forward, put her hand to the barrier, and found herself stumbling away, dizzy. "Oh, I can see it."

"That was incredible!" Hani exclaimed. "You just manifested a shroud to protect all of your people. Is that what it was like when you created that jungle and the sun above it? I've been wondering since I saw—" Hani cut off his stream of excitement when he saw the look Yawin was giving him. "In any case, that was very impressive. I supposed we should be on our way now? Zerinley, lead the way." They headed off holding hands and Hale followed with a glance at Eowen.

"She does that sometimes," Zerinley whispered once she and Hani were out of earshot.

"Does what?"

"Makes stuff, but not on purpose."

Hani thought about that for a moment, then asked: "How?" Zerinley shrugged and pulled him along.

As they combed the void, spread out in a wide arc, Hani would carry Zerinley on his shoulders or swing her forward with one arm while she made noises like a monkey. Hale kept them in sight, but had largely relaxed. Ne and Genia walked slowly, whispering to each other, and Yawin walked with Eowen. Eowen had not requested his company and, in fact, had been very intentionally trying to give cold enough shoulders that the others would leave her alone.

"He asked about you last night," Yawin said without inflection.

"Is that so?" Eowen tried not to sound curious.

"He wanted to know about your creations, the oasis and the sun."

"Hmm."

"It's understandable, the scale of those creations are very impressive. Anyone would be curious."

"Of course, anyone would be," Eowen mumbled.

"He also asked why you are traveling with us and not

with your own people." Eowen's shoulders tensed and her palms began to sweat.

"What did you tell him then, Yawin?" Something in Eowen's tone was sharp and saw-like, her question pregnant with a different meaning she'd been too afraid to voice. *What are you going to tell your own people about me when we find them?*

Yawin did not need Eowen to explain all of her feelings to pick up on them. "I told him that one's past is their own to tell, and that yours is not to be asked for." The old mountain man gave her a loving smile which Eowen found herself shyly returning despite her attempts to remain frosty.

"Thank you," she whispered, and Yawin responded to the thanks by elbowing the girl, who elbowed him back till they were affectionately shoving each other around. Eowen smiled openly and laughed for the first time in days, her head held up a little higher.

Yawin glowed, enjoying every little victory he achieved against his charge's despair. Eowen and the other children under his care were no longer mysteries to him. He knew that Eowen felt some resentment towards him for how things had gone with her own people, since the creation of the sun had been partially inspired by his advice. He also knew that she placed most of the blame on herself, and that she did not blame her people. While he felt that the priestess, Mein, was in the wrong, he accepted that it was not his culture and therefore not his right to question how things had gone. In Eowen's mind, her people had been the victims of her incompetence, which objectively had some truth to it. Yawin felt the good she'd done should have outweighed that, but he also knew she wouldn't listen to such reasoning. He'd decided to be patient with her though; it was his purpose now in this new world to make sure the children he'd found himself caring for were safe. He wanted to make sure they knew they were loved. He wanted them to know that, despite it all, they still had a life ahead of them.

* * *

Zerinley was the first to spot the other mountain folk. The settlement Eowen's companions were from had long since been cleared of its bodies; like with Eowen's people, the dead had been collected and gathered in one place to deal with later. The party passed through that empty place and found the mountain folk's main settlement within hours. In the distance figures could be seen, underlit by the starlight from below. Everyone's reactions were slightly different; Zerinley jumped up and down and started running, Hale followed at a jog with Hani. Ne froze in place, his eyes skating over the distant apparitions. Genia put her hands on his shoulders and whispered something in his ear. He looked up at her and nodded, then marched forward with his sister behind him. Yawin walked forward confidently and calmly, Eowen at his side.

"Don't worry," he said to her while his hands shook. "I'll stay right next to you."

Eowen's skin felt like it fit wrong, she was all nerves. "No, I'll be ok. You go on ahead." She pushed the old man forward and he stumbled a bit, coughed, cleared his throat, and then put a hand over his eyes.

"Oh! I thought I was ready." The old mountain man choked down a sob and wiped at his tears. Yawin was all fear and joy in that moment and couldn't hope to untangle them. "I'm sorry, Eowen, I might be the one that needs some courage." Eowen shuffled to his side, tugged his hand away from his chest, and held it tight. The old man took some deep breaths and wiped his nose on his sleeve. "Thank you."

"Are you two coming?" Genia called. Ne ran back and took Yawin's other hand. The children had found their courage.

There were hundreds of them, perhaps several thousand, scattered in clustered camps with buildings of stacked stone. They wore clothes like those Eowen's friends had first made, out of fur and wool. Hale and Zerinley were already explaining themselves when the stragglers arrived. Hani waited patiently to the side; word was spreading fast and mountain folk from across the settlement were gathering. The party was jostled, hugged, whispered about while questions and answers rippled through the settlement. A few mountain folk, older than Yawin, had arrived and were consulting with him, asking quiet and hurried questions about who they were and how and why they'd come to arrive just then. Yawin kept his promise and didn't leave Eowen's side. The words savior, teacher, and friend began to circulate regarding her, while words like traveler, powerful, and unknown circulated regarding Hani.

For many minutes there was an energetic sternness to the reunion that consisted primarily of serious questions with serious answers, but that tension broke like a wave when someone recognized them.

"Genia! Over here girl!" a woman cried, pushing her way through the crowd that had encircled them.

"Aunt Preh!" Genia cried when she spotted the woman, and the crowd split for them to reunite. Genia pulled Ne along with her, and when the little boy saw his aunt his serious demeanor finally broke. He tackled her, almost tipping her and Genia over.

"Hale, is that you?" Another voice rang out, a tall warrior man, the tallest mountain folk Eowen had seen, striding through the crowd which parted for him. Hale rushed forward, prepared to salute, and was instead swept up in his arms.

"Woah! Hello captain," she got out as he spun around and sent her legs flying. More warriors followed with their rough greetings. A stern old man found Zerinley and struggled to pick her up in arthritic arms. Finally a woman around Yawin's age came sidling through and locked eyes with the old man. He squeezed Eowen's hand painfully, but she didn't complain.

"Yawin," The woman said, moving tentatively forward with her hands out as if to take or give something, but they were empty, and he had nothing to offer.

"Riauni..."

"When I found Phya, and you weren't there—"

"I-I couldn't do anything, I—"

"I don't blame you, Yawin!" The woman named Riauni held him by the shoulders. "I was afraid and confused and I didn't know what had happened to you, but it wasn't your fault." She and Yawin were shedding tears now, his one hand in front of his eyes and his other still holding Eowen's tightly. She realized she had never known the name of Yawin's wife; he had never spoken it. "Yawin, do you hear me?" Riauni continued. "I don't blame you. It wasn't your fault. Yawin, listen to me."

She continued repeating those words until he was brought to his knees. Riauni came down with him and they held each other like that with Eowen standing over them. Many eyes were on her, many whispered voices spoke of her, but for once the attention did not bother her. Eowen stood vigil beside her friend as he allowed himself to weaken in grief for the first time since the fall, and it felt right.

* * *

The next few hours were a blur for Eowen. As the reunions commenced, Eowen and Hani found themselves watching from the sidelines along with the various leaders of the mountain folk. It seemed they were being led by a duo of ancient men that might have been twins. A younger man who assisted the leaders asked Eowen and Hani questions. Her grasp of their language impressed them, and she was able to give them a satisfying sense of what had transpired since the fall. The two elders appreciated her honesty when she revealed that she had been exiled from her own people, though she only told them it was for bringing outsiders into her people's midst. She emphasized how, despite her part in saving her mountain friend's lives, they had been the ones to stay by her and had invited her to come with them home. Her account of Hani was only to say he was passing through and appeared to be trustworthy. Yawin, after collecting himself, corroborated her claims, but he included that he would like to officially adopt Eowen as one of the people. Hani politely followed the proceedings as much as he could by tone of voice and body language.

The two elders announced that a special celebration for the return of their lost people should take place. The young man assisting them listened to their whispers and made gestures of polite welcoming to Hani and Eowen.

"The Patricians have decided a small affair for the close family and friends of our returned people will be held at the center hall." He gestured to a stone building constructed like the others that was much longer and several times wider. "We will gather our makers that are most skilled at food for the event." Eowen translated for Hani, and he performed a gesture for thanks as best he could.

The new arrivals were shown to massive gender-separated baths with huge fires beside them to heat water and pump it in. Genia, Zerinley, and Hale washed each other in the bath, and the simple activity, despite the unfamiliar setting, tools, and people, was achingly familiar to Eowen. No matter what village Eowen had been sent to apprentice in or how long she was there, the women and girls bathed together in the cold mountain springs and the men bathed in the lakes and ponds. The water was too warm at first, and she found herself lightheaded such that, all in a rush, her weariness caught up with her. The mountain girls were excited and joyful, taking the celebration in full swing, but Eowen could only smile faintly and nod.

After the baths they were given heavy, soft robes of wool and animal fur, then shown to the hall for the feast. At the hall, Eowen was interviewed more closely, and Hani was given an updated map that would lead him to the closest site the mountain folk estimated was in the direction of Port Disoke. Yawin supplied answers and clarification where Eowen's language failed, and after a hushed and lengthy discussion between the Patricians, they seemed to approve of the story and announced that the feast would commence.

It was not like the feasts Eowen's people had, with everyone dancing and singing, scooping food from huge communal bowls as you wished. It was a quiet and formal event with seating at a long table and no music. The food was delicious but overly sweet to her, though her friends were overjoyed to have a more traditional meal that they themselves could't replicate. Eowen was given one dish after another to try and an extremely sweet honey-flavored drink that burned her throat pleasantly. She did her best to keep up with conversation, but the warm bath, snuggly clothes, and full meal were making her drowsy fast. That combined with the cold atmosphere the mountain folks maintained put her to sleep in the middle of the feast. Zerinley and Ne were unconscious as well, and together they were moved to beds of animal skins. Yawin carried Eowen to his new residence with the woman named Riauni, who turned out to be his sister-in-law, and Eowen did not wake for some time.

****

[Listen, for you cannot hear me yet]

IT WAS THE CAVE OF AH'OM, BUT THE CAVE WAS NOT AT AH'OM MOUNTAIN.

****

Eowen's fumbled to rub her eyes, which felt fused closed. She shifted in the thick robe she'd slept in and groaned.

"You must be thirsty." Hani's voice cut in, fully waking her up. She looked around, noting the interior of a stone mountain folk home but closed her eyes again as the soft light made her head hurt terribly.

"What are you doing here?" she said, groggily.

"I'm also staying with Yawin till I leave, don't you remember?"

Eowen did not bother answering. She didn't remember much of anything from before the feast.

"I bet you've got quite a headache."

Hani sounded like he was smiling, and so Eowen found the strength of will to peek an eye open to see if it was a mocking one. It was. She cursed under her breath at him while creating some water to float into her mouth. She lost control of the water and splashed it onto her face.

"Ugh." A glup's worth made it into her mouth, but it tasted like moss and ash. She wondered why her subconscious had added the nasty taste to her water when she realized it wasn't the water that was bad, but the taste of her own mouth. "What's wrong with me?" she asked Hani.

"Well, it seems the mountain folk brew a strong and famously sweet mead from mountain bee honey."

"What's mead?"

"Alcohol from honey."

"Mountain bee alcohol?" Eowen muttered, then recalled that huge, furry bees used to nest in the mountains and buzz down to the jungle flora for pollen. Their honey was a rare treat that Eowen's people used to trade for, but they'd never considered turning it into alcohol.

"Seems you had more than a few sips... and needed the sleep because you've been unconscious for almost thirteen hours."

"What!" Eowen jumped out of her bed but wobbled back down, feeling as though a spike had been put through her eyes. "I can't have slept that long, I need to—" Eowen searched for the next part of her statement but came up with nothing.

What do I need to do? She knew there had to be something for her to do, some responsibility or chore, some task or purpose. There had never not been something she had to do before.

"Well, I don't know what you need to do but there's a lot to see around here. Want to join me?" Hani held out his hand to Eowen. She eyed it, created another gulp of water for herself that made it into her mouth, then stood without taking his hand.

"Food first," she grumbled.

Outside Yawin's residence, Hani created a stone table and seats with a casual flourish. The island boy set the table with an assortment of dishes from his home and what looked like some mountain folk dishes. Then he finished by raising a tree up with wide leaves that cast shadows as though filtering bright sunlight, despite there being none. In moments he had created a relaxing, tropical atmosphere, and Eowen noted that even the air tasted hot, fresh, and briny. It reminded her of the few times she'd visited the ocean with her family, before Tavo had left. A few mountain folk passing by had stopped to watch Hani's display of creation, and he flashed them a bright smile. The mountain folk smiled back nervously and wandered away, except for an elderly woman seated outside another home who glared at anything that crossed her path.

"Huh. I thought they would like a bit of a show of manifestation. That whole feast last night was like a performance the way they created it."

"He's a bit of a show-off, isn't he?" Genia came around a corner smiling at Eowen.

"Genia!" Eowen hugged the girl from her seat. "Join us, please?" Eowen said. "He thinks people will like a display of creation."

"I see. No, it turns out our people have adopted a

ceremonial association with creation. While we were gone," Genia said.

"What are you saying about me?" Hani asked, as they'd been speaking in the mountain folk's language. "I heard my name there."

"She was saying you should tone it down a bit when creating. It's treated ceremonially here," Eowen said with Genia nodding to back her up.

"Oh, of course." Hani settled down, humbled but not offended, and paid closer attention to the mountain folk about him.

"How did you know to show up just when I woke up?" Eowen asked Genia.

"I had Ne wait to come get me. He's off playing with some children now." Genia got a faraway look in her eyes. "I'm glad he can act like a kid again."

The three of them ate and Eowen nursed her first hangover away. After their meal, Hani dismissed the seating, tree, and remaining food back into non-existence. A man passing by gasped and stared at Hani with his mouth open.

"Did I do something wrong again?" Hani asked. Genia chatted with the man, who calmed down and left them alone. "I didn't think that was too showy."

"It turns out they didn't know that was possible, making things stop existing," Genia explained, then she looked at Eowen. "Seems we have a lot to teach them." Eowen didn't respond, but privately she thought it would be a terrible idea. "Come, there's something I want you to see." Genia took Eowen's hand and led her along past Yawin's house. Hani started following but Genia held up her hand. "I'm sorry Hani, I'm taking Eowen somewhere that only our people are permitted to visit."

"Oh, I'm sorry. Of course." Hani took a step back. "I'll see you later?" he asked Eowen.

"Uh, maybe?" Eowen said before leaving quickly with Genia. "Genia, why is Hani still here?"

"What do you mean?"

"He is looking for someone, that captain, and trying to get to that place, Port... something. Why is he still here, and why is he trying to spend so much time with me?" Eowen asked when they were out of earshot.

"Well, if it were a boy trying to spend time with you in the old world, I'd say he was courting you." Genia poked Eowen's side and smiled conspiratorially.

"Courting?" Eowen tried out the unfamiliar mountain folk word.

"Trying to become husband and wife."

"Oh..." Eowen was not amused, but she thought about it for a moment then shook her head. "We're not in the old world though. And... I'm not sure how to properly describe it, but I don't feel that's his motive."

"No?"

"No. I've seen people try to marry others before. Uh, court them. He is looking for someone, that captain, and he wants to get to that place. I doubt he'd stop his quest to try and marry someone after just meeting them."

"Port Disoke, that's the place."

"That's right." Eowen nodded confidently. "They already updated his map before the feast last night, so why is he here?"

Genia gave it some thought. "It might have something to do with how powerful you are."

Eowen stopped walking. What Genia had said made some sense; Hani had followed her this far due to her power, but she could not imagine what he'd want her power for when he was already so capable.

"What do you mean by that?" Eowen asked.

"I don't know. Maybe he wants to create something big and impressive with you?" Genia continued leading Eowen, who was now deep in thought, her mind awash with memories of the sun hanging over the oasis. There was the feeling she and Hani had felt when they'd first met and their auras of subconscious potential had flowed against each other. She recalled the time she'd tried to create something communally with the mountain folk and had nearly taken over their dreaming auras to fuel a flood of unintended chaos. She had no idea what Hani would want to do with a combination of their potentials, but she was certain that should they try anything it would result in an incomparable catastrophe. "We're here."

Genia's voice brought Eowen back to the present. They stood before a building of stone and wood, more well and intentionally crafted than the residences and feast hall. It was a massive complex with a wall of tight fitting stone bricks that stretched out at least a quarter kilometer to each side of a tall, wooden gate. A guard next to the gate wore what looked like ceremonial garb, the animal skins cut into patterns with an artful arrangement of faces, teeth, and claws.

"Where is here exactly?" Eowen asked, glancing nervously at the guard as Genia led her through into a wooden room with candles, a basin of water, and a door at the opposite end. Genia washed her hands in a particular way, and showed Eowen how to as well. The savannah girl had never felt water so cold and gasped as goosebumps ran up her arms. Genia seemed to find Eowen's reaction funny and rubbed their hands together till warm again. A woman entered through the door, made a gesture Eowen was not familiar with to Genia, and after a pause where she looked Eowen over, gestured to her as well.

"We are where our dead have been placed," Genia whispered as she took Eowen through the door.

True to her word, beyond the vast wall that stretched to either side of the gate was a field of shelves with the dead on them. Eowen's breath fogged, which she had only ever seen on the coldest and most humid nights at home, for it was much colder past the door. The facility was massively long and the bodies were stacked six high on shelves. Names had been inscribed on the wood to denote who was who, though many shelves were empty of people, names, or both. Further down there were no shelves at all, but workers stalked through the place creating more of them, identifying bodies off to the sides with tearful families, and carrying identified bodies to their resting place. Eowen saw all that was being done and all that had been done and breathed a sigh of relief. Nothing in her future with the mountain folks felt certain or safe, but this was familiar, a common experience, a uniting thread between all people.

"Come," Genia said, tears forming in her eyes. "I want you meet my and Ne's parents."

Through the paths between shelves they went, their breath like smoke as they passed body after blanket covered body. Frost was on all the surfaces, and Eowen snuggled into her thick robe. She could have increased the temperature of her atmosphere but she intuited that the cold had some importance, for it was much more pervasive here than in the rest of the settlement and Genia did not seem concerned by it. Eventually, at the very end of the shelves, they arrived at one not yet full with only three bodies in it. One blanket covered a body the size of a baby, the other two were adults. Genia pointed to the names of the adults, symbols made of straight lines and dots that Eowen did not understand.

"What does it say?" Eowen whispered. Her words did not go far, swallowed up by the cold.

"Kaia, Bokka, my mother and father." Genia passed her fingertips over the names two, three, four times till her hands were needed to wipe away tears. "The, um." She sniffed, wiped, and pointed to the workers moving bodies. "The morticians need help to identify the bodies. That's what Ne and I did earlier while you were asleep. Yawin was here too, but I don't think Hale or Zerinley have come yet. I don't think they're ready." Eowen only nodded, patient and calm. Genia cycled through a pattern of meeting Eowen's eyes, looking around, fixating on something, spacing out, wiping away tears or snot, then repeating. Eowen's nerves were unusually calm and she waited patiently beside her friend.

Maybe it's the cold, or maybe it's the quiet, but I like it here. It's peaceful.

Eowen touched Genia's arm softly, then held it, then slowly and stiffly the two wrapped themselves around each other till they embraced to share their warmth and company. Genia wanted to say something but had no words to express what was in her to Eowen. Eowen didn't need the girl in her arms to speak to know how to comfort her. The girl from the jungle and savannah tribes ran her hand up and down the mountain girl's back and took deep breaths with her.

* * *

Eowen and Genia snuffled back to the entrance with slow and deliberate steps. Genia didn't seem to want to leave, but she didn't seem capable of staying; her spirit was drained. When they reached the door, Eowen saw two great statues flanking the exit that she hadn't noticed before. One of an eagle and the other of a large cat. Genia noticed her staring and stopped to explain.

"They are sacred animals to us; the copper-back eagle and the wild snow cat. They are the beasts of heaven and earth."

"I see. So your cemeteries in the old world would have had statues of these in them as well?" Eowen asked, and Genia looked very sad.

"No... for a funeral, the heart would be removed and left out for an eagle to eat, and the liver left out for the cat."

She searched Eowen's face for some recognition or judgment of their funeral practices, but Eowen only listened politely. She'd never heard of funeral practices other than what her tribe did, but it didn't feel wrong to her or strange. After a moment Genia continued.

"The heart carries the divine aspect of love, given by the gods so that humanity can know what it is to better themselves beyond their earthly trappings. The liver carries courage, the earthly aspect, given by the gods of the earth, who renounced pure divinity so that humanity will still serve the world. The eyes carry the collective spirit of humanity so that we can know the world outside our own minds. These three parts must be removed and eaten by their respective entities so that they may be returned to their sources to be given again." Genia recited all this very formally and with a particular cadence, having heard it many times during religious events. "Then the body is cremated after these parts are devoured so that the ghost does not carry love, courage, or sight, as those would be bad things for an eternal spirit to have." This part was said with a less religious intonation and more of one belonging to an adult trying to convince themselves they are no longer afraid of the scary stories from their childhood.

"So the statues are here to represent those things since there aren't any eagles or cats anymore?"

"Yes, that's the idea, though no one can truly be laid to rest without them, so this," Genia gestured all around them, "is the best we can do for now." Genia's tone suggested a helpless discomfort with this. They passed through the gates, waved goodbye to the guard, and in moments it was out of sight behind the stone homes.

"I see," Eowen said. She was lost in thought, thinking about how she had, in fact, created animals herself. It had always been by accident though, and the animals had run off and died almost immediately after. She dismissed the idea of doing so for the mountain folk immediately.

Better if they can't perform their funerals properly than if I accidentally hurt someone trying to make it possible. Still, it's sad. Being unable to mourn properly because of what is missing.

Eowen thought of the bone herons her own people needed for their funerals and the wrongness of her people's inability to perform their own funeral rites. It made her think of her mother, and the painful knot in her chest twisted.

Maybe I'd have been able to mourn her, if we'd had the trees and the herons then maybe I'd... What? Feel better?

Eowen shook her head out of the thoughts of her people, a weight of guilt and bitter disgust at herself making her hunch over.

I wonder if one day someone will be able to create an eagle and cat to eat the hearts and livers and eyes... Wait—

"Genia, did you say what eats the eyes?"

"We do of course."

"What?"

"They come from the spirit of humanity."

"What!" Eowen shouted, then covered her mouth, embarrassed. Genia doubled over laughing at her. She had a bright, tinkling, beautiful laugh that Eowen had rarely heard. "I'm sorry! I didn't mean to imply there was anything wrong with that!" Eowen said with her hands up.

"It's alright, sister. I forgot that it would seem strange to some outsiders." Then a sly expression crossed Genia's face before she settled it into pious seriousness. "Of course, you'll have to eat our parents' eyes to be considered one of us." Eowen glanced between Genia's deadpan expression and the cemetery behind them.

"I-I suppose we should get it out of the way?" Eowen turned around, but Genia cut her off with a snort.

"Ha ha! Stop, you don't have to eat anyone's eyes, I was joking."

"I hate you, truly!" Eowen smacked Genia on the shoulder, but both girls were alight with joy.

"Ah, that's a good one eh? I bet no one else will get a chance to prank someone like that. No, even among family some find eating the eyes distasteful and leave it for others, no harm in that. Besides, Ne and I ate our parents' eyes earlier while you were asleep. They preserved very well without air and in the cold."

"Oh, you did? Alright, I suppose that's... fine?" Eowen shook off some chills that went up her spine as she imagined Genia daintily plucking an eyeball from its socket, slurping it in like a grape, and chewing it thoughtfully while Ne slopped a messy handful of eyes into his mouth beside her. Genia giggled and put an arm around Eowen's shoulder.

"Didn't you know? We're having my uncle and aunt's eyes for dinner! Then you'll officially be part of the family!"

"Oh of course, and you can have a necklace of my toenails. Don't worry, it's what all sisters give each other in my culture," Eowen said with a laugh, but instead of laughing with her Genia's smile became shy and a tear formed in her eye. She wiped it away and when she spoke her voice cracked.

"That's the first time you've called me sister," Genia said. Eowen looked away. Her face felt hot and she knew she'd overstepped. Eowen knew the mountain girl had been wanting Eowen to consider her family, but she felt she'd crossed a line in her own heart. To distract Genia from her embarrassment, Eowen pointed to a decorative looking obelisk with four sides and writing.

"What's that for?"

"It's to help people figure out where they are. We had them in some of our larger settlements in the old world. There should be eight of them representing North, South, East, West, and the directions between them. That way, when everyone's house looks the same, especially under snow, they can tell you which obelisk to go towards." Genia began pointing out details and decorations on the obelisks and residential homes, explaining them all to Eowen as they strolled through the settlement. She saw children at play, young and old telling stories as best they recalled. People wearing ceremonial robes of deep blue wool were creating huge wooden beams that would be carved, painted red, and assembled into gates, some of which already stood in the settlement. A small part of Eowen nagged at her, saying that they should just create the beams already carved and painted, or better yet, create the gates already constructed. It seemed there was still a mental block for many people in the new world to create things fully formed rather than in their component parts to be assembled later. They passed by warriors training with mountain folk weapons, hand to hand combat, and carrying stones while performing athletics. Hale was among them, but Genia said not to bother her.

Eventually, they arrived back at Yawin's home. The settlement had grown darker, and Eowen wondered if some kind of light effect had been created to simulate night and day, but she realized it was the people themselves. The starlight from below, which followed people and grew brighter in response to creation, combined to affect an overall sense of daylight across the settlement due to the condensed population. Hours passed, and as people grew weary and retired to their homes less light was put out, effectively creating a day-to-night cycle organically timed by the population's internal clock. A few stragglers remained, but it was almost as dark as night in the old world, and Genia was looking weary. They'd stopped for food while visiting Zerinley at her grandfather's home before returning to Yawin's. Neither Yawin nor Hani were present and Eowen looked around, feeling lost. This was supposed to become her home but it felt alien, and she was sure it would never feel like a home to her.

"You'll be ok," Genia said, rubbing one eye. "He'll be back shortly. I suspect he was out looking for you."

"I'm sure you're right."

"Hani's gone, too."

"I noticed."

"Maybe he left for that adventure." Genia made a neutrally dismissive gesture. Eowen knew that wasn't true. She could sense him just at the edge of her dreaming aura, probably further out than anyone else could detect. The mountain girl pulled Eowen in for a hug. "I'll see you tomorrow," Genia whispered. "Sleep well."

"Sleep well, Genia," Eowen said as the older girl walked away, and then she was alone. When no one was looking, she created a stone seat outside of Yawin's residence that she hoped fit in and waited for him. She wasn't tired; the thirteen hours of sleep had made sure of that. So she just sat, taking in the village around her.

* * *

The settlement was almost completely dark when Yawin appeared, sauntering between the stone houses. Eowen watched him from her seat, darkened by the lack of starlight. There was something different about the way he moved, a quality to his body language that had shifted. Yawin wasn't exactly a graceful man, but he'd always conducted himself with a certain care and precision. He never tripped, or knocked things over, or even stumbled, but among his people and the home they were making she saw a different side to the old man. His hands would casually reach out to brush against walls, sometimes leaving things like hanging decorations slightly crooked things in his wake. The direct and efficient way he'd move from one place to another was replaced with a wandering and relaxed trundle. Eowen saw now that what he'd been for her and the other children, an unshakably consistent fixed point, was not the true state of the man. When he was close enough, she saw in his eyes why he'd survived into this world instead of perishing like the rest of their settlement. The man was a dreamer, taking in the world around him while, in the background, his subconscious wandered where his waking mind could not hope to follow.

"Hello Yawin," Eowen said as the old man pushed open

his door. He snapped back from his daydreaming and looked around till he noticed Eowen on the dark bench. "Welcome back."

"Eowen? I thought you'd be asleep."

"I got plenty already."

"That's right, you were out a long time."

"Genia said it was thirteen hours." Yawin confirmed this with a nod, then gestured for Eowen to move.

"Nice bench, scoot over."

"Don't stay up for me, I'm sure you're tired."

"I've still got business to attend to." Eowen moved and he took his seat next to her. Sweat broke out on his forehead and he wiped it away with a sleeve. "The air is always so warm around you and smells of the jungle."

"Really?" Eowen sniffed herself. "I hadn't noticed."

"Of course, how would you? That's normal for you. How does it feel and smell here?" Yawin gestured around them. "Hmm, we should really name the settlement. We could just name it after our largest city from the old world, but that feels wrong. It's a different place."

"It smells like stone, dust, and it's always cold. And the air is so... thin?"

Yawin smiled. "Dry, the air is dry, and yes, thinner. I suppose you've experienced dry air in the savannah, if not the jungle."

"I always thought the sun dried out the air, though. There's not much sun on top of the mountains, they're always covered in clouds. Or were..."

"It's the cold. All the water in the air freezes into ice and snow."

"Oh, yeah. I've never touched real snow." Eowen felt suddenly nostalgic for when she'd first arrived in the new world and had created intentionally for the first time before meeting the mountain folk. Barely two months worth of time had passed, but the landscape of her life was incomparable. She brought herself back to that time, the dreaming part of her mind that knew what snow was in that subconscious way. The starlight flared beneath her and the shadows writhed, and then there was snow, like she'd made it before, in a clump on her hand. "It's like this, right? I made some before ever meeting you."

Yawin took the clump, though his hand mostly passed through it. Like before, it was as cold as the mountain streams that fed her jungle, but insubstantial like a cloud. The clump floated on her hand and could be wafted around, denser than fog, but not a solid.

"Fascinating. No, snow's not like this at all."

"What?"

"I can see why you'd think it was like this, having never touched it and only looked from so far away."

"Then... what is it like?" Yawin shook with silent laughter at her. Then he closed his eyes and held out his hands. Eowen felt the moving of his subconscious, the balancing of intent and stray thought which he'd described as lighting a fire with a stick and bow while trying to catch that fire with your hands. The creation formed, and in his hand was a clump of snow that looked almost exactly like Eowen's, only it slumped more, sank between his fingers, and, when observed very close up, had a crystalline structure. Eowen touched it and it was just as cold as hers, but her finger sank in, leaving an imprint rather than passing through. It was no cloud but a soft, fluffy, and very cold thing that took shape and melted to water at her touch.

"It's more like this, though there can be different types of snow and ice. This is the most common form after it falls from the sky."

"Why is it so fluffy?" Eowen mused, poking it again.

"It falls like this." Yawin created again, and above his hand a little cloud formed, dropping gently drifting snowflakes that melted before they could build up. His brow furrowed and he stared at the snowflakes, concentrating very hard. A few of them stopped falling, suspended in space. The air around them became very cold and Yawin leaned in close, gesturing for Eowen to do the same. "It's really just tiny stars that gently cluster together, see?" Eowen did see, and it was the most beautiful thing she'd ever seen. She stared at the snow crystals as closely as her naked eye would allow until her body heat overcame the cold Yawin had brought on to preserve the snow, and their beauty was whisked away into formless drops of water.

"I had no idea," she whispered. Something shifted inside her. She could feel it in the far recesses of her mind, like a new current being added to the ocean of her subconscious, one that begged to be explored.

"Come, we'll have plenty of time to learn about snow and such later. I've got that business to attend to, and it involves you." Yawin pushed Eowen out of her seat, shaking her from daydreams of frozen patterns and drifting beauty.

"What?"

"The Patricians want to meet with you and I privately." They started through the buildings towards the hall where they'd had the feast.

"Why? Did I do something wrong?"

"No, of course not. It's about the matter of your adoption."

"Oh... I thought that was already settled. Are the others going to be there too?"

"No, they've already been taken in by what remaining family or close friends they still have. Eowen, how do your people handle adoption?"

"It's not unusual. My parents took in my cousin, Tavo, when his parents died from disease. We didn't have to meet with any leaders, we were just the closest family to him, and one day he was just living with us."

"I see. Know this Eowen; adoption is taken very seriously among our people. Everything must be approved by the Patricians. That's where I've been most of today, discussing the matter with them. It seems we've largely abandoned the ceremonies of adoption because there are... so many who need families, the chaos has made it less of a priority to do so ceremonially. Still, almost every child taken in after the fall has met with the Patricians about it. We'll be going through the full formal process because you are not originally one of our people. Tonight is the first step and it will take about a week. Hmm, I wonder how we'll perform the ceremonies that are done during certain phases of the moon?"

While Yawin mused over the adoption process, Eowen was very quiet. She wanted to cry, or hide. It didn't matter to her that she'd spent so much time with her mountain friends or that Yawin was fully prepared to take her in. She still had to go through steps that others didn't to be adopted, steps that no one else had to go through because she was not one of them. She knew what it would really mean for her when all was said and done. She wouldn't ever be one of them. She'd always be the one they had let in, a stray they would tolerate so long as she behaved. Eowen knew it in her heart; she'd be kicked out the moment they felt she was more trouble than she was worth. For three years it had been that way, and in the new world it would be no different.

They arrived at the hall and Yawin held the door open. Eowen shuffled in with her head down, trying to be as respectfully quiet as possible. The Patricians waited at the end of the hall where they'd sat during the feast, though the great table had been removed. Yawin and Eowen approached, flanked by two warriors in ceremonial garb similar to the one at the cemetery gate. Yawin gestured respectfully, and Eowen followed suit. The assistant to the Patricians spoke for them; the ancient men seemed perpetually exhausted. The conversation mainly consisted of informing Yawin and Eowen of which ceremonies and preparations they would and would not be required to do. Certain ceremonial garb, face paints, and sacred psalms that bound people together as family would have to be observed. It was a similar process as marriage, as Yawin explained, but different in connotation. The assistant declared, by the decision of the Patricians, that ceremonies which required certain times of day and phases of the moon would be performed between the other appropriate steps at a suitable time to be determined. All in all, it would take about a month of time with ceremonies done almost every other day's worth of time.

Yawin took it all in stride, nodding and hmm-ing when appropriate until, over an hour into the meeting, both the Patricians were asleep. They decided to call the meeting to a close when one Patrician interrupted the proceedings with a snore that shook his chair. The assistant looked behind him, blushed, and apologized on behalf of his masters. He dismissed Eowen and Yawin, gesturing respectfully to both. As they walked back, Eowen tried to recall anything she was expected to do but came up blank. It all had passed right through her head and she was feeling stupid and disoriented.

Yawin noticed the dizzy look to her and patted her head affectionately. "You feel ready?"

"Ahhhhhhhhhh... Yes?" Eowen tried very hard not to sound as though she were asking a question.

"Oh good, because you'll have to recite that all to the Patricians later."

"What!"

"Ha! Joking." Yawin slapped Eowen on the back, grinning ear to ear.

"I felt like I was going to die, you bastard!" Eowen pushed him away.

"Don't worry about a thing, it seems like a lot, but really it'll be a few minutes of your time every other day or so. Anything you need to recite will be whispered to you. Oaths on certain gods and the binding of your spirit to certain spirits and such."

"Ah, mmhmm." Eowen's shoulders relaxed a bit, comfortable with the familiar feeling of going through unfamiliar ceremony. It seemed to her that, for all the geographical and cultural differences between her people and the mountain folk, ancient and tedious ceremonies were a common thread.

They arrived back at Yawin's home, where Ruani was waiting with dinner in a pot. They ate together at a stone table built into the floor and spoke of what they had done that day. It was mundane, but in the cozy stone home with Yawin's sweet sister-in-law, Eowen felt a bit of what she'd been missing with her own family for many years. Simple expressions of love and company without guilt or expectation.

It did not feel right though, not for her. When Eowen lay down to sleep in her new bed, her new guardians wished her sweet dreams. She wished them the same as convincingly as she could, but once they'd turned away Eowen cast a shroud of silence over herself. She curled into the fetal position under her blanket, and she cried and cursed at the unfairness of it all. That she should feel homesick for what she hadn't had in her own home for many years. That a family that wasn't her own should give her the kind of care and love she had only ever wanted from her mother, and had not been given in many years. She did not entirely know that this was why her heart beat painfully and her stomach turned on itself. All she knew was pain based in the terrible wrongness that was to be her life from that point on, and the knowledge that this was as good as it would ever get.

****

[Listen, for you cannot hear me yet]

IT HAD FOUND A WAY TO ME.

****

The next day Yawin let Eowen sleep late again. A lethargy had taken hold of her, but he did not see the need to break her from it. When she did wake they toured the settlement, met old friends of his, and presented themselves before the Patricians as in the evening before. They were more alert this time and managed to preside over the first step in Eowen's official adoption. First, she had to be accepted and acknowledged as a friend of their people before she could be considered one of them. They painted marks on her face and shoulders in reference to the service she had done for their people, and chanted in words she did not understand. Eowen's conversational grasp of their language left her ignorant to almost everything said in the ceremony, save for when they thanked her and explained that they'd be able to give her the actual mark of friendship to their people later. Yawin explained it would be a talisman depicting a hand with an eye in the palm, a symbol of offering which the mountain folk believed connected all humanity to each other.

They returned to Ruani and Yawin's home, but after dinner Eowen wandered outside. The old man followed her out.

"Eowen? It's time to sleep, we have another important day ahead of us tomorrow." Eowen waved him off and avoided looking him in the eyes.

"I'm going to stay up a bit longer," she said. "I had so much sleep before that I'm not tired now."

"Alright." Then, very much in the way her father had done before, he said: "Don't go too far, and don't stay out too late." She did not want to hear that from him, and because of that it was awful to hear. She nodded and ducked around the corner with her barriers up, feeling sick in her stomach and her spirit.

How far does he think too far is? Eowen wondered. The settlement was a few kilometers wide. She'd have to try to get lost. *How can I stay out late? Night and day don't exist anymore.*

She found herself wandering in a direction that felt randomly chosen till she reached the edge of the settlement and looked up from the stars beneath her feet to see a pinprick of light far, far away. It was the sun that hung above the jungle oasis, her sun, her oasis.

"I still want to know how you did that."

Eowen yelped. Hani seemed to have materialized next to her.

"Why did you scare me like that?" Hani seemed to find her surprise plenty amusing.

"I didn't mean to, I promise! I noticed you were out here away from the center of the settlement and got curious. I've been practicing making myself less noticeable, so I suppose it worked."

"Genia thought you'd left already."

"But you didn't?"

"I could tell you were still around." She moved the flow of her dreaming aura against his to illustrate her point. "I just wasn't paying attention when you approached just then."

"I've been working on that. I call it blending. I match my aura with those around me so that it's harder to notice me."

"Most people can't even sense you when you're not 'blending' You're too far away." Eowen frowned. "Or they just don't know what to sense for."

"Sounds about right." Hani looked up as though trying to remember something. "You know, I don't think most people understand how things work here."

"And you do?" Eowen looked him up and down.

"That's... a good point," he conceded with a shrug. "I definitely understand better than the rest of my people do." When he said this, a pang of empathy struck electrically through Eowen.

He might have been exiled, like me. What happened, what did he do?

"Hani, why are you here?" she whispered softly. Hani shrugged and gestured around.

"What else am I supposed to do with myself? I don't

really know your mountain folk friends very well, nor the language. Not many people around here speak our language so I'm out here alone, whittling away the time. Besides, your other friends are off reuniting and such. So, I decided to wait around for you so we could spend time together."

"Spend time together?" Eowen crossed her arms.

"Yes! I haven't met someone that understands manifestation and the nature of the new world so well."

"I'm not sure I do understand it all that well," Eowen trailed off in thought. "But I have thought that maybe what some people get wrong is assuming the things we create are still the same as the things we remember from the old world."

Hani stroked the peach-fuzz on his chin, pretending it was a beard. "Elaborate."

"I don't know! I was just saying whatever came to mind. I don't make sense to myself." Hani had gotten her thinking though, and the more she did think about how things worked, the more she wanted to understand. She was still too self conscious to continue musing about it out loud, so Hani took over.

"I think I understand what you're saying. Most people will manifest a... a piece of bread." Almost too fast to see the creation happen, a loaf of bread, warm and fresh, appeared in his hand. "And they will think: this is a piece of bread because it looks and feels and tastes like bread. But it can't be, not really."

"Exactly!" Eowen's confidence surged back up as another person put to words what she had never been able to, or was never brave enough to say out loud. "The traits that make it bread are very strange when you think about it. It's a soft and squishy thing with a hard but flexible crust outside. You make it from a combination of crushed plants, water and heat, and somehow it becomes what it is. No one questions it because it is so mundane, so common."

"Right! If it wasn't so familiar to us because it had existed in the old world it would be impossible to imagine, ridiculous even. But we can believe it is possible to exist because we have known it to be real."

"And then you eat it and it keeps you alive! In a way. It's just such a strange thing without the context of the old world." Eowen couldn't help but smile at the absurdity of the situation she was in to be having the conversation she was. Hani tore off a piece and handed it to her, then took a bite for himself.

"But this bread, even though it's so like how bread was in the old world, is still not real bread. No plants were grown, nothing was crushed into flour and no mixing with water or baking happened." Hani said this while looking his loaf over carefully. "It's made of the stuff of this place, the shadows and light and... ourselves?" He looked at Eowen for confirmation, but she could only shrug.

"All I can tell or feel makes sense is that when we create things here, they're not really the things we think they are from the old world. They can have all the traits of them, even being food that fills our belly and keeps us from starving, but they're still... different. Something else."

"It's not a loaf of bread but a manifestation of my belief that there is now a thing in my hand with all the traits of a loaf of bread." Hani smiled at her. "Something like that?"

Eowen nodded slowly, paying attention just enough while the rest of her mind was far away, wrestling with abstractions. Something pinged her and she reeled her attention back.

"What's that word you keep using? Manifestation?" The

word belonged to Hani's islander dialect and was unfamiliar to her.

"Oh, it's a word that means... to make known or obvious, I suppose. To uncover maybe? It's usually used when referring to the workings of gods in the stories about how they created the world. We, on the island, started using it when referring to making things in this world." Hani pulled in shadow and light to his palm with his usual ease and control. He gazed into the swirling depths of potential, both fully present and lost in the possibilities of the subconscious. With a twist of reality and a wry smile he flicked his eyes at Eowen, and the gathered power in his hand became a red fruit with a waxy skin and almond shaped leaf on the stem. "From nothing, it is made known, like the works of the gods." Eowen was silent after his little show and he had the decency to look embarrassed after a moment. "Not that I'm suggesting that I'm like a god! Just that the way this all works resembles our stories about them."

That's not how gods do things, they can't create things, Eowen thought, but she did like the sound of the word and its meaning, which seemed to touch on an aspect of how creation in the new world worked.

"The gods can't create things," Eowen said, drawing on what she recalled of her people's religion. "They bestow knowledge of the future but they can't actually do anything." She gathered her thoughts, then recited: "From one to many they split and carry the knowing of what will follow in the happening of all things. Listen and understand." Eowen said this with a kind of meter that suggested it was a common phrase, the meaning of which was less important than the memorization of it. Hani made a face.

"Maybe that's how the gods are where you're from, but

our gods are powerful and created the world. Their demi-god children rule over the elements of the world, embodying things like volcano lava, snow, the ocean." Hani said this matter-of-factly, another piece of knowledge that was worth more memorized than understood. "If they were ever real, that is," he said with a casual gesture of dismissal.

Eowen had to think about that for a moment, as she'd never encountered the idea of the gods she'd been taught only being her gods and that other people had their own different gods. She knew that other people had different assumptions about the world, like the mountain folks' ghosts, but she'd assumed that all people worshiped her gods, just in different ways.

What did he mean by 'If they were ever real'?

"Gods can't do things, Hani, that's crazy," Eowen said, but she sounded less certain. "They exist in and as a part of the things that happen, bestowing knowledge to those that can listen, but they can't control what happens. They don't have... agency. They just have knowledge about what comes next by conversing with other gods." Eowen had grown more quiet and contemplative as she spoke. "Even children learn the basics of listening to them," she said, almost as a whisper, lost in thought. Hani just shrugged again.

"If you say so, but let me ask you this; assuming they were real, do you really think they're still around anymore?" He gestured in a circle, encompassing the whole of the new world in one motion. "Nothing happens in this new world except what people make happen. Where then do the gods, yours or mine, exist?"

He might be right. Everything in this world is made by the intent of people. Aside from the chaos when I lack control that is. The bitter thought ran through her mind as Hani continued.

"I already had my doubts about their existence in the old world, but when the fall happened... I just assumed that even if there ever had been gods, they weren't here anymore." He put his hands out with the palms up, as though holding something large in them. "It's just us now, isn't it?"

Eowen tried to remember if Mein had shown any signs of communion with the gods since the fall, and could not. "I think... that I know how things used to be, but that doesn't matter anymore, does it?" Eowen stared at her small hands. "It really is just us people now, isn't it?" Hani nodded but stayed silent, sensing that Eowen had more thoughts to go through. She was mulling over the significance of a world without what she had been raised to believe when her thoughts returned to her original unanswered question for Hani. "Wait!"

Hani jumped. "Sorry, what?"

"You never explained yourself. Why are you here?"

"For... conversations like these? I think?"

"No, not here right now with me, I mean here instead of at home with your people?"

"So suspicious! It can't be that I want to become friends with many interesting people across the new world?" Hani's smile was bright and friendly, but it didn't quite reach his eyes, and Eowen did not look convinced. After Eowen silently held an expression of doubt long enough, Hani gestured placatingly. "Alright, I'll tell you the truth. I'm looking for my father." Eowen's heart skipped a beat, her breath caught, and she leaned in to hear more. "He disappeared a long time ago, long before the fall," Hani said.

He's like me!

"My decision to leave wasn't exactly a popular one. No one really believes he's still alive. But I know he is. I just can't believe he wouldn't be." Hani looked at her, his face open and genuine now, but he was on the verge of tears. "A dreamer like him? He can't have died!" Eowen looked at Hani very gently now. She sat down cross legged and gestured for him to sit in front of her. When he complied, she created a campfire, the perfect size for telling stories.

I created this campfire, but Hani would say I manifested it. She tasted the word in her mind, and decided she liked the flavor.

"Tell me about your father. Why did he disappear so many years ago?"

A strange energy came over Hani. His expression was of one who has carried a burden heavier than his years imply, and he practically buzzed with the excitement of getting to talk about it. "It's a story that started many years before I was born. A tale of pirates, heroes, kings, and adventure." He sounded as if he'd rehearsed this. Eowen resisted the urge to roll her eyes. "For centuries the islands were ruled by pirates, but during all that time none ruled over all the islands. Instead they warred with each other, taking and losing territory often. By the time I was born, a pirate captain had, for the first time in history, become king of all the pirates in the islands. My island had been targeted and owned many times over by sea captains both benevolent and cut-throat, but we were further away from the biggest ones that the pirates wanted to build forts on, so we were usually left alone. Then one day, a cruel captain under the command of the pirate king took many of our men as slaves for their ships. My father was one of them, and I was six years old." Hani's voice dipped down at the mention of his age, and a weariness in him surfaced. Eowen wanted to say something to comfort him, but before anything came to mind Hani was ready for the next part of his story.

"You might think that's when he disappeared, but no! Instead of staying as a slave, he organized a revolt on the ship and named himself captain! He earned the respect of the other slaves, and they became his crew. The king heard of this rogue, and sent his minions to hunt them down. My father and his crew fought bravely, but when only he and a few of his crew were left, the pirates captured them and brought them before their king. His name was: The Dreaded Knife-Eater Besantu!" Hani paused for dramatic effect, but Eowen had never heard of The Dreaded Knife-Eater Besantu. She tried to look suitably impressed but failed. Hani cleared his throat, then continued.

"Besantu ruled his own island and commanded his fleet of cut-throats from there to rule most of them. My father thought he was going to be executed, but do you know what happened when he met with King Besantu? The king was so impressed by his bravery and leadership he offered my father a ship of his own to command in his fleet! He promised no one would ever raid our island again if my father would sail off for him to the most distant and dangerous lands and bring him treasures."

Hani got quiet then, his energy receding. He still seemed excited to be telling his story, but there was a certain melancholy lurking behind his eyes. He tried to hide it, but it leaked out all around him in the shadows that swirled with his subconscious thoughts. "He was gone for... many years after that, fighting bravely and collecting treasure, no doubt! The last time I saw him was when I was eleven, then he had to leave again. I decided I would join his crew once I was old enough, or march up to the pirate king and demand a crew of my own, but then..." He gestured all around them. "This happened. The pirate king died and all leadership fell apart.

I made sure my island would be safe. Air, food, water, all that. Then I left to look for my father." Hani paused for a long time and looked very intently at his hands. "I know he's alive out there, somewhere. We were getting reports about him up until a few months before the apocalypse. He is a dreamer, like me, so I've no doubt that he survived and is making a name for himself as we speak! I... just have to find him."

They sat in silence, save for the crackling of the campfire. Eowen knew for sure now what felt familiar about Hani. His search for his father had initially reminded her of her own search for her cousin Tavo, but now she knew that Hani wasn't like her; he was like Tavo. Something in her stirred then, a feeling she hadn't known she'd given up on when the fall had interrupted her own quest. A hope that Tavo was still alive. She knew her old life would never be restored by finding and bringing him back, but with how many people had died she hadn't even considered that Tavo might not be among them. She hadn't thought about him being dead exactly, but the idea of continuing her original search hadn't occurred to her. It was simply too outlandish to hope she'd find him out in the void.

And yet, Hani still has hope even though it's been longer since he last saw his father than it has been since I saw Tavo.

Hani stared into the flames, smiling faintly to himself, imagining the swashbuckling adventures he'd expected in the old world, and wondering what adventures awaited him in this one. There wasn't a trace of doubt he would find his father though, and it showed on his face. Eowen was mulling over his story, what it meant to him, and what it might mean for her.

Maybe I can hope, too. Maybe I've still got family out there, somewhere. Real family who won't turn me away and won't cast me out, but will be overjoyed to find me and will never let me go.

"So, you'll be leaving soon then," Eowen said, quiet and even.

"Hmm, what was that?" Hani emerged from his daydreams. Eowen looked at him and saw that the shadows which hung at the edges of them both had taken on the shapes and implications of their daydreams.

"You haven't left yet. You wanted to have this... conversation with me and now we've had it. How long do you intend to stay here when your father is out there, somewhere, waiting to be found?"

"Why? Do you want me gone?" Hani frowned and Eowen shook her head. "Do you want me around then?" he said with a wry smile, to which Eowen rolled her eyes. "You have a point, though. I suppose I'd hoped to meet people along my journey that would join me for their own reasons. I wanted to put together a crew of adventurers, like my father did. I suppose... when I felt the creations you were doing and saw them in person, I'd hoped the one responsible might be the first member of my crew." He looked back at the fire. "Not that I expect you to uproot yourself and join me. I'm not even going to formally invite you now that I know you're staying here. I wouldn't take you from your new family. Still, I'm curious how you created that sun and the whole jungle. I tried asking your people when I arrived there but... I promise, I'm not trying to be rude, but they weren't very friendly." He gestured apologetically. "Not that I blame them, hard to know who or what to trust in this world." Eowen's stomach twisted, she felt sick. "I asked them who made everything but they refused to answer and asked me to leave. They must have been very protective of you."

Hani stopped speaking and waited in silence. He left the conversation open for Eowen to interject, clarify, or change the subject if she wished. Eowen was weighing her options in her mind. On the one hand, it seemed like she was building a new friendship, one where she could tell her side of the story and be believed. On the other, she felt a responsibility to properly own up to the harm she'd done and the potential for harm she still had.

Hani will be leaving soon anyway so it doesn't exactly matter what impression I leave him with, good or bad. And he's told me so much about himself it would only be fair for me to do the same.

"Hani, how did your people react to you creating, um. Manifesting things? What did they think when you left home?" The island boy looked up into the darkness above, tracing the path of their campfire's cinders as they glowed, then winked out.

"That's a good question. I'll have to remember it when I'm traveling and looking for crew members, very good way to assess how comfortable they are with what I can do and what we might encounter. My people appreciated my ability to manifest things. You may have noticed, but I'm quite fast and accurate!" Hani put his hands on his hips, openly proud. "I can do small and simple things easily and accurately."

He stood, breathed in through his nose, then gestured a few times through the air, not quite dance-like. Around them, a hut roofed with broad, tropical leaves swayed into existence. Trees laden with fruit emerged, followed by a beach with waves of water that spawned from thin air, pushing onto the sand then pulling away. Finally, a wide-brimmed woven hat curled smoothly into reality upon Eowen's head. Hani returned to himself in time to casually adjust the hat on Eowen's head before whipping it off onto his own.

"See, small things. I tried teaching my people, and they

can make basic things, but even this stuff evaded them for a long time. By the time I left they could do the basics, but none of them could create larger or more complex things, like when I created a volcano for us to properly deal with our, uh, dead." Hani seemed uncomfortable when talking about the dead. He dismissed his creations except for the hat which he twirled on a finger. "They were... worried when I left, but they could take care of themselves without me. They threw a party for me, but my mom didn't show up for it. I know it's because they want to protect us and for us to stay as their babies forever, but a man has to make something of himself, doesn't he?"

"What's a... volcaano?" She worked around the unfamiliar word.

"It's... a type of mountain on an island, I suppose. With liquid lava and fire and smoke inside." Eowen gave him a blank look. "You really haven't heard of one before?"

"It sounds made-up," Eowen said. "What's lava anyway?" Hani sighed, but thought privately that maybe this was for the best. He'd need experience explaining things to foreigners if he was going to travel the new world.

"Right, so lava is liquid rock—"

"What!" Eowen looked at Hani like he'd just said that the men on his island birthed children and the women had retractable tails.

"You've really never heard of this?"

"You're lying, liquid rock? Is it cold like water?"

"No, it's hot, very hot. So hot that when it meets the air and water it cools and becomes solid rock." He smiled awkwardly and shrugged. "It's a thing that happens."

Eowen shook her head. "Let's say I believe you, what about the... water-rock, the lava. What does that have to do with preparing your dead?"

Hani shifted uncomfortably. "So we dig ditches where the lava is going to flow and leave the bodies there to get covered by it when it cools." He shrugged. "I made a temporary volcano and directed the lava to our dead." Eowen put her hand to her chin, pretending to understand, but she couldn't picture it.

"This still sounds ridiculous," she said. "Also, why did you make the... volcano—" Hani indicated that she'd pronounced it correctly, "—temporary? Wouldn't your people have felt more at home with a permanent one?" Hani brightened up.

"That's why I was so eager to meet you! It's not just the scale of your creations or how impossible they seem, but that they are permanent! I can't do that with difficult manifestations. Watch, I'll show you what a volcano is."

Hani faced away from the mountain folk's settlement and Eowen, recognizing when things could go terribly wrong, put up a barrier wall as high and wide as she could between them and the settlement that would make their side invisible to the mountain folks. Hani looked at the barrier, sensing it was there but unable to tell what exactly it was.

"Did you manifest something there?" He reached out and passed his hand through the barrier.

"It's a wall of sorts, no one on that side can see what's on this side."

"Really?" Hani passed through it and turned around. "Wow! You're gone!" He passed back through. "Why did you do that though?"

"You're about to create some kind of fire mountain next to a quiet and peaceful settlement. You'll terrify them."

Hani looked like he'd never considered that massive creations could frighten people, but he conceded that Eowen knew the mountain people better than he. He prepared himself again, stretched out his arms, reaching forward as if to grasp something. He closed his eyes and his dreaming aura thickened around him, shadows rising up like some great wave that might crash upon the land. There was a thick feeling of anticipation, a pull of power in front of them, and for a moment, Eowen thought the wave would crash, spitting out a chaotic storm of creation as it did for her when she attempted something of this scale.

"Hani!" She backed up and gathered her own power to do something, though she knew not what. When she'd shouted his name, Hani's lips twisted into a half smile, his eyes flashed open, and lit up as the starlight below burned through the amassed darkness before them with an intense, clean light. The potential became creation, and the boy from the southern islands bowed with a flourish as a burning island settled into existence.

"This," he held his hand out to Eowen, "is a volcano." The lava oozed out, far different than she'd imagined. She'd thought liquid stone would be the color of the stone, with browns and grays and veins of minerals, but it glowed, red-hot like embers in a fire. She could feel the heat from some distance and stepped past him without taking his hand, watching as the lava flowed hypnotically down. She saw that where it cooled was smooth, black rock, she stepped onto it and the dried lava crunched underfoot.

"How is this possible?" she muttered.

"These did exist in the old world, you know," Hani teased. "But manifestations like this, and like yours, make you think anything might be possible. Don't they?" Eowen didn't know about that, but Hani's confidence was inspiring, infectious, and made her want to explore and experience. It made her want to create.

The volcano shimmered as though it were a heat illusion. Eowen lost her footing and fell on her back.

"Ow! What happened?" Hani helped her up. His hand was sweaty and he had a forced expression of effort.

"I told you, it's difficult for me to maintain." He paused to huff. "I can't keep anything of this scale up for long."

Eowen turned her senses to the fading volcano, and with it her dreaming aura followed. She felt herself flowing over, into, and through the volcano, the shadows of possibility moving with the flow of the volcano's existence in the way they had flowed with Hani's dreaming aura. Something happened to her then, a rushing in her ears and a distortion of her vision, an explosion of taste and an unplaceable smell. Her skin crawled, then felt like it was walking, even sprinting, all of her senses struggling and failing to keep up with what she was experiencing save for the sense of her dreaming aura, which could feel the true nature of things around her. Her power was in Hani's volcano such that she was beginning to understand, intuitively, what it was meant to be; its forms, possibilities, and flaws. She couldn't perfectly dissect all of it in that moment, for it was Hani's creation, but she could feel the cracks in it, the implacable aspects of reality that Hani had needed to bind the manifestation together in order for it to become a self-reliant creation. She could feel Hani's power, immense like hers but accurate and precise, holding his working together, but for all his skill he had missed those fundamental parts of the construction. Eowen could feel them though, somehow. She knew what was needed.

Instinctively, entirely without intent, her power flowed into the volcano, and the cracks began to fill. Eowen fell into a trance, her waking mind drowning under the waves of her subconscious as the Storm of her spirit flared. Hani watched her, trying to understand what exactly was occurring until the strain of maintaining his volcano slacked and the flow of Eowen's power started becoming chaotic. Eowen fused Hani's collapsing creation with fresh shadow and light, welding the cracks in the volcano's metaphysical structure together. Hani released his grip on it, and the volcano settled.

"That," he said, short of breath but beaming, "was the most amazing thing I've ever seen! Eowen, how did you—" He was cut off as a flare of her power spun a scattering of flowers, music, lightning, and a bird into existence beside him. "Eowen?" Hani stepped toward her as pressure surged out from her, pushing him back from the girl lost in the storm of her dreaming.

****

[Listen, for you cannot hear me yet]

I ASKED THE CAVE TO SPEAK AGAIN, FOR THEIR VOICE, THOUGH GRAND EVEN TO GODS, WAS TOO SMALL FOR ME TO HEAR WITHOUT LISTENING CAREFULLY.

****

Hani fought toward Eowen, erecting barriers not of sight and sound, but of force. Manifestations of Eowen's power flowed over him, depositing nonsensical realities around as he deflected the effects. "Stop it Eowen!" Hani reached out, touched her hand, and felt what was in her spirit, the Storm upon her ocean.

****

[Listen, for you cannot hear me yet]

THE CAVE TOLD ME OF LOVE AND OF THEIR QUESTIONS AND OF WHO LOVE WAS, SO FAR AS THE CAVE KNEW TO TELL.

****

"You can't stop this," Hani realized, and Eowen's power flared again, ripping out of her, a tidal wave of ipseity alchemizing the oblivion around them into a mad rush of everything that dwelled in the depths of Eowen's subconscious. Hani lunged forward and grasped Eowen's hand, holding on tight. Like a jolt of static through his system, he could feel her spirit for himself as it spooled out as a torrent of shadow and light, sculpting creations without intent. He did not lose himself into it though, and when he reached with his own power to stabilize the girl the way he had when he'd held his volcano together, Eowen's spirit responded.

****

[Listen, for you cannot hear me yet]

THIS WAS NO EASY TASK AS THEIR VOICE WAS SMALL AND HARD TO HEAR, AND TO CALL UPON MY NAME CAN SHAKE A CREATOR'S SOUL TO PIECES.

****

"I can stop it!" Hani was alight, glowing between the streaks of shadow as the stars below moved under his command. "I can stop this!"

The island boy planted his feet, gritted his teeth, and bent his will against the powers before him. He could feel that the forces raging within her were not insurmountable. He dipped deep into his own subconscious, which was like a grand mountain range to be climbed. He only needed to persist until Eowen regained mastery over herself. The two remained locked in this stalemate for seconds that stampeded into minutes, and minutes that threatened to become an hour, till at last, the Storm abated.

****

[Listen, for you cannot hear me yet]

I WAS INTRIGUED, AND SO I AGREED TO MEET THIS LOVE AT AH'OM, THOUGH I WAS NOT CONFIDENT THAT WE WOULD BE ABLE TO SPEAK AND KNOW WHAT THE OTHER SAID.

****

Eowen's rampage was hooked, bound, tethered, subdued, and finally quelled. She collapsed onto Hani, who crumpled under her weight, and the two fell away from one another, rolling to the foot of the volcano. Hani coughed. He felt as though he'd dropped out of a tree and hit one too many branches on the way down. Yet, despite the discomfort, he buzzed with exhilaration.

"Eowen, are you ok?" The boy pushed himself to his knees and crawled to her. "Wake up. Let me know you're alright... Now!" She was unresponsive. A cut from her fall seeped blood down her arm and another on her forehead looked worse than it was. Hani gritted his teeth and slung the girl over his shoulder. "Come on, let's get you to Yawin."

He staggered away from the volcano and through the barrier, which had kept their activities invisible. He sampled it as he passed through, and managed to create a shroud of his own to conceal them as he made his way through the settlement. Eowen awoke to the discomfort of his bony shoulder on her ribcage and squirmed.

"Put me down." She sounded woozy and hungover.

"You're ok!" Hani knelt down and set Eowen on the starfield.

"I feel like shit."

"You were incredible, and you're mostly fine." Eowen looked and patted herself over, discovering the minor injuries.

"I hit my head." Eowen's skull ached, her mind in a fog similar to that of being awoken from a deep sleep.

"You fell," Hani said, though he was beaming. "But you're

ok. I don't even know what was happening, but I managed to stop it." That statement struck a chord in Eowen's mind, and the jumble of her thoughts began to organize.

"Where were you taking me?"

"To Yawin. I couldn't think of what else to do with you." Hani shrugged apologetically.

"No, that's perfect. Let's go find Yawin." Eowen started in the right direction while Hani scrambled to his feet to follow. They paced through the settlement, weaving between houses that all looked identical to Hani. There were some mountain folk awake, walking around, washing up with manifested water, preparing food for their families. No one noticed Eowen or Hani, invisible and silent with layered barriers around them. Hani stared at her, burning with curiosity and a desire for an explanation of what happened.

"Eowen."

"Yes?"

"I'm trying to be sensitive and patient." Eowen stopped and faced Hani, her expression one of intense focus. Eowen's mind was alight. She felt both awake and more in tune with her subconscious than she could ever remember feeling.

"What is it, Hani?" Her voice had a strange, heavy quality.

"Ah, it's just that I've told you a great deal about myself, just about everything there is to tell really, and I was hoping you could explain... anything about what just happened. What we're doing now, or why..." He gestured to indicate that what the 'why' referred to didn't matter as long as there was a 'because' somewhere in the next few minutes. Eowen's mind was organizing itself into a new hierarchy of priorities and possibilities where she might join Hani, become a member of his crew, find her cousin Tavo, and use him as a way to safely control her manifestations along the way.

Not that I'd be using him, we'd be assets to each other, she corrected herself. *But this could work!*

Eowen could feel that something had changed for her. Possibilities and hope existed that hadn't before. She had to test them though, and she knew where and how she wanted to do it.

"Do you know why I'm here, being adopted by Yawin?" Eowen started walking again, but slowed so that Hani could walk next to her.

"I know a bit... I know you saved him, those two girls around our age, and those two kids from dying."

"And you know we met at that dirt patch with the stream next to it, but that we traveled together back to my people."

"Yes, I figured out that much."

"And there I created the jungle oasis and the sun, then left with the mountain folk."

"Right. I suppose I assumed that you'd just come to feel very close to them and wanted to leave..." Hani seemed to come to a conclusion that brought tears to his eyes. "O-or that the rest of your family didn't... Oh. Oh no, Eowen?"

She shook her head. "They're not all... dead." She swallowed the lump in her throat that followed the statement. She kept walking and soon they arrived at Yawin's home. Eowen faced Hani, gestured for him to stay there, and took a deep breath. "My father's alive, Hani, but I very nearly killed him, along with the rest of my people."

Hani shot her a look of shock, which transitioned into confusion then curious sympathy. Never did it pass through fear, mistrust, or blame though, and for that, any doubt she could trust him was gone. Eowen smiled sadly and pulled Hani into a hug that he managed to return once he'd organized the new set of questions in his mind.

"Be right back," she whispered, then glided through the animal skin that hung over the entrance.

The stone house had low ceilings, cool floors, and an economic use of rooms. They each had their own room with animal skins hanging over them connected to the central room. She moved silently, her power ensuring it, and brushed aside Yawin's animal skin. The old man lay sleeping, and by the aura around him his dreams were gentle. Eowen shook him awake and he jumped to a sitting position. "What is it, what's wrong? Eowen?"

"Yawin, listen to me carefully. I think I've discovered something. Maybe a few things, but I need to test them out first. I need you to do something for me, alright?" Yawin listened, looking only a little suspicious as the sleep faded from him.

"You're planning to create something, aren't you? Something big." Eowen was surprised. "Is this something you need to do?" His tone was practical, not afraid or accusatory. Despite the harm she'd done before and could still do, he trusted her.

"No... it's nothing I have to do." Eowen squeezed her eyes shut and her hands together, as if in prayer. "It's not something I have to do, but at the same time it is." She opened her eyes again and Yawin was already getting dressed to go out.

"So what's it going to be?" His eyes twinkled. "Not another jungle? I'm not sure that would go over so well with mountain folk." Eowen laughed. Tension poured out of her and she leaned her head on Yawin's shoulder.

"You really trust me don't you?"

"Oh my. You're still a child, despite it all. Yes, Eowen, I trust you. You saved our lives. More than anyone, you understand the costs and the risks of what you can do. But it's also who you are in some way. I have come to know in my heart that the reason we are here is to dream things into this new world." He smiled sadly. "We will fill it with the contents of our souls, we who are left. Of course there are to be risks and unexpected consequences. We are in unprecedented times. But I have come to believe, my dear, that people like you will be the ones to show us the way."

Eowen embraced him. She didn't know if she agreed with all of that, but he'd always had that confidence in her, and at that moment she needed it more than she needed humility.

"Come, you have some task for me," Yawin said. "Make it known."

"Right." Eowen tried to control her expression to make it serious and official, but the silly, joyful, relieved smile was ruining it. "I need you to get the others and bring them to the cemetery." Yawin raised an eyebrow but nodded and headed for the entryway. Eowen tackled him with a hug from behind before he could get any further and didn't let him end it early. "You are my second father, Yawin. I'm so lucky you and the others found me." Then she let him go and rushed past him out of the house.

"Ready—woah!" Hani said when Eowen grabbed his hand and pulled him along at a jog toward the cemetery. "Where to now, don't we need Yawin?"

"He's meeting us there."

"Where? Oh." Eowen pointed to the walls of the cemetery, spreading out as they passed through the settlement. They slipped past the guard and froze nervously when the inner door creaked loudly, but the guard didn't notice and they slipped in. "Eowen," Hani whispered, despite the barrier still up around them, "what are we doing in the mountain folk's resting ground? Isn't this place... sacred? Or forbidden."

"Not yet it isn't," Eowen whispered back. There were a few mourners and workers there even in the depths of the mountain folk's night. They didn't go far in, stopping almost immediately after the door to face the two statues flanking it, one of the eagle of heaven, the other of the wildcat of earth. "Tell me, Hani, have you heard of the bone herons?" Eowen asked. "You might have seen them with their young on the southern beaches in late summer, before the monsoons." Eowen thought for a moment. "I suppose the beaches would have been north of you since your island is so far south."

"I've heard of them. Huge birds with long beaks. They collect bones from the savannah after the monsoons and then fly north, or so I've heard." He looked to Eowen for confirmation and she nodded. "Not sure why they do that though."

"It's for their nests," Eowen said. Hani was surprised but kept his mouth shut. "You might have noticed when you came across my people that none of our dead were prepared in any way."

"I... suppose I did. I don't like to think too much about it, though." Hani shifted uncomfortably, glancing at the bodies all around him. Eowen hadn't pegged him as squeamish around the dead, the way he'd talked about how his people place their deceased under the lava flows. Eowen realized then that she had developed a comfort around death that others might not have. She considered that by being bounced from one village to another throughout her youth, she might have attended more funerals in thirteen years than any of her people ever had. In her culture funerals were not just for family but for the whole population of the village to attend.

"The reason we couldn't prepare their bodies was because, among my people, we remove the skeletons and lay them at the foot of the bone trees. Those are the trees that bone herons nest in. The flesh is planted beneath bone tree saplings to help them grow." Eowen's hands curled into fists, her chest swelled with purpose. "My people couldn't perform the funeral rites because the herons and trees don't exist anymore, and I'll never be able to help my people like you did by manifesting the volcano, even temporarily, because I was banished."

"What?" Hani looked to see if Eowen was joking. When she turned to face him he saw there was no lie.

"I can't control my manifestations like you can. It's like a force starts moving through me and I can't stop it."

Eowen gritted her teeth. *I am not crying here!*

"You admired the jungle I created and the sun I left floating over it, but they came with a cost, and that cost was that I hurt my people, I destroyed my father and I's hut, and he nearly died!" Immense currents of dreaming force writhed around Eowen, boiling with potential beneath the surface. Hani's breath caught in his throat and he swayed under the weight of it. "For that, for bringing outsiders into their midst, and for abandoning my people even before the fall, I was excommunicated. Hani, I can never return."

I will not cry, I have cried enough!

Hani searched for the right thing to say, but there is little one can say to comfort someone who's world has collapsed twice in as many months. He decided that saying anything would be better than saying nothing. "Maybe someday—"

Eowen put her hand up to cut him off. "I will never return, understand? I can't, not ever." She stared him until he nodded and kept his mouth shut. Eowen looked up at the eagle and cat statues again. "Maybe someday, someone will recreate the bone herons and the bone trees... Without hurting anyone," Eowen whispered. "Without them, my people will hold no funerals and be unable to truly grieve, but that isn't my concern anymore. I've lost that right." At that moment, Yawin, Hale, Genia, Ne, and Zerinley shuffled through the wooden door into the makeshift cemetery. The guard behind them seemed interested in the group but let them past, and once the door was closed Eowen undid her barrier and waved them over. "But it's not too late to do something for them," Eowen whispered to Hani.

"Eowen!" Zerinley sprinted for her and Eowen picked her up.

"Hello there."

"Hi Hani! This is very mysterious," Zerinley whispered to Eowen conspiratorially.

"It is, isn't it?" Eowen kissed the little girl on the cheek.

"You needed us?" Hale asked, all business.

"Yes, I suppose so. Mostly I wanted you all here for this." Eowen handed Zerinely to Yawin, who put the girl on his shoulders.

"Their guardians were worried about why I needed them," Yawin said. "They probably only let me bring them all because of our history, but we can't stay out too long."

"Right, we'll get to it. Genia, can you tell Hani what you told me about mountain folk funerals?"

"I suppose." Genia took Hani aside to one of the wooden shelves of bodies and began explaining to his great discomfort.

"Hale, can you make sure no one interrupts us?"

"Should have told me there might be a fight, I would have brought my ax."

"Do you even need it?" Ne asked. Hale flexed her bicep at the boy and patted it proudly.

"Children, let's please be respectful here," Yawin said, but he seemed overjoyed to have everyone back together, even for some secret purpose in the cemetery. Hale took up a position some meters away watching the workers, the door, and the other mourners. The workers in deep hoods and masks took notice of the large group but left them to their devices. Eowen and Hani stood out, and while they'd heard of the jungle girl that was going to be given an honor of friendship to be officially adopted, few had heard much of anything about a boy from the southern isles. One shrugged and decided it was none of his business, while another decided to investigate. Hani returned from his cultural lesson looking slightly sick.

"So, do you get the idea?" Eowen asked.

Hani eyed the eagle and cat statues, uncertain but with a growing interest, his mind working out what it would entail. "I've never created a... living animal before."

"I have, never on purpose though." Eowen held out her hand. "I think I can remember how I got there, though. Genia's going to help too."

The mountain girl pointed at herself and looked between Eowen and Hani. "Me?"

"Remember when we tried creating together as a group in your tent at the oasis?" Eowen asked.

"It didn't go well, things got out of control."

"You're right, but Hani here can keep it under control." Eowen patted him on the back.

"I can?" Eowen shot him a look that said to shut up.

"Of course you can, like at the volcano."

"What volcano?" Genia asked.

"His volcano, he can create volcanoes," Eowen said. Unlike Eowen, Genia had an idea of what a volcano was, but the volcanoes in the mountains were different from Hani's gently flowing island ones and tended to be extremely large and destructive. She'd seen one go off from hundreds of kilometers away, but had felt the earth shake and saw the way the ash exploded outward.

"Did you make a volcano here?" Genia looked over the walls of the cemetery, expecting to see a smoking peak pop up out of nowhere.

"Yes, but..." Eowen began. "It's not important."

"I think that's very important!" Genia threw her hands up. The worker had gotten close enough that Hale was forced to stand in her way with her arms crossed. Ne ran up to join his sister.

"Did someone say something about volcanoes?" He'd heard of them but had been too young to remember the eruption from Genia's childhood and thought they were the most exciting thing he'd ever heard of.

"No one said anything about volcanoes!" Eowen shouted at Ne. Genia and Hani shared a look and the cemetery worker decided to make a half-hearted shoosh before leaving the strange group to their devices. Eowen glared at Hani and Genia, took both their hands, and with a flare of her dreaming aura fully captured theirs and the group's attention. "We're doing this now!" Eowen said with far more confidence than she possessed. She took a deep breath, let go of reality, and fell into the dream, trusting her friends to catch her. Shadows thickened and danced around her with more purpose than ever before. Genia and Hani accessed their own dreaming minds in their own ways. Synchronizing as best they could, they stepped onto that stage with Eowen, where reality had yet to be determined.

******

[Listen, for you cannot hear me yet]

SO THE CAVE TOLD ME THE WAY THERE; NORTH OF HERE, WEST OF THERE, TEN PACES FORWARD, AND THREE LOOKS BACK.

******

The cemetery seethed with the combined shadows of the three dreamers. They flowed out in a great tidal wave that coursed through rather than breaking against the shelves and walls. Within the shadows were everything and anything that the three could birth from the depths of their minds. Half-heard, half-seen, half-felt, the onlookers' senses were awash with possibilities, and none could tell which would become and which would merely fade. Eowen's friends strained to watch through the darkness, waiting to see if this would be chaos as it had in the past. The workers and patrons of the cemetery backed up against the walls, trapped by the shadows with nowhere to run. Genia was breathless as she shared in the synchronizing power of the two dreamers.

"This is what they experience?" she whispered to herself. "Every time?" It was the most exhilaration she'd ever known, and the most fear as well until then the light broke in. Like uncountable arms with too many hands and more and more fingers every second, the light reached through the darkness and caressed the statues. Genia looked to her right where Eowen stood holding her hand, and past her at Hani. Their eyes were open but unseeing, their mouths moved as if to speak but no human sound came out, so deep in the trance of creation as they were. She let go, followed them into the dream, and found the great hands of light and currents of shadow were her own as well. Like clay, the light dredged up the shadows and layered them upon the statues, both creating and converting them into something else.

Then, through a break in the shadows, the onlookers saw things moving. A great wing, larger than any living eagle's from before the fall, shook off the dust of its previous form. The wild cat stretched and yawned, exposing fangs larger than a man's skull. The power surged and thickened around the two statues, though they were no longer statues. Life, bloody fleshy and thick, coalesced upon their forms. They shifted, flexed, breathed, and as the seconds passed into minutes, the darkness continued to pour into them.

Ne was closest to the trio and the first to see them fully through the shadows. All in a rush the vague shapes of tailfeathers, clawed paws, and glinting eyes gave way to their full forms. The boy staggered back and fell on his butt, but he could not look away from the beasts before him. Larger than the statues had been, larger than any living version of them could have ever been in the world before, the sacred beasts of the mountain folk emerged. They had been given a true life of a sort, but somehow the powers that had done so had made the creatures greater than life itself. It had only existed for a few seconds, but the eagle's eyes were clouding with ancient knowledge. The wildcat's were timelessly young. They were nobler and grander than life could have ever allowed, seeming to shine in the darkness as if light were being shed upon them from all angles.

Hani could sense the need for the manifestations to come

to a close and guided the last of his partners' powers toward their opus. Lights and shadows funneled away from the three of them, weaving the last of Eowen's power and Genia's cultural associations into the fabric of their being. He tied down the last loose strands of existence and came back to himself to admire his work. The creatures eyed the world around them, people, corpses, buildings, and the void beyond. An intelligence burned within as they regarded their new home. They exchanged a glance, seeming to converse. Then they locked onto the people below.

Hani grinned. "Yes! We did it!" He threw his hand in the air and turned to share his success with the others, but paused when he caught sight of Eowen. "Oh, no," he whispered.

Eowen's power had not dissipated, nor had it been completely drawn into the creatures as he thought it had, but was thick around her. He reached out to take her hand again, but there was a density that wouldn't allow him to pass through. He tried to erect a barrier and push past, but his own power seemed to dissipate and smear around hers. The light bent to the silhouette of her form and seemed to be blurring as if by a heat illusion. Eowen's skin, hair, and clothes were streaking out from her at the edges, like wet paint being washed off, her being appeared to be getting watered down, thinned out, and gathered up behind her.

"Eowen... What's happening?" Hani stepped back and looked to her mountain folk friends to see if they knew what was occurring or how to stop it. None of them were looking at Eowen. They were fixated on something behind Hani. The island boy felt breath on his neck from a creature far larger than he was and froze in place, shivers running up his back. A pair of massive wings crushed the air beneath them and the eagle dropped next to Genia, talons carving arm-sized divots into the stone. Genia was wide-eyed, on the verge of panic. Yawin held Ne and Zerinley close. The eagle clicked its beak; it was large enough to make them look like mice. The wildcat huffed on Hani's neck, purred like an earthquake, and padded around him. Hani's head reached to the beast's knee.

Hani and the mountain folk had never felt such fear in their lives, not when faced with wild animals, nor natural disasters, nor the cruelty of other people, nor even when the fall had brought their world to an end. The power of the beasts was not of the world they knew. It was active, intelligent, and unassailable in a way that had only ever been described as divine. Despite effectively birthing the beasts, neither Hani nor Genia had any clue what these creatures would do next or what they were capable of. Hani glanced around at the helpless mountain folk and knew he had to do something. His power had brought these things into being and he felt that perhaps only his power could stop them. He ran past the beasts and put himself between them and the others.

"Everyone, get out of here!" He gathered his dreaming power up around him, prepared to do something, though he did not know what, he had never used manifestations for violence before. The eagle twisted its head to the side and locked him in place with a deep black stare, its eye a bottomless well. The wildcat crept around it, muscles bulging through its fur as it tensed as though to pounce. A growl rippled through the beast that shook the buildings, the ground, even the starfield below seemed to dance. The eagle responded in kind and screeched at a pitch and volume that sent the onlookers to their knees with their hands over their ears. It sounded like the heavens splitting open. All across the settlement, mountain folk awoke to the eagle as it rent the air and the wildcat as it shook them from their beds to the floor. Hani's power and courage abandoned him, he took a step back only to fall to his knees, death seemed imminent.

Then Eowen stepped in front of the creatures, and the moment changed. Grave-like calm and silence settled in like a cloying fog. Hani tried to look at her, but the strange smearing of light around her shape made it nearly impossible to focus. Instead, he and the others' eyes would slide up and behind her where Eowen's edges flowed into some unknown shape, some inhuman silhouette. Certain details made it through to the onlookers, a form that was bipedal, long-necked, and very tall. Eowen reached out a hand and placed it on the wildcat's cheek. She had to stand on her toes to reach it. Hani tried to shout 'No!' or get up to save her from certain death, but his voice would not come and his legs would not respond. It was unnecessary though, for when Eowen touched the cat its aggression melted away. Under her hand the sacred beast of the earth lay down, looking at her as though it were a cub. She turned to the eagle, which twitched its great head in that jerking way birds do. Eowen made a gesture and bowed to it, and the eagle settled in comfortably on its talons. No one moved, no one dared breath too loud, save for Eowen who turned to face Yawin.

[Yawin.]

The old man jolted up, blinked rapidly, and pointed to himself.

[Bring your wife.]

Her words did not make a sound, did not travel through the air at all, but were in his spirit as a whisper in which there was no language, only comprehension. He left Ne and Zerinely with Hale and hurried to the shelf where his wife lay. He gathered her up in his arms, wrapping the cloth around her tight, and carried her to Eowen. A cemetery worker appeared next to them with a knife in hand, called by Eowen's silent instructions as well. He handed the knife to Eowen, then backed away with his eyes on the beasts. Eowen uncovered the body to reveal an elderly mountain woman. She was naked, had long gray hair, and was already eyeless. Eowen took Yawin's hand and placed the knife into it.

[They are ready to feed.]

Yawin nodded, and with great and deliberate care he cut into his wife's chest where the divine gift of love lay caged. He pried apart the ribs, and there was a crack followed by a few careful incisions. Eowen took the heart from him and he put the knife back in, lower this time, shifting about in her abdomen to extract the liver.

Eowen stood Yawin up and guided him to the wild cat. Even laying on its belly the creature's head was higher than Yawin's. The old mountain man looked over the beast, noting its claws and its fangs. He swallowed his fear, closed his eyes, and held out the liver with both hands. The people behind him gasped, certain it would devour him as part of the offering, but all he felt was the brush of lips and fangs against his arms, then the scrape of the cat's sandpaper tongue on the bottom of his hands. He opened his eyes in time to see the cat swallow, then it curled up and yawned. Yawin shivered; three of him could have fit inside that mouth.

Eowen then pulled him to the eagle, which settled in on its talons, hunching over them and puffing its wings out so that it became a great arch of feathers with a beak for a capstone. With far more courage this time, Yawin offered the heart of his wife up to the eagle of heaven. It was not as gentle as the cat, opting to snap up the heart from his palms cutting into one. Yawin hissed and pressed his shaking hand against his robe to stem the bleeding. The beak had not gone to the bone, but a long strip of skin was missing.

Yawin looked up from his hands when the eagle shifted, and with a beat of its wings that nearly knocked him over, it climbed into the sky. Those that had been present watched it glide away over the wall of the cemetery and out of sight. Something in them knew the love of Yawin's wife was being carried back to heaven. Yawin turned around, weeping, and reached for Eowen to embrace her. She sagged against him, her arms and head hung like a stringless puppet, the silhouette around her was gone leaving only the girl.

"Eowen, are you alright?" Yawin patted her cheek gently but her eyes did not open.

"I'm tired, Daddy," Eowen whispered. "Can I sleep a little longer?" Yawin's tears ran over his chin and he cradled the girl to his chest.

"Of course you can, my girl, as long as you like."

****

[Listen, for you cannot hear me yet]

SO I WENT AND ARRIVED UPON AH'OM, AND IT WAS A SHORT JOURNEY, AS ALL OF MINE TEND TO BE.

****

Eowen and Hani were seated in front of the Patricians. One was already asleep, but the other was unusually alert. He was speaking quietly with his assistant as they conferred over how, exactly, to handle the situation. Yawin was present, as was Hale, but others were barred from the current proceedings. After the moment of hushed discussion, the Patrician who was awake fixed his unblinking gaze on Eowen. She felt a similar force behind it as a snake coiled in the sun, attentive but not necessarily on guard. The Patrician's gnarled hand extended one crook of a finger and gestured for them to approach. Eowen and Hani looked at each other, uncertain, then to Yawin for guidance. He stood and tilted his head in a 'follow me' motion. Hale stayed where she was as the three approached the Patrician, standing just shy of a meter away. He whispered to his assistant who spoke.

"The Patrician wishes for you to come closer so he may speak to you himself."

The ancient man nodded and waited patiently as Eowen, Hani, and Yawin crowded around his seat as best they could. Yawin was practically on the sleeping Patrician's lap. The assistant backed away with a look that said: 'Whatever he wants, he's the boss.' The Patrician patted Yawin's hand affectionately and spoke to him first.

"Yawin is your name?" His voice was smoother than

Eowen and Hani had expected for one who needed to whisper. Raspy in the way of two river-smooth-stones being rubbed against one another, each word pleasantly hissed with a little pebbly clink on the hard consonants. "I remember you child," the Patrician said to Yawin, who was nearly seventy years old. "You married one of my grand nieces. Her name..."

"Amphya," Yawin finished for him.

"Yes, yes. Little Phya. She is dead I hear?" Yawin confirmed with a stoic nod which the patrician mirrored. He then panned over to look at Eowen. "This one and two others made the eagle and cat?"

"Yes, with Hani and Genia." Eowen spoke up and gestured to Hani and to the door.

"Hmm, Genia is one of our names."

"She is of our people your honor, a girl of... seventeen I believe." The assistant spoke up, surprising them. *He must have excellent hearing*, Eowen thought.

"I remember now, you told me as much, Assistant Ugin. Why is she not here?" The assistant looked panicked and glanced at Yawin.

"Ah, she was not invited, your honor."

"Bring her, now." The Patrician never raised his voice in anger or applied any aggressive tone, but there was no space in his tone for disobedience. His assistant made a complicated gesture of deference which Eowen recognized as being similar to a gesture which, in a more casual version of the mountain folk's gesture-speech, meant: 'You're right and I'm wrong'. Then he scurried off to find Genia. The Patrician settled back in his seat even further than he already was and sighed with his eyes closed. For a moment they thought he might have fallen asleep like his partner, but he spoke up with his eyes closed. "I understand, jungle girl, that you were to be adopted as a mountain folk. This is correct?" The Patrician used a word for mountain folk that Eowen did not know. Yawin quickly explained that it was an old word that translated closer to: Those closest to heaven.

"Umm." Eowen's darted to Yawin and he gave a nod. "Yes, your honor," she said as formally as she could.

"Not merely honored as a friend of our people?"

"She was to become my adopted daughter, your honor," Yawin said. He avoided looking at Eowen and his face fell. "Those plans have since changed." Hani was fidgeting, clearly impatient to know what was being discussed.

"So you have rescinded your place as a mountain folk," The Patrician said.

"Yes, your honor. I..." Eowen looked at Hani for guidance; she didn't feel she had the right words in the mountain folk's language to explain herself. The island boy had sounded so certain, so authoritative when telling the story of his father and declaring he would find him. Even confused, fidgeting, and politely silent, Hani seemed to radiate the kind of adventurous spirit that, until Eowen had met him, she had only sensed in her cousin Tavo long ago. "I am not going to be a, um, close-to-heaven-person." She tried to work out the word the Patrician had used. "I will leave with Hani, who is looking for his father, and I will be looking for my cousin, Tavo."

Behind them, the door opened and Assistant Ugin led Genia into the hall. She and Hale exchanged a confused look. The Patrician gestured them over incessantly as Ugin began to announce them. "Your honor, I present—"

"No." It was the most aggressive the Patrician had sounded and the first word he'd said above a whisper. "Genia, come here."

The rest of the group backed up so she could approach the thrones. The Patrician took Genia's hand and attempted to sit up fully, swatting away his assistant when he tried to help.

"We..." He looked to his partner, glared, and backhanded the equally ancient man on the chest. The other Patrician startled awake, gasped, choked on his spit, and hacked until his lungs were clear.

"You bastard's son, I'll have my liver and eyes left in to haunt you!" The formerly sleeping Patrician noticed the group gathered close and transitioned to quietly cussing out his partner.

"We," the first Patrician started again, "are rescinding our position." Everyone present gasped save for Hani, who looked around wondering what all the hubbub was about. Hale was leaning in to try and hear the proceedings, and the recently awoken Patrician sighed with relief.

"Finally," the groggy Patrician said before promptly returning to his nap.

"Your honors—" the assistant began, but the now former Patrician cut him off.

"My partner and I are hereby to be referred to only by our names. We are no longer the Patricians, and our final decree is for our position to pass to Genia."

The assistant was speechless. Yawin listened to the proceedings with amused interest. Genia looked as if she'd been slapped in the face.

"M-me?" Genia pointed to herself, and the ancient man nodded. Hani tugged on Eowen's sleeve, he could not stand being left out anymore.

"What have you all been saying?" he whispered to her.

"Ah... So the Patrician that was awake was asking about me being adopted and then deciding not to be adopted. Then he asked about the eagle and cat and we mentioned Genia, and then he asked for her to be here, and now he just declared her the new Patrician."

"Oh..." Hani glanced around at everyone gathered. "Alright, I think I can follow from there."

The Patrician drew himself up, infusing as much energy as he could into the moment. "My assistant gave me a full report of the events which led to the creation of the eagle of heaven and the wildcat of earth in this new world." Everyone in earshot looked to the assistant for confirmation, who bowed to Genia.

"I was in the cemetery when you performed the creation. I gave my wife and three daughters their last rites a few hours ago," the assistant said.

"I was informed as to your part in the creation of the eagle and cat, Genia. Our friends," He gestured to Eowen and Hani, "played significant roles in that, but I understand that you ensured that the beasts became what we needed them to be to perform our funeral rites?"

"Well, I don't know if I really did all that." Genia blushed and looked at her feet and Yawin stepped in.

"That is exactly what happened. Even Eowen and Hani confirmed that it was Genia who ensured the creations turned out the way they did. Your hono—I mean... great uncle, it was Genia who embodied the spirit of our traditions and brought them into the new world." Yawin gestured to the two children. "It could not have been done alone, but without Genia it could not have been done at all." The elder peered at Genia, then Hani, then Eowen.

"We are in debt to all of you, yet there is no true way to pay this debt. All that you could desire of our people, you can bring into the world of your own power." He shook his head and rolled his eyes. "This new world... we are not suited to lead our people through its ways." He flung his hand at his sleeping partner, almost smacking him again. "We were retired before the fall, you may have known that. We were brought back into service as the Patrician at the time; our successor perished in the fall. We have our wisdom, our experience, but we are too old to lead our people. Heh, we were too old ten years ago! Genia." The Patrician fixed her with his unblinking stare. "Our people require one who understands the workings of this world, one who knows our most important traditions, and is young enough to carry the mantle for an unknown stretch of time. We have struggled to stay aware of the status of our people, but in the time since the fall, no news has reached me of one so capable in all these aspects as you." Genia was holding her breath during his speech and let it out once he paused.

"But your honor! I—"

"There is no arguing! The seat of Patrician cannot be declined. Several witnesses have already heard my decree. You are the Patrician now, a position that can only be given up through a chosen successor or death. Do you have a successor chosen?" Genia was panicking, looking for help, but no one had any to offer.

"N-no, how would I have one?"

"Do you intend to die?"

"No!" Genia backed up with her arms wrapped around her. Hale could not hear what was being said, but saw Genia panicked and rushed forward.

"Whatever you're saying to her, stop it! I don't care if you are the patrician, you can't treat her like this!" The former Patrician grinned, exposing more gum than teeth, and laughed until he gasped for breath.

"You did not have permission to approach!" Assistant Ugin said.

"Genia!" The elder spoke louder than he ever had in the memory of all present. "Do you wish this warrior girl to stand beside you right now?" Genia nodded, wide-eyed at the ancient man. "Assistant Ugin, the Patrician has accepted this girl's approach, show respect." Ugin glanced around, uncertain, then gave up and bowed low to Genia.

"My apologies patrician Genia."

"But I can't—"

Hale interrupted Genia with a hearty pat on the back. "So you're the Patrician now! Who would have thought? Excellent decision, sir." Hale nodded to the man with the mischievous, gummy smile. He gestured for Genia to approach and took her hand when she did.

"Listen to me, child. Experience such as mine does not lie and does not make mistakes, but my age does. If you are truly unfit to lead, then someone more suitable will make themselves known in time. When that time comes, I trust you to know that person and step down, but until then you are our Patrician. Worry not, you will have our guidance as long as we are here to provide it." The old man looked at his sleeping partner and huffed. "Such as it is. And do not forget Ugin. As much of a sour fellow as he is, there is no one who knows procedure and ceremony better." Genia smiled shyly at Ugin, who looked at her not with dislike, but rather a mournful commiseration as if to say: 'welcome to my life'. He bowed to Genia, respectfully rather than differentially, and Genia bowed back.

Yawin, Eowen, and Hani watched and waited till the bow. Yawin put an arm around Genia's shoulder and gave her a hug from the side. "There's no one more suitable, great uncle.

Genia has adapted better to this world than almost anyone I have met, and indeed knows our ceremonies and traditions well. She is kind and fair, loyal and perceptive." Genia was blushing fully and seemed to find her feet more interesting each moment. "You will serve and lead our people well," Yawin said to Genia, then stepped back to gesture deferentially. Hale did the same, but with a mocking smile that put the new Patrician at ease. Eowen placed a hand on Genia's elbow, and followed suit when she had her attention. Copying everyone else, Hani mimicked her as best he could. Genia immediately lifted them both by their shoulders and brought them in for a hug.

"No, you two don't bow to me, ever, understood? You don't bow to any of our people." Genia turned to her new assistant. "Assistant Ugin, my first, uh, decree as Patrician is that these two," Genia gestured to Eowen and Hani, "are to be treated with high respect by all our people. They, um, don't need to bow to anyone and are to be given the respect I am given."

"Respect but not authority," the former Patrician said.

"Right, everyone should respect them as they do me, but that does not mean they have my authority." She smiled at the ancient man.

"Good enough for a first decree, girl, sets the tone. You have to be very precise with this man, though." The former Patrician pointed a thumb at Assistant Ugin. "He will serve the word of your law, not necessarily the spirit." Ugin rolled his eyes, but stepped forward and removed a wooden cylinder from a sleeve.

"A beautiful display of friendship, your honor, and a good transition to another matter at hand." Ugin handed Genia the cylinder. She cradled it in one hand and lifted it open longways on hidden hinges. Within was a piece of metal twisted into shapes with no known meaning to Eowen. Genia looked it over, a puzzled expression on her face.

"I recognize this, but I don't know from where," she said.

"That is understandable." Yawin approached, looking at them closely. "I only ever met one person branded with this symbol. It is the mark we would place on an outsider of friendship with our people. If they accept, they would be branded with it."

"I have heard of this! Why branded though? In the story of Barrith the northerner, he was given a medallion with this symbol to carry."

"That's true in the old story, but that was hundreds of years ago. We implemented this when a medallion was stolen and the thief used it to kill some of our people who housed him as a guest and take their belongings. You cannot steal someone's skin." Yawin grimaced when he looked at Eowen and Hani. He spoke in Eowen's language now. "Hani, this symbol is branded onto the skin of friends of our people so we may know them as such. You need not do this, our people are gathered in one place and will never forget you as long as you live. It is the old way, and we have a new Patrician." Eowen and Hani listened but were somewhat lost in thought, drawn to the metal symbol which pulled them in as though it were magnetized for them. Genia found herself reaching in and stroking it as well, largely without thinking.

"I will take it," Eowen said and she looked at Genia. "I would be honored to. Even though I cannot be your sister, it will be a privilege to forever be marked as a friend of the mountain folk."

"Me too." Hani bowed to Genia, but she was staring at Eowen, and her expression was growing progressively more angry.

"Not my sister?" Genia said, and Eowen, unfamiliar with the harshness in her tone, took a step back.

"Uh, no? I'm not staying after all."

"I know that!" Genia snapped the cylinder closed with a harsh clack. "I made my peace with it when you told us last night. If Ne, or, or, someone important to me like Tavo is to you had gone missing but might be alive, I'd go in search of them too. I understand why you're leaving, Eowen, I respect it and I will make my peace with it, but you think that after all we've been through I wouldn't call you sister? " Genia advanced on Eowen who backed up into Hani.

"I can't be, right? I never finished the adoption ceremonies to be a member of the mountain folk." Eowen checked Yawin for confirmation, but he seemed as concerned about Genia's attitude as she was.

"I don't care!" Genia shouted, making the former Patricians jump in their seats where they'd been dozing. "I've already lost so many people, we all have! It's the one thing we all have in common, and it still hurts, but Yawin found us! Me, Ne, Zerinley, Hale, and you! We became a family, maybe only because we had to, but we did! Who knows if we would have even been friends otherwise, but even so, we did become a family, and you're a part of it!" Genia quieted down. "I know that sometimes you don't really feel that way, but it's true, and I need you to know that before you leave because... I know you'll be alright, but it feels so much like I'm losing you. So..." Genia looked around, searching for some answer to some question, then locked eyes with Assistant Ugin and arrived at it. "I declare that Eowen of the jungle and savannah tribes is also one of the people closest to heaven. I will not accept any criticism on this judgment. It is final. Understood?" Assistant Ugin looked like he very much wanted to argue with this as his respect for authority and his encyclopedic knowledge of tradition and procedure grappled with each other. He gave up after looking to the former Patricians for guidance, only to find them both asleep.

"Ah, I see, very good Patrician Genia, it will be made known publicly this very day." He managed to somehow sound both defeated and professional at the same time. Genia shook her head though.

"No, the announcement will be publicly made only after Eowen's departure." Genia smiled at her, sadness in it, but also pride and love. "Eowen doesn't like being the center of attention. We will make the announcement after she leaves, but when she returns she will have family here, no matter what." Eowen's instincts were to distance herself from Genia and deny that she could ever feel the same kind of familial bond, but she fought those instincts. Eowen rushed into Genia's arms, burying her face in the older girl's shoulder to hide her tears.

"Why are you making it so hard to leave?" Eowen whispered just for Genia.

"So that one day you'll come back," Genia whispered in return.

****

[Listen, for you cannot hear me yet]

LOVE FELT THEIR WORLD SHAKEN WHEN I ARRIVED, FOR I WAS LARGER THAN ALL OF AH'OM, TOO LARGE TO EVEN REALLY KNOW OF MY PRESENCE SAVE FOR THE PRICKLE ON ONE'S NECK OF BEING WATCHED.

****

Eowen stayed for one more night in the mountain folk's settlement. Her dreams were vast and strange as always, but they faded away as they always did. The previous night they'd held a feast to say goodbye to Eowen and Hani attended only by the mountain folk friends she'd saved, their family, the previous Patricians, and Assistant Ugin, who tried to insist that him joining for such a feast was hardly proper. Genia found herself giggling behind her assistant's back whenever she made him uncomfortable with her decisions. During the dinner, Ne raved about his sister's greatness and swore he'd become worthy of replacing her. Genia appointed Hale as her personal guard and Yawin as one of her counsel. Ugin was relieved to have some help managing the young woman, but Hale flatly refused. She had not finished her training before the fall and would not accept any such position until such a time as she was deemed worthy by their highest ranking warrior. Eowen pointed out that there was not likely to be much violence in the new world as there were no resources to fight over, not to mention how difficult finding people was at all. Hale had said that wasn't the point and spent over an hour disseminating the long and noble history of the warriors of the mountain folk.

After the feast, they'd all returned to Yawin's house to spend the night. No formal announcement about Eowen and Hani's involvement nor of Genia's new position had been made. The mountain folk they passed stared at them, muttered rumors, and sometimes gestured with deference. It seemed word had gotten around anyway. Eowen traced the lines in the stone of Yawin's ceiling with her eyes, finding nostalgia and significance in everything. It didn't matter that she'd only been in the mountain folk's settlement a few days worth of time. Her leaving now left her feeling the weight of every moment she'd spent with them.

She rose slowly and carefully from her bed on the floor of the main room where they'd fallen asleep in a pile, much like when she'd been a child among other children. Yawin was in his own room with the curtain open, awake and staring at the ceiling. He noticed Eowen rising and waved. Eowen waved back, then tiptoed her way to the entrance and stepped outside. She sat on the bench outside Yawin's home and he soon followed with Zerinley, who climbed onto Eowen's lap and yawned. She pulled Eowen's arms around herself and leaned against them.

"Are you eager to go?" Yawin asked. Eowen shrugged.

"I don't know, I don't feel excited exactly. I was when I first heard Hani's story about his father. He... reminds me of Tavo," Eowen trailed off. Zerinley tugged on her sleeve.

"Who's Tavo?" she asked. Eowen patted her head.

"He's my cousin. I was looking for him when I found you all. It's why I left home originally. We all thought he was dead when he disappeared three years ago, but then I heard some stories about him from a traveler." Eowen looked into the darkness beyond the settlement.

"That's why you're going away again," Zerinley said, matter-of-factly.

"That's right."

"What if he doesn't want to see you?" Zerinley's question put a tension in the air that woke Eowen up. She'd never really considered what it would be like to find her cousin.

"What made you ask that question, little girl?" Eowen said.

"I just thought that, because he left a long time ago, maybe he doesn't want to see anyone from home because if he did he would come back." Zerinley explained this carefully. Yawin looked down sadly at his feet.

"Well," Eowen began. "I suppose I'd just come back here. I never really considered whether he'd want to see me or not until you said that, but I have to try. He's family."

The only real family I've got left.

"Since being banished, I feel like I've started to understand why he left." Eowen smiled at Yawin, but there was pain behind it. "Tavo was more adventurous than other kids, he liked outsiders more, and would make friends with merchants and travelers. That would make my mom and his master angry, because he was going to be a very important person among my—among the jungle and savannah people. He was going to be like the leader of your warriors, but for our people."

"Wow," Zerinley said. "Was he a good fighter?"

"Of course! He was good at everything; hunting, tracking, foraging. He knew all the animals and their habits, and medicine, and could make a trap or a shelter, or a weapon anywhere in the jungle or savannah. He was the greatest. But he still left, and we treated him like he was dead. I suppose... I need to know why, and I need him to know that, after all these years, I still consider him family even though, after he left, no one else did."

Eowen smiled her shy smile and stared at her booted feet. She missed her sandals and the heat of the savannah, and her light yellow clothes that didn't need animal fur to resist the cold. She didn't know what climates and people she'd encounter on her journey, but she supposed it was possible she'd have to wear all kinds of different clothing to deal with all kinds of places. She had no idea how or if she would make it through the empty world, as it was filled with unknown things.

"Eowen." On her lap, Zerinley was trying to get her attention again.

"What is it?"

"I'm not sad you're leaving. We'll see you again." The little girl saw her statement as so simply true that Eowen somehow found herself accepting it.

"Oh? Is that so?"

"Mmm hmm." Zerinley nodded to herself, completely certain, and Yawin laughed under his breath while shaking his head. Genia and Hani emerged from the house.

"What are you three doing out here? Aren't you tired?" Genia asked.

"No," Zerinley answered for them before yawning. The five of them chatted idly, mostly interviewing and teasing Genia about the terrible job she'd no doubt do as Patrician. Soon Hale and Ne joined them, and they passed the time together till the settlement noticeably glowed with wakeful people.

"So," Hani said with a clap. "I suppose we should be on our way?" Eowen nodded. "We still need our brands though. Not that I'm looking forward to that exactly, but I was expecting my adventures to leave me covered in scars and tattoos anyway, so this is a start! A brand of friendship to a foreign people, it's the perfect thing to mark the beginning of my journeys."

Hale rolled her eyes and Ne nodded approvingly. Eowen felt a small ache in her heart though, for in a way he sounded just like her cousin in her memories, all excitement and bravado no matter what was ahead. They moved to the great hall, where Genia woke up her assistant. He stoked the fire and summoned the creator who had manifested the metal seal. It was a bald mountain folk adult of indeterminate age, who drew in Eowen and Hani with an aura of strange depth and magnetism. He didn't seem more powerful than Genia at first, but the uncannily dense quality of his dreaming aura pulled at them.

Assistant Ugin lined everyone up in a ceremonial fashion, with Eowen and Hani standing before the fire. Genia, the crafter of the brand, and Ugin faced them from the other side of the fire, and the other mountain folk were behind them in a line. Genia clasped her hands in front of her and looked to Ugin for guidance.

"Eowen of both the savannah and jungle people and now of those closest to heaven, will you accept the brand that marks you as a trusted friend of the mountain folk?" Ugin said.

"Yes I will."

"It will burn and forever mark you, but with it you will be trusted among our people and treated with the utmost respect. Hani of the southern islands, will you accept the brand that marks you as a trusted friend of the mountain folk?"

"Absolutely!" he shouted eagerly. Behind him Zerinely and Ne sniggered while Hale muttered something to herself.

"Present your hearts, for the love you have given and will receive is a heavenly thing, and thus the mark of our love and trust will be placed there."

Eowen hadn't actually known where the brand would be till then; she'd assumed it would be on a part of the body she chose. She had wanted it to be somewhere fleshier, like her shoulder or leg, as she'd heard from those among her people that had them that brands and tattoos were more painful on bony parts of the body. Hani undid his robe enough so that he could pull it off his shoulders and arms, letting it drape around his waist. Eowen followed suit and they both stood with their chests bare, trying to convince themselves that they were breaking out in a sweat because of the heat of the fire. As the brand was pulled from the coals by the unknown mountain folk that had crafted it, they glanced at each other, exchanging a look that asked: 'This is worth it, right?' Hani faced forward again, flushed in the face, and adopted an expression of intense concentration. Hani's chest was even bonier than Eowen's, which wasn't saying much, but she decided that if he had the courage for this then she did too. Ugin gestured to the creator of the brand.

"This is Agwe. He has been responsible for creating many ceremonial objects since our arrival in the new world. He is among our most capable creators." Ugin approached and held out sticks wrapped in several layers of fabric. "For your mouths." Eowen unclenched her jaw and accepted it, as did Hani.

Agwe stepped forward, brandishing the seal, and when he looked at Eowen and Hani they experienced something strange. It was as though he could see past their skin and flesh, even past their organs to some vast beyond, the way one could see the sky through gaps in the leaves above them. He presented the brand to Eowen first. It was glowing almost white. He put one hand on Eowen's shoulder to hold her still, and she could feel some power from him knife straight through her dreaming aura and clamp onto something beyond her body, some aspect that was her 'self' that she had not yet fully identified. Agwe's expression was blank when he spoke:

"Grit your teeth."

****

[Listen, for you cannot hear me yet]

WHEN I ARRIVE AT A PLACE ALL NECKS PRICKLE.

****

Eowen awoke, gasping and covered in sweat to a terrible aching, throbbing, stinging pain in her chest. *What?*

The answer to her question came with swift and unpleasant memories; hot metal melting into her breast, the smell of her own flesh burning, and then the sudden lack of any feeling at all. The brand had somehow pushed her perspective up and out of her body, and for a moment she had hung there, feeling nothing. Agwe had not been looking at her body. He'd been looking at the part of Eowen that had been pushed out of her body. He'd held the brand to her chest only for a few seconds, but the moment she hung there had felt like an eternity. When the brand had been removed Eowen had fallen back in her body, flooded by all the pain at once.

Eowen shook her head, hissed in pain, looked down at her chest to see the brand on her breast, then lay back gasping. She noted that they were in one of the back rooms of the great hall.

"Oh, you're up," said Hani's haggard voice to her left. Eowen looked over at him and resisted the urge to vomit when she opened her mouth.

"Did you—"

"Out of my body, yes."

"How?" At that question, Hani grinned, then laughed, which turned to groans of pain.

"I suspected, ever since I saw that sun above the oasis you made, that there are people who can do things even we can't dream of," he rasped. "People that can imagine and understand things that we, no matter how powerful we are, can't ever. I think he's one of them." Hani raised a fist up to the ceiling. "Ahhh, I can't wait to meet more of them, people like you and me and him. This new world is amazing, Eowen, we don't even know what kinds of things we're going to see!"

"Hani." Eowen's tone did not convey any amusement, which Hani failed to pick up on.

"Yes, Eowen?"

"You're not allowed to talk until this stops hurting."

Hani laughed again, but quickly transitioned back into moaning and groaning on the floor.

* * *

Genia bowed respectfully to Hani, and the others followed suit. Eowen tried to bow to her, but was pulled in for an embrace. "You'll be back to visit someday, won't you?" Genia whispered in Eowen's ear.

"I think so."

"Will you be able to find your way back?" When Genia asked, Ne tugged on her sleeve.

"She will, I made this," Ne said, and held out what looked like a flat, black, river-smooth stone. "Hold it, see what happens." He was clearly proud but was trying to keep a neutral expression. Eowen took it and immediately felt something move her in a direction. Not in the way of being pushed from the outside, but in the way where you lose your balance and find yourself swaying from within. She widened her stance to steady herself and was able to tell the purpose of the stone.

"Oh! It moved me back to the settlement. Ne, this is a very clever thing." She mussed his hair and the little boy swatted her hand away.

"Off! Thank you, I'd hoped you would approve." He crossed his arms and tapped one foot impatiently. "We've talked a lot about how easy it is to get lost so I thought something like this would be good. It took more than ten tries to get it right!"

"Really? What did the other attempts do?" Yawin asked. Ne dug a lump covered in cloth out of his pocket and revealed a stone like the first, careful not touch it with his bare hand. Yawin picked it up and the stone started tugging toward the center of the settlement. The tighter he held it the harder it pulled until he fell over to Zerinley's delight. "I see." Yawin got up and dusted himself off.

"Other versions just make you dizzy or don't point the right way at all. One always points to me," Ne said, and Genia put an arm around his shoulder.

"Oh, can I have that one?"

"No! I destroyed it." He grinned at her.

"Fine, I'll just make my own. I've a right as Patrician to always know where my little brother is."

"Yawin! Genia is abusing her power!"

"Yes!" Zerinely chimed in. "Abusing it!" Eowen knelt down and hugged Ne tightly.

"Thank you Ne, it's a wonderful gift. I'll miss you." The boy held back his tears, convinced he was too tough for such things.

"Yes, well, you'll be back sometime anyway. And I'll create

things more amazing than that, so you've got to come and see them."

"Absolutely." Eowen let go, then she picked up Zerinely. "You'll be good, won't you?"

The little girl shrugged. "Grandpa says I ask too many questions, but he says grandma was like that, and sometimes people say my questions are bad, so I don't know if I want to be good because instead I can be like grandma, and grandpa says she was clever!" Zerinely grinned with only half a mouth of teeth, all mischief and intelligence. Eowen approached Hale next with her arms open, but the warrior was gone.

"Where's Hale?"

"She's with the guide that will be escorting you to the furthest waypoint we have," Genia said. "I can't go with you, I need to attend to my duties here." Genia looked to Assistant Ugin and the man gestured for confirmation. Genia's shoulders hung, but Ne held her hand and shook her arm.

"You've got to send friends off with a smile," he said.

Together they walked to the edge of the mountain folk's settlement where Hale and the guide, a warrior man a few decades older, waited. The mountain folk they passed bowed respectfully.

"I don't think I'll get used to that," Genia muttered.

"Good, a leader with a big ego is of no use," Yawin said. They exchanged one more round of goodbyes, and then it was Yawin's turn. He and Eowen embraced and the old man took a few deep breaths, trying to control himself until he couldn't. Eowen felt him shake silently with repressed sobs.

"It's ok, Yawin. You don't need to be worried about me, I'll be ok." Eowen stroked his back.

"Worried? About you? Where'd you get an idea like that?

Two kids going alone into who knows what? What could even happen, what's there to be worried about? Nothing at all, right?" Eowen couldn't help smiling into his chest.

"That's right old man, nothing at all." Hani, Hale, and their guide waited patiently. Yawin stepped back with his hands on Eowen's shoulders.

"Alright. Keep track of time out there, you never know how much has passed if you don't check."

"I will."

"And eat properly, I know you can make any food you want but it can't all be sweets."

"Understood."

"And get plenty of sleep, not that you have trouble with that... In fact, maybe you should sleep a little less—"

"Cut it out old man!" Hale gestured her annoyance at him and Yawin blinked at her.

"Right, right." He let go of Eowen's shoulders. "Go on, then."

Hale gestured smartly and stepped behind Eowen and Hani. They started off into the empty lands beyond the settlement, the only visible landmark being a stone waypoint in the distance that the guide was heading for. Eowen felt for the gift from Ne and felt the comforting tug that would take her back to the mountain folk. Yawin picked up Zerinely when she patted his leg and held her arms up. She cupped her hands around her mouth and shouted after them.

"And don't die!"

Genia broke down laughing and gestured her approval. "Thank you Zerinley! I should make you one of my council, that was already better than all of Yawin's advice." The old man opened his mouth to argue, but shrugged and kissed Zerinely on the cheek instead.

"She's right."

"Of course I am," said Zerinely. Genia grinned and shook her head.

"I've got a new decree; the rest of you aren't allowed to leave, ever."

Eowen, Hani, Hale, and the guide dwindled out of sight, and as they reached a certain distance, a kind of threshold passed through the group watching them. It was the range of Eowen's dreaming aura, massive and powerful. They'd been living within its radius for so long that once it was beyond their perception the change was like night and day. An intense, but also comforting and familiar weight no longer on them, like a blanket that had gotten too warm. The air of the settlement, which had always been cold and smelled of stone and snow, had been intermingled with the aroma of humid air jungle earth. Now gone, the mountain folk's settlement felt more like their home from before the fall and less like the one they'd made after.

Genia took a deep breath of the crisp air and felt her own power flower out more than it ever had before. A strength welled in her that she hadn't known was there, one she hadn't needed to cultivate when adjacent to a power such as Eowen's. Her power had truly awoken for the first time during the creation of the eagle and wildcat, and now she could feel that it would continue to grow. Genia turned around, head held high, tears dry, and gestured for the others to follow her back. As they walked, Yawin's heart swelled with pride, for the girl looked grown up. She looked like a patrician of the people closest to heaven.

* * *

It took a few days to reach the final waypoint. Their guide, a man named Lagat, had placed the waypoints himself, as he'd been in the first party to seek out and gather the scattered mountain folk and deliver them to the settlement they now occupied. As they walked, Lagat spent most of the time telling stories about the first weeks after the fall. It turned out he'd been responsible for creating most of the stone houses as well until he'd taught others such creation. Hani had been picking up some of the mountain folk's language and he insisted Hale and Lagat teach him more.

"Why do you even need to learn it now that we're leaving?" Eowen asked.

"You never know who you'll encounter out there, it's important to be able to speak with them if you want to form bonds and get information."

"But if they don't live in the mountain folk's region, won't they know the language of whatever place they're living in?" Eowen asked.

"There's a difference between speaking to and speaking with someone." Hani raised his eyebrows meaningfully, and Hale gestured that she agreed. "Oh! Next I want to learn that gesture speech you use."

"I don't think so," Hale said. "It's really only for us." She winked at Eowen.

"Oh, sorry for trying to copy it," Hani said.

"It's not insulting for you to try and copy, but we still won't teach you. Besides, it definitely won't come handy anywhere else."

When they rested, they would share stories and play games. Hale and Lagat would try to regale them with legends about mountain folk heroes. "It was a hundred years ago..." Lagat began.

"No, three hundred," Hale cut in.

"It doesn't matter, a hundred years ago makes the story more interesting because it makes it feel like less of a legend. You can meet someone who was alive for something that began a hundred years ago."

"But what if they asked someone about it? The former patricians are over a hundred years old, they would remember if Kaikoura the stone-foot was alive then."

"How would they ask? We're leaving the settlement, the Patricians will probably be dead before they return."

"How dare you say something so disrespectful!"

"You called them sour bags of chalk-dust yesterday!"

"I did so respectfully." Hani enjoyed listening to their banter and used it to test his ability to pick up on their language. He practiced by egging them on in their language at times.

"Hello, two people. Hale and Lagat, patrician men, ahhh. One know story better?" Hani said in broken mountain folk.

"You're asking which patrician would know the story of Kaikoura the stone-foot better?" Hale asked in Eowen's language.

"Yes!"

"It's obvious, former Patrician Gissler," Lagat said.

"Which one is Gissler?" Hale asked.

"You can't even tell which former patrician is which?"

"Can you?"

Lagat held up a finger with his mouth open for a long moment before giving up. "You could tell a few decades ago, before they stepped down."

"That was before I was born!" Hale protested. Hani sat back and manifested a warm drink to sip while Eowen placed a barrier of sound over herself and went to sleep.

****

[Listen, for you cannot hear me yet]

SUN TOLD LOVE THAT I, A GIANT, HAD ARRIVED.

****

Five days later, they were camped out at the final waypoint, a fire burning and the darkness beyond feeling like a curtain around them. Lagat had made his best guess as to where Port Disoke was, but he had not sounded confident. Eowen lent him the stone Ne had made for her and he walked in a wide arc, trying to get a feel for the position of the city. When he returned he pointed in a direction and manifested two arrowhead shaped stones the size of his feet pointing the way. "Somewhere in that direction, I'm sure." He did not sound sure, but no one argued with him. The darkness beyond pressed upon them, stifling the spirit of curiosity and adventure.

Eowen found her eyes drifting away from the fire and out into the void. She had never been in the Elder Mountains before the end of the world, but she had been to the ocean. She hadn't been interested in playing in the waves with the other children, but preferred to stand on the grassy dunes where even the high tide couldn't reach. As a child she had stared for hours out to where the water got dark and deep. It was like that for her now, a murky beyond that made her heart ache with fear while her spirit craved to know what was in it.

Hani finished his meal, sipped the hot tea he'd often manifested, and took stock of the dour mood. He considered trying to egg Hale and Lagat into an argument, but they didn't seem to be in the spirit of it. After a long moment he stood, lit by the fire and his own glowing starfield, and moved so that the dark beyond was to his back.

"Jhona the Sage spent his life seeking the answers that his fathers, and his father's fathers failed to find. Who were the mighty gods that first stoked the fires of creation? Why did they cache it beneath the earth? Where have they gone? And why did they create our world to begin with? Jhona asked the sages of each island, but they called him a fool for wondering over such things for which there can be no answer and reprimanded him for lacking devotion to the demigods that preserve life.

"This did not satisfy him, and despite what the other sages said, Jhona was most wise, and could speak with all the animals of the world, great and small. He asked the birds first, as they saw and exchanged information further and faster than any creatures of the world, but the birds have poor memory and could only tell him of current affairs. Next he consulted the beasts of the land; stalking predators, wild tree-climbers, skittering and slithering scaled ones that hiss, and cowering burrowers. They did not know either, too wrapped up in their constant battles for life and death to concern themselves with the history of the world. You would be uninterested in such things as well if each moment you existed you were only concerned with eating, being eaten, or finding a mate.

"Finally he took a craft out into deep waters during the season of the great beasts of the sea for which such trivial matters of life and death are no concern. Not the fish or the crustaceans of the ocean, for they are caught in the cycle of death and life just as those of the land are, but the great serpents of the deep who, unassailable as they are, only die when beached by the workings of the demigods. The demigods themselves don't know, of course, for they are younger even than the animals of the world.

"After twenty days and nights a great serpent, whose enormous black back was as large as an island unto itself, rose up beside Jhona to ask why he lingers in the domain of time where creatures of land do not belong. He told the great beast he sought the answers of the beginning of time itself. The serpent saw that he was a great sage and would not use such wisdom for ill, but admitted that even it, a creature young for its kind but still older than the demigods, did not know of such a time, nor would its elders.

"Jhona despaired, for the answers to the questions of his father and his father's fathers would never be answered. The serpent took pity on him though, and told him it could not tell him of the beginning of the world, but it could tell him of the end. Jhona agreed to be given such wisdom, and the serpent took him to the bottom of the world's waters where a great hole sucked them and the sands of the ocean's depths out into the world below with no sky and no up and no down. The serpent told Jhona, the sage, that while the fires were the workings of the unknown gods who created the world, the waters were the workings of the gods who would bring about the end of it. One day, the waters would quench all the flames of creation, wash all the land of the world into sand, and the sand would trickle out through the hole at the bottom of the world along with the world's waters, and all that once was would be no more.

"Jhona thanked the serpent for the wisdom of the end-times, and was returned to his people. Thereafter, the great sage taught the secrets of the depths to the people of the islands, but few believed him. None now know if his story was true or if it was the madness of one who spent too long at sea, where creatures of land do not belong."

Hani locked eyes with each of his listeners as he finished the story, then cracked a smile. "Well, I suppose now we know."

After a suitably dramatic pause, Lagat began clappin. He turned to Hale.

"Can you translate that for me?" the guide asked, and Hale laughed at him.

"Not a chance! You want me to remember all that?"

Eowen breathed a sigh of relief as their bickering began. Hani sat down next to her and sipped his drink.

"Can I have some of that?" She pointed to his cup. Hani held out his empty hand to her and in a twist of shadow and light a steaming cup was in it. Eowen took a sip and stuck her tongue out. It was bitter in the way of dirt and medicine, but also fruity in a way that made her think it was ok until the after taste of more earthy bitterness came in.

"Don't like it?" Hani looked amused. "It's an acquired taste, a tea that's supposed to bring a calm mind, the drink of the sages. It's made from... or was made from the bark of the makahuni tree. They live a long time and can survive fires from lava flows, so they supposedly have some kind of special properties."

"If they're always drinking this and talking to animals I can see why they'd do absurd things like waiting around in the ocean for a serpent to take them away." Eowen stuck her tongue out and threw the rest of the drink into the fire.

"Ha! Maybe. I thought I'd find out if there was anything to it though, so I've been drinking it since we arrived at the mountain folk's settlement."

"Is it working?"

"Hmm." Hani took another long sip, swished it around in his mouth, and with obvious discomfort, swallowed. "Ugh, I don't think so."

"What was the point of that story anyway?" Eowen asked.

"No point, I was just sick of the silence."

"But... who told you that story?"

"My grandma did, but it's not a totally uncommon one. Why do you ask?"

"I know you didn't make up such a story yourself." Eowen raised an eyebrow at Hani who put a hand to his chest in mock offense.

"You think I have no imagination? A dreamer such as myself, capable of feats the likes of which this world has never known?"

Eowen thought about this. "Isn't every new manifestation a feat the likes of which this world has never known?" As an example, she held out her palm and in a surge of light and shadow produced a purple flower with a tough brown stem and long petals that leaned out and over her hand. Hani eyed it suspiciously, then reached out a hand and poked a petal.

"It's... a flower?"

"Yes, but it's purple."

"Huh, well done jungle girl." He sounded decidedly unimpressed.

"No, you don't understand. This flower only blooms in orange and yellow. I made one that has never existed before!"

"Well, I have to admit. You did just do something that no one else probably has."

"When you put it that way it doesn't sound impressive."

"That's because it's not!" Hani said and stuck out his tongue at her. Eowen rolled her eyes and lay back on the starfield.

"You just lack the imagination to appreciate my manifestations."

"Is that so?"

"Let me see that flower then." Hani held his hand open expectantly. Eowen eyed it suspiciously but couldn't think of what kind of prank he'd try to pull, so she handed it over. Hale and Lagat had finished their banter and were quietly sharing a drink that had their cheeks flushed. They watched Eowen and Hani through the flames. Hani sat up straight, focused in on the flower, and for a long moment nothing happened. No shadows stirring, no light creeping up from below. Hale held her breath but after almost a minute let it out to take a sip. With her mug in front of her she missed what happened but heard a quick, high pitched whistle from Hani followed by the gasps from Lagat and Eowen.

"What did he do?" She sat up from her slouch and pointed at Hani. "Do it again." Hani shrugged but his eyes shone with pride.

"I don't know, should I?"

"What are you teasing her for?" Eowen snatched the flower away. "Here, I'll do it." Eowen held the flower out just beyond the fire's reach, then flicked it in. The petals curled and crisped immediately, the stem let off a puff of steam, then blackened. Eowen held out her hand and the shadows and light of her dreaming collected and scooped into the fire, like a spoon, but nothing happened. The ashes of the flower danced in the air from the disturbance. "What? But I used my power in the same way." She looked at Hani accusingly. "I felt what you did." Hani looked quite proud of himself, and, without even looking at the fire, held out his hand and whistled like before. His power responded, and from the flames and ashes the flower returned, fully formed and perfect.

"I attached the whistle to the flower. If you don't do the whistle, it won't come back."

Eowen crossed her arms. "Well that's not fair, I can't whistle." Hani slapped his leg and laughed at her. "You can be awfully rude, has anyone told you that?" Eowen huffed. "Besides, who cares if I can't whistle?"

"That's exactly why it's funny! You can make jungles and suns and giant magical creatures, but you can't whistle!"

Eowen closed Hani off in a barrier of silence and rolled up in her blanket. "Doesn't matter if no one can hear you anyway. I'm going to sleep now, Hale, Lagat."

It took Hani a moment to notice no one was responding to his voice and another to extend his senses and understand what Eowen had done. Hale and Lagat could see him speaking and gesticulating, but no sound, not even from his movements, left his presence. Eowen had a cocky, satisfied smile as, with a gesture, she manifested a stone tent around herself when Hani tried to reach for her.

"A few months ago I would have asked what you put in my drink after seeing the things I have this evening," Lagat said. Hale chuckled and finished off her drink.

"Those times are gone." She lay down with her hands over her stomach and closed her eyes. "Things are only going to get stranger." Lagat followed suit, and soon enough was humming a relaxing mountain folk tune that Hale joined in on. Hani spent some time straining against the barrier with his power, giving up, then trying again. Eventually he accepted the silence and drifted off to sleep as well.

Eowen did not sleep though, as tired as she was. The wall of darkness beyond their campsite called to her even while out of sight. The emptiness of it seemed to have a craving to be filled.

* * *

Hale turned over, rubbed the crust from her eyes and saw Eowen standing some distance away, facing the direction of her journey. Hale rose, stretched, and joined her, Eowen was sipping something that steamed from a small cup. "What's that you're drinking?"

Eowen looked at her cup, still full except for one sip. "Want some?"

Hale took it and spit it out as soon as the drink touched her tongue. "That's terrible!" Hale handed it back. Eowen looked at the cup and grimaced.

"Yes, it really is, I heard it was an acquired taste."

"Why would you want to acquire terrible taste?" Eowen shrugged and tossed the cup away. "So, you're ready to go then?" Hale asked, and Eowen looked at her feet and nodded.

"I'm going to miss you Hale," she whispered.

"You're going to miss everyone else more." Hale said this but was smiling. She put an arm around Eowen and rubbed her shoulder. "I'll miss you too, kid."

Eowen glared. "You're shorter than me."

"You're younger than me."

"You're less powerful than me."

Hale flexed her arm that wasn't around Eowen. She'd been training daily since her return to her people and had regained muscle that had faded during her first weeks since the fall. "In some ways."

Hani stirred behind them. Eowen leaned in close and whispered in Hale's ear.

"I took down the barrier of silence a few minutes ago but left one that doesn't actually do anything, pretend you can't hear him." Hale chuckled and faced directly away from Hani towards the void of darkness beyond. The only light around them was the gentle glow from the stars below.

"My, what a beautiful morning it is, Eowen," Hale said, which made Eowen giggle and slap her shoulder.

"Eowen!" Hani called, but she and Hale didn't react. He checked with his senses for the barrier, feeling one in place. He walked around in front of them and they reacted with surprise.

"Oh, Hani? I didn't hear you get up," Hale said, making Eowen laugh more.

"Of course you didn't, this... child put—"

"Sorry, what was that? Speak up." Hale put her hand to her ear and Eowen had to turn away with her hand over her mouth to stop from laughing at him out loud. Hani opened his mouth to speak again, paused, and moved so he was directly in front of the girls. He put his hands together as if in prayer and mouthed: 'please.'

"What—" Eowen paused to giggle. "What do you think he wants Hale?" The warrior girl fixed an innocent look on her face.

"Hmm, breakfast maybe? He should just make it himself." Hani fixed as happy and polite an expression on his face as he could manage.

"Very funny, I'm going to drown you in your sleep," he muttered between teeth clenched in an unconvincing smile.

"Well that's an overreaction," Eowen said.

"Then take down the shroud already!" Hani shouted and threw up his hands. He held them above his head as he processed the last few seconds. "I see." Eowen laughed in his face but undid the false barrier. Hale nodded approvingly. "Fine, that was good. Come, let's eat."

With a wave he manifested a stone table and four seats. Then he focused carefully, gathering more shadow and light than Eowen thought necessary for a meal. When he did combine them and their food appeared it was a diverse spread of islander, jungle and savannah, and mountain folk dishes.

"Wow, this looks very appetizing," Lagat said as he sat down.

"I've been practicing replicating every new food I eat. If I've got all the world's dishes in my memory, why should I ever have a boring meal again?" Hani said, and picked up a steaming cup, like the one Eowen had shared with Hale and took a sip. He frowned as he choked down the bitter liquid. Hale leaned in and whispered in Eowen's ear.

"Is that what you were drinking this morning?"

"Yes."

"He likes it?"

"I don't think so." Eowen took a bite of grilled fish glazed with something sweet and spicy.

"Why does he drink it then?" On cue, Hani took another sip and grimaced.

"I think it's a personal challenge to... become more sage-like." Eowen used the word for 'sage' in hers and Hani's language. She took another bite of the fish and focused on memorizing it to recreate later.

"What's a sage, Hani called the animal-talking man in that story a sage didn't he?"

"It's a wise person, I think they have to be old." Hale shrugged and dug into the mountain folk dishes.

"Not terrible, kid," she said to Hani with a gesture of approval. They finished eating, then Hale embraced Eowen again and patted her shoulders approvingly. "Till next time."

Then she turned her heel and marched off back toward the mountain folk's settlement.

Eowen's heart ached as she watched the warrior girl go. She felt a slipping away, as though the ground under her feet was tilted. She took a step back, faced the direction of their travel and started for the city of Port Disoke.

"That was less emotional than I expected," said Hani when he caught up with her. Eowen sniffed, but no tears formed in her eyes.

"Yes, well, Hale isn't as sentimental as the others, but I know she cares." Her shoulders drooped, so Hani patted her on the back and manifested a light the size of his head to shine above them. Its light, combined with the bright stars from below, cut them out of the darkness.

"Come, let me tell you about how my father discovered an ancient temple in the frozen southern seas where an octopus-headed god had once been worshiped. The inhabitants were long dead and the dust of ages lay heavy on the place. He sailed up in midsummer with his crew when the ice was at its thinnest and—" Eowen let him prattle on, allowing herself to be distracted by the tale of adventure and daring.

Behind them, Hale walked blindly with a sleeve over her eyes as tears streamed out. Lagat patted her back and kept her on track.

"You sent her off well, child. Now let's both of us get home," he said.

* * *

Manifested lights hovering over their heads, Eowen and Hani walked for hours without landmarks. They often had to readjust their pace as Hani would unconsciously speed up, almost to the point of jogging, while Eowen would go slower and slower so she could carefully look around. Eowen first noticed Hani's habit an hour in when she found him almost four meters ahead of her.

"Hani, wait up." She jogged up to him. "Did you spot something?"

"No, not yet."

"Why are you going so fast then?"

"I'm not going that fast," he said.

"Look at how fast your legs are moving while you walk." Eowen pointed but Hani slowed down once he looked down. "No, you were walking like this before." Eowen stomped off in an exaggerated speed-walk with her arms flailing. Hani crossed his arms.

"I do not walk like that."

"It doesn't matter what you look like, we need to slow down or we might miss something."

"We're not going to miss anything, do you know how many people lived in Port Disoke? Over twenty thousand! We can't miss them." Hani held out his open hand, but just Eowen put her hands on her hips and raised an eyebrow at him.

"Twenty thousand people in one place?"

"That's what my father told me, and he sailed there many times." Eowen repressed the urge to comment that fathers often told tall tales to amuse their children.

"Either way, you're walking too fast for me, so slow down." She turned and continued the way they'd been going to the best of her knowledge.

"I don't know why you have trouble keeping up," Hani said when he jogged up beside her. "Your legs are as long as mine."

"What did your father say about Port Disoke?" Eowen asked to change the subject and keep him moving at her pace.

"It's amazing! Or was. It was the biggest port city in the world, built on stony slopes that stretched for dozens of kilometers inland. Apparently it is actually three port cities that are connected by enormous inland roads that are wide enough for fifty people to walk next to each other without jostling. Each city controls a port that can hold over a hundred large sailing ships. Apparently people from all over the world have settled there, it's the most diverse place in history."

"Wait, I thought the people of Port Disoke were the Britchen?"

"Oh... that's right, but it's also people from everywhere?"

"Why would people from everywhere be able to live where the Britchen do?" The two lapsed into silence. They had never encountered a non-homogenous culture. The only difference between them was that Hani had heard stories from his father. All Eowen had heard up to that point was that there were people on the other side of the mountains called the Britchen.

"Well... I'm sure they worked it out somehow," Hani finished lamely. Eowen tried to imagine what such a settlement would be like, how the buildings would fit or what they'd look like at the edge of the ocean. She imagined the huts of her people blown apart by ocean storms. Then she imagined the stacked stone of the mountain folk, but that would sink in the sand and collapse. They moved largely in silence, deep in thought, stopped to eat when hungry, and after many hours made camp to sleep. Eowen and Hani erected barriers while they slept that made them virtually undetectable. Hani called the barriers he made shrouds, and while the effects were almost identical, Eowen's were somehow stiffer, like a membrane, while Hani's were more like a blanket. They were careful and left markers shaped like arrows in the direction they had been heading, but the passing hours had left them uncertain as to whether they were going anywhere at all or entirely in circles.

A full day passed, and while they did stop to rest, Eowen again could not sleep. They grew quieter and quieter as one day stretched into two, and the darkness and silence began to weigh upon them. Their conversations became shorter, more irritable, and as their minds were left with nothing to occupy them, their dreaming auras became more and more unstable. Eowen's manifestations had always been accompanied by unintended effects, the excess ballast of her subconscious escaping when she opened the doors of creation. She'd begun to master the ability to ensure these excess effects were temporary and innocuous such that, for simple creations, they were hardly noticeable. Things like a distant sound, a whiff of some scent, the barest of physical material fluttering out with it, a slight change in the texture of her atmosphere. Time wore on and the emptiness and lack of sleep drew more and more out of her subconscious, until the effects were anything but innocuous.

Their third full day passed, but it felt like twice that, for Eowen had not slept when they'd stopped. She nodded off and jerked awake as they walked, and she'd stopped trying to slow down Hani and he'd stopped trying to keep track of her. She simply followed the light he kept above his head knowing that, eventually, he'd stop for food or to relieve himself, and she would catch up. They were weary of trekking, and Eowen's creations were leaving strange and motley trails of landscape and dilapidated things behind her.

Small creatures and distant chants flowed from the water she made to drink, and she found herself pulling food up from sticky shadows that shed soil, static electricity, and cloth that wrinkled into familiar faces.

Hani was having his own troubles with creation, but for him the tendency for them to be incomplete was creeping into even his weaker ones. The blanket he slept in would shrink with each toss and turn until it had disappeared, his food would taste real but disappear after swallowing, leaving his stomach empty and painful. Even the atmosphere he kept around him felt thinner while Eowen's had become terribly heavy.

Their fourth day drew to a close, and Eowen had still not slept. An incessant insect buzzing she was barely aware of surrounded her. They did not bother making a cheerful campfire; neither felt capable of doing so successfully. Hani sat close to Eowen, for her quality of air was better than his now, but the buzzing bothered him. Eowen focused herself on the task of manifesting some simple bread, and through the buzzing, the pressure in her atmosphere, and the sleep deprivation, minutes passed. Shadows and light gathered, but the shadows were like a thick mud that her creation was stuck in. Frustrated and hungry, Eowen waved her hand through the starlight till it was coating her skin and pawed through the darkness as though excavating something, sending strange creations tumbling into reality.

Hani watched flowers made of animal fur, songs that smelled like urine, and a scarf that shimmered with heat tumble off of Eowen's shadows. The scarf landed on the hem of her mountain folk robe and the acrid smell of burning animal fur filled the air.

"Do you mind?" Hani muttered.

Eowen turned and a sound like the squeal of wood under pressure drifted off her, the annoyance on her face was so fixed it could have been carved from stone. Hani put his hand up as an apology and looked away. Eowen flicked her hand at the scarf and a small wave of water manifested out from her side, washing it a few paces away. The water steamed from the heat and the steam congealed into a black and white bird that cawed, took flight in a rush, and soared away. It made it a few meters to the edge of Eowen's atmosphere, then plummeted to the starfield, twitching till dead.

Eowen and Hani grimaced, looked at each other, and silently agreed not to bring up what had just happened. Eowen finished brushing the shadows from her bread, which strangely tasted like raw frog, but at least was filling. Hani snapped his fingers and a perfect little loaf rushed into being on his palm. He took a bite, chewed, chewed, and then stopped chewing. He opened his mouth and there was no more bread in it at all. His stomach growled and he turned to Eowen sheepishly. "Um, Eowen. Can I have some—" She dropped the other half of her loaf on his lap.

"You're taking first watch," she muttered.

"Thank you," Hani whispered, then he took a bite of the bread and spat it out. "Why does it taste like swamp and raw bird?" Eowen didn't answer with words, but her dreaming aura, saturated with raw potentiality, flared against Hani's, cowing the boy and physically pushing him back. Hani flushed with anger, but just as quickly slouched down, exhausted. He didn't have the energy for much else besides apathy, so he choked down the bread and sat back for his watch. He neglected to wake Eowen for her watch; the silence and stillness sent him to sleep before he'd finished chewing. Exhaustion caught up with Eowen as well, but she could still not sleep, only drift through states of unfocused consciousness.

* * *

Three hours of sleep later felt to Hani as though he'd nodded off for only a moment. He kept to his watch for a bit but fell back asleep, and what felt again like only another moment was five more hours. When he awoke again, his sense of time had evaporated but he figured the watch had gone on long enough and reached for Eowen to wake her.

"I'm not asleep," she said before he could touch her. She sat up and looked around blurrily. Hani considered laying down, but didn't feel tired enough in body and yet felt terribly weary in his spirit.

"I'm not really feeling like sleeping, Eowen. Maybe we should keep going?"

Eowen stood up and walked around in a circle, then manifested a bright light above her head that made Hani squint. They ignored the sound of thunder that accompanied the light. "Hani, where's the arrow?"

"What arrow—Oh no!" Hani scrambled to his feet and looked around desperately for an arrow-shaped stone to denote which way they'd been heading, but neither of them had manifested one before resting. Eowen stared at him too incredulous to be enraged.

"You didn't make one," she said.

"You didn't either!" Hani whined. Now Eowen was angry, literally burning with fury as her dreaming aura swaddled her in flames that became trees that exploded into beetles and other swarms of discord. The Storm from within and beyond her threatened its emergence, howling wanton destruction.

"I didn't either? I didn't? Who was on watch Hani?" Eowen's breath smelled like a tree rent by lightning and her hair snapped out of her two braids. Hani backed up. He tried to summon his power around him to match and suppress, but it had abandoned him many hours ago and even basic manifestations were beyond him. However, for the first time in days he was fully awake, alert, and actually looking at Eowen.

Her skin was tight and dehydrated, her eyes were seated on deep bags, and her fists trembled at her side. Her mouth was twisted with rage, but her expression was frightened, her shoulders hunched. She didn't look like she wanted to fight, she looked like a fight was being dragged out of her. Hani took three deep breaths, gathered what courage he had, then manifested a veil of armor against Eowen's Storm and marched right up to her.

"What are we going to do now?" she said, and though her voice echoed louder and deeper than her natural one, suffused with power and threat, he listened for the exhausted and frightened girl beneath. "This was all your idea, and I was stupid enough to go along. We'll be lost out here forever, and maybe even that would be ok if it hadn't been your fault!"

"You're right," Hani said. "I'm sorry."

Eowen stared at him, breathing heavily until she dropped her head in her hands. The power around her clung, but Hani felt clear of mind. He reached out with his own power and, like cutting a rope under tension, undid the Storm around Eowen. It burst out without becoming anything, and Hani sat down in front of her. He manifested two cups with a hot drink in them and motioned for her to join him.

"We haven't been working together, and that's been our

mistake. We work well together, remember?" Eowen nodded, sighed, and took a seat. She lifted the cup and sipped.

"Ugh! Not this shit!" She tossed the cup at Hani's head and he ducked under it, grinning now. Eowen smiled back and wiped at her eyes. "I'm sorry, I don't know why I let things get like that."

"This... emptiness is affecting us both. If we were staying in one place or were traveling with a larger group, or had found any evidence of people, it wouldn't be so bad." Hani gestured around them. "But all this moving through nothing, it's driving us crazy."

"It really is, isn't it? You haven't even been able to manifest things well. I'm sorry, I hadn't even thought about how that's affected you, it was just annoyingly inconvenient to me."

"Thank you and you're right, I can hardly maintain anything right now. Look at the cup you threw." Eowen leaned to the side to see around Hani but couldn't locate the terrible cup of tea she'd thrown.

"I see, you couldn't even keep that up."

"No." Hani shook his head. He held out the hand that had been holding his own tea, which was now empty. "Who knew this could happen, days of nothing breaking apart my ability to do... anything. It's maddening. I've never been without stimulation in my life."

"I experienced something similar to this," Eowen said. "In my first days in the new world I was all alone. There were times I did think I'd gone mad, but I had my little dirt island. It was lonely, but that at least kept me centered till the mountain folk found me. All this walking through nothing though, I can't take it, I feel like I'm drowning." Eowen rubbed her eyes with both hands. "I've barely slept in days, Hani."

"Why? What have you been doing when I take watch." His tone was gentle. Eowen shrugged.

"Thinking."

"About what?"

"Nothing... I suppose I'm not actually thinking, my mind is just wandering." They lapsed into thought, both puzzling over what to do while avoiding the spirals of thought that had almost brought on disaster.

"I have a suggestion," Hani said, and Eowen gestured for him to speak. "I think we should spend one full day's worth of time right here. Make it as familiar, comfortable, and fun as we can, really fill the space, do you understand?" Eowen brightened a bit.

"We'll lose progress though, and we still don't know which way we actually need to go."

"That's alright. The point is to get ourselves healthy again, then we can figure something out. After all, we're the two most powerful dreamers in the new world, what can't we do?" Hani flashed a heroic smile and posed with his chest puffed out, fists on his hips. Eowen waved him off, but there was a much softened look in her eye.

They set to it right away, working together to manifest a sizable patch of earth that was a strange mix of jungle and island soil. A beach surrounded it with waves of seawater that appeared from nowhere and coasted up only half a meter before coasting back out into nonexistence. They planted all manner of flora, fully grown, and in some cases fused to produce jungle vines that bloomed with island flowers and island grass that rooted like jungle trees. Hani manifested a hut on stilts of fibrous material, stacked and bound together. Eowen's hut was of the clay and fiber mixture she was familiar with. When they'd finished, Hani's psyche had recovered enough that he manifested a large meal for them that only partially disappeared, and Eowen had calmed the Storm of her mind enough to lay a comforting atmosphere upon the island full of the scent of rich, living earth and clean ocean air.

They ate their fill in silence, satisfied with their progress thus far, and retired to their huts. Eowen's was almost exactly like she and her father's had been, both in the old world and the new, before she'd destroyed it. She felt terribly homesick, but in the bitterness of it she found herself reminiscing upon sweet times she hadn't thought of in a long time.

"I almost forgot," she whispered to herself, "when we visited family near the ocean, how much I loved the sound of the waves on the beach." Eowen drifted off as the sounds of the waves outside conjured her mother, father, Tavo, and her other cousins from a village across the savannah near the ocean. Her cousins had played in the water while she had stood upon a high dune, staring out at the dark and deep beyond.

****

[Listen, for you cannot hear me yet]

LOVE LOOKED ALL AROUND THEM AS BEST THEY COULD TO TAKE ME IN, BUT THEY COULD NOT, FOR THEY WERE TOO SMALL AND I TOO VAST.

****

Hani awoke hours before Eowen, and neither knew how long they'd slept, but it had been enough. Eowen stumbled out of her hut and rubbed her eyes clear.

"Hello," she muttered.

"Hello." Hani was standing in the water wearing new clothes he'd manifested that resembled what he'd worn when they had first met rather than the robes of the mountain folk they'd been traveling in. "Look what you did." Hani pointed behind Eowen. She turned, squinted at the foliage of the island, then realized what had happened. The island had expanded in her sleep, like how the oasis had expanded on its own.

"Do you think it's going to keep going?" Eowen asked.

"No, it stopped once you woke up."

"Hmm. That's fine, I suppose." Eowen looked over Hani's clothes again and got an idea. "Be right back." She returned to her hut and shed the mountain folk wool and furs she'd been wearing. They were comfortable and warm, but in the atmosphere they'd created on the island they were hardly appropriate. She set to manifestation, trying to keep herself steady so that a Storm would not emerge again. It turned out to be no trouble at all as shadow layered obediently in front of her and starlight stitched across it. Within seconds, new clothes in the familiar yellow she wore were folded neatly in front of her. She donned the skirt, top wrap, and head scarf. There was something special about her garments though, some quality that was like the barriers she manifested, but with a purpose she could not yet identify.

I'll figure it out later, she thought, and joined Hani in the water.

"Ah, just like when I met you," he said.

"You too."

"So..." Hani looked out from their island and scanned the empty dark. "Any idea where we should go?"

"Actually, I did have a thought about that." Eowen retrieved the stone Ne had given her.

"That only points back to the mountain folk doesn't it?" Hani asked. "I suppose going the opposite direction of it wouldn't put us entirely in the wrong direction, but it seems like it'd be imprecise."

"You're right, but I figured we might be able to make something similar, only instead of pointing to a specific place or person it could indicate where people are in general." Eowen gesticulated vaguely, having no idea what form such a creation should take.

"A person-finder thing? Interesting."

"It could tell us how far away they are, how many, what direction, things like that." Eowen started pacing in the water. "Maybe it would, um, talk to us? It could say things like:" Eowen put on a deep, serious sounding voice, "'Three people, four and a half kilometers away on your left.'" Eowen stopped her pacing. "I'm not sure even we could manifest something so specific that also does what it's supposed to every time and without strange unexpected side-effects. What do you think?"

Eowen had turned to Hani for his input, but he was busy shuffling his feet back and forth till they were covered in sand. "Try this, it feels very nice."

"Can you please be serious?"

"We do our best when we're relaxed and when we don't focus on things too hard. Remember what we talked about at the volcano, about how it all works? What we manifest aren't things that ever existed before, even if they look like things from the old world and do whatever those things did.

The shapes we give them emerge because they're familiar and we can believe they exist like that."

"Well, yes," Eowen said, then kicked some water to spray at Hani's shins, "but shouldn't we try to keep in mind what we are trying to do for something this complex and specific?"

"Are you asking me because I'm usually successful at manifesting specific things?"

"I guess I am."

"Hmm, for me it's like... I can see what something might be like far in the distance, and I have an idea of what it would be like to reach that thing, and if I've reached it before then I definitely know what it'll be like. But until I actually try to create it, I don't know what I'll have to overcome or understand to craft it. That's why the more difficult-to-understand things I sometimes can't finish. I can see what the final form and function should be, but I remain out of reach." He held out his hand to Eowen. "That's why I use the word manifest. I don't think you jungle and savannah people use it much because of your gods, but for us it refers to when gods reveal things." Eowen shifted from one foot to the other, but did eventually stand next to Hani and take his hand. He grinned at her. "That's why we work well together. You seem to have no trouble getting to places with your manifestations, you just can't always guarantee where you'll end up at!"

"Are we going to try this?"

"First, bury your feet in the sand."

"Why?"

"It feels nice, the sand feels warm even without the sun, but it's cool underneath." Eowen frowned but did as he suggested. The soft layers on top shifted aside easily and she dug her feet into the damp sand beneath the way Hani had so that the warm, loose sand would cover them up.

"Let's give it a try now," Eowen insisted.

"Does it feel nice?"

"Yes, now please, you're getting on my nerves," Eowen said, but a smile fought to be seen. Hani seemed satisfied and closed his eyes. "Last time we did something like this, Genia made sure it turned out right, we were just the..."

"Laborers?"

"Close enough. It was also something with precedent." Hani laughed at that. "What?"

"Eowen, those things may have looked like a cat and eagle, but there has never been anything like them. We... we practically made a pair of gods together, just the three of us."

Hani opened his eyes and his atmosphere of dreaming rushed in like a tide that never rushes out. Eowen was worried for a moment since their powers had been at odds the past few days, but even though they'd only performed creations together a few times, the shifting, dream-like implications of their subconscious minds met each other with familiar compatibility. Eowen felt a tension in her shoulders relax and let go of the present and the past for a moment to simply enjoy the rush of power between them.

The shadows came in slow, rising up around them like waves they were sinking beneath, and when the levels overcame them they found themselves submerged in a dream. Hani had described it well; when he let go of his conscious mind he knew where to go in the dream, for the end result was obvious in the distance, like the peak of a mountain. When he reached for it and the starlight below reacted to him, the darkness piled on, absorbing the light, combining to become something. As he attempted something greater or more unfamiliar, the fathoms of unknown layers within the shadows slowed his progress. He couldn't reach the summit and make his creation known. At least, not on his own.

Eowen's power rushed in like an oceanic current and proud winds pushing a massive ship in full sail. Her power moved itself, and she, more often than not, found herself abandoning any attempt at control and could only hang on for the ride. When these two forces merged, Hani found himself buoyed up to the peak in a rush and Eowen found herself sailing towards a clear destination. The sea of shadows around them vortexed into the space between their clasped hands, passing through a gate of light that shredded, spun, and wove the darkness into a new wonder the likes of which the world had never seen.

****

[Listen, for you cannot hear me yet]

THEY LOOKED HARDER AND HARDER, THEY STRAINED AND LISTENED, THEY FELT WITH ALL THEIR MIGHT, SKIN, AND BONES, THEIR FACE SCRUNCHING, THEIR NECK TENSING, THEIR HANDS FLEXING, TILL LOVE REALIZED THAT NO MORTAL SENSES COULD TAKE ME IN.

****

Hani opened his eyes to find his hand empty. He looked to his left, where Eowen still stood with her feet in the sand, holding what looked like a handle with a ball the size of a child's fist on one end. It all seemed to be made of one piece of polished wood, and aside from a comfortable looking grip, had no particular design elements to it.

"Is that it?" he asked.

"I think so." Eowen held it out with the ball facing upwards, then held it above her head, then turned her wrist so the ball was facing down. "I think we might have made a handle that doesn't do anything." She pulled her feet from the sand and washed them in the water.

"Let me see it." Hani held out his hand and Eowen handed it over, the ball side still pointing up. Hani moved it around, shook it, then wiggled the fingers of his other hand at it. "Aaaaand work! Find people. Uh, how many that way?" The handle did not respond. "We can try again, I suppose." He flipped it in the air, caught it, and held it out to Eowen again, but this time the ball was pointed directly at her. Hani's arm jerked down and the handle dropped out of his hand. "Woah! What was that?"

"Why'd you drop it?"

"It suddenly got really heavy." Hani said as he pulled his feet from the sand. Eowen picked up the handle and pointed it to Hani's left, then she slowly panned it towards him. The moment the ball end was pointing at Hani it became extremely heavy in her hand and she almost dropped it as well.

"Oh wow, it works! Hani, it works!" Eowen jumped around full of joy. "We did it, it works, it finds people, I can't believe it!"

"Ah! Stop splashing me! Here, let me see it." Eowen handed it over and he ran some yards away, keeping it carefully pointed to the stars below. He pointed it at Eowen and his hand jerked down, but he kept it steady. "It's not nearly as heavy here!"

"Run further away!" Hani did as she said and Eowen ran in the opposite direction. They stopped and faced each other.

"It still works!" Hani shouted, then they both ran further till they were well off the island. "Still works!" They went even further, running for almost a minute till they were just specs to each other. Hani shouted something unintelligible.

"What?" Eowen shouted back and he started running toward her. She met him back at the island, both short of breath.

"It, huff, still works!" He handed it back to Eowen, who held the stone Ne had given her and faced the mountain folk's settlement. She scanned it away from the settlement, then back towards it, noting the slight increase in weight.

"So it works even far out of sight. So even if we've gone far off course since leaving the mountain folk's settlement..." Eowen turned the opposite direction of the mountain folk and scanned back and forth. "Then the closest people are..." She honed in on the direction that felt heaviest, though the difference was very slight. "That way." The direction she faced looked no different than any other, but the weight in the handle suggested there were people.

"What are we waiting for?" Hani splashed through the waves and started running through the darkness, glowing as the stars beneath lit him up. Eowen folded up her skirt to give her legs more room and tore off after him. They ran till they were out of breath, jogged to catch it, then ran some more, outdoing each other in turns. Eventually Eowen couldn't keep going and had to rest, hands on knees and gasping.

"Hold, huff, hold on! Wait, please!" Hani was out of earshot and didn't check behind him till he was a spec in the distance. As he turned around and made his way back to her she scanned the distance, trying to find the heavy point again.

Unfortunately, Hani was in the way. "Move, I can't find anyone with you in front of me."

"Maybe I should carry it since I'm faster."

"Rude, just for that I'm not letting you." Eowen pushed him behind her and scanned again, finding that the closest person was to their left. "We're a little off course, but we are closer already."

Eowen started in the correct direction at a walking pace to keep the finder steady. She let Hani take it after a half-hour when her arms tired, and they traded off throughout the rest of their day's worth of travel. As they went they made sure to stop for good meals and manifested familiar comforts from home. Whether it be more jungle and island, familiar buildings, or simply a sun-like light above their head and a dome that resembled the sky from beneath, they made sure to break up the monotony. They didn't walk apart from each other anymore, and while conversation still dwindled in the empty expanse, they supported each other through it. Hani made sure Eowen wasn't getting too lost in the ocean of her mind by gently bringing her back to the present with soft words or a brief touch, and Eowen made sure Hani kept himself centered on something by handing him the detector and letting him guide them most of the time.

* * *

Many hours passed in their excitement to reach their destination, and eventually excitement became determination, which transitioned into habit, and finally, sixteen hours in, morphed into stubborn persistence. Though they were weary, the detector had gotten heavy enough to mean the people would be in sight within a few kilometers, so they persisted. Hani walked with poor posture, head down, and stared at the finder which he held with both hands. Eowen walked similarly, holding onto the hem of his sleeve to keep track of the boy. Their eyelids felt like stone and Eowen, not for the first time, fell asleep on the move. Her molasses thoughts managed to conclude that it was time to stop. "How're you doing, Hani?"

"Fine." His responses had been monosyllabic for the last hour and a half.

"You sure?"

"Yeh."

"That... um." Eowen rubbed her face to try and wake up enough to form a sentence. "That wasn't a, ah... what's the word?" She blinked a few times and yawned. "Word. That's the word." Her yawn was contagious, and Hani's yawn was big enough that he had to stop and fix his posture for it. Eowen bumped into his back.

"We're so close, though."

"I think we should be rested before we meet the people, right?" Hani struggled to comprehend her words, but as soon as he did he dropped the people finder.

"Ok." He collapsed, falling to his knees and immediately keeling over to lay prone. Eowen, still holding his sleeve, tumbled next to him and landed on the people finder, bruising her side.

"Ah! You monkey shit," she muttered and dug the finder out from under her. Hani was already fast asleep and snoring. Eowen passed out, chuckling under her breath.

****

[Listen, for you cannot hear me yet]

I GREETED LOVE, THOUGH I DID NOT EXPECT A RESPONSE, FOR NONE SO SMALL AS THEY HAVE EVER BEEN ABLE TO HEAR ME, FOR THEIR EARS ARE TOO WEAK TO DISCERN MY VOICE FROM THE NATURAL TWISTING OF THEIR UNIVERSE, AND THEIR VOICES TOO SMALL TO HEAR OVER THE BURNING OF STARS.

BUT LOVE DID HEAR ME.

****

Eowen kicked Hani awake and he jolted out of his dreams. He looked at the girl, still asleep and perpendicular to him, and scooted away, manifesting a basin with cool water to wash his face. After that he provided himself with a meal, a comfortable seat, and a light that shone warmly on him like the sun. Eowen mumbled in her sleep and rolled away from the light. Hani manifested a half-tent over her to block out the light, then leaned back to doze in the sun, whistling to himself.

He was later woken by flecks of water being flicked onto his face. "Ah!" He sat up and wiped his face off.

"Ready to go?"

"No, I've just woken up," he said with a yawn. "Again, that is. Are you ready, have you eaten yet?"

"Yes." Eowen was scanning with the people finder and, once she found her bearings, started forward. Hani grumbled as he hopped out of his comfortable seat to follow her.

"You're rather serious today," he said when he caught up with her.

"I've been thinking that there's a few problems."

"Like what?"

"Do you know anything about the Britchen people?"

"Not much besides what I've told you."

"Which is almost nothing," Eowen pointed out. Hani opened his mouth to retort but had no counter so he stayed quiet. "I'm worried about how they'll receive us, or what they'll think of us. We don't know their customs or culture. We might insult them terribly without even realizing it."

"I don't think it will be much of an issue."

"We don't even know what they eat, what if their food makes us sick?"

"Why would their food make you sick? They're just people like us, they probably eat the same things we do."

"The mountain folk eat dishes neither of us had before. You made food I've never had before."

"Obviously, there's different plants and animals everywhere. What I mean is they will still eat meat and plants just like we do."

"But maybe they eat raw meat that we need cooked, or poisonous plants that are harmless to them." Eowen's eyes got wide. "I've heard stories, Hani, of cannibals in the north that eat human flesh to get witches powers, and when they run out of captured victims they eat their own children." Eowen marched on with the finder held out, but her hands were shaking. Hani walked up beside her so she could see his face and spoke to her very gently.

"Eowen, you believed stories like that? Those are stories for scaring little babies! Are you saying you're a scared little baby?" Hani poked her shoulder, and with a flick of her wrist she manifested a splash of water that caught him full in the face along with an unintended fish that slapped his eye on its way past. "Ah! That was an overreaction."

"Hmm, don't be rude then." Eowen fixed her eyes on the direction of the finder again. "Fine, those stories might be fake, but my point still stands; we don't know what we're going to encounter out there or what these people will be like. Do you even speak the language of the Britchen people?"

"No, but remember, there are people from all over living there. I'm sure some will speak a dialect of our language or the mountain folk's language."

Eowen was suspicious of this, as her people largely lacked a concept of the cultures beyond the southern islands and elder mountains. Eowen had never been taught to consider people beyond those that bordered the jungle and savannah as distinct. Her people didn't even have much of a concept of how many different people or places there had been in the old world, let alone what their lands, languages, or cultures were like. The policy of the jungle and savannah tribes was to be ready for news of war or disease that might spread to them but to otherwise avoid interacting with the outside world at all. In her mind, the word Britchen conceptually encompassed every human beyond the elder mountains.

"I hope you're right," she said.

After some time, Eowen handed the people-finder to Hani to take a turn navigating. His hand swayed as he initially took it. "Oh, we've gotten a lot closer, we should run into them in no time!" They increased their pace, scanning the darkness for an enormous mass of people, seeking out buildings or landscapes underlit by the starfield's glow. Eowen imagined that if Hani was right about the population it would be even brighter than the mountain folks' settlement. In her mind, a great town filled with buildings that were a combination of the stacked stones of the mountain folk and the packed clay of her people stretched out for kilometers under the shade of tropical foliage.

Maybe they have a sun like I made, only better. Maybe they're so powerful and skilled at manifesting things they've recreated the whole world and everyone can go back to living in it.

"Eowen!" Hani's call broke her from her daydream. "Over here!" He was about twenty meters to her left, so she hurried over.

"Sorry, I didn't realize I'd gone off course."

"I don't think you have, you were walking perfectly straight. It was the finder, it started leading me off to the left as if we'd gone around them." Hani scanned with the handle, then gave it to Eowen for confirmation.

"You don't think it's... broken? Or never worked in the first place?"

"No, it seemed to work fine before, I don't see any reason it would stop now. It's just the way it was leading us was as if we'd already walked around their settlement, but there's no way we wouldn't have seen it." They scanned the darkness together, looking for towering buildings, trees, landscape, anything.

"Maybe there aren't as many as you thought?" Eowen suggested.

"No, even if my father exaggerated there'd be many more than the mountain folk."

"Hmm. Maybe they can hide themselves," Eowen mused.

"You mean they were able to construct a shroud large enough to hide thousands of people?" Hani seemed unconvinced, and Eowen had to agree with the sentiment. She didn't know what feats people were capable of throughout the new world, but she doubted they truly rivaled what she and Hani could do.

"No, you're right. Besides, if such massive manifestations were being performed I think we'd feel it. That's how you tracked me, isn't it?"

"It is..." Hani tapped the people finder on his chin as he thought. "Well, no way to find out but to go forward." With that he set off in the direction it led, which veered sharply to the left of the direction they'd been going. They kept scanning for a large settlement and Hani had trouble keeping the finder on course, until Eowen realized where it led.

"Stop."

"Do you see them? Where?" Eowen took the people finder from him and pointed solemnly down. Out in the dark, just barely visible by the light of their starfields, was a prone figure. "Oh, we've been tracking one person," Hani whispered.

Eowen started forward and Hani followed. She lit up the space around them with a bright light that floated above her head. Eowen slowed as she approached, dimming the light into a more intimate circle around them.

"Hello there," Hani said with a wave. "Are you alright— Oh." Hani stopped short, but Eowen knelt down next to the body. "They're dead, aren't they?" Hani whispered.

Eowen nodded. It had been a mountain folk, a man in his early twenties, now a naked and emaciated corpse that had left a trail of his own filth as he'd crawled from wherever he'd started in the world to his dying spot.

"He never figured out how to make clothing." Eowen's voice was soft, observational but not callus. "He probably couldn't make much air either."

"Or food," Hani said, keeping his distance. Eowen shook her head.

"No, look." She increased her light's output and pointed back along the trail he'd left of waste. Among the trail were the remains of food, some in puddles of water, crudely manifested and likely not very filling. "He could barely make anything, and he lasted as long as he could." Eowen gently turned the body onto its back. It had stiffened some time ago.

"Wait! You shouldn't just move it around like that!" Hani waved his hands at Eowen but kept his distance.

"It's fine," she said without looking at Hani. "I know what I'm doing. He's one of m—the mountain folk after all."

Eowen knelt with the corpse perpendicular to her. Hani shifted from foot to foot and glanced around self consciously. "Is there something I can do, or should do? We can't just leave him there. Or maybe we could?" Eowen turned to look at him, and he felt his face get hot. "I'm sorry, I just don't know what to do here."

"It's alright." Eowen's voice was even and warm. She sounded older than her age. "This is not for you to do, Hani. Give me some space. I'll be done in a moment." She turned back to the body.

[After I lay him to rest.]

Hani paused. He hadn't heard her speak, but he knew she had told him something. His mind struggled to hold the wisps of it as it faded, but he could not. He shook his head and hugged his arms around himself. "Alright, I'll be... over here if you need me." He left Eowen and the corpse behind, glad to be away from it.

The lone mountain folk corpse was withered, naked, his weeks of suffering sunken into the grotesque state of his body. Hani looked back once more before settling some distance from Eowen. He felt a strange quality around her again, like at the mountain folk's cemetery. A shape, or a silhouette that seemed to coalesce not from light or shadow, but from Eowen herself. It was too incomplete to be identified, but Hani could tell it stood over her, that it shrugged some kind of shoulders, and had a very long neck. He watched the savannah girl as her form seemed to smear like charcoal rubbed over a smooth surface, and the smear spread into whatever the shape around her was.

Hani felt a rush of power, immense but brief, which fused the torrent of light and shadow into Eowen's hand. She'd manifested a knife, like the ones the mountain folk used to prepare their bodies. Eowen brought the knife up slowly over the body's chest, then plunged it into the dead man's chest. Hani heard it cut into bone. The silhouette around her moved, shifted, its form still unclear, but it seemed to have an eye fixed on Hani. He promptly turned around and marched away, putting up a shroud around himself that would keep him from seeing or hearing anything happening where Eowen was. He manifested a cup of bitter tea and splashed a bit on himself as he took a sip. "I—I'll ask her about that later."

Eowen had not meant to strike so hard into the body with her knife. It had been as if the knife had moved her. She could feel a strange buzzing in the arm that held it, not unpleasant but unfamiliar. The knife felt like it was more than its shape implied, but she ignored the question of why and instead focused on her task. She removed the heart, cutting like she'd seen Yawin do, then set it aside. She removed the liver the same way, then carefully cut out the eyes. She hadn't seen this done, but the knife seemed adequately designed for all three removals, the curve of it following the shape of the socket. She manifested a small pouch with preserving qualities to put the eyes in, then set it and the knife aside, focusing instead on the organs.

Eowen closed her eyes, knowing what she wanted to make but also knowing it should be special. She didn't know what chaos would ensue in trying to manifest something with power without Hani's help, but there was no one around to hurt and she wanted to do this on her own.

No, I need to do this on my own. I don't know why, but I can feel it is right.

Eowen's power thickened, gathered, rose and descended upon her, only this time it did not roil as a Storm, but grew about her person; a tree of shadow with roots of light. The shadows and light grew heavier, fattened with implication, then gradually gathered together on the tips of two leden branches of darkness filled with thick, sap-like light. Eowen opened her eyes and held out her hands. The manifestation hung over her from the umber branch, and she plucked it and set it aside. A twin manifestation hung down as well, and with it she did the same, plucking it from the dream and introducing it to reality. The remaining darkness and light snapped out of being, then softly faded away into nothing, no unintended effects, no accidental manifestations. Before Eowen were now two stone urns, wide enough to accommodate the organs she'd removed with a stone eagle cap on one and a stone wildcat cap on the other. Eowen could feel a density to them, a power that had its own gravity in the way the brand had before it had been placed on her.

The girl lifted off the lids, and with a sense of reverence mimicked from Yawin as he'd offered the courage and love of his wife to the great beasts, she placed the heart and liver into the jars. She set the lid back on the jar with the eagle, and there was a sealing sound. Eowen tested it, and though she was not particularly strong, she could tell that no human strength would budge it. The barriers infused into the jars were unlike any she'd made before.

[They will last beyond mortal reckoning, until it is their time to open.]

The words slid out of her, unguided and unbidden, and their meaning was lost to her even as they were said, leaving her only with an assurance that the jars would be safe. She set the liver into its own container, then sat before the body. The silhouette around her shimmered, shuffled, and faded. A great weariness took hold of her and she slumped over the body.

"Oh, wow," she said, picking herself up. Eowen looked at the dead mountain folk, and held the body's hand. "They'll find you someday, and bring your heart and liver to the beasts they belong to." She blinked slowly, struggled to open her eyes again, and shook her head. "Ok, almost done."

Eowen stood and prepared for her next manifestation. It wasn't difficult, just kindling for a fire large enough to dispose of the body. She walked around it, trailing dry sticks and grass in her wake, along with an assortment of other random but undisruptive manifestations. She pushed the kindling under the body from all sides, then set them on top and around it as well. She smiled to herself.

Like tucking someone into bed.

Finally, Eowen manifested a flame into her hand and knelt down. She put the flame to the edge of the bed of kindling, and it took to the dry material with a hunger. She stepped back as the flames swam through the larger pieces of wood, eating up the grass until they were large enough to become a proper blaze. Eowen left the flame to its work and went to Hani. She sensed the barrier he'd made and walked through it, surprising him.

"Oh! Are you all done then?" He stood up, brushing some crumbs off himself.

"Yes, well, almost." Eowen glanced at the pouch. "Hani, have you ever eaten... eyes before?" She held up the pouch with a grimace. Hani stared at it, wide-eyed and disgusted. Then he looked over Eowen, noting the gore that went almost up to her elbows and the knife she still held.

"How about you wash up," he said, gingerly taking the knife and pouch, "and I'll try to figure out something to do about that." Eowen nodded gratefully and swayed.

"Thank you, I'm a little tir—" Eowen didn't finish the last word as she collapsed. Hani caught her head before it hit the ground.

"Woah! Alright, that took a lot out of you." He set her down and manifested a blanket to lay over her. "That's fine, you can sleep," he said, mostly to himself. "I'll do... something with these." He looked sick holding the pouch. "Hmm, maybe I'll just toss them in the fire and make some kind of... little orb of meat," he whispered. "I could slather it in sauce, she'd never know the difference."

"Nooo," came Eowen's sleepy moan.

"Weren't you asleep?" Hani asked.

"Gotta—" Eowen's eyes were still closed. She smacked her lips together and tried to gather her thoughts, but she felt like they were moving through tar. "Gotta do it right, have to eat them. Emmm," she trailed off, now fully unconscious.

"Alright," Hani said with a shake of his head. "I'll cook up these eyes for you." He walked away and manifested some equipment for the task. "I can't believe you were worried about the Britchen food making you sick."

******

[Listen, for you cannot hear me yet]

HOW, I KNOW NOT.

******

A bowl of reddish stew that smelled of unfamiliar spices sat in a bowl on Eowen's lap. Poised in her hand was a piece of flatbread with a pouch to scoop with. Hani was waiting patiently as he watched her lean in, sniff it, dab the bread in once, twice, and taste the sauce on the bread with the tip of her tongue.

"You're not even going to be able to tell the eyes are in there," Hani said. "Arainam sauce is what we islanders use to cover up the taste of anything, you could put raw fish and fresh fruit in there and never tell."

Eowen nibbled off the saucy corner of bread and smacked it in her mouth. "It's not exactly bad. I don't hate it, but it's not good either." She took a sip of water. "It's more that it's... intense. Hot but not too hot, my mouth feels... fuzzy?"

"That's exactly how it should be, I tasted some myself before mixing in the eyes. Trust me, this'll do the trick."

"I do trust you, I can see why this sauce works but it's not the taste that's bothering me." Eowen gave the dish a wary look. "I'm not sure I can handle the texture of eyes in my mouth."

Hani looked a bit sick. "It was disgusting preparing them, I'll tell you that. I just squished them, minced them, and mixed them in." It was Eowen's turn to look sick. "If it helps I'm fairly certain there isn't much texture left." Hani smiled encouragingly and shrugged. Eowen looked skeptically at the bowl once more then let her shoulders slump, resigned.

"Down the gullet." With that, Eowen dipped the bread and shoveled a large scoop into her mouth. She chewed hard and fast, scooping out everything she could get out of the bowl then washing it all down with several liberal gulps of water. Hani nodded his approval.

"You've done the mountain folk a great honor here, I think."

"Ugh!" Chills ran down Eowen's back. "I had no problem cutting out that man's innards but I will never eat eyes again if I can help it!" She manifested another gulp of water and floated it to her mouth, but this one was too big and it splashed all over her face. "Wonderful, if I wasn't awake before I am now. Do you know where we go from here?"

"I think so." Hani stood and scanned the distance with the people-finder. "It feels light in just about every direction. The closest person is that way." Hani pointed in a direction that, after checking the stone Ne had given her, Eowen could tell would continue taking them away from the mountain folk settlement.

"Can you tell how far we are from the mountain folk from here?" Eowen asked. Hani held out his hand and she put the stone in it. He lined himself up with the mountain folk's settlement and leveled the finder in the same direction.

"They're both far enough that it feels faint, but I'd say that the next closest people in our direction of travel are about as far from us now as we are from the mountain folk. Or maybe more, it's very hard to tell so far away."

"And it took us... how long? About five days to get here?"

"I stopped keeping a close track of time, honestly. It couldn't have been more than a week could it?" Hani looked concerned, and Eowen made a gesture to indicate her own uncertainty.

"I suppose we should get going. We still have a few more days of walking ahead of us." Eowen stood and approached Hani, waiting for him to lead the way.

"There's a lot of nothing out there between us and the next person we find, though," Hani said.

"I suppose."

"It's possible we're not headed towards the Britchen people at all, but another mountain settlement, or..." He glanced meaningfully at the smoldering pyre behind them. "Do you know how far the mountains ranged in the old world?"

"No, hold on, what do you mean how far?"

"You know, how many kilometers would you say the mountains used to extend for? How far away were the Britchen from your people? I've heard mountain ranges can stretch for thousands of kilometers. I'm no expert though."

"Hold on, I don't think I understand..." Eowen tried to remember seeing a map or hearing anything about how far the mountains went, and realized that she had no idea. Her whole life she had imagined the Elder mountains as more of a wall a few mountains deep, not as something that stretched out in every direction like the jungle or the savannah. "Oh! Oh no. I had no idea the mountains could go so far. We would have been going up and down in the old world, but here..."

"I take it you have no idea how far the mountains went."

"No, not really. I guess there's nothing to it, we just have to keep going." Eowen started in the direction Hani had indicated.

"I had an idea about that," Hani said. "I don't know about you, but I'm getting sick of walking."

"You sound like you have a solution for that," Eowen said with her hands on her hips.

"I was thinking we could ride something!" He beamed at her.

"Do you mean one of those... riding animals? I've heard of them, but never seen one."

"No, I was thinking we could manifest a ship!" Hani held out his arms as if waiting to receive applause.

"Hani."

"Great idea, isn't it?"

"There's no water here." Eowen gestured around them, but Hani didn't look the slightest bit discouraged.

"Oh Eowen, when has a lack of something ever been a problem for us?" Hani's smile faded as he closed his eyes and his face took on an expression of deep focus. Shadow and light flooded around him, rose, pushed forward towards Eowen, and crashed over her. She instinctively put up her hands to guard herself, but the shadow and light passed by harmlessly, causing only a rush of Hani's subconscious to flood her own mind with unfamiliar dream-like impressions. It was not quite that she felt, or heard, or tasted the texture of Hani's inner self as it flowed over her, but that in an instant she felt an intuitive sense of his inner workings. She felt the restless, optimistic craving for adventurous discovery and the certainty that his journey would bring new friends and foreign experiences flood her mind. Eowen knew then that those certainties and desires were like the heartwood of Hani; everything else about him had grown outward from that core. When the wave of potential was past her it ceased to be only light and shadow, and in a crash of both became a wave of water that held its crest for a time before collapsing into a wall of spray and disappearing. Hani returned from his dreaming and gave Eowen an expectant look, clearly proud.

"Alright," Eowen said, steepling her fingers. "This might work."

They assembled the ship quickly, but they did not manifest it all in one go. Hani had suggested that they do it piece by piece to give each section of it a greater fortitude, anchoring its existence into reality on multiple layers. They started with the frame of it, a wooden skeleton that, as with past manifestations, Hani provided the structure for while Eowen provided the dreaming fuel. Then they manifested the outer shell, levels, rooms, and other miscellaneous parts, curved wood seeming to dance into existence. Within an hour they had a ten and a half meter ship with two levels of polished, cream-colored wood that smelled of the island air Hani carried with him. Eowen paused at the rudder and sails though, disrupting Hani's flow.

"Is there a problem, do you need to rest?" Hani asked. Behind him the illusions of a great mast and sails shuddered as they waited to be made.

"Does it really need a sail or way to steer? Won't the water you manifest just... guide it where you want it to go?"

"No, it... Huh. I never thought of it that way." Hani let the partial manifestations dissolve. "I admit, it doesn't need those, but don't you think it looks wrong without them?"

Eowen surveyed the ship. She'd hardly ever seen any in her life, and the few times she had, the sails had looked more awkward than anything. They'd always seemed to her like big bulbous bubbles of canvas held by shaved trees, perpendicular to the otherwise graceful shape of the craft beneath. She knew they served a practical purpose, but to her that's all they did. Hani, who had grown up on the great ships of his people, knew how they connected one to the sea and the sky. With no real sky above, Hani let the need for a mast and sail on his ship go.

"We're ready to embark then." Hani slapped the side of his vessel proudly. The ship lay tilted on the curve of its hull, effectively beached. They climbed aboard using a rope ladder Hani manifested and he positioned himself at the stern, directing Eowen to the prow. "You guide us while I manifest the wave."

Eowen held onto the lip of the prow as water bloomed under them. The ship groaned as it shifted. Hani laughed joyfully, then summoned more water as the ship buoyed up, rocking back and forth as it settled. Eowen's insides reeled, sickeningly.

"Ready, Eowen?" Hani called and she waved a hand over her head, hoping he'd settle the waves on their little patch of sea before the churning in her stomach got the best of her. "What's wrong?" he called again, and Eowen vomited over the side. Hani heard her retching and solidified his manifestation into a calm, flat bubble of seawater that the ship rocked more gently on. He rushed to her side and put a hand on her back, rubbing gently. "I didn't know you were one to get seasick, are you alright now?"

"No, no I'm not." Eowen looked haggard. "Is this what it was like in the old world? Why would anyone ever go on the water?"

"Not exactly." Hani couldn't help smiling, but he kept his tone sympathetic. "It's normally much smoother when actually sailing. It was only that upsetting because we had to get the ship upright."

"So it'll be better from now on?" Eowen said between breaths.

"Yes, definitely. Normally we'd have to worry about reefs and storms, but that's not a problem here." At the word 'storms' something in Eowen shuddered, and the atmosphere around her became heavier, denser, as if charged. The air around them moved as though wind were picking up, and Hani saw the calm bubble of sea the ship rested on develop waves against his will. Eowen waved Hani off and stood.

"Enough, I'm fine now. Let's, ugh, let's just get going." The sudden weather effect dissipated and things calmed again, so Hani returned to the stern.

"Alright then, point the way." He started up the water under their vessel into a gentle wave that, after only a minor lurch, began to carry them smoothly forward. Eowen's stomach turned again, but she was better prepared. She held out the finder, scanning it till the weight brought her toward the closest people.

"I've got it, this way!" she called back. Hani adjusted the wave and they pressed on.

Their ship sailed, or rather flowed, smoothly along for several hours, stopping so that Hani could rest. The strain of a constantly maintained manifestation was not unfamiliar, as the very air they breathed was maintained this way, but the wave was one that required more active attention. Still, they were in high spirits, as they'd covered more than three times the distance than walking would have. Eowen even noted that she could feel the weight of the finder increase as they flowed forward, while previously the change had been almost imperceptibly small.

When Hani stopped the wave, he kept the water calm so Eowen could jump off first. She swam out of the small bubble of sea water, which collapsed and disappeared into spray, leaving the ship on its side once more. Eowen extracted the water from her person by floating it off while Hani climbed down. They ate and rested in companionable silence, content to relax after the hours of concentration necessary for Hani to keep the wave going and for Eowen to resist vomiting. They spoke of small things as Eowen manifested an island similar to the one they'd camped at before to rest on. They drifted off to sleep in their personal huts, content that the pace the ship set allowed them to take it easy.

****

[Listen, for you cannot hear me yet]

MAYBE WITH THEIR HEART, MAYBE THEIR SOUL, OR PERHAPS—

[!]

****

Eowen was wrenched awake as a sensation coursed through her consciousness like a bolt of lightning. Her world felt disrupted, off kilter, it was more arresting than an earthquake.

"Hani!" Eowen shouted, crawling as her senses reeled from the change she was still grasping with.

"Y-y-you too?" He staggered out of his hut at the same time as Eowen, eyes wild and trembling. No distinct forces of manifestation were working around them, but something had happened that affected them, possibly the entirety of the new world. They could sense the shape of the change making more sense as they adapted to it. It was like a demarcation of sorts. Eowen and Hani could feel it through their entire beings, something like instinct, only foreign and new rather than ancestral.

"What's happening?" Eowen yelled, though there was no sound to overcome. She felt as though the new experience was drowning out all her other thoughts and senses.

"How should I know?" he shouted back. "It—it feels like—"

Eowen was also starting to understand what was happening when another wave of the same washed over them, the world suddenly and unstoppably demarcated again. They both reeled, balance and sense overcome, and tumbled onto the sand. They gritted their teeth, waiting for the experience to pass, but it did not. It seared itself into their minds, bodies, even the powers of their subconscious like the brand of the mountain folk had. Their muscles locked in tense curls, shaking and sweating, but as the seconds ticked past, they acclimated. The experience didn't fade, but eventually they somehow integrated into it, and soon they understood exactly what had occurred.

"We're... in the southeast," Eowen said, then looked to Hani for confirmation. He nodded, stood, swayed, and planted his feet more securely.

"North." He pointed in roughly the direction their boat was. "East, west, south." He turned, establishing each of the cardinal directions, and Eowen knew he was perfectly correct because she could feel the compass as well.

"The world has... direction now," Eowen said after standing and dusting herself off.

"I know."

"How?"

"You already asked that."

"But... How!" Eowen threw her hands up, mirroring the fear in Hani's expression.

"I don't know, it just... is now."

"What do we do now, what should we do about—" Eowen waved her arms over her head. Hani thought about it for a long silent moment, then pointed to the people-finder at Eowen's waist.

"Does that still work?" Eowen lifted the finder from her waist and pointed it the same direction their boat was pointing, north and slightly east. She nodded. "We keep following then, don't we?"

"But... how can we? The world, everything is different, this is—I don't know what, but we can't just ignore it!"

"You're right, ignoring it is definitely impossible, but what else can we do?" A manic look spread across Hani, and he bounced on the balls of his feet before jogging over to the ship. "It had to be the work of someone, right? A dreamer, like us."

The implication that someone like her could have changed the world in such an immense and unignorable way seemed impossible to Eowen. It constituted an act so immense and impactful that all manifestations she had seen or performed felt like party tricks in comparison. Hani seemed completely unconcerned, reveling in the new feeling of clear direction, while Eowen staggered to the ship, barely keeping her balance.

"Besides, this will make it easier to find people!" Hani whooped. "Now we'll know if we ever veer even slightly off course."

"The finder did that for us anyway." Eowen stopped in front of the ship as Hani established the bubble of water for it to float on.

"Yes, but the directions seem to roughly align with the old world. The Britchen were north of us in the old world, and they're north of us now, aren't they?" Eowen held out the finder in the relevant direction to confirm this. "That means we can use these directions to find other people in other settlements, assuming they're arranged in relatively the same way as they were in the old world."

"How can you be so sure they will be?" Eowen asked as she readied herself to swim to the ship. A stream of water flowed out and under Eowen. Instead of flooding her sandals it stiffened under her, the surface tension as solid as stone, and with a slight lurch she found herself being lifted up to the ship's edge by the water, completely dry. She looked at Hani, who was lost in concentration, his dreaming power reaching out around him to guide the water. She stepped aboard and favored him with a bright smile, impressed. He bowed with a flourish and Eowen laughed; she was nearly acclimatized to the directions now, and Hani's excitement was contagious. A determined glint in his eye and eager expression on his features seemed to promise adventure and excitement ahead.

"I can't be sure, of course I can't, but I can't wait any longer to find out. This is what I was talking about, Eowen; the world is changing, filling with amazing things because of people like us. I have to see it all!" Eowen shook her head, but she was feeling eager as well, like a flame in her belly. She pointed the people-finder and motioned for Hani to start the wave, which sent them rocking forward such that Eowen had to catch herself on the lip of the prow. Her stomach turned, but not enough to be sick, the ship's motion no longer juggling her organs. Not since the first day of her quest to find Tavo, when she'd first crested Mount Joramu, had she felt so thrilled.

"Faster!" she cried, hardly believing the word had come out of her mouth, and Hani's power surged around her, clear and direct. The wave crested beneath them and the ship's prow lifted into the darkness ahead. Eowen raised a great light above her head, as wide around as she was tall, to shine their way. It shed birds of ice and ribbons of song as it burst into creation.

* * *

The progress they made was incomparable to their first foray on the ship, and Eowen's seasickness was soon completely drowned out by the new sensation of cardinal directions in her mind. After only an hour, Hani slowed down. "Do you need a rest?" Eowen asked as the ship came to a stop, but Hani didn't look tired, focusing intently on the distance.

"Do you feel them?" He pointed in the direction they'd been heading. Eowen searched with her aura of dreaming, but couldn't sense anything.

"No, not yet. You found them, then? The Britchen?"

"There's definitely people that way. Let's go, you'll feel them soon."

"Do you need the people finder anymore?" Eowen held it up for him to see.

"Are we still going the right way?"

"Seems so."

"You can put it away then, I can follow my senses now."

The wave rose and the ship started forward once more.

Eowen sat on the deck with her back to the prow's lip. She found that being on a ship was much more comfortable when she didn't have to balance being the navigator with being seasick. They sailed for some time in silence, Hani locked on to what his senses had found in the distance. It only took a few minutes for Eowen's dreaming aura, many kilometers wide as it was, to catch up with Hani's range, and when it did she immediately perked up.

"Hani!"

"You feel them now?"

"There's so—oh wow. There's so many!" Eowen peeked over the stern and squinted. She could just barely make out a glow in the distance that indicated the presence of people lighting up the starfield below. For how distant the glow was, Eowen noticed it was extraordinarily wide such that, from her vantage, it seemed to almost stretch across the whole of the new world. She could feel the interplay of more dreaming auras than she'd ever felt before as they drew closer. Eowen flushed, eager to finally reach her destination, to find Tavo and meet him for the first time in three years. She turned to show Hani her excitement, but found him grim-faced and tense. "What's wrong?"

"Look." He pointed back to the glow. Eowen searched for what Hani was referring to, but nothing stuck out to her save for the mass of people that seemed to just keep growing without end. Her eager smile shrank and she grew nervous, hands gripping the ship's edge tightly.

"There's too many people. It's impossible, there couldn't be that many people!" Eowen turned to Hani, now fully unnerved.

"No, it's about what we expected, give or take a few thousand."

Eowen was dumbfounded. *The thousands of people wasn't an exaggeration? How can there be that many people in one place, where do they grow food and relieve themselves and... live?*

"It's not the number of people I'm worried about, it's that." Hani pointed again, and this time Eowen followed his finger to the darkness above the mass of people. Eowen squinted. It seemed to her as though nothing were out of the ordinary, just the inky blackness like a starless night sky save for some clouds in the distance.

Wait, clouds? "Is that... weather?"

"I think so." He slowed the ship to a complete stop, his voice calm and measured but the lack of enthusiasm betraying his worry.

"It looks like a storm." Eowen walked back to where Hani stood. The people were still too far to see in any detail, just a line of light in the distance, certainly too far to notice Eowen and Hani unless they had the ability to sense things in the distance as well. Behind the people were indeed clouds, but in this strange new world they seemed like a wall that shifted and swirled in the darkness. If one looked from the very edge of the settlement's light, they'd see a layer of hazy gray where clean starlight met a fogbank of sorts, hardly noticeable if you weren't looking for it. They followed the fog upward till it faded into darkness, only visible by the light from below which was carried and scattered among the clouds above, creating the effect of textured darkness. Above, or behind the settlement, Eowen could not tell, an enormous Storm churned out the clouds that billowed and twisted about. Looking at it made Eowen's skin crawl; the way the Storm moved wasn't like the weather of the old world. To her, it more closely resembled the way a great jungle cat's muscles rippled under their patterned skin, ready to punch.

"Eowen." Hani patted Eowen's shoulder and she emerged from her thoughts. "I don't think we should go any further right now. Would you be alright with me stopping for now?" Eowen just nodded and stepped off the ship, lowering herself to the starfield with a stream of water that she could stand on. Hani let the water dissipate and climbed down as soon as it settled on its side. Eowen couldn't tear her eyes from the Storm wall behind the settlement. Hani stood next to her, similarly entranced. There was a strange sort of tension in their combined atmosphere, a twist and twirl to it, as though it were not only the dreaming auras of the two mingling, but a third presence cutting in.

"Do you think it's a person doing that?" Eowen whispered.

"I don't know, I didn't think one person could make something that big and... heavy. Can you feel it from here?" Eowen nodded and took Hani's hand, as slick with sweat as hers was, and even clammier.

"Maybe it's not one person," Eowen suggested, her voice cracking.

"Maybe it's not a person at all," Hani suggested. A shiver ran through them both which extended to a tremor through their dreaming auras. They felt a discordant wave pass over their spirits that made their stomachs' turn but that the third presence resonated with. Hani gasped and the hair on his neck stood up. Eowen looked deeper into the distant clouds, and something in them changed, a shape or quality. The clouds seemed to react to them, even at such a distance, like a living thing.

"It's looking at us," Eowen whispered, and Hani did a double take between her and the Storm. Her eyes grew wider and her expression contorted as if to scream. The atmosphere around them began to move with force and intensity, a threat of immense and uncontrollable creation close at hand.

"Eowen, stop looking at it, close your eyes!" Hani stepped in front of the girl and gripped her arms tightly, locking eyes with her. "Close your eyes!" he shouted, trying to ignore the feeling of something stalking him from behind. Eowen complied but her anguished expression didn't diminish even with her eyes screwed shut.

"It's still looking at us Hani, I can feel it!" The forces around them picked up. Wind was raging, their skin tingled with static, and a roar like some beast too large to be real sounded in the distance. Eowen and Hani sank to the starfield and surrounded themselves in their own power, but the foreign presence whipped their own defenses into a frenzy. Eowen screamed and her voice disappeared in the twisting energy, Hani looked left, right, up, and down, casting about for some inspiration. He turned back to the settlement with the Storm behind it, and his stomach dropped; inside the roiling clouds were the shapes of teeth.

Hani grasped onto the wild strands of power around them and his spirit staggered under the strain as though it would be ripped from his body. He felt something rising within him, like when he'd dip into the working of a manifestation he knew was beyond his scope, only instead of climbing up to it, he was looking down from above. He decided to trust the strange feeling, and abandoned all pretense of control to follow the impulse.

{Why have you come here?}

Eowen stopped screaming and looked at Hani. She thought he'd said something. She couldn't remember the words, only an impression of words, a meaning left echoing in her mind. Hani had an expression she'd never seen before, something akin to detached benevolence. She felt compelled to answer the question that still echoed in her spirit, so above the din she shouted:

"To find Tavo!"

Hani nodded. His eyes were not the ones she knew. They were like holes in the world. Hani opened his mouth and a sound emerged that was like singing, which drowned the Storm in one clear note. The song grasped at the roiling potential around them and manifested something that curved up around them. It was a shelter of sorts, seemingly made from perfectly smooth stone that arched into a dome overhead. The strange, foreign presence was cut off, leaving Eowen and Hani in the abrupt presence of only themselves. Hani collapsed into Eowen's arms, unconscious.

"Hani! Hani, are you alright?" Eowen shook him, fear and anguish scrawled on her face. In the fresh silence she could hear him breathing, but just to be sure she pulled his chest up and placed her ear against it. His heart beat fast but after a few seconds slowed to a more natural pace. Eowen choked down a sob, took several breaths with her head on Hani's chest, then laid him down. She sighed, shifted the boy so he was closer to the wall of their little shelter, and turned to see an entrance behind them. There was nothing covering it, just a smooth arch in the stone of their tiny shelter. Eowen scooted closer to it and, tentative, reached out her hand. As soon as her fingers crossed the threshold they tingled as the power of the third presence bit in like a snake striking. She pulled her hand back in, flipping it over and back to examine. No marks showed, but she had felt it out there, whatever it was. Inside the shelter they were protected, but

Eowen could also no longer sense anything beyond it with her dreaming aura.

She looked over at Hani, who was fast asleep, then reached with her senses to try and identify how the shelter worked. It was incomprehensible to her, disorienting in its layers of power, so she lay back on the cool stone, manifesting a folded blanket under her head.

"As long as we're safe," she whispered to herself. Hani twitched in his sleep, but otherwise remained as he was. Eowen breathed in, then out, and with the exhale let go of a great deal of tension. She felt weary in her spirit, the adrenaline from the strange assault upon them wearing off, and the weariness was spreading to her body.

Hani, what did you do, and what happened there?

Eowen tried to stay awake and keep watch, but her body pushed itself into sleep before she knew what was happening.

****

[Listen, for you cannot hear me yet]

**LOVE ASKED WHY THEY COULD NOT PERCEIVE
ME PROPERLY, AND I WAS SURPRISED
TO HEAR THEIR VOICE CLEARLY,
FOR IT DID NOT COMPETE WITH THE BURNING
OF STARS OR THE RUMBLE OF TECTONICS.**

****

Eowen awoke to the smell of food. Hani was laying out dishes. He inclined his head to acknowledge her. Eowen rolled into a sitting position with her legs crossed. She acknowledged him with a small wave.

"I've never been attacked before," Hani said. Eowen waited for more of an explanation, but instead Hani was looking at her expectantly.

"Neither have I," she said, and took a bite of an unfamiliar bread-like thing.

"Actually, I have been attacked before."

"Ok."

"But never like that."

"Right."

"Some bigger boys tried to wrestle me down, they started it, see?"

"Mmm."

"Just kids being stupid... My island was attacked by pirates, but that was only when I was little, before I was born. What I'm saying is I don't remember it." Hani looked for Eowen to pick up the conversation, but she didn't feel there was anything for her to add. "So... what I'm getting at is that what happened before was a new experience for me." Eowen chewed and thought.

I don't think anyone has ever experienced that before the fall.

"Do you remember making this?" She gestured at their shelter.

"Oh, no." He seemed to notice it for the first time. "I thought you'd made it." Eowen shook her head and took another bite. "Hmm, I suppose it does feel like my power, but also not my power."

"Exactly."

"How did I do it?"

"I don't know." Eowen put down her food and stared hard at the floor. "What are we going to do?" she whispered.

"We're going to that Britchen settlement, obviously." Hani stood up and stretched, his head almost touching the ceiling of their shelter.

Is he joking? Eowen thought. "There's no way, the moment we step outside that power grabs us."

"Really?" Hani moved to the entrance and slowly put his hand out. Eowen saw him flinch and pull his hand back as if he'd touched a hot coal. "You're right, that's strange." He rubbed his hand, turning it over and looking surprised not to find any marks. "What should we do then?" He looked expectantly at Eowen, who frowned and shifted uncomfortably.

"How am I supposed to know?"

"You're always full of good ideas. You made that people-finder, you thought to create the sacred beasts for the mountain folk, you even made that sun-moon thing for your people." Eowen did not like being reminded of the heavenly body hanging above the oasis she'd made, but Hani didn't seem to notice her discomfort. "It's your talent, it seems, coming up with creative solutions."

"I don't have a solution here, Hani," she whispered, refusing to meet his look.

"That's alright, we just need to think about it for a bit." Eowen's chest flushed with heat and she faced Hani, glaring.

"How about you figure out the creative solution! Huh? Whatever happened before—I've never been so scared in my life except when the shitting sky fell and I almost died, naked and alone!" Eowen shouted, eyes wild. After a stretch of silence she backed up and hid her face in her hands. "I'm sorry, Hani, you saved us and I'm acting like this!" Eowen's voice cracked and she groaned.

"It's, uh, it's ok, Eowen." Hani scooted next to her and tentatively patted her back. "You don't need to figure anything out here. I'll get us out of this one."

"No, we'll do this together, I just... Hani, when whatever that thing was had a grip on us it felt like when..." Eowen shook her head. "It felt like when I lose control of my manifestations, but worse. It felt the same as when I hurt my people. I almost killed my father, Hani." The boy's expression grew grim. "What if I'd killed you yesterday? What if I'd... I don't know! Hurt all the people in that settlement? That Storm, I've felt it in me before, but now it's out there waiting!" Eowen hugged herself into a ball and squeezed her eyes shut, her banishment playing through her mind: her people's fear, Mein's face twisting crueler and colder in Eowen's memory. She imagined her father crippled and her dead mother miraculously revived and cradling her broken father's head while glaring at Eowen, eyes ablaze.

"What do you think we should name the ship?" Hani's question broke Eowen from her spiraling and she looked up.

"I'm sorry, what?"

"The ship, every good ship should have a name."

Eowen's mouth hung open. "I don't care!"

"Well, I do, so help me out." With that statement, Hani stepped out of the shelter.

"No wait!" Eowen lunged forward but she wasn't nearly close enough to stop him. Hani was outside the shelter and fully in the influence of the entity. She watched in horror as he shivered, gooseflesh running up his skin, then he squeezed his eyes shut, lifted his arms and shook them in the air.

"Wow, that feels weird!" Hani shouted. Eowen's mouth hung open, her eyebrows came together and she sat back up straight.

"Are you ok?"

"I'm fine. Feels strange. That power is all around us here, but it's not too hard to resist once you know it's coming." He flashed a winning smile and offered Eowen his hand. "Come on, I believe in you. You're Eowen, one of the greatest dreamers of the new world. This is just some new, strange thing, but it's nothing compared to you, I promise." Eowen eyed the space around him suspiciously, as if expecting to see some monster waiting to pounce on her. "Just a hand at first, alright?" Eowen looked at Hani, as young and almost as naive as her, but swelling with confidence. She reached out and took his hand, her skin prickling as soon as she crossed the threshold.

"Ah!" She flinched but kept her hand out of the shelter, acclimating to the feeling. It was not as bad as she'd thought, just strange, certainly unpleasant, but resistable.

It just took me by surprise. That's all. It took us both by surprise, but we know what to expect now. I know what to expect now.

Eowen stepped through the entrance, reacted in much the same way Hani had, but found she was otherwise fine. She smiled through the discomfort at him, and he reflected it back.

"See, no problem." He glanced at the settlement, then immediately looked away.

"Let's avoid looking at the Storm again though," Eowen said.

"Agreed. Now, the first order of business is naming our ship!"

"Fine, but why? Shouldn't we make our way to the settlement first?" Eowen turned toward the Britchen people, carefully keeping her eyes downcast. "I noticed this before, but didn't think to say it. That Storm is definitely behind the settlement and they don't seem affected by it."

"It certainly feels that way from here," Hani said as he climbed up the ship. "We can't just arrive without a name for the ship, people are going to ask: Ho, traveler, what is the name of such a stout vessel that has taken you across this starlit land?" Eowen rolled her eyes but smiled. His antics in the face of the previous experience was a relief. She felt that, somehow, if Hani wasn't worried, Eowen could not bring herself to be.

"Do people care about the name of a ship?"

"Of course they do! Everyone in the islands knows of famous ships and their captains. The Serpent Hunter, fastest in legend. Under-Blow, which had the tallest sails. Pearl's Seed, the most beautiful ever crafted and its captain the miserly Yushkt! My father's vessel was called the Gale-Catcher." Hani manifested the water for his ship, and though the Storm's presence did make itself known with gusts and random twists upon his manifestation, the island boy kept it under control. "Eveytime a ship came to port, the children of the island ran up to see the name and get stories from the sailors. Then we share stories we heard from past sailors with them. They sometimes even give treasures from distant lands in exchange for news they wanted to hear." Hani lifted Eowen to the deck as before so that she didn't have to use her power. Even though she was not immediately being possessed by the Storm, she still felt more comfortable not manifesting while under its influence. They started forward at a good pace, and Hani was careful not to draw on too much power so that the Storm couldn't affect his manifestations more than he could control.

"So you want to find a good name for yours so that news of your quest can spread with it?"

"Of course," Hani insisted. "The name of a ship will spread further than any man's name." Eowen weighed this claim beside the fact that she'd never heard of ships having names at all. She shrugged and curled up on the deck, feeling alright despite the Storm, the rocking of the ship now soothing rather than sickening.

"How about Star Boat?"

"No, that's terrible."

"We are sailing on stars though." Eowen patted the floor of the ship.

"Maybe, but it's still a terrible name."

"Then you come up with it, captain." Eowen was knocked a few centimeters in the air as the boat hit a small wave that had manifested in front of it. "Watch it!"

"Sorry! That was an accident." Hani was grinning at her. "I just really like the sound of that. Captain Hani! It has a lovely ring to it, doesn't it?" Eowen looked him up and down and arched an eyebrow.

"You need to grow into it," she said. Hani opened his mouth to respond but something in the distance caught his attention and he pointed. Eowen got into a crouch and peeked over the prow. "Wow," she whispered.

"This is it!" Hani shouted. "The final stretch to Port Disoke!" They were close enough to see buildings now, with people moving among them like ants on a hill. The settlement was more technologically advanced than any they'd seen before. Aqueducts webbed out across the massive settlement, delivering water from a massive jar perched on a tower that perpetually poured out water. The buildings, which looked to be of sandstone, were stacked haphazardly in every conceivable way, but maintained their structural integrity. Pulley systems spiderwebbed the entire place, acting as elevators, delivery systems, and transport between the tops of buildings. The place sparkled with bronze embedded everywhere. There were doors with hinges, stakes driven into sandstone, wheels and pulleys, and tiles everywhere. Even at a distance, it seemed wondrous.

Eowen found that a horrible, prickling feeling was moving across her skin, something akin to many ants crawling on her as she sensed more and more of the dreaming auras in the city. She grimaced as they drew closer, but Hani was starry-eyed.

"This is amazing! Eowen, have you ever seen this many people in one place?"

"No, and they're so... close together." Eowen looked for some sign of discomfort in Hani's expression, but he was loving the experience, till something caught his attention and he frowned.

"A powerful dreamer in the city is on the move towards us, hold on."

Eowen wrapped herself around the lip of their ship, hands white-knuckled as Hani increased speed. The ship swayed as Hani led it in a wide turn to circle around the city rather than head directly for it. Eowen glanced up at the city and couldn't help noticing the Storm behind it. It felt like it was watching them again, patiently. Eowen gritted her teeth and Hani kept silent as Eowen's aura of dreaming twisted about her, repressed but disturbed.

"Don't make anything, don't do anything, keep calm!" she whispered under her breath, focusing on their immediate surroundings rather than the Storm in the distance. Abandoned attempts at settlements and manifestations ringed the city, left behind as the scattered people had congregated. There were no dead in sight though, and when Eowen did open her eyes, the lack of them made Eowen wonder if they'd been able to properly perform funerals or if they had disposed of them some other way.

The approaching dreamer was wreathed with power that laid a thick, oily layer of subconscious potential upon them. Hani tried to match Eowen's pattern of power and morph the combined result so that they would feel unthreatening to their host. The two great auras of power, the stranger's and the combination of Eowen and Hani's, met like two waves crashing from opposite directions. They did not mingle and coalesce as Eowen and Hani's had soon after meeting. Instead the stranger's power seemed to prod and grapple with theirs, trying to disarm or immobilize them somehow. It felt unpleasant to their extended senses, like wrestling with an invisible snake. They resisted the urge to push back aggressively, and soon enough could see as well as feel the dreamer who was flying toward them on a flat platform of sorts.

"Do you feel that? How powerful they are?" Hani called to Eowen, slowing down the ship.

"Should we do something? I don't know any Britchen customs or language."

"Neither do I, but they're familiar with people south of the mountains. I'm sure we've got nothing to worry about," Hani said with a smile he hoped was reassuring. Eowen was not reassured but watched the approaching figure, taking interest in their mode of transportation.

"How are they doing that?" she asked.

"I don't know, let's ask!" Hani slowed the ship to a stop and it rocked from side to side gently, making Eowen feel sick again such that she curled up on the deck, groaning. "Stop acting like a baby, we need to make a good first impression," Hani hissed. Eowen made a rude gesture and hauled herself to a kneeling position.

The flying figure was rushing forward, but turned sharply to circle around them at a wide radius. Hani waved and Eowen nodded to them, trying to look as though she weren't about to upend the contents of her stomach.

"Hani," Eowen whispered, "have you ever seen anyone that looks like that?"

"No," he whispered between teeth clenched in a smile.

The being approaching was on a mat of some kind, cloth-like but thicker and covered in swirling designs and colorful patterns. They sat cross-legged, piloting it by no obvious means. They wore a bronze helmet with a visor that covered their eyes and bronze armor on their shoulders, elbows, and knees. Their clothing under the bronze was loose and white, flapping in the wind. They shouted in a language neither of the southern children knew.

"Hello!" Hani called. "We seek to approach—Woah!" The figure stood on their mat, raised a hand, and with impressive speed manifested three enormous spheres of bronze that breached from the starfield below like beasts from the ocean. They moved over the ship and hovered there, held floating by the person. "Please, wait! We mean no harm!" Hani held up his arms as if to show he had no weapons.

The gesture prompted the stranger to shout in their unknown language and snap their raised hand into a fist, crashing the bronze spheres together above them. The bell-like toll was deafening, and Hani fell to his knees with his hands over his ears. Eowen instinctively put her barrier of sound over herself the moment her ears hurt, but even that small act of manifestation caught the attention of the Storm that still prickled on her skin.

Violent winds rushed in around them, crackling with a static sort of power that lifted the hairs on necks and arms, but the barrier held. Eowen looked up in time to see the panicked eyes of the stranger behind the visor. They shouted, but their voice couldn't penetrate the barrier. The ship had stopped rocking, so Eowen stood to try and communicate. The stranger seemed to think this was enough and brought their raised fist down. Eowen's eyes went wide, she looked up to see the bronze spheres descending fast with no time to respond.

{We are protected.}

Seawater rained down on Eowen. The bronze spheres had burst as a rush of power that felt both like Hani's and somehow something beyond him speared into them. Eowen's mouth hung open as she stared at him, wondering how he'd done this or if it really had been him at all. The island boy was blank faced, his mind hardly present. He looked between Eowen and the stranger then collapsed, the strange power that had possessed him gone. The ship shuddered as the water he'd been maintaining flowed out as if to collapse and disappear. Eowen reached out and grasped the manifestation with her own power, and the ship steadied once more. She settled a part of her mind on maintaining the bubble of sea beneath them and collapsed on the lip of the ship, relieved and exhausted.

The stranger glided slowly closer, their hands clasped in front of them, a gesture that Eowen took to mean they wanted to peacefully parlay. The stranger's head moved as if they were speaking and Eowen undid her barrier of silence.

"You're not going to attack again, are you?" Eowen asked.

The stranger paused, thought for a moment, then spoke again.

"You are... you, not this?" Eowen struggled to understand them; they were speaking a broken dialect of her language she could barely understand layered under an accent foreign to her.

"I'm not sure I understand," Eowen said, then switched to the mountain folk's language. "Do you understand this language?"

"Oh! Yes, you speak the mountain words very well."

"Uh, thank you... You speak it well too. Are you going to attack us again?" Eowen crossed her arms.

"I—you're not possessed by the Storm, are you?" The stranger pointed at the Storm again, which at this distance Eowen could now clearly see was on the other side of the city, not attached to it at all.

"No. It tried to take control of us before, but Hani stopped it." Eowen gestured to the boy and noticed the awkward position he'd landed in. She hurried to his side and settled him in a more comfortable way, manifesting a folded blanket under his head.

"I will apologize for the aggression," the stranger said, "but it was not without reason. We have been besieged since soon after the fall. Many have been taken by the Storm, possessed by it, and used to mount attacks on us from all sides. You're not the first outsiders to reach us, but few approach without becoming tools of the Storm." The stranger's head tilted to the side and they scanned Eowen up and down. "You two are different though. We felt you from a great distance."

"We felt you, too," Eowen said, and the two stood in silence for a long moment, regarding each other. Eowen was unsure of how to proceed and decided it would be best to let the stranger take the lead. The stranger stayed in deep thought until a bright light, crimson red and flickering, burst into sight above the tower that held the ever pouring jug. The stranger turned and lifted their hand, manifesting and launching a similar green light above their head that Eowen had to shield her eyes from. The light faded out, and the stranger regarded Eowen once more.

"Who are you and why are you here? A jungle girl and boy traveling alone in this... creative way." The stranger gestured to their ship.

"We're, uh, looking for the Britchen?" Eowen shrugged. "We heard they were this way."

"Why?"

"Oh, we're looking for—" Eowen paused.

How would Hani phrase it? He always seemed so ready for this sort of thing.

Eowen flung her arms out. "We come on an epic quest to locate our loved ones... uh, for him, his name is Hani, he seeks his father, captain..." Eowen tried to remember the name of Hani's father and failed, "... his father is captain of a ship! And I seek my cousin, Tavo. We have traveled far on foot and on our ship the, um, Star-Boat." Eowen crossed her arms and nodded, trying to affect confidence. "My name is Eowen, and he is Hani. He's from the southern islands, not the jungle and savannah tribes."

"I see," the stranger said, then they cleared their throat and turned on their mat to face the city. "My name is Nolyi. This is what remains of those that once inhabited the Britchen city of Nopt Shisoke. If you come in peace, I offer you hospitality and safety from the Storm behind our barrier." Nolyi looked to Eowen for an answer.

"Um, we're looking for Port Disoke, actually," Eowen said. Nolyi seemed confused, but recovered quickly enough.

"Others call it... Port Disoke in their own language, the Britchen call it Nopt Shisoke. The old Britchen word for port is nopt, but I don't know why Shisoke became Disoke.

"Oh, well, we accept, please lead the way." Nolyi nodded and their mat moved smoothly forward, carrying them back from whence they came. Eowen grappled with the water under Hani's ship, attempting to make a wave like he had and wishing she'd paid more attention. The boat swayed wildly as she started forward, and Eowen had to stop and start a few times before getting the hang of it. Nolyi slowed down to match Eowen's pace and much to her relief made no mention of her bumbling. Eowen could feel the dreaming auras of thousands in the distance, along with three particularly significant ones that stood out as being similarly powerful to Nolyi.

As they drew closer, Eowen found herself increasingly overwhelmed by waves of unfamiliar things assaulting her senses. Smells she had no comparison to permeated the air, some making her salivate and others making her feel sick. The din of voices, carrying music, conversation, and a dizzying assortment of languages rose up like a flood. Eowen had to establish a barrier that filtered some of the sound to keep her focus. It was another half an hour before they reached the city, and by then a large crowd had gathered. Eowen had never seen so many people in one place, nor so many different types of people. Skin tones ranging from pitch black to cloud white, some people's eyes were dark and others were every color in the rainbow. Some had hair that stood up in tight, springy curls, or hung down to their knees perfectly straight, waves of red, green, black, blond, and a thousand other shades. The clothing was even more diverse than the people, with weaves, furs, patterns, colors, and cuts that she'd never known to imagine. Eowen didn't even realize she'd been staring until Nolyi cleared their throat to get her attention.

"Eowen, was it? We have reached the border. You can dock here." Eowen shut her mouth and nodded.

"Of course. Could you help me, though? I can't lift him." Eowen pointed at Hani. Nolyi stepped aboard and scooped up Hani into their arms as if he weighed nothing.

"Here, step onto my carpet. I'll take you in." Eowen followed to the edge of Star-Boat but hesitated, eyeing the carpet suspiciously. Even though Nolyi had flown on it, the vessel still just looked like a thin, woven mat to her. Hundreds of eyes were watching her, muttering, so she swallowed her nerves down as best she could and scooted from the lip of Star-Boat onto the mat. It was coarse but soft and held firm under her weight, cushioned by air. It felt something like how she imagined it would be to sit on a cloud, and she grinned at the wonder of it. "Are you going to leave... Star-Boat on the water like that?" Nolyi asked.

"Oh, thank you for reminding me." Eowen relinquished maintenance of the water as gradually as she could, allowing it to fade into nothing. The ship settled to lay on its side next to the city, and Nolyi turned to face Eowen.

"The barrier around the city rejects the Storm, so when you go through it the Storm will be... filtered out of you." Nolyi turned toward the city again. "It may feel strange."

Before Eowen could ask 'Strange how?' the carpet started forward. The moment they passed the city border, denoted by stalks of silver bamboo that ringed around it, Eowen felt a change. The atmosphere seemed to suction at her, pushing into and through her without physically moving her body. Hani squirmed in his sleep, and Eowen could feel something leaving her. It was like having a splinter removed from every part of her at once, a splinter that kept getting longer. The membrane bowed inward with Eowen and Hani as they flew for the first few meters. Then, with a shudder that went through her spirit and body, Eowen felt the presence of the Storm leave. She groaned and rubbed at the gooseflesh that now covered her body.

"I have never felt anything like that before! I didn't even know the Storm was... in me like that." Eowen shuddered, thinking how slyly the foreign power had wormed its way into her spirit.

"That's how it captures its prey. Most don't even know that the Storm has taken root inside them. Then, the more creation they try to use, the more the Storm can infest them until they become like that." Nolyi pointed out over the city towards the roiling clouds that buffeted against the membrane.

Eowen squinted, not sure what she was supposed to be seeing until they drew a few meters closer. Inside the churning clouds, a flash of lightning lit up a silhouette that stood at the edge of the barrier. It looked at first like a tree, but as they got closer Eowen saw that it had previously been a person, sprouting branches from which, instead of leaves, the Storm poured out in thick, black clouds. Eowen felt it looking at her, even at their distance across the city she could feel its stare filling her mind, pushing out the rest of the world and drawing her closer, she was meters away, centimeters, she could see the texture of the bark through the clouds, she could feel—

"No!" Nolyi smacked Eowen on the back of the head, and she was cut from the illusion.

"What happened!" Eowen rubbed the back of her head and blinked rapidly.

"Even with the barrier, the Storm is insidious. It cannot reach us here, but it can warp everything outside, everything within its influence. It can make it so you think you're there, next to it. You must remain vigilant, else it will take you." Nolyi's tone left no doubt that they'd seen the Storm do exactly that many times.

"Thank you."

"It's alright, you'll still be safe in here. It can't actually take you. Unless you let it."

They flew for the tower that housed the great jug, which was situated at the edge of the city bordering the Storm. It was even more massive than Eowen had thought at a distance, and she had to keep readjusting her sense of scale as they approached. When they were finally beside it, Eowen felt like an ant, her imagination conjuring the foot of the great being that the jug would have been hefted by. Nolyi noticed her gawking.

"Amazing isn't it? That's Aiyano's work, you'll meet her soon." Eowen noted how tender Nolyi's voice got when they spoke of Aiyano.

The rug coasted in under the jug, passing by the ever-flowing spout of water that put to shame even the grandest waterfalls Eowen had ever seen. Under the jug's platform were arched entrances wide enough for several people standing side-by-side. In one of them was a round woman wearing some kind of white robe with a flat skirt to her ankles and tight fitting sleeves. She was only a little taller than Eowen, around Nolyi's height, skin of light caramel with brown hair bound into a tight bun. Her brow was creased with worry, but she brightened when Nolyi greeted her in a language Eowen did not know. The room past the arc was several meters high, at least seventy meters across and shaped like an octagon. It was completely empty save for people milling about at other arches, some with rugs like Nolyi's, but they all turned to see the new arrivals. The moment they landed, several people of various cultures, but all dressed like the robed woman in white, approached.

Nolyi handed Hani to them, issuing instructions. The one carrying Hani began to leave, but before they could take a step Eowen lunged off the rug towards them.

"No!" The group tensed, their dreaming auras drawing up shadow and light with a tension to them, words flew around her in various languages. "He stays with me!" Eowen grasped the sleeve of the one carrying Hani and a shock threw her hand off. The crowd moved to apprehend her, but Nolyi cut them off with sharp orders.

"Eowen, please be calm, they only want to give him medical attention." Nolyi approached gently, but Eowen turned on them, shadow and light rushing to her service in a startling amount.

"He stays with me or I'll—" Eowen cut herself off. She still had no idea what she would do, or what she could do if forced to fight, but she was prepared to find out if they took Hani. The first woman, the one Nolyi had greeted, stepped forward, speaking quickly with Nolyi. They exchanged a few words, and then the woman gave the one carrying Hani an order. Hani was deposited in the woman's arms and the robed people were dismissed.

Nolyi gestured to the woman. "It's alright, we'll all stay together. Eowen, this is Aiyano, my spouse, the greatest medicine person in the new world, and the primary creator of this city." Then Nolyi spoke in the unknown language again, but Eowen heard her and Hani's name and understood that they were being introduced. Aiyano nodded her head and Eowen followed suit, adding a mountain folk gesture of greeting for good measure.

"Can you tell her that the city is impressive and we appreciate your hospitality?"

"You can tell her yourself in a moment," Nolyi said, then gestured at their rug, which rolled itself up against the wall. Then they removed their helmet for the first time and Eowen saw who her assailant and host was. Nolyi was easily the most beautiful person Eowen had ever met, clearly of the same race as Aiyano but with shorter, darker hair. They had an androgyny about them that Eowen was unfamiliar with. They hung their helmet next to the rug and removed their armor as well. Nolyi saw Eowen staring and smiled at her. "The armor protects me from the effects of the Storm and sometimes the powers of others. Come, we've got a special room to talk in."

Eowen hesitated. She was in an unfamiliar land among entirely unfamiliar people for the first time in her life, other than when she'd gone to the mountain folk's settlement. This was it, the moment she'd been anticipating since leaving to look for Tavo before the world had ended, the moment she would make her first impression on the world outside her tribe without another to present her. She felt that the confrontation with Nolyi hadn't counted as a true introduction, merely lead-up. This was not like with the mountain folk where she'd known the language, culture, and some of the people before arriving. For the first time, Eowen was truly in a foreign place among foreign people and she felt the need to show confidence. She desperately wished Hani were conscious. She cleared her throat.

"Le-ead the way," her voice cracked and she stood stock still, sweating.

Nolyi started towards the center of the room without a change in expression. Aiyano was beaming at her, and said something in her own language that Eowen took to mean: 'Follow me.' Nolyi took them down a massively wide flight of stairs in the middle of the octagonal room, which split to the left and right at the bottom. They took the left path, and inside the tower Nolyi led them through corridors of perfectly cut sandstone with smokeless torches to light the way. Eowen tried to keep track of their progress but almost immediately lost any sense of direction. They crossed paths with many people of various races, ages, and presentations, most wearing the same garb as Aiyano, who greeted them as they passed. Eowen had never been in a building so large, let alone one with more than a few rooms, and it was making her feel nervous. She tried to look for windows or doors to the outside in the rooms they passed but every room was closed off by dark curtains. Eowen did note that the inside of the tower was largely unadorned save for markings above the doors of rooms and at splits in the hallways.

They went down several more flights of stairs smaller than the first, and arrived at a room that looked no different on the outside than any other. It was the first with a door rather than a curtain covering it. The door was of a heavy, dark wood, polished to a shine. It had a bronze ring embedded in it and had three thick bronze hinges that were sunk in the wall which it hung on. Nolyi held the door open and Aiyano shuffled in sideways to keep from hitting Hani's head on the wall. Eowen followed and looked around. The room didn't seem to be special in any way. It was circular with a round table a few centimeters off the floor in the middle surrounded by cushions. It could seat about fifteen.

Aiyano lay Hani on the table and took a seat. She began poking and prodding him, taking stock of his condition. "Will he be alright?" Eowen asked Nolyi.

"He's perfectly healthy, my dear," Aiyano responded in the unknown language. "Come, sit, we've much to discuss." Aiyano gestured to a cushion next to her as Nolyi took the one on the other side of Aiyano. Aiyano continued her assessment of Hani, but Nolyi was smiling strangely at Eowen, as if there were some joke she was not in on. Eowen took her seat, trying to look polite, serious, controlled, and worldly at the same time. The combined effect of her efforts made her look constipated.

"Eowen, why don't you ask Aiyano some questions about the creation of the jug and the city?" Nolyi was giving her that strange smile again.

"I'd love to, but maybe it can wait till your friend wakes up." Aiyano sat back and looked tenderly at Eowen. "He will wake up, won't he?"

"I think so? He did last time this happened but it's only happened once before when we—wait, I can understand you?" Eowen looked at Aiyano for an explanation. The woman had been speaking her own language, Eowen was sure of it, yet she had understood the words. Nolyi laughed and slapped their leg.

"Impressive, isn't it? This is the work of a man named Ordwell. He's on his way." Nolyi spoke in their own language as well, words that Eowen did not know, yet the meaning reached her.

"You mean this Ordwell is somehow... making words understood?" Eowen asked.

"Yes, we have so many people speaking different languages that it seemed prudent to make a way to translate," Aiyano said. "Look." Aiyano pointed at the ceiling, where half a bronze sphere was embedded. "He's been making those for a few weeks now for as many homes as he can. They work better in an enclosed space because if you hear people speaking from a distance you'll understand them even if you can't hear the words properly. It makes conversation rather confusing." Aiyano nodded approvingly at the sphere. "It's quite impressive, isn't it?"

"Not as impressive as you." Nolyi put a hand on Aiyano's shoulder, whose cheeks colored ever so slightly, but otherwise didn't react.

"You'll see, Eowen, we've adapted quite well to this new world." Aiyano turned to face Hani again just as his eyes flicked open, not a trace of sleep in them. The three were silent as he took stock of his surroundings, sat up, and looked to Eowen for guidance.

"It's alright Hani, we're safe here," Eowen said, hoping it was true. "These are two of the dreamers we felt the presence of."

"I see," Hani sat up and offered his hand to Aiyano and Nolyi. "Hani of the islands. The, uh, southern islands." Nolyi took his hand first.

"Nolyi of Nopt Shisoke."

"You're not speaking a dialect from south of the mountains, how can I understand you?"

"He picks things up quick, eh?" Aiyano gave a look of approval.

"Thank you... Do I have to sit on the table any longer?" Hani asked and Eowen gestured to the cushion next to her, which Hani slid onto.

"That was impressive what you did at your ship," Nolyi said.

"Again, thank yo—Wait!" Hani jumped up, an accusing finger pointed at Nolyi. "You're the one that attacked us!"

"Sit down, Hani, I'll explain," Eowen said, swatting Hani's hand and pulling him down. She took him through the events since his lapse of consciousness, careful to paint Nolyi's attack as an unfortunate accident and highlighting how impressive their manifestations and city were. She described the situation with the Storm, the translator, and how they'd come to be in the room they were in. She asked Aiyano and Nolyi to fill in the details they better understood and came to learn that Aiyano was effectively the head of their settlement, at least according to Nolyi, though Aiyano refused to acknowledge any such thing. They also told Hani that Aiyano was largely responsible for the creation of the entire city, especially the great tower they occupied with the everflowing jug of water and the aqueduct system.

"It just seemed like a more elegant solution," Aiyano explained. "We could have gone into every home and manifested a personal water source, but that would take a very long time. Instead, we have a centralized source that can be diverted to provide for any number of people."

"That's brilliant!" Hani exclaimed. "I just established a weather system so it'd rain on a consistent basis with my people, but they still have to collect it."

"That's still a clever solution though, and the rains have a sacred quality in the southern islands, if I'm not mistaken? You've managed to provide for your people in perpetuity and retain some of the old world's culture," Nolyi said, nodding her approval.

"But the fact that Aiyano manifested all this by herself is

incredible, the scale is incomparable!" Hani insisted and gestured with his arms wide.

"Ah, that wasn't all me," Aiyano said. "I indeed created many of the... effects here, such as the never-emptying quality of the jug, and many rooms with properties we use for healing. Nolyi is the architect behind the scale of our manifestations." Aiyano took Nolyi's hand and squeezed it. "My spouse is immensely powerful, if a little single minded sometimes," Aiyano said with a wry smile.

"I've already apologized for attacking them and they accepted my apology. You accepted it, correct?" Nolyi said

"No ill will at all," Hani said, magnanimous despite having been unconscious for the negotiations. "What I want to know is how you consistently solidify such immense creations, I couldn't do it without Eowen's help, you see—" Hani launched into an academic conversation with Nolyi on the matter of manifestation that had them leaning across Aiyano and Eowen seated between them. Eowen didn't mind, though the context of their situation was miraculous to her. That they could be seated there, casually discussing deeds that in the old world could only ever have been attributed to gods, was making her feel heady. She scooted her cushion back to get some space and noticed Aiyano favoring her with a sweet, protective expression.

"They'll go at this for some time. Nolyi rarely has anyone to discuss manifestation with other than Ordwell and I. It's interesting, but I'm not as suited for such talks as they are."

"Neither am I, Hani and I discuss it sometimes, but it's enough for me to know someone understands... after a fashion. He always wants to know more though." Eowen couldn't help smiling back, bubbling warmly inside. Aiyano's presence was undeniably soothing. Her voice somehow filled one with a feeling of soft clarity and healthy, wakeful energy, and she always seemed to be speaking in a deliberate, unhurried way.

"Here, let's sit on the other side, give them space to have their fun." Aiyano suggested and stood with Eowen. Before they could move to the other side of the room a young woman, dressed as one of Aiyano's healers and lighter of skin than Eowen had ever seen, stepped in followed by a tall old man.

"Respected Aiyano, Respected Nolyi, Ordwell has arrived as requested." The young woman lifted her long skirts and bowed, then stood aside for Ordwell.

Eowen had never seen anyone like Ordwell before. He looked somewhat like a jungle and savannah tribes-person by the shape of his nose and chin, but was too light of skin. His eyes were wider and rounder than Eowen's people, like those of Aiyano and Nolyi's. His lips were hidden under a long mustache, the only facial hair he had, and his gray hair lay flat on his head. He was extremely tall, taller than anyone Eowen had ever seen, and without any muscle tone. His stick-like arms and legs along with soft, uncalloused hands indicated he'd hardly done any labor at all in his life. He was dressed similarly to Aiyano, with tight sleeves and a skirt, but his outfit was dark brown and had a hood that he let down. The strangest thing was the seeming lack of a dreaming aura he exuded. Eowen could passively feel the presence of many people moving in the building along with the entirety of the city, which she'd largely blocked out as background noise. Ordwell, however, put out almost no dreaming signature at all. Eowen found it hard to believe he had created something as miraculous as the translator above them.

"Greetings friends. These are the two causing a stir I take it?" He held out his hand for Hani who shook it enthusiastically.

"Hani of the southern isl—" Hani froze as soon as he touched Ordwell's hand and the old man's mustache shifted with a smile underneath. Eowen detected a change in Hani's aura of dreaming, but the boy gave no indication of what he was experiencing other than to look Ordwell up and down with wonder. "Respected Ordwell, it is truly a pleasure to meet you." Hani had never sounded so reverent nor had he, in Eowen's memory, used such formal language. Their hands separated and Hani stared at his palm for a moment before hurriedly gesturing to Eowen. "This is my companion, Eowen of the jungle and savannah tribes." Hani gave Eowen an encouraging look and Ordwell's eyes twinkled. She tentatively reached out to clasp his open hand.

"Nice to meet you."

"Likewise."

Ordwell took her hand, and the universe disappeared. Eowen had looked upon the starfield below many times since arriving; it was the new bottom of the world, a vertigo-inducing floor that, if stared at too long, one might feel they had fallen into. No one ever did though. The bottom of the world held firm, save when creation rose up from it. Still, Eowen had idly imagined at times what it would be like to fall into the stars below. Usually, she'd hurriedly retreat from these thoughts when nausea struck, but in the instant Eowen and Ordwell's hands clasped she somehow knew what it was like to have not only fallen into that deep black ocean of stars, but to be floating peacefully in it, alone in the universe except for Ordwell. Face to face, they drifted in a place of dark and empty save for tiny stars all around them, a twinkling autumn of light frozen in the blackness. Ordwell's mouth moved as if to speak, then the moment broke and Eowen was back in the room, hand empty.

"I know, it is rather dramatic, isn't it? You get used to it when it happens to everyone you meet." Ordwell patted Eowen's shoulder. She tensed but nothing happened. "Don't worry, it only happens when I first meet someone. Don't know why. Noyli's got their theories, but it's none of my concern."

"Which is infuriating!" Nolyi threw their hands in the air.

"I need to hear everything you've ever thought about that power!" Hani slapped the table.

"That's more like it!" Nolyi responded. "You see, it definitely has to do with how his dreaming power works best when dealing with how people connect to one another, that's why his dreaming aura enveloped you when meeting and—" Nolyi and Hani dove into their conversation while Ordwell, Aiyano, and Eowen took seats on the other side of the table.

"Could you bring some refreshments please," Aiyano said to the young woman that had arrived with Ordwell. "I'm sure our guests are getting hungry."

"Of course, Respected Aiyano." The young women hurried off, then Ordwell stretched and sighed.

"Thank you Aiyano, I'm exhausted." He looked at Eowen. "Been installing those and other creations of mine into homes all day."

"What other kinds of things?" Eowen asked. She was resisting the urge to stare at her hand and had to reign her mind into the present moment.

"Things to connect people. Orbs that let people talk to each other in different places, rings that when two people wear them and shake hands they can tell if the other is to be trusted. It's what I've found my calling to be. I think everyone finds a calling in this new world, but those of us with a bit of power do find them faster." He winked at Aiyano. "I'm eager to help you and Hani, Miss Eowen, I hear you're looking to meet with some lost family in the city."

"Yes..." Eowen said. *Aiyano and Nolyi were right,* she thought. *This city is amazing, they've adapted so well. Finding Hani's father and Tavo will be easy, especially with this Ordwell person.*

"Well," Ordwell began. "I will help you, it is no trouble." He blinked slowly and when he opened his eyes they looked terribly sad, his smile was not gone but it reached no further than his lips. "Only... we may not ever find them. I need you to understand that may be the case."

"Ordwell!" Aiyano gripped his shoulder. "Please, let's not talk as if there's no hope, they've only just arrived, and they're so young." Aiyano glanced at Eowen, pity in her eyes, and Eowen realized what, despite their powers, she and Hani looked like: children. Overeager, awkward, and naive children. She'd wondered why, despite stating their purpose, no one had asked who exactly they were looking for. It seemed that Aiyano and Nolyi had been trying to protect them by avoiding the issue.

Something inside Eowen flared up at that notion, a righteous need to assert herself. She took one of Aiyano's hands in both of hers, straightened her back, and fixed the woman with an unwavering stare that brooked no other option but to meet it.

"Aiyano, despite your hospitality, I feel we have not properly met." Eowen's voice was quiet, unheard by Noyli or Hani in their conversation, but it carried through to Aiyano and Ordwell with steel. Some kind of power was gripping her that felt greater than herself, and she decided to let it speak its mind. "I am Eowen of—well, I am one of the few left alive. I arrived in the new world alone and survived by my own power. I have borne witness to more death and desperation than any of my ancestors, held in my arms grieving men, women and children. I have enacted great creations and faced the death of my own moth—" The word stopped in her throat. Eowen shut her mouth, swallowed, and tried again. "I have faced the death of many of my own. We have traveled far to find our missing loved ones. We are prepared for the worst because we have seen it already."

The healer had tears in her eyes and took her hand back to wipe them away. The young woman returned with food and drink, laying it out with the help of two others. Ordwell sipped something with a satisfied expression, Hani and Nolyi transitioned seamlessly into a conversation about food, and Aiyano sighed. "I'm not sure I'll ever get used to children like you. I know we all saw terrible things after the fall, I was in the midst of it as a healer, but the way children have had to grow up..." Aiyano looked Eowen up and down. "It's not right." Eowen wasn't sure how to respond, so she decided that a casual shrug and a change of focus to her meal was the best option.

"Don't think poorly of Aiyano. Her heart is simply too tender," Ordwell said, draining his cup.

"We'll look for your lost loved ones, I promise," Aiyano said. "If they were in the city at any time, someone would have heard of them."

"Thank you," Eowen said. She was internally overcome again at the strangeness of her situation. Somehow, eating with foreign leaders and discussing personal quests felt more bizarre than even the fall had. It felt like she was living someone else's life.

"Who's your lost one?" Ordwell asked.

"Hmm?" Eowen emerged from her thoughts. "Oh, it's my cousin, Tavo. He disappeared three years before the fall, but I know he was here at some point."

"Haven't heard of him, but that's not saying much considering how many people once populated Nopt Shisoke. Aiyano?" The healer shook her head.

"No, I'm sorry Eowen, and if I haven't heard of Tavo then Nolyi probably hasn't either. Who was Hani looking for?" Aiyano looked across the table at her spouse and the island boy. Their conversation had dwindled into stories from the old world, mostly involving recreational activities such as cliff jumping and mountain climbing.

"I'll... let Hani say. It's his business," Eowen said. Aiyano shrugged and Ordwell nodded. "Even..." Eowen began, licked her dry lips, then took a sip of water. "Even if Tavo is dead or possessed by that Storm, I'd like to retrieve his body." Aiyano put down her food, she was staring at Eowen but the girl's eyes were in her hands and she didn't notice. Ordwell had gone stiff. "If he's dead, I want to give him a proper funeral. I wasn't able to do that for... any of my people..."

And I'll never be able to.

"... So I'd like to at least be able to do that for him." Eowen waited for a response, but none came. She looked up to see Aiyano staring at her grimly. Ordwell was deliberately looking away, uncharacteristically uncomfortable. "Did I say something wrong?"

Aiyano sighed and shook her head. "No, no you didn't say anything wrong. It's just that..." Aiyano dropped into a whisper. "If your cousin died outside these walls, or was taken by the Storm, then I'm sorry but his body is lost." Aiyano held Eowen's gaze for a moment, her expression grim.

"What do you mean? If his body is out there in the Storm, I have to get it back."

"Eowen, we can't go in there. It's dangerous enough for Nolyi to travel outside of the city even with their armor."

"What's that about me and my armor?" Nolyi called across the table.

"She's explaining why Eowen can't go into the Storm," Ordwell supplied.

"She's absolutely right, no one is leaving under any circumstances." When Nolyi said that Hani and Eowen reacted as one, their dreaming auras merging indignantly in response.

"What do you mean we can't leave?" Hani shouted, slamming the table.

"Hani, calm down." Eowen's voice was even, but there was a harsh edge to her aura. "I'm sure they'll explain themselves. Couldn't we bring some of those silver bamboo shoots around the city, they make up the barrier, don't they?"

Nolyi and Aiyano froze. Ordwell just shook his head.

"That bamboo barrier," Nolyi began, gritting their teeth, "was not our doing. It was the work of a monster, one that drew us in with promises of safety. She made the barrier in exchange for hundreds of our people and took them to die in the Storm." Nolyi's hand had curled into a tight fist that shook.

"You know it's not that simple," Ordwell muttered.

"Is that so?" Nolyi turned on him. "Why don't you tell them what you felt when you met her then?" Nolyi gestured at Eowen and Hani. Ordwell glared over his cup at Nolyi, who met his gaze for a long, tense moment. Eowen and Hani desperately wanted more context, but there was no room for them to speak as Ordwell stood up, casually manifested a square of cloth, and quickly packed some food into it.

"I'm not doing this, Nolyi. Let me know when you've cooled off." Ordwell strode purposefully out of the room without a backwards glance, leaving Nolyi opening and closing their mouth, retorts primed and canceled. Aiyano sighed, brushed off nonexistent crumbs from her lap, and stood.

"Eowen, Hani, eat your fill. Hollu, the young woman who brought Ordwell, will show you to accommodations. Nolyi and I need to get some fresh air." Nolyi opened their mouth to respond, but closed it once again. They groaned, lacking the words for their frustration, but stood and left the room.

"It was a pleasure speaking with you!" Hani called after Nolyi. "I'm sorry... I hope we haven't offended?" Hani said.

"No, no my dears." Aiyano shook her head as she made her way to the door. "It's complicated, but I promise to explain everything later. We have been through much, Nolyi more than Ordwell or I." Aiyano said this very quietly, not secretly but somberly. "You must be exhausted after your travels and the exciting meetings we've had. Please get some rest." She looked at Eowen and Hani, a sweet warmth radiating from her as before. "You're not prisoners, I promise. You are our guests, but please please don't leave. The Storm cannot be faced." Aiyano gave them both a small bow and left. Soon after the young woman, Hollu, entered.

"When you are ready to be shown to your rooms I'll be outside." Then Hollu left them in privacy.

"Eowen."

"Hani?"

"What do you think they meant by the creator of the barrier being a monster?" He sounded more curious than worried.

"I don't know. They have to be a person, right? Just

someone who can manifest in the new world better than the average person."

"Maybe, but I've been thinking about something. It has to do with this Storm, that monster-person, and also what happened with me when I passed out during Nolyi's attack." Hani locked eyes with Eowen. "It also has to do with some of the things you've done. I've been wondering if there are other things in this new world."

"What do you mean?" Eowne pressed her hands together in her lap, curving her shoulders in, something about the way Hani was speaking sent chills down her spine.

"I don't know, it's just a feeling, like sometimes we're being watched by things that aren't people."

"You mean things like animals?"

"No, I mean things that aren't... alive, at least not in the way we or animals are." Hani scratched his head, exasperated. "I don't know how to describe it. It's just an idea I've been playing around with." Hani stared at the wall opposite as if seeing something far away. "The way it felt when that Storm was trying to control us. It wasn't a person."

"The Storm is probably just a manifested thing with traits it shouldn't normally have, like the eagle and cat we made. There was nothing in the old world like those, this Storm is like that only..." Eowen thought back to when the Storm had almost taken her, the way its power wormed into her. "Bigger," she finished, but somehow Eowen knew the implication that a person was behind the Storm was impossible. Hani didn't look convinced either, but he had no other theories to present, so he shrugged and swigged down the rest of his drink.

"I suppose it doesn't really concern us. I'm just curious is all." He tried to look encouraging. "We've got our own quest, right? First we should get some rest like Aiyano said. Next, we are going to look for your cousin Tavo and my father. That's our priority. It's why we came all the way here, right?" Eowen blinked, shook her head, and gave Hani a weak smile.

"You're right, we've got our own things going on." She stood up. "I'm not hungry anymore, but I think Ordwell had the right idea. Let's pack some of this up."

Eowen sighed out of pure relief. The tension had broken, they'd made it to their destination, and they could finally get some rest. They packed up some food and followed Hollu to a pair of rooms, but opted to share one. Once inside, they manifested a curtain to separate it and tubs of hot water for each of them. Hani took the bed that was padded with sand, eager for every bit of new culture he could encounter, while Eowen manifested a more familiar one. They both touched up the room with the sounds and smells of islands and jungles. Their weeks together had begun to blend their tastes such that their manifestations would organically pull from each other's sensibilities to balance what they brought into being. The scent of rich jungle earth and island flowers merged with the hum of rainforest insects, somehow fitting with the distant crashing of waves.

Eowen fell immediately asleep, exhausted and eager to let time pass, but Hani couldn't relax. There was too much of interest to him: a new culture he'd only heard of, the mysterious Storm, a monster-woman that could create barriers against it, and hidden somewhere in the city, the first clues to finding his father. It upset him that the people of Nopt Shisoke were trapped in their city, besieged by a power they believed was insurmountable. He stared at the ceiling, annoyed that he had to stay put when he too had the power to resist the storm.

"I made that shelter for Eowen and I, don't see why I couldn't do something like that again," Hani whispered to himself, ignoring the fact that he couldn't even recall how exactly he'd performed that deed.

"Go now, find The Nagirr'Om in the Storm, and you will find your father."

A detached, formless voice appeared within the depths of Hani's ears, somehow bypassing sound itself. It had no pitch, accent, or language and was so unidentifiable that Hani could only assume it was his own thoughts.

Aiyano and Nolyi will never let us go into the Storm, but I'll never find my father staying here. Besides, I can't trust them, they're content to let their people live in a prison like this.

Hani glanced at the curtain separating him and Eowen.

I'll just have a quick look into this Storm. No reason to take Eowen. It's not safe for her.

While Eowen slept, Hani put up shrouds of silence and invisibility, then crept out the door and down the hallways. He didn't know the way, but a voice in his head that he took for his own whispered in his mind.

****

[Listen, for you cannot hear me yet]

I TOLD LOVE THEY WERE TOO SMALL TO PROPERLY PERCEIVE ONE SUCH AS I.

****

Eowen did not wake gradually, but bolted upright and rolled out of bed as reverberations of energy hummed through her. Her mind was alight, bright sparks of thought glowing in the blank darkness of sleep, which ignited her senses. "Hani!"

Calling for him like that was merely habit; she could already feel he was gone from the room. She couldn't tell how long she'd been asleep, let alone how long Hani had been gone. Shadows perched around her, shifting as she dashed through the curtain towards the door. A quick twist of power and the darkness danced around her, manifesting yellow robes held by a sash and a head-scarf that gathered up her hair. She pushed open the door and looked both ways, the compass directions in her mind no help as she couldn't remember which way they'd come from.

"Greetings, Eowen." She jumped. The voice was deep and spoke in her language. She turned to see a man's face poking around the door. He was short, perhaps in his thirties, and looked to be a member of her tribe, though he wore the garb of Aiyano's healers.

"Hello?" Eowen stepped fully out of the room and the man smiled pleasantly.

"My name is Isana," he said. "I'm to bring you to Aiyano when you are ready. Have you and Hani rested well?" Eowen was caught off guard by the familiar language, though it was a slightly different dialect.

"Are you from the jungle and savannah tribes?" Eowen asked.

"To the far east, bordering the ocean." He looked around her into the room and Eowen grappled with what to address first. "Is Hani not here?" Isana asked and she focused her attention back on that.

"No! He wasn't here when I woke up."

"Ah, he must have been led to Aiyano and Nolyi already. I only just relieved the previous attendant a few minutes ago."

Eowen wasn't sure she believed him. She didn't think Hani would leave her alone like that, but she also didn't want to suspect them of foul play as they'd been gracious thus far.

Besides, she thought, *who would even be powerful enough to capture Hani? Even if someone here was capable of doing so, the struggle would have surely woken me up.*

Eowen relaxed and gestured for Isana to lead on. "Alright then, take me to Aiyano please."

It's alright, he's alright. He probably did go to meet with Aiyano and wanted to let me rest.

Eowen followed Isana through the hallways, making a more concerted effort to memorize the way. Staff and visitors, who bustled past them, seemed to be following bronze markers embedded in the walls. Without knowing the language and with her terrible sense of direction Eowen had no luck creating a mental map.

"Eowen?" Isana had asked something but Eowen hadn't been paying attention.

"Sorry, what was that?"

"I was just wondering from which cluster you're from?"

"Cluster?"

"Of the people." The word he'd used for 'the people' was the jungle and savannah tribe's word for person, the word for non-outsider, a word that Eowen knew did not apply to her anymore.

"I-I'm..." The words faltered, Eowen's throat felt rough. "I am... not of the people." She looked away from Isana's questioning expression and cleared her throat. "What do you mean by 'cluster'?"

"Ah, you must be from far to the west then, I've heard our people to the west don't leave their villages often. How many clusters of villages are there west of you?" Eowen tried not to look skeptical or ignorant. Clearly what Isana was saying made sense to him, but there had been no village clusters to the west of hers in the old world. There had only been the villages of her tribe and a few outlier villages far to the east.

"There were none to the west in the old world. You're from an eastern outlier village then. It makes sense that I haven't heard of you being exiled. News from the east rarely came to us." Eowen spoke confidently. It cheered her somewhat to see that a fellow exile or runaway had made a good life for himself. She didn't want to accuse him of abandoning her people, so she had assumed his fate to be similar to hers. Isana looked confused though, his eyebrows pressed together, but after a moment something seemed to occur to him.

"Oh, I see. I've heard of the people farthest to the west, but never met any. Your villages kept to themselves, hugging the steepest mountains, densest jungle, and harshest savannah." This described the villages of Eowen's tribe perfectly, but it had never occurred to her to put such descriptions to them at all. It was simply the way they had been. "It makes sense you haven't heard much of the people beyond your cluster," Isana continued. "To the far east of your cluster there are at least seven other clusters of villages."

Seven? Eowen contained her shock. She'd been rapidly learning how large the old world had been beyond the jungle and savannah, but to think she hadn't even known how big her own tribe had been. "Hmm," was all she said.

"The further west, the more they keep to themselves, or rather, kept to themselves," Isana went on. "This is amazing.

I've never met someone from the cluster furthest west. I am from the cluster furthest east, our totem is the groskmu."

Eowen knew what the groskmu was; a massive crocodilian reptile that nested in estuaries and ventured upriver. It could grow to the length of three men, was covered in scales and webbed spines, had jaws almost a third of its body length and two prehensile tails. It was a lazy but vicious beast. Even with that recognition, Eowen was beginning to feel well out of her depth with all the new information being thrown at her and was rapidly growing tired of that feeling. She didn't like being so ignorant. She didn't think Isana was trying to mislead her, but the fact remained that she could be lied to and would never know. Her mind raced for some piece of information she could latch onto, something she could share with this Isana to put them on similar standing, but came up with nothing. Insana waited for her to respond, but when she stayed silent he continued speaking.

"Well, you should know that in the clusters far to the east we had frequent contact with Nopt Shisoke and the Britchen. The mountains are small there and the paths are well tended." Isana slowed his pace as they arrived at a room, different from the meeting room from the previous day. "I don't know too much about what it was like in your cluster. I just want you to know that many of the people have settled in Nopt Shisoke." He smiled gently. "You're not alone here." He stepped back and gestured for Eowen to enter.

Eowen tried to match his expression, but it came out more as a grimace. She knew he was wrong; however it had been in the old world where he was from, however similar his cluster of the people had been to hers, she was still alone. Hani might be her friend and some people might speak her language, but they were not truly her people, they never would be. The only one of her people left was Tavo, and he was somewhere out in the new world, waiting to be found.

"Thank you for your guidance," Eowen muttered before ducking into the room. Inside, Aiyano was seated on a floor cushion in front of a long rectangular table facing the door. On the table lay a young man, bloody bandages wrapped around his head that Aiyano was gingerly removing. There were five others seated around the man dressed like Aiyano, and they all turned when Eowen entered. They were mostly caramel skinned Britchen, but there was one of the pale people Eowen had seen and someone who looked to be of the jungle and savannah.

Isana was right, they really are common here.

"I'll be with you in a moment, please take a seat," Aiyano said to Eowen without looking at her. Eowen didn't see Hani in the room and desperately wanted to ask about him, but something important was clearly going on.

Offending and disrupting will get me nowhere, Eowen thought as she took a seat to the side.

She scanned the room, noting diagrams on the walls of people and their bodies with labels. There was a bronze sphere in the ceiling, no doubt Ordwell's work, and the gathered people were all young adults, except for one ancient man that smiled toothlessly at Eowen. Aiyano finished unwrapping the bandages and almost immediately blood seeped down the man's forehead from a gruesome gash. No one reacted and Eowen glanced from face to face to see if she was missing anything, but the group was only watching silently. Eowen looked back and noticed, with some interest, that the blood had stopped flowing out of his head. Eowen sharpened her senses, felt for the man's aura of dreaming, and her eyes widened. Aiyano's aura of power was present in the man's body as well, but so gentle and so controlled that one would hardly notice if they weren't looking for it. Aiyano had a hold on his blood and was keeping it from leaking out.

"Koh, take over the blood." Aiyano didn't look up when she spoke, and the oldest man unfolded his hands from his lap. He reached out towards the patient on the table, hands shaking, and muttered to himself. Eowen could feel his dreaming aura reach out to match the patient on the table. Koh had less ease and grace than Aiyano, but she seemed satisfied and retracted her influence as he took over. "Good, now try to clean it." Koh nodded and his powers moved in small sweeps, gentle and precise. The blood was thinned away, disappearing like water from a hot rock, and evaporated into nothing. Koh's power wavered for a moment, causing more blood to seep out, but eventually the gash was cleaned and exposed. The patient, for his part, looked like he was enjoying himself, and grinned at everyone seated around him, including Eowen. "Can you close it?" Aiyano asked Koh.

"No, teacher, I'm quite certain I can't."

"You'll have to learn to do so with your power. Your hands are too shaky to apply stitches."

"Yes, teacher." Koh didn't sound embarrassed. His respect for Aiyano was obvious.

"Another day, then. Release. I'll take over." The transfer of power was so smooth, so seamlessly done that if Eowen hadn't been paying attention she wouldn't have noticed it at all. Aiyano scanned her students, then stopped at a young Britchen woman. "Rewol," was all she said, and the woman named Rewol nodded. Rewol's power rushed in, a little too eagerly, and the patient flinched as the force of it played against his and Aiynao's without harmony.

"Ah! Too rough!" the patient complained.

"Talk again and I'll put you to sleep," Aiyano said to the patient. "Fix it, now." Aiyano did not raise her voice, but there was a powerful clarity to it. Rewol flushed, nodded, licked her lips, flexed her fingers, and bobbed her head to some rhythm in her mind. Her power focused, clarified, and took over Aiyano's hold. The blood did not flow, and before Eowen's eyes, the gash closed without a scar and in moments was no more. "That'll do. Replace the blood, confirm no more injuries under the surface, and send him to get checked for a concussion."

"Yes, teacher!"

"The rest of you, dismissed." The students, save for Rewol, stood and bowed to her before shuffling out of the room. Aiyano finally looked at Eowen, and all the seriousness she'd maintained while teaching immediately dropped into warmth. "Greetings Eowen, I hope you slept well." Eowen stood and mimicked the students bow, but Aiyano waved it off.

"Yes, thank you, I'm sorry but I need to ask you abou—"

"Oh! And did you meet Isana? He's one of my top students."

"I—yes, he led me here, but where's—"

"Charming lad, I knew it would be best to have a guide you could speak to. Don't worry about a language barrier as we go about the city, Ordwell is working on something especially for that."

"It's fine, but Hani, where is he?" Aiyano looked to either side of Eowen as if the island boy should be there and she simply hadn't noticed him till now.

"He's not with you?"

Eowen felt a flutter of panic but tried to keep her cool. "No! No, he was gone when I awoke. Isana said he was probably taken to see you before I awoke."

"Oh! That would make sense."

It would?

"I was asleep till a little while ago. He's probably with Nolyi touring the city," Aiyano said, and she certainly seemed confident in this theory. Eowen decided not to question it and accept what the woman said. It was her city after all, surely someone like Hani didn't disappear without her noticing.

Unless she made him disappear.

Eowen shook off the thought, reminding herself that a fight couldn't have happened without waking her, and even so they wouldn't have been able to stop Hani. Aiyano was back to observing her student's work. She gave the approval and the patient rose from the table, thanking first Aiyano, then the woman Rewol.

"Come, I'll take you to get checked for a concussion." Rewol led the patient out of the room. Aiyano shook her head at them, frowning, but there was joy and pride in her body language, a loving gentleness in her eyes.

"They're my least capable batch of students, but I love them all the same," Aiyano said once they were out of earshot, and Eowen found it impossible to imagine this woman threatening anyone, let alone Hani.

"You still seem very proud," Eowen said, and Aiyano shrugged.

"They're good people, and really that's what matters most, isn't it? Doesn't matter how powerful or skilled you are; if you don't want to do good, no good is going to get done. Come, let's find my Nolyi and your companion."

Aiyano led Eowen out of the room and through a few hallways till they reached a great spiraling staircase with huge landings that opened to other floors. She greeted and spoke with her followers in several languages Eowen did not understand, but never broke her stride. Aiyano was clearly master of this place, but it operated well without her as hundreds of workers moved to tasks on their own. It gave Eowen the impression of an ant colony. When they'd descended several floors and passed by the busiest areas, Aiyano took out a chain with two bronze spheres on it, not unlike the translation spheres set into ceilings. She handed one to Eowen and held the other.

"How's that?" Aiyano spoke in her language.

"Clever, it's not translating anyone else's speech. Did Ordwell make these too?" Eowen asked, turning the sphere around in her hand.

"No one else seems to have such a knack for crossing the border between people. Do you know he's made ways for people to share emotions, pains, pleasures, and power? He's even working on ways to share memories."

Eowen was amazed. In less than two days she'd been introduced to more possibilities of creation in the new world than she'd ever considered before. She gripped the bronze sphere and felt for its power, its traits. In it she felt an echo of the moment when she and Ordwell and shaken hands. Everything she'd experienced of the new Port Disoke felt fresh and new, blooming with untold possibilities, yet it was hemmed in by the Storm.

As they reached the bottom of the stairs and exited the tower, Eowen found herself drawn to the north of the city where the clouds turned patiently, small flashes of lightning betraying the power within, though no thunder could be heard. Aiyano watched the Storm as well, accustomed to the existential threat of it but newly disturbed with fresh eyes at her side.

"I can tell you're full of questions. Feel free to ask, we've got all day," Aiyano said as she guided Eowen.

"Alright." Eowen paused to consider where to start. "You specialize in healing, like how Ordwell specializes in connecting people?"

"Yes."

"Does Nolyi specialize in anything?"

"Not really, they're good at assisting others though, making their dreams a reality. They were an acrobat in the old world." Aiyano always carried a tender expression when speaking of Nolyi. "That's how we met. I was a healer in the old world as well, and Nolyi was the fool that kept requiring my services."

Maybe I'm like that too, the way I help Hani complete his manifestations. Maybe that is my speciality.

"I see... Do most people become good at something specific?" Eowen asked.

"Not that I've seen. I think those like us, the truly capable creators, tend to notice a speciality sooner or later. I think Nolyi will discover theirs in due time. Do you have a specialty?"

"No, I don't think so, or perhaps I just haven't found it yet. I'm good at helping others make things, like how you described Nolyi." Eowen looked around, totally lost except for the massive tower that could be seen over any building, pouring its water into the aqueducts that stood over everything. "How do you know where Nolyi is? Are they in the same part of the city all the time?"

"I was wondering when you'd ask." Aiyano held up her

left hand to show a ring on it. "We will always know where the other is so long as we wear these. Ordwell made them, of course, but with Nolyi's help."

"I have something like that!" Eowen exclaimed and fished around in her pockets. She revealed the stone Ne had given her. "One of my mountain folk friends, a little boy named Ne, made this for me. It will always lead me back to their settlement."

"He might have a talent for Ordwell's style of creation," Aiyano said, nodding approvingly. She led on, and as they passed from narrow streets into wider ones filled with activity, people greeted her constantly. Some stopped to bow respectfully, and a few even genuflected till their foreheads were on the ground. Aiyano responded with brief waves and quick words, but didn't pay them much mind.

"You're... very well received," Eowen commented, smiling awkwardly as a stranger bowed to her as well.

"We should be. Noyli and I are largely responsible for saving the entirety of Nopt Shisoke." Aiyano's hand tightened on the bronze sphere and her round face creased into pinched lines. "Save for what the Storm claimed, that is."

Eowen didn't want to touch on pained topics so soon into getting to know her host, especially with how it had gone the previous night, but there was a question she desperately wanted an answer for. "Do you know what the Storm is?" Eowen asked.

Aiyano sighed. "No. I don't know if it's a natural part of the new world, or some creation a dreamer lost control of." Aiyano's voice got low and heavy. "It grows within people, though. It takes over their manifestations, and then it uses them as a puppet to bring itself into the world. No person has ever been able to resist it forever." Eowen thought about this.

"Except the one who made the silver bamboo," Eowen said simply, and Aiyano flicked a glance at Eowen, who held her expression in check. "Nolyi called the bamboo maker a monster, and Ordwell walked off while they were talking about it." Eowen smiled nervously at Aiyano, but she was feeling unusually bold. She cleared her throat and tried to sound authoritative, channeling Mein's body language. "I don't want to pry, there's clearly some... issue with the bamboo maker. But that Storm nearly took me, and Nolyi nearly killed Hani and I because of it. If we're going to be trapped here, I'd really like some answers."

"... Of course," Aiyano agreed with a nod. "Ask, and I'll try to answer."

"Oh, well..." Eowen floundered for a question. She'd been expecting more resistance. "Why, um, was Nolyi so upset yesterday?"

Aiyano stopped walking. She scanned the street, looking for something, and locked onto a building with a canvas awning dyed green, pulling Eowen towards it. "Let's talk about this before we see Nolyi. Are you hungry?"

Eowen hadn't been thinking about her bodily needs, but when Aiyano brought it up she found she was. They were on another wide road that curved to the north east. As with all the wide roads Eowen had seen in Port Disoke, there was a bustle of activity as people of many cultures manifested things, presented things, and shared things. It seemed that the whole city had adopted a system of creation and sharing, though few of the creations were particularly impressive in scale and none possessed special properties from what Eowen could sense. Active manifestation had simply become part of everyday trade. They stepped inside the canvas-awned building, passing through sandstone into a food stall lined with a smooth, tan material that curved gently as though molded from clay. Green fabric hung from the walls to add color, and bronze circles were set into them here and there, shining as though sunlight were streaming through them. The city was lit up from below with wakefulness in the same way the mountain folk's settlement was, only on a much grander scale.

Aiyano left Eowen at their table and spoke to a woman behind a counter, over which delicious smells wafted. She rejoined her and leaned in close. "We'll have a bit of privacy here, but we should still speak quietly. The topic of the Storm and… what's happened before you arrived gets mixed reactions, but you deserve to know." She patted Eowen's hand encouragingly. "You're a good sort, dear."

"I can give us more privacy," Eowen said, then established a barrier of silence so that they could hear out of it but their words would not reach others.

"What's this?" Aiyano asked, waving her hand through the invisible barrier and detecting it with her dreaming aura.

"No one can hear us through it," Eowen said

"Interesting…" Aiyano gave Eowen a searching look, but didn't ask more about it. "Well, to start, you have felt the Storm, so you know how it feels when it pulls upon you?" Eowen nodded. "Here is what we know: It seems to invade some people more easily than others. Usually those with less power are more susceptible. The Storm uses them, and they are effectively dead if it ever leaves them."

"How would it leave them?"

"If they were on this side of the barrier when it was made." Aiyano's tone was dark. "It creates itself using them, but it can only make as much as itself as the power of the people it's possessing. It craves capable dreamers, because then it can make more of itself. Even without powerful individuals, it can still do much damage with many people under its thrall." Eowen nodded. She could imagine the volume of people and power it would take to maintain the Storm at the size it was.

"So what happened to make the barrer, and why does it upset Nolyi?" Eowen asked. Their food was delivered to the table, a fish Eowen had never seen before smelling delicious and foreign. Her stomach grumbled and Aiyano gestured for her to dig in, taking only small sips of her soup as she spoke.

"The Storm was taking over, quickly. Nopt Shisoke was once three city states, and those of us that were left after the fall came together as one city. Then the Storm appeared and spread like a disease through it. Nolyi and I resisted it well enough in those early times and provided for others as much as we could. That way, the Storm couldn't get a grip on the weaker dreamers around us, as they didn't have to do creations with our support.

"The dreamers we couldn't help as easily fell, though. It grew in power, and seemed like it would batter down Nolyi's and my resistance to overtake us all." Aiyano paused to slurp from her bowl. "This was less than a month ago. We thought all hope was lost, but then she showed up. A... thing, I hesitate to call it a person. They looked like a person though, like a woman of the Britchen but from some inland city, not Nopt Shisoke. She was heavily pregnant and naked and wore a white veil with thick silver embroidery over her face. She rode a strange creature that I am certain never existed in the old world." Aiyano paused to collect her memories. "It was large enough to perch on my tower and cover the entire roof. It was like a bat, but also not like a bat. The fur and nose and feet were... wrong, and it had six wings. The being on it, the pregnant woman-looking thing, called themself: The Nagirr'Om."

The barrier of silence did nothing to stop the utterance of the name. It echoed past Eowen's power. Gooseflesh raced across Eowen's skin, and she saw that Aiyano had reacted the same. It was eerily quiet as though the whole room, perhaps even the entire city, had gone still. Eowen felt eyes on her and glanced around to see that, to the contrary, no one was looking at her or Aiyano. Rather, everyone was very distinctly looking at anything but them. Aiyano cleared her throat, took a big, loud slurp of her soup and clacked the empty bowl on the table. The spell was broken and, after a collectively held breath was let out, the city came back to life.

"The thing, I'll call it a woman, seemed to be a dreamer in some way. She could manifest things very well, but her greatest trait was full immunity from the Storm. She carried three tools. A hammer that sprouted bamboo, yes, the same bamboo that protects us. It... repels the Storm somehow, and she would cut it with a knife that transformed the bamboo into an arrow. The last tool was a bow that could fire the arrows. No other bow could. The woman arrived in a fury, drove the Storm off with arrows, and planted the bamboo that barricades us from the Storm."

"Then shouldn't everyone love her?" Eowen said when Aiyano paused. "And where is she now?"

"Some do still love her, and some, like Noyli, have reason not to. You see, when she established the barrier, she called for volunteers to fight the Storm. She gave the volunteers, in groups of three, her tools. Apparently only she could wield all three. She called them her acolytes, and those that volunteered treated her like a god, as did many others. As some still do. Then she marched them into the Storm to root it out." Aiyano leaned back and closed her eyes.

"What happened then?"

"Nothing."

"Nothing?"

"They haven't been seen since. That was three weeks ago." Aiyano opened her eyes and looked at Eowen, a resigned, sympathetic sadness in her expression. "Nolyi's little sister was among them." The statement was like a gravestone being set, heavy and certain.

"Oh," Eowen said.

"Mmm," Aiyano responded. "Nolyi... they've lost hope, and if I'm honest I don't believe any of the acolytes are still alive. But without their sister's body to mourn, without knowing for sure, Nolyi has become bitter. I have to believe the Storm-fighting woman had the best intentions. I can't ignore that she saved our city, but she took over a hundred of our people into it to die." Aiyano couldn't seem to decide between anger or resignation, and it seemed to Eowen that she'd been struggling with those feelings since they spawned. "The people of this city have been through so much since the fall. As many have, I'm sure, but our spirits are growing thin. They try to be thankful for what they do have, our current safety and security, but we are prisoners. I can feel the spirits of my people wearing thin each day." Aiyano paused. "Especially Nolyi."

Eowen nodded. "So, we don't bring up the bamboo woman around Nolyi."

"No, we don't." Aiyano looked toward the door and held up her hand with the ring. "Finish your food, Nolyi's headed here now." Aiyano left the table to chat with some of the other patrons, as she seemed to know everyone. Eowen finished the food and sat back, watching the way Aiyano spoke, politely but with utter confidence. She didn't act like the ruler of a city, but there was no doubt that the people of Port Disoke had the utmost respect for her. After a half an hour, Nolyi showed up along with Ordwell, saw Aiyano's back turned as she chatted with someone in the corner, then spotted Eowen and headed her way.

"Greetings, Eowen," Nolyi said in the mountain folk's language. Ordwell spoke in a different language and Eowen took his words to be a greeting and motioned for them to join her.

"Here, take this." Eowen handed the other end of the bronze ball and chain to Nolyi.

"That's better. I've never liked the mountain folk's language, but my father facilitated some trade with them in the old world and insisted I learn," Nolyi said. Ordwell put his hand to the middle of the chain and Eowen could feel his dreaming aura thickening, shadows walking up the edges of the table to his hand. In a quick and gentle threading of starlight, the chain linked off into a third direction with another ball on the end, which Ordwell held.

"How has your morning been, Eowen?" he asked.

"Fine, thank you. Um, are you two not angry with each other anymore?"

"Ordwell? He's my best friend, I can't stay upset with him." Nolyi slapped the old man on the back.

"Besides, we have so many creation projects together," Ordwell said. "We spend almost every day on alterations to people's homes adding whatever they can't create on their own."

"I see." Eowen looked past Nolyi and Ordwell to the door. "Where's Hani?"

"He's not with you?" Nolyi said, and tremors flowed out from Eowen. Heavy, powerful disruptions that heaved her spirit and sent ripples through every soul in Nopt Shisoke. Held things were dropped, voices went silent, and children began to cry. Many turned to the Storm, thinking it had somehow broken in. Eowen stood, fists clenched, wreathed in bitter shadows and glass-sharp starlight.

"He's not with you?" Eowen's voice was deeper and wider than it should have been. It burned her throat, empowered beyond her body. Her shadows curved toward Nolyi with a terrifying implication of sharpness, weight, heat, violence close at hand. "I was told Hani was with you, so if you don't tell me where he is right now I'll—"

Nolyi's eyes widened, tensed for a confrontation, and flared their power up against Eowen's.

"Not here!" Aiyano placed her hands on Nolyi's shoulders. Ordwell touched Eowen's hand, and she was brought back into that place of stars and silence where only she and Ordwell existed.

"We have done nothing to him," Ordwell said. Eowen's question burned all around her in his galaxy, but there was no lie in Ordwell's words; he had not seen Hani. He also communicated that Nolyi had been with Aiyano, then Ordwell all day. Hani's disappearance had nothing to do with them, and they did not know where he was.

Ordwell let go and Eowen took deep breaths, dismissing her power as much as she could, though there was still a panic in her spirit. Aiyano and Nolyi were speaking in the Britchen language. No one was holding the bronze spheres anymore. Ordwell picked his up and handed Eowen hers.

"When did you last see him?"

"When we went to sleep! He was there, I swear."

"Maybe he's in the city hiding his presence," Aiyano said, picking up the third sphere and holding it with Nolyi.

"Seems unlikely, we'd have noticed his presence."

"He can hide it," Eowen said and the three looked at her, surprised. "He can hide his presence very well. He calls it blending. Hani is almost impossible to notice if he doesn't want to be." The four of them went silent, unsure of what to say next or how to proceed. Thankfully the proprietor of the building approached and, in the Britchen language, asked if everything was alright. They finally noticed the many eyes locked on them and the crowd gathered outside. A baby's wail cut through the silence.

"Everything is under control," Aiyano said, stepping forward to address their sudden audience. "We have business to attend to in the tower." The crowd immediately parted for the party, though they did seem suspicious of Eowen. A wave of muttering spread out as the four passed. Nolyi pulled a bolt of dark red and gray patterned cloth from where it was strapped to their back and shook it out.

"Get on," they said. It floated like the rug from before and was nearly as wide, but the thinness of it made Eowen nervous. Ordwell and Aiyano stepped on confidently, so Eowen followed suit, gripping Ordwell's sleeve. The cloth took off for the tower at an incredible speed and Eowen threw herself flat, desperately clinging to the sides despite how the others stood. They landed at the top as before, and a few of Aiyano's people rushed in, asking questions. She brushed them off, speaking rapidly in the Britchen language. They walked toward the stairs, Aiyano and Nolyi chatting in their own language without holding the bronze sphere anymore. Ordwell still held his end with Eowen, so she spoke to him.

"Where are we going?" Eowen asked.

"A room we created to find people," Ordwell said. "We don't need it often anymore, but with such a large population it was indispensable after the fall to reunite families."

Eowen was led through the twisting hallways till they arrived at a very empty, dusty one. Down two more turns and they faced a stretch at the far end of which was a solitary, arched entryway with no door. Aiyano, Nolyi, and Ordwell entered first, followed by Eowen. Inside was an empty, circular room entirely bare, save for a bronze statue in the middle. The statue was humanoid but otherwise lacked distinguishable features. No eyes, ears, or even fingernails, just blank. One thing did stand out, which were the arms, outstretched as if offering to be held. As Eowen approached, it took on a strange quality of personhood. The light that reflected off it curved and colored, taking on more distinct shapes. When Eowen was within touching distance of the extended hand, the statue no longer looked like a statue, but a person with extremely familiar features that constantly changed as soon as she felt she'd identified who it was.

"What is this?" Eowen whispered.

"One of my pieces," Ordwell said.

"A wonder," Aiyano chimed in with some reverence. Eowen could understand her again and glanced up to see a bronze translation sphere in the ceiling.

"It takes on the appearance of people you remember. It should be shifting and changing right now," Nolyi said.

"Yes, it is." Eowen tilted her head and began to pick out specific features of people she knew all jumbled together and ever-changing. There were Mein's hands, an old teacher's eyes, Hani's feet, her father's shoulders, Zerinley's elbows, and many more, all shifting as soon as they were named.

"You need to focus your mind. Think of only one person,

remember them, and it will take that form. Once you do, touch one of the hands and you'll know where they are. A visage of you will also appear to them and you can speak with each other." Nolyi smiled at Ordwell. "It is truly a marvel like none other." Ordwell bowed slightly to show his appreciation, but kept his expression fixed.

"It works, and for that I am satisfied," he said simply. "Focus on Hani. We can't see who you are seeing, so only you will know if it is working as intended."

"Right," Eowen said, and tried to focus on the image of Hani in her head, but it was difficult. The constant shifting was hypnotic, and the closer to it she stood the more she could feel the dense, electric power that made up the wonder. Gradually, she began to hone in on Hani's features; his long, thin eyebrows, easy smile, knobby joints, sun-kissed skin, and dark eyes. In moments, a person very near to Hani's appearance was before her with a few traits still off. "How exact does it need to be?" Eowen asked.

"Just enough that you can identify only one person, though there will always be slight shifts. The mind is not an exact thing, but the heart can be trusted," Ordwell said, and Eowen felt a fluttering in her chest. She was terribly worried for Hani, but the wonder of the creation before her was thrilling.

Nolyi was right! Eowen thought. *This is a marvelous thing! It's utterly unlike anything the old world had ever known.*

It only then occurred to Eowen just how well the city of Port Disoke was adapted to the new world. Aiyano had said as much, but Eowen was beginning to feel that the wonders she'd been shown were only the start. Eowen reached out for the statue's hand, Hani's hand.

Amazing how great this city had become with only three dreamers working to create it. Four including The Nagirr'Om

The tower shook as though an earthquake had gone through it. The statue's store of power flared out, hot and cold and sharp and weightier than anything Eowen had ever felt other than the Storm. Eowen didn't know The Nagirr'Om's name would invoke her even in one's thoughts the way it had when Aiyano had said it before. The light around the bronze statue solidified into flesh and blood, and a person Eowen did not know appeared before her. She knew who it was from her host's description; naked, caramel skinned, long wild brown hair, veiled face, and heavily pregnant. Eowen's heart hammered and her mouth became immediately very dry as the entity before her suffused the room with power. It smelled like burning flowers and animal musk, it tasted like dried blood and sickly sweet honey.

"How did she summon her?" Ordwell said.

"Get rid of her!" Nolyi shouted. Eowen looked to them but they were averting their eyes; they could see The Nagirr'Om too. Eowen looked back over the visage and noticed its features were still shifting, so she sought out something, anything that would resemble Hani. The visage's head moved, just a fraction but with the force of a glacier, carving out the space it occupied. Eowen had not been told if the statue could move or not, but she suspected it wasn't supposed to. It opened its mouth as if to speak, and that's when she saw it, the lips changing just for a moment into lips she recognized. Eowen grasped onto the memory of them before she was even fully aware of who it would become. In a flash, The Nagirr'Om transformed into a different woman, older, clothed, darker skinned, and stern. Eowen lunged for one of the hands before it could transform back, and was transported.

Eowen stood in a horrible, familiar place amidst throngs

of bodies. She looked down, and the knot in her chest she hadn't felt in weeks twisted like a heart attack. She pressed her hand against her sternum to try and dull the pain. It did not help, but as before, no tears came. She glared at the corpse before her, blood boiling and stomach in ropes.

"I—I'm sorry, I didn't mean to come back here," she whispered to the body. "My friend is missing." Eowen could still feel her corporeal body holding the statue's hand and she let it go, sending the image of her mother and the cemetery back into oblivion.

When she returned, Aiynao and Nolyi were talking about who remembered Hani's appearance best. Ordwell was standing next to Eowen and noticed when her hand fell. "How did you bring her here?" he asked, and the other two went silent. "You've never seen her."

"I-I thought of her name, just her name," Eowen said, deliberately trying to not think it again, and judged by the expressions on the other's faces that they were doing the same.

"At least you managed to stop it, who knows what would have happened. Did you find Hani?" Ordwell asked.

"No... Someone else," Eowen said, barely loud enough to be heard. "I've got it this time." She focused on the statue again but Nolyi objected.

"Absolutely not! We're not letting you bring her here again!"

"I suggest we avoid discussing a certain something in case a certain name is thought of again." Ordwell put out his hands to stop Nolyi, speaking carefully. "And I suggest we let her continue. Our familiarity with certain unwanted subjects might make us more likely to commit such an accident now." Nolyi gave up but glared at Eowen.

"Don't let it happen again," Nolyi growled, and after a pause: "Please," they said more gently. Eowen saw more fear than anger in Nolyi's eyes and tried to adopt a confident and encouraging expression. She looked more sick than anything, but faced the statute again. The knot in Eowen's chest tightened, immediately conjuring her mother in eerie detail.

No, Eowen thought and locked onto a feature, the ears of a mountain folk she'd seen but never learned the name of. The image changed, and from there she changed it again and again until she found a trait of Hani's. She secured the image of the island boy, and before anything else could happen she lunged for his hand.

The Storm was everywhere. The wind ripped at Hani's clothes in a fog so thick that Eowen could barely see. He was a silhouette amidst the chaos, but a familiar one.

"Hani!" she screeched, and the silhouette turned its head.

"E-we-n?" His voice reached her, chopped by the gales around them.

He really went into the Storm, that fool!

"What are you doing, come back!" Eowen pawed at the clouds but her hands were intangible and she was stuck at a set distance from Hani.

"W—?" He called back to her, but she could only hear the tone of his voice, not the words.

"Hani, get out of the Storm!" Something changed, shifted, the mention of the Storm seemed to bring Eowen to its attention, and the winds began to blow against her.

It's alright, she thought. *I'm not really here, it can't get me.*

That should have been true, for that was how Ordwell's creation was intended to work, yet when the winds shifted towards Eowen, she could feel them. She could even feel the

Storm within her as before. The clouds broke apart unnaturally, mulched and resculpted till they took on terrible shapes; an eye, a mouth, many teeth, and a very long neck. Eowen was certain she'd die. The Storm was entering her corporeal body through her spirit in defiance of The Nagirr'Om's barrier.

Just as the great, monstrous head, carved from wind, rain, and lightning, fixed its eye on her and opened its mouth, something disrupted the power. A bright flash of cold, silver light shot through the side of the great Storm-beast's neck. A roar like a thousand waves crashing at once upon the shore rattled through Eowen's bones. The sound was cut off as another silver flash struck the Storm, followed by another and another. Eowen looked up through a gap in the clouds to see a black-winged form, barely more than a speck in the distance, rise up, pause, and launch another silver flash. This time, the light did not go into the beast but seemed to grow brighter in a fraction of a second till it blinded Eowen and she flinched away, eyes closed.

There was terrible pain in her chest and the silver light was still present. Eowen opened her eyes to see a silver bamboo stalk coming out of her chest. Her incorporeal body was pierced through, but she could still feel the pain, greater than any she'd known. It was intense enough that for a moment she didn't even know it was pain, only the obliteration of her thoughts.

Eowen's corporeal hand dropped from the statue in the tower and the Storm, Hani, and the black spec in the distance vanished, replaced by the room from before. Eowen stumbled back into the arms of Aiyano who was shouting, face twisted in panic. Eowen could not hear her though. The pain was pushing out her other senses. She looked down to see a silver bamboo stalk in her chest, blood pouring out. She coughed and spat red.

Why can't I taste the blood, why can't I hear Aiyano, why is it getting so dark, why doesn't it hurt anymore—

****

[Listen, for you cannot hear me yet]

LOVE ASKED WHAT I WAS.

****

Eowen's eyes shot open and saw Aiyano kneeling over her, only this was not the same woman from before. The sweet host and the stern teacher had been replaced with a thing greater and stranger. A weight and quality of power was about her that reminded Eowen of when Hani had protected them from the storm and Nolyi. Aiyano's hair had unraveled from its ties, her eyes pupil-less windows to some incomprehensible beyond, and all around her was an atmosphere suffused with more dreaming power than Eowen had ever experienced in one place. Aiyano's aura poured into her, forcing life through Eowen's body, crashing like a hammer on the stones of death that sought to drag her down.

Eowen looked at her chest where the bamboo was still sticking out and shuddered. Pain from the arrow, pleasure from the healing, the lingering effects of the Storm, and The Nagirr'Om's power all warred within her amidst images of her mother's corpse and Hani in the fog. With all the experiences vying for attention, Eowen found herself in a strangely clear state of mind. Colors were more vivid, touch was electric, sounds felt like great drums that sent her heart beating madly.

"I—" Eowen coughed up blood, which tasted surreal. "I saw him!" she choked out as more blood frothed from her mouth. She wouldn't die from loss of it. Aiyano was healing her faster than the blood loss could kill her. If anything, Eowen felt overfull of life.

"You're alive!" Ordwell said, coming into view.

"Don't, speak!" Nolyi was kneeling next to Aiyano now. "I've never seen her like this," they said to Ordwell.

"She's never treated someone so close to death," he responded.

"I found Hani!" Eowen shouted, then she pushed herself to a sitting position, slapping away the hands that tried to keep her down.

"Stop! We can't remove the bamboo, Aiyano is the only thing keeping you alive," Nolyi said.

"She is coming, I can feel her," Eowen said, and she could. The bamboo felt as though a thread were tied to it, one that shook with the wingbeats of The Nagirr'Om's great black mount. Nolyi's eyes flashed and they bared their teeth.

"She? You mean—"

"Yes, The Nagirr'Om." Saying the name was more powerful than thinking it, and the statue surged with the Nagirr'Om's image once again. Eowen glared it down till it became her mother again, then met Nolyi's eyes and held them. "I need to get to the top of the tower. Help me."

"You're insane!" Ordwell tried to intervene, but Nolyi shouldered past him. "You can't move her like this, she'll die!"

~None have died under my power, and none will.~

The three stared at Aiyano. The healer had spoken. Her mouth had moved and something like sound, but much greater, had come out so that meaning had been imparted on the three of them. Aiyano scooped Eowen up in her arms and began carrying the girl through the halls.

"Wait!" Nolyi called after them. "Stop, she'll die!"

"I—" Eowen hacked out more blood. "I won't." She studied Aiyano's blank eyes, fogged over as if she were blind, as she glided purposefully through the meandering halls. "I don't think I can die right now." Ordwell rushed up next to them and manifested a bronze sphere, one of his translating kind.

"You're not going to the landing bay, are you?" Nolyi said as they ran up beside them, frightened of what was coming and what was happening to their spouse. "My love, please explain so I can understand."

Aiyano paused, her eyes clearing a bit. Eowen gasped and clutched at the bamboo as searing pain rushed in.

"We need to face her, Nolyi, though I don't know why," Aiyano said. "Something is going to happen, though I can't say what. I think it will banish the Storm." Aiyano's power was tense around her, as if she could snap back into or fully out of the blank-eyed state that had been keeping Eowen alive. Eowen felt the injury killing her again as Aiyano's power faded, and she flailed at the healer's collar. Nolyi had tears in their eyes and they shook their head silently, but directed Aiyano's attention back to Eowen. Aiyano's eyes clouded over again and her power flared, life surging through Eowen. Even with a spear through her heart, she had never felt healthier.

Aiyano pushed through the halls, her aura of power knocking aside the students that got too close. Indignant shouts and questions fell on deaf ears as Ordwell and Nolyi followed. Soon, a caravan of people were following them to the landing bay. They ascended the last flight of stairs and could see the Storm beyond its barrier to the north. The strange tree below it had grown taller and the elements of the Storm were raging harder against the barrier. More lightning, rain, and the shapes of great heads with curved teeth churned within, fixing their eyes on Eowen.

Is the world ending again? Did we lose the old one only to lose this one?

They moved to the entrance where Nolyi's flying rug was, and Nolyi ran to the cubby where their armor was stored. "My helmet! That boy stole my helmet, I can't believe it! He really did go into the Storm by himself."

"He's not by himself out there," Ordwell said. "He's with her, isn't he?" The old man turned to Eowen for the answer.

"Yes." Eowen's eyes were glued to the clouds. "I saw her when I found Hani."

The next moment, a weight descended upon the city of Nopt Shisoke, a pressure like being under water. The feeling was familiar to every being present other than Eowen, and even within the aura of Aiyano's power she felt as if she were suffocating. Her heart began beating faster, her breath was pained, and the blood that had been streaming constantly from her wound came out faster. Aiyano was soaked red and a pool of it was around their feet, but still the healing held. Eowen squirmed, but Ordwell caught her hand and squeezed it.

"Just breathe child, breathe normally." He glanced at the spear protruding from her chest. "As normally as you can."

Eowen did as he instructed, and the extra oxygen supplied by Aiyano kept her going.

A sound like a great tree felling cracked across the city, echoing into fragments between the streets. A blinding light burst through the clouds at an incredible speed, blasting them apart and shredding the remains into an inert cyclone. Through the hole in the clouds, a massive, black, many-winged beast emerged, its rider a mere speck shining with silver light. The pressure mounted, the power that the silver light commanded more terrifying and intoxicating than anything Eowen had ever known. She understood then why so many had followed her into the raging elements beyond the city, why some still trusted her. The Nagirr'Om was like the gods and demigods Hani had described, entities with power that commanded respect, inspired worship, and were credited with the creation of the world.

The Nagirr'Om wheeled around in the air and loosed five more arrows into the tree-person from which the Storm flowed, and a great screech erupted from it. The winds and clouds broke, scattered, and dispersed, no longer besieging the city. Eowen felt nothing save for the bamboo in her chest, as though in that moment she did not exist and was only an extension of the entity now flying towards her. She looked to Nolyi, whose anger was gone, replaced only by fear. She looked to Ordwell, who stared at The Nagirr'Om evenly, though the sweat soaking his neck betrayed his feelings. A mixed cheer and cry of terror went up across Nopt Shisoke as the great black beast soared over the city. It swooped in, directly towards the entrance where Aiyano, Nolyi, Ordwell, and Eowen waited. Eowen was in a trance where nothing but the silver light felt real, but when the claws of the beast, each as long as she was tall, locked onto the sandstone, she snapped out of it.

"Nagirr'Om!" Eowen shouted, pushing more blood out her throat. "Wh—" She stopped to cough. "Hani!"

The beast lowered one wing for The Nagirr'Om to dismount, and the being who fought the Storm set foot in front of them for Eowen to finally see in full. She was even more beautiful, strange, and terrifying than the image conjured at the bronze statue. She stood almost two heads above the tallest person Eowen had ever seen, her skin the Britchen's dark caramel but glowing silver and flawless. She was indeed pregnant, her belly swollen and breasts full, but she walked like the weight didn't exist, like she wasn't even touching the ground. Dark brown hair canopied around her, and her veiled face scanned the gathering. Even through the veil, Eowen could feel the gaze upon her as though The Nagirr'Om's eyes were spears as well, piercing Eowen's spirit and pinning it there. A silver bow hung from her hand, a silver hammer was in the other, and a silver knife was sheathed in her belt.

Like when Eowen had met other powerful dreamers, her aura of power flowed out and against the Nagirr'Om's. This time she wasn't alone though; Ordwell, Nolyi, and especially Aiyano's joined in. The five of them stayed in silence for a moment as shadows and light, saturated with more potential that Eowen had ever experienced, danced among them to the rhythms of their deepest selves. Eventually, a harmony was struck, despite Nolyi's resistance, as Ordwell's presence passed a sense of wordless understanding through the group.

The Nagirr'Om stepped forward, an inhumanly fast blur, and wrenched the bamboo from Eowen's chest. Eowen cried out in pain and relief as the power left her and Aiyano's healing finally closed the wound with a sucking sound. Eowen's blood arced overhead as the last of it shot out of her lungs, painting the ceiling of the landing bay. The Nagirr'Om pointed at Eowen and Nolyi, then spoke.

"You and you will come with me." The voice was similar to when Aiyano had spoken before, suffused with power, its meaning clear and memorable.

"Why?" Eowen asked.

"Never!" Nolyi shouted, and their power broke from the cohesion the five of them had found. "You took my sister!" Shadows and light crashed together with a violence Eowen had never known was possible. The burst of it sent a shockwave out and everyone near Aiynao, Nolyi, and The Nagirr'Om were sent flying. Eowen's fall was broken by one of Aiyano's students. Ordwell was helped up by another.

"Calm yourself, Nolyi. We have a greater purpose to serve here."

Nolyi screamed something in their own language and the world erupted; the sandstone crashed apart as massive bronze spikes, like teeth, plowed through air and stone at every angle to crush The Nagirr'Om. Without a move or gesture, the bronze spikes crumpled against some invisible barrier, not a single one reaching the veiled woman. Nolyi cried out, arming their hand with shadow and light, which blazed a pure expression of destruction and hate before becoming crimson flames. They lunged for The Nagirr'Om, but faster than any human movement, the silver bow was strung with the same bamboo that had pierced Eowen. The arrow loosed, the bamboo flashed, the flare of Nolyi's attack strobed, and a sound that no person has ever heard severed the barrier between sound and soul, like nails on a chalkboard if the nails were an earthquake and if the chalkboard were the sky.

Aiyano stood between the two demigods, one hand holding the shining arrow, the other holding Nolyi's wrist. The healer dropped the arrow, let go of Nolyi's hand, and all the power, the tension, the danger in the moment melted away. Aiyano faded, returned to herself, and swayed into Nolyi's arms. They held each other as Nolyi collapsed and pushed their sobs into Aiyano's shoulder.

"Shhh, my love." Aiyano sounded tired, her voice was ragged. "Nagirr'Om, is Nolyi's sister alive?"

The veiled woman lowered her bow and watched the scene in a detached, clinical way. It shook its head. **"She perished with many others."** Nolyi cried harder, their body twisting against Aiyano's in grief. Eowen's heart swelled as she watched Nolyi, the image of her mother playing in her mind, twisting at the knot in her heart. Aiyano continued comforting her spouse while glaring at The Nagirr'Om.

"Why then would we go with you only to become another sacrifice in your hopeless war?"

"To finish my and your sister's work, which was impossible until the boy and the girl arrived."

All eyes turned to Eowen. It was no mystery who the boy and girl were.

Until we arrived? Why would we be able to help? Why did The Nagirr'Om say I had to come with? Surely Hani, Nolyi, and Aiyano are the only ones powerful enough to fight beside her.

"You manipulated her!" Nolyi's shout was muffled by Aiyano's shoulder. "You controlled her and dragged her to her death!" For the first time, The Nagirr'Om relinquished some of her inhuman beauty. Her skin's silver glow faded, her shoulders drooped and she placed both hands under her belly, her weight no longer supernaturally supported.

"She fought valiantly, Nolyi, and died a hero. Without her and all the others that came with me, Nopt Shisoke would have already fallen. Now, it can finally be saved. The missing elements are here." The Nagirr'Om looked directly at Eowen, who squirmed under that veiled gaze. The silver glow brightened back up, and The Nagirr'Om again stood as though their feet touched the ground by choice alone. **"We must leave now, before it is too late. Decide, Eowen and Nolyi, if you will fight with me now to subdue the Storm of Nopt Shisoke, or if it will one day consume you."**

The Nagirr'Om stared at Nolyi, who stood, glared, ground their teeth, but nodded. Then The Nagirr'Om turned to Eowen, who was on the ground, eyes wide like prey before death, and shaking her head.

"I can't! I can't help you! The Storm will take me. You have to get back out there, Hani needs your help." Eowen looked around in a panic, seeking sympathetic eyes that would back her up. Aiyano was exhausted and barely awake in Nolyi's arms. Nolyi glared between Eowen and The Nagirr'Om, who watched Eowen impassively. Aiyano's students watched with bated breath. "I-I can't!" Eowen whimpered.

Ordwell reached down and took Eowen's hand. He lifted her to her feet, and with an arm around her shoulder, walked the shaking, stumbling girl to The Nagirr'Om.

"Your friend needs saving, Eowen. There's no time to waste, now is there?" Ordwell said softly to her. Eowen looked into his eyes, calm seas of understanding. "Go on. Don't lose anyone else."

Still shaking and stumbling, Eowen left Ordwell's arms

and approached the great black beast. Nolyi had already climbed on, a look of disgust on their face. The Nagirr'Om did the same, moving with that impossible grace, and took her seat straddling the beast's neck. Eowen approached last, crawling up on her hands and knees before Nolyi pulled her up and helped her get settled. Every fiber of Eowen's being screamed to run from the beast and its terrifying master, to hide deep in Aiyano's tower and never leave. She tried to convince herself that Hani would be fine, that anyone else would be a better choice to bring into the Storm.

"Don't worry," Nolyi whispered in her ear. "I won't let anything happen to you."

Eowen didn't respond, clenching her teeth and grabbing fistfuls of black hair as the six massive black wings stretched out, flexed, and pushed down, crushing the air beneath them and pinning the people behind The Nagirr'Om against its back. Within seconds after the beast's launch they were across the city, hurtling towards the Storm. Eowen was terrified of the heights and the danger ahead and the monstrous woman that had convinced her to face both. But Hani was lost in the chaos before her, and if Eowen was needed to save him she would dive into such terrors.

He's the best friend I've ever made. I can't lose him now!

They passed through the barrier and immediately Eowen could feel the Storm entity seeking a new foothold in her spirit. Shadows and light followed her, begging to be manifested into chaos. Eowen's mind turned against her as the entity that was the Storm whispered of the things she could create, the wonders she could bring into the new world. Endless jungles, revived loved ones, towers like Aiyano's to her glory, only greater. The clouds parted for the black beast, and Eowen felt the protection of The Nagirr'Om.

Behind her. Nolyi pulled Eowen closer and shouted in her ear above the howling winds.

"This is what it was like before the barrier! It was like this all the time, only it's stronger now!"

The elements seemed to hear them and it twisted with rain and cloud and lightning into great maws that tried to crush them. The Nagirr'Om was vigilant though, and the bamboo she'd pulled from Eowen's chest warded the Storm away, shining as a blinding silver beacon when she raised it up. The Nagirr'Om's mount was faster than anything Eowen had ever experienced, its body rolling like ocean waves as its six wings pulsed through their rhythm. Eowen had her face pressed to the creature's fur, terrified to see how high they were or how fast they were really going. Nolyi, who held Eowen tight and had no such discomfort, pulled at Eowen's middle, trying to get the girl upright. Nolyi said something in the Britchen language, but without one of Ordwell's translators present Eowen couldn't understand.

"What? Are we almost there?" Eowen asked in the mountain folk language through clenched teeth.

"No, but you must see what I see," Nolyi responded in the mountain folk's language. Eowen shook her head but Nolyi pulled at her insistently.

"Fine!" Eowen said, and took some quick breaths that pulled dark, musky fur into her mouth. She leaned back to spit it out and Nolyi pulled her fully upright. She went ridgid with terror as a Storm maw with lightning teeth and icy eyes rushed them, only to be obliterated by The Nagirr'Om firing the bamboo spear that had been in Eowen through it. They were surrounded by the Storm on all sides, clouds boiling, cyclones raging, wind, rain, ice, snow, and lightning. Eowen looked over the side of their mount and saw the trees from which the Storm was emerging. There were hundreds of them, few as large as the one that had been at the border of Nopt Shisoke, but all seemed to have once been people. Their legs had been fused, their arms turned into branches, and from the branches streamed clouds that surged into the violence around them. "Why are they all trees?" Eowen asked, but no one answered.

There was constant noise around them, screeching wind and vast, borborygmus thunder. Without the silver bamboo in her hand, The Nagirr'Om could no longer ride straight through the attacks and had to maneuver around and through them. She gave no warning and Eowen was whipped to the side, almost losing her grip on the fur before Nolyi pressed them both flat to the beast's back. The creature tucked, rolled, dipped, swooped, and dove at speeds that almost caused Eowen to vomit on herself and Nolyi.

After less than a minute of these maneuvers the flight was over. The Nagirr'Om's mount swooped and glided just above the starfield, then flung all six wings open, slowing to an abrupt stop. Their halt had brought them through another barrier, like the one which protected Nopt Shisoke. The beast landed, extended a wing to let its passengers off, and The Nagirr'Om all but floated down, as light and powerful as before. She filled the space around her with the kind of pressure and power Eowen had felt before, their aura suffusing the place.

"Come on girl," Nolyi said in the mountain folk language as they pulled Eowen to her feet.

"I don't feel well," Eowen moaned. Nolyi was keeping Eowen up with one arm wrapped around her as the girl stumbled down the wing. The world was dancing around her dizzily and it was difficult to focus on any one thing. The barrier was not fully closed on all sides. They had entered from one side that was secure, but Eowen could feel the presence of the Storm leaking in from straight ahead.

As Eowen's vision and stomach settled, she managed to take in the people gathered around them, or rather, around The Nagirr'Om. She saw the acolytes of the woman who fought the Storm firing arrow after arrow into a terrible form ahead of them. Here, the Storm was not like the one that had besieged Nopt Shisoke, nor like what they'd flown through to get there. It was an otherworldly, entropic presence for which Eowen had little comparison. Higher, wider, more awesome and grand than Eowen had ever known possible, the roiling clouds coiled and layered upon themselves. They were green and black, gray and blue, a twisting nest of monstrous heads that whipped out and slammed into the starfield, opening great serpentine maws to spew lighting, fire, cyclones, ice, water, or gritty black ash and dust. Eowen tried to count the heads but lost track after twenty. The writhing form of the Storm seemed an endlessly collapsing and reforming hydra of elements. Eowen had felt that The Nagirr'Om was the most powerful being in the new world and represented the apex of what a dreamer could achieve, but now she knew how horribly wrong she had been.

"This is worse than I ever imagined," Nolyi whispered in their own language.

The Nagirr'Om strode past them towards her acolytes, a line of small figures in the distance that Eowen could see moving back and forth. Nolyi followed the glowing woman, pulling a stumbling Eowen along. When they got close enough, Eowen could see who, exactly, made up the acolytes of The Nagirr'Om. She'd expected grand heroes with rippling muscles and scarred faces, but they were an eclectic collection of largely average folk, mostly Britchen, and presumably all citizens of Nopt Shisoke. They wore white robes, and were of many ages and genders, from a child younger than Eowen who looked to be of her tribe, to a middle aged woman with bone-white skin and red hair, to an old Britchen man. All of them bore one of The Nagirr'Om's weapons, but none carried two, let alone three. Those with the hammer had silver embroidery on their robes depicting a medium length line with a square at one end. Similarly, those with the bow had the long curved line, and those with the knife had the short straight line. Aside from the white robes, the only thing they all had in common was the white veils they all wore and their clear reverence for the glowing woman standing before them. The veil of The Nagirr'Om depicted all three embroidered lines, the symbols of those who fought the Storm. There were not nearly a hundred acolytes that Eowen had been told about, perhaps only forty.

Eowen and Nolyi waited to the side as The Nagirr'Om addressed her followers. The silver woman shouted over the Storm, commanding her troops as they sprouted bamboo by hitting their hammers on the ground, cutting it into arrows with their knives, and firing the stalks with their bows. Eowen fully disengaged herself from Nolyi's support and took a seat on the starfield. Nolyi's dreaming aura of light and shadow felt eager to spring into action as it folded and twisted all around them in dense, dangerous implications.

What, exactly, does The Nagirr'Om expect us to do? I can't fight, I can barely protect myself. And where is Hani? What's the plan here, there should be a plan.

She got her answer soon. **"Nolyi, Eowen! To the front!"** The Nagirr'Om's voice reverberated through the bones of all in earshot, nailing itself directly into their skulls.

Nolyi pulled Eowen up and ran to the chaos at the front of the fray. Acolytes sprouted bamboo to create barriers, but the Storm was too strong here, pressing against silver plants and ripping them up. Archers fired into it, but their arrows rarely did serious damage. This close, Eowen could see the true source of the Storm: a massive tree, easily three times taller than Aiyano's tower and pouring out filthy, violent clouds into the mass they fought. The tree was a gnarled and twisted humanoid shape like the others. Many of the elements which poured from its branches were not assaulting the archers, but instead were linked with the many smaller trees around it as if taking root and growing like a banyan grove.

"**Now is the time. You must do what I have brought you to do!**" The Nagirr'Om shouted above the din, loosing five bamboo arrows in quick succession.

"You said you'd bring me to my sister! Where is she?" Nolyi said in Britchen. Eowen did not understand what Noyli said next to The Nagirr'Om, but from the latter's responses she put the conversation together.

"**I will bring you to her body when the Storm is quelled! You will fight now!**" The Nagirr'Om growled, its voice inhuman. Nolyi didn't move, their aura of dreaming crackling into shards of light and dark and twisting glass-edged arcs of power that burned and severed the air around them. Eowen feared another fight would ensue amidst the chaos without Aiyano to stop it. She pulled on Nolyi's sleeve but let go when a flare of power burned like fire through Eowen's hand.

"Where is she!" Nolyi screamed.

The silver glowing woman paused with an arrow knocked on her bow, looked at Nolyi through the veil, then, for the first time, lost her balance as a massive serpentine head crashed through the barrier, scattering acolytes. The army battled it back, every weapon clashing against the beast, but just before they could push the head away and reestablish the barrier, it caught an acolyte in its jaws. The poor man, an archer, did not scream long as the teeth of ice crushed his chest and his fragmented corpse was flung into the air, landing somewhere near the massive tree. The Nagirr'Om's power flared as never before, now a shining silver beacon that seemed to grow taller and more pulchritudinous. The Nagirr'Om, more god than woman in that moment, slammed their hammer down, sprouting the largest bamboo stalk Eowen had yet seen. They slashed with their knife, cutting it perfectly, and caught it on their bow string before it could fall to the ground. The Nagirr'Om bent their bow into a harsh arc, brought the string past their cheek, and there was a moment when The Nagirr'Om held their breath that even the Storm was silent.

Then the arrow flew, a gasp off the string, a comet that clove the winds aside, and met the Storm beasts with a rending shock that felt more violent than the end of the world had. The light faded, the power waned, and The Nagirr'Om collapsed onto its side, the silver glow of its skin all but gone.

Eowen rushed to its side, checking for injury. Eowen had tended to pregnant women before, but none like this. She manifested pillows, blankets, water and cloth. "Nagirr'Om, can you hear me? Are you alright?"

Nolyi stood stone still, frozen between old hate, new fear, respect, and confusion. Eowen reached for the veil to check on the woman, but the Nagirr'Om caught her by the wrist the moment she touched it. A feeble version of its silver glow returned, barely present. It pointed to the battle, beyond her soldiers.

"She is there, Nolyi of the Britchen. Will you foolishly run in for a corpse? I have exhausted myself, and by the time my power returns my acolytes will have perished, as will Nopt Shisoke." Nolyi faced the Storm, but all the bravado that they'd faced The Nagirr'Om with was gone.

"We can't defeat that!" Nolyi shouted.

"How did you think you would retrieve your sister without defeating the Storm?"

"I wasn't going to fight it for you at all! I was going to get her body, take her home, and ignore your foolish crusade!" Nolyi was twisting in on themself. Their dreaming aura no longer spoke of power, only flight.

"Know this once and for all: You can join me against it, or wait for it to do its work and bring the ruin of all." With that ultimatum, the silver glow left the veiled woman completely and it collapsed onto the pillows.

"Wait," Eowen said. "You haven't told me where Hani is!" Eowen shook the Nagirr'Om but received no response. "You were supposed to take me to him! Wake up!" Eowen was speaking in her own language, but Nolyi heard and understood Hani's name. They pulled Eowen to her feet and pointed to the battle, then spoke in the mountain folk's language.

"There, wearing my helmet!" At the front of the fray, battling with silver bamboo spears in his hands, was the boy. Spears of lighting, twisting cyclones, and elemental teeth closed in on him. In the space between two beats of her heart, Eowen's mind capsized into the ocean of her subconscious.

****

[Listen, for you cannot hear me yet]

I TOLD THEM I AM A GIANT.

****

Eowen's aura of power rose, whipped up, and manifested curls of drum music, cats made of fire, ice that glowed golden, and a hundred other impossibilities. But most of all, Eowen manifested the jungle. She streaked forward on a wave of creation that plowed aside acolytes and Storm alike till she was next to Hani. She emerged from the sudden trance and embraced the island boy, still resplendent with power.

"Eowen? What are you doing here?" Hani pulled back to look at her, and Eowen glared at him through tears.

"Don't you dare ask that! You foolish, reckless fool!" The Storm was worming into Eowen's subconsciously, whipping her own power into its service, but Eowen didn't care. "We're supposed to be a team, and you left me behind!" Hani's expression was twisted with guilt, but on all sides they were still beset.

"Later, we've got to stop this now!" Hani shouted. Eowen's response to this was to push Hani to the ground, grab him by the collar and shout in his face.

"Don't you get it? I can't do this without you! I can't find Tavo, or travel to foreign cultures, or even manifest properly without you!" Now Hani was paying attention.

"No, you—"

"And you can't do it without me, either!" Three great heads of the Storm pointed themselves at the two fighting children. They coiled their necks like snakes ready to strike, and flashed forward, each mouth opening like a glacial chasm with teeth larger than a grown man. Arrows struck them but were not strong enough to divert the attack. Hani noticed too late, Eowen didn't see them at all, and before either could respond, a maw snapped down on them.

It had only closed over them a fraction of a second when a spear-length bamboo stalk, shining silver and burning with crimson fire, blasted the serpentine head apart.

"Get up!" Nolyi roared, hauling Eowen to her feet by her collar. Nolyi burned with red flames fed by shadow and light, and wore a new set of leather and bronze armor. They put a hand to Eowen's head and a helmet like Hani's manifested around it, immediately cutting off the Storm from Eowen. "That monster—" Nolyi pointed to The Nagirr'Om, "—isn't the only one that can resist the Storm!" Nolyi's eyes glowed orange-red and they fixed a grim look upon Eowen and Hani. They spoke in the mountain folk's language. "Are you going to squabble like children or are we going to destroy this thing?"

Hani jumped up immediately, pulling a bamboo spear from the starfield to use as a weapon. He struck left and right, enthusiastic but unskilled. The boy had clearly never done more than play-fight, but the helmet and the spear he'd pulled up were acting as a barrier for the moment. Eowen stood in a gap in the barrier and manifested layer upon layer of barriers she could only hope would resist the forces. Nolyi leapt and rolled, striking with their crimson-fire staff. Nolyi did not move so much like a warrior as they did a performer, their acrobatics effective enough to fight with. The massive tree, wreathed in the Storm, sent lashes of elemental violence at Nolyi but they were untouchable, sliding belly flat under or vaulting over heads and through gnashing teeth.

Nolyi and Hani were making their way steadily toward the tree with the acolytes planting new barriers to keep their progress up. The Britchen acrobat, vested in the bright red flames, slammed their staff into a former person turned tree-slave to the Storm. The dry timber flashed a fountain of detritus and cinders that looked to Eowen in the moment like a flare of victory. For a moment, Eowen believed they would make it, that she hadn't really been needed to defeat the Storm. When the soot cleared though, Nolyi stood still, staring ahead at something on the starfield. Eowen saw a body clad in a robe of The Nagirr'Om's acolytes. There were acolyte bodies strewn all over, but this one had stopped Nolyi short.

No!

"Nolyi, move!" Eowen screamed, but the winds batted her voice aside as the Storm surged past her. Eowen dipped back into her dreaming mind, trying to focus only on her barrier to protect as many as she could. Hani heard Eowen's warning, saw Nolyi, and the Storm readying to spring upon them.

"That idiot!" Hani charged forward, bulling through an avalanche of clouds to reach Nolyi. Eowen saw him shout something but couldn't hear it over the wind burning her ears. Hani grabbed onto Nolyi's shoulder, shaking them, but the acrobat hardly seemed to notice. The island boy closed his eyes and his manifestation surged, establishing a barrier around them that repelled the Storm. Nolyi finally came back to their senses and flinched back as Hani put his hand into the flames on their staff. Eowen's barrier broke when she saw

Hani's hand enveloped in the flames, blisters bubbling on his skin. She could not hear his roar of pain, but his mouth was wide open and he shook. Nolyi forced him off their staff and shouted at the boy who'd fallen to his knees. Sweat poured down his brow, but as he staggered to his feet the same crimson fire that Nolyi used to fight the Storm burned on the surface of the barrier around them. Hani grit his teeth, his expression twisted into a smile.

Shadows thickened, blotting out even the Storm around Hani and Nolyi, as starlight below shot up in massive geysers that blinded Eowen. The dense powers all coalesced on the young island boy. Amidst the surge, Eowen saw Hani lift his ruined hand above his head, two fingers fused together grotesquely. Upon his palm a ball of fire spawned, dense with the compressed material of manifestation. He closed his eyes, tilted his head back, and the burning sphere rose up, growing in magnitude and intensity till all had to shield their eyes. It was like the sun Eowen had manifested above her oasis, only built of Nolyi's flame. It grew to an enormous size, shedding a light and heat that made Eowen sweat and which the Storm could not encroach on. Nolyi gazed in awe along with the archers until, with another surge, Hani swept his upraised hand toward the tree, sending the great flame bowling forward. The Storm beasts coiled in front of the gnarled trunk, catching the flames even as they disintegrated. The fireball eroded the defenses, sending shredded wisps of elemental detritus flying out for kilometers, stinging the watchers' nostrils with the smell of burning air. The Storm surged against it, Hani pushed, Eowen and the acolytes cheered, and the fireball touched the bark of the tree, sending thick, black smoke streaming out. It was taking too long though, and while the others cheered, Eowen's triumphant smile fell.

He can't maintain his manifestations!

Eowen got up from the gap in the barrier she'd been maintaining and sprinted forward. The fireball shimmered like a heat-illusion. Hani fell to one knee, his teeth grit. Nolyi had knelt next to their sister and was cradling the corpse which, as Eowen approached, she could see had lost most of the left half of its body. Eowen reached forward with her dreaming aura, trying to synchronize with Hani's, trying to help him maintain the attack that would end things, but she was too late. The flames died like coals with sand shoveled upon them. The sudden change in pressure made Eowen's ears pop, and Hani collapsed face-first on the starfield. Eowen scooped up his body and established a barrier just as the onslaught of the Storm raged down upon them again.

A maw of unrelenting violence closed over her meager defense. Teeth of ice and ash and fire and lightning knifed into her powers. Despite the helmet, the pressure from the Storm both within and without was immense. The acolytes of The Nagirr'Om rushed in to aid the three, the focus of the Storm having been diverted by Hani's assault. Hammer's slammed, bamboo was cut, and arrows flew from bows to bolster Eowen's barrier. Eowen hugged Hani closer and redoubled her efforts, dipping deep into her dreaming to keep the barrier up with the acolytes' help, but the beast had its teeth on the throat of her spirit. Behind her, Nolyi sobbed over the body of their sister, the fight having left them. Eowen could feel the grief like dust upon her skin. It felt like when she'd prepared the body of the lone mountain folk she and Hani had found, like when she, Hani, and Genia had manifested the sacred beasts. It felt like the knot in her heart when she looked upon the body of her mother and could not cry.

Eowen set Hani aside, made her way next to Nolyi, and all around her shadows and light danced. The power thickened into the outline of a silhouetted shape, a frottage of manifested subconscious that exposed feathered wings, stick legs, and a spear of a beak. Hani opened his eyes and recognized the shape, but to Nolyi it was utterly new, and their weeping paused as the young woman from the jungle and savannah approached, dense with this strange power. Eowen's eyes were vacant and she remained only vaguely aware as a presence emerged within her. It wasn't the Storm, but something else. It resembled the silver glow of The Nagirr'Om, or the forces Aiyano had poured into Eowen's body even on the brink of death. Eowen knelt next to Nolyi and held out her arms. Nolyi glanced between the two girls, one her deceased sister and the other the stranger one they'd only just met. Nolyi looked into Eowen's eyes, and the girl's vacant expression solidified into a present one, soft and teary.

"You want me to give her to you?" Nolyi whispered. The Storm was still raging against Eowen's barrier but was rendered silent, banned from interrupting the moment. "I can't! I can't lose her again."

Eowen could feel the knot in Nolyi's heart, so like and so unlike her own. It could be undone though. Eowen knew it could. She only needed to figure out how. She looked at the sister of Nolyi, a girl that couldn't have been much older than herself. The half of her body that was missing spilled viscera and gore, sticking to Nolyi's arms and clothes, though most of the blood had long since dried. Eowen could see what the girl had once looked like, or an approximation. Gentle, leisurely shadows moved in like a viscous oil, dripping from above onto the body's ruined parts. Light, soft as feather-falls, settled onto the formless clay of the shadows. Nolyi started, jerking the body away so that it was pressed against their chest, but the manifestation did not stop.

"What are you doing?" they asked, but the answer came soon enough. Within moments their sister was physically whole again, the damage undone in an act of creation. "Cynna?" Nolyi whispered their sister's name in disbelief. They checked the body over, shook it gently. "She's still... d—" Nolyi choked on the word.

"I can't bring back the dead, Nolyi. I don't think anyone could, not even Aiyano." Eowen whispered, and her voice seemed to echo, seemed to come from far away and vibrate from the bones within her body rather than the chords in her throat. **"I can hold her though, until you've done what you must."**

Nolyi shook their head with their eyes closed, they rocked the body and pressed their face against its face. They wiped their tears on their shoulder and stared into Eowen's eyes, their expression morphing between a glare and a plea.

"You will?"

Eowen gave them a measured nod.

"Ok."

Nolyi unfurled their arms and passed the body into Eowen's, who cradled it close. When the corpse passed through the silhouette of power around Eowen, something happened to it.

****

[Listen, for you cannot hear me yet]

LOVE SAID THAT THE CAVE HAD TAUGHT THEM THAT GIANTS ARE BEINGS GREATER THAN THOSE WHO CAN SEE THEM, AND THAT SINCE LOVE COULD NOT SEE ME, I WAS THEREFORE NOT A GIANT TO THEM.

****

The silhouette was no longer merely that, but a full form standing regally over Eowen. The bone heron raised its wings and there was a thick, utter silence, the silence of bated breath as a tomb is sealed. The bird was not a mere creature of creation like the eagle and wildcat that Eowen, Hani, and Genia had manifested for the mountain folk. It was a being greater than that, something transcendent. The creature's simple, animal movements refracted into impossible, divine grace as it stalked behind Eowen's back.

****

[Listen, for you cannot hear me yet]

I ASKED LOVE WHAT I WAS TO THEM.

****

Eowen looked upon the body that had once been Cynna, sister of Nolyi and acolyte of The Nagirr'Om, and the look in her eyes was that of a mother watching their sleeping child.

There could be no doubt in Nolyi's heart that they had entrusted Cynna to the right person. The bone heron brought its wings down, and a shockwave of power effortlessly pushed back the Storm in a wide radius around them.

****

[Listen, for you cannot hear me yet]

DO YOU KNOW WHAT LOVE SAID TO ME NEXT, TO ONE SUCH AS I, WHOSE PRESENCE HAS NEVER BEEN INSIGNIFICANT?

****

Nolyi knelt before Eowen and looked between the buffeted elements and the girl cradling her sister. They gritted their teeth, fixed a glare upon the tree that hatched the Storm, then looked back to their sister. They noticed something, and reached forward to lay a hand on the face that had once belonged to Cynna. It was the previously ruined side that Eowen had remade, and upon touching it, Nolyi frowned.

"She had a scar here since childhood," Nolyi said, caressing the non-existent path of it on Cynna's flawless cheek. Eowen had reconstructed the face well, but she hadn't truly known what it had looked like before. Nolyi did not resent her though, and Eowen knew this. Eowen took Nolyi's hand and there was a charge between them, a dense current of power that felt to Nolyi like it could do anything, create anything, destroy anything. Instead, it trickled out of the space between their touch and onto the face of the corpse in Eowen's arms. An old, faded scar that could have been from a fall or a fight or anything at all bloomed into the skin. Nolyi nodded. "That's better." They stood with their bamboo spear in hand, new flames crackling into being along its length. "Be right back," Nolyi whispered.

They took off, sparks flying from their bare feet, flames streaming from the gaps in their armor. The forces of the Storm were still trying in vain to crack the barrier around Eowen, but with the arrival of the heron Eowen's barrier became perfectly impenetrable. The Storm hardly noticed Nolyi streaking towards the tree that was its source. Nolyi got closer, a dozen meters away, then half that, then only a few strides, then, with a leap, they plunged the bamboo spear into the great tree.

The Storm paused, like a beast holding its breath, then the flames rushed out into the gnarled wood, racing through the wrinkled bark to the lowest roots and highest branches. The Storm roared, louder and harsher than ever, before crying out utter distress and pain in the throes of its demise. Nolyi's eardrums burst and blood trickled out, they clenched their teeth and a molar cracked. The elemental forces wheeled around to throw themselves at their assailant, but Nolyi could not be stopped. Their power coursed through the wood, rending the presence of the Storm from it and lighting up every dip and curve with harsh flames that glowed like coals. The tips of the branches, where leaves should have been and from which the Storm emerged, erupted into a black and crimson autumn of fire and smoke. The wind, rain, and thunderous lightning gave up, and were swept away on waves of heat that emanated from their erstwhile source. The roaring stopped, the clouds disappeared, and finally, there was peace.

Nolyi's hands unclenched and they fell from the tree onto its roots. The acolytes held their breath, but into their midst strode The Nagirr'Om, its silver light still faint but no longer totally gone.

"The Storm here is quelled at last. We are victorious." The Nagirr'Om's acolytes lifted their tools and a cheer went up. **"Still, it infects this world and will find new hosts to crawl in through. So we, my followers, will range out far and wide, bring more into our cause, and root the Storm out wherever it may emerge."**

Nolyi lay heaving on the ground, hearing the silver woman's voice in their mind in that strange way in which it bypassed sound. They glared, picked themself up, and curled their hands into fists. Hani had recovered enough to stand beside Eowen, and he eyed the bone heron with a combination of recognition and awe. Nolyi marched toward The Nagirr'Om, stumbled, but carried on, their fists becoming enveloped in more red flames. Eowen cradled Cynna's body close to her chest with one arm. She tried to stand but her limbs would not move. The power she'd been commanding was fading out. A voice came through her from somewhere else.

[Hani, help me. I must go to Nolyi and The Nagirr'Om.]

Hani felt the voice within his spirit and he nodded, hooked an arm around Eowen, and stood with her, forcing her limbs into moving. The bone heron followed behind, one long stride for three of Eowen and Hani's staggered ones.

Nolyi approached The Nagirr'Om, and The Nagirr'Om

turned to face them, drawing their silver knife. "**You are a fool, Nolyi. A useful tool, but a foolish one. Come, I am weaker than I have ever been, try for your revenge while you can.**" Nolyi roared a wordless battlecry and charged forward. The Nagirr'Om braced stock still with its knife pointed at Nolyi's chest.

Before more bloodshed could ensue, the bone heron swept down between them, flung its wings wide, and sent gusts against Nolyi and The Nagirr'Om. Hani and Eowen, still cradling the body of Nolyi's sister, stepped between them.

[Nolyi of the Britchen. I would enable your revenge should it serve your grief. But your blame of The Nagirr'Om will only wound your heart more.]

Eowen turned on The Nagirr'Om.

[You will not depart from here until you have gathered your fallen comrades and delivered them back to Nopt Shisoke to receive their rites. This will be so.]

The power that moved through Eowen, hammer and anvil to their wills, forged onto them an ordained obedience. None spoke up in opposition, and even the veiled face of the perfectly poised Nagirr'Om seemed subdued. Eowen looked between them, her eyes not her own, her spirit that of a greater being moving her, but it was not like how the Storm did. This was, from what Hani could sense, an expansion of Eowen, an overflowing of herself, the source of which he could not account for.

When Eowen seemed satisfied that her will would be done, she approached Nolyi. Eowen passed the body back over to its rightful mourner, and collapsed, the power gone but the ordinance remaining. Hani lifted her up and shook his head, an expression of awe on his face. He looked at Nolyi, who was staring at their sister's reformed face, something purer than grief, but not unlike it, pictured there.

"She's right, isn't she, Cynna? I need to get you home." Nolyi readjusted Cynna's body in their arms and flexed the hand with the ring on it that matched Aiyano's. They started walking in the direction of Nopt Shisoke, pointedly ignoring The Nagirr'Om as they passed. The Nagirr'Om called in their great beast and climbed aboard. The acolytes collected the bodies and deposited them on The Nagirr'Om's mount. It began to fly them back to Nopt Shisoke in several trips, and while it did that, Nolyi manifested a flying carpet so that they, Hani, and Eowen could ride it back together.

****

[Listen, for you cannot hear me yet]

THEY SAID IT DIDN'T MATTER WHAT I WAS TO OTHERS, BUT THAT THEY WOULD APPRECIATE HAVING MY NAME, AND THAT PERHAPS I COULD THEN BE THEIR FRIEND.

****

When Eowen opened her eyes, she was in a room she didn't know. It wasn't like those in Aiyano's tower, nor the sort she and Hani had made for themselves. Her head pounded and her limbs felt overly stiff, so she lay with her eyes closed for a long time.

Eowen tried to recall the details, but they were fading fast, as if parts of it had all been a dream. She remembered the fight, The Nagirr'Om, and the discovery of Nolyi's dead sister; the image of the young woman's destroyed body was easy to recall. Towards the end of the conflict her memories thinned more and more, like rubbed out charcoal.

Then I took the body from Nolyi and...

This was where Eowen's memories became fuzziest. She knew that at some point she had taken the body of the girl, then handed it back to Nolyi. It had been as though her body were controlled by strings, and as soon as she'd been entrusted with Nolyi's sister the strings had pulled and her mind had been pushed out.

"We beat it, though. The Storm is gone," Eowen whispered, and this made her smile. The bone heron settled down next to her and nipped at her hair.

There was a fraction of a second where Eowen didn't question what the huge bird was doing next to her. In the next fraction, she yelped and scrambled away from it, joints popping and head throbbing. The bird was nonplussed and proceeded to fold up and sleep.

"What are you doing here?" Eowen rubbed her eyes and blinked, but the bird was still there. "Did I manifest you?" The heron did not answer.

Eowen's heart rate slowed and she took stock of her surroundings. She was in a massive, round, wooden room, four times as wide as she was tall, its wooden walls soaring upwards. She had been in a round bed on the floor piled with animal skins and blankets. There was a stone bath taking up most of one corner and shelves along the walls. Next to the bed was a silver spear of bamboo, glowing faintly. It was the first familiar thing in the room, so Eowen moved to it for comfort. She reached out to pick it up, but when her hand touched it a harsh, burning ache shot through her chest that sent her to her knees.

"It's the one that was shot into me. But I remember The Nagirr'Om shooting it." The name of The Nagirr'Om still carried the thrum of its power, but it felt lesser to Eowen. She gritted her teeth, touched it again, and the pain acclimated, fading into a reminder of the power that had pierced her and the power that had kept her alive despite it.

Eowen used the spear as a walking stick and lifted herself up, looking around the room for a way out. Eowen located the door behind her and, glancing at the heron as she approached it, made to slip out. However, as soon as her hand touched the door handle a rush of wind accompanied by the sound of wings passed over her. She didn't need to look back to know the heron was standing over her.

"What do you want?" Eowen didn't look at the heron. She was remembering the other creatures she'd accidentally manifested, the ring of death around her oasis from their mad and confused dash. "I'm sorry for making you. I know it must be confusing, but please don't hold it against me."

She knew that in the old world, bone herons had been bringers and purifiers of death. *But I am not afraid of death,* Eowen thought, and knew in her spirit that it was true.

Eowen turned and faced the heron, expecting something to happen, but nothing did. It was like a normal creature of the previous world, perhaps more beautiful and graceful, but there was no obviously strange quality to it like there was in the eagle and wildcat she'd manifested. It smelled of the jungle and the sea, for that is where they flew to find mates and nest. Its feathers were resplendent; glossy blacks, grays, blues, and whites layered in waves. Its beak was a bright orange spear, and Eowen found she wanted to touch it. She reached out, shy and careful, to lay her hand on the beak, and the bone heron held its head still, only shifting a wing and its feet in response. Eowen smiled and ran her hand up and down the beak, eventually moving to the creature's neck.

"Your feathers are so soft. I never knew bone heron feathers were so soft. No one ever got close enough to you in the old world for that." Eowen thought about her statement and frowned. *Were they this soft in the old world? There's really no way to know. After all, this is only how I dreamt a bone heron to be, I've never touched one. I don't know any more how one should be than I did snow.* Eowen found it hard to be bothered by a lack of inaccuracy. The creature was beautiful and endearing, and when it butted its head against her chest she laughed and stroked its feathers more.

The door behind her opened and someone bumped into her. "Oh! You're awake!" Aiyano hugged Eowen from behind and lifted the girl off the ground. "I'm so glad you're alright! In the old world we might have thought you would never wake up." Aiyano looked behind Eowen. "Ah, the bird. Still with you, then."

"Woah, hello," Eowen said after the healer put her down. "Where am I exactly?" Eowen gestured around the room then locked eyes with Aiyano. "And where's Hani?" Her voice had a warning in it.

"Don't worry, I actually do know where he is at the moment. Eowen, I heard what happened. If you hadn't been there, my Nolyi wouldn't have come back." Aiyano beamed at Eowen. "Come, let's reunite you with your friend, follow me." Aiyano waved over her shoulder and left the room.

Eowen looked at the heron, which offered no opinion. It did take the silver bamboo spear from her hand and tucked it away under a wing, where it disappeared.

"Alright, you can have that if you want," Eowen said, then she went to follow Aiyano through curving, wooden hallways, the bird on her heels.

"Is that thing going to follow you everywhere?" Aiyano asked, and Eowen looked back at it, stalking along half a meter taller than her.

"Yes." Eowen was surprised at how confident she was in her answer, but somehow she knew it to be true. "How long was I asleep?" Eowen asked.

"A week," Aiyano responded, and Eowen stopped following, stuck with surprise. She looked at the heron, which looked back, then rushed after Aiyano.

"A week?!"

Around a corner they approached a massive archway through which light filtered in. When they passed through, Eowen finally saw that she was standing a great height above the starfield on a porch that wrapped around some wooden, naturally curving tower. It took her a second of looking around to realize she was inside the great and gnarled tree from which the Storm had once emerged. They stood on a platform wide enough for five men to walk abreast that encircled the tree and seemed to have been grown out of it. The burned cracks in the tree from Nolyi's attack had been filled in by bronze veins that hummed with Ordwell's power, translating Aiyano and Eowen's words.

"I guess... a lot can happen in a week," Eowen muttered.

"And a lot more is going to happen! We decided to turn the tree into the center of our new city," Aiyano said, sweeping her hand across the thousands of people who moved like ants across the starfield below. Eowen could already see that the new city would be less cramped and more glorious than before, built of rich dark woods and sparkling marble. The dull sandstone and utilitarian stacking of buildings was a thing of the past, born of their need to huddle together in the barrier that protected them from the storm. Aiyano gazed over the foundations of her city with such pride that she seemed to be glowing. "The sandstone was familiar and easiest to manifest, so that's what most people built with before. But the palaces of the old world were made of many rich and beautiful materials, and once the Storm was gone, people's spirits lifted and their dreams opened up. We've been weighed down by fear of it for as long as we've known this new world that I don't think we realized how much the layers of ourselves were repressed. But, Eowen, look at them now, my people."

And Eowen did, for without the oppression of the Storm the people of Nopt Shisoke were absolutely thriving. The city sprawled for dozens of kilometers, featured beautiful architecture she hadn't known was possible even in the old world, foliage of the kind that must have been common before the fall, and thousands of people relishing their freedom. Manifested buildings soared up with glazed mosaics in colors that Eowen hadn't known were possible to make in the styles of more diverse cultures than Eowen had known existed, just as Hani had promised. Games were being played by huge teams, parties were being thrown with food, decorations, songs, and dances. There was an especially large crowd to the northwest of the great tree.

"That's where Hani is," Aiyano said, following Eowen's eyes. "Shall we go?"

Aiyano unrolled a carpet like Nolyi's that was strapped to

the wall and floated up on it. She offered Eowen her hand, but the bone heron stepped between them and gave Eowen a piercing, animal look. There was a moment where Eowen and Aiyano looked at each other, wondering what the creature wanted. Then, it bowed low, genuflecting before its master and spreading its wings wide.

"Uh, I think my... bird wants to take me," Eowen said.

"I suppose so," Aiyano said politely. "Can it... Can it carry you?"

Eowen looked at the bird, large but hardly strong enough, in the old world, to fly with more than the weight of a small child. She felt something from the bird, a sourceless yet apodictic confidence. Eowen stepped onto the heron's back, grasping its neck to keep her balance, and to her amazement and satisfaction, the creature held. She took a seat, cross-legged, and wrapped both hands around the heron's neck. It was completely unperturbed by her presence, and as it straightened, Eowen felt a weightless strength like the one she'd seen from The Nagirr'Om. Aiyano shrugged and nodded, impressed. Then she directed her carpet and it rose up and over the railing, sailing out to Hani's crowd. Eowen expected her heron to immediately follow, but instead it waited patiently.

"Can... we follow her?" Eowen whispered to it. The bird opened its wings fully, and with one powerful yet leisurely flap carried Eowen up and over the railing to follow Aiyano. Eowen's stomach turned and she gritted her teeth as the world rushed beneath her, the only thing keeping her from plummeting to it being the feathered body she sat on. Eowen gripped the neck hard enough that if it were a real heron she might have crushed its windpipe, but the creature was unaffected. "S-sorry," Eowen said just to be safe as she tried to relax her tense fingers.

They swooped over the city and reached the crowd, which cheered as they flew overhead. Soon, Eowen saw why the crowd was gathered; Hani had a new ship, and it was a truly grand thing. Towering two stories high and three times as long with a mast and sails, just as the boy had said he'd wanted. This time, however, the ship didn't float on water but in the starfield itself, partially submerged in the sky beneath them. Hani was on the prow, shouting and gesticulating, pretending to fight as he danced about. From what Eowen could hear over the crowd he was recounting the battle with the Storm. When he spotted Eowen and Aiyano he shouted and pointed, whipping his audience into deafening cheers. Eowen didn't dare let go of the heron's neck to acknowledge them, grinning awkwardly even as she dipped her head to avoid all the attention. She and Aiyano landed on the ship and Eowen got off her mount with shaky legs.

"You're finally awake!" Hani rushed in to hug her, sweeping Eowen into a spinning embrace.

"Yes! Yes, I'm a-awake, and you made a new ship, and everyone is here and, and..." A pressure in Eowen's stomach she hadn't noticed gave way and she buried her face in Hani's shoulder, too relieved to care about the many eyes on her. "...And you're alive! You're ok, everyone's ok!" She wept joy and the island boy laughed, a tension uncoiling from him as well.

"That's right. Everyone is alive and well." Of course, not everyone was. Many had died suppressing the Storm, Eowen and Hani had seen some of them, but his meaning was understood: 'we are still alive, the majority of Nopt Shisoke is still alive, we faced terrors and they were not the end of us.'

Aiyano smiled at the children, letting them have their moment, before she turned to the crowd and flew over them on her carpet.

"Off now, you've been hearing this story all week, you all know it by now," Aiyano said.

"I haven't heard it yet!" a man called.

"You will later, off with you!" Aiyano shooed the crowd and they gradually trickled back to their friends and family for more celebrations, re-buildings, or simply to be content in their safety and prosperity. Hani pulled back from Eowen and led her toward a staircase that went into the depths of the ship.

"You'll never believe this either!" Hani said, disappearing below.

"What?" Eowen lagged behind, giving Aiynao a look. The woman smiled warmly, gestured for Eowen to be off, then glided away.

"I found where my dad went next!" Hani's voice echoed up.

"That's amazing!" Eowen's heart soared, she followed with a skip in her step. *Hani's quest to find his father is bearing fruit, and that might mean...* She didn't quite dare to think that she too would find Tavo, but the hope was still there, a little glowing ember inside her. Then, Hani said this:

"And I found where your cousin Tavo went." Eowen tripped on her way down the stairs, tumbling onto Hani's feet. Her heart beat painfully. Hani was speaking but she couldn't hear him.

"W-what?" Eowen took his offered hand and gasped for breath, trying to still her heart. Her hearing returned in time to hear Hani explain.

"—found where he's gone. It's definitely him, Tavo of the

far western cluster of the jungle and savannah tribes. Grew up in a savannah village, just like you. He stayed with some of your tribe living here before the fall. Are you alright, do you need a moment?"

"Keep talking!" Hani was taken aback by her aggression, but did as she asked.

"He left before the Storm got so bad and headed northwest. Well, now it's northwest, he left before the compass directions appeared in the world. But he was heading towards where other Britchen settlements should be. Which would still have mostly been northwest in the old world." Hani led Eowen to a common room in the ship's hull and sat them down at a table. He manifested some of his awful tea for them to drink and Eowen downed hers without tasting it. "Eowen, what's wrong? I thought you'd be happy about this."

Eowen gritted her teeth and forced, as best she could, an expression of gratitude. She looked constipated. "I just didn't... Uh—"

I didn't believe he was really alive, didn't believe I'd ever make any progress, didn't think you'd be the one to find a clue first, didn't... want to believe too much, only to be disappointed. I had hope, but I didn't have faith.

Eowen couldn't say any of this, couldn't get out another word, too much had changed in too short a time, but Hani seemed to understand. While Eowen stuttered through her feelings, poorly converting them, Hani nodded, smiled, frowned, chuckled, and held her shaking hands.

They sat like this for minutes, which stretched into an hour. Eowen told Hani more about Tavo, how his parents had died of a lung disease and her parents had taken him in, sick from the same. How she and Tavo had been inseparable since the moment he'd joined her home. The talent he'd shown, the pride her parents had in Eowen, until he'd disappeared. Every lesson Eowen held dear, everything of worth she felt for herself she could trace back to a time with Tavo. He'd seen her wandering mind as a beautiful thing and encouraged her to tell him what she saw in her daydreams. He'd defended her against bullies and taught her the skills to defend herself in the jungle and savannah. She'd even gained a decent reputation merely by proximity to Tavo, the next in line to become ranger. Her life had been oriented and purposeful with her cousin to define and defend her worth. There had even been rumors that she'd become the next priestess after Mein. But after Tavo had left, it was as though all her aptitude had disappeared as well. The years of association with Tavo, which had cultivated her good reputation, now tainted it. Her life had transformed into the endless apprenticeships and disappointments, until she'd received news of her cousin from a trader who'd come over the mountains. Some of this was new to Hani, some was reiterated, but he received it all with appropriate alternations between silence and questions.

Eventually, Eowen fell silent, drained and hunched over. It was then that Hani spoke up to tell her everything that had happened while she slept. He explained that after Nolyi had flown them home, Aiyano had mobilized the entirety of Nopt Shisoke, determining immediately that the tree should be the center of their new city. She'd started work on it right away with Nolyi, and together they'd already made a larger and more effective version of their old tower. The Nagirr'Om and its acolytes had gathered their dead and delivered them to the citizens of Nopt Shisoke, as promised.

"Where did they leave the dead?" Eowen interrupted to ask. Hani did not know, and Eowen resolved to find out.

Hani explained that news traveled fast, and he'd found that he liked telling the story of how they had defeated the Storm. He then explained to Eowen her exact part in it and the dramatic conclusion Nolyi had wrought. Hani could not describe the words Eowen had said when she'd taken Cynna's corpse from Nolyi, only that she'd spoken with authority and power, similar to when they'd created the sacred beasts for the mountain folk together. Eowen chewed on the inside of her cheek, privately wondering why that seemed to keep happening, with her, Hani, Aiyano, and The Nagirr'Om. Powers that displayed their ability to rival the Storm but could not be fully understood or remembered. She stored those questions away for later and let Hani continue.

It was while regaling the population with a dramatic version of the events that had led to their liberation that Hani slipped in bits of his and Eowen's history. In doing so, he had attracted the attention of those who had seen or heard of his father, one of whom was a pirate scout under the service of The Dreaded Knife-Eater Besantas. His father had indeed visited to trade and dock in the past and he'd left to sail far to the north some years ago. Hani had a direction to sail, an idea of where his father was and was eager to be on his way, but wouldn't leave till Eowen had information on her cousin. It was only a couple days ago he'd gotten just that.

"Tavo stayed with this family, some people from your tribe who'd settled here," Hani relayed. Eowen opened her mouth to argue that her people would never settle outside a jungle and savannah village, but remembered her conversation with Isana. "This was almost three years ago, long before the fall and only for a few months, then he left to travel through the other Britchen lands. That family... died in either the fall or the Storm, but their neighbors remembered

Tavo. He had returned to Port Disoke almost three years later, just before the fall, saying he was trying to get across the mountains to your tribe. He was looking for a caravan that could take him safely over the mountains."

"He was trying to come back home?"

"That's what they said."

"Then... Why? Didn't he come home after the fall? He could have finished journeying back to us, but he left to travel northwest?" Eowen whispered.

"Good question, no one knows. After the fall he learned to manifest food, water, the other usual basics, then left heading northwest. Isn't that wonderful, though? He and my father went in similar directions! We can depart tomorrow."

Hani was full of vigor, standing up and pacing as he described that they already had a crew: Ordwell would be joining his adventure, along with a mysterious cloaked person who went by Strife and a Britchen woman named Kelt of no current renown. Eowen wanted to know more about Tavo, but it seemed Hani had already told her all the information he'd gathered. She asked how he had made the ship, massive and impressive as it was, floating in the starfield itself. Hani put a hand to a timber, stroking it with a wistful look on his face before answering.

"Something changed when I found out where my father had gone. Port Disoke here was the only clue I had, but now I knew he sailed north to other Britchen settlements and beyond." He seemed already older to Eowen, his energy, both in body and dreaming aura, more contained and focused. He moved with a subtle certainty and his aura of power hung about him like well-fitting clothes. "When I learned where I was going next, a place called Long Grass by the Britchen, I knew I could do things I had never done before. It's like my problem with manifestations was cured." As he paced around the hold, Eowen could feel his aura melding with it and the hold seeming to meld in return. It was like Hani's blending technique, except that he and the ship were doing it with each other, as if the ship was a dreamer unto itself. "I fell into my manifesting state of mind as soon as I found out where my father had gone, and when I awoke this ship was here. It's a part of me, more than anything I've ever manifested. I call it The Stormwake." When he said its name, the ship shimmered. Its timbers tremored and bent as though it were taking a great deep breath and swelling with pride. It reminded Eowen of the way The Nagirr'Om's name seemed to call upon her, even at a distance. Hani grinned and looked over Eowen's shoulder. "Like your bird."

The bone heron was still behind her, standing in the shadows by the stairs. Upon being inspected, it adjusted its wings and snapped its beak, making a sharp, quiet click.

"A part of me?" Eowen felt no melding of her spirit with the creature like what she felt from Hani and his ship.

"Trust me, I can see it, or feel it; you're connected. That bird wasn't merely a manifestation of yours, it emerged from you as a part of you. Like my ship." He sounded so certain that Eowen found herself nodding despite not feeling anything of the sort. When she reached out her senses to the bone heron she could identify its general presence and qualities as a manifestation, as she could with most other things, but felt nothing like the connection Hani spoke of. It tugged at the knot in her chest though, and Eowen pushed down the thoughts that feeling conjured up.

It's not my home anymore, they're not my people anymore... They're not my family anymore.

Hani saw her troubled expression and shrugged. "We've been a team since we both started our journeys, Eowen. Together, we'll surely discover the secrets of this world and fulfill our quests." Then he bounced on the balls of his feet and ran down the hull of the ship towards a door at the back. "Follow me! I'll give you a tour."

She smiled, glad to see her friend hadn't lost his childish enthusiasm in the last few days, and allowed him to show off his ship. It was a graceful thing, moored deeper in the starfield than it had seemed and filled with luxurious cabins. They were largely unadorned so that the crew members could alter them as they wished. Even Hani's cabin was largely empty, save for a bed and shelves.

After the tour, Hani took Eowen through the new city that was being built. It was to be named Nolano in honor of Aiyano and Nolyi, who would be honored as its founders. They walked through the streets, and while they attracted some attention with Hani's new fame and Eowen's bird stalking behind them, most of the citizens of Nolano were busy with the joyful work of celebration and rebuilding. They passed by Ordwell manifesting the same rings he made for Aiyano and Nolyi in front of an enormous crowd, giving them to families, friends, and lovers so that they could know where the other was. She met one of the new crew members, Kelt, who was sweet and shy and had little power but simply wanted to explore the new world and help Hani on his quest. Eowen saw that there were still a few acolytes of The Nagirr'Om around. Hani explained that as soon as their dead had been gathered, the silver woman and most of her retinue had left. Many acolytes stayed, but the ones that didn't were traveling in groups of three to root out the Storm in the rest of the new world.

"So it really is still out there," Eowen said. "I... It's not like I know how it worked or what it was, but I thought the Storm was being brought in by that tree."

"Aiyano, Nolyi, and I have learned a little bit by exchanging information with a few of the acolytes," Hani said. "The Storm seems to grow stronger and infect others more easily when it can emerge through a powerful dreamer. Until it can do that, it's always there, waiting in some... place beyond our senses. I know I'd felt it even before getting here. It was lurking at the edges of my mind, we just didn't notice it much till we were close enough to be in its manifested presence. It's still out there though, waiting."

Eowen thought about all her chaotic manifestations; the oasis, the sun, the way even her simplest ones carried unintended consequences. She'd felt at times as though a force or entity had been watching her, disrupting her powers. Now she knew for certain it had been the Storm.

"Don't worry, the Storm can't touch my ship or crew as long as we're on it. The Nagirr'Om herself confirmed it."

Eowen looked skeptical. "How can it do that?"

"I... don't actually know, but who would know better than her?"

Eowen shrugged. She had to admit that no one else would know as well as that strange being. Eventually, as they wandered through its budding streets, the city retreated into an artificial night, like that of the mountain folk's settlement. The collective brightness from the stars below faded to the barest of glows as the population moved to sleep. Eowen waved and made for the tree to sleep, but Hani insisted she pick a cabin on his ship. A thrill went through her, reminding her of their sailing together before arriving at Nopt Shisoke. It had only been a short time, but it already felt like an era of her life.

That was less than a week ago. Eowen felt dizzy when she considered all that had happened in so short a time.

Hani showed her to a cabin that was cozy and smaller than the rest. He knew she'd prefer that to a larger one, and upon walking into it, it manifested a recreation of the savannah's scent and atmosphere. Eowen thanked him, pretended to be very tired with a big yawn and stretch, and said goodnight. Hani casually manifested a bed for her and left for his own cabin.

Alone, she lay on her bed, a perfect replica of the one she'd used on their travels together. She tried altering the scents and smells of the cabin, changing the walls to look more like they were of her tribe's construction, but it never felt quite right. She considered that it might have been how much she'd already slept, or the excitement around her, but somehow the cabin felt wrong in a way she couldn't put her finger on. Like Hani had their first night in Nopt Shisoke, Eowen crept out while her companion slept, restless and dissatisfied. She moved with barriers of silence and sight and did her best to meld like Hani did. Her whole body surged with a craving to do something, some very specific thing, yet she could not clearly puzzle out what it was she felt so inclined towards. Eowen wandered away from the ship, agitated, melancholy, and convinced that there was still something undone that needed doing. Something more personal to Eowen, yet vast and widely pertinent.

She wandered the city like a ghost and sought out scenes of joy, celebration, and love, thinking that perhaps she needed reassurance that the people of Nolano were truly saved, or at least felt saved. There were parties going deep into the night, joyful and content moments between families, and the many projects in progress, abandoned for the night except by those most dedicated workers. She even heard a song of her own people, not a special or ceremonial one, but the sort of thing sung when drunk, with lyrics and a melody almost impossible to make a mistake with. She crept close to a fire surrounded by seven adults from the jungle and savannah tribes, who were doing their best to challenge the ease of the lyrics with inebriation. Several children played inside, eating sweets, permitted to cause a ruckus. Eowen saw Isana among them, and knew she could join in if she wished, as Isana would introduce her. Even without him, she knew that her new reputation as co-savior of their people would likely make her welcome anywhere in the city. For one beat of her heart, she undid her barriers and stood among them, just outside the fire's warmth.

"Hmm, what was that?" a man said when Eowen suddenly appeared a few meters away. He blinked and she was gone, her barriers back up. She'd already run far away. The man rubbed his eyes, forgot the mirage that had appeared on the other side of the fire, and got back to the task of trying, and failing, to outdrink the old matriarch of their group.

Eowen returned to The Stormwake, but didn't board it. She sat on top of a blueish marble building that had been gracefully created to look like colliding ocean waves. She hugged her knees to her chest and shivered, the cold unintentionally manifesting out of her. She forced it into dry savannah warmth, and sprouts from the grasslands emerged from the stone. It did nothing to settle her nerves.

Something happened to me when we were fighting the Storm, something important, Eowen thought. *And I have to know what it was because I feel that... if I don't figure it out now, I never will, that it will fade. Like my dreams when I wake.*

She stood and her heron stood with her, having shown up without her noticing. "Why are you the thing I made during the fight against the Storm? What makes you so important?" Eowen muttered.

"It represents something in your spirit."

Eowen turned in a circle, looking for the source of the voice and finding no one near her. The voice had been detached from any source. It hadn't even seemed to use sound but inserted itself directly into the depths of her ears, as if it's spoken from inside her head. It wasn't like the voices that had emerged from Eowen, Hani, and Aiyano in the past, nor the voice of The Nagirr'Om. It had definitely been a human voice, but somehow entirely lacking in features. Age, pitch, accent, even language hadn't existed within it, only the meaning of the words as a sound directly in Eowen's ears. A moment passed and Eowen thought she might have imagined it. Slightly unnerved, she decided to give up on her musings and go back to The Stormwake. She approached her heron, which bent low to admit her, and climbed on.

"Wait."

That wasn't her imagination. "Who said that?" Eowen stood, her heron unperturbed, and did a double take. No one was present until, suddenly, someone was, standing a few paces away on the roof with her. Like the voice, Eowen could not identify much of anything about this person. They were impossible to look directly at for long, as her eyes seemed to slide off them. They seemed tall, then shorter than Eowen, portly, then emaciated, clothed, then naked. Nothing remained consistent, and even when Eowen directed the sixth sense of her dreaming aura upon the person she felt nothing, as if they weren't there at all. "Are you... someone?" Eowen asked, squinting to try and identify the being on the roof with her.

"I am called Strife."

"Oh, I—I've heard of you, I think?" Eowen said. The being solidified a bit more, not enough to be identified, but enough for Eowen to see that they were cloaked, all features hidden in the shadows of the massive hood.

"I have been beside Hani."

"I... see. We're both part of his crew, then." Strife gave no indication of an opinion on this, which annoyed Eowen. "It's nice to meet you." She was unsure of what gesture for greeting she should do, her's, the mountain folk's, or the Britchen's she'd seen while in the city. Eowen settled on a simple nod, but Strife offered nothing of the kind.

"It's not his fault, The Nagirr'Om knew outsiders would come. Outsiders that she... it, needed for its purposes. It took steps to ensure Hani would follow into the Storm."

Strife spoke so matter-of-factly that Eowen found it hard to feel any sort of emotion about it. "Why are you telling me this?" Eowen flexed her dreaming aura, trying to make it dense and dangerous, letting it flow over Strife. The strange entity didn't seem to notice at all. The people in the building below, however, did notice, and Eowen's power woke them up. She melded her power back into obscurity when she heard the voices from below, embarrassed and annoyed. Strife didn't seem to care and continued speaking.

"You're angry at Hani."

"What do you know!" Eowen shouted, her anger suddenly flashing hot in her. She flinched back from her own ferocity, stung by the venom in her voice. Strife stood still and was silent.

Am I angry at Hani? No I can't be, because...

Eowen's train of thought stopped at 'because' and refused to move.

"You have a right to be upset. You thought it was his fault for leaving you alone. It wasn't though, I want you to know this. He was drawn into the Storm by powers that were beyond him. He values you."

Eowen was confused as to why Strife felt the need to tell her this, and was annoyed to discover she was indeed angry with Hani. She looked at The Stormwake and the feelings quelled and retreated. When she imagined Hani's face she did feel angry, but also meek and compliant. There was a sour, horrible mistrust in him, like something in her that refused to distinctly feel anger.

Why? He's my friend, my partner! We're a team, we trust each other. I do trust him... and I can't be angry with him because... because he's all I've got now.

Eowen swallowed down the lump in her throat.

Because I can't lose that again.

Strife noticed the change in Eowen's expression, and their

voice took on something resembling a real texture for the first time.

"Hani is a good person, actually good. I don't know if I've ever known a person to truly be good till I saw Hani. That is why I follow him now. I needed you to know that before you continued following him as well."

With that, Strife disappeared so completely it was as though they'd never existed. Eowen was left with only her thoughts, her feelings, the lingering sting of Hani abandoning her to run into the Storm, and the revelation that it hadn't been entirely his fault.

There's been all kinds of strange powers influencing and affecting us in this new world. I suppose we can't be held accountable for every strange decision we make, Eowen thought, but the sting didn't abate. She felt there was still something wrong with her, something wrong with the world, and Hani wasn't it. Then, she remembered the first thing Strife had said to her.

"Wait! Strife!" Eowen called out. No response. She couldn't sense Strife at all and had no idea how powerful they really were. "Strife, please! I have one more question for you!"

The strange being appeared before her again, cloaked and ever-shifting.

"Ah! You scared me! Do you have to sneak up like that?" Strife did not respond. "Strife, what did you mean when you first spoke to me, about my heron representing something to me?" Eowen gestured to the bird behind her, which curved its great neck around so that its beak was cradled in Eowen's hand. Strife stared at Eowen silently, then disappeared again.

Before she could protest, their voice filtered into Eowen's ears.

"The ship is a manifestation of Hani's quest for his father. It is his purpose. So too is the bird for you, though I know not what it represents. Only that it is of importance to you."

Eowen looked at the heron, then at Hani's ship, then at the empty space where Strife had been. "But my purpose is to look for Tavo. Why would a bone heron have anything to do with my quest for Tavo?" she muttered. The brief thought arose that it might be because Tavo was dead, but she pushed the thought away.

The bone heron had been important to my—the jungle and savannah people's burial rituals, but that doesn't mean Tavo is dead. It could mean any number of things... Any number of things that have to do with death. But, Hani said that the silhouette of it appeared around me a while ago, before we ever arrived at Port Disoke.

Eowen sighed, exasperated, and looked at Hani's ship again, a truly beautiful vessel, as much an expression of his inner self as she could imagine. She considered the other powerful dreamers she knew: Ordwell and his wonders that brought people together, Aiyano and her healing, The Nagirr'Om and...

"I'm not going to try and understand The Nagirr'Om. Hmm. I wonder if this Strife person's shrouds that hide their identity are a manifestation of something. Maybe it means they're afraid of being known and are looking for someone they feel safe being known by?" Strife was still in earshot, but no one perceived them tripping over their own feet when Eowen said that. Eowen shook her head. "What do I know?" she whispered.

Behind her, the bone heron stretched its wings and shifted its feet. Eowen looked it up and down. Of all the powerful dreamers who'd manifested aspects of their self into the world, hers was the only one that was alive, or had a life of its own in some capacity.

Except for The Nagirr'Om's bat-thing... maybe. But all the heron has done so far is follow me around and fly me where I want to go.

Eowen stroked the creature's neck and it hummed under her touch. Touching the creature and giving it attention made her feel weightier, yet stronger. Eowen patted the heron's back and before the thought had fully formed in her mind, it knelt to let her mount up. She climbed on, still white-knuckling the neck for balance, and sat cross-legged. The heron took off weightlessly, its grace an impossibility that no creature of the old world could have ever achieved. Together they glided around and around the city, a few flaps taking them high above it. Eowen saw Nolano as its citizens would likely never be able to. Even while in progress, it was a lovely place with soaring towers and elegant ground dwellings. Flora colored the place and bronze glittered throughout. Ordwell's works upon the place no doubt encouraged a spirit of interconnectedness while the great tree of Aiyano and Nolyi presided. Something was still off though, but Eowen could not tell what until she spotted the first stump.

The thousands of trees that had once been people were almost all gone. They'd been chopped down, leaving only stumps embedded in the starfield. Eowen did not know where they'd been taken, but it made her uncomfortable. She scanned the city, looking for even one tree. All the trees near the massive one that Aiyano and Nolyi had made into their palace were long-since removed. She managed to spot some at the outskirts of the city. Eowen flew towards them and saw a small squad approaching one such outskirt tree. She followed their progress as they applied ropes and saws until the tree was brought down. They loaded the tree onto a long cart full of other trees and pulled it along some path out of the city. The squad was heavily cloaked, featureless beneath their garb. Eowen followed them as they progressed through the void, their way guided by floating lights set within stone lanterns. It took hours, almost a whole Nolano night, but Eowen was not tired and neither were the laborers bringing the tree, formerly a person, to its destination.

They reached the previous dwellings of the citizens of Nolano, Port Disoke, and turned to the left to avoid going into the actual city. It was still a massive sprawl that Eowen could see many still lived in, though whether they would move eventually she did not know. The tower continued to spill its water and the stretch of the city went beyond Eowen's sight. She hadn't spent more than a day in the sandstone city, but was certain that a week wouldn't have been enough to see it all.

The tree-carriers skirted around the border of the city, heading in a direction Eowen had seen the least of, the opposite side from where the tower was situated. It took another hour just to reach that end, but Eowen didn't mind. She enjoyed flying on the heron and was curious about what they were doing. Another cart joined with the one Eowen had been following with lumpy, oblong sacks in the back. Eowen saw an arm sticking out of one of the sacks and realized the carts were transporting the dead.

"Of course. The trees were people, so they must be taking it where they take their dead." She assumed that the many varied cultures of Nopt Shisoke would pursue their own practices. *Maybe they're stacked on shelves like the mountain folk did before we manifested their sacred beasts.*

What Eowen saw when she reached the other end of the city was not a dignified storage courtyard where the dead awaited their final rites, nor a field with the dearly departed laid out to mourn. There was only a squat, square, stone building with a wide set of stairs climbing up from the side to a front entrance that glowed orange. Out the other side was a massive field of gray and white sand. As Eowen approached overhead, more sand spewed out the back of the building, away from Port Disoke.

Eowen felt that something was wrong here, and strangely enough, she could feel a remnant of her own manifestation present. The heron brought her down lower, gliding above the group transporting the tree. With a mounting sense of dread, Eowen watched the group drag the tree, a former person, a victim of a manipulative otherworldly force, up the stairs. Without ceremony or care, they dumped the tree into the glowing opening of the building and watched as it slid down a ramp into the light. The orange glow flared up, Eowen felt a gust of heat, and within seconds more sand spewed out the other side. Only, of course, it wasn't sand.

"Ash. They're just burning them all," Eowen muttered. She grimaced as the transporters left, no words spoken, no dignity or acknowledgement at all that the particles being shunted away from them had once been a person. The other cart, one with actual bodies, followed to do the same, no difference in treatment for the dead of any kind.

When both groups were out of sight, Eowen landed at the edge of the mountain of ash, the dust of countless corpses. Hani had said to her that Port Disoke once contained over twenty thousand people before the fall. Only a fraction had survived, and now Eowen knew what had become of the ones that hadn't. From above, the ash field was massive, a single hill being piled upon and gradually spilling down under its own weight. There were still bones among the remains, too hardy to break down from the flames that undid the flesh. Standing next to it, the ash seemed like it could go on forever, fading into the darkness beyond the light of Eowen's starfield. She balled her hands into fists and looked left and right for someone to direct her displeasure at, but she was alone save for the several thousand around her that could not answer.

She could still sense a creation of hers, and rather than dig through the ashes for it, she reached out with her dreaming aura, enveloping the entirety of the ash field. Eowen dipped back into her dreaming, trusting her subconscious self to navigate through it and identify what was hers. The heron stood patiently behind the girl as seemingly random, dispersed ashes separated themselves from the rest and coalesced before her. Eowen came back to herself, looked at this small pile of ash, and frowned. She had never manifested ash before, and everyone burned here had been people. *And I know I've never manifested a person.* But with the bits of her creation all collected in front of her, she could tell they'd undeniably been her work. So she dipped back in her dreaming and undid the damage to it, returning the ashes to their original form. When Eowen opened her eyes, half of a girl lay before her, severed down the middle by impossibly massive jaws, an old scar on her face.

"Cynna," Eowen whispered.

She didn't understand. Nolyi had been so relieved, so thankful to Eowen for restoring the missing half of their sister so that they could say goodbye. Now Eowen was recalling more of the battle with the Storm. She had sensed the need in Nolyi for ceremony and dignity. It had been like a beacon inside Nolyi, the need for their sister's body to be treated as a relic of the life the girl had lived.

"Why then are you here like this?" Eowen whispered. The rest of Cynna's body, her real body, which had not been of Eowen's making, was somewhere in the mound, reduced to a scattered form beyond the reach of her power. If all the ashes of Cynna were laid before her Eowen felt that she might be able to reconstruct them, but mixed with the others it would be impossible. Eowen's lip trembled, and she began pacing around the artificial half of Cynna's body, kicking up clouds of ash. She crossed her arms, gesticulated meaninglessly, then stamped and pulled on her braids.

"Why would they do this to you?" she said to the field of ash and bones. "This isn't right, it's unfeeling, unloving, there's no dignity or care or ceremony, there's..." The knot in her chest was tight and painful, the image of her mother laid out amidst the rest of her dead people as present in her mind as the thousands of deconstructed bodies before her. Her own people's dead were awaiting their ceremonies. They were laid out because there was not yet a way for their last rites to be fulfilled. "But Port Disoke has powerful dreamers, fully capable of manifesting the necessities to perform such funerals! So why haven't they? There's no... life here."

That was it, life. Eowen didn't completely understand why a proper ceremony of death meant life, but it felt right and true and necessary. She'd seen the relief in the mountain folk when they had the sacred beasts to give the hearts and livers of their lost ones to. She felt in her heart that to deny death was to deny life.

Eowen took one last look at her recreation of Cynna's

body. It might have never been the real thing, but in the moments before defeating the Storm it had been real enough to the person who'd needed it to be. She mounted up on the heron which was already waiting, looking at her as if it knew what she wanted and was going to do. It shot off, one beat of its wings carrying them far away without disturbing any of the ash.

They arrived long before the hooded groups with their body-collecting carts and landed on the outer platform of the tree where Aiyano had shown Eowen her new city. Nolano was rousing, its late-night revelers going to sleep as its primary population got to their life of building, eating, celebrating, and manifesting the world around them. It was lively and joyful. But when the hooded figures came shuffling through, people avoided them as though they carried a plague. The hooded ones responded in kind, pulling their hoods lower, avoiding the eyes of others and choosing whatever paths were the least populated. While Eowen watched this unfold, Aiyano emerged from the tree with Nolyi to see her at the railing.

"Eowen! What a surprise." Aiyano approached with her arms wide. "I would have thought you'd be with your crew." Eowen shrugged and continued watching the hooded figures, save for a glance at Nolyi who nodded back. Nolyi looked like they hadn't been sleeping much.

"I had a question for you, Aiyano," Eowen said, and her voice reverberated, almost as if echoing against itself to become wider than it should have been. It was almost, but not quite, like when The Nagirr'Om would speak. "Who are those people down there?" Eowen pointed at the cloaked figures. Aiyano went to the railing and her magnanimous demeanor shifted into immediate discomfort.

"Just some... workers. They clear up refuse, that's all. Makes it easier for people to figure out where to settle. There's all kinds of leftover campsites and such from the early days after the fall. Lots of food scraps and obsolete dwellings and poorly manifested clothes and such. You should see my favorite new designs in Nolano, there's a young Edeltraunt man with a knack for stone manifestations."

"So that is how you treat the dead here." Eowen's tone still contained its power, but there was no rage in it, only a frank sort of sadness. Aiyano opened her mouth to ask what Eowen meant but the heron silenced her with a look. Energy and a density suffused the space. To Aiyano and Nolyi, the girl before them seemed to be building up to some great statement or revelation. It was only a short silence, but it felt weighty as a dying breath. "Nolyi."

They jumped at their name. "Yes?"

"Do you know what happened to Cynna's body?" Eowen's voice went past their ears and minds, directly into the spirits of her listeners. Aiyano's smile became like stone. Nolyi's eyes were harder.

"L-let's not talk about such unpleasant things!" Aiyano said. Eowen was not surprised by the healer's reaction; Aiyano was the most effective combatant of death she had ever met. It seemed to Eowen that Aiyano drew her inspiration to heal from a denial of death.

"For what you did before," Nolyi said, their voice low and dangerous, "I'm letting you off. But don't you dare mention my sister again." Nolyi turned and stomped away, their aura of dreaming like a wall of stone around themself.

"They'll be alright," Aiyano said, turning to follow Nolyi as she smoothly transitioned to a more palatable subject.

"We'll be sure to see you all off before you leave on your quest. You're taking our dear Ordwell with you, after all." She hurried off.

Eowen felt desperately alone. The power that had been gripping her fled, leaving her exhausted and self conscious. She swayed against the railing before her, dizzy, so the heron snaked its neck around her, pulling the girl upright.

"Why did I do that?" she whispered to the creature. Eowen felt like she was emerging from a trance of sorts, as though she hadn't really awoken till just then. "Is this what you're here for? To fly me around and keep me upright?" The heron didn't respond and showed no indication of intelligence beyond that of an animal.

The sleepless night suddenly caught up with Eowen and she desperately wanted to rest. She considered her options for where to sleep, but both returning to the room within the tree and her cabin aboard The Stormwake felt distasteful to her. She climbed onto the heron's back, curling into the fetal position, and trusted that it would carry her somewhere suitable.

"Maybe that is what you're here for. To take care of me," she muttered into its feathers. The bird took off, and the gentle sway of its flight as it circled around Nolano put Eowen almost immediately to sleep.

When it finally landed, the heron stood before a home belonging to the jungle and savannah people that Eowen had encountered the previous night. Its main resident was an old woman, bent and sharp eyed. She emerged from her home to see the heron seated in front of the entrance, Eowen fast asleep on its back. The old woman smacked her gums and adjusted her hands on her cane. She scanned the heron and girl, well aware of who they were and cognizant of the power they possessed. She looked unimpressed though, having the expression of one who has seen it all.

"You're not to squat on my stoop. Come, come, get in," she whistled through two of her remaining teeth as she shuffled aside to admit the heron and its cargo. The outside of her home was made of the graceful wood and stone of the new city of Nolano. The inside, however, smelled like the jungle, and the light that filtered in seemed to dance through a canopy. The heron nested itself in a corner beside a shelf with seashells as the old woman laid a blanket over Eowen.

****

[Listen, for you cannot hear me yet]

**I TOLD LOVE THAT I DIDN'T THINK MY NAME
WOULD MAKE SENSE TO THEM,
FOR THEY WERE TOO SMALL.**

****

Eowen woke up to the smell of herbal smoke. The old woman was on a bench on her stoop, puffing away. Based on the light, Eowen had slept through the day and almost all of Nolano was asleep again. Eowen got up and joined the old woman.

"Hello."

The old woman grunted in response.

"Um, I'm not sure why I'm here."

"Your bird."

"That makes sense... My name is Eowen, respected elder."

"I heard of you. Don't call me that. Call me Gran," Gran said, sucking on her pipe.

Eowen smiled, It felt good to hear her own language, albeit in a different dialect. "Thank you for your hospitality, Gran."

"Huh! My hospitality is usually taken, drinking and singing all night on my stoop. Never letting me have a moment's rest. It's nice to give some hospitality for a change." Eowen had to grin; she'd seen Gran singing and drinking along with them the previous night.

"Thank you all the same. Should you visit them, please treat my dwelling as yours as well, respected Gran." It felt wonderful, better than she'd known it would, to be among her people, speaking the same language together, and performing small formalities she'd begrudged having to learn in her youth.

"Huh. Don't you know your manners. Where you from, Twig?" Gran chose Eowen's nickname and poked the girl's thin arm.

"Um. My—the village I was born in didn't have a name, but I'm told it was in the cluster furthest to the west in the old world."

"Huh, far from home." The word 'home' stung Eowen and conjured images of her mother's body, her father's exhaustion, her expulsion by Mein. It was a pain she was becoming familiar with, one she was becoming more able to push aside.

"Aren't we all," Eowen whispered.

"Speak up!" Gran's shout made Eowen jump. She leaned in toward Gran's ear.

"I, um, said: 'Aren't we all.'"

"Eh." The tone of this grunt sounded like approval. "Why d'you have a bone heron with you?" Gran asked.

"I think it helps me perform funerals." Eowen again surprised herself with the confidence of her response. Hani had said that the visage of the heron had appeared around her during all her workings with the dead. She hadn't even thought of the answer before she'd said it, but it felt true.

"Yeh, might be." Gran's unflagging nonchalance put Eowen increasingly at ease. She found herself smiling easily in the old woman's company. "Haven't seen a funeral in Port Disoke in all my years, was born here too."

"I thought that might be the case."

"You're a thinker, Twig." Gran's tone almost made the statement sound like an insult.

"I... suppose so."

"Huh. Good, need those. Too many doers about. Too much doing, not enough thinking."

"You must also be quite a thinker, respected Gran."

"Huh! Wrong, Twig. I'm no thinker, I'm a doer, I get things done, always have." Gran stamped her cane and tapped the side of her head with her pipe. "Not a thought up here 'cept things to do. Huh. Too old to do things now. Huh. Terrible thing being a doer in a body only good for thinking."

"Seems like you've given that a lot of thought," Eowen said, and Gran barked out a laugh that turned into a hacking cough. A short, portly, middle aged member of Eowen's tribe scurried around the corner from another house.

"Are you alright Gran?" The woman was dressed in yellows, like Eowen, and had bags under her eyes. "Oh! Who's your guest, Gran?" The woman got her answer when the bone heron stalked out of the old woman's home and stood behind Eowen, framing her. The woman took a half step back, fingered her skirt, unsure of how to react.

"This Twig is Eowen," Gran said

So she does know my name, Eowen thought.

"She thinks we should be doing funerals," Gran declared and Eowen turned to Gran, mortified that she'd so casually make such a claim about her.

"O-oh," The woman responded, trying to smile politely. "I see."

"I wasn't going to do anything." Eowen put her hands up. She didn't know if this was true. She'd felt that she was meant to do something, but what exactly that was she hadn't puzzled out.

"Huh! Course you weren't, thinker you are, you were just gonna think about it till someone had you do it. That'll be me." Gran heaved herself up on her cane with a grunt.

"What?" Eowen and the portly woman said in unison.

"Come with me, Twig." Gran shuffled off, and Eowen could only shrug at the woman and follow the old doer. They moved past a few other buildings with jungle and savannah tribe features inside, eventually arriving at a small courtyard within them where jungle flowers grew. "Made these, that's what I'm good at," Gran said, taking a seat on a bench.

"They're beautiful," Eowen responded, joining Gran, unsure why they were there but curious enough to be patient.

"Couldn't plant a garden in the old world, not enough ground. Would have needed someone to go get jungle plants."

"I see."

"Couldn't do it after the fall either, that new Port Disoke was too cramped. Here works fine though." Gran paused, and Eowen waited patiently, enjoying the atmosphere. It reminded her of her former home, and she quietly manifested more into it, thickening the air to a proper jungle-like quality and scent. "The others brought me here from Port Disoke. A lot of us got no family left, but we treat each other as such. Better city than the last, nice to not have that Storm around too." Eowen nodded politely. "Couldn't bring everything with us. Course, we don't exactly need to. Can make most things, can't we?"

To demonstrate this, Gran fixed her posture and dipped into her dreaming. Her shadows and light painted a new, orange flower into an empty patch in the courtyard next to its twins.

"Beautiful," Eowen said.

"Huh. You can do better," Gran said, and Eowen shrugged. It was true. "I did leave something at my home, something I can't make another of. Can you bring it to me?" Gran asked

"Maybe." Eowen was immediately suspicious. Gran had said she'd help Eowen perform a funeral, and though the prospect did excite her a bit, the actual doing of it seemed unlikely in a place like Nolano. *After all, almost all the dead's already been turned to ash.* "Depends what you need me to retrieve," Eowen said, and Gran answered immediately.

"I saved my great-grandson's body in my old house."

Eowen's mouth fell open. She had not imagined the old woman would have a corpse stashed somewhere. "Your great-grandson?"

"Hmm. Aiyano's collectors came for the rest of my family, saying some nonsense about dead bodies making you sick. I traveled back to the jungle in my younger days for funerals. I've taken out my father's bones myself. Huh. I may have lived in Port Disoke all my life, but I'm of the people. I know our rites. They got to the rest of my family; my three children, my five grandchildren. Only had the one great-grandchild left because I hid him." Eowen stared at the old woman, who sat chewing on her pipe as though she were discussing something as mundane as the weather or breakfast. "Most a-my family died in the fall. My eldest and her son followed that pregnant Britchen with the bat-thing to fight the Storm." Gran fixed an eye on Eowen, her stare intense. "I'm proud of them, they died heroes! Huh. Huh. Huh." Gran sucked on her gums and settled into herself. Eowen didn't dare respond to anything, didn't know how, but Gran was full of the energy of a doer and was more than happy to do all the talking. "Don't know what happened to them. Fighting Storms, naked silver Britchen women on bats. I've seen stranger even before the fall, not much stranger, mind you." Eowen could not fathom what would have been stranger than what Gran just described but held her tongue. She couldn't help commenting on the one thing she was now an authority on.

"They burned them," Eowen said, and Gran went silent. Even her gum-sucking and smoking paused. "There's a building outside of the new Port Disoke. Bodies and the trees that people were turned into are thrown in there. Then it spits out the bones and ashes." Eowen looked at her hands and chewed on her cheek, her eyebrows furrowed. "They're all just ashes, as far as the eye can see." Eowen looked at Gran to see what she thought of this, but the old woman didn't seem affected. They lapsed into silence for some moments till Gran broke it without ceremony.

"Go on then. Fetch my great-grandson."

"Go now?" Eowen asked, to which Gran gestured with her cane. "To fetch your great-grandson?"

"Huh."

"Gran, I don't know where your old home is."

"Huh, suppose you wouldn't. Take me with you then, that magic bird can carry us both, can't it?" Eowen looked at her heron. It hadn't seemed strong enough to carry Eowen, yet it had managed without strain.

"Let's try then," Eowen said, getting excited. She suddenly had purpose, a thing to do with this strange heron and this restlessness she felt about the dead. The heron didn't object to Gran's approach but stared at Eowen instead of crouching down. "Hello, bone heron. I humbly ask your permission to carry Gran and I," she said. The bird gave Eowen a look very much like Gran's, but folded its legs to admit them.

"I like your bird, it's got the right attitude." Gran got herself settled with her legs hanging over the heron's neck and patted its head. Eowen scooted up behind her and sat cross legged as before. It was a tight fit but there was just enough room for the both of them. Eowen did not have to issue any commands or requests. The heron understood, as it always seemed to, and took off. The creature rose up, weightless, and Gran grabbed its neck in a stranglehold, her whole body tense. Eowen laughed under her breath, enjoying the old woman's broken composure.

"Are you alright, Gran?"

"Shut it! How do you make this thing go where you want?"

"It knows," Eowen said.

"Humph. Smart bird, I like it."

It was a much shorter trip back to Nopt Shisoke with the bone heron flying at full speed, only a matter of minutes. Eowen manifested an immense light, almost as large as the sun she'd created for her oasis, and lit up the dark city below so that Gran could see. She had a moment of pride at easily creating such an impressive thing without losing control. She idly wondered what she'd be capable of in the future. When they arrived, they circled the city with Gran scanning the buildings for her old dwelling. After two full passes Gran grunted, exasperated.

"I'm not used to seeing things from here, I just know it was in the south of the city."

"Maybe you'll recognize things if we fly closer to the roofs."

"Huh."

"Gran, out of curiosity, do you know how the compass directions became a part of the new world?"

"Haven't a clue. That's you being a thinker, asking questions." Eowen thought that it was probably a question most people had, not just thinkers.

It was eerie being in the city Eowen had been introduced to only a week before now completely abandoned. Without a population bringing their light from below, it was full of the darkness of the rest of the new world. Eowen's great light floated high above cast strange shadows, and things seemed to lurk around every corner. They glided down to float just above the roofs to the south of the city and soon enough, Gran spotted a street she recognized.

"Down that way. Now left. Another left." Her directions continued till they arrived at a stack of sandstone buildings and landed in the street. Gran stayed on the heron and pointed to one of the dark doorways in the sandstone. "There. He'll be behind a sandstone brick with three lines scratched into it."

Eowen dismounted and looked at Gran, the dark

entryway making her nervous. The shadows of her subconscious aura seemed to pour in there, lurking with possibilities. "Don't you want to come in with me?" Eowen muttered.

"What? Speak up, Twig!"

"Nothing! Be right back!" Heat rushed Eowen's face and she strode into the shadows. "What am I doing asking her to come in with me like I'm afraid of the dark? I'm not a kid, I can just make more light!"

Eowen did just that, manifesting a small, floating light above her head. The room was plain, but for the collection of sea shells on shelves. *I suppose Gran manifested them all. I thought she was more interested in flowers.* Eowen remembered the shells in Gran's new home on one small shelf next to where she'd slept. They'd hardly meant anything to Eowen at the time, but now she knew they had importance to the old woman. They were, after all, the only decoration she had. Eowen manifested a bag and pushed the shells into it, scooping them carefully but underestimating some of their fragility. She winced as a heavier one crunched into a shell already in the bag. "Sorry Gran," Eowen whispered, but continued till they were all in her bag. Then she looked for the brick with three lines.

It wasn't hard to find, but if you weren't looking for it you'd not suspect it had any great significance, let alone a hidden corpse. Eowen stood before it and extended her power into the brick, moving it with the will of her subconscious, a dreamt sort of telekinesis. She lowered it softly to the ground, and inside was a small form, wrapped in a blanket. Eowen hadn't considered the age Gran's great-grandchild had been when he'd died, but it was a child's body inside the wall cavity. Eowen knelt before the hole. The brick had been as long as her arm and half as wide and tall. She found herself relieved that it was a small child, as she wouldn't have been able to lift an adult body by herself. She didn't know why, but despite her power to float the body, she felt that wasn't right. Something in her knew that she had to touch the body, to carry and cradle it.

"I should do something before I leave, give it something..." Eowen muttered to herself.

Give it what? Dignity? Care? Service? Love?

None of those words felt right, but the need to do something was still there, so Eowen simply said: "I'm sorry for disturbing you. You didn't know me, but I'm going to take you to your Gran."

She retrieved the body. It was both heavier and smaller than she'd expected once she could feel its shape through the blanket. It smelled musty of sandstone and the wool of the blanket, but also the sweet of rot. Decay didn't happen properly in the new world, Eowen knew that. Without heat, plants, animals, or air, most of the dead didn't decay right. There was some bloat and some rot, but no one had died from disease or injury, and so, most bodies were intact and suspended. The child in her arms, however, had been in the atmosphere of Gran's home for some time, albeit sealed in a cool chamber behind sandstone. Eowen stood, cradling the body the same way she would for a living child, and left the home.

Gran watched Eowen approach and nodded her approval. "Took long enough. Give him here." She patted her lap.

Eowen gently set the bundle on Gran's lap, expecting the stern women to finally cry, or wail, or to break in any way. Instead, the old woman flipped back the blanket to reveal the corpse's face and nodded again.

"That's him," she said, and it was impressive she could tell. The eyes were open and milky, the face bloated and red. Foam had leaked from the nose and mouth, but the blanket had soaked up most of it. "Let's go."

Gran flipped the blanket back over the baby and waited for Eowen to mount back up. Eowen did, acutely aware of their taboo cargo and worried the whole flight back that someone, somewhere would know and stop them. Eowen didn't think what they were doing was wrong but she recalled the furtive body collectors, the unspoken law of suspicion and avoidance around them. Flying high above with a small, well-wrapped bundle all but ensured they wouldn't be harassed. Still, Eowen didn't want to be exiled again, even from a place she was planning on leaving anyway, especially for trying to do something good.

Fortunately the flight was swift and uneventful. The heron brought its passengers gently into the floral courtyard from which they'd left. Gran scuttled off as soon as they landed with Eowen hurrying to help her. "That's the only way to travel, huh. Have to make myself one of those. Unless you'd be inclined to." Gran took a seat on the same bench as before.

"I'm not sure I could," Eowen admitted. "I think this was a one-time thing. I might be able to make another bone heron, but it wouldn't be like this."

"Gran!" The woman from before ran into the courtyard. "Where did you take our Gran?" The woman stood in front of Gran protectively. Eowen shrank back against her heron which curled its neck around her. Despite its exceptional qualities, the bird had a living warmth, which it pressed into the girl.

"Stop you fool!" Gran swatted at the woman. "Huh! Huh! Insulting a powerful hero like that, insinuating she'd kidnapped a poor helpless old woman for devious purposes. Insulting insinuations is what that is!" Gran pulled the woman on the seat beside her, continuing the lecture with things like: "You should be ashamed!" and "No sense of hospitality in the youth." and more creatively "You're a soft-toed spider-eater!" The woman, who in Gran's rant Eowen had learned was named Crueen, nodded along with Gran as the old woman got worked up, becoming more at ease the more she was lectured. Gran finished, huffed, and crossed her arms.

Crueen patted Gran's lap and favored Eowen with a smile. "Yes dear, you're right of course." Gran nodded her approval and winked at Eowen, who decided to speak up.

"I apologize for taking Gran, though I do promise it was at her request and for... non nefarious purposes."

"Of course it was my idea! You think I'd ever climb on some great bird if it weren't my idea?"

"I'm sorry for my reaction, Eowen. I've been taking care of Gran for some time. I overreacted, but I can see by how energetic she is that nothing bad happened."

"Not much to get excited about!" Gran countered. Apparently the Storm, relocation, newly spawning city, and the mere presence of being such as The Nagirr'Om hadn't qualified as exciting. "Put out the word, to all the people in Nolano and whoever is left in that new Port Disoke. We're having a gathering."

Eowen and Crueen were taken aback. "A gathering for what?" Crueen asked. Gran threw her eyes up in exasperation.

"Huh! A gathering, a village gathering. Huh. We are gathering together for an important purpose!" Gran sucked her gums impatiently. "You young folk, born in that Britchen city, never properly learned how our people do things!"

"I see..." Crueen looked to Eowen for clarity, but Eowen only threw her eyebrows up and shrugged. "I'll put out the word then. When is this meeting?"

"Tomorrow night." It was already dark.

"That's not enough time to gather everyone!" Crueen complained.

"Huh. That's alright, don't need everyone. Just put the word out." Gran nodded to indicate Crueen should go. "They'll be drinking and singing on stoops all night, go around to them." Crueen shared an exasperated look with Eowen, but kissed Gran on the forehead and left them alone in the garden once more.

"Yes, Gran." Crueen passed by Eowen and leaned in, whispering. "After the fall she became our elder by default. But one must respect their elders, yes?" This small moment of shared familiarity, of connection back to her culture, being spoken in her own language, sent an electric, but also sour, thrill through Eowen. Crueen was already out of the courtyard before Eowen could pull herself enough together to nod or respond.

"She's a good girl, that Crueen." Gran stamped her cane with approval. "Respects her elders no matter what, and believe you me I've tested that."

Eowen smiled. *Of course you have.* "What's the meeting for, Gran?" She indicated the blanket-wrapped body on the bench next to the de facto elder of her tribe's Britchen chapter. "To decide what to do with your grandson?" Eowen spoke simply and flatly about the body, in a tone she thought Gran would appreciate. The old woman shook her head though.

"No, that's when we're holding the funeral." There were several long seconds of silence that passed in which Eowen could hear the distant drinking songs and revelry of the Nolano night.

"The meeting is for the funeral?"

"Can't tell anyone what it's for, else they might not show up."

"What?" Eowen broke out in a cold sweat.

"Don't want that Aiyano to catch wind of it, else she might try to stop it."

"I thought I was going to do the funeral for your great-grandson though?"

"Huh. You will. Impressive woman that Aiyano, but scared of the dead she is."

"No, Gran, I thought I'd be helping you do the funeral just for you!" Gran fixed Eowen with a powerful, authoritative look, and the girl was immediately put in mind of the elders in her old home. An expression of uncompromising certainty that their will would be carried out. It was a look Eowen had always folded to, and here she was folding again. "I-I suppose I can try to do it."

"Eowen, do you know why our people are celebrating on stoops and drinking all night long?"

"Because they're happy to be free from the Storm?"

"Huh. Not as such. It's because they've got no ceremonies. That was something we started to lose, living in Port Disoke, even before the fall. No jungle and no savannah meant no ceremonies that needed those environments unless we traveled around the coast or crossed the mountains to do so. We no longer lived in our villages where rivers for marriage abound. There were no bone trees or herons for funerals." Gran patted the bench for Eowen to join her. "Even before the fall these things were true, but that was how it was supposed to be. We lived in Britchen land, so we lived by many of the

Britchen ways. But this is new land, in a new world, and though this city is named after Aiyano and Nolyi, it is no one's land except what we make it to be," Gran said, sounding more contemplative and soft than Eowen had known the old woman to be in their short time together. Gran patted the bundle. "Our people need ceremonies to tie us together and remind us what is important in life, and what is important in death." She leaned back against the small courtyard wall that the bench was flush with. "Huh. I don't think we'll keep to the old ways. That's fine, new ceremonies will spring up in time. I only mean to give us a place to start. Hmm." She sucked thoughtfully on her gums. "Maybe I'm wrong and this isn't the way for our people to find their place in this new world, but they put me in charge so I'm going to do what I want!" Gran shook her fist at no one and nothing in particular.

"Does it have to be me though? In front of all those people..." Scenarios played in Eowen's mind; blundering as she removed the child's bones, fumbling the skeleton, or trying to manifest something necessary and failing to do so amidst an awkward silence.

"Oh, I don't know. Someone else could probably do it, but you're going to. I've decided." Gran shrugged. The conversation was over. "Now help me get home, I'm hungry and tired." At the mention of food and sleep, Eowen found she too was famished and exhausted.

"Come one then, Gran," Eowen said, helping the old woman up.

I don't have to do the funeral, I could just leave with Hani. He's probably been ready to go all day today and I held him back by spending all my time with this lady.

Eowen felt a slight pang of guilt at this, but not as much as she thought she would, and it quickly faded as she and gran shuffled off into the dark, the bone heron toting the bundle of the dead child behind them. They settled down in Gran's home to sleep, the sounds of jungle and savannah people singing and talking, only broken up as Crueen interrupted to invite them to Gran's meeting.

****

[Listen, for you cannot hear me yet]

**BUT LOVE INSISTED,
AND ASKED WHAT TO CALL ME.**

****

The false night of the new world passed and Eowen had slept, but not well. She greeted the rising underlight of starfields with a frown, the darkness above with a glare, and finally, the sleeping form of Gran with a sigh. Her instincts were screaming to run away from the responsibility Gran had placed on her. Eowen knew no one would be able to find her if she hid, nor catch her if she fled, and no one was powerful enough to force her to do it regardless. Hani, Aiyano, and anyone else would protect her from Gran's imposed purpose. But a part of Eowen did not want to run. Against her instincts, a growing part of her wanted to do the funeral, to own the moment as, in a way, it had been her idea. It felt like righting a wrong, restoring some semblance of balance, or perhaps just fulfilling a need in herself. Eowen sighed, fortified her resolve and walked out of the dwelling.

"I suppose I'd better get started," she whispered, and the heron looked at her as though it agreed.

Nolano was still in development and the buildings were spread apart quite a bit. Eowen selected a spot near Gran's home that was relatively clear of settlers and buildings. She marked the area off with a low wall of simple sandstone that she manifested in a ring. Then she set about making the tools.

Her people had used sharpened stones for millenia, but bronze knives had been a recent and infrequent addition to their ceremonies. She began to manifest one, and the place became heavy with her power. It drenched the atmosphere with shadows that dripped down and light that dredged up. She felt in her subconscious ocean for where the tool was, sailing her waking mind on the waves and the winds of her inner self. The heron curled up around her, patiently offering its company and warmth.

The random manifestations that accompanied Eowen's creations barely emerged this time. Shadow and light, dense with her inner self, kept largely to their purpose, and in moments a bronze, unadorned knife with a simple wooden handle lay before her. Eowen's discomfort waned as she hefted the tool, dense and leden with her infusion of power, yet light to move. It felt as though she were not lifting it with her hand so much as moving it with her spirit.

"This will do." She looked up to see that a small audience had already gathered, mostly jungle and savannah tribe, but also other people, drawn by the display of her power. *Hani will have noticed, Aiyano and Nolyi too.*

"Huh. Not too subtle, but I supposed that's alright." Gran's voice approached from behind. Eowen stood to greet her and Crueen, who was helping Gran along. Gran carried her bundle under one arm, which Crueen seemed unconcerned about.

Which means Crueen is also very casual about this, or Gran hasn't told her.

Assuming the latter, Eowen greeted them and hid the knife from Crueen's sight in case she recognized its purpose. Eowen manifested a comfortable chair for Gran, letting Crueen fend for herself. Crueen was no great dreamer but was capable enough to produce refreshments while she and Gran chatted idly.

Eowen sat down before her stone wall, preparing for her next manifestation. Her power gathered, the shadows flowing out and moving in a graceful, creeping vortex that implied the presence of some great, tall thing within the wall. It danced out at times, hands of darkness reaching for hands of starlight, desperate for a partner to beget creations beyond Eowen's scope of intent. Her heron presided over the proceedings, its sharp glare and ruffled feathers cutting off the coryphee of dreams that craved to manifest out of control. Eowen knew that trees and even much larger things were within her scope, but she felt that this needed to be special. It was to be a bone tree, and the bones of Gran's great-grandson would become the first nest atop it. Whether or not anyone else chose to have a funeral performed here in the future, Eowen had resolved not to fail Gran. It felt, to her, like a kind of recompense for the harm she'd done to her people. It felt like something resembling redemption.

I may not be of the people anymore, but I have been asked to do this for one of them. I must do it right.

"I was wondering where you went." Hani's voice severed Eowen from her dreaming such that the shadows and light burst like a bubble, becoming nothing. Eowen returned to herself and blinked the blur out of her eyes to see Hani standing next to the sandstone wall. He smiled, but it didn't reach his eyes. "Were you hiding from me? I didn't feel your dreaming till a few minutes ago." The steadiness and undercurrent of confident energy he now had was still there, but so was the very real insecurity of a boy whose friend had been avoiding him. Eowen stood, and in her Hani saw a similar look, a conflict between uncertainty and a sharpened sense of purpose around her.

"Let's talk in private for a moment," Eowen said, and instantly manifested barriers that left them undetectable. People, not just Gran and Crueen, had been present, and the disappearing children were a surprise, but far from the strangest thing they'd seen. While the audience moved on with their day, Eowen faced Hani inside the barrier. "I'm sorry I haven't been around. I had to do something, but I didn't fully realize what it was till recently."

"I... Think I understand," Hani hazarded. "It just worried me is all." He looked at his feet and kicked at the stars beneath them. "Did I... do something to offend you?" He stopped kicking his feet and glared at them.

Eowen froze, for this was a heavy question, one that could not be answered with a simple yes or no. She considered saying: 'Besides abandoning me to run into the Storm like a fool?' but that wouldn't truly answer to how she now felt. It had been true when she'd found him in the Storm, but after the events since waking up it was no longer true. She wanted to tell him this and explain the transformation of her feelings, only she wasn't completely certain of how or why she felt different. Eowen considered saying: 'I was angry before and scared because I thought, after we'd come so far and come to understand so much together and about each other, that you leaving me like that meant you didn't really want me by your side. It made me feel that we weren't the friends I thought we were.' This didn't seem right either though, It would dredge up a conversation she wasn't ready for, one where Hani would profess the certainty of their bond, name her his best friend, and declare that he couldn't face this world without her, that he considered her family already, all of which Eowen knew would be no more than false flatter. She found that didn't feel particularly angry at him for running off into the Storm either. She had when she'd found him in the Storm, but after the fight and her conversation with Strife it seemed that hadn't been his fault. Eowen didn't know what power had compelled him so, but she felt somehow inclined to trust Strife. Their words felt inexplicably credible, as if she couldn't even conceive of opposing them. Either way, all that was true was that Hani had hurt her, but he had also protected her, supported her in her quest, and sought her out.

The boy cooked eyeballs for me, how could I doubt his friendship?

Hani was waiting for an answer, but Eowen was lost in thought and daydream. He sat down and manifested some of his bitter sage tea, and in a cup manifested some fragrant fruit juice for Eowen. The discord in the scents broke her from her thoughts and she blurted out:

"It doesn't matter now." Hani felt the torrent coming from his friend's spirit and he downed his bitter tea. Eowen let go of a breath she'd been holding. "Things have been a little strange the last few days."

"Stranger than a giant pregnant woman riding a bat monster and fighting a living Storm?"

"Well that's not a fair comparison!" Eowen cracked a smile, but it faded fast. "No, I'm talking about some more recent strangeness. It started when I met Strife."

At the mention of their name, the space over Hani's left shoulder shimmered, though neither of them noticed.

"Wow! I'm surprised Strife showed themself to you. They're very... shy. What did you talk about?"

"I'm going to do a funeral for Gran's great grandson." Eowen gestured to the old woman. "She requested it from me specifically." Hani froze.

"That's a strange thing to request from a kid." His statement abruptly put their lives into stark perspective. She was, after all, just a kid, and Gran's request was a strange one to make of a child. Eowen was about to voice that she agreed when Hani followed his statement up with: "But there's really no one better than you for this sort of thing."

"You... really think so?" Eowen whispered.

"It's been rather obvious since the eagle and the wildcat that you're good with... dead people things. Those manifestations were your idea, after all, and you handled that dead mountain folk we found quite comfortably. It makes sense that others would notice eventually." Hani's confidence in Eowen made her swell inside.

"One of the first things I thought was really... true and important after the fall was that we needed a way to perform funerals properly. It felt like, among all the things missing from the old world, this was one of the most important. I don't know if it is all that important to everyone else, but it feels important to me."

"That's good, isn't it? And it's for a member of your tribe. At least you know how it's supposed to be done."

Eowen looked down and away. Hani had never really understood the full extent of what her excommunication meant. "That's true." Eowen was quiet when she said this. They were not her people anymore, and that was part of the problem. Gran, Isana, Crueen and the rest were technically not of her village cluster at all and did things very differently. By this logic they had never been of her people, the ones she'd been excommunicated from.

But they are still of the jungle and savannah tribe. They speak the same language, they look like my people, and they hold funerals the same way. They are of the people that I cannot be considered one of anymore. I never knew that the world beyond my villages would be so complicated.

Eowen knew from Gran and Isana that they didn't feel the same way her people did about many things, and she wondered if they were different enough that interacting with them wouldn't count as a breaking of her exile. "I think it will be alright," Eowen whispered, and Hani clapped her on the shoulder.

"Of course it will! Now what needs doing? I'll help you."

Eowen shook her head, though a part of her dearly craved to have Hani by her side at this most pivotal of moments for her. His steady dreams and newfound mastery made her feel like she'd be invincible if he were behind her. *That's probably why his new crewmates want to follow him. Hani makes others believe in their own quests and dreams, like he did for me.* The certainty in the power he now held about him was clean, clear, and generous. It felt limitless with a loving will behind it that sparked at the prospect of fueling other's dreams. Hani was standing at the edge of Eowen's barrier of privacy now, observing the space in which the funeral would take place, possibilities crackling almost into reality at his edges. Eowen undid her barrier, moving to stand next to Hani.

"Thank you Hani. I appreciate all you've done for me, but this time I need to do it alone." She took his hand and squeezed it. "There's much I couldn't have done without you up to this point, but this cannot be one of those things." Eowen shivered. "Though I wish that wasn't the case."

Hani grinned at her. "You've never needed me, but I'm glad I was there when you felt like you did." He let go and turned to wave at Gran who was still seated in her chair, attracting the attention of other jungle and savannah folk who stopped by to speak with her. Gran narrowed her eyes and munched on a berry of some kind. "Can I come to the ceremony?" he asked, and Eowen shrugged.

"Ask Gran, it's her great-grandchild." Hani skipped over to the old woman, introducing himself with enthusiasm and a flourish. Eowen faced the empty circle of sandstone before her, smiling as Gran tore into Hani for his lack of manners and stupidity, how could he just skip and wave to an elder such as her, and what an idiot he was for asking to attend an event his close friend was guiding.

Eowen dipped back into her dreaming to the comforting sounds of Hani's enthusiastic conversation and Gran's no-nonsense attitude. The world around her faded, the shadows and stars dredged up possibilities from the dark places within and beyond her waking mind. She sailed out into the waves and winds of her subconscious, and found the things she'd need, the manifestations of a funeral. The tree would be easy, albeit massive, and she found the place in her subconscious where it was waiting for her. Eowen made for it within that ever-shifting darkness, and brought it into the light.

To Eowen, it was the work of a moment, the time spent in the dark of her dreaming to manifest the bone tree only a few seconds. To those of Nolano, however, many hours passed as Eowen stood in her trance, all but invisible inside her aura of power. The shadows dripped down and thickened from the furthest reaches of Eowen's dreaming aura, which stretched for dozens of kilometers. All in Nolano, but especially the most powerful dreamers, felt Eowen's aura flow around theirs, unignorable by the sheer volume of potential it was gathering. Over the many hours, the full extent of Eowen's spirit washed over the entirety of the city, then pulled to coalesce in the courtyard where she stood. Like a viscous flow of lava, her gathering of power moved down towards the point where the tree was to be manifested. Many felt the movements of the power and were drawn hypnotically to the source of them. By the time of the great manifestation not only were the jungle and savannah tribe present, but so was most of Nolano. Normally the light in Nolano would have faded by then, but the audience lit the place brighter than day. As the power coalesced, the people of Nolano felt in their spirits the notes of sweet sorrow at the heart of Eowen's. It was a feeling that promised a ceremonial catharsis that had been sorely lacking in their lands since long before the fall.

The people of the jungle and savannah tribe were closest by, and Gran moved beside Eowen with Crueen at her side and the small bundle under one arm. The power was gathered, dense, its potential unknown. Behind Eowen stood her heron, and in its presence the shadows and light were kept dedicated to the purpose Eowen had for them. Eowen, in her trance, plunged herself into the sea of her dreaming, and the manifestation began.

****

[Listen, for you cannot hear me yet]

LOVE COULD NOT PROPERLY HEAR ME, THIS WAS ABSOLUTELY TRUE, YET THIS COULD NOT STOP THEM FROM UNDERSTANDING ME, AN ENIGMA.

******

The darkness silhouetted the impression of the bone tree, a massive one, even from the standards of the old world. Then, with deliberate grace and unerring precision, the starlight that fogged around Eowen washed up against the shadows like waves on a shore, smoothing away footprints. The waves of light cleared away the darkness, leaving only the ghost-white bark and barren, twisting branches. The tree was almost as large as Aiyano and Nolyi's, not nearly as wide but close to the same height. When Eowen emerged from her trance of creation, she felt she could remember hearing something, words larger than knowing could account for and the deep well of melancholy that they'd been drawn from. It aggravated her, the dreams she had with their ever-close feeling of a presence greater than herself that she could still not grasp.

Gran approached, Crueen next to her, and knelt with the bundle on her lap. "Huh. This'll do," was all Gran said.

Eowen felt certain of what she was doing and why, as though she were no longer a mere observer or participant but had become a part of the moment itself. The funeral was her domain. Power flowed between Eowen and her heron, smearing her edges as had happened in the past. Instead of a vague silhouette painting itself around her, the Heron stood clear to all onlookers, a defiant banner of Eowen's authority in this place and moment. On her chest the brand of the mountain folk, given for such service, burned anew, a badge of her qualifications. She shrugged her robe off one shoulder to expose the brand shining over her heart. Only a few understood the full significance of the bone heron, and even fewer the symbol on Eowen's chest. In that moment it hardly mattered. All understood them as evidence of her authority as master in the proceedings to follow.

During her travels with Hani, Eowen's personal clock had brought her to what, in the old world, would have been her fourteenth year of life. Eowen did not look any older than that; a short, skinny twig of a girl, dwarfed even more by the tall bird and massive tree behind her. Yet despite these things, when she stepped forward to receive and unveil the bundle on Gran's lap, her presence was like that of a giant.

Gasps and mutters came from those who could finally see why they were all gathered there. When Gran felt the time was right, she stood and faced the small chapter of her tribe and addressed them.

"Huh. The Britchen of Port Disoke have hidden death for their people. For generations they stole the evidence of it away in the night, burned it to ashes, and put those ashes out to sea. You have all felt the wrongness in this. In the jungle and savannah, the bone herons hatched their young on the bones of person and beast alike. The young then carried the souls of the dead to the ocean to be purified. Huh, Huh." Gran sucked on her gums. "Now, we will reclaim the spirit of this cycle." Murmurs passed through the crowd and Crueen stared at Gran, aghast at the reason for the gathering. She stood by her elder though, and the rest of their tribe followed suit.

Word spread that the gathering was a funeral, that a body was the reason for all the fuss, and that it was a child's body, no less. It spread to people who pushed to get closer, people who turned and stalked away in disgust. It reached children who pulled on their parents for an explanation. Some children were told what was happening, some were not, and some were simply held to bear witness. Eventually, it reached Aiyano and Nolyi on their balcony that a massive public funeral was taking place for a child. Aiyano, the careful architect of her perfect society of healing and death-denial, rushed around the balcony, looking for a carpet to fly down on and stop Eowen. None could be found though; an unseeable and unhearable being had hidden them all away. Nolyi only stood and watched, the memory of their sister being carted away by Aiyano's disposal people being the last time they'd seen Cynna.

Eowen ignored the fuss and took the bundle from Gran, holding it between them. Eowen then whispered words that were only, in that moment, for Gran to hear, but they reached beyond, her voice now as powerful as The Nagirr'Om.

"Life is a burden, forever beyond the strength of those who carry it. Your burden is gone, little one. Now we will carry it."

She lifted the body of the dead child into her arms, and something passed through the hearts of the people of Nolano. They saw themselves as the child, cradled in death by a loving and unafraid servant, here to honor their body as a relic of the life they had once been burdened with. Eowen laid the child down and drew out her brass knife, which hummed with power. She offered it to Gran, but the old woman shook her head.

"My shaky old hands with that thing? Huh. You just cut him up, Twig, I'll pull out the bones." Eowen smiled a crooked smile and wondered if the old woman had some hidden power to resist the mood around her, granting her immunity to the emotional waves the city of Nolano was riding on.

Gran waited for Eowen to continue and the girl set her knife to the tiny body before her. She had seen such ceremonies performed many times, for she had attended many funerals. In the jungle and savannah tribes it was the whole village, and any from other villages who wished to, that gathered for a funeral. Eowen had been sent to many villages, been apprenticed to many and made many friendships, however brief. It only occurred to her at that moment that in all likelihood, no one her age had attended as many funerals. The thought briefly put Eowen in mind of destiny, but the twisted knot in her heart reminded who the true orchestrator of her life was and had always been.

I suppose I've got Mom to thank for this then. I wouldn't have been sent to so many different villages if not for you.

Her knife cut perfectly, though the hand that wielded it did not. Eowen slipped more than once, making some unnecessary mess of the tiny corpse, but not too much of one. She otherwise managed to cut in most of the right ways and places. The body stank, for it had not been attended to as soon as was normal among the jungle and savannah people. His abdomen was discolored and distended, his veins were like solidified roots throughout his body, and his orifices purged fluid. Gran pulled the bones from their extraneous cartilage and tissue, setting them aside after a quick cleaning on the blanket that had held him very nearly since the fall. It was hours of work, made slower by Eowen's extreme care and Gran's arthritic hands. They finished though; the soft parts of the body all unseamed like a thing the child had only been wearing over his real self, the bones removed and set aside. The skull had been hardest, it being integrated with so much. It too rested with the child's skeleton, removed of all that had made it a face.

Eowen gathered the soft parts in the blanket, and when she stood and turned, the starfield around the bone tree manifested into loamy, dark earth. She pushed and pulled it aside, making a trough for the contents of the blanket to rest in. She lay the whole bundle into the hole, and pushed it closed with her hands as well. The bone heron nipped at her ear, then stalked away, drawing her attention to the edge of the crowd that had remained, a mixed smattering of jungle and savannah tribe, and other folk.

The crowd parted for Aiyano, who marched toward Eowen shouting something. The healer's voice did not reach Eowen though, and her advance was abruptly cut off by something rushing in front of her. The bone heron stood before Aiyano, who found she could not move as the creature locked eyes with her. She opened her mouth to speak, but her voice was gone, seemingly snapped up in the great bird's beak. Aiyano tried to reach out with her power, but it was effortlessly buffeted aside by a flap of the creature's wings. The bird stood full-height before her and every bit of its body language communicated the same, crystal clear message: Only one has power here, and it is not you. Eowen did not watch Aiyano glare, turn, and march away. She had more important things to do.

She and Gran gathered the bones, not all pristinely clean, not all completely unblemished by Eowen's blade, but all perfectly loved. They laid the bones around the tree and stepped back. The ceremony seemed over, the girl and the old woman coated in crusted gore up their arms, laps, and torsos. Gran turned to say something to Eowen, but the girl held up her hand. There was still something missing.

The atmosphere around Eowen moved with her, suddenly dense and suffused with a power that rivaled even the Storm. Eowen's power was quiet, gentle, and certain, and until that moment few in Nolano had known that such power could be just as peaceful as it was violent. They felt a promise in Eowen's presence, of the stillness after life leaves, the peace all are due. Eowen was the very embodiment of the serenity of the grave. The girl directing the funeral held out her hand, as if to them all. Her heron answered, the beast resonating not as a mere creature anymore but as the embodiment of her will, power, and self. It flapped its wings and lowered its beak into her hand. Eowen gripped the beak and drew her hand back, seeming to pull something from the heron. Like an unraveling ribbon, Eowen carried the strands of power she'd pulled from the heron to Gran, placing them in the old woman. Then, she manifested something with the sweep of her arm that appeared as a silhouette around the old woman, smearing Gran's features. It stood beside her, another bone heron, this one mundane compared to the one that followed Eowen around but still weighty with a divine sort of presence. It acknowledged its creator, Eowen, then bowed to Gran, who 'Huh'-ed at it. Then it turned to the bones at the base of the tree.

"**It is done, Gran,**" Eowen said.

As the new heron stalked over to the skeleton, poking around the small bones for the ones it desired, Eowen's spell over the place ended. Her power, which had made the space of its influence like another world unto itself, snapped off. The people of Nolano swayed. Aiyano shook, afraid of exactly what, she knew not. Nolyi wept bitterly, and they were not the only one. Eowen very nearly collapsed onto the starfield, but her heron was there to catch her. Gran sighed and rubbed her back, squatting to pick up her cane.

"Took longer than I thought it would, Twig. Suppose that's fine, though. Not the sort of thing to be rushed, huh. Huh. Huh." The old woman hobbled over to Eowen, who was breathing heavily, barely conscious. She was sinking into the feathers of her bird, fighting against the mental undertow of exhaustion that dragged at her.

"Gran. Uh, I've got something. It's, it's for you." Eowen pushed against the heron to get herself upright, but her arms shook and her eyes refused to stay open.

"Huh, you're barely on your feet. Give it to me later," Gran said as she pushed Eowen against her heron. "Foolish girl."

"No, wait." Eowen reached around the heron for a bag she's stowed in its feathers. It wasn't where she'd left it on the heron's back, but when Eowen pawed around for it her hand sunk into some impossibly deep pocket of space in the heron's feathers. She felt the bag in the space, pulled it out, and filed away the question of how that was possible for later. "Here, it's for you."

Gran huffed, but took the bag, clinking with its contents, and pulled it open. Inside were seashells, many broken but plenty intact, clattering against each other with every small shift of the bag. They were nothing special by the new world's standards, but when Gran recognized them, great fat tears ran down the well-worn canals of her face. She looked at Eowen who was asleep where she stood, leaning against the heron. Gran wiped the tears from her face, smearing the gore from her great-grandson across her cheeks.

"Oh! I'm a mess thanks to you! Look at me. On then, we're getting washed up." Gran leaned on her cane and shuffled back toward her home, the heron in tow with Eowen slung over its shoulders.

"Well," said Crueen, sidling up next to Gran and putting her arm around the old woman. "That was... something."

"Huh, was a funeral for my great grandson is all. Don't know why there was such a fuss." Crueen resisted the urge to point out that it was Gran who'd invited hundreds of people for the event.

"Here, I'll take that bag for you," Crueen said, but Gran whipped it away.

"No one touches the bag!" she growled, and Crueen shrugged. She was as well accustomed to the old woman's quirks as anyone. Hani sidled up next to them from the crowd as they entered it. Many were still watching and waiting for something more, though they didn't know what.

"How are you feeling, Gran?" Hani asked.

"Tired and old."

"I meant emotionally, that was a very dramatic event and it lasted hours." Hani glanced at Eowen's arms, then kept his eyes off her and Gran entirely. "I was sweating just by proximity, though maybe that's because I'm more sensitive to death than the average person. Do you think everyone felt the same thing?"

"Anyone tell you that you talk too much?" Gran spat. Hani thought about it for a moment.

"My Aunt Zagu used to say—"

"Shut it!"

"How'd you know?" Hani grinned. He couldn't help it, he was full of joy and pride for his friend, and he enjoyed Gran's company, though she mostly complained at him.

Gran rolled her eyes and continued on in silence till they reached her dwelling. By then, the remaining onlookers had largely dispersed, save for the small crowd that used the old woman's stoop for their nightly revelry. They followed with a somber air, a wake of sympathetic grievers gathered to stand vigil outside the old woman's home. An unspoken agreement had passed through them that no one would bother Gran tonight. Once Gran was alone in her home with only Eowen, Hani, and Crueen, she closed her door, shuttered her windows and manifested an orb of light. Then, she manifested a screen across half the room and a bath with steaming water.

"That side of the screen, lad." Gran pointed and Hani took a seat out of sight of the woman next to the shelf of seashells. Crueen helped Gran with her clothes and did the same for the sleeping Eowen, getting them both into the bath and sponging off their grime. She'd done this plenty of times for Gran before, though not for such filth as coated the old woman and the young girl now.

"She'll be alright, won't she?" Crueen asked when Eowen remained entirely limp in her arms during her ministrations. Gran was silent, for she truthfully did not know and feared answering in such ignorance. She'd become comfortable in her role as matriarch, and in her opinion that role did not include admitting you weren't an expert in anything. The girl seemed devastatingly drained though, no aura of dreaming detectable in the least. Fortunately, Hani answered.

"Yes, she'll be fine. It was like this when I manifested The Stormwake. I was asleep and drained for a day and a half." Though the creation of The Stormwake had not been so public, nor taken as long, he recognized the quality of power and the texture of significance that had possessed Eowen during the ceremony. He'd woken different after that creation. Not changed into someone else, but elevated into a being that was somehow more himself than he'd been before. "She's just resting, Gran," the island boy said. **"She's waking up."**

****

[Listen, for you cannot hear me yet]

I SAID TO LOVE THAT I WOULD TELL THEM MY NAME, THAT PERHAPS THEY WOULD BE ABLE TO CALL ME BY IT, AGAINST ALL LOGIC, AGAINST ALL ODDS.

****

"Who is Love?" Eowen whispered when she awoke, but no one answered and her voice was terribly dry. She manifested water that floated up from the stars below and into her mouth. She coughed as it flowed down her throat at an awkward angle. **"Who is Love?"** she tried again. The voice of power was now close at hand, relatively easy to access, but still, nothing answered.

She sat up. It was dark within Gran's house, but she could hear the sleeping breaths of three people inside and many outside. Hani's familiar aura, massive and eager within his dreams, blended even in his unconscious state. Eowen could still detect it through Hani's subtlety. In fact, she could feel everything more completely than before. Eowen's senses moved at her whims to identify things in a clarity that had previously been beyond her scope. A few dozen kilometers away, a child was learning to manifest food for himself because he was hungry and did not want to wake up his mother. Closer was a middle-aged man who'd always wondered what fire would feel like if it did not burn, and manifested some that he could touch without harm. It didn't matter to him that the question in the old world was unanswerable, because in this one it felt like feathers made of sun-hot sand. Far to the west, Eowen could feel the mourning of a boy around the same age as she and Hani. He'd lost his first love in the fall but the rest of his family and friends were still alive. He wallowed in the loss, but also in a keening guilt, for though his family told him to be thankful that they had lost so little, he could only feel that it was still too much.

Eowen could not perceive all these things in such detail but in a kind of wordless knowing, a subtle understanding. It was difficult for her to keep looking through her senses like this, putting a strain on her like craning one's neck for too long.

I wonder if Ordwell's power makes it easy for him to connect to and perceive people at distances like this?

Upon thinking about him, she found she could sense the old man's aura of dreaming, larger and more developed as it was. Eowen rose from the bed and noticed for the first time that she was dressed in some of Gran's clothes that were far too big for her. They were patterned in purples, grays, and blues with shining beads and tassels. She reached out her senses for her own clothes and found they'd been burned, their ashes in the fire outside that Gran and her friends drank and sang around.

Eowen put barriers up that made her undetectable and approached the door of Gran's home. There were men asleep on the stoop that she didn't want to disturb. She faced a wall with no one on the other side and felt the creation of it. She felt the matter of the wall for what it truly was; not the stone of the old world, but dreams. She touched it and felt how it was only power, a solidified dream, as alterable by her own abilities as any creation. She pushed her hand and her will into it, and the stone dreams became nothing to her. She took a step forward and her leg passed through. Then another step and Eowen was on the other side, as though the wall hadn't been there at all. The heron followed, moving as though it hadn't even noticed the wall in the first place.

"You'll follow me anywhere, won't you?" Eowen asked the bird, which nipped at the cloth on her shoulder. She looked down at her clothes and, with a twist of power, they were her yellow robes again.

Hani stepped through the wall next to her and she jumped. Even with her new senses he was still exceptional at hiding his presence.

"That's impressive, Strife had to show me how to move through things." He patted the wall.

"Strife did?"

"They're amazing, everything we've ever learned about hiding our presence or resisting the power of other's manifestations, they were able to do almost immediately. Even the Storm can't touch them."

"That's... very impressive. Why didn't they stop the Storm then, if they are so powerful?" The two started walking through the city, largely unnoticed by those they passed in the sleepy, early hours.

"I wondered the same thing, but it turns out Strife can barely manifest anything. They are untouchable, unperceivable, and unaffected by any powers that they do not choose to be, but they can barely maifest air, food, or water. I think they had to cling to others and steal to survive right after the fall. They haven't told me how they actually survived, that's just my theory." They were moving towards The Stormwake, and Eowen could feel Hani reach out and touch his senses upon Ordwell, who reacted and began moving towards them. "How are you feeling?" he asked, but he had a knowing smile, his eyes twinkling with the starlight that glowed under them.

"I... feel like I could know things about anyone in Nolano right now if I wanted." Hani nodded for her to continue. "I think I could manifest just about anything I want, no matter how big or complex or strange. But... uh." Eowen frowned and brought her eyebrows together. "However...." She gestured vaguely, trying to put into words what she was only just comprehending.

"It's not that you feel more powerful or capable than before, but that you feel as if you know your own power and abilities for the first time?" he supplied, and Eowen gestured her assent, for he'd captured the feeling perfectly. "Kelt helped me to understand that." Hani swelled, his crew a greater source of pride than even his own abilities. "Kelt isn't terribly powerful, not like you and I, but she has incredible control. She really seems to have an intuition about how things work." Hani jumped as soon as The Stormwake came into view, his dreaming aura resplendent with joy. The smile on his face and the lightness of his steps infected the entire world around him, coloring and texturing the very alley they walked down with an implacably friendly aspect. Eowen wondered if Hani could have done this in the old world: make any part of it feel like a cordial place.

Ordwell rounded a corner and waved to the children.

"Hello kids. I hope you both slept well." The skin around his eyes crinkled when he smiled.

"Of course!" Hani skipped forward and hugged the old man. They'd become so close in such a short time, Eowen was a bit jealous. It had taken weeks and dire circumstances for her and Yawin to get so close. There was a keen pain at the thought of him, and she felt for the stone in her pocket that Ne had given her.

It's alright. I can find my way back to them if the time ever comes.

"You stirred things up quite a bit last night," Ordwell said to Eowen, and she felt her face heat up. "No, don't let there be any shame, I think much needs to change for the people of this new world. I don't know what exactly, but whatever happened yesterday, I think it's on the right track." He patted Eowen's shoulder.

"Have you said your goodbyes?" Hani asked him, and Ordwell nodded.

"Yes, so has Kelt. I assume Strife has as well?"

"I'm not sure they had anyone to say goodbye to." Hani and Ordwell looked at Eowen then. "I suppose you'll want to say goodbye to that lady, Gran?" Eowen looked between them, and felt a sharp disturbance deep inside her.

"I'm sorry, why would I be saying goodbye to her?"

Hani shared a look with Ordwell. "Because we're ready to leave. You did what you needed to do, didn't you? That funeral for Gran. Now we're ready to go, to find my father and your cousin Tavo and add to our crew as we go along."

"I'm not going with you," Eowen blurted out before she realized what she'd said. Her voice was quiet, but just loud enough to be heard. Hani and Ordwell were frozen, either unsure of what to say next. Eowen realized with a stark clarity how true the statement had been and continued. "I can't leave yet, there's more I have to do here." Eowen gestured towards Nolano behind them. "I can feel... others who need me. Some of them don't know it yet, it's still too soon, but they will."

"For... funerals?" Hani asked, and Eowen nodded.

"Exactly, there's people who need the means to grieve, perform their ceremonies, and let go. They need to feel safe doing so and they need help performing their rites, as you saw before." Eowen was growing increasingly agitated, though Hani's joy was draining from him.

"You already did that, though. The tree and the other bird will still be here when you leave."

"No." Eowen shook her head. "That won't be enough. The people here have only just come to accept the idea of a public funeral, they need to feel safe actually performing it. Hani, do you know what they've been doing with their dead here?"

"I don't see why it matters, that's their business, their culture!"

"No, it isn't! It's... the opposite of a culture. It's a thing that's being ignored and shut away."

"Eowen—" Hani flailed his hands, seeking an idea to grasp onto. "You're part of my crew!" Eowen's eyes became steel hard then.

"Is this an order then?" Her voice was a dangerous hiss, her aura of dreaming separated from its normally comfortable blend with Hani's to become jagged and dangerous. Hani quelled. He hadn't meant to invoke aggression, only to stop from the desperate feeling of loss that Eowen's words were leaving him with.

"No! That isn't what I meant, I'd never order you to do anything. Eowen, you're in my crew, you were the first member of it. I haven't even been thinking of it as my crew, it's ours, and you're the most important part of it." He looked to be on the verge of tears, his mouth opened and closed with newly formed, then abandoned remarks. Eowen looked away, locked her eyes on her feet, and bit her lip, keeping her hands in fists. They stayed like this for only a moment but it felt longer, each tick of silence painful. "I can't do this without you," Hani whispered. Eowen locked eyes with the boy and glared.

"Yes you can!" She didn't let him respond. "You've never needed me for your quest. Hani, you're the most stubborn and foolhardy person I know, nothing's going to stop you even if you went by yourself. But you're not alone, you already have amazing people who want to come with you and who believe in you." Eowen gestured at Ordwell, who was watching with a strangely satisfied expression on his face. "You'll make friends everywhere you go, like you always do. Believe me, you've never ever needed me... but for a while I was the one that needed you. No, don't argue with me, I needed so many people's support to get here, the mountain folk that helped me find my people then took me in when they exiled me, you to convince me to find Tavo and travel with you across the void, this whole mess with The Nagirr'Om and the Storm to make me what I am now." Eowen looked at her hands and saw in their lines and callouses what her life had been until now; a never-ending series of uncertainties and desperate attempts to be of worth to someone, anyone. *To my mother.*

"Does this mean that you've given up on finding your cousin?" He searched her eyes, looking for something in there, and Eowen shook her head.

"No, I'm still going to search. He's alive out here in the

world, I'm sure of it, and he's my only family left." Hani opened his mouth to say that he was her family too, but Ordwell sensed the nature of the response and put a hand on Hani's shoulder to stop him. "I'll find him. I just have to be here for now. I know it, just as you know you have to leave to find your father." Eowen gave the boy a sad smile. "You've already been here too long waiting for me, haven't you?"

Hani seemed to teeter in his mind. He knew Eowen was right, but he'd developed an expectation in his mind for all the many adventures he'd have in the new world, and in all of them was Eowen. She had to smile, for all Hani's power, his senses and his wisdom, the island boy was still an excited and idealistic child with grand expectations. Even the end of the world had done more to encourage than hinder him. Eowen felt for Hani, for the lesson of disappointment he was going through was one that she knew all too well.

Ordwell stepped between them and offered his hands. Tentatively, both children placed their hands into his, and he pulled them into the power of connection and understanding he commanded. There was a moment like when Eowen had first met Ordwell and shaken his hand. She was in the space outside of bodies with only the mind present, and Hani was there too. Ordwell hosted the space of supernatural understanding and their minds met, knowing each other without barriers. Hani saw her regret, great but dwarfed by her new sense of purpose and duty. Eowen saw how he truly felt she was a member of his new family, the first he'd found, only to lose. Then, in the blink of an eye, they were back. Shadows and light from Ordwell's power curled around their fingers and coalesced in their palms, depositing a small, brass ring into each of their hands.

"You both recognize these, don't you?" His voice was soft,

deep, and wide enough to hold the two children. "Wear the ring and you'll know where the other is. Many have them. Aiyano and Nolyi were the first, but Nolyi wears another that is the match to mine." He held up his own hand to show a brass ring on his pointer finger. "I've already said my goodbyes. With this, I hope it will be easier for the two of you to do the same. The rings lead back to each other, but only work if you two are the ones wearing them. Wear them, and you are assured to reunite one day, even if one of you should perish. " The children looked at the rings, then at each other.

"Ok," Hani said, and wiped at his nose.

"I'm glad you approve, Captain Hani," Ordwell said with only a bit of mocking. Hani smiled again, pushed his hair back and stared up into the darkness above.

"Fine! That's it then, the matter is settled." He looked between Ordwell and Eowen. "Thank you, First Mate Ordwell. That make you jealous enough to rejoin, Eowen?" She rolled her eyes and pushed him in the direction of The Stormwake, their joy restored for now.

"Leave already! You're long overdue."

Hani had wanted to make announcements to the whole of Nolano, throw a massive party, and generally go off with style. His mood had shifted after his conversation with Eowen, and by the time they reached The Stormwake, he was ready to depart right then.

"Are you sure? You don't have to go immediately. Aren't there... preparations to make? Some kind of ceremony for a ship departing?" Eowen asked.

"Not that I know of. We'd usually hold a party on my island, but we've been doing that for the past few days all over Nolano." Hani looked out over the city from the deck. "Everyone's here. Strife and Kelt already started living on the ship." At the mention of her name, Kelt showed up and Eowen finally met her, a thin, tall Britchen with a shaved bald head. She approached and snapped her fingers, a steaming pastry of some kind manifesting perfectly in her hand. She had a pinched, severe look, but offered her hand to Eowen.

"My, you really are just a little strip of a girl, aren't you?" They shook hands and Kelt sniffed and moved her pursed lips around in a version of a smile. "You've been of good to my city, it's an honor to make your acquaintance. A friend of mine joined The Nagirr'Om, I'd thought them dead till you and Hani showed up and made quick work of it. I saw that funeral as well. Messy, but earnest, I suppose. Keep up the good work, I'm eager to work beside you." Kelt finally let go of Eowen's hand.

"She's not coming with us," Hani said, and Kelt gave him a look with one eyebrow raised.

"Well, didn't you seem so certain? Listen to Ordwell next time. Honestly, why we're following a child into the void is beyond me!" Kelt turned on her heel and strode back down the stairs. "A pleasure, Eowen. Till next time." With a wave she was gone, Eowen and Hani looked at each other and he shrugged.

"She asked to join. I wasn't going to say no."

"Not who I'd expect for a crew of adventurers," Eowen responded.

"Turns out she was quite a skilled sailor in the old world and missed the feel of it." A moment of silence passed between them before Hani lunged forward and embraced Eowen. She squeezed him back tight and the two swayed, holding each other. "Till next time, Eowen the funeral master."

"Bye, Hani. You'll find your father, nothing can stop you!"

Eowen thumped his back with her fist and Hani did the same to her. They separated, and Hani turned away, wiping some tears. Ordwell put a hand on Eowen's shoulder and leaned in close to whisper.

"You're doing the right thing. I know you understand this, but let it be said by an old man who's seen many years as well."

"Thank you." Eowen nodded.

"And maybe, while you're here, you could check in on Nolyi for me?" He glanced at the great tree behind her. "They're a tough one, but... well, what can I say? They're my best friend." Eowen nodded again and Ordwell patted her shoulder. "That's that. Where's Strife? They should meet Eowen before we head out."

"We've already met," Eowen said. Then she stepped onto her heron's back, and with one push of its wings it gusted up and coasted down to the starfield next to The Stormwake.

"Strange one, that Strife," Ordwell said. "Are they even on board?"

"They're here," Hani said. The island boy stood at the helm of his ship, rudder in hand, and wind without origin surged up around him, pushing the sails taught and sending his hair and robes flapping. For the first time, Eowen saw Hani as he likely saw his father; a noble figure atop a worthy vessel, the open expanse promising to make a legend of the worthy such as he. Then, Hani turned to Eowen, waving and grinning like the foolhardy child he still was. "I bet you I'll find my father before you find Tavo!" he called down as the ship creaked forward, listing away from Nolano.

"That's not fair! You're leaving before me!" Eowen called back. Hani barked a laugh at her over his shoulder, and in seconds The Stormwake was a receding dot in the vast darkness beyond. Eowen watched till she could see it no longer, but she could still feel Hani's dreaming aura at the edges of her own. She stayed standing at the edge of Nolano's new barrier of silver bamboo until the last threads of Hani's presence were beyond her own. She'd known it would feel terribly lonely, just as it had to leave the mountain folk, and before that her own people, and before that when Tavo had disappeared all those years ago. The loneliness of goodbyes all had the same sting, but for the first time Eowen felt ready for it, the sharp pain in her spirit a side effect of her own choices rather than a symptom of a life without agency.

Sleepy citizens just waking up had begun to notice the departure and were streaming toward the place the ship had been. Eowen became imperceivable and skirted around the crowd as the great city stirred to life. She made her way back to Gran's, buzzing with an eager energy to take her next steps in providing people the funerals their hearts yearned for while entirely unaware of where to get started. She was brainstorming ways to tactfully find out if anyone had hoarded the corpses of their loved ones away from Aiyano's collectors, which ranged from enhancing her voice enough to advertise her services to the whole city to knocking on doors to do the same.

Both proved unnecessary when she arrived at Gran's home. There was a bustle of activity around the old matriarch, who was seated on the bench on her stoop. Several of the men who'd fallen asleep there were still present, discussing something amongst themselves. Crueen was waving people off of Gran as they vied for her attention, looking very annoyed. The causes of the hubbub were hidden from Eowen till she got close enough to see two teenage

Edeltraunt boys pleading with the men and Gran. They looked to be a few years older than Eowen, and carried between them a long, awkwardly bent bundle wrapped in blankets. Eowen heard the word 'mother' from one of the boys, and confidence surged in her veins.

People have already come to find me themselves!

Buoyed by this, she undid her barriers and strode forward, shoulder back and chin held high. The heron followed in much the same way. Gran spotted the bird approaching and banged her cane on the ground for silence. Once she had it Gran nodded to the approaching Eowen, drawing the other's attention to her as well.

"There, huh. She's the one you want. Now get off my stoop!"

****

[Listen a little longer.]

LOVE WAITED, WITH MORTAL EARS AND A MORTAL MIND AND MORTAL SOUL, ALL THINGS UNABLE TO HEAR ME, ALL THINGS NORMALLY BROKEN BY MY PASSING, BY MY BREATH, AND CERTAINLY BY MY NAME.

****

The Edeltraunt, the name of their people being a portmanteau of their words for 'The People Upon Hills,' hailed from across the ocean of the old world. Their funeral practices were simple; to bury their dead in hills and sing a long hymn to their ancestors on top of the hill. The boys that had brought their mother's body to Eowen did not know the words of the hymn, but Eowen would not turn them away. She accepted the body of their mother and told them she would protect it till such a time as they were ready to perform the ceremony properly. The boys agreed, though they looked scared and unsure. If the boys were any indication, the Edeltraunt looked a great deal like her own people, only with a tendency to be much taller and wider-shouldered. They towered over Eowen, but still somehow gave her the impression of small, frightened animals. She took their hands and urged them to ask others of their people for the hymn, though usually it was performed by a holy man or woman who knew it all. They told Eowen they would be fine with a jungle and savannah tribe funeral, but she could feel this was untrue and sent them away.

This was the first of many Eowen met in Nolano to perform services for. She had no idea how long she'd be in Nolano, nor how many funerals she'd be called to do. After meeting with the Edeltraunt boys, Eowen made it her business to be prepared for whoever requested her. Over the next six months, Eowen learned the funeral practices of the varied demographics that had settled in Port Disoke. Slowly and with many mistakes, she performed over a hundred ceremonies. No one had known or would have suspected that so many bodies had been hidden from Aiyano's disposal unit, but when a few came out of hiding with the vessels of their former loved ones, more followed.

There were, of course, the Britchen, who made up the majority of the population and had left the disposal of their dead into anonymous hands for generations. There was little to learn from them save for the discomfort that many of them held in Eowen's work.

Her former people's own practices were already well known to her, and after only a few such funerals, Eowen's hand no longer slipped when cutting to the bone. She became comfortable guiding the hands of the mourners that were in her care, and the funerals proceeded well under the protection of her bone heron.

She already knew the ways of the mountain folk, and told them of the manifested beasts she, Hani, and Genia had made at the settlement. One family of mountain folk that had saved some bodies of their loved ones recited prayers from the faith of their old world, and the eagle and wildcat responded to them. They arrived out of the dark from the direction that the stone Ne had given her pointed to. They were perfectly capable of performing the rites themselves, but requested Eowen preside over it all the same, and she complied. She felt compelled to protect their ceremonies and provide, if nothing else, a place of comfort to perform them and mourn. The great beasts ate the offered organs, then disappeared back into the darkness. The trait that allowed them to be called by prayer was not something Eowen had known they would possess, and it left her wondering how many other manifestations had hidden qualities deposited into them by the dreamers from which they spawned.

Other practices were not so easy to learn, and at times there were other barriers in the way of her work. Aiyano tried to intervene a few times, but was always rebuffed by the bone heron. Eventually, she changed tactics by treating Eowen as though she were some visiting dignitary. Aiyano would send her students with messages inviting Eowen to the great tree for civil discussions. Eowen had fully moved in with Gran and now sought the old woman's advice for virtually all her social graces in Nolano, to mixed results.

"Pah! Off my stoop, you pidgeon!" Gran shouted at the messenger, who checked the placement of their feet and took a step back despite not being on the stoop in the first place. "Huh! You tell that stuffed up Aiyano she can come here herself."

"Um..." The messenger wasn't of the jungle and savannah tribes, but spoke enough of the language to have been given the job. Isana was no longer available for the position as he'd relinquished Aiyano's robes to spend more time with his people. "Aiyano is very busy," was all the messenger said, which was not untrue. She had thrown herself into her work, visiting home after home, manifesting personal water and food sources and imbuing them with healing and bodily fulfilling properties. In her city, no one would ever want for any of the necessities of life. She was also mounting expeditions with Nolyi and the acolytes of The Nagirr'Om that had stayed behind to find more Britchen and either bring them to Nolano or provide them with livable conditions in their own settlements. Gran did not appear impressed by this, and sent the messenger off. What exactly would impress the old matriarch was a topic of some debate among her people. The most common assessment was that even a full recreation of the old world by a single dreamer would warrant little more than a sniff and a nod.

It took months, and there were moments of bitter work. Eowen constructed the elaborate pyres of the far eastern river folk, the smallest demographic in Nolano. They required that very specific leaves be plucked fresh and coated in a very specific, flammable resin. Then the leaves had to be stacked around the body, and burned as the body was set upon the river. The resin burned green and the leaves burned white, and the effect was beautiful and haunting as the river folk wailed their mourning cries and beat their fists on the ground beside the river. Eowen had manifested everything for their ceremony, as their people couldn't quite get it right. There were only twenty five river folk in Nolano, and they all attended every ceremony.

Eowen manifested valleys for the nomadic valley people to bury their dead, special marble for the jars in which the Carrulians placed certain body parts, and even a volcano for southern islanders like Hani. Some would try to insist that Eowen did not need to be so specific with her manifestations or her role in the ceremonies, some were cruelly insistent upon everything being perfect, but to all of them Eowen offered the same patience. The young girl, within weeks, had eclipsed her own legend associated with the banishment of the Storm by her care for the dead. Sometimes she would perform or preside over several funerals a day. Other times she dedicated herself to longer processes. For one ceremony, she spent an entire month perfecting a manifestation of something from the old world she did not know and could only try to make from descriptions.

Aiyano and Nolyi spent more and more time away from their city, connecting to other Britchen settlements. Nolano began to take on geographic features from the cultures that had left their lands behind even in the old world to live there. The result was a mottled cornucopia of biomes, almost all of which were used as places for mourning and reflection. With each ceremony, Eowen grew more secure in her identity, though the strange voice in her dreams that told her to listen still eluded her in the waking world.

By the time five months had passed, Eowen had a full

mastery of the commanding power that The Nagirr'Om spoke with always. And though her regular manifestations were still accompanied by unintended effects, her power was almost perfectly under control when she performed funerals. The Storm still raged, its influence growing through distant beings and rooting in the spirits of those who crossed the barrier of silver bamboo. But the acolytes of The Nagirr'Om became valued guards for caravans of people wishing to seek out family and friends who lived far away. After some time, a persistent fog enveloped the world outside the bamboo, and those who stepped into it without protection were quickly invaded by the Storm. The people of Nolano and its neighboring settlements learned to fear it once more, but not so much as before, for now there was organized resistance to its corrupting powers.

It was in Eowen's fourth month in Nolano when she found out that many people had affixed an epithet to her name. On a particularly dark and sleepy night, Eowen was sitting on Gran's stoop, staring into the darkness above, allowing her waking dreams to dance in the ebon without the urge to become. She sensed a presence moving toward her with intent, a powerful one that was familiar and full of turmoil. Eowen stood and clasped her hands in front of her just as Nolyi turned the corner. They faced each other, their auras meeting and playing against each other as it was known that powerful dreamers did in each other's presence. Eowen was far more powerful than Nolyi by this point, but the true extent of it remained in the bounds of her ceremonies. Nolyi broke the tension by relenting, shrinking the force of their presence away and gesturing their respect to Eowen in the way of the mountain folk.

"Greetings, Eowen Mortician."

There was a tremor through the world, or perhaps through Eowen's world, as the name Nolyi had called upon her with sent waves with eclectic immediacy into Eowen's being. Gooseflesh pinched across her body and a chill ran down her spine along with a blushing heat that rose up from her belly to the top of her head. Upon being called by that name, Eowen could feel a new sense emerge, one that tied her to all who had need of her. The connection was almost imperceivable, a thin strand from those who were unaware of the title and a less faint thread for those who called her Eowen Mortician actively in their hearts, an electrically alight tether now tied to each individual. She had not known the full extent of her influence till that moment, as she'd had no reason to look into it. There had been much work to do, and there was still work to do. But upon becoming aware of her epithet, Eowen could feel the pull for her presence far outside her dreaming aura. Her name had spread to the many settlements of the Britchen and even to some beyond, carried on the caravan routes of The Nagirr'Om's acolytes. She realized then why speaking or even thinking The Nagirr'Om's name all those months ago had called the being to her. The name had taken on a power of its own. It had been affixed an aspect of connection, power, and summoning by a collective manifestation of those that had come to know and associate the name with the being. It wasn't that the name had inherent power, but that thousands had given power to the name.

"Um, Eowen? Are you alright?" Nolyi's question broke Eowen's attention. The sudden awareness of her widespread identity was a labyrinth she could easily become lost in.

"Yes, sorry, hello Nolyi." Eowen gestured for Nolyi to join her on the bench. "It's nice to see you. It's been a while."

Nolyi took the space Eowen offered and they sat together, staring into the darkness.

"It has been a while. I've been... busy." Nolyi glanced at Eowen, then glanced away, they bit their lip and twiddled their thumbs. "Eowen... I—"

Nolyi cut themself off, looked to Eowen and gestured at her vaguely. They wanted Eowen to make the offer, to save face and to make the meeting easier. Nolyi already felt uncomfortable enough having come to Eowen like this, but Eowen did not respond. She only stared at Nolyi, silently waiting. Eowen had come to understand that her work, which followed death, was not meant to be easy or hard for the living to experience. It was meant to be gone through, and you could not do so when carried by another. So Eowen waited, and Nolyi gathered up the same courage that had brought many to Gran's stoop in the dead of the night.

"Please, perform a funeral for my sister, Eowen Mortician. I know Aiyano has been... difficult, and that I have been no better, but I've seen the change in my city. I don't know how to put it into words exactly, but I'll try. It's like a weight has been lifted. I think that is how we Brtichen have viewed the dead for a long time, as a burden to be removed as soon and efficiently as possible. That was wrong though, and I don't know how it started, but you have changed that, and it needed to change. So please." Nolyi lowered their head and awaited Eowen's answer.

Eowen no longer felt embarrassed by such praise, nor by Nolyi genuflecting. It came across to her as a natural result of her work, not a thing she herself deserved. Thus, when Nolyi, the powerful, fire wielding co-master and founder of the city of Nolano, presented themself like this, Eowen felt comfortable saying: "No."

A beat passed. Nolyi held the bow, glanced up at Eowen, sat abruptly upright, and glared. "What do you mean, no?" Eowen held up a hand for silence, but Nolyi was riled up. "You think I don't deserve to say goodbye or, or, whatever you have people do? You think I'm not good enough? Why? Why won't you do it!" Eowen didn't speak up, didn't try to interrupt them again, only waited while Nolyi's heart broke. "After everything I've been through, you won't do this one thing for me? You arrogant death-monger! Do you know what they say about the great Eowen Mortician? They say you stink of bodies, that you lay with them! That you eat them! Do you? Huh? Answer me you pathetic, self righteous child!"

Nolyi struck the wall of Gran's home next to Eowen's head with their first, releasing a burst of crimson flames that singed Eowen's hair and burst through the minor cracks in the stone. Gran threw open the door, cranky, wild-eyed, and hastily dressed.

"Huh! Huh? Huh!" The old woman's breathy exclamation and dagger-glare managed to shut Nolyi up. Gran sucked on her gums, taking in the full scene: Eowen sitting with a look of calm and empathy, Nolyi baring their teeth as tears ran unbidden down their face. Gran chewed on her gums and spat, the wad landing square on Nolyi's foot. "I was sleeping!" Then she slammed the door shut.

A few quieter clacks followed as the neighbor's windows and doors were closed as well, and Eowen and Nolyi were left alone once more. The fight went out of Nolyi and they deflated, now leaning against the wall they'd struck.

"I'm sorry," Nolyi whispered, and took their seat next to Eowen again. "I'm sorry, you don't deserve to be treated like that." Nolyi dropped their head in their hands and stayed there.

The truth was, Eowen had heard as much from others already. Four months of performing funerals had brought people to her at their worst moments. Each small mistake of hers had been met with the full range of comforting sympathy to enraged degradation. Some people were even glad for Eowen to make mistakes, for it meant that a person, fallible and sincere, was taking care of their loved one. Eowen knew that Nolyi's harsh words weren't their own and that they'd likely been heard in passing from others. Eowen scooted closer and wrapped her arms around Nolyi, and they, without hesitation, leaned into Eowen.

"It's nothing to do with you, or anyone else," Eowen whispered. Nolyi looked up, anger gone and only a question in their expression. "Nolyi... Cynna's body has already been destroyed. It is fragmented beyond any restorative power I know. If it can ever be reformed and recovered from the ashes, it will not be by me as I am now."

"But... couldn't we do a ceremony of some kind anyway? You know the words and ways of so many people now, can't we do something?" Eowen shook her head.

"You know that the words and sacred beasts and settings of other peoples would not serve the weight you carry." Eowen was gentle. She took Nolyi's hands and kissed each one before pulling them into an embrace. "The Britchen have no ceremonies for the dead. You, Nolyi, have no ceremonies for the dead. Your sister has already been burned, and her ashes lay with thousands of others." Eowen paused for a moment, and changed. She spoke with her power, for what she needed to say Nolyi needed to understand from one of authority. **"I cannot provide for the needs of a heart that knows not what they are."**

She pushed Nolyi away then and smiled, a sad and

crooked smile of one who understands the pain before them. "I was never able to perform a funeral for my own mother. None of my people received their rites before... I left. And now I will never be able to do that for her. Hmm, rather, I mean that I'll never be able to do the funeral of my mother for me. I too carry this weight, Nolyi, and in a way this is what death means, doesn't it? That the burdens of the dead will be carried on by the living who are left behind... and that certain opportunities are forever lost." Eowen forced herself to breathe through the knot in her heart, which was hard and painful, but she'd come to accept it would always be there. She touched her chest, feeling the scar of the mountain folk's seal above it, love and pain layered together. "But perhaps, if this weight cannot be lifted from our shoulders, we can learn from it. And maybe what we learn will be good, and it'll be something we can do some good with." Eowen squeezed Nolyi's arms. "That's... all I've been trying to do, really. So for you to come to me like this, well, I must be doing something right." Eowen kissed them on the forehead. **"Grieve, hurt, but do not be alone in your suffering. Let your pain motivate you to engage with life once more."**

Eowen's eyes had clouded over for that statement, but they returned to their dark, brown to see Nolyi shake themself out and stand up straight.

"Fine, I understand. It's aggravating and it's unfair and a part of me still wants to blame you! But I won't." They stepped back and rubbed at their face as if trying to wake up. "I'll talk to Aiyano, though. I want to change her mind. She's fine with your work being done, she just doesn't like it... She might also have been convincing other Britchen not to come to you. Though I don't know if any of us have any bodies of our loved ones left." Eowen made a small gesture of thanks, but it was noncommittal, a clear lack of expectation. "I'll... come by to visit again. We'll have a more pleasant conversation. Would that be alright?"

"I'd like that," Eowen said, and they shared an expression of, if not love, certainly affection, the kind all people are capable of sharing, if only in those rare moments where even the most divided find common ground to stand upon.

Nolyi left, disappearing back into the thick dark of the sleepy false night. Eowen dropped to her seat in a deep slouch and let out an exhausted and aggravated sigh. Gran kicked open the door and blew a stream of smoke out it.

"Thought they'd never leave. Huh," she muttered. "Get in here, Twig. You look tired."

"I caaan't," Eowen moaned. "I'm supposed to have a chant memorized for a Nemsto funeral tomorrow. I had it perfect, was reciting it in my head, but then that all happened and now it's gone."

Gran spit and shrugged. "Huh. Get to it then." She tapped out the contents of her pipe onto the stoop and retreated back inside.

Eowen sighed a deep and weary sigh, rubbed her eyes, and manifested some water to drink and splash her face with. She retrieved a small cube of light wood from her pocket and pressed her thumb over a piece of glass embedded in one of the faces. A voice emerged, as if the speaker were the box itself, reciting a long droning chant in a twisty language. She sat up straight, and after the chant finished began reciting the words back. It was a language she didn't know for people she'd only just met the day before, but the chant was only performed by designated holy officiants, and the old man and middle aged son had decided Eowen could fulfill that role. After several hours of recitations, Eowen nudged her heron where it sat curled up next to the bench.

"There, how was that?" The heron opened one eye and Eowen groaned at the look it gave her. "Alright, again."

* * *

Four entire months and a week's worth of time in Nolano had passed when the two boys who'd approached Eowen with the body of their mother returned. She was sitting beneath the bone tree, her heron curled around her. She could feel the shifting subconscious of the entire city. She held the stone Ne had given her in one hand, its comforting tug toward the mountain folk a reminder of where she could always go to be treated like family, even if she was not. She felt the tether of the ring on her other hand, a guideline to an adventure she would always have a place in. She was also familiarizing herself with the web of dreamers that knew her by the title of Eowen Mortician. She could feel when they wanted her, when they needed her, when they simply knew of her or were thinking of her, or when their spirits sang for her workings even if they did not know it in their minds yet.

The final object of her meditation was the path that would lead her to Tavo. How far he had gone in the new world and whether she could ever catch up to him was an entirely unknown factor. Inside her spirit she felt as a ship without rudder or sails, pulled in too many directions and only kept from going adrift by anchor. It was in this state of contemplation that the Edeltraunt boys approached Eowen. To them, she seemed like a great, if very young sage, as a dense serenity hung about her. Eowen was still only a strip of a girl, but seated beneath the massive tree, surrounded by the many skeletons and stroking the head of the bone heron, she seemed much more than that.

"We greet you, Eowen Mortician," the older boy said, bowing to her.

"Yes, we do greet you, Eowen Mortician. Uh, the honorable." The boys both stumbled through her language, clearly having learned this small bit just to meet with her. Eowen opened her clouded eyes, her dreaming self extended far beyond where she sat. Her eyes cleared as she returned and gestured for them to sit down. Eowen pulled one of Ordwell's brass spheres from a pocket and manifested a table with a divot to place it in.

"Goma, Suka, no need to be so formal. Sit down, have you eaten today?" The boys shook their heads and joined her.

"We're actually here about our mother," said the older boy, Goma, still trying to keep things professional with Eowen. "We've been working with other Edeltraunt in Nolano to remember the hymn, and we've almost got it all."

"Have either of you eaten today?" Eowen asked, and the younger boy Suka's stomach growled. "I haven't eaten in many hours, got too distracted. Can you manifest some of your favorite dishes? I've never had Edeltraunt food. Here, I'll make some from my home."

Eowen manifested familiar bread, fruit, and a roasted fish from the rivers of the old world jungle. The boys looked at each other, muttered and discussed whether to try and manifest something special they'd only eaten a few times in their life, or something familiar they were more likely to get right. They decided on the latter, and soon the table was covered in flat breads, large roasted invertebrates, and nutrient-rich grasses with an astounding variety of flavors. The boys picked and twisted various grasses together, arguing over what combination Eowen would like the most. She let them bicker as they relaxed into well-trodden conversation. They ate and Eowen forced herself to smile and nod politely, as the weave they'd picked was overstimulating.

When they'd had their fill, Eowen gestured to the starfield to her left. It moved aside at the touch of her power, and the wrapped, preserved body of their mother emerged to rest next to the table. "Where will the funeral be?"

The boys brought her to a hill the Edeltraunt of Nolano had manifested on the outskirts of the city. It was a minor landmark by the standards set by Eowen's massive bone tree and the valleys and rivers of other cultures. There was an arched entrance cut into it, and the two boys marched in to deposit the body of their mother.

They emerged uncertain of what to do next, and Eowen directed them with confidence. She sent them to retrieve other members of their people who would attend or assist, and soon they arrived, all taller than Eowen save for the little children. She was invited to sit with those who were most familiar with the funeral hymn. Three adult women, one adult man, and a girl who could not have been more than seven years old when the world had ended. Eowen wondered what the little child's life must have been like, even before the fall, for her to know part of a funeral song that the adults present did not.

They recited it to her as best as they could, an appropriately haunting song that would drone on for a half an hour when recited in full. It took almost two hours to fully assemble their collective recollection of it for Eowen. The little girl knew a stretch in the middle that to Eowen sounded less like singing and more like a ghastly wail, but no one corrected her, and so it remained. Eowen repeated it back to them over and over, making many mistakes, yet her and their patience did not falter.

The main problem with the hymn was that the Edeltraunt people had an entirely separate language used by their arcane religious figures, and thus they were attempting to recreate the song exclusively by memory of the sounds. None knew the holy language, and so none knew what the hymn actually said. Eowen recorded the most complete version they managed to assemble on a glass bead which could be placed into the wooden cube, like the one she'd used to learn parts for other funerals. She sent the gathered people away for the night, promising she'd have it memorized by the end of the next day. They left, bowing, waving, and appreciative, yet Eowen could sense a lack of confidence. They would let her perform the rite, their people had no restrictions against outsiders becoming religious figures, but they knew the hymn was incomplete. Their mourning ritual would be done as best as it could, but Eowen knew it would be unfulfilling in the end, and this certainty itched at her. She recited for several hours, but the feeling of discontent didn't abate.

Eowen took a break and sighed. "It doesn't have to be perfect, it just has to be enough," she whispered to herself.

The bone heron stalked around her, looking down its spear-beak at the girl. She craned her neck to see it and huffed.

"Easy for you. You can't speak, and even if you did they wouldn't ask a bird to do it." The heron adjusted its stance but stayed locked onto her. "I can't just ask them for more time, that's not the issue. We could fly to the east and try to find a holy person that knows the entire hymn, but the chances of that are... Fine, I also don't want to go flying to the east." The heron sat down and lay its head in Eowen's lap.

She ran her fingers through its feathers absentmindedly. "I know I've been here a while, but I can't just go off in the opposite direction of Tavo. I still intend—"

The heron nipped her hand and she glared at it, repairing the scratch with a snap of manifestation.

"I will find him, but I also want to serve the people here. I can feel it, they still need me. Hmm, they probably need a lot more than just me, but what they need from me I'm going to give."

The heron was asleep by all appearances now, and not for the first time Eowen wondered just how divine of a creature it really was. At times it seemed to speak to her, communicating some wisdom beyond mortal ken, but other times it seemed little more than a dumb bird. A few months ago Eowen had been beside a manifested river with fish in it. Her heron had been stalking through the water while she rested her feet in the cool current. The heron had seemed like no more than a normal bird, but when it had struck for a fish, something in the quality of it, the light it reflected or the grace it held, had been transcendent. Eowen had turned the memory of the event over in her head since, and wondered whether she had been meant to interpret some wisdom from it, or if she were a fool on the edge of sanity for trying to do so. Eowen turned the thought over in her head again, but the well trodden memory only served to lull her to sleep.

****

[Listen a little longer.]

AND I SAID MY NAME OF—

Why must I listen to this? What is the point? Who are you, and why have you been in my dreams?

[…]

You've spoken through me before, I'm starting to remember now. Why did you? Are you like the Storm, are you something else?

[…]

Are you just a dream?

[…]

Alright, I'll listen.

[Just for a little longer.]

I SAID MY NAME OF YAWNING FIRE THAT IS ONLY RED AND HAIR TIPS THAT CAN FEEL AND THE SHIFT OF A FOOT UPON SAND UPON STONE AND PERFECT FINGERNAILS AND BELLS THAT CANNOT BREAK AND A FEELING FOR WHICH THERE ARE NO WORDS TO DESCRIBE, BUT IT IS SIMILAR TO THE FEELING OF SINGING SO BEAUTIFULLY THAT THE HEARTLESS WEEPS AND IS NEVER HEARTLESS AGAIN.

****

"Oh! She's awake!" Suka, the younger brother, called to the other Edeltraunt. Eowen sat up from where she'd fallen asleep the previous night, the heron was still on her lap. "Greetings, Eowen. How, uh, was your rest?"

"Oh, I'm fine." Eowen sat up a little too fast and dislodged the heron. It glared at her and fluttered away. Eowen wiped an embarrassing amount of drool off her chin and took stock of her surroundings. Suka was seated next to her, very tactfully ignoring the disheveled state of his substitute holy person. The other Edeltraunt were seated nearby, speaking quietly amongst themselves. Their body language gave off the impression they'd been discussing something at a normal volume before and were now muttering furtively. Goma rose to join his brother and Eowen and Suka tried to smile confidently at her. "Why are you all here so early?" Eowen asked when Goma sat down with them.

"Honorable Eowen Mortician, we have been here for some hours. You've slept through most of the day."

"No!" Eowen jumped up and straightened her robes. "I'm terribly sorry, let us begin the ceremony right away!" Before she could move, Goma caught her by the wrist and pulled her back to her seat.

"No. We," he gestured to the others he'd been speaking with, "have decided not to hold the ceremony. We will travel with a caravan to find the Edeltraunt to the east, whatever is left of them. Even if there are no holy people left who know the hymn, we may be able to piece it together with the help of others that have heard it." He bowed his head. "Thank you for the time and effort you have given to us. It is enough."

He lifted his eyes to Eowen, who met and held them for a long time. She searched his expression, then turned to Suka, who looked away immediately. Eowen stood up again, slowly, and she held her head high and proud. Eowen felt the weight of her history then. It had taken her entire life and all she'd been through to not feel embarrassed in this moment. Today, she would stand before a people that she'd let down and not be crushed under the feeling of her own failure. Eowen felt something, the remnants of her dream with the vast voices of power within it. Her own voice of power had been infantile in comparison, but just large enough to join theirs. She felt their weight, their texture, their presence, and she smiled.

[Follow me.]

There was no way to resist the request, for it tapped into the desire within the gathered people to be led, to have an authority to rely on. Eowen moved up the hill, practically gliding, her presence heavy with significance yet physically weightless. The Edeltraunt of Nolano looked at each other and saw in their fellow's eyes something they had all but lost in the fall, something that few managed to find again: Faith.

Eowen stood upon the rise above their dead and spread her hands wide as if to embrace them all. The people before her, especially the two boys, had been the first to approach her to honor and care for their dead. Eowen felt that she was not herself in that moment. The greater voice that spoke in her dreams was guiding her, and she was eager to let it. Her dreaming aura thickened around them as starlight shot up in great pillars that propped up a ceiling of darkness. They stood within a temple of power and potential. Then the heron landed, craning over her as Eowen's visage smeared and flowed into it. The preparations were complete, a firmament of ceremonial loss and acknowledgement. Eowen opened her mouth for the voice to speak through her again, but before it did, she interrupted it.

"**Wait. Suka, take this.**" Eowen handed the boy her wooden cube with its ability to record sound. He activated it, and held it out with both hands like an offering. Eowen smiled, and from her, or perhaps through her, a presence spoke.

[The hymn for the dead.]

The song came, plucked from beyond time and space by a presence not wholly bound by either, channeled through a mouth that had never known its words. The voice that spoke could not be held in the mortal minds of those that listened, for it was too vast and too powerful. Despite that, its words could not be misconstrued. None present knew the entire hymn, nor had they ever known the true meaning of the words before, yet as the great voice spoke they understood it all. Later, after the spell of the moment had worn off, the listeners who had been given this unique view into the secret holy language understood why it might have been kept secret.

It was a hymn of duty and loss, of the gifts the gods give us all and the secret ones that even we may never come to understand. The voice sang of the terrible ache of those that loved the deceased, of those that could have come to love them, of those that had once loved them but had long since died as well. The hymn also claimed that the singer, as one in tune with the gods, was familiar with a divine sort of grief, and therefore their own suffering was worse than the actual loved ones. The hymn also begged the gods to forgive the foolish and sinful dead and living for their many transgressions against them. Finally, the song's last ten minutes were spent exalting the infallible, divine mathematics that the gods used to calculate the worth of all things, thus extolling their wisdom in balancing the universe. This might have been a rather cold end to the funeral if the hymn did not conclude with one final assertion: That their beloved dead would be with the gods forever, where pain could not exist.

It was a simple promise. The Edeltraunt afterlife was not complex, and few people in the new world still believed in their old religions. Still, the promise of everlasting life without pain, seated beside the greatest beings of the universe, was a comfort when spoken by a voice that, to those listening, was the closest they'd ever come to meeting a god.

The ceremony ended, and the firmament that Eowen, or the presence that had worked through her, had established washed itself away. The gathered Edeltraunt emerged from the dream to find Eowen Mortician asleep on top of the grassy hill.

****

[Listen a little longer.]

THAT IS MY GREAT NAME.

****

Eowen sat in Gran's home some days later with Suka, listening to the wooden cube as it spoke with Eowen's voice in a language neither of them knew. The Eowen of that moment spoke clearly with confidence, authority, and mourning, but not with the power she had then. Ordwell's brass sphere could not translate the words from the box, as they were not being spoken by a person but by an inanimate recording. Suka had assured her that the ceremony had been perfect, that no one had ever heard the hymn more flawlessly performed even in the old world. It seemed there was a unanimous and intuitive agreement, despite no one actually knowing the entire thing, that Eowen, or whatever had possessed her in that moment, had done it perfectly. Thus, she was grateful she had recorded it for their future use, but it frustrated her that only her voice emerged and none of the power that had been in it. Eowen glared as her past self droned on into a third listen of the hymn. Suka yawned and Eowen glanced at him, her expression still a glare from her annoyance with the results.

"My apologies, Eowen Mortician." He slapped himself awake and sat up straight. Eowen sighed, stopped the recording, and shook her head.

"You're right to yawn, it is boring. Thank you for humoring me." She stood and gestured that Suka could leave. He got up and dipped his head to pass through Gran's low doorway.

"Goodbye then, Eowen. Goodbye, Gran." He waved to Eowen and the old woman smoking on the stoop, then was gone, though they could see the top of his head bobbing over the low buildings.

"Tell him not to come back," Gran said when Suka was out of earshot.

"Did he offend you?" Eowen took the seat next to the old woman.

"Huh. Too tall." Gran exhaled and it drifted toward Eowen, so she manifested a small breeze to blow it away.

"All the Edeltraunt are tall, Gran."

"Why? They stretch out their babies?"

Eowen opened her mouth to respond, but not knowing the answer shut it again. "Why do you smoke?" she said instead.

"Hmm?"

"Is it pleasant? Smells terrible to me."

"Hmm. Huh. Makes me look distinguished. Can't be a respected elder if you don't smoke." Gran sucked on her pipe, then her gums, then her pipe again. Eowen closed her eyes and leaned back. She liked Gran's stoop. It had felt more like a home to her than anywhere in years, even before the fall. She knew her time to leave was soon though. She just didn't know exactly when it would be.

* * *

The answer came in her last month in Nolano, after she'd been inactive for almost two weeks with no work left to do. Roughly six months worth of time had passed after she'd arrived with Hani. Eowen received another invitation from Aiyano, but this time the woman came in person. Eowen was seated beneath her bone tree when the healer approached. Eowen was stroking her bird's neck and testing its strange ability to store things in its feathers, pulling out and putting in clothes, wrapped food, tools, and even an entire door, though that had been awkward to finagle. Aiyano approached with her hands clasped and smiled at Eowen.

"May I sit with you?"

"Of course." Eowen gestured and continued feeling into

the feathers till she found her old people-finder stick. "So that's where I left it. What can I do for you?" she asked.

"Nothing for me, exactly. I wanted to invite you to something." Aiyano had her hands out, trying to seem unthreatening. "Nolyi and I, mostly Nolyi, came up with an idea that we were hoping you'd be present for."

Eowen cocked an eyebrow. "You do realize what I'm usually requested for?"

"This isn't that... Well not exactly that."

"So you're fine with what I do now?" Eowen manifested a cup of water to drink. She felt awkward and needed something to do with her hands.

"I've..." Aiyano thought for a moment. "I've been fine with you for some time, mostly thanks to Nolyi. Funerals seem to me like celebrations of death, but people appreciate having them. So, yes, I'm fine with you. Your work might be the opposite of mine, but it's important to you and some people." Aiyano shrugged and waited for Eowen to respond, her expression resigned but open. Their dreaming auras pushed against each other, two powerful pressures that had once easily commingled but were newly strangers. Eowen tried to settle down and make her body language as nonchalant as possible.

"Of course, Aiyano, I'd be happy to attend." Eowen gritted her teeth, hoping her voice wasn't too stiff. Aiyano seemed to understand that the awkwardness between them wouldn't disappear at that moment and smiled warmly.

"Follow me then, we'll be starting soon. If you're not doing anything else?"

Eowen did, in fact, have several plans for the day, but they were all just to keep herself busy and were easily abandoned. She mounted the bone heron and Aiyano unrolled her floating rug. They took off and flew over the city, out past the barrier, and into the stretch between Nolano and the first settlement of Port Disoke. Eowen could feel the Storm once she passed through the barrier, but it was faint and distant. She knew the power of it could still come through her if she let it, but without a strong host present it wasn't nearly so dangerous.

They arrived at the former city of the Britchen, the new world's Port Disoke, now sparsely populated by previously scattered peoples that had been brought by caravans. They continued past it to the ash field and landed by the incinerator building, where Nolyi was waiting.

"Hello." Nolyi nodded to Eowen. They fidgeted, seeming full of an excited energy. "I'm glad you came. I think you'll like what I have planned."

"I'm still not sure we should be doing this," Aiyano muttered.

"What exactly am I here for?" Eowen spoke formally in the mountain folk's language. Somehow it felt more proper than using the formalities of her own, and she'd continued practicing with the mountain folk living in Nolano.

"Just watch and tell me what you think afterward," Nolyi said, then turned toward the expanse of ash. It hadn't grown much since Eowen's last and only visit, but there hadn't been many more bodies to burn. Nolyi held out their hand for Aiyano, who, with great discomfort, took it. Nolyi closed their eyes and began to dip into their dreaming. The usual signs of it followed, shadows, light, and the tension of a great deal of potential present, but it also felt as if Nolyi were waiting. The power mounted its peak presence and even Eowen's own aura of dreaming was entirely pushed back. though she wasn't resisting. Nolyi felt fully prepared to do something, yet still they waited for a long minute to pass before groaning. "Aiyano, please."

Aiyano stiffened, adjusted her hold on Nolyi's hand, but did not contribute her power to the manifestation. "I just... I don't understand why we must do this! Things are fine, our people are happy, safe, prosperous. They don't need anything to change and we don't need to be here!" She gesticulated, getting worked up, but Nolyi pulled her close with their entwined hand and placed their other one on Aiyano's cheek.

"I know. I know my love. Maybe it is too much, and maybe things don't need to change, but it can't really do any harm and... Can you do this with me? For me?"

Aiyano and Nolyi shared a few looks that transitioned from playful glaring, to pouting, to grinning, then to fixed love. Aiyano closed her eyes and faced the ash once more. She leaned into Nolyi and they let go of each other's hands so that they could wrap their arms around each other instead. Nolyi still held their power at the ready, and this time Aiynao added hers. The two immensely powerful dreamers, one who had once defeated the Storm and another who'd awakened the same kind of strength The Nagirr'Om, Hani, and Eowen had displayed, merged their dreaming selves into a mass of shadow and light Eowen had never before been present for. It rose and rose, a great wave of merging possibilities that blotted the entirety of the new world from Eowen's vision. She stood back and let the sheer volume of the unreality obliterate her senses and replace them with awe. Then the collected power tipped forward, spilling and breaking over the ashes, pushing them out for dozens of kilometers. Pure force which, as Eowen watched, transmuted into a great crashing wave that was briny and crisp. No longer did a sad, collapsing mountain of ash tower before them, for now it was a beautiful beach, glowing with silvery-gray mist. There was a new sea before them, stretching far beyond the eye and alight with its own cloud-soft glow. Waves pushed and pulled the ashes of the dead in and out.

It wasn't a funeral, exactly, and it wasn't an established start of a new tradition for the dead, nor a continuation of an ancient ritual, but Eowen could feel why Nolyi had wanted her there. There was something about the sea before them, constructed from Nolyi's feelings for their sister, for the goodbye they'd never gotten. Eowen sensed a cleansing aspect about the water that purified the spirit, and took a few steps forward to let the water wash over her feet, spreading thick, damp ash and a few scattered bones. She could feel something in her when she touched the water, a deep cleaning in the marrow of her substance, a washing of dust from the old pains in her heart. The knot in her heart was still there, solid and stiff, but something in the ashen beach infused her with a feeling of promise that one day the knot would be gone. Eowen grinned, totally unbidden, and laughed, the joy of hope unlocking a child-like energy. She turned to see how the creators of the beach were doing in time to see Nolyi leapt past her with a shout and splash into the water. They breached, laughing and continued running and splashing.

"It's amazing! It's perfect!" Nolyi declared for no one other than themself. Eowen looked at Aiyano and saw that the healer looked joyful and confused, as if their positive feelings were supposed to be wrong yet couldn't help enjoying them.

"Well, Aiyano," Eowen said with a wry smile. "Is it amazing? Is it perfect?" Aiyano shook her head, but she was smiling.

"What do you want me to say?" She made a gesture of resignation and turned on her heel, making her way back to the floating rug. "If Nolyi is pleased, then it must be." When Eowen stepped off the beach no ash clung to her as dust or wet sand, it peeled off as if there were a barrier only the living could pass through.

"It is a wonder," Eowen whispered, for though the physical attributes were simple, the effect on her spirit had been real and powerful. It wasn't exactly a new funeral tradition and didn't fall entirely under her domain of power, but what Aiyano and Nolyi had done was near enough that it might one day become part of a death ritual for the Britchen. Nolyi emerged from the water, shaking it off and laughing. They passed the barrier and all the ash that had gotten on them from their swim sprang off to rejoin the rest. They approached Eowen and held out their hand which Eowen clasped.

"I can see it. You felt what I felt when the water touched me." They squeezed Eowen's hand and shook it.

"Many will feel the same. You've started something here and I've no doubt it will change things for the better among your people." Eowen let go of Nolyi's hand and stared out across the waves. "I couldn't feel the Storm in there either, which means you've made a safe place away from it." *And your own power has matured enough to resist it in the way Hani, Aiyano, The Nagirr'Om, and I can.*

"The sea goes further than you might think too." Nolyi pointed to the most distant crests. "I can't sense that far, but when I was making it, with Aiyano's help I thought I could feel the people who'd been on the other side of the sea in the old world. The Edeltraunt, that is. I think the sea reaches them, and that it can be safely traversed." Nolyi flashed a smile. "We'll find out someday!"

Eowen mounted her heron and Nolyi joined Aiyano on the rug as they flew back to Nolano, taking their time. They watched the moving people far below; caravans bringing refugees to Port Disoke, acolytes setting down paths with barriers. The two leaders followed Eowen to the bone tree and landed there to speak. Nolyi leapt off the rug, still full of energy.

"So, Eowen, that was a very nice funeral for my sister and everyone else's ashes there. Don't you think?" Nolyi patted the bone tree and looked to Eowen expectantly.

Eowen smiled at them, but it was a sad one that looked forced. Nolyi noticed and both their faces fell. Eowen teetered for a moment, deciding whether she wanted to lie to them, but she'd never gotten better at that, since her expression usually gave her away. So, she decided on the truth.

"It... was a beautiful manifestation, Nolyi, and a wonder of creation, but that was not a funeral."

"Why? Didn't it have all the qualities of one, wasn't there, uh, ceremony and an emotional experience? We were all uplifted, right, weren't we?" Nolyi looked at Aiyano for confirmation and she nodded enthusiastically, but otherwise didn't look as though she agreed in any way. "I just want to honor my sister, and say goodbye to her properly. Why isn't all that enough? What was missing?" Nolyi dropped onto a root of the bone tree, their question not directed at anyone. "What do I have to do?"

Aiyano moved to embrace her spouse, but Eowen gestured for her to stay back and knelt next to Nolyi. "Nolyi, I can feel how you wish for this, and I promise I understand. We've spoken about that before, remember?" Nolyi didn't look Eowen in the eyes, but they did nod. "I don't know what the answer is, I only know that wasn't it. Your people don't have such ceremonies, and substituting another won't do. You must discover your own and understand it. I think that sea and that beach may well become part of something for you, but it is not yet."

Eowen flexed her fingers against each other, thinking back to her years and years as an apprentice, how she'd felt for so long that she'd never be able to speak with authority on anything. She wondered, not for the first time, if even now she had the right to speak of death and funerals with any kind of expertise. Eowen knew her insecurities were habit, not evidence, and they would not hold her from speaking truths she could feel in her spirit.

"My approval will not appease the need in your spirit. Seek it no longer."

Eowen took Nolyi's hand and stood them up, then brought them to Aiyano, who embraced them. Nolyi took their seat on the rug and gazed up at the bone tree.

"Why do I want this so badly?" they whispered, but they were asking themself, and so Eowen did not answer. Aiyano stood next to Eowen and sighed, looking quite exhausted.

"I know we'll always be at odds because of the work we do, but I'd still like to spend more time with you. Aside from all this—" Aiyano gestured at the bone tree "—I think you're a rather pleasant person."

"Why do you think our work puts us at odds?" Eowen's question seemed to confuse Aiyano.

"Because, I serve life and you serve death. They are the two most opposing forces there are." Eowen considered this and couldn't help her expression becoming amused and a touch mischievous. "Is something funny?" Aiyano asked.

"In a way. I'm not a killer, I don't bring death or harm, so your claim is a little off. We don't serve opposing forces,

Aiyano, we both work with the body for the sake of the spirit. My part just... come after yours." Eowen laughed and nudged Aiyano with her elbow. The older woman rolled her eyes, but didn't deny what Eowen had said. She looked at Nolyi, waiting on the rug, and decided she'd give it some more thought.

"Either way, come join us at the tree sometime. We'll honor you."

Eowen made a simple gesture of respect and stepped back. "I'll do that."

Aiyano joined Nolyi and they took off, back to the tree and the work that awaited them. There were still, after all, many many people scattered and alone in the new world, and Aiyano was determined to try and save them all. Eowen waited till they were entirely out of sight, then started back to Gran's place. She didn't fly on the heron this time, but walked slowly through Nolano. It was not a long walk, but the city was alive and active. She passed many people, most of whom waved and greeted her, and it occurred to Eowen how many lives she'd touched and how many she'd come to know. Even with Ordwell's translator, she now spoke five languages with some fluency, knew hundreds of games that children played across the cultures of Nolano, and had tasted more flavors than anyone in her former home even knew existed. As she passed through the city, a group of old men invited her to gamble with them, some children asked her for a story, and a woman manifested the ingredients for the breads she baked because she insisted the smell from the oven was the best part. In only that short walk Eowen passed more people whose names, likes, and dislikes she knew, more than she'd ever known even among her former people before the fall.

She arrived at Gran's house, and there the old woman sat, smoking like always.

"Saw you on that bird," Gran said. "Felt something big happen. Not gonna be a bother is it?" Eowen grinned at her and shrugged.

"Might be, honorable Gran." The old woman glared, her beady eyes boring into the girl.

"You don't talk that way to me, huh, you Twig of a girl. What's gotten into you?" Eowen looked around, hoping for a distraction to forestall the moment, some passerby she could strike up a conversation with, but they were perfectly alone.

"I thought I should give my elder some respect before... I leave."

Gran removed her pipe and sucked on her gums for a long, thoughtful moment, looking Eowen up and down.

"Huh! I'm no elder of yours, you just been hanging around my house. Why haven't you left then, eh? You were waitin' around for something, I thought."

"I was."

"Got what you were waiting for then?"

"No, but I think that's alright. I thought I had to be here till everything changed and I'd completely made things right, but I think if I tried to do that I'd be here forever." Eowen sat next to Gran. "Things can always keep getting better, can't they? Eventually, one has to decide things are good enough and move on, don't they?"

"Huh. You think too much. Are you leaving or not?"

Eowen covered a laugh with her hand. "Yes, Gran. I'm leaving Nolano to search for my cousin. He's been going northwest, or at least that's the direction he left a few months ago."

"Then shift off. Wasting time here, huh."

"Well, I wanted to say goodbye to you first."

"Course you did, got all your manners." Gran pointed away with her cane. "Go on then, said it didn't you? Huh." Eowen wrapped her arms around Gran's frame and kissed her on the cheek.

"Goodbye, Gran. Thank you for letting me stay with you, for giving me a place where I felt safe. You've done more for me than you know." Eowen held the old woman as she 'huh'ed and glanced around as if worried someone would see their tough old matriarch doing something so tender.

"Course I did, little Twig like you couldn't hang around here without my help, huh. Off now." Gran disengaged from Eowen and pushed her off the bench. The bone heron stretched its wings and danced from foot to foot. It seemed eager to be gone as well. Eowen gave a last little wave and mounted up, sitting cross legged as she usually did. The bird flapped its wings and floated up and off the starfield, hovering above Gran's roof. "Eowen!" Gran called to her. "Come visit next time you're around!"

Eowen opened her mouth to respond, but stopped short as she realized. The heron took off while Eowen was speaking, and in seconds she was out of earshot. "You didn't call me Twig!"

In the time it took Gran to refill her pipe and light it, Eowen was out of sight. Crueen came out of the house, where she'd heard everything. She sighed and sat next to Gran.

"Well, it's going to be quiet around her now, isn't it?" Crueen said.

"Oh, shut it," Gran muttered around her pipe.

"I know you'll miss her. No need to be so sour about it." Crueen patted Gran's back and leaned into the old woman.

Gran eyed the caretaker next to her, then pulled out her pipe, wiped the mouthpiece off, and offered it to her.

"Huh. You know how to smoke, Crueen?"

"Me? No, nasty habit. Smells like poison."

"Learn." Gran forced the pipe into Crueen's hands, who held it pinched between two fingers away from herself.

"Why?"

"It's an order from your honorable elder." Gran closed her eyes and leaned back against her house. Crueen glanced at her, manifested a cloth to wrap the pipe in, and slipped it into a pocket.

"Of course, honorable Gran." The old woman was already snoring, so Crueen retrieved a blanket from inside and laid it over her lap.

* * *

Eowen's latent fears of traveling alone into the unknown were assuaged within her first weeks outside of Nolano. On the soft back of her heron the going was easy, and she could spend hours marveling at the beauty of the new world from her high vantage. Settlements twinkled in the distance, each spot of light within the endless dark a promise that the people were finding a way to thrive. The new world no longer felt vast and inhospitable as it had when she'd first arrived or when she'd traveled with Hani. Her senses were vast enough that merely being in sight of a settlement was enough to feel the overall status of the people there. So it was that Eowen passed by many of the first populations on her way without stopping in them. They were the auxiliary habitations to Nolano, full of the scattered people from formerly inland Britchen cities and towns. Eowen already knew a bit about these settlements from the caravans that went between them and Nolano. In the half a year she spent in Nolano, there was little of greater interest to the citizens than news of the world beyond, and that usually meant news from the other Britchen cities.

They had managed to survive the Storm in the early days because of The Nagirr'Om's efforts. The silver glowing woman was rumored to have originated from a Britchen city far inland. The Nagirr'Om had flown from place to place, killing powerful dreamers that showed signs of falling to the Storm. It was a brutal tactic, but it had kept most Britchen settlements from being besieged like Port Disoke had. Unfortunately, the development of these settlements had also been hobbled by having all their most powerful dreamers executed. Eowen flew past them, seeing how small their cities were compared to Nolano, how their manifestations were not as grand or as clever. There was less power in these places, but there was also less discord. The Britchen people had been well spread out in the old world, their territories stretching far up the eastern coast of the continent and deep inland to the west. None of the new world settlements were as diverse as Nolano though, as its predecessor, the old world's Port Disoke, was a three-city-state-port in the old world that brought people from everywhere.

Eowen saw that in some places, landscapes were being manifested to recover a feeling of the old world. There were forests, rocky deserts, marshlands, and many rivers the further west she went. The aid Nolano had provided since the banishment of the Storm had done a great deal to help the far cities, but even without Aiyano and Nolyi, Eowen could feel that nearly all of them had achieved something Nolano had not: care for their dead. It seemed that the

Britchen didn't normally burn their dead and dump them into the sea, as in the old Port Disoke.

A few days into her trip, Eowen approached a settlement during a funeral to observe, though she kept herself hidden. She could feel that they did not need her, but she was curious. As it turned out, other Britchen did cremate their bodies and pour them into their rivers, similar to how Port Disoke put the ashes out to sea. The difference was in how publicly the ceremony was performed. After the family had collected herbs, flowers, and wood, they'd bring the body to the beach where many in the town waited. It still lacked much in the way of ceremony that other cultures partook in, but it was real, and it faced death with courage. She listened as a figure with some authority recited a small piece of a larger speech honoring their dead: "Your life was given by the rivers, and they are the veins of the world. Now you are given back so that you can rejoin the flow that gives life to the world." Eowen hadn't known till then the Britchen word for river, but when they spoke it she heard the word 'Britck,' and her translator from Ordwell made it known to her.

Britck. Britchen. Their name for themselves must be an old word for river-people, or of the river. Maybe that is why the people of Port Disoke became so distanced from their funerals; they no longer lived on the rivers. Maybe it was all the other cultures that moved in, pushing them away from their collective traditions. Who knows, the change might have happened so long ago that even in the old world there were probably no records.

Eowen left the mourners and continued on, noting how the Britchen funeral seemed to lack any religious implication. She wondered if that had always been the case or something that had changed after the fall.

In those first weeks away, Eowen swooped close to

settlements while keeping to a northwest heading. She could feel the pull for those that would benefit from her work everywhere, even beyond her dreaming senses, tethered by the identity of Eowen Mortician. The pull to the Britchen cities was weak, as none of them lacked funeral rites the way Nolano had. Thus, Eowen continued on past these places, knowing that she was not needed. She slept when tired, ate when hungry, and only sometimes felt lonely. When those times came, she could not bring herself to move for many hours.

The tethers Eowen could feel to those that would benefit from her work served to remind her that there was a place for her in this new world with people she could ingratiate herself to. At times it was discouraging to know that the bond she felt to mourners would always be one-sided, a thing only she could feel. Eowen knew that wherever she went, she'd have to earn her worth through what she provided. Even in the old world, when her mother had declared her worthless and sent her away to a new apprenticeship, they'd still welcomed her with open arms. No matter how useless she'd been before, or how poor her reputation, she'd still been one of the people. It had been a security she'd always believed would be there no matter how much of a disappointment she was, so long as she eventually came back home. That security had been long gone now, though Eowen was still unsure how she would approach totally new people that had never heard of her. The new world held few threats for her other than the Storm, but somehow strangers felt almost as threatening.

After a few weeks, Eowen would occasionally stop to get news and rumors, or simply for a break from the back of her bird. She kept her bird out of sight and tried to be as unremarkable as possible as she asked after Tavo. Eowen described him as a young man of about twenty, hailing from the jungle and savannah tribes and traveling northwest. People from her background were rare in these parts but not unheard of. Her inquiries yielded few results until Eowen learned from a family that had taken him in for a few nights. She learned that her cousin was traveling alone. Eowen tried to contain her relief in learning that he was still alive, but as soon as she was alone she found herself short of breath and the heron had to carry her away.

"He's alive, heron! He's out there!"

Tavo had left Nolano before the Storm had been banished and therefore before the caravans had become common. She started to hear more rumors of him as the days progressed, and learned he was regarded as a powerful dreamer capable of wonders. As he'd traveled, Tavo had provided manifestations in exchange for hospitality. Simple but impressive things like ever flowing fountains of water, plants that regrow plucked food instantly, and basic domestic things. Eowen met people with tools that never broke and clothes that never wore out, smelled bad, or stayed dirty. From what she'd heard, he'd passed through the outer Britchen settlements only about five months prior with a consistent northwest heading. On her heron, Eowen was quickly closing the gap.

Sometimes when Eowen stopped to ask about Tavo, she received other news instead. Hani and his crew were sailing north through the starfield, his ship immune to the Storm and his crew an impressive collection of powerful dreamers. They were making quite a name for themselves, and many hoped The Stormwake would visit them one day. Children played pretend that they were members of Hani's crew or other already mythic figures like Aiyano, Nolyi, or The Nagirr'Om.

Sometimes the people Eowen met would speak of The Nagirr'Om, who inspired hope and terror in equal measure. In all her travels through the Britchen territories, Eowen heard more news of Nolano than of anything else. Everyone seemed to have an opinion about the powerful founders who ranged out with caravans to provide infrastructure and aid.

Eowen was surprised to find that even her own legend had made it out of Nolano, though her story didn't inspire nearly as much interest. The strange small girl from the jungle and savannah tribes that served the grieving, or by some stories, the dead themselves, was a touchy subject. In some rumors, she'd played some part in stopping the Storm. In others she was a secret servant of it. A generally positive impression of Eowen's funeral work spread, but she was still spoken of in hushed tones, as if they were afraid of attracting her attention. One consistent part of her growing legend was how she had stayed in Nolano in defiance to its founders, a detail that carried many implications. Sometimes the stories said that she stayed for its people, but most suggested she was a dreaded, though not necessarily antagonistic, associate of Aiyano and Nolyi.

Eowen never stayed in one place long; she didn't want to make new enemies or friends, as they would only slow her down. Sometimes she wouldn't even be seen at all, moving with barriers that were all but impossible to perceive through settlements and landscapes. Like this, she made excellent progress, and within a month had arrived at the border of the Britchen lands. The fog that had blanketed the world was still tinged with the presence of the Storm, but she could resist it well enough, which gave her confidence. Eventually, Eowen landed near a settlement that was one of the farthest Britchen settlements from Nolano. She put up barriers and slept outside of the city on the heron's soft feathers, undetectable to those inside. The sounds of human activity, even at a distance, were relaxing and lulled her to sleep.

Travel had been easy with the heron, but Eowen craved people to be in the proximity of. The silence of the new world was a disturbing thing, and without people nearby she could rarely sleep. The Storm still pulled at her manifestations, but she kept her power bent towards simple things like food, water, and light. Her life had become relatively straightforward and predictable, yet still her spirit felt as though it teetered on the edge of a knife. Eowen pushed down the directionless anxiety that kept her heart beating just a bit too hard and her stomach in too tight of a knot. She nestled into the heron and let its warmth and jungle aroma lull her to sleep.

Deep asleep, Eowen's dreams flowed through the logicless currents that emerged from the dark of her mind. Small, temporary manifestations flowed off of her. Nothing big, or complex, or powerful, but at the edges of her manifestations was the Storm, looking for a way in. The bone heron nipped at the threads of chaos that sought a hold in its master. The creature managed to keep the entity away, for a time.

****

[Listen, for you cannot hear me yet]

I do not want to listen any longer without understanding. Who are you and why are you telling me these things?

[...]

AND THOUGH IT KNEADED REALITIES ABOUT ME UPON THEMSELVES, AND THOUGH IT SHOOK THE FIRMAMENT OF AH'OM, AND THOUGH NEITHER THE SUN NOR THE MOON COULD SAY MY NAME BACK TO ME, LOVE SOMEHOW COULD.

****

Eowen confirmed with the people of the settlement she'd bedded down next to that Tavo had indeed passed through roughly four and a half months ago. They were so far away from Nolano that no caravan had visited them yet. They had, however, met Hani and his crew, which was now made up of six people. They'd sailed down through the starfield, telling stories and following the path Captain Asobrab had taken through the largest rivers of the old world after going north up the coast. Eowen checked her ring and felt the direction Hani was in, and for a moment it made her feel less alone. She was still bound north and west, while Hani had left a month ago to venture south.

Hani's crew had shared their stories from Nolano, so the villagers she met knew of her even though no caravan had reached them. Eowen learned that the crew was currently rooting out the Storm with a few of The Nagirr'Om's acolytes. The Nagirr'Om's influence was increasing, as well. The strange, silver being picked up new followers wherever it went. Eowen had not passed through a settlement without at least three acolytes in it, one for each of the silver woman's tools. Ordwell, Strife, and Kelt were still members of the crew, and Eowen learned the names of the new members, Nasem and Lokah. Nasem was a woman in her fifties who had powerful sensory abilities that ranged far beyond anyone's. She was a cartographer of the old world and was attempting to map the new one. Lokah was a young boy who manifested instruments from the old world and could learn to play them with ease. It seemed he created things through the music he played and could sway the emotions and spirits of all that heard him. The news of Hani made Eowen smile. He was fulfilling all of his dreams and it made her goals feel even closer at hand.

When Eowen mounted the heron to continue on her journey, she decided that after she had found Tavo, she would reconnect with Hani and introduce them. The heron took off, surrounded by Eowen's shadows, which shifted into a myriad of illusory futures where she, Hani, and Tavo sailed through the new world together on adventures.

* * *

When Eowen left the Britchen settlements behind, the expanse of the empty starfield became immediately less densely populated. She could feel the threads of people's need for her work in all directions, though often only faintly. It was an itch she could ignore for the purpose of her quest. The world's compass in her mind kept her heading the right direction while her people-finding tool kept her headed towards the next closest population. She traveled faster on the heron than she ever had on her and Hani's ship, yet it still took a month's worth of time to reach the closest people that Eowen detected. She slept most of the time, and each time she slept there was creation, unbound and beautiful, that would writhe out. Manifestations would branch from her like vines climbing a cliff face, evidence of her power's growth but also of the Storm which lurked within and without her. During that time, Eowen awoke to landscapes, buildings, objects, scents, lights, and sounds. The myriad of her subconscious was being dredged up by the power that sought a foothold in her spirit. Each hour, the fog lay heavier on the new world, and upon each waking Eowen found it clinging to her. She pushed it away as it whispered of wishes it would grant her, power she'd have, anything if she but let it in.

The Nagirr'Om had not visited the lands Eowen now flew through, and the Storm here was a more wild thing that ate through the weak as it sought an anchor in the strong. Eowen passed many dead and destroyed settlements in those days, thousands that had perished in the fall, and a lesser number that had been obliterated by the Storm. Eowen kept her wits about her for an attack from a powerful host, but in all the lands she passed through it was clear that a grater dreamer had not yet been corrupted.

There were dead everywhere, and Eowen did what she could for them by performing rites if she knew their heritage, but for many she did not. In those cases, she took to storing dozens of bodies inside the starfield itself. They'd be preserved there, in a space only she could access, until she was certain of what to do.

Eowen found some Britchen corpses and suspected they'd been traveling before the fall, but most people she found were of a people called the river folk. They were not the same as the caramel skinned, brown haired Britchen who had once called themselves the river-people, they were a tribe of lighter haired and dark-brown skinned people. Their hair curled while the Britchen's were usually straight, and Eowen knew they'd been nomadic before the fall. As a people, the river folk had already been in caravans such that few had been close enough to the more powerful dreamers to survive in those first minutes. Even those that had survived had mostly been overcome by the Storm without opportunity to grow strong enough to resist it. They had no Nagirr'Om in their lands in the early days, and the losses were incalculably more devastating than anywhere Eowen had been.

Eowen did not weep in those silent, foggy days as she flew through lands devastated by the fall and the Storm. She did her work, and grew slowly and silently angrier. Each body she secured added another coal to the low, hot fire in her belly. Her dreaming self was becoming more influential upon the world, the fragile stuff manifested in her sleeping times becoming more permanent and saturated with potential. Senseless artifacts of her subconscious mind littered the void in her wake, leaving landscapes, sounds, illusions, gasses, waters, fires, and a kaleidoscope of other manifestations with unintended staying power.

The heron tried to nip away the Storm as it reached for its master, but it was becoming unmanageable. The fog that begot chaotic manifestations were more present than ever, and it was all the heron could do to keep itself at Eowen's side and serve her. It avoided her ire, but as time wore on, the creature began to fray at the edges. Her sense of those that needed her power grew more and more distant as a wordless rage at the deaths around her rose up. Eowen had never felt so angry over deaths, only empathy for the living, but the further she flew the more the whipping waters of her subconscious turned to blind enmity.

After some weeks, she no longer heard the strange voice

in her dreaming that told her to listen, only the rush of the Storm. Eowen had even stopped performing rites collecting the dead. The fog was too thick, the wind in her ears too strong, and it was all the heron could do to keep in the air.

* * *

At last, after a month of flying, she arrived at the closest living settlement beyond the Britchen territories. It was a majestic place from the outside, with a massive dome of flowing water that covered the whole city. It was about half the size of Nolano, and rivers emerged from the stars below and fed the wall from all directions. She landed at the city's edge, where a great gate of stone stood embedded in the wall of water. A few strange creatures skittered around the outer edges. They were shiny, black, chitinous, possessed of too many limbs, about the size of a person, and when they spotted Eowen they chittered at her, their carapaces clicking.

I wonder if these are creatures from the old world, manifested here?

The creatures seemed repelled by the water, which also pushed against her own dreaming aura. It stank of a resistance to her that she found offensive, as though the water and gate had been meant to specifically repel her. She approached on the heron, gaining the attention of the skittering creatures, of which there were dozens. A few tried to leap at her, and Eowen's features twisted with disgust. She unleashed a few waves of manifested force, and the creatures closest burst apart into random manifestations. They looked like large insects, but they bled red. Eowen grimly appraised the bodies with satisfaction and approached the wall of water.

Eowen dismounted from the heron, and when she set foot upon the starfield it moved like ocean waves around her, cresting into bursts of light. The fog around her twisted into harsh shapes and crackled with potential. The heron followed, its eyes darting all around at the clouds, but it could do nothing about the Storm rising up in Eowen. Hate, power, and the need to use it steamed off Eowen, her tiny frame warping the world around her. Eowen approached the gate and raised her fist. Her hand seemed to eat the light from the stars below, shining in a strange and unnatural way. The darkness of the void and the starfield below curled upon her hand, the density of potential distorting the space around the girl. It reached a tipping point and when Eowen exhaled wisps of fire and sprigs of electricity jumped out. Her eyes became clouded over by roiling gray and flashing white clouds.

Eowen opened her hand, placed it on the stone gate, and for a moment the world seemed to stop. Then, the gate burst. The sound of it was like a mountain cracking in twain. All through the settlement glass shattered, ears bled and screams of fear and pain rang out in the aftermath. Light burst from the splits as the barrier crumbled to the ground before her. Unintended manifestations writhed out from the point of destruction, leaving mismatched pieces that spread into a thousand shavings of chaos.

Eowen bared her teeth and smoke seeped from between them. She ascended into the air without the aid of her heron, and set herself down atop the rubble of the gate to face the cowering people before her. Almost all of them were river folk and Eowen glared, the very figure of a dread god as they cried out, clasped their hands and fell to their knees. Between the mass of cowering people, five men and two women, all elderly and wearing richly embroidered and beaded robes, hurried to the entrance.

"Please! Great One, why have you come here? Does your master require more offerings?" The first of the robed ones, an old man, cried, which finally gave Eowen pause.

What does he mean by offerings?

"I am here because of this!" Eowen opened the starfield below to where she'd been collecting and storing the bodies as she traveled. Piles of them spilled out around her in great mounds, corpses twisted in the pain of suffocation and ruination of the Storm. The dead poured into the city around her, and Eowen stood among them like a conquering queen. The poor citizens before her who dared to look up quickly returned their eyes to the star field below, but the robed ones before her stood, shaking. Three vomited when the bodies appeared, two looked like they might, but the first to speak kept his composure as best they could. "You let them die like this!" Eowen shouted. "You left them unattended!"

"W-we could do nothing, Great One," One of the robed women said.

"Nothing?" Eowen growled, her voice not her own, too deep, too strong, echoing against the stars below. The robed figures cowered as Eowen floated up, her power crackled and burned the air around her.

"We have needed to stay for our safety!" the first man that spoke to her said. "Please, we'll give you whatever you wish if you leave us! We have to repair the gate!" Eowen intended to ask more questions, but a voice belonging to one of the citizens interrupted her.

"Mother! Oh my mother!" The person was a young man, one ear bleeding from her initial attack. He rushed forward and climbed into the pile of corpses behind Eowen. The young man pulled the body of an old woman free and wrapped his arms around it. The woman had not died to the Storm, but in the fall, and the moment her son touched her Eowen felt the pull to serve him as mortician. It was like a splash of cold water, dispelling some of the hazy fog that had been filling her spirit. Eowen shook her head and tripped forward, falling from the rubble of the door and onto the back of the heron, which swooped in to catch her. The Storm's influence tangled itself inside her and warped her powers outside. She pushed at it, but even in resistance it twisted her powers into crackling manifestations.

When did this happen? How did I not notice it getting such a hold on me?

Eowen gasped as the struggle in her subconscious sickened and disoriented her. One of the robed elders approached, glancing at his fellows for support. "Uh. Great One? Miss, is everything alright?"

"No!" Eowen shouted, the churning power and rage still there, along with the need to use it. She knew the people of this settlement didn't deserve her wrath, but she was suffused with the power of the Storm, and it begged to be used. She could feel it pulling at her shape, trying to transmute her into something else, a vessel for it to emerge. A cry went up from the man who had climbed the hill of corpses, which echoed through the city.

"The Great One is here with his horde!" The man shouted, and as though a switch were flipped, the city collapsed into panic. The citizens ran from the entrance, hid in their homes and shut the doors while the robes figures cowered behind their people.

Eowen grabbed the man closest to her before he could leave and dragged him to the top of the rubble mound. Over it she saw who their Great One was. A mass of black shelled creatures, like the ones she'd destroyed on her way in, were crawling across the starfield toward them. In their midst stood a creature like the rest of them, save for its stature. The thing stood over four meters with chitinous limbs as large as Eowen's entire body. From the gaps in its shell leaked a smoke that coalesced into a great serpentine head of roiling elements.

"The Storm," Eowen hissed, and as her aura of power met the approaching forces, the Storm within her synchronized with it. The power surged in her, seemed to speak to her, whispering that she was greater than the creature that approached, urging her to dominate it.

"Y-you know the Great One?" the robed man asked, caught in her grip.

"This is what you've been giving offerings to?" Eowen said, her voice leden.

"Yes, it left us in peace in exchange for one offering every week."

"What were the offerings?" Eowen asked, knowing the answer; the creatures she'd destroyed had red blood and followed the one from which the Storm leaked. It was like the great tree at Nolano, a once powerful dreamer taken over and warped by the Storm, spreading out and morphing other people as well. The settlement behind her could resist the Storm, but it seemed that fear of it had driven its people to give it offerings in exchange for safety. The robed man did not answer her, for he could see the rage in her eyes. He bowed his head and begged her forgiveness, but Eowen didn't care. She was still full of the Storm herself, full of its power, and she wanted to use it. She dropped the man and stood to meet the army of carapaced beings before her.

Pathetic, twisted into a monster by powers you can't control. I can control them, though. I am better than it.

Eowen neither knew nor cared if her thoughts were her own. She rose in the air, a node of destruction that burst apart the bodies of the carapaced creatures closest to her. Waves of the smaller creatures charged but were annihilated before they could reach her. Finally, the leader charged, a screech that no living creature had ever made erupting from it. Eowen didn't wait for its attack and lunged forward to grasp its shell with one hand. She crushed it and gripped onto an exoskeletal vertebrae. Its massive arms flailed at her, but they merely bounced off a barrier around her. Eowen grinned madly and slammed it down against the starfield. She opened her mouth and a high, bitter laugh came out of her, sending drops of molten metal bouncing off her teeth.

The Storm head above the carapaced creature never moved to defend it, but slowly, deliberately, abandoned its host. The tendrils of power leaked from the creature in Eowen's grip until, without her finishing the job, what life was left in it departed. Eowen shook the empty vessel, disappointed at the lack of sport. In her state, she failed to notice the great serpentine mass of elemental power coiling around her, feeding on the power she was generating. Eowen's mind fogged more than ever, her thoughts were submerged into the deep of it, and the great beast of smoke, ice, and lightning seemed almost to grin.

Eowen was almost taken, but her heron could no longer wait. Long legs burst through the clouds and sunk their talons into Eowen's shoulders, knocking her to the starfield. Eowen cried out and the Storm around her coiled to strike. The bone heron lifted one wing up, revealing something that shimmered in its feathers. Eowen, her mind slightly clearer, felt a sudden, terrible fear of whatever was in the heron. She squirmed and covered her eyes from the bitter light, but the bird caught her wrist in its beak and forced her hand onto the shining thing in its feather.

A horrible, stabbing pain burned through the center of her chest. Her bones felt as though they were cracking in the heat, her organs like they were melting. She screamed, waves of power pouring out of her, shadow and light becoming manifestations of chaos that twisted the city and starfield around her for dozens of kilometers into subconscious abstractions. The pain sharpened her mind, and she recognized the source of it. The girl reached into her heron's feathers, and grasped the silver bamboo spear that had once pierced her chest. Her hand went numb and the scar on her chest was blindingly painful, but Eowen drew it out from the heron with both hands. Finally she felt how deep the Storm had gotten into her. Its roots were in her mind and her spirit, its teeth deep in her dreaming. Holding The Nagirr'Om's power, Eowen hefted the bamboo like a javelin and aimed for the great coiled head above her. It roared and lunged, but she let fly, and the streak of silver light met the thing. The clouds fled, the fog burned away, and the elemental forces shattered, their hold upon her gone. The spear fractured when its target was destroyed, sending silver shards raining down around her. Eowen, exhausted and empty, fell upon the heron.

"Thank you, bird," she gasped through the pain in her chest. She clung to the heron with the last of her strength, and stared through hazy eyes at the field of dead things around her. The Storm had taken the carapaced creatures' lives with it when it attempted to invade her, leaving them empty. *Were they really even alive though?* The rage was gone, and even exhausted, her mind was more clear than it had been in weeks.

How could I have thought I was safe to travel the void alone? I cannot resist the Storm like The Nagirr'Om, or Hani on his ship.

The heron lifted her up and she curled up on the creature's back. It reached its head around to nuzzle her, and she accepted the warmth gratefully. It stalked back to the settlement where the robed council waited on the rubble. When they saw her approaching, they fell to their knees.

"Great One! You have banished our terror. Our lives are yours." The heron stood over them, its piercing gaze daring them to look up. Eowen petted the neck of the bird and pulled herself into a sitting position. Once more, she was upon the rubble of the settlement's gates, looking down on the city, surrounded by corpses. It had felt so right and satisfying before, but now it only felt terribly wrong. Everything that had occurred set a great and weary sadness in the pit of her stomach. She could feel that the elders were not dreamers of any great ability, and were full of fear. One of the elders, the woman who hadn't spoken to her yet, looked up. "Um, Great One—"

"**Eowen.**" Her distaste for the false title brought out her voice of power and a quick flash of rage. "Just Eowen. Please," she whispered, frightened by the instability in her own emotions. She checked herself for the influence of the Storm, but it was gone. Still, it had gotten deep into her mind and her spirit and had left scars there, unseeable grooves through which the effects of its influence now flowed with ease.

"Uh, great Eowen, we, the council of seven, are your humble servants." The woman was rising to her feet now, a waxy smile plastered on her face. Eowen faced her, and what she sensed from the woman made her stomach turn. "As the hero of our people and the source of our new peace, our city,

Waterwall, is yours!" She turned to her compatriots who had risen and were nodding and muttering their assent. Eowen's face twisted. They disgusted her, and she was exhausted.

"I don't want your city," she said.

"Ah." The man who had first spoken to her stepped forward. "You wish for... offerings then?"

"**No!**" A flash of rage again, of hate. The council cowered and backed up. Eowen's blood surged with the feelings she knew could carry her to violence, feelings remnant of the Storm. The heron turned to look at her and she took several deep breaths.

"Please, tell us how we can serve you!" another robed man shouted. His cry spread to the rest of the city, and they fell to mutterings of devotion and pleas for mercy.

Eowen scanned the place, and her heart fell for she felt how frightened they were. Never in the new world had she encountered such frightened and desperate people since the mountain folk had come crawling naked up to her island in the first days. She wanted to help them, somehow, but knew it could never work. They would treat her as a monarch, a conqueror who'd freed them from their old master only to become their new one.

"How many?" Eowen whispered, and the closest of the council approached.

"I'm sorry, uh, great Eowen. What was that?"

"How many did you give to it?" Eowen said. She wrapped her shaking arms around the heron's neck, and it rose to its full height.

"It's—we did not record such a thing."

"How many!" Eowen shouted, but her voice carried no power of command now. It was a cry from the scars in her heart. The council did not answer her, and retreated into the folds of their robes, into muttering and reasoning, their self-service hidden beneath subservience. Eowen looked at them, incredulous. "You don't know, do you?" She wanted to shout more, to cry, to run away, but caught between these feelings she did nothing but stare at them, her mouth set in a hard line, her jaw clenched.

Someone spoke up though, the young man that'd rushed to his mother's body in Eowen's piles of dead. "Forty!"

The council rounded on him, but their responses were deafened by a barrier of silence established with a swift gesture. "Forty people?" Eowen asked the young man, who averted his eyes.

"B-between thirty and forty. I don't know for sure." Eowen's expression softened from her frustration into a weary sadness.

"Thank you for telling me." She spoke very quietly. Only the young man and the council he'd moved to stand beside would have heard her. She turned to the council and looked each in the eye, and to her they seemed like selfish, weedling rats. Yet they'd kept their community relatively safe, even if in such a terrible way. "You still wish to serve me?" Eowen asked them, dispelling her barrier of silence.

"Of course! Anything, great Eowen! You destroyed our oppressor, we are forever in debt to you!" one said.

I didn't really kill them, they were as good as dead the way they were. Eowen thought, though the truth of it brought her little peace. "This is what you will do; you will properly dispose of these dead," she indicated the piles to either side of her, "in your people's way."

"Oh. Uh, of course," a council member responded, confused at the lack of a demand for service to Eowen herself.

"Then, you will do the same for all of them." Eowen

gestured to the carapaced beings behind her whose life had been dragged out of them when the Storm had tried to take her over.

"Them! But they're not—"

"People?" Eowen interrupted the robed speaker.

"Ah, uh, well—"

"They were people, once, as much as they were once people." Eowen gestured to the dead on either side of her. She looked out over the city, the frightened, secluded place ruled by frightened and self-serving people. She hoped it would be alright, but she couldn't bear to stay any longer. Her heron lifted her off into the air and she settled on its back. "Do this, and I will not need to come back." A hollow threat, but by the looks in most of the council's faces she thought it would stick. The heron flapped its wings and wheeled around, carrying her away. "And rebuild the gate!" she called over her shoulder.

In moments the settlement was out of view. Eowen wrapped her arms around the heron as it flew onward. It tilted its head to look at her and she met its eye. "I know, it's not safe to travel like this anymore, I just needed to get away from there. Find somewhere safe to land, then we'll take it slower."

She pressed her face into the feathers, and with nothing left to distract her the horrible confrontation played out in her mind vividly. She remembered the strength she'd commanded, the pleasure at using it, the craving to let the roil of the Storm obliterate who she was and make her into something else. It almost had, and Eowen could still feel the way her form had tugged, almost shifting into whatever shape she would have become. Harsh shudders wracked Eowen's body, and she buried herself further into the heron's feathers. For once its warmth was not enough.

* * *

The heron flew for just less than a full day but covered hundreds of kilometers. Eowen awoke on its back amidst fog and darkness. She manifested a light above her, but it did little to cut through, throwing strange and unnerving shadows instead. The Storm was all about her, driven out but looking for a way back in, always.

Eowen extinguished her light and curled up against the heron, trying to fall asleep again. She hadn't dreamt of the great voice that told her to listen for weeks. Eowen had never known what the meaning of the voice was or why it would speak with and through her, but it had become a comfort for her. The great presence of it had left her feeling small, but not diminished, and greater attunement to it had always followed advancements in her abilities. Now, without it, she felt more lonesome and directionless than ever.

Perhaps the Storm is blocking it.

Eowen snuggled into the heron, but still found little comfort in it. She felt alone, beset, and as though she lacked some fundamental understanding of how to face the challenges ahead of her. In the jungle and savannah of the old world, there had been plenty of animals, plants, and natural disasters that could have killed her, but she had been taught how to deal with them. There was no instruction for outer entities invading one's heart, mind, and spirit. She seemed out of options, and found herself wishing she'd gone with Hani after all.

At least on his ship I'd be with friends, and not in so much danger... and not so terribly frightening.

The months of work to help the people of Nolano and her

quest to find Tavo felt distant and insubstantial compared to the cloying mists around her. She erected barriers of familiar scents, sounds, and temperatures for comfort, but all her manifestations sprained entropically away. Eowen barely managed to do enough to calm her spirit some, and pushed herself back into sleep.

The heron will take me somewhere safe. It carried The Nagirr'Om's spear, it has always served me exactly as I've needed it to. Eowen believed that, and so she abandoned all will, intent, and dreams, and let the heron fly on.

* * *

"Run! They're coming!" Eowen awoke to a child's panic.

"It's alright, you're safe now. The ravel cannot reach you with us." An old man's voice cut in. Eowen sat up and scraped the salty crust from her eyes, then surveyed her surroundings. There were four people gathered in the light of a ghostly lantern that hung from a shepherd's crook. Three of the people Eowen recognized as river folk, but she wasn't sure if the one holding the crook was a person at all. It appeared to be a man, with chalky white skin and beady black eyes sunk deep in his skull. He stared at Eowen, and she found it difficult not to stare at him as well. He was wearing a loose black capote with a hood up that clung to his bald head and framed his gaunt features. He was hunched, his body curved in a C with unnervingly long limbs and massive hands and feet. He stood only a head taller than Eowen, but it seemed to her that if he were to straighten his spine and fully unfold his limbs he'd stand twice as tall as her heron. The child, no more than five years old, glanced fearfully between Eowen on her heron and the strange lantern man. The old river folk man, short but with excellent posture and an open, kind face, patted the child's back and smiled at Eowen.

"Finally awake, are you? Your heron landed among us some hours ago." Beside the old man was an old woman with similar features, though they were marred by terrible scars from her throat up to her hairline. "This is my sister, Bolye, she is a mute. And this is our host, who may also be mute." He gestured to the women and the lantern man, then smiled at Eowen. "My name is Bolyu. Our parents were not clever, I'm afraid." Eowen glanced at the gathered people, wondering where to begin and what to ask for first. "I'm sorry, bird girl, do you understand me?" Eowen shook herself.

"Yes, sorry, I do." She spoke in her own language, but the bronze sphere she still carried translated all the languages of those in its vicinity. The three river folk's eyebrows went up and the small child's mouth fell open.

"Old man, I could understand that!"

"Yes, so could I. How curious," he said.

"Um, where am I exactly?" Eowen asked as she dismounted her heron. The lantern bearer stopped staring at her and turned slowly to look at the child, who squirmed in discomfort and whined.

"Shh, shh, child, you're alright. We are safe in the light of this lantern." Eowen could tell Bolyu was right; there was no fog in the light of the lantern, no feeling of the Storm at all. She couldn't even feel her own power, and when she looked down, even the starfield was gone. It was as though the space the lantern lit existed under the rules of the old world, but though its glow covered a radius of a few meters, everything beyond it was perfectly black, including the ground they stood on. "To answer your question," Bolyu continued, "we are between settlements, in the wilds of the ravel."

"The... ravel" Eowen turned the meaning of the term the man had used around in her head. "Is that the same as the Storm?"

"I suppose it is like a Storm in some ways, though ravel is what I and mine have always called it. It unravels us into something else, but it cannot reach us so long as we stay close to our host." He gestured to the strange, pale, person-thing with the shepherd's crook. "You must have been frightened, little one." Bolyu addressed the child again. "You are safe now. What is your name?"

"Okuz. It was scary! It was like water but black and it stuck to me and followed me!"

"Were you alone?"

"No, I was with Mommy and Daddy, but they went to the safe building. The scary outside stuff can't get us there, but it ruined all the other houses!" The child was working themself up into tears, so Bolyu shushed them again, and held them close.

"You're safe now, and Mommy and Daddy are safe in the safe building, aren't they?" The child nodded. "Don't worry, we'll get you back to them, won't we?" He directed this question at the lantern bearer, but the strange man did not react, not even a twitch. The child did calm down and Bolye knelt down to stroke their hair and smile at them, sweet looking despite her scars. Bolye pulled at her brother's sleeve and pointed at Eowen. "Oh, of course. What's your name, bird girl?"

"Eowen. I'm previously from the jungle and savannah tribes. Uh, we can understand each other because of this:" She held out the brass sphere.

"What a wonder! Did you create it?"

"No, it was someone else."

"I see, and what about that bird?" The heron nipped at Eowen's sleeve and she looked up to see the lantern bearer had gotten up, perfectly silent, and was on the move.

"I think we need to go."

"Oh, yes, time for chatter later." Bolyu hefted himself to his feet with the child in his arms, groaning as his old joints fought him. Eowen stepped forward and helped him up. "Thank you, Eowen."

"Of course. Okuz, was it?" Eowen smiled at the kid who was staring at the heron over her shoulder.

"That's a biiig bird," Okuz informed them as they shuffled along after the light of the lantern.

"Would you like to ride it?" Eowen asked, and Okuz nodded enthusiastically. The elderly siblings seemed amused by the idea, so Bolyu handed his small charge over to Eowen, who sat them on the bird's back.

"We're quite a merry band now, aren't we?" Bolyu asked his sister, who shrugged but seemed happy. Bolye walked beside the heron, nodded at Okuz's chatter and made the appropriate expressions to egg them on. "Lend me an arm won't you?" Bolyu reached out to Eowen, who supported him, though the old man seemed to be perfectly able to walk without her help. "It's slow going following that lantern man, but it's safe. We never really know where we'll end up though."

"You mean you don't know where he's going?" Eowen asked.

"I've been in his company for a couple weeks now. What you've seen is about all you'll get out of him."

"So why are you following him?" Eowen asked.

"Ah, it's my daughter. She married into another caravan before the fall. I've been making my way to where it might be, to... hopefully find her and my grandchildren." Unspoken was the phrase of all people who'd been separated from their loved ones before the fall: 'If they're still alive.'

Bolyu began updating Eowen on the few things he had come to understand about their guide and the region of the new world she now found herself in. The Storm, which went by plenty of names; ravel, distortion, chaos, ruin, roil; had been gaining in power and influence across the new world to the degree Eowen had come to expect. Its presence ebbed and flowed, capturing some powerful dreamers, ripping its way through weaker ones, and butting against various barriers and defenses that other powerful folk had created. It was clear from his descriptions of other settlements that Bolyu had not seen The Nagirr'Om or Hani's crew. This didn't mean they hadn't passed through the areas he'd described, but Eowen was able to surmise that they largely hadn't passed through the part of the world she was currently in. Bolyu described how he'd effectively been trapped in the first settlement he'd found himself in till the lantern man had shown up. Others had come with, but they'd found other settlements to stop in along the way. Eowen described the one she'd been at with the wall of water, which Bolyu recognized.

"Distressing place, that. A council of weak cowards ordering everyone else around just because they were important in the old world. They haven't done much of anything to help except tell others what to do." He leaned in and whispered so Okuz wouldn't hear. "Did you know, they convinced their people to give sacrifices to a ravel being in exchange for safety?" Eowen stiffened and avoided his eyes.

"I didn't stay long," was all she said, and Bolyu never pressed her for details. It was very slow going compared to her bird, and the lantern man had a strange, gangly way of walking that was somehow too slow for a jog and too fast for a stroll, forcing his caravaneers to constantly adjust their pace. This frustrated Eowen immensely, for she had become accustomed to a much higher quality of travel in the new world on her heron. She would have ridden the bird and let it do the walking, but she'd given that seat away already, and so was stuck skipping awkwardly between a stroll and a trot. Eowen came very close to shouting at their guide, but Bolyu reined her in and distracted her with stories and jokes.

It went like this for over a day's worth of time, periods of silence between chatter, stories, and speculation as to where they'd end up and what was to come. Eowen shared much of her time in the new world, but omitted her mortician status and the part she'd played in removing the Storm from Nolano. She felt normal among the small group and was enjoying the novelty of it. They didn't know her past mistakes or achievements, and within the lantern's light none could feel her power. The time seemed to stretch strangely, but none of the party complained about being tired, hungry, or even wanting to stop. Eowen knew her sense of direction wasn't the best, but after the many hours of walking, she was beginning to wonder where exactly they were. She reached for that universal sixth sense of all new world residents, the compass in all their minds. It wasn't there though. When Eowen looked for it she found... nothing.

"Bolyu, is there... I mean, do you have a, and this will sound strange, but do people in this part of the new world know in their mind where north, south, east, and west are?"

With the sense gone, she felt like it had all been a dream, and trying to describe it now made her feel crazy.

"Yes, of course," Bolyu said.

"Why can't I feel it now though?"

"Oh, I forgot to tell you! It's one of the most interesting things about our guide here." Bolye patted the pale man's back like they were old friends. The lantern man paused his strange gait and turned to stare at the old river folk. Bolyu beamed at him, and the lantern man showed no emotion at all, just stared for a few seconds that felt much longer. The strange guide turned away and started into the dark again. "See, in the light of his lantern, no other powers exist. You probably felt that. Not even the greatest dreamers could create things here, and the ravel cannot reach us. Have you noticed that you're not tired or hungry either? That's because we can't get tired or hungry with him! Isn't it miraculous?"

Eowen stared wide-eyed at the lantern man. She'd never encountered such a power or creation with a rule as absolute as the lantern's. The closest she'd encountered was Strife's untouchability by the powers of others if they did not wish to be.

"It is miraculous," Eowen muttered. "You wouldn't know how the compass directions happened, would you?"

"No clue!" Bolyu laughed. "I think it will simply be one of the great mysteries of our new world."

They did not stop walking for days, and they took turns riding on Eowen's heron, but as promised they did not hunger or tire. As such, they made relatively good time in reaching the next settlement. Once they were just outside of it, their guide put a cloth over his lantern, cutting off its light and plunging them back into the world. It was a fascinating place as the people had collectively manifested an enormous, lush valley. It smelled perpetually of clean earth, petrichor, and flowers Eowen had never encountered. The most interesting thing about the valley was that, because those that had manifested it did not know how to actually warp the starfield below as Eowen had come to learn and as Hani could do with his ship, the valley actually rose up out of the starfield instead of dipping down into it. The settlement was primarily of the valley tribes, people from far to the west in the old world whose lands had previously criss-crossed with the river folk's.

Eowen and the rest of the caravan entered the town, but the lantern bearer merely walked through it as though it did not exist. Bolye explained that the lantern man would wait for a bit, especially if a new person joined, but would otherwise continue moving. If they wanted to journey with him, they had to catch up before he got too far away.

As soon as Eowen left the lantern's radius, all her senses returned. It was disorienting at first, feeling the dreaming auras of so many around her and sensing the pull for her work as a mortician. Eowen had somewhat enjoyed her time with the small caravan. She had felt like a normal person again, one without power and purpose. It wasn't bad having her power back, though. The break had invigorated her, and she headed for the first person she could feel attached to her inner threads. She knew they needed her, and she had the strength to act, so she would.

The valley tribe preserved their dead and mummified them with special embalming materials that the average person did not know how to produce. Then, the body was to be staked through the heart on the valley wall facing east till the sun and the falling rain had purified it. Eowen had learned this in Nolano from the few members of the valley tribe there, and so she recognized the signs in the valley. As few could travel through the unprotected lands, her small caravan attracted quite a bit of attention, and a crowd gathered around them. Most every settlement was now protected from the Storm in some way, but there were few travelers. Eowen moved directly toward a couple that she was pulled to, drawing some attention. They were stony eyed, hardened, but still together with love. She stopped before them, and they looked at each other, confused, but she knew what to do, what to say. Eowen opened her mouth, and spoke with power welling up within her.

"You have lost, and you feel petrified in your grief. But you are not stone. You are parents who must say that most fearful thing." She returned to herself, just a small skinny girl with tears in her eyes that mirrored the tears in those of the couple whose hands she held. "You have to say goodbye." Eowen squeezed their hands and met their eyes, pained, disbelieving, but no longer stony. "Come, I'll help you."

She soon learned that their baby had died in the fall. Their grief, over a year old now, had become a stale and familiar companion. They had not yet performed the rites of their people as many other valley tribe people had done. Other bodies had been mummified with materials manifested to have similar properties to the true materials of the old world, but none of the attempts had been very accurate. The family with the infant had preserved their child as best as they could with their powers, but they could not bring themselves to stake their baby to the valley wall with the rest of the dead. Their neighbors did not blame them, and so they were left to calcify in their stagnant, incomplete grief.

Eowen spoke with them for many hours. She told them

stories of the valley tribe in Nolano, described what she knew of their practices, and manifested the relevant materials as proof of her abilities. They were hesitant, not out of a lack of trust in her, but for fear of change. Even the old, stale pain of things left undone can seem preferable to facing its source head on.

Eventually, after her presentation and a long conversation in private, they agreed to a ceremony and presented their child to Eowen. She cradled the baby in her arms, and they knew they'd made the right choice when they saw how gentle the foreign girl was despite their child being long past the point of harm. Eowen performed the embalming in sight of them, her moves sure and smooth but slow enough for them to track. Hours passed that felt like seconds, and when Eowen finished she faced them with a question in her eyes: 'Do you wish to be there for the next part?'

The child's mother covered her mouth and pressed herself into her husband, shaking her head. Eowen nodded, then turned and left them to their privacy. She ascended the valley wall on the back of her heron to a cut path, where many dead had been staked. She held the infant against the wall and pushed the bronze stake into its chest, then hammered it into place. The ringing of her strikes tolled out to all in the community what was happening, and many bowed their heads in prayer. When she finished, Eowen looked to her left and right to take in the hundreds of bodies given their final care as best as their community had been able to. Then, she too bowed her head and spoke.

"Life is a burden, forever beyond the strength of those who carry it. Your burden is gone, little one, now we will carry it."

She did not wash her hands till she had returned to the

couple. She rinsed before them in the couple's own basin, a final seal on the ceremony that left no question to them that it had been done. They did not speak to her and she did not speak to them, all settled in a professional sort of silence.

When Eowen left them, she wandered for some time through the valley, garnering looks and mutters until she ran into Bolyu again. He raised his eyebrows at her and patted the seat next to him, where he was sharing a meal with his sister Bolye, Okuz, and a few people from the settlement. Eowen took a seat and he passed her a plate of some delicious smelling thing covered in gravy. "So, Eowen, who did you say you were again?"

****

[Listen a little longer.]

FROM THEIR MOUTH, EACH SHAKING SYLLABLE, WHICH MAKES EARTHQUAKES MEEK AND STAR-DEATHS SHY AND ARMAGEDDON BOW WITH DEFERENCE, BECAME AS SOFT AS THE LAST HEARTBEAT OF A LIFE WITHOUT REGRETS.

****

Eowen stayed in the settlement for a few more funerals, letting the caravan go with the two elderly siblings and a couple new faces. Okuz had been given to a family that would look out for them and bring them home if the opportunity ever presented itself. After a few days, Eowen had done all the work she could, and even found evidence that Tavo had passed through. He was, in fact, partially responsible for the formation of the valley itself. Eowen learned that he had continued northwest, while the lantern-bearer's caravan was going mostly west and slightly south. Still, it was the only way she had to travel safely, and after finishing her work she braved a few hours of the Storm on her heron to rejoin them.

This was how the next few months' worth of time passed, with Eowen staying to perform funeral rites to those that needed it, then catching up with the caravan after. She never stayed out in the Storm long enough for it to affect her. The caravan gained and lost members, rarely having more than eight people at a time as it passed through various lands. They mostly encountered river folk and valley tribe settlements, but very rarely they met with Britchen people and another demographic Eowen had seen very few of: Carrulians. They were so named after their deity, Carrul, and believed that all their people were descended from that being.

Eowen met people with strange and amazing powers in those days. Some had even awakened voices of power and specific talents that rivaled her abilities. She met a blind, middle aged, half-mountain-folk-half-valley-tribe woman who was one of the very few that had not lost anyone in the fall. Her family had already been dead before the fall, and she'd lived alone as a hermit for years. She shaped clay creatures, pushed fire and power into them, and brought her statues to life. It was not a true life though, nor a dreamer's life that the people of the new world lived. Still, it was a strange and incredible ability Eowen had not seen before or ever considered.

The settlements were becoming more common and denser

as they reached places that had been more populated in the old world. Sometimes more powerful dreamers with a resistance to the Storm even organized smaller caravans between close settlements, but few braved the distances the lantern bearer could traverse. Eowen felt good to be doing her work, and there was always some need for it wherever she went, even if only to manifest a more accurate version of a sacred object. It was a fulfilling time, but as the lantern bearer brought them further south, Eowen found her path diverting more and more from Tavo's.

After passing through a number of settlements, Eowen could find no news of him, and had to face the decision of continuing with the lantern man, who traveled consistently but was no longer going in the desired direction, or waiting for another opportunity. She decided on the latter and bid her erstwhile friends and companions goodbye. Bolyu had become chummy with nearly everyone he'd caravaned with, his bright charisma having convinced many to join him in the first place. He and his sister were sad to see Eowen go, but it was not a tearful goodbye. Bolyu and Bolye were too positive for such things.

"I've said too many tender farewells in my time. It was a joy traveling beside you, that's all I'll say on the matter."

"I understand. Be well, Bolyu, Bolye."

"Keep doing that strange work of yours, Eowen Mortician." Bolyu winked at her, and Bolye patted Eowen's cheek. The lantern-bearer uncovered his miraculous tool, and in a flash they were gone.

It was lonely at times in the settlement Eowen had landed in, for it had once been a town of the valley tribes entirely populated by a secret religious order that kept to themselves. A valley had been manifested for them to live in, but there were also high towers of stacked stone, graceful bridges, fountains making art of water, and no doors. It apparently mirrored designs from the old world, though not anything that had actually existed, as it was all inspired by an architect who had never gained the support to build his wondrous temples. Thus it was named Tnomleb, in honor of the architect whose designs had been regarded as divine but impossible.

Eowen often sat atop the high towers, heron beside her as always, gazing out into the fog and clouds beyond, catching flashes of movement and activity. Once, she could have sworn she saw The Nagirr'Om as a great, dark shape moved through the clouds, light shining through the gray.

****

[Listen a little longer.]

PERHAPS THAT WAS THE TRICK.

****

Eowen was not the only outsider in Tnomleb. There were refugees rescued from the Storm, caravaners who had come with the lantern man or braved the lands between, and there was one particularly strange person. When Eowen met the strange person, they looked like an incredibly tall, beautiful woman of no race Eowen recognized. They claimed a menagerie of traits that she had never seen before. One bright green eye, one violet, hair that curled like Eowen's people, but was bright red like the valley tribe's. Caramel skin of the Britchen, Carrulian freckles, she seemed an impossible being that stood out more than even the strangest manifestations. Eowen saw her walking through town at times, but the strange person suddenly disappeared after a couple days. Then, Eowen met a new person whose dreaming aura felt the same as the woman from before. Eowen felt that they couldn't have been the same person, as they looked very much like a jungle and savannah tribe child, a nameless little boy that she had seen the like of a hundred times.

Eowen approached the child, making them jump as she appeared without warning, presence hidden. "Who are you? You have the same presence as that tall woman from before with the red hair."

"You recognized me?"

"Your form is different, but your power is the same."

"This has never happened before! Follow me!" They took Eowen to a private corner where they showed that they could not only look like any sort of person, but like anything at all. To prove it, they transformed into a large, unfamiliar predator, then a tiny rodent, then a bird that landed on Eowen's shoulder. The heron chased the bird off and the person assumed a human shape again. Eowen wondered what their original shape was, but they refused to show her and their language was not one she knew, so she could not extrapolate from that. They also refused to give their name, but spoke with Eowen for some time about the nature of their new world, of manifestations, and what created things really were. In their conversation, they said a thing that stayed with Eowen.

"People think the body is only a physical thing, and in the old world that might have been true, but the soul has always had no shape. Here we are, in a world where all that exists is what we bring out of our souls. Why then should our bodies be considered different? So I become what I am inside, a formless nothing, and then I pull out what I am to be from within." That was the last Eowen saw of the shifting stranger before they disappeared from the settlement.

****

[Listen a little longer.]

PERHAPS ALL WORDS BECOME GENTLE WHEN NO CHAINS HANG FROM THE HEART.

****

It was months later when another caravan finally arrived, this one escorted by acolytes of The Nagirr'Om. They brought with them news that their master had arrived in the lands around them and was banishing the Storm everywhere she flew. They were new members, two were of the valley tribes and one Carrulan. Neither hailed from Nolano. Eowen asked if they would take her into the north west. She learned that they were heading back east but would be sending several other caravans, one of which would be going in that direction.

As Eowen waited for the caravan that would come and take her further on her quest, she was practically vibrating with excitement. She was so eager for entertainment that she attempted to teach the shy members of the religious order some mountain folk games to get out her excess energy. In her time there and with the lantern man's caravan, Eowen felt as though she'd reclaimed the bit of herself, a part that had been healing since the Storm had nearly taken her. She no longer felt so afraid, and being able to perform her work over the last few months had made her swell with confidence. The dreams with the great voice had also come back, though she rarely slept anymore. Eowen had tried to mimic the power of the lantern man and preserve herself with her own power rather than needing food, water, or sleep. After achieving a similar result, she rarely ate or drank unless invited to, for she no longer required food. Her impatience made the time before the caravan arrived feel much longer, but it was only a few days worth of time before Eowen was able to continue her journey.

In the ensuing months, Eowen went with many caravans of acolytes from settlement to settlement. She performed her work, providing for funerals in the places she landed, and her reputation for it grew. In some places she was immediately feared and respected, as the terrifying stories that named her Eowen of the Dead had reached them first. According to some, Eowen of the Dead cursed those that did not honor the fallen and arrived with hordes of corpses to punish entire cities for the sins of a few. In other settlements, she was already known as Eowen Mortician, the quiet and giving girl who knew your pain and mourning better than you did yourself. According to them, Eowen Mortician soothed the spirit and served the grieving by providing for the dead.

Both rumors traveled faster than she did, but so did news of others in the new world. Hani and his crew had made a name for themselves as the second most effective force at fighting the Storm, and were currently sailing through the starfields far to the south of Eowen. Rarely, she'd see things that reminded her of them, and a feeling akin to homesickness would wash over her. Ordwell had truly become the patron of interconnection, and his translators were now common in most settlements, though few individuals owned them. Ships, either made by Hani himself or crafted in his style, had become the most coveted form of transport through the new world as it was faster and safer than an escort from The Nagirr'Om's acolytes.

Eowen herself still could not safely resist the Storm unless it was part of her practice, and in only two instances was she responsible for transporting the bodies of the dead between settlements. She never again gathered the fallen out in the world without being requested to do so, for the Storm had made her do that. Few knew much about Eowen aside from vague rumors, but those that did came to respect and even trust her. By most, she was largely treated as a distant figure, a foreign being of power that served a purpose but was not to be approached lightly.

In this way, Eowen's reputation had inspired a certain reverence, and more than once she saw men and women wearing yellow robes like hers, telling stories of her deeds and power. This was a rare thing and she avoided them. Formal terms of respect, genuflections, and the like felt strange and unfitting. Sometimes it allowed her to do her work without having to prove herself first, and it made it easier to ask for rumors about Tavo. Other times it impeded her, as would-be followers put themselves between her and the people that needed her services.

The Nagirr'Om and Hani's crew had more and grander stories spreading, with many even declaring them gods of the new world. A kind of pantheon was starting to form that labeled the powerful dreamers who safeguarded the world as its members. Aiyano and Nolyi were not spoken of this far from Nolano, but Eowen suspected they had achieved a similar status across all the Britchen territories. Hani's crew included names that had earned great renown all on their own. Ordwell had been given the epithet: of the Union. Lokah, the young boy who manifested through his music, had expanded his power to create instruments that allowed others to exceed their usual abilities. He could also facilitate immense creations through musical harmony with large groups. Butra, a strange woman who called into being great and powerful beasts that had never existed in the old world to her bidding, had earned a reputation as a Storm-hunter. Nifroht, an armored warrior from the far, far northwest was supposedly the follower of an even greater warrior who could single-handedly defeat anything, even a powerful Storm entity with greater ease than The Nagirr'Om. Eowen doubted that legend, as no one had proven themselves more powerful than The Nagirr'Om in fighting the Storm, but took it as a testament to the warriors abilities. Nasem, the cartographer of the new world, was still with them, and there was a trio of The Nagirr'Om's acolytes that traveled with them as well. Eowen assumed Kelt, the Britchen woman who cooked, and Strife were still in the crew despite a lack of news about them.

Eowen was lonesome at times, but tried to carry it proudly, as she felt she was supposed to be alone. Though these thoughts came with pain, a certain satisfaction was derived from them as well. Satisfaction from feeling she was on the correct path for herself, and a grim pride in the abandonment of personal joys and comforts for the sake of her quest and her work.

After all, it is the life I have chosen and the life I have earned. It is the nature of my work and the nature of myself.

In meditation, she'd reach out with her senses into the world, feeling out where the need for her power was, but also looking for Tavo. She'd come to recognize the signature of his dreaming from his manifestations, but finding someone's power from their creation was much more difficult than the other way around. It was like trying to identify an artist by their works when you have not ever witnessed them making any. No matter how much of it you see, the person is difficult to derive from the creation.

Amidst her meditations were daydreams about mythical figures from old world stories that brought her some encouragement. In the old days, she loved to hear about heroes accomplishing great feats of strength, discovering hidden places or powers, and moving through foreign cultures with ease. Those grand parts of the tales held less interest to her now that she'd achieved as much and more. Now what captured Eowen's imagination were the hard parts of the old heroic legends; the sacrifices, the trials, and the scars.

Once in a while, when she was feeling particularly lost, Eowen would daydream about what life would be like once she found her cousin. It would be the reward for her quest, the justification for all her own trials and scars. She was convinced they'd immediately be a family again, and they'd journey to find friends and adventures, just like Hani. They might even link with Hani's crew, reach distant lands, rooting out the Storm and becoming heroes. For now though, Eowen was resolved to travel alone, paying her dues.

* * *

Eowen always tried to embody the gentler persona she'd gained, and without her many would never have been able to perform proper funerals. She served whatever the wishes, needs, or cultural traditions were, learning new ones along the way. Many ceremonies required Eowen to recite the same chants, manifest the same landscapes or materials, and bear witness to the same pageantries of death repeatedly. Her empathy never wavered, though. Even with most of the new world's dead being from the fall, Eowen never met a soul whose grief felt the same as another's. The spirits of mourners called out to her, and she treated them as though their losses were the most important in the world.

Many were not in need of her, and many who did spurned her. There were rumors about a variety of things in the new world, and Eowen of the Dead was the most public epithet that carried a negative connotation. Eowen knew there were worse things being said about her, but the rumors of the strange girl who followed the dead were the least of people's worries, so she let them be.

When she arrived somewhere in her caravans, Eowen seemed to be little more than a strange, small girl from the jungle and savannah tribes. She'd quietly find those souls calling to her, and speak with the voice of Eowen Mortician. When she met a mourner's eyes, they saw that she was one who would never claim to understand their pain, but would serve the need to face it with them so as to reach closure. When she left a place, spirits were lighter.

She made every ceremony she conducted a little different, adjusting it intuitively to the needs of the person. Only one common thread tied the ceremonies she performed together, which was a single phrase she'd say to the dead. In that voice of power, Eowen would whisper the words which had come to her in the first funeral she'd performed in Nolano for Gran's grandchild. **"Life is a burden, forever beyond the strength of those who carry it. Your burden is gone, little one. Now we will carry it."**

****

[Listen a little longer.]

LOVE CALLED MY NAME, AND THOUGH I WAS STILL TOO GREAT TO BE PERCEIVED BY THEM, I LIFTED THEM UP TO HEIGHTS THAT HEAVENS PRETEND THEY REACH, AND LAID OUT ALL THAT WAS IN MY GRASP BEFORE THEM. WHICH TO ONE SUCH AS I COULD HAVE BEEN SAID TO BE ALL THAT THERE IS TO ONE SUCH AS THEY.

****

Many months later, Eowen found herself on a caravan heading toward settlements that belonged to people who, in the old world, had been of the far western coast of the continent. She'd been able to keep on Tavo's trail and was now only two months behind him. The Nagirr'Om, seeking to establish safe and consistent paths between settlements, had filled the land with acolytes as she rooted out the Storm. It might have even been safe enough for Eowen to travel alone, but she dared not risk it. The people warped by the Storm were less in number by a great margin, but the ones that had remained, lurking out in the fog beyond settlements, were powerful, strange things that The Nagirr'Om did constant battle with.

Defenses against the Storm were becoming more impressive as well, and with the Nagirr'Om gaining followers across the new world, everywhere was becoming safer. Cities were grander and more sprawled out, and some even covered a greater area than Nolano. They were full of wonders: floating structures, gates one could walk through that would take them to distant portals, and great statues that moved at the commands of their creators.

Following Tavo had become easier as time went on by the rumors he left behind, always an extremely powerful young man from the distant jungle and savannah tribe who passed through the Storm-lands without the need of a caravan. Occasionally, Eowen could find where he'd gone by the signature of his power, which she was trying to become more familiar with. He'd manifested some of the grandest towers, strangest objects, and largest acres of sweeping landscape she encountered in the new world. Wonders followed in his wake and Eowen sought them all out, trying to better understand her cousin. She encountered buildings bigger on the inside, fruit from a crystal tree that made one apparently unkillable by injury when eaten, and a pool of water that if one bathed in, they would lose all their memories. Eowen did not know why Tavo had created these things, but all of them were leden with power.

Tavo's manifestations never seemed to follow any theme, a trait Eowen had assumed the most powerful dreamers had in common. Their abilities had always seemed to display themselves in a way that related to some specialty, yet nothing about Tavo's manifestations indicated he had a specialty. Eowen was eager to learn what new rule of the world Tavo had mastered that made him an exception to the rule.

* * *

Eowen had just left a small settlement that had manifested a massive, dense forest to live in. It was a serene place with a false sky above it that moved through a day and night cycle. At times, the trees seemed to have moved when no one was looking. It made it difficult to find the people settled in it, and just as difficult to leave. Tavo had helped to manifest the forest, and Eowen was close behind him now. He no longer seemed to be going north anymore, only west. He was headed directly towards some of the more dangerous areas that The Nagirr'Om had not yet been to. Eowen had not seen more than a distant sighting of the silver woman in weeks, gliding through the clouds.

She was currently traveling with a group of eleven; a trio of acolytes, five trying to find loved ones in distant settlements, two adventurous souls inspired by stories of Hani's crew, and a fairly powerful man named Ennik. The acolytes were a quiet, serious sort, chosen and sent to the lands they now traversed by The Nagirr'Om itself to lay the groundwork for its eventual approach. The two adventurers were sisters named Trung and Setili. Both were in their twenties and had come all the way from a rare Britchen settlement far beyond where Eowen had believed such territories ended. They carried up the rear as the acolytes lead.

The caravan trudged steadily through fog heavier and more oppressive than Eowen had encountered in over a year. Ennik stood in the center, talking with the non-combative members of the caravan.

"No reason to be nervous, you've the next greatest warrior in the world with you. I've fought alongside The Nagirr'Om herself! Who wants to hear the story of the legendary battle at the settlement of Hule?" The only ones that raised their hands were the two newest members of the caravan, who hadn't heard it yet. Ennik glanced around victoriously, as though it'd been a competition. "I arrived through mist denser and colder than this, lightning flashing in the distance. I moved through the Storm on my own, without the need for a caravan, for the Storm couldn't touch me. Such is my power, the power to wrestle even gods!"

"Weren't you carrying a knife you found off a dead acolyte to resist the Storm?" Trung spoke up from the back. The knife had been a part of Ennik's story before, but it seemed he'd edited that out for his new audience after people had reacted poorly to him looting the dead.

"What was that, girl?" Ennik marched right up to her, disrupting the caravan. "You want to interrupt me? Then prove you can, right now!" Ennik flexed his muscles and his power, glowering over the young woman. Her sister, Setili, stood beside her for support while the acolytes waited for the conflict to pass. Ennik's dreaming aura was impressive by most standards, and by the old world's standards he cut an imposing figure. It was clear that the sisters were weaker than he as his dreaming aura bore down on them, flattening their powers beneath the force of his. "Anytime you want, I'll even give you the first strike." He tapped his chin, inviting the sisters to fight.

A shadow shaped like a heron passed over Ennik and he turned around to see the great bird towering over him with Eowen beside it. "I'd like to hear the rest of your story,

Ennik." Eowen said, just loud enough for everyone to hear her. "It gets better with each telling."

Ennik narrowed his eyes and flexed a burst of his dreaming aura at Eowen, but it buffeted harmlessly against her like wind on stone. Despite Eowen's words, the challenge was obvious. But Ennik was unsure if he could take Eowen, and as long as she wasn't openly trying to start a conflict he wasn't going to test it. He forced a smile and left the sisters alone, saving as much face as he could.

"See how even the dreaded Eowen of the Dead respects my greatness?" he postured to the rest of the caravan. "She, who is worshiped like the great heroes of Hani's crew and The Nagirr'Om herself, respects me!" He kept eye contact with Eowen, practically begging her to argue with him. "Is she really so great, though? She who needs the protection of these acolytes, unlike myself who is here for their protection?"

The acolytes did not deign to respond, and instead turned away to continue moving. Eowen matched his stare, her eyes seeming to change in the light to look like her heron's; inhuman, unblinking, and predatory. When Ennik received no response to his questions, he huffed and continued on with the rest of the caravan. He restarted his story, but the mood was tense from that point on. Eowen fell to the back of the group and the sisters approached her.

"Thank yo—" Eowen cut off Trung's words with a gesture. Ennik was watching them between glances as he monologued. Eowen manifested a barrier of sound and her heron moved in front of her so that she'd not be seen speaking.

"Why bother irritating him?" Eowen said. "You know what his temper is like."

"He's an infuriating, pompous bastard!" Trung said.

"Yes, but he's a bastard who could kill you," Setili said. "Thank you, Eowen Mortician, for your support. My own temper is too short for her own good."

Eowen waved off the thanks, walked away, and dropped the barrier. Over a week ago their caravan had been made up of the sisters, the acolytes, Eowen, and Ennick, but all the other travelers had been different. Among the former group, a young man, tired of Ennik's attitude, had challenged him. Ennik broke the young man's arm, then nearly killed him with a strike of manifested force. Eowen had stopped him by blocking the attack and redirecting his rage by congratulating him on his victory.

Since then, Ennik had carried a chip on his shoulder around Eowen, and at times it seemed like he wanted to challenge her, but he never did. There was an unspoken understanding between them. Ennik knew that if they fought, powers against powers, he'd be woefully outclassed. The big man wouldn't dare to be seen losing to a girl that looked no older than fifteen. However, Ennik also knew that Eowen was trying to keep a good reputation, and that violence on her part would spread faster than any peaceful or charitable actions. There was also a dangerous mystery around the possibility of a violent confrontation with Eowen. In all her travels she had rarely, if ever, been known to fight, and whether she could withstand the full onslaught from another powerful dreamer was still unknown. Power to power, she outclassed every dreamer she'd met in her travels, but just as with real combat, how one used their abilities was just as important. So an awkward balance was struck between her and Ennik, where she disallowed him from harming others while openly helping him keep face. Ennik liked to test the limits of her patience constantly, and Eowen put up with him.

He can make his remarks, so long as I can continue my journey.

* * *

They passed through several small settlements over the next month, most of which had never seen a caravan at all. The settlements were hardened, suspicious places that had only resisted the Storm through rigorous upkeep of barriers. Their advancements in manifestation had almost exclusively been put towards the development of countermeasures. These places lacked beautiful architecture and sweeping landscapes, and they did not waste their powers on festivities, food, music, and other simple pleasures. Their manifestations could too easily be warped by the Storm. As such, few if any of them had been able to hold funerals of any kind, let alone collect their many dead that lay unattended out in the fog. Eowen felt the pining of many spirits to have her aid them, but these calls were muffled behind calloused souls and stony hearts.

The people she encountered were still largely of the valley tribes, but among them were Carrulians, various coastal tribes, and even a few that hailed from islands to the west. The Carrulians tended to be tan with icy blue eyes that tilted up at the corners and were often covered with freckles. They were a people few and far between who kept to themselves. Most of them were from a land that had been far across the western ocean in the old world. Those that had found themselves in settlements that did not belong to their people were often looking for ways out. They sometimes stirred up trouble, arriving at settlements in forces that could resist the

Storm to retrieve their own people. Otherwise, they had kept to themselves since the fall.

During their stays with these far western settlements, the acolytes of Eowen's caravan would establish barriers for their hosts to earn their trust. Eowen constantly blended her dreaming aura so as not to attract attention, but the heron was hard to ignore. In these new suspicious lands that had never heard of her, Eowen wanted to maintain a neutral reputation. Ennik seemed to see it as his duty to disrupt that possibility. At times he claimed to be the leader of the caravan, the only one among them keeping them safe from the Storm, keeping Eowen in check. In addition to extolling his virtues, chasing women, and occasionally challenging someone to a fight, he would spread rumors about the others. By Ennik's words, the acolytes were spineless devotees of The Nagirr'Om, which he described as a nightmarish monster only slightly less evil than the Storm itself. He characterized the adventuring sisters as stupid, airheaded thrill seekers, implying that they were diseased whores that should not be trusted. Finally, Ennik claimed that Eowen was a dark entity that laid with the dead and the corpses of children. He claimed she was a witch that stole bodies to perform evil magics and to keep their dearly departed far away from her. The rest of the caravan became largely ostracized in the settlements they passed through because of him, and it was always a relief for the poor, beset people when they finally left.

The question of why Ennik was traveling with them came up, and he revealed that he was seeking a man who'd attained a reputation as the most powerful warrior in the new world. It was the same legend Eowen had heard some months ago, which was tied to the armored warrior in Hani's crew, Nifroht. Nifroht hailed from a land that had once been far across the ocean to the west, and the fabled warrior who Nifroht served and Ennik wanted to challenge was rumored to be even more powerful than The Nagirr'Om. Ennik wished to prove himself by joining the man's ranks.

As time went on, Eowen found it more difficult to ignore Ennik's pompous attitude and constant challenging of anything he perceived as a slight. She might have been able to put up with it if wasn't also disrupting her work with false rumors. Eowen spent a great deal of time meditating and convincing herself not to retaliate against Ennik, but the sisters felt differently.

"Why haven't you put him in his place?" Trung asked after some weeks. They were in a settlement nearer to the coastal tribes but still made up primarily of valley people. "You're much more powerful than he is... Aren't you?"

"Because she isn't a bastard like he is," Setili said. Eowen smiled at them and manifested food and drink to share.

"Believe me, it's tempting, but even if I did, and I'm not sure I could, what good would come of it?"

"He'd stop tarnishing our names and making me consider murder!" Trung said. She was the younger sister and had a tendency towards righteous fury. Setili was more level headed but seemed to largely follow her sister's lead, letting Trung set the pace and always backing her sister up.

"It's true, he's a problem wherever he goes and you are his superior, Eowen Mortician." Setili raised a glass to Eowen, who made a gesture of appreciation. They had joined the caravan after Eowen had helped them perform seventeen funerals. They had lost every member of their extended family to the fall and the Storm and were the only ones left. The sisters had been the most powerful people in their settlement, and had defended it until acolytes had arrived to establish barriers. Eowen had helped them gather and take care of their dead, as she had for many others in their community. After her duties were done she had left them behind, fully expecting never to run into them again. The sisters, however, left soon after to travel on their own, intent on exploring the far west, and had run into Eowen in a settlement some weeks later. Eowen ate and thought about how to respond to their praise and their concerns.

He's not as bad as he seems.

This wasn't true.

He does help us fight the Storm.

This was not incorrect, as he was a dreamer whose power had an identity, though that identity seemed to be entirely about and for himself. There was evidence that Ennik's abilities were tied to his ego.

Perhaps that's why he hasn't tried to fight me, because if I don't challenge him or give him enough reason to challenge me, he won't actually be strong enough to at all.

They had encountered a few Storm entities in their travels, both at settlements and while traveling between. The acolytes were usually effective enough to fight them off, but with Ennik they were able to make quick work of them. Eowen always relegated herself to bolstering barriers, and for some reason this made Ennik angry. He'd glare at her, sometimes demand to know why she hadn't fought as well, sometimes insult her as a coward, but Eowen would not rise to his barbs.

Why do we put up with him?

Eowen sighed. She knew why.

"We could at least leave him behind at some settlement," Trung said. "Abscond in the dead of night."

"No, then he'd just be their problem, and he'd take it as a huge insult," Satili responded. "He might even pursue us through the Storm just to make us pay for insulting him or whatever excuse he ends up with. But I do think you should do something, Eowen. Not to presume, but you're the only one around who can."

"It's... not that simple. Maybe I could, but I truly don't know, and things would surely get much worse for us or others if I did." Eowen frowned, and her brow wrinkled. "It's a bigger issue though, one that goes beyond us and Ennik. I'm not sure how exactly to put it in words but... He's not the enemy." Eowen looked at the sisters but saw that they didn't quite understand. "See, no matter how insufferable or problematic he is," *no matter how much he impedes my work,* "the Storm is the one true enemy of our world, of life in this place. For however devastating the fall was, there has been no real threat in the new world save for the Storm. So long as he is not possessed by it, and so long as he is not threatening lives himself, I have to accept he is not the enemy." Eowen grimaced. "Even if it makes me feel ill to say it." Trung laughed and raised her cup.

"Fine, here's to the Storm! Without it, Ennik would be the worst thing in the new world!" Setili was grinning while she shushed her sister and glanced around to see who was listening. Eowen cracked a smile and raised her cup as well; she'd long since gotten into the habit of establishing barriers of sound around them, as their conversation often became about their problems with Ennik.

* * *

Their caravan changed out most of their members, gaining those few desperate enough to brave the Storm and seek loved ones. The core members of the acolytes, the sisters,

Ennik, and Eowen stayed the same, and the tension between them continued to grow. The acolytes kept more and more to themselves, serving their purpose only, while Eowen kept with the sisters. As their other members became fewer and fewer, Ennik found himself alone and irritable, bouncing between annoying the acolytes and the sisters. He rarely confronted Eowen directly, but when he did it was masked as an attempt at conversation. "Your creations are dull, girl."

"Please call me by my name, Ennik. I might start considering 'girl' to be an insult."

Ennik rolled his eyes and spit to the side. "I don't like your name, jungle girl."

"Actually, I grew up closer to the savannah—"

"I don't give a shit where you're from!" Eowen didn't know how to respond to this, so she opted to watch him silently. "You think it matters? You corpse fucking gir—" Eowen cut his voice off, making it so that the sounds simply couldn't escape his throat.

"Try saying it, Ennik. We might get along better if you treat me like a person." Eowen undid the block to his voice, and there was a long moment of silence where he glowered and shifted uncomfortably. Eowen sat facing him, her heart beating painfully hard despite her outward calm as she prepared for a possible confrontation. She couldn't really be sure what would set Ennik off. He seemed to use most any excuse to fight, but he also always picked on those weaker than him. So Eowen was nervous but kept patient, since she knew him well enough that he wouldn't make a move unless he was sure to win. Finally, he sat down in front of her and spoke.

"Your creations... They're pathetic, and the way you use your power is a disgrace!"

Eowen was surprised. The topic he'd brought up was the one he actually wanted to speak about, even if his style of conversation had much to be desired. "Can you elaborate?"

"Your creations are dull and wasteful. You have so much more power than you display, yet you only use it for basic things." It was true that Eowen had used her power for little else than simple manifestations in a long time. The Storm was still a threat, and she could feel it reaching for her spirit whenever she was outside a barrier. "And your disgusting obsession with the dead, it's off putting and makes a bad name for the rest of us." Eowen smiled, and it was thin but triumphant. She'd managed to start a conversation with Ennik, which meant she might be able to find common ground.

And if that happens maybe he'll become less insufferable.

"Are you insulting me, Ennik?" The man glared and gritted his teeth. It was so clear that he wanted to put Eowen in her place, but he was not a fool.

"No, I was not insulting you. I am making... observations. Your reputation used to precede you, so people respected you, but they didn't realize how poorly you use your power. You've never stayed in one place long enough for people to develop an opinion of you, like I have, and I think you know that. You have... some power, but the way you put it to use is an insult to all of us who are blessed with it in this new world!"

Eowen's heart skipped a beat. Ennik clearly didn't know about her time in Nolano and the good she'd done there, except perhaps by rumor. His opinion was skewed, certainly, but it hit her in a way she hadn't expected. Mein's banishment was fresh in her mind now, her mother's glare from the many times Eowen had been sent home after a failed apprenticeship swam before her. Eowen was caught in a brief loop of child-like helplessness, resentment, and the self confidence she'd attained. The feelings strobed through her spirit, disrupting her dreaming aura which wavered, thinned and shrank in ways it had not in years. It had been Ennik's tone, his disdain, his certainty. To Eowen, this man, far from her home and long after she'd left it, had for a moment perfectly embodied the enmity of her mother.

Ennik watched as Eowen looked away from him, her face twisting into a pained and meek expression. His lips lifted into an oily smile and he shivered with pleasure as he felt her dreaming aura fade. His eyes gleamed and seemed to say: 'Ah ha! There's always a weakness, and I've gotten closer to finding yours.' He fixed his expression into a more neutral one and stood with his hands clasped behind his back. When Eowen refocused and looked back up at him, Ennik had adopted a stately manner. Eowen cleared her throat and adjusted her sitting position.

"Thank you for your honesty. Rest assured, I have my reasons for what I do, and I highly doubt my actions reflect on you. Now, I'd appreciate it if you left me alone."

Ennik considered taking his small victory, but was enjoying his moment of control too much to stop. "I have hardly seen any of your manifestations, at most you make simple things or create invisible effects like your pathetic barriers while I accomplish great things! I have created weapons empowered with fire and lightning, I have fought the Storm beside The Nagirr'Om and have defeated many powerful warriors before and after the fall. I have built towers, created jewels of such beauty that none in the old world could rival them! I have laid down mountains upon this new world, girl!"

His use of 'girl' snapped Eowen back to herself. Her spirit was still off balance but newly focused on disdain for the man before her rather than the scars of her past.

"I am as a god in this new world!" Ennik bellowed so that the rest of the caravan, which only had two members other than the original ones, heard him. His dreaming aura was flaring with power, and none could approach. "You do nothing compared to me. Actually, it is worse than nothing, because your power goes only to the dead or to mundanity." Eowen chewed the inside of her cheek and crossed her arms. "You are a disappointment and an insult to me!"

Eowen felt a dark burning in her gut, like coals beneath the ashes. She very slowly rose to her feet and stood before Ennik, though at her height his navel was level with her chest.

"So, Ennik, just to be clear. What you're saying is that no matter how powerful I am or what I use my powers for, I am inferior to you because my creations aren't flashy and shiny enough?" Eowen's voice was low, dangerous, but it was still the voice of a girl. Her spirit still wavered, so Ennik grinned with all his teeth and arched over her.

"That's the right word for you, girl." He leaned close enough that Eowen could taste his hot breath through her nose. Her feet wanted to get far, far away, but she held her ground. "Inferior," he whispered.

His words were like a tick in her ear, his presence would require a bath. Eowen wanted very badly to strike him, to use her power in the way the Storm had used it through her. The prospective satisfaction of it was tantalizing, and as the seconds of their standoff stretched, Eowen dearly wished to scratch that itch. She didn't though, for she could feel the Storm at the edges, waiting, watching, hoping, and whispering that to put this man in his place was not only the right thing to do, it was the only thing to do. The heron, which had been curled up behind her, unfolded its neck and nipped at the back of her leg.

Don't worry, I know.

With great effort and several deep breaths, Eowen calmed herself enough to be sure that if she opened her mouth no fire would spew out. Then, she smiled at Ennik, a strange little smile that was crooked and thin and playful all at once. Ennik took a half step back as he felt Eowen's power reassert itself. She whispered, "Don't call me girl."

Eowen wasn't sure of what she was going to do, but she knew what Ennik wanted and she hoped that simply refusing to fight or cow to him would be enough. The rest of the caravan waited, fearful and helpless as the two demigods had their standoff. Then the wind picked up. At first, Eowen thought it was Ennik, and she readied to call up barriers, but then Ennik reacted as if it was her.

"Is this wind supposed to intimidate me? If you want me to call you by your name, make me." He took the flash of fear in Eowen's eyes as him gaining the advantage, until she stepped to the side and looked past him.

"It's not me." Eowen pointed to the north, and the rest of the caravan turned to see what it was. No one was surprised that severe rains and burning clouds were approaching. Amidst the clouds were tornado columns that stretched up to bear a turbulent firmament of electric death and icy brutality. To the caravan, this kind of elemental savagery was familiar and merely meant the approach of a Storm-being. What did inspire fear, as they looked more closely, were the massive proportions of the encroaching threat. The cloying mists that permeated the new world had at some point receded like the ocean on a beach before a great wave comes crashing in. Eowen struggled to comprehend the magnitude of what approached, for it was more than she'd ever seen. The darkness above was already roofed by the outer reaches of the anvil cloud, the world to their left and right encircled, as though the Storm were trying to trap them first. Lightning flashed, but it took a full thirty seconds for a tiny rumble of thunder to reach them. For there to be so much power before them at such a distance represented a danger that Eowen had known the Storm was capable of, but only in theory. Necks upon necks, heads upon heads of its serpentine manifestation squirmed in the roil before them, snapping with jaws that would burn and freeze, tear and crush.

Eowen glanced behind her and saw that the encircling clouds had almost pinned them in, pulled like curtains by two great Storm-beasts. "There!" The others looked. "We can still escape!"

Ennik pushed Eowen down before she had any time to react. "Even now you are a coward!" he roared at her. "We stand and fight!" Eowen's heron screeched at him and fluttered to her side. She let it help her up and struggled to find the words to respond to such stupidity.

"You can't be serious!" Ennik marched to the acolytes, glancing back at Eowen only to flash her that same look of disappointment he'd had before.

"Ready a barrier, coward, we'll hunt this Storm ourselves!" Eowen couldn't believe what she was hearing.

Surely the acolytes aren's fools enough to try this!

Yet there they were, hammering bamboo stalks out of the starfield and cutting fresh arrows as their archer eyed the entity. The sisters and the two poor caravan members cowered behind them. Eowen approached with her hands out.

"Come, we can still escape! Acolytes, you can get us out of here, but you cannot fight that!" The Storm was rushing closer, Eowen could hear the thunder clearly now, feel as the teeth of the wind bit at her clothes. The hammer and knife acolytes continued fortifying, but the bow wielder turned to Eowen. He was a young man, more a boy really, with curly black hair and brown skin. The longbow was taller than him, but the look in his eyes said he'd seen horrors, the set of his shoulders said that he'd faced them.

"We have respect for you, Eowen Who Follows Death." This was an epithet she had not heard before. "We've heard of how you aided our master far to the south and east, and for that you will always have the respect of The Nagirr'Om's acolytes. But this," he gestured at their impending doom, "is our purpose."

Eowen stared at them, horrified, but they only continued their preparations. Ennik glared at her, spit at her feet, then strode to the front of the barrier to face the Storm first. The newest caravan members were an elderly husband and wife who looked back and forth between Eowen and the acolytes. The elderly couple were shaking with fear, and the sisters were trying to look brave but failing.

"Eowen, what should we do? We'll follow your lead, just say the word," Setili said. Eowen looked behind them and saw that the Storm had already fully encircled them kilometers away. She considered making a run for it, trying to break through the thin point while protecting the caravaneers, but dismissed it.

Without my domain of power around me I can't do such deeds, and the Storm may take control of me if I am away from the acolytes for too long. She looked back at the servants of The Nagirr'Om, all more powerful dreamers than most of its servants, hand picked by the silver woman to scout the hostile lands they were currently in. *Maybe they can actually do it, maybe they'll be powerful enough to defeat the host.*

Eowen's dreaming aura had grown vast and covered a massive radius around her, but the Storm had stayed mostly outside of it, cleverly sensing the girl's capabilities as it hunted her. It no longer had any reason to keep up pretense though, and just as she was debating what to do, the thundering clouds stampeded in from all sides. The whole of her, mind, body, and spirit, were submerged in the weight of the powers around them. She fell to her knees, clutching at her throat as if she were suffocating. It was like her first seconds in the new world all over again. She felt helpless, naked, weak, alone. Then, a silver bamboo stalk slammed into the starfield next to her and broke the illusion. Eowen looked up to see the archer boy standing over her, pity and steel in his eyes.

"You're strong enough to hold one of these, yes?" Eowen bobbed her head, and he made a curt, militant gesture before returning to the front. Eowen grasped the bamboo and pulled herself to her feet.

"We stay," Eowen said to the caravan, as though it were a choice. "And I'll protect you," she said, as though she could.

Rain began pittering on them. Then splatting. Then slamming down upon them, flooding up to their ankles and drenching them in seconds. Eowen stood over her caravan, one hand on the bamboo and another on the back of her heron. The bird was attempting to shield them from the rain, but it was insufficient. The elderly couple began to pray to the gods they'd long since stopped believing in, the sisters held each other and whispered their love.

Eowen closed her eyes, slipping through the veil of

consciousness into the depths of her dreaming ocean to seek the sort of power that would get her and those under her protection through this ordeal. She pulled what barriers, enhancements to the acolytes powers, and resistances to the Storm that she had out into reality and braced for impact. Her powers were impressive, dying the atmosphere around them with her dense aura of potential made manifest. For a moment, it seemed like it would be enough. The rain bounced off of her barrier, the winds parted around it, and even a stray branch of lightning broke on her powers. For the moment, even Ennik was impressed and the company felt safe.

Then the flood came. Water, increasing at first by centimeters, then suddenly jumping a meter high flooded in and crashed into Eowen's barrier. She responded by manifesting a platform of stone under them, which rose several meters into the air. The acolytes began to fight, firing their arrows into the elements before them. It worked to repel the Storm for only seconds before it reformed around them. Great serpentine heads emerged from the waters and winds, with maws like valleys and teeth like forests of lightning, ice, and fire. Eowen was fully in her dreaming, divorced from reality to maintain the powers to defend her party, but the Storm was trying to drag her back. It crashed into them again and again, armageddon with teeth. Bamboo barriers ripped out of the platform or exploded from the sheer pressure upon them.

Ennik was proving his worth as a maw sunk its teeth into the platform and, bursting with the strength he was so proud of, he wrestled it off. The Storm creature was all water and wind, but where he gripped it, it became physical, and he could slam it down. The man was fighting a losing battle, treading water that coursed with electricity and horrors.

Eowen found the strength to raise up another platform under Ennik to get him free of the water as the acolytes supported him with their arrows. They were indeed among the greatest followers of The Nagirr'Om, fending off the powers that beset them with more skill and ferocity than Eowen had seen since she'd helped drive the Storm out of the Britchen lands. They were not pushing it back, but it seemed as though they might hold out for a while, perhaps till The Nagirr'Om herself or a company of her acolytes could show up.

Or maybe even Hani, Eowen thought. The thought was desperate and far-fetched, but nonetheless, Eowen hoped it would come to pass.

Things did not stay the same, though. Shapes stirred in the clouds that hastened towards them. A body, humanoid by the loosest definitions, cut through the gloom and latched onto Ennik. The creature was like a person flayed open, empty eye sockets leaking smoke that joined the clouds, teeth too large for its mouth and an emaciated body with arms as long as it was tall. It shed blood that screamed into fire, screeched out a call that riled up the Storm around it to greater strength, and from the center of its chest, a heavy black chain dragged behind it. Ennik grappled with the creature, a slave of the Storm, slamming it down. A bamboo arrow found its skull, and it died to an outpouring of fire and lightning. Ennik had no time to celebrate his victory as two, then five, then dozens emerged. They grappled on him, biting and clawing and pulling, and though he fought valiantly, their sheer numbers pinned him. Dozens more, over a hundred clambered up Eowen's platform, pounding on her barrier as the Storm continued to lash out with its great elemental heads and violent strikes. Eowen couldn't hold.

One finally ruptured her defenses, skinless fingers dripping burning blood next to the caravaneers. Eowen fell to her knees, the heron shielded her, and a great serpentine Storm head of water, ice, and lightning rushed through the gap in the barrier, plunging them into the deep. Eowen surfaced from the water, gasping and fully out of her dreaming. All her companions were out of sight, and the water was eroding her platform as it churned into a whirlpool. Flayed creatures reached for her limbs to drag her under, their flecks of blood blistering her skin. The water was ice cold and electrified, the heron under her the only thing keeping her afloat.

Then they stopped, their thick black chains, each link wider than Eowen's arm, pulled taught. The serpentine heads pulled back like a dog being called to heel, and the sudden stillness was deafening. From somewhere beyond the fog, a thing wrenched on the chains embedded in the hearts of the Storm-cursed, and they fell away from the caravan. A voice of power, more gargantuan than any Eowen had thought could be, rippled through the world, shaking all that it touched.

"Cease. There are some among them I want."

It emerged from the gloom, a being similar to the chained creatures in the way a pebble is to the moon. High as the tree of Nolano, flayed and shedding drops of blood as large as ponds, holding thousands of chains in its hands, the lord of this Storm approached. Fires as large as Eowen's entire village burned in its sockets. The things teeth jutted out from its lipless mouth, each as large as a mansion. One hand held all the chains, while the other dragged on the starfield. The massive serpentine heads coiled around it like pets adoring their master, but Eowen could feel the truth. The Storm was the master, and there was nothing left of the person this giant entity had been.

Ennik rushed it, but was dragged away by a Storm serpent of oily smoke and fire. The elderly couple were nowhere to be found, the sisters lost to Eowen's sight in the chaos as well. The flayed behemoth lifted its empty hand from the starfield, and reached out towards one of the acolytes in the water, the boy with the bow. He fumbled for an arrow with shuddering hands, managed to knock and loose it, only to miss the target entirely. The thing extended its pointer finger, the digit easily three times the size of the boy, and pressed it to his chest. The boy shook, and Eowen could feel his dreaming aura as the Storm rushed in and through his spirit. His eyes steamed, then exploded with fire. The finger pulled away, bringing a black chain out with it that peeled the boy's skin off. He clutched at the chain, trying to drag it back in, and his arms warped out into the elongated ones of the other chained creatures. He screeched in pain and his teeth jutted out, expanding like the others. The being passed the chain to its other hand and the thing that had been the boy turned to face its former companions. It lunged at them, but its new master pulled it back.

"Wait until I am finished."

The two remaining acolytes held each other and wept. One of them, a boy around the age of the newly flayed one, cried out, and their grief reached Eowen. She watched and felt as a new thread, invisibly connecting her to a mourner, strung itself between them.

She wrapped her arms around the heron, and it launched them to the acolytes' side. The entity reached for another acolyte, but Eowen Mortician was in her power now. She struck out, splintering the entity's arm up to the elbow, sending gouts of blood as large as houses that exploded into bonfires wherever they landed. Eowen shimmered as shadow and light danced under her will, the space around her evacuated of all other influence. She knelt beside the acolytes, took their hands, and shared with them her own tears.

"**I am sorry,**" she whispered, her voice of power kept low in their company. "**It is only at times such as these that I can resist such as the Storm.**" The expression on the face of the boy acolyte who'd cried out transitioned from helpless loss, to hate, to pleading, to an expression of such hopelessness that it very nearly overcame even his grief in that moment.

"We know," the other acolyte, an older woman, said. "The story of you and The Nagirr'Om reaches many acolytes."

Eowen nodded, and turned to face the towering being again. "**That one is mine.**" She pointed to the newest addition to the entity's army. The arm Eowen had destroyed was already reforming as serpentine heads of fire, ice, and lighting wove into the flesh, making it anew. The entity gestured with the hand that held the chains as if to say: 'go ahead, I will have you soon enough.' Eowen glanced at the former acolyte and her power locked its movements, severed the chain, and levitated it back to its grieving companions. "**Who he was has died, but you must deliver his true death.**"

The acolytes understood, and despite shaking hands and tearfilled eyes, their hands were steady as they guided their tools to the workings they had committed their life to. The boy with the hammer struck the starfield, and a great, shining stalk of bamboo erupted from it. The woman brandished her knife and cut a spear larger than the one that pierced Eowen long ago. They held it together, and with their warped companion immobilized by Eowen's power, plunged the point through the chain in its chest. The presence of the Storm hosted in the body fought, squirmed, but in the silver light of The Nagirr'Om's power broke so that only the ruined corpse remained.

The acolytes breathed heavily, their expressions pained and their shoulders hunched. Eowen removed their hands from the spear, and when she'd done that she removed the spear from the body, and knelt next to it with the mourners. There was a terrible moment of uncertainty between them all as, for the first time in a long time, Eowen did not know what to do next.

"I... think I can make it look like him again," she suggested, but the boy shook his head.

"He died already, serving our master's will," the acolyte boy choked out. "Pon would be proud to be laid to rest in whatever form that left him."

The flayed giant waited its turn, for as soon as Eowen's work ended, she'd be unable to defend anyone. Ennik watched, horrified and enraged as Eowen attended to the body.

"Do you know how Pon would have preferred to be laid to rest?" Eowen's voice shook. There was no more power in it, only fear.

"This power is gone once the funeral is over, isn't it?" the older acolyte asked, and Eowen nodded. "Shouldn't we delay? We can hold off until our master arrives and bring the others under... your... protection..." Eowen met the acolytes' eyes and she studied Eowen's expression. "You can't?"

"No."

"Why?"

Eowen was slow and deliberate when she spoke, her voice

still colored by fear, but lucid and explicit. "Because this power only exists to serve the ceremony, the body, and those that grieve. I can't prolong it, I cannot cut it short, I can only have this power while I perform my work as best as I can." She looked to the young acolyte, who was holding their flayed companion's hand through their sleeve, for the boiling blood would still blister.

"We gave up our old ties when we joined The Nagirr'Om. The trio becomes our family and... our master does not teach funeral practices. I think... most of us are left where we fall, but—" the boy shook the monstrous hand and looked from his fellow acolyte to Eowen and back, helplessly, "that does not feel right though. I am not questioning my master, she is wisest and most powerful, but I cannot... I will not leave him like this!"

Eowen reached down and took the body's other hand. Her skin burned and blistered, but she was in her power, and could repair it as quickly as it was damaged.

"Something simple, for the acolytes of The Nagirr'Om do not hold to any traditions. Something here, where he fought till his life was forfeit. Something that will last and serve to tell of who he was."

The young boy nodded at each of her declarations, so Eowen began her work. It was simple and quick; she manifested a stone rectangle for the body to be placed in, not merely on top of the star field, but embedded into it. The stone glowed silver in the way that The Nagirr'Om herself did. Next to it, she manifested a lid that glowed the same, and upon it was the symbol of The Nagirr'Om. Three lines, one short for the knife, one medium with a square for the hammer, one long and curved for the bow. Eowen manifested liquid silver that she had flow into the bow-line and solidify.

"Will this do?"

The woman nodded, and the boy swallowed his sobs. "It is the most fitting any of us could receive," the woman said.

Eowen then manifested a robe, like the one the dead thing had been wearing when it had been a person, and wrapped the body in it to lay in the coffin. Eowen carried it over, for it weighed nothing. The boy still held the hand, and the woman stood by with hers clasped. They set the erstwhile acolyte to its final resting place, and the boy leaned in to whisper his goodbye. He kissed the forehead, despite it being flayed and despite that the blood burned his lips. Then he too stood back, waiting for Eowen to finish it.

"That'll do, I think." His voice was hoarse. Eowen levitated the coffin lid and paused before placing it over it.

"After I seal him in, it's over. I'll... try to stop it, by myself I mean. With my own power. And when I do, the Storm might take me instead." Eowen found herself stalling after all. She tried to stay in the moment, tried to think and feel only for her work as she said her next words, but it was impossible and her power was breaking. "So... be ready." She met their eyes and saw that they understood. "There won't be much time."

Eowen brought her attention back to the coffin lid and moved it so that it was almost in place. She lowered it, and with only the barest hush of stone on stone, the body was sealed, the funeral over. A short, simple affair befitting of the one it had served. Her power over the place faded and the giant reached out to her chest. Eowen prepared to fight the thing, but as she faced her demise, her dreaming did not come. She could not fall into her subconscious, for she was locked in the reality before her by a terrible, painful knot in her chest.

Every survivor of the fall had faced their death, and many had seen it as a rebirth, but Eowen had come to feel that she was largely above the threats of the new world. For all its dangers, the possibility of her demise had become a theoretical thing. In a way, Eowen felt that her near-death experience at the fall, naked and alone, yet still capable enough to survive and protect others, had been a way of paying her dues to the new world. She'd crossed the threshold, honored the entry fee, and found her place. She did not feel owed anything, save for the opportunity to pursue her work and her quest. Hani had inspired her of this conviction long ago, and she'd carried it with her. Yet now, facing a power that would end her, all that certainty melted away.

This is it, then.

Her thoughts were of grim, broken acceptance, her feelings were of disappointment. The flayed finger, three times her height and width, pressed against her chest and she could feel the Storm entering her spirit. Eowen gritted her teeth as it fought and bit and writhed for a way in, moving through the scars of her past possession and feeding on her power. She gritted her teeth as the chain started to form in her chest, the links struggling to manifest, for the Storm was deciding whether to enslave her to its current host or emerge anew through her. Eowen could feel that the dreamer who'd become the flayed giant had been immensely powerful, and that they spoke with the voice of power indicated they'd awakened a jurisdiction before their possession.

Eowen's mind was pushed aside. Her dreaming held no sanction, for it was now home to the entity. She fell into profound unconsciousness, a dreamless empty where even the great voice that told her to listen would not reach, though Eowen thought she heard it calling.

I'm dead.

Were her last thoughts.

****

[You are not.]

****

Something ripped the flayed giant from Eowen with such acute severity that the shock paralyzed her, and she fell woodenly to the starfield. Voices in a language she did not know bellowed out battle cries. The flayed giant roared like a hurricane and sent its swarms and Storm serpents to the source of the cries, which emerged from the west. The heron slipped itself under the girl and lifted her enough to see some of what transpired before exhaustion took her.

A company of armored warriors emerged through the mists, cutting down Storm beasts with sweeps of their swords and thrusts of their spears. Their armor and weapons glowed with golden markings that seemed to repel the torrent before them. The flayed giant kicked through their ranks, sending them flying, but the warriors picked themselves up as if nothing had happened and rushed back in. Eowen passed out to the pained screeching of the giant as the armored company swarmed over it like ants, hacking it to pieces with strikes that clove through it like butter.

****

[Listen a little longer.]

I ASKED WHAT LOVE WOULD HAVE OF ME, WHAT QUESTIONS I COULD ANSWER, WHAT REQUEST THEY WOULD MAKE OF ME.

******

Eowen's eyes flicked open. Her mouth moved as if to speak, but no words came out. Her throat was too dry, so she manifested some water to drink. She felt the heron under her head acting as a pillow, and she took stock of her surroundings. She was in a small camp with her caravan next to Pon the acolyte's grave. The elderly couple had miraculously survived and were asleep next to each other. The two remaining acolytes were standing to the side, watching something in the distance. Trung cradled Setili's body in her lap. A serpent of the Storm had gotten Setili in its jaws. Half the young woman's torso and face were gone. The body had been cleaned and wrapped with a blanket. Trung was soaked in her sister's blood and tissue. Eowen felt no thread from Trung, no call for her work. The young woman's eyes were far away and her hand stroked Setili's hair absentmindedly.

"Trung," Eowen said, sitting up with the help of her heron, and upon hearing her name the young woman's eyes flicked back to the present and locked onto Eowen.

"I trusted you," Trung said, and Eowen felt sick. "You were powerful and kind and didn't let Ennik push you around. We had a bet going where I thought someday you'd put him in his place, but Setili thought your patience would never run out... I thought we'd be safe with you."

"I... Trung—"

"I'm not blaming you. Or... I'm trying not to. Setili wouldn't have. She said we shouldn't rely on you or the acolytes like that, because we needed to become strong and independent on our own. It's just..." Trung looked back down at her sister, readjusting the blanket to better cover the ruined half of Setili's face. "We were the only ones left out of all our family, do you understand? But we survived, we were safe. I just... stupidly thought that because we'd lost so much already we had—"

"Paid your dues," Eowen whispered, the knot in her chest twisting itself tighter. Trung nodded. Eowen forced herself to stand despite her stomach threatening to be sick. She sat next to Trung and held the young woman's hand.

"It wasn't Setili's idea to leave our settlement, that was all my idea. She was happy about it, though. She told me all she wanted was to follow me wherever I felt like going, so long as we were together." The young woman wasn't mourning yet. It was too soon, there was still too much shock. An aimless despair colored her dreaming aura, which washed over Eowen. "I don't want you to do anything for her. Or, I mean, me? A funeral, I mean." Eowen knew; there was no thread connecting them, but she let Trung speak for herself. "I want to do it all myself. I've seen you perform some funerals, I think I can do it." Eowen only nodded, squeezed Trung's hand, and shared her company in silence for some time.

Eowen glanced away to see what the acolytes were watching. The company of warriors that had saved them were camped some distance away, and Ennik was with them.

The moment Eowen directed her attention at him, Ennik felt it and turned to her. Hate, smugness, and a strange sense of triumph radiated off of him. He said something to the armored man he was speaking to, then marched towards her. The acolytes sighed, and the boy with the hammer looked at Eowen.

"He was telling them how we only survived because of how he held off the Storm till they arrived," he said. Trung wilted beside her, all the fight entirely out of her.

"Proving me right all along, Eowen corpse fucker!" Ennik shouted as he approached. "I saw the whole thing, your pathetic defenses, which failed! All your supposed power and status, yet you were useless to prevent these... awful losses!" Ennik seemed to be suppressing a smile. He shouldered past the acolytes, grasped a fistful of Eowen's robe and lifted her off the ground. Trung made to rise, but Eowen held out her hand to stop her. The acolytes watched from the side and the elder couple, who had woken up, were cowering together. "Where's your righteous attitude now? Huh?" He shook her by her robe.

Eowen's blood was boiling. She glared openly at him and her breath was coming fast and hot. She wanted to do something to him, something that would hurt the vile man disrupting their peace. He leaned in close.

"You're a pathetic, vile, disgrace and I should have put you in your place a long time ago."

He tried to throw her to the ground, but Eowen was immobile. He tried again, but Eowen took his huge, meaty hand in her tiny, thin one, and pulled it away from her.

"Let go—"

With a thought, Eowen cut off Ennik's words with her power. He gathered his own power and suffused his body with it, grinning madly, for finally she was fighting back. He tried to move to grapple her, but found his body paralyzed. Uncertainty flashed across his eyes, quickly followed by panic as Eowen floated off the starfield, carrying him up by the collar of his shirt. Eowen's tiny form was crackling with such an excess of power that her muscles creaked and her bones shuddered as she threw Ennik back.

"Trung," Eowen said, her voice low and dangerous. "That bet with your sister, you win."

Eowen flew forward and landed in front of Ennik as he was getting up. His mouth opened and closed like a fish, but Eowen was still blocking his words. She pinned him in place with a grip like stone, and he squirmed against her, trying to escape. Eowen's power was pouring out and around her in a vortex of shadow, light, and manifestation, the chaotic likes of which hadn't happened since she'd manifested the sun at her oasis.

"So I should use my power, Ennik? Fine! **I will!**"

The starfield below lifted in heavy, cresting waves, as though a stone the size of a mountain had been dropped into the ocean. Eowen's lips reformed into a serene smile that was for Ennik alone, and he desperately scrambled to get away from the girl, crying out silently. Eowen decided, for once, to completely let go of all the control she'd been carefully balancing for so long. She felt as though she needed to. She wanted the satisfaction. The Storm wasn't present enough to possess her, but the grooves it had left in her spirit, pathways to strength and violence, were there for her to use now. Eowen was sick of feeling weak despite her strength, humiliated at her impotency despite her power, disappointed in herself. None of these feelings would have made her act the way she was. Eowen attacked Ennik because it felt so, so good. Ennik fought back, launching all his power at her, but couldn't even touch the girl. He was a fly, buzzing around the edge of her perceptions. Eowen leaned in close. She decided that she would show him, show everyone the part of herself that she kept down. Eowen howled an inhuman sound and left the world behind. She capsized into her dreaming and let come what lurked in the deep of her deepest mind.

Creation erupted. Inexorable waves of landscape careened into fires that screamed. Towers of wings, oceans of faces, songs with hands, lanyards of technicolor flesh, and beasts that blotted the sky. All became glass, became sand, became stairs, became beetles, became anything, and on and on. Wonders abstracted the world of darkness and stars into a kaleidoscope of dreams wrung from the twisted parts in Eowen's spirit where all her hurts had been healing.

****

So this is what I am.

[Is it? Or is it only how you are right now?]

Trying to offer insight now?
It's too late to set a precedent for that.

[I've only ever said what you could hear.]

And how have you been deciding
what I can and cannot hear?

[I haven't made any such decisions, you have.]

Why are you so full of insights now? Don't you think there were other times when I needed to hear from you?

[It's never been about what you needed to hear, only what you could.]

What do you mean?

[Listen a little longer, and you'll find out.]

LOVE ONLY ASKED THAT I WOULD SPEAK WITH THEM, CARRY THEM TO FAR PLACES, ANSWER THEIR QUESTIONS OR FIND THOSE THAT COULD, AND TO SIMPLY BE THEIR COMPANION.

****

A gauntleted hand glowing with golden runes curled around Eowen's wrist.

"I think that's enough, don't you?" A gruff voice shouldered its way through the speaker's thick beard. Eowen didn't react for a moment and the warrior pulled at her wrist again, managing to move it just a bit, though several of the glowing runes whined under the strain and cracked.

There was a tense standoff as Eowen looked at herself, what she was doing, and sighed. She returned to herself, eyes clear and power settling down again. The starfield ceased its churning and the uproar of unbidden manifestation ceased, evaporating as Eowen dismissed her creations far and wide.

She dropped Ennik, who scrambled away. He had his voice back but was not using it.

The warrior let go of Eowen's wrist and huffed. "Such a lot of fuss." He began to trundle back towards his company, who hefted their weapons and gear, ready to leave for the next battle.

"You're a Nemsto person, aren't you?" Eowen called after the man, and he turned to address her.

"Strange that I can understand you, girl."

"Eowen." She put iron in her voice.

"Eowen the strange, then." He smiled under his beard, then looked out across the dark of the new world. "Not the strangest I've seen out there, though. I'm Glasgow. We're warriors of Nemsto. We've been pursuing that giant for many months. It emerged among the Carrulians and fled from us, accruing strength. It might have one day surpassed our strength had your company not slowed it down. This one claims to have been responsible for that, though after your display I have my doubts." Glasgow glanced between Eowen and Ennik.

"He, well." Eowen thought about how to phrase her thoughts. "In some ways, Ennik was more effective than I."

"That so?" Glasgow glanced around Eowen. "I think I've got the idea. Ennik said he was going to join us." Glasgow gestured to Ennik, who was still collecting himself. "Not sure about it. Don't know what's between you two, but I want no part of it in our company."

"Are you going east?"

"That's right."

"I'm going west, so you'd be taking him in the opposite direction."

"Would you recommend him for my company, then?"

Glasgow's beady eyes scanned Eowen up and down through the tufts of blond hair and his helmet. Ennik was getting indignant as Glasgow interviewed Eowen for his credentials.

"Don't listen to her, she—"

Glasgow grabbed Ennik by the collar and pushed him toward the rest of his company. "You want to join us, you'll keep quiet when your superiors are talking!" Ennik glared darkly, ground his teeth, but did as he was told and stalked away. "Hmm, trouble maker that one. Well, I've got a few with fouler attitudes under my command. So long as they can follow orders and fight."

"He can do that," Eowen said. "Ennik was strong enough to survive that attack without weapons or armor like yours. You'd be doing a favor to us anyway, keeping him in line."

"Good enough for me. I need warriors, their attitudes can be dealt with. We've picked up a few not of our people along the way. Battle forges bonds beyond origin." Glasgow offered Eowen his hand, and she took it. "Safe travels, Eowen the strange."

He walked back to his company, calling for them to get ready to move again. Eowen manifested a link from her voice to Ennik's ear such that she could whisper and only he could hear.

"Think about why you do what you do, Ennik." He jumped when her voice dropped in, his expression and body language vacillating between fearful hatred and righteous indignation. "I keep myself in check, always. Because if I don't, terrible things may happen." Ennik slowly turned to face Eowen, and for once his countenance opened. The same helplessness Eowen had just inspired in him was mirrored in her eyes. It echoed in her voice. "I don't want to hurt anyone," she whispered.

Eowen gave a slight bow to Glasgow's company, then turned on her heel and returned to the remnants of her caravan. Questions would need to be answered, such as: What do we do next? Where are we going next, and who will we be going with? The greatest source of the Storm in the lands they were in had been dealt with and so, for a time, it would be much safer to travel. Eowen could not bring herself to think through some kind of solution at the moment, so she manifested a tent big enough for herself and her heron. The fight was out of her, the brief pleasure she'd felt giving into the deep of her power to embarrass Ennik was gone. She felt lonely, cracked, hollow, and hungry in her heart. She wanted to be left alone, to be held, and yet she knew that neither would soothe what was happening in her now.

I thought that when I found purpose and work that was my own, I wouldn't feel this way anymore. For a time, I was right. So why didn't it stay true?

The acolyte boy with the hammer approached the tent and reached out to get Eowen's attention.

"Come back here," his companion said.

"I just wanted to check on her," he said.

"Leave her alone." The acolyte woman sighed. "She's got a lot on her mind. So do I, so do we all. Don't you?"

* * *

It took a week to reach the next settlement, and it was a week without the fog or the oppressive force of the Storm upon them. Like at Nolano, its effects had largely been removed from their location after its host had been destroyed. They kept their wits about them though, for it could always find a new host. Eowen felt the presence of it at times, playing at the edge of her subconscious, too weak to invade her as it currently was. The settlement was well fortified, having developed a barrier to the Storm that was even stronger than The Nagirr'Om's, though it did require a rotation of dreamers to keep it active. It was small by most standards, but the people there lived well. There were none among them that could not manifest most things effectively, so they taught each other their discoveries and were excited to meet newcomers who could show them new things.

The acolytes were popular as they described their master and the powers she'd bestowed upon them. They were inundated with offers to replace their fallen companion. The boy with the hammer had accepted the need to become a trio, but hid away while the woman tested people's ability to carry the weapon.

The elderly couple decided to settle there without so much as a goodbye to the rest of the caravan members. They hadn't been in the caravan long, and hadn't bargained on the kind of turmoil they'd had to deal with.

Trung settled into a small shelter she manifested with the body of her sister, waiting for a caravan that would take her back east while Eowen waited for one to take her west. This did not take long. Ships inspired by Hani's Stormwake were becoming more common, and one was already docked at the settlement when they'd arrived. It was going south, and so Eowen and Trung had to wait till another arrived. It was a day and a half before one did. During that time Eowen spent it manifesting effects onto Setili's body that would preserve it for the journey home, make it lighter to carry, keep its smell from leaking. Eowen offered to help Trung in any other way she could. Trung did not need anything else though. She had simply steeled herself for her next steps.

When a ship going west arrived, neither Trung nor the rest of their former caravan saw Eowen off, except for the acolyte boy with the hammer. He nervously gripped his weapon and stood before her amidst the crowd that cheered as the ship prepared to leave.

"Thank you for seeing me off," Eowen said. The boy nodded, looking at his feet.

"Do you think that... I'm doing the right thing, serving The Nagirr'Om."

Eowen was taken aback. She'd never heard of an acolyte doubting their master. "I don't know. Do you not think you are?"

"I never thought about it at all till Pon died. My partner said he didn't die in vain because it happened serving The Nagirr'Om's work, and because we're still here to carry on the work." He held out his hands in an expression of helplessness. "What is The Nagirr'Om's work though? I know it is to hunt the Storm, and that is good for everyone, but why does she want that? Is she doing it for the good of the world, or is there something else? She celebrates when the Storm is killed but, Eowen... I don't think she cares when people die." Eowen knew The Nagirr'Om didn't care, or at least that the silver woman hadn't back at Nolano.

"I can't say what your master's reasons are and I don't know if anyone's even asked her. Who knows if it—she—would even give an answer." Eowen shrugged.

"Exactly."

"But that doesn't really matter does it?" Eowen said, and the boy looked up, confused. "You want to protect people, with or without serving The Nagirr'Om, don't you?" He paused for a few seconds, but nodded. "And Pon wanted to protect people from the Storm, right?"

"He did, Pon was the best of us."

"And that lets you do it." Eowen pointed at the hammer. "Is that good enough?"

"I suppose, for now. Safe travels, Eowen Mortician."

Eowen gave him a small bow and climbed aboard the ship. Her heron glided up, landed beside her, and the crew cheered at it. They'd been drinking and celebrating just about everything for almost an hour. A few minutes later, they had cast off into the starfield on winds manifested from dreams amidst songs and chants. There were quite a few passengers with them, and some were on deck making merry, but a few like Eowen were hiding below in the dark. She curled up with her heron, put up barriers that would make her imperceivable and would block most of her own senses as well. She was properly alone again.

As I should be.

She meditated on what it meant that she had found her purpose, that at times she could speak with such confidence about things yet still feel the same insecurities she always had. Eowen had thought that finding a purpose and some authority would free her from everything that had once weighed down her spirit. Yet, somehow, she now carried both the strength and certainty of her purpose and the scars of her past. They were not mutually exclusive, and Eowen did not know if this was reassuring or terribly disheartening. Eowen snorted.

Maybe it is both. Maybe life will only ever be more, rather than old exchanged for new. I'm not sure how I feel about that.

* * *

She dozed, dreamt, and meditated as they passed through

the starfield going west. They would soon reach settlements belonging to people who, in the old world, had lived on the coast of a great ocean. The ship made excellent time and covered dozens of kilometers each day. Eowen emerged only if she sensed her work was needed, but otherwise kept to herself. Her reputation had some presence this far west, but only in vague tellings of her deeds, her appearance largely unknown. Her heron, which had once been a dead giveaway, made her stand out less and less the further west she went. Far more eccentric accouterments were becoming more common in the territories of the coastal tribes. People dressed in fine fabrics, precious metals, and vibrant colors. Manifested animals were also becoming more common, with terrifying reptiles and large carnivores being the most prevalent. With the oppressive Storm presence gone for the time being, the far western valley tribes and the coastal folk were in full celebration, traveling and sharing their culture and developments as caravans flocked in to connect the previously quarantined peoples.

Tavo had not passed through any of the settlements she visited, but his name was rippling through them in every direction as news spread far and wide of some massive and wondrous landscape he'd manifested. After almost a month, the ship Eowen had found was set to arrive at the very place, along with dozens of other caravans. Eowen was restless the last few days before reaching the landscape. From what she'd heard, it had appeared only a month and a half ago. *Tavo might still be there!* Eowen thought when she encountered a story teller on a stage, advertising the wonders of the far west.

She sensed the outer borders of the lands a day before they reached it, and the enormity of it was staggering. They sailed in and, as the hours passed, a green line appeared in the distance through the dark and gloom, getting longer and longer. Eventually, they could see grass, hills, trees, flowers, and a great city of red marble rising up. The lush landscape before them extended so far north and south that the edges could not be seen from the ship. The port city rose up on stacked tiers, but at the very top where it should have become a point, the city continued spreading out wider and wider into a giant hourglass-shaped wonder of marble and light. Hanging poles upon which hovered soft yellow orbs that glowed like little suns lit the place, and the red of it glowed like an inviting fire. Gravity had been inverted on the upper part of the hour glass, and people walked upside down there. Eowen's ship and several others passed through a massive portal at the edge of the landscape, with statues on the left and right depicting figures of power and significance. She saw a man in Nemsto armor, The Nagirr'Om bearing its tools, a child with their eyes closed and a third eye open on their forehead, and others that Eowen knew not the meaning of.

One particular statue caught her eyes and held her attention. It was a young man who looked to be of Eowen's people, his smile joyous and open, his eyes sculpted to express wonder, and his hair long and braided in the Nemsto way. Though she had no proof yet, her heart told her it was undoubtedly Tavo. It looked a bit like how she remembered him, but also not. Eowen had thought about how he'd change over the years, had considered alterations to his height, hair, and general physique. Eowen couldn't put her finger on it, but something about the statue was far different than her imaginings had accounted for. As their ship found a dock and was moored, one of the crew saw her staring.

"I've heard of that Tavo boy, amazing he could do so much while so young." The sailor nudged Eowen's arm. "Not so impressive to you, eh? Being even younger."

"He doesn't look that young, he's got a beard." Eowen said, and then it occurred to her. The statue had a goatee, and a mustache. His jaw had widened, and there were small lines around the mouth and eyes. The depiction of Tavo wasn't elderly, but he'd been sixteen when he left the jungle and savannah tribes. Eowen considered that the statue might not be perfectly accurate, yet those details couldn't have been a mistake. Her cousin was a man now, almost twenty years old. New thrills and worries sifted through her heart as she finally pulled herself away from the statue.

I believe he's become a good man, but I don't know what kind of man he's become. What if... he doesn't consider me family anymore? What if he doesn't even remember me? What if he's been away too long?

Eowen glanced back at the statue, at the artist's rendering of Tavo's eyes, wide and full of that awe which yearned to see the world beyond what it was seeing now. Eowen put her hand to her chest and settled herself.

If some random artist captured him like that, then he's still the Tavo I knew, in some ways.

Eowen departed the ship, and immediately asked the first person of authority she found if they'd met Tavo or knew where he might be. This person turned out to be the captain of another ship that had just arrived and Eowen slunk away, blushing furiously as the lady laughed at her and explained that she too had just arrived. So Eowen went further into the city, which was packed with constant activity. People were manifesting, performing, talking, arguing, playing games, and rushing to the new arrivals. There were mostly coastal folk, but the city had been pulling in a massive diversity of people for months. Eowen encountered waves upon waves of sounds and scents she was familiar with from various cultures, but which were layered upon each other in ways she hadn't known possible. It was an intoxicating sensory overload, but also disorienting.

Eventually, she found someone standing on a podium in beautiful blue and purple robes patterned and embroidered with gold. The man on the podium was more richly dressed than those around him, and seemed to be talking about something important. Eowen got closer and heard him shouting about honoring the true lord of their land, and though few were listening closely, he did seem to be confident.

"Excuse me," Eowen knocked on the stone stage he was on. "Can you give me some directions?"

"See! Even the young and freshly arrived intuitively understand the glory of our lord Ahn! Yes, my young pilgrim, I shall guide you and all who seek his wisdom to the temple of Ahn!"

"Sir, I didn't want directions to some temple, I'm looking for Tavo." Eowen pointed to the statue. "That man." The man on the stage glared at her fiercely and stamped his foot, practically kicking her away.

"I've no time for heretics declaring false lords as their masters! Tavo the supposed creator, the girl following death, the cruel Nagirr'Om, and the wandering crew of false hero gods; these are not true lords, they demand your souls for their workings! They steal your children to fuel their magics! Do not be swayed by them!" Eowen backed away from the platform and quietly made her way into the crowd. A few sympathetic eyes caught hers, but there were some listening with rapt attention and glaring at those that weren't.

Eowen wove through the crowds, her heron stalking behind her. It was becoming oppressive for her, the sights, sounds, smells an overpowering constant, and though she was trying to blend her dreaming aura through the mass of spirits, most in the city were not on similar wavelengths. Eowen found that in trying to keep herself innocuously merged between the dreaming auras around her, the clashes and bursts of the place jerked her extended senses around. There were other people on stages advertising their own followings, encouraging people towards other well-known dreamers, old world religions, new world ones, or the abandonment of them all. One woman was even advertising for Eowen, but not in any way Eowen found flattering. She rushed past, seeking out a mostly unoccupied spot. When she did, she swung onto her heron and let it carry her far out of the city.

Once at a distance, Eowen felt she could breathe. She cast her senses over the entire city and understood it better. While inside it, the place had felt as though it were in constant conflict with itself, but this was not exactly right. The city was more like a boiling stew, all full of disparate ingredients that were jumping around in the heat and motion. Eowen found that from far away, she loved the feel of the city, as it gave off waves of creativity and passion. She was, however, quite content to never go in again.

She flew up into the atmosphere above Tavo's land and extended her senses even further, trying to find people she could speak to in a less disruptive environment. The land had not just been manifested with landscape and air, but also a sky with a bright sun shining in it. The sun never moved though, and it was gradually transitioning from blinding white to a soft yellow as night descended. Eowen identified several smaller settlements scattered far and wide. There were also cities of comparable size to the hourglass one, though they were far away. In all her searching, she could not find the edges of Tavo's landscape. It was truly the most massive single manifestation she had ever encountered in the new world, and it teemed with layers of effects which she could not identify. Eowen's heart beat out an eager staccato, and she pointed past her heron's head to the closest settlement.

"We'll start there, come on!" The heron shot forward, carrying her towards abodes many kilometers outside the city. They passed over hills and flew by woodlands, alighting upon a collection of homes next to a marsh. Eowen's heron landed to an excited greeting as little children swarmed around her bird. A woman with white hair, light skin and freckles scolded the little ones.

"Ah! Down! Get back with you tiny monsters." She pushed the children aside with a shepherd's crook until they'd dispersed enough to give Eowen some breathing room. "Now, what are you doing here, girl?" The woman chewed on some kind of grass and tapped her foot impatiently.

"I don't mean to bother you, I'm just looking for Tavo. The man who made—"

"I know what that Tavo fellow did around here." The matter-of-fact way the woman spoke about the very ground she stood on put Eowen off a bit. "I don't know where he's gone off to. Last I heard he was a few towns over, south and west of here, staying at Luu's place."

"Thank you! Who is Luu?"

"I don't know much about the woman herself, keeps quiet. Her kids are always up to something. Someone's always stirring things up one way or another." The woman gave Eowen an accusatory look. "You gonna stir things up around here?" Some children still watching giggled and the woman hissed at them.

"I, uh, don't intend to." The woman sniffed and turned her nose up in a way that said she doubted it.

"That way." She pointed with her crook. "There's some hills, but your bird'll take you over that, now won't it. They're settled in a cliff."

"On a cliff?" Eowen asked, but the woman only narrowed her eyes, as if the most Eowen could have done to insult her was have the audacity to question her.

"In the cliff! Innit! understood?

"Thank you." Eowen patted her heron and it floated up into the air on a gust it summoned.

"Don't come back here!" the woman called as Eowen sailed off.

She found the hills the woman had spoken of, but they stretched on in many directions for many kilometers. Eowen flew over them, looking for a cliff, and had to fly southwest for half an hour before some of the hills inclined sharply. They never became mountains, but one hill did rise up high and steep only to be cut off on the other side into a sheer cliff face. Eowen spotted a charming cabin situated on top of the cliff and landed there. *Why did that woman say 'in the cliff'?*

Eowen approached the house and knocked on the door. She heard voices inside, and after a moment a young man opened it. The young man was of the coastal folk, short haired and stern. He hardly looked at Eowen, instead locking onto the heron.

"Um, hello," Eowen said to get his attention.

"Who is it!" The voice of an old woman shrieked from behind the man.

"It's a big bird, ma!" The young man finally looked down. "A girl's with it."

"Well what do they want?"

"What do you want?"

"I'm uh, looking for Luu?"

"Wrong place!" The young man slammed the door in her face too suddenly for Eowen to flinch back from it. She heard them arguing inside and she backed up, glad that it had been the wrong place.

"Then what's the right place..." Eowen jogged over to the edge of the cliff and peeked over with her heron. From her vantage she could just make out a roof jutting from the rocks at the bottom. "In the cliff, innit. Alright then." Eowen mounted her heron but it did not take off. She waited for it to move, but it only swayed from foot to foot and readjusted its wings. "Why aren't you going?" Eowen pulled on some feathers. The heron snaked its neck around and gave her a look. "I don't know, maybe everyone here is crazy and rude! We're still going." The heron made a head shake that seemed to mean: 'Whatever you say, you're the boss.' Then it leapt off the cliff and glided down to the entrance at the bottom.

There was, indeed, a cabin built into the cliff, and in front of it a large garden overflowing with plants Eowen did not know. There were two windows with frosted glass from which gentle orange light glowed through. The sun above was a lazy red and seemed as if it would go dark any moment. Eowen wasn't afraid of the dark, the whole world was surrounded by a pervasive empty darkness, but something about the encroaching night felt different in Tavo's land. It felt as if when night descended, something would wake up.

Eowen approached the door, through which the sounds of many voices filtered. She knocked and the voices stopped short. A pair of feet rushed to the door, swung it open and a hand yanked Eowen inside.

"What are you doing out this close to dark, you fool!" A tall woman with a mane of brown hair and dressed for working outside immediately sat Eowen down on a stool next to the door. "Honestly, you children are all reckless. Except for Rennick, you could stand to get out and about more, kid."

"No thank you!" a young boy, presumably Rennick, answered.

"Who are you!" a little girl shouted at Eowen from across a table. Eowen managed to gather herself to take in her surroundings. She assumed the woman that had pulled her in was Luu, but she'd been wrong once already and didn't want to assume. The dwelling was paneled with clean planks of wood, the room Eowen was in stretching back about ten meters. There were toys, tools, clothes, furniture, and decorations everywhere. Most of the possessions seemed to belong to or have been made by, or for, children of various ages, and the home had plenty of them. There were five people in the cabin other than the woman that had pulled Eowen in; a young man on the verge of adulthood, a girl around fifteen or sixteen, and four others ranging from preteen down to a child no older than ten.

Eowen was trying to take everything in as the children threw questions at their mother and the oldest boy attempted to mediate, smiling apologetically at Eowen. Her heron had followed her in and was standing beside her stock still, as though it too wanted to avoid being the center of attention. As the family was getting worked up, continuing their previous arguments and conversations, demanding to know when they'd have dinner and asking about their guest, the door opened with a creak again. Eowen paid it little mind since there was so much else going on as, through it, a tiny girl no older than six walked in. The girl walked right up to Eowen and put her arms on Eowen's lap, making her jump.

"Hello," the girl said, smiling up at Eowen.

"Uh, hello," Eowen said back, noticing the door was still open.

"Are you a friend of my mommy?" the girl asked as something moved in the dark beyond the door.

"Is that your mommy?" Eowen pointed at the woman who'd pulled her in.

"Mmm hmm."

The movement in the dark outside the door became more solid. A long, black, segmented, exoskeletal leg with a wickedly sharp point slowly reached through the open door and pinned itself into the wall above the little girl's head. Eowen gasped, pulled the girl behind her and pushed a barrier into the open door. The thing didn't seem to care about her barrier as more and more legs, some five times longer than Eowen's body, chitined through.

"Get back!" Eowen shouted, and the dwelling went silent. More and more legs, long, short, thin thick, but all black with many segments, pointed and spider-like, pulled into the room through her barrier. Eowen prepared to launch more power against it, but stopped short when no one else in the dwelling panicked. The girl Eowen had pushed behind her got out of her grasp and walked right up to the emerging source of the legs, pouting.

"That's Legs-Friend, stupid!"

The source of all the legs seemed to have no central form, but a black, vaguely spherical, and ever-shifting source of the legs did eventually pull itself in. Eowen looked closer at the limbs that emerged from Legs-Friend. They uncurled from around the center of their source, gained as much length, girth, and segments as it seemingly needed to reach whatever it would reach for, then pulled itself forward. Legs that had finished moving curled themselves back in, disappearing into the center of the thing. It climbed the little girl, lowered itself onto her shoulder, and folded up until it was small enough to fit in the palm of Eowen's hand. Only a few tiny legs remained to anchor it to the girl's cloak. Eowen looked around at the people in the cabin, who were watching with everything from sympathy to amusement to exasperation. Finally, Eowen could think of nothing else to do but turn to the woman of the dwelling and say:

"Please tell me you're Luu."

"That's me, what do you want?" Luu didn't sound offended or suspicious, just direct. It wasn't a friendly greeting like Eowen would have liked, but she'd take it.

"I've been looking for my cousin, Tavo, and I was told that you were the last one to see him."

"Your cousin is Tavo?" a boy shouted from the table.

"Yes, I haven't seen him for years before the fall, but I've been looking for him since." Before her family could explode into more questions and conversation, Luu grasped a walking stick from next to the door and banged it hard on the ground.

"Alright, alright! We're sitting down, having dinner, and doing nothing else till that's done! Have I made myself clear?" The children muttered their yeses, and the little girl with Legs-Friend on her shoulder took a seat next to the oldest boy, who gestured for Eowen to join them at the table. Eowen shook her head though.

"I'm not going to stay, I really just need to get going so I can find him."

Luu eyed Eowen and her heron. "Can you go through the mist-lands?"

"Do you mean where the Storm is?" Eowen asked.

"Hmm, that the stuff that changes people, brings on foul weather and such?"

"Yes."

"We call it the strange-mist around here."

"Well, I can't travel through it safely. I've been moving with caravans that can resist it."

"He's already left through the mist-lands some two weeks back. You won't catch up without a caravan, then."

Eowen sighed, made a gesture of respect to the people before her, and made to leave. "Then I'll need to find one. Forgive my intrusion, I'll be on my way."

"Can't go out after dark in these lands. This your first day here?" Luu said, placing her hand on the door.

"Well... yes. First couple hours, really."

"There's things out in the dark here, part of the landscape I suspect. They're strange, dangerous things."

Eowen glared, feeling impatient and annoyed. This was the closest she'd ever come. She stopped blending and let her power be felt, saturated with potential such that it weighed upon the house, making the residents stagger and the timbers creak.

"I'll be fine." Eowen took a step forward, but was blocked by her heron as it dove in front of her. Legs-Friend had unfolded faster than her eye could catch and had pierced her heron, three in the chest and one in the neck. The little girl sat glaring, entirely unaffected by Eowen's display of power.

"Legs-Friend doesn't like when you're mean to mommy." The girl's voice was unnaturally dark and low. Eowen released her power, and the legs released her heron. She checked its side, but the wounds were already closing, no blood, no flesh, just darkness and stars inside it.

"Alright enough!" Luu shouted. "You damn children are making trouble every minute of my life! Nathalie, keep Legs-Friend in check! You!" She pointed at Eowen. "Sit down and eat dinner!" Eowen immediately shuffled over to the table and took a seat. Nathalie pouted and the other children sat giggling at the two in trouble. "We're having a lovely dinner right now. We'll talk about you and your cousin later." Luu marched over to a cookfire. "Rennick, bowls."

The oldest boy leaned over and spoke to Eowen in a conspiratorial tone. "She's not usually so harsh, you just came on a bad day," he whispered. Eowen was going to ask what made it so bad when Luu sat down, held out her hands and closed her eyes. Everyone at the table clasped hands with the person next to them and closed their eyes as well. Nathalie held one of Legs-Friend's appendages and nudged Eowen to take one for herself. Eowen did, shivering as she grasped the black insectoid segment as lightly as she could. Luu took her other hand.

"Miles?" Luu said, and her eldest son started speaking, his voice deep and his accent lilting musically. The meaning of his words translated through to her, but in his own language the words danced as poetry.

"With humility, we accept the food before us, for it is food for the body and the spirit. With love, we accept the transformations that bridge life and death, for that is how such changes come to be. With grace, we gather as family to the table, for to share in this meal is to share in our spirits. With ju—I'm not done, Eria!" Miles shouted at one of his sisters, a pre-teen, who had ladled a spoonful into her mouth.

"You were going to do all twelve lines?" Eria complained.

"Yes, we have a guest that we've already made a terrible impression on, which you've just made worse!"

"Miles, darling." Luu picked up her spoon as well. "You're not doing all twelve lines unless we get to eat while you're talking." Miles scoffed, but picked up his spoon with the rest of the family. They continued their chatter and arguing, but it was more civil and loving now. Luu grinned at Eowen and gestured to the stew. "Simple stuff, but I made it all myself. Minimal creation powers involved."

Eowen smelled it, earthy and bitter. She tasted it and there was no bitterness at all, but delicious animal fats and something thick that coated her tongue and made it tingle. It was bland compared to much of what she'd eaten in the new world, not a manifested masterpiece of culinary perfection achievable only in the new world by the power of dreams. Just a simple meal made well for a large family. Eowen found tears in her eyes as she took another spoonful, and more welled up. The flavors were unfamiliar, the setting new, the company strangers, but not since before the fall had she shared a family meal made by hand like this. She wiped away the tears as tension in her shoulders she'd been carrying for weeks loosened. Eowen wolfed down her food, sniffed as her nose dripped and sat back. Luu scooped up her bowl and refilled it before Eowen could say anything.

"That's better, isn't it?" Luu asked, and Eowen could only nod and eat more. Eowen had hardly eaten in months, hadn't needed to as she fulfilled her bodily needs by her power alone. She hadn't thought she would need food again, but it was her spirit rather than her body craving it, and she fed it well.

After they'd eaten, three of the children were already asleep at the table. Miles and Luu carried them to their beds. The other two quietly played a game with stones on a grid together. Eowen had been given a seat by the cookfire where, soon enough, Luu and Miles joined her.

"Thank you," Eowen whispered. "For the meal, and for accepting me into your home."

"It's the way," Luu said simply, and sipped something that smelled like honey, herbs and alcohol. She passed it to Miles, who took a sip, and then passed the drink back to his mother, who gave it to Eowen.

"Isn't she too young to drink that?" he said. Eowen hadn't bothered about her appearance much in her life, but at his comment she held out her arms and ran her eyes down her shoulders, chest, hips, and limbs. She knew she hadn't gotten any taller, and her body was still that of a thirteen year old girl, skinny with a few bits of baby fat holding on, but she hadn't realized how little change had happened in her physically since the fall.

"She's older than she looks, I reckon," Luu said, her eyes locked on Eowen's in a searching way. "How old are you, kid?"

Eowen played the past few years through in her mind: months and months of traveling, being stuck in settlements, performing her work, and avoiding danger. Seeking Tavo, meeting friends, losing them, and always finding herself alone again.

"It's been almost three years since the fall?" Eowen muttered.

"Two months short of three, by my count," Luu said.

"I'm... I must have turned sixteen about a month ago." Eowen stared into the fire as the volume of time sunk in. Luu handed her the drink, which she took, sipped, and almost immediately coughed back out.

"Heh, old enough but not experienced." Luu rubbed Eowen's back as she regained her breath. "So, you're that Tavo's cousin." Eowen cleared her throat and nodded. Miles brought her some water before she could manifest her own. "And you're looking for him."

"That's right. I've come... very far."

"Hmm. Why're you looking for him?" Miles asked this time.

"That's rude, kid." Luu flicked her son's ear.

"No, it's an understandable question," Eowen said.

"You're our guest, and as long as you're passing through your business is your own. If you were staying longer, then we'd have to talk. Point is, you're here for information that we might have. Who told you Tavo had stayed with us?"

"I don't actually know her name. She was a white haired woman next to a swamp near that big, upside down city."

"Not many folk knew he'd stayed with us. Not like it was some big secret, he just hung around here making things for a few days." Luu leaned forward, gazing into the fire, and Eowen could see the coals glowing in her eyes. "Then, one day, he got a wild look about him, a kinda distant one, and stood outside before the kids'd woken up. I was outside with him. That Tavo said he could do more, much more, and then he rose up in the air." Luu let out a deep breath, and Miles nodded, his eyes wide. "I tell you, I've never seen anything like it. Not from a person or the mist-lands or some self-named god or anything. As far as the eye could see, the starfield glowed bright and shot up. Then the dark got thick." Luu locked eyes with Eowen. "You know how the dark feels empty when we're not filling it with our dreams? How it seems like it might just go on and on, nothing hiding in it, nothing there at all?" Eowen didn't move, but Luu seemed to take the look in her eyes as an answer. "It stopped being like that. It was like one big ceiling coming to crash on down. And that Tavo, he was shining and flickering in it all. Then all that fuss came together and all this came out of it." Luu swept her hand at the door to indicate everything outside it. "There's strange things out there now. Flowers that remember what you say and say it back, pools of water that show you people in your memories, trees that when people touch them they... appear hours later." Luu took another sip of her drink. "He put a sky over us. They loved it in the cities, threw a party for him. Then he left the next day." Luu's tone hadn't been frightened or accusatory. She'd spoken very evenly.

"He wasn't controlled by the Storm though," Miles added. "The Storm hasn't been able to threaten these lands for some time because of our protector."

"No, no, he certainly wasn't, not that I could tell. I'm not sure what he was doing, though, or why. I can't say I'm worried. Strange isn't necessarily bad, it's just hard to understand sometimes. Well, as long as you're intent on searching for him, know that he left a bit ago and that you'll need a caravan before going west."

"Thank you," Eowen muttered, thinking. "I suppose I'll have to wait again. I've spent so much time waiting around, I wish I knew why he's been going west."

"We didn't spend a lot of quality time with him, but he did say he was trying to get back to his family. Apparently he'd left them to travel before the fall."

"I know about that," Eowen whispered. "He left us three years before the fall. He was from the jungle and savannah tribes, far to the south and east of here, below the Elder mountains... or whatever you call them in your language." Luu was giving Eowen a strange look. "Uh, you might not know my—the jungle and savannah people or where they're from so... uh, do you know of the Britchen?"

"That's not it, kid, I know where your tribe is from. Tavo was trying to get back to his family in the east, past the Nemsto lands in a place called, uh, what was it?..."

"They're the Niude," Miles supplied. "Don't know much about them, except that they live in a frozen desert on a plateau past the mountains over there."

"What?" Eowen whispered as her heart dropped like a stone.

Luu and Miles froze when they saw the expression on Eowen's face. Luu spoke gently as though to a scared animal.

"Kid, your cousin's got a family, a wife and a baby out there. He's trying to get back to them. Are you alright?"

"Mom," Miles chimed in, "Eowen said that Tavo left the jungle and savannah tribes three years before the fall. I'm not sure she knows much of anything about him."

"I do know!" Eowen shouted. The children playing their game on the other side of the house paused, and someone in a bedroom woke up and called for Eowen to be quiet. Eowen settled down, embarrassed. "I'm sorry I just... didn't know that about him."

Eowen's thoughts moved through all she'd heard of her cousin: the scattered reports from her search, the brief mention of him from a traveler even before the fall. A brave young man that had crossed an ocean and a continent several times over for adventure, but the question of exactly why

Tavo had been in the Britchen lands before the fall had never been answered. It had been so obvious to her that his wandering had simply brought him close to their tribe by chance, and that the fact he was still alive was the more important miracle. Yet, the question had always been: Why had Tavo not tried to reunite with them after the fall? He'd been so close, and arguably it would have been even easier for Tavo to reach his tribe without the elder mountains in the way, yet always his progress had been north and west.

"Or, I thought I knew him," Eowen whispered. "But then why did he leave his... wife and baby behind before the fall? He was in Port Disoke before the fall, that's far to the east."

"I can't say," Luu muttered. Miles seemed to have a theory he wanted to suggest, but his mother shook her head at him. "That's really all we knew about him. That he arrived from the east, and had a family he was trying to return to out west. He was powerful, for sure. He made all this, then he left." Luu put a hand on Eowen's shoulder and shook her gently. "I'm sorry we can't be of more help." Luu rose and stretched. "I'm going to sleep now, you two can stay up. But Miles."

"Yes, mom?"

"Let's let Eowen think things over herself for a bit. Yeah?" Miles gestured his compliance. Then Luu marched over to the kids that were still awake and scooped them up, one under each arm.

"Mom! We're in the middle of a game!" one protested while the other squirmed, but Luu's arms were strong.

"Tomorrow, kids. And I'll give you a chance to play me two verses one." The kids moaned a bit more about it, but relented and allowed their mother to deposit them through a door in the back of the home through which a hallway connected to several other rooms.

Miles and Eowen were alone, the only sound was the crackling of the fire. Miles was turning over the conversation in his mind, trying to find some comforting thing to say to the girl that wouldn't pry into her. Eowen was stuck in a spiral, reviewing everything she thought she knew about Tavo, his likes and dislikes, his tendencies and teachings, but her data was all from childhood, woefully outdated. The five, almost six year gulf that'd shaped the two cousins into who they were now had never felt wider to Eowen than it did in that moment. Rumors and stories were no help either as, until now, all she'd learned from them were the vaguest things. Tavo is a kind young man, charismatic, and knows his manners in several cultures. He's powerful, helpful, a little strange, but such descriptions were all Eowen had ever gotten. Finally, unable to carry her thoughts any further, Eowen stood.

"Thank you for your hospitality." She made a respectful gesture to Miles.

"You should probably stay the night," Miles replied. "Like mom said, the landscape is full of strange powers. It would be better if you had a guide, it's dangerous to wander around."

Eowen shrugged. She didn't feel like sleeping. She didn't feel like doing much of anything except dwelling in ever deepening spirals about her work, her quest, powers, friendships, and her banishment. Somehow, in that dark quiet night, it all seemed to tie back to Tavo, even the years she'd spent failing her mother before the fall. Yet all that time he'd been thousands of kilometers away, living his own life for the past five years, which Eowen hadn't had any impact on at all.

"Do you think he'll even want to see me?" Eowen

whispered to Miles. She was desperate for someone to respond with authority, and reassure her. Though she knew Miles was no such person, he was the only one around.

Miles blinked, looked into the fire, picked up a metal poker, and sifted the coals so that they glowed a little brighter. "That's not what you really want to know," he muttered, and Eowen glared.

"Are you making fun of me?" she said, and her power thickened around Miles, just a touch. He shivered, but otherwise kept himself composed.

"You're not searching to get one outcome or another, because either way you'll still have to figure out what to do with your life." He looked at her with a strange, distant expression before speaking again. A new power rose up and brushed the pressure of Eowen's away. **"You seek so that you can know, for without the pursuit of mysteries we forfeit our work's meaning."**

Eowen's mouth hung open and her eyes were wide. She readjusted her expression as the great presence Miles had summoned up faded to a jejune level. "You can speak with power," she whispered.

"Sometimes, when it feels right or when it feels true." Miles hid a shy smile. "I've been calling it the true voice. I try to use it sometimes when I'm alone."

"You're not alone right now."

"You're a stranger. I don't want to use it around my friends and family yet. Or maybe it just hasn't felt right to. I know it means something, but I'm not sure exactly what yet. Do you understand?"

"Yes. I can speak like that too, sometimes. I've known others that can. You said something about the mysteries."

"Yes, like why the fall happened, or where the compass

directions in all of our minds came from, or what the Storm really is." Miles shrugged. "Those are the big ones, anyway. Everyone has their own mysteries that their spirit needs answers to. It's just that, from what I've seen, people so often think they want a particular answer when what the heart needs is an answer, no matter what it turns out to be."

They lapsed into silence, staring into the fire and musing on their personal mysteries. The hours drifted by, and the girl and the young man grew drowsy in their chairs. Miles shrugged himself deeper into the soft folds of his clothes and Eowen stroked the head of the heron on her lap. When she drifted off, Eowen slept more soundly than she had in a long time, and she dreamt deeply, listening to the mysteries within her.

****

[Only a little longer.]

A SIMPLE REQUEST FOR ONE SUCH AS I. IT GAVE ME JOY TO GRANT IT, BUT GRANT IT I WOULD NOT WITHOUT AN EXCHANGE.

****

When Luu found them the next morning, they were still asleep in their chairs. She puttered around the room, quietly tidying up. The morning shrank much of Eowen's anxieties, though it did not banish them completely. When she cracked an eye open, the light filtering in the window seemed hopeful to her. Eowen smiled, feeling warm and loved and free, even amongst strangers she'd only just met. She snuggled into her robes and pulled the heron's head closer, pressing its warmth against her belly.

The mysteries will only be answered when I am done pursuing them. Until then, I might as well enjoy the journey.

Eowen dozed back into half-sleep, but soon enough one of Luu's daughters emerged from her room, marched over to Miles and poked him. He stirred a bit but didn't wake. "Let them sleep, Eria-Leck," Luu whispered.

"You never let us sleep in," The girl whined.

"Fine, you can wake Miles, but leave Eowen alone, she's a guest. We don't bother guests. Now scoot kid, you're shadowing Thurmin for the day."

"It's such a waste of time!" Eria-Leck's complaining was loud enough to wake Eowen and Miles up. As they stirred, Luu rolled her eyes at her daughter.

"Go get your siblings up, you're good at that." Eria-Leck grumbled, but did as she was told. Eowen could hear scuffling and muffled arguments from the other rooms. "Good dreams, kids?" Eowen noted the meaning of the word for 'kid' Luu used carried a very familiar, familial meaning. Eowen gestured respectfully.

"I slept well Luu, thank you. Your hospitality is much appreciated." She used as formal a tone as possible, trying to put some emotional distance between herself and the woman. *I'll be leaving soon anyway.*

"I've got breakfast. We'll have eggs from Thermin's coop. If they're edible." Luu's oldest daughter emerged from the back along with the rest of the family.

"They'll be fine, probably," Thermin said as she headed outside to gather them.

"It's alright, I won't be staying for breakfast," Eowen said. "I need to be on my way." She adjusted her robes and the heron stood up beside her.

"You sure you don't want to rest up here for a few days?" Luu had one hand on her hip while she tapped a wooden spoon on the table.

"No, I can't miss the next caravan heading west. I'm unable to travel through the Storm lands alone."

Luu chewed on a thought for a moment as she laid thick, fatty strips of some animal's flesh on a skillet over the fire and filled the pot next to it with a pale grain and water to boil. "There's three major cities around here that caravans go through. You'll be looking for the one on the western side. They call it Gonda after some old world ocean god that islanders out there used to worship. If there's a caravan going west it'll be going through there."

"Thank you for your advice." Eowen made a gesture of respect again and moved toward the door.

"Ah, but you don't know where Gonda is. You'll need a guide. Stick around, one of the kids will show you the way." Eowen knew she could find it on her own by flying around and asking for directions, like how she'd found Luu. Luu probably knew that as well, but a guide would still be more efficient, and the smell of her cooking was having a similar effect as the previous night. Eowen looked to Miles, who only motioned for her to sit at the table with them. Eowen gave up, and joined them as Thermin returned.

"You caught us a bit off guard last night, but let me actually introduce you to everyone," Miles said. "I'm the oldest—"

"And the ugliest!" the second youngest girl at the table chirped up, making the youngest child, Nathalie, giggle to hiccups.

"That's Rose, she's nine years old and the artist of the family, but not the smartest," Miles said. Rose had blocky, rough features, but an extremely expressive face that she used to great effect when mocking her siblings. "You already met Nathalie and Legs-Friend." Nathalie seemed to glow, a tiny spritely thing that looked exactly like her mother. Eowen smiled at the little girls. Rose responded by flipping her eyelids inside out while Nathalie whispered something to Legs-Friend on her shoulder. A spider-like limb unfolded itself from the tiny coiled form on her shoulder, extending across the table till it was in front of Eowen.

"Legs-Friend wants to shake hands," Nathalie said very seriously. Eowen took the limb and moved it up and down, then let go. It folded back into the center, and Miles continued introductions.

"That's Rennick, he's ten years old but he's already an accomplished historian of the old world." Rennick was a tiny strip of a boy, deep in thought as he consulted a scroll, but he lifted a hand when Miles called to him. "Thermin is sixteen. She manifests animals and creates new ones, either for domestication or companionship, or just because people want strange beasts around." Thermin shrugged as though it were no big deal. She looked the least like the rest of her family, with paler skin and lighter hair than the rest of them.

"People like strange things, not my business why," Thermin said.

"You had to think of all the weird stuff to make it, though!" Eria-Leck said, trying to heckle her sister.

"That's Eria-Leck, thirteen, and a pain in everyone's ass," Miles said, but Eria-Leck didn't seem to mind. She had a certain rapport with her brother, punching his shoulder while grinning.

"I see the world and I say what I see," Eria-Leck said. "Call me Eria." She offered her hand to Eowen, pulled her in close when she took it, and whispered conspiratorially. "Did you know that some of the creatures Thermin makes are used for sex?" Eowen glanced at Thermin wide-eyed as Eria chuckled.

"We're not having this kind of talk at the table." Luu slammed a place of food down between Eowen and Eria. "Now eat up. You've all got big days." They discussed with their mother what their plans were and she issued advice and commands, juggling several conversations at once. Her children finished their meals at their own paces and left for their activities till only Miles, Eria-Leck, and Luu were at the table. "So, Miles, you'll show Eowen to Gonda?"

"Of course."

"Can't I go with them?" Eria whined.

"No, you'll get them distracted and off track. Now either go shadow Thermin or go visit Delilah." At the mention of Delilah, Eria shot out the door, cussing.

"Oh, I didn't tell you about Delilah," Miles said. "She's the second oldest after me. She lives at the temple of Ahn, the great protector of our lands, serving as one of his acolytes."

"So Ahn is the reason you haven't been threatened by the Storm here," Eowen said.

"That's right, he's incredibly powerful and has been keeping us safe this whole time. He's widely worshiped around here."

"I still think they shouldn't treat him like that, he needs to live like a normal child," Luu said as she cleared the table.

"He's a child?" Eowen asked, and Luu stopped her work.

"That boy, Ahn, was no more than two years old when the fall happened, but he was already powerful enough to manifest air and all kinds of other things within hours. There's some secret to how he keeps the barrier around the land up, but his attendants keep him locked away from the public in that temple." Luu made an exasperated gesture. "Can't be any good for a child, being kept away like that. There's some trick to his power, I'm sure, but it's a secret."

"It's strange for sure, but as long as all this good is being done, what's the harm?" Miles asked.

"I don't trust it when you can't get a straight answer out of people." Luu gave Eowen an expectant look that made Eowen shift in her seat. "Well, you're off now, aren't you?"

Eowen stood and bowed to Luu deeply. "I supposed I am. Thank you, Luu, for your hospitality. It was some of the... warmest I've received in a long time." Luu waved her off, but that same, strange, expectant look was on her face, as if Luu had noticed something obvious that she was waiting for Eowen to bring up.

"Just come back if it doesn't work out," Luu said. Eowen looked at Miles, who shrugged and led her out the door. They started down a path west with Eowen's heron following behind.

"What did your mom mean by that?"

"Who knows? She sometimes gets ideas that she doesn't want to let go of, but sometimes she's got a certain sense about things." He breathed a laugh. "She calls it her mother's sense, and says that having more kids makes it stronger. There, see that huge tree there?" Miles pointed at a conifer rising up in the distance.

"Mmm hmm."

"Gonda's in that direction. It'll take a day's walk to get there." Miles started forward.

"You don't have to guide me all the way there, these

directions are enough," Eowen said. "I'm sure you have better things to do?"

Miles laughed. "To be honest, I genuinely don't. Till you showed up I was planning on wandering around and finding a nice hill to nap on. Trust me, this is a much better use of my time."

"In that case, no need to walk, since I wasn't planning on it anyway."

"What do you mean?" He was answered when Eowen climbed onto her heron, scooting forward and patting it's back for him to join. "No!" He put up his hands in protest, and Eowen grinned. "It can't hold us both," he insisted.

"You'd be surprised," Eowen said.

"I absolutely would be!"

"We'll get there in a few hours if we fly."

Miles eyed the heron, which matched his look evenly. "You're sure?"

"I've carried five people on here before." It was a lie, but the truth was her heron probably had no carry limit.

"Really?"

"Really."

"... Fine." Eowen helped Miles on and he reached around her, gripping the heron's neck tight enough to strangle a normal bird. "Just give me some warning!"

The heron took off as smooth and perfect as it always had till they were high enough to see the landscape laid out beneath them like a flat map. Miles was hyperventilating and Eowen was laughing.

"Be ready to give me more directions when we pass the tree!" Eowen said, and the heron shot forward. It was only a two and a half hour flight to reach the city of Gonda, but Miles spent the first twenty minutes rigid in fear. "You could have told me you were afraid of heights," Eowen said.

"I'm not! This isn't heights! This is something else!"

He relaxed after a half an hour, and then they enjoyed the flight. Miles pointed out villages and locations of interest, describing people he'd met and strange things he'd seen. People that told stories from the old world, that manifested potions which could give powers, who worked with Thurmin to create strange creatures, and a grove of black trees that sometimes bent into portals to other places. After two hours, the edge of the landscape could be seen, a snaking line where color and atmosphere stopped and the empty began. Miles pointed towards what Eowen saw as a spec of gray.

"There, that's the city."

"You said this landscape has only existed for a few weeks, how do you already know so much about it?" Eowen asked him.

"Well, I've probably seen more of it than anyone. I was already wandering between all the settlements in our area regularly, bringing aid from my mother. She isn't particularly powerful, but most of us kids are, and she's always helped us figure out what to do with our abilities. I'm not suggesting we were the only source of aid early on, nor the most significant. That title goes to Ahn. We just did what we could, and as the oldest I always escorted my siblings or delivered their creations. So I already knew the layout between the settlements before Tavo ever showed up. After he created all this, I spent every day either escorting my siblings like before or exploring."

Eowen thought about this, and began to wonder what Miles's power most lent itself to, for if he had developed the voice, it must have been tied to a specific designation. *Perhaps it's just mysteries and exploration, similar to Hani?*

"Miles, how do you—"

"We're here!"

The heron had just flown over a gray, stone plateau, which Eowen had taken for Gonda at a distance. She now saw that the city had been built into the side of the plateau facing away from their flight the whole time. Its dwellings seemed to have been grown out from the stone, which crescented around a massive harbor of starfield. Then the gray stone of the plateau's buildings cut off sharply into wooden dwellings that teetered and leaned against each other irregularly. The stone half of the city looked sculpted by the hands of a giant, masterful mason, while the wooden half looked arbitrarily thrown together by an army of toddlers. They skimmed down out of the air and landed in the great starfield bay that the crescent shape embraced. There were already many ships moored there, floating in the stars like how Hani's ship had. Other ships of different designs could be found, but not all of them operated like The Stormwake. Some floated on manifested waves of water, others were effectively beached on their side, and a few were more like houses on flat platforms with enormous wooden legs under them.

"This is excellent! I'll be sure to find a caravan going west."

They dismounted from the heron and stretched out their stiff limbs. "I'm surprised there aren't more," Miles said. "Before the mist lands became a greater threat around here, Gonda was famous as the primary port to stop through. Even in the old world, the city that used to be here was the main one used on the Green Seas." Miles pointed west, away from the city.

"This is more than I've ever seen in one place." Eowen gazed around her at the variety of vessels.

"Makes sense. There's plenty of people out east since there was a whole continent there. But west..." Miles paused and stared out west. "In the old world, the Nemsto people commanded the entire coast of the continent across the Green Seas, but aside from a few islands it was empty." There was an uncomfortable gravity to his voice, and Eowen did a nervous double take between him and the darkness to the west. Miles noticed and put on an unconvincing smile. "It's alright! Fewer people means less threat from the mist, right? It's just... a long way without people." The heron's head was leaning over Eowen's shoulder, and she absently stroked its beak. Miles's brow crinkled, deep in thought, so Eowen nudged him with her elbow.

"Come on now. How should we do this? Walk up to ships and ask around?"

"Uh, no, there's actually a system. Follow me."

Miles began to lead her to a building at the innermost part of the crescent curve. The entire city crawled with as much diversity as Eowen had ever seen, but in front of that building was a truly dense and eclectic collection. The people wore feathers, skins, barrels, robes, leaves, water, clouds, anything. Some were nude, some floated, some were covered in moving tattoos, and some had piercings everywhere. There were plenty of people dressed in ways that Eowen had seen among the cultures she'd passed through, but there were plenty who'd seen fit to explore the new world's possibilities for expression. Some had fire in their hair, some had an extra set of arms floating from their shoulders, and some had animal traits growing from them.

Upon entering the building, Eowen saw that it was little more than a single, massively long desk with a roof over it. Behind the desk was a single man receiving the attention of every person without any sign of being overwhelmed. He was a short, balding, portly man in his fifties, wrapped in a robe that was three sizes too big and served as more of a blanket than clothing. He had an unconcerned air about him, and seemed on the verge of falling asleep.

Miles brought Eowen away from the bulk of the crowd that surrounded the man to a far side of the building. The man at the center was seated on a well cushioned chair made of the same gray metal as the armor of the Nemsto warriors Eowen had met. More of that gray metal was in the desk itself, as one long bar embedded in the wood ran its entire length. Metal disks were attached to the bar at every arm's length or so, and Miles had an amused look on his face as he gestured for Eowen to touch one. She narrowed her eyes at him, but reached out and pressed a finger to it.

"Joining or hosting?" Eowen jumped back as a gruff, tired voice that matched the man at the desk perfectly lit up in her mind.

"Miles, he talked in my head!"

"Don't worry about it, just touch the iron again." Miles seemed extremely amused.

"But how did he do that?"

"I'll explain later, just answer his questions."

"But he asked... if I was joining or hosting?"

"A caravan."

"Oh." Eowen eyed the iron disk, then Miles, who leaned against the bar, whistling. Eowen carefully put her hand to it again and the voice popped back in.

"Joining or ho—you were here already." The man's eye flicked open and locked directly onto her from dozens of meters away. His mouth had not moved.

"Uh, yes, I was just surprised by the—I mean, your voice

in my head." Eowen experienced the equivalent of an exasperated sigh in her head, which sent gooseflesh down her spine.

"Are you trying to join a caravan or host one?" Eowen had not known a voice in her mind could be so impatient and sassy.

"Joining," Eowen said out loud.

"You don't need to speak out loud," Miles said, enjoying all the expressions on Eowen's face.

"You could have warned me about how this would work!"

"He really should have," said the voice in her head.

"See, even the desk man agrees!"

"Name's Harod."

"And his name is Harod!" Eowen shouted at Miles who was backing up with his hands up. There was laughter in his eyes and a gently mocking smile.

"Let's get back to your journey," Harod said in her mind. "Joining, in which direction?"

"Uh, the Nemsto and the lands beyond them. So... to the west?"

"Nemsto are west and northwest."

"Just west I think."

"Traveling preference?"

"Soonest possible?"

"Understood, take the token." The disk Eowen had been pressing her hand to rose out of the wood and separated from the rest of the iron bar. From what she could tell, it had been infused with some of the man's power, but was otherwise a plain metal disk. "When a caravan is heading the way you're wanting to go, the disk will let you know."

"Thank you..." Eowen turned it over in her hand.

"Fair warning, we don't get many going west. It's empty and dangerous out that way. The monsters born of the mist get out of hand easily. You've heard of that lady on the giant bat with the silver bamboo out east?" Eowen nodded. "We don't have anyone like her out here. We've gotten a fair number coming from the west, not many going." The man's tone had gotten gentler in her mind.

"Thank you."

"Don't lose it!" Eowen jumped back as he screamed in her head.

"T-thank you." Eowen backed up, then put the disk into her heron's feathers. "Well, that was strange."

"It works very well, and he's been doing that work by himself for a while now," Miles said.

"You were having quite a lot of fun at my expense." Eowen glared at him.

"It's amazing isn't it? The mind-speak," Miles said. Eowen tried to look unimpressed, but it was interesting.

"I've never met anyone that can do that."

"Apparently Ahn was the first to do it. Some have learned it from him, and they mostly stay in his temple, but some, like Harod, take their skills elsewhere."

Eowen looked back at the man behind the desk, who seemed entirely at ease. He was juggling dozens of conversations in his mind as the crowd around him cycled through people gaining and leaving with disks of their own.

"So, should we head back to mom's for now?" Miles was tentatively reaching out to touch the bone heron. It watched the young man, unblinking, but allowed him to stroke its neck.

"I'll drop you off there, but I think I'll wait around here for my caravan."

"Are you sure? Did he say when a caravan might be going west?" Miles asked, and Eowen shook her head. "People almost never go west. You might be waiting for days, or longer. When a signal is sent out, they usually give a few days for everyone with a token to assemble from across the land. You can fly from Mom's place in a few hours, there's no need to wait around here."

"I'd rather not take the risk if it's all the same," Eowen said, then she made a gesture of respect to Miles. "You and your family have been of great aid to me. Thank you, Miles." The young man returned the gesture, but he looked saddened.

"Mind if I ride in front this time?"

* * *

They arrived in a bit less time than it had taken to reach Harod. Miles had sat with his legs hanging over the heron's shoulders and Eowen had sat with her back to his. He pointed out more things in the landscape that Tavo had left behind, places in the distance rather than what they'd passed over, but many minutes were spent in silence, enjoying the sound of wind in their ears. They landed to a quiet house, save for Luu in the garden, harvesting and planting.

"Huh, wasn't expecting you back till tomorrow at the earliest," Luu said. "Strong thing, that bird."

"Apparently Eowen's carried five people on it before," Miles said.

"That so? Did you find a caravan?" Luu wiped some dirt from her hands and faced Eowen.

"Not yet, but I have a token. Thank you for your hospitality. I'll be returning to Gonda to wait for a caravan."

"Right then, off with you," Luu said. Miles gave his mother a look of confusion, but she ignored him. Eowen gave a quick bow of her head, then mounted her heron and took off. She waved to them and was soon out of sight.

"I thought you were going to offer for her to stay again," Miles said when Eowen was out of sight.

"Eh, I've already made the offer, she can take it or leave it. Now help me in the garden since you've got the time." Miles groaned, but rolled up his sleeves and knelt in the dirt.

Eowen returned to Gonda, settling on the lip of the plateau that overlooked the bay. She was eager, pulling the disk out of her heron every few minutes to see if it had signaled her. Eventually, her checking stretched out to every half hour or so. Then every few hours until it was dark. She paced and meditated and even played fetch with her heron to pass the time, but grew bored in the dark. Eowen did not need to sleep and she did not feel properly tired, but the day and night cycle of the place was affecting her. She curled up on the heron's back, clutching the token to her chest, and let her power slack so she could become tired, expecting the token to wake her up any moment. Eowen did not dream or listen to any voice in the dark of her mind. Her sleep was too light and troubled.

* * *

Eowen awoke the next day in a panic, thinking the medallion might have gone off in her sleep. She pushed her startled bird to the cliff-edge and rushed down to the desk on it, pressing her hand to the iron in it. "Harod! Did I miss my caravan in the night?"

"Did the medallion alert you?" he asked.

"I don't know, I was asleep."

"You'd know. Trust me. It's impossible not to notice if you're anywhere near it."

"What's the signal then, so I'll know?" Herod sighed and opened one eye. He looked annoyed, but somehow also sympathetic.

"Loud, buzzing vibrations, enough to make a whole house shake but only for a few seconds. Trust me, you'll know. It'll only shake for you though, won't bother anyone else." He winked at her and smiled with one good tooth. "Clever, don't you think?"

"Very clever," Eowen muttered. She returned to her camp on top of the plateau and tried every method to pass the time, but her meditation was unstable. She considered going out to perform funerals, as she could feel a few threads pulling her to people in the lands, but they were all farther away than Gonda, and she didn't want to be away from the port. She spent most of the time sleeping, but even that became boring. She flew around and around the area, dipping low and back up high. There was little to appreciate near Gonda, and the time dragged on. Finally, nearing the end of her third day she returned to the desk. She approached the far outer edge, away from the constant crowd.

"Hello, Herod?" she said in her mind after touching the iron.

"I told you before, girl, there's been no caravan going west yet, you'll know when there is."

"It's not that. I heard from someone that even when a signal goes out the caravan will wait a few days before leaving so everyone can assemble."

"That's right, save for a few exceptions. A caravan straight west is rare, though. I'd suspect one would wait a full week.

Not many people trying to go west either." Herod looked Eowen up and down from the middle of the bar. "There anywhere else you're trying to go?" Eowen shook her head.

"No, there's nowhere else for me to go." Harod sighed, stood up for the first time that Eowen and apparently anyone else had seen, and waddled over to her at the end of the bar. There was silence and muttering as the crowd watched the harbormaster and the girl with the heron.

"You got a place to stay?" he said out loud, and it felt strange that the voice she'd only heard in her mind was the same she was now hearing with her ears.

"I, uh, think so."

"Good, get settled in." He knocked on his bar. "And stop bothering me. I got my hands full here." Harod waddled back to his seat, closed his eyes and clapped for attention. "Hands back on the iron," he commanded, and the activity proceeded as before.

Eowen looked at her heron, feeling sunken and resigned. She climbed on and flew back to Luu's place. The heron took its time. They glided for hours till the night was deep and the land was still, save for strange stirrings in the dark. Eowen thickened her robes around her and snuggled into them, frustrated, tired, and feeling cheated.

"I'm so close. He was so close," she said to her heron, which tossed its head. "It's not fair!" The heron didn't respond. "I know, I'm acting like a child, but I just want things to go right for once. Not like they've been going wrong exactly, but I want this one thing to go right." The heron did move this time, it snaked its head around to fix an eye on her and seemed to say: 'You know that's not what you're upset about.' Eowen crossed her arms and frowned at the heron. "I know Tavo hasn't actually been running away from me. He doesn't even know I've been searching for him. It just... feels that way. Like he's choosing his new family over his old one." Eowen turned that thought over in her mind. "I supposed he made that choice a long time ago, but I didn't get to make that choice. I didn't ruin things with Tavo. Not like I did to get banished."

Or when I wasn't there to keep mom from dying.

Eowen couldn't let that thought out, but the knot twisted hard in her chest and a feverish heat flushed up her neck. "I don't know why I'm this impatient. I was never this impatient before." Eowen scanned the dark landscape around her, feeling with her dreaming aura as it gave off waves of power and implication. Tavo's presence suffused the place, yet it was still just an artifact of her cousin's passage. She yearned to meet the real man that her cousin had become and bond with his dreaming mind as she had done with many others. "Maybe it's just because I'm surrounded by all this and saw that statue of him when I arrived. I feel like I've been able to put together a real idea of Tavo in my head for the first time. It's like I can almost see who he is, and it's wonderful!" Eowen had begun smiling, but her face quickly fell again. "But I just don't know for sure." She snorted a laugh. "I guess Miles was right about seeking mysteries. We really just want some kind of answer."

The heron had been gliding steadily down for some time, and as Eowen finished that thought, it alighted in front of Luu's home. She ran her fingers through the bird's feathers for a long while before dismounting. She couldn't hear any activity from inside, but it was very late. She approached the door and, as quietly as she could while still trying to be heard, knocked. There was some shuffling inside, and

Nathalie opened the door, Legs-Friend unfolded around her with many limbs poised for a threat.

"Shhh." Nathalie held a finger to her lips, and Legs-Friend mimicked her with a limb three times Nathalie's height. "I'm not supposed to be out of bed." Eowen fixed her expression into a very serious one and put a finger to her lips too.

"Me neither," she whispered. "Can you wake up your mommy and tell her I'd like to see her?"

"No." Nathalie looked at Eowen like she was stupid. "I'm not supposed to be awake! You can come in though, brother Miles and Mommy said you might visit again."

"I don't think I should come in without your mother inviti—Oh!" Eowen was interrupted as several of Legs-Friend's limbs curled around her and pulled her inside. The little girl's strange companion deposited Eowen into a chair at the table, and Nathalie climbed into the chair next to her.

"Want a cookie?" Nathalie offered one to Eowen.

"Uh, why not?" Eowen took it and they munched together in silence.

"I like your bird," Nathalie said, very seriously.

"Thank you."

"What's her name?"

"I... haven't given her a name." Nathalie looked very disappointed with Eowen.

"I've got one."

"Is it Bird-Friend?"

Nathalie nodded and munched on another cookie through a big yawn.

"Let's think of something else, shall we?"

"Ok." Nathalie's eyes were drooping, and after a few seconds of swaying she teetered over. Legs-Friend smoothly caught the girl and laid her head on the table. Eowen sat back and observed the strange creature, looking for its center and finding only legs and more legs curled in on itself. Behind it, she spotted someone leaning in the doorway to the back rooms. It was Luu, watching them with some amusement. Eowen stood quietly to greet her host, but Luu waved for her to sit back down.

"I put an herb for sleeping in the cookies, otherwise she'd be up all night. Can't be awake to watch her every night." Luu sat next to her daughter and kissed her on the head. "Take her to bed, will you?" She directed the request to Legs-Friend, and the strange entity scooped the little girl up, spidering its way silently to the back rooms. It even closed the door after itself.

"Greetings, Luu."

"No formalities." Luu slouched in her chair and watched Eowen with dark eyes that seemed to take in more than they saw. "Make something warm for us to drink, will you? I don't feel like getting up. Those kids run me ragged."

"... Alright." Eowen manifested two mugs of a dark, sweet drink with the flavors of dried spices in it. She had no idea what the old world ingredients would have been, but the taste was replicated from the creations of others.

"Mmm. That's good. Be better with spirits in it."

"So, Luu. I'd like to accept your offer of hospitality until a caravan going west is ready."

"Good."

They sat in silence, sipping and watching the fire. Luu didn't initiate any conversation after that, and Eowen didn't feel inclined to speak either. The woman's company was relaxing, and the time passed in a comforting haze. Eventually, the first light of day glowed in through the frosted windows, and Luu got up.

"Come with me." She led Eowen out of the house to a spot of soft, spongy grass nearby. Luu laid down on her back and gestured for Eowen to follow suit. They looked up at the sky, a false one, but at that moment it felt as real as any Eowen had seen in the old world. The sun never set in the horizon but hung in the middle of it, transitioning from the black it had been in the night to a deep, sleepy red. The sky was going from dark navy to powder blue. "Sometimes, in the old world, I'd see a sunrise or sunset that made me think it meant something," Luu said. "Danger, or love, or the future. Things like that. It's all just feelings and thoughts in my head, but it feels real sometimes. This sky though, it was made by that cousin of yours, you understand? A real person who had his own thoughts and feelings when he made it." Luu nudged Eowen. "I like to think we might be able to feel what those feelings were by looking at it. What do you feel looking at this sky, kid?"

Eowen stared at it, the sun gradually becoming too bright to look directly at and the firmament around it becoming a more and more perfect blue. "Hope," Eowen whispered.

"You seem like the type," Luu said, and Eowen turned to her with a look that said: 'What does that mean?' "See, it makes me feel annoyed every day. Why doesn't it set like in the old world? It just hangs there. Seems to me that Tavo lad thought he knew better how things should be and made it that way. But see, that's the thing." Luu chuckled at Eowen's defensive expression. "A person made that sky, and he definitely felt his way about it, but here we are feeling our own two ways about it. Just goes to show, it's all in our heads, isn't it?" Luu got to her feet, pulled Eowen up, and made her way back to her house. "Come on, every day's a big day. Time to get it started.

* * *

With Luu's family, the weeks flew by, and, as promised, every day was full. She held a philosophy that her children should be as active as possible, pursuing fulfilling work and discovering their talents and passions. Eowen joined them for much of this, as she had little else to occupy her time. She'd accompany Miles as he escorted his youngest siblings to their activities or help them with projects. Every meal was the time to discuss and debate plans and accomplishments, and Eowen had been easily integrated into their habits.

It was after a month and a half that Eowen finally met Delilah. The day started like usual, with Eowen seated beside some of the younger children. She'd be going with Miles to take them to their activities.

"What do you think?" Rose said, showing Eowen her most recent design, a collection of flowers with bones for stems and skull shapes in the petals. "It's based on the mythological flowers of the Haiden underworld."

"It's totally inaccurate, Rose," Rennick muttered. "The Haiden, or the people of the mossy forests, don't have flowers like that in their religion."

"It doesn't need to be the same!" Rose reached across Eowen to smack her brother, who glared at her and looked at his mom for help.

"Just because you're right doesn't mean you need to be rude about it, Ren," Luu said to her son without even looking at them to address the conflict.

"Ha! See!" Rose shouted.

"Mom!"

"Don't argue with your brother when you've got better

things to do." This was Luu's favorite advice for her children. It seemed they always had something better to do. "Go wash up, Miles is ready to go. You're meeting Mr. Jit today."

Rose got up with a huff and stuck her tongue out at her brother, who was staring angrily at a scroll. "I do have better things to do!" Rose said as she marched off imperiously.

"You do. Go, be safe and have a nice day, I love you," Luu called out.

"I liked the design," Eowen said to Rose before she left the room.

"Thank you!" Rose called back. Rennick was muttering to himself about his mother's favoritism, so Luu came around to give him a hug from behind, which he stubbornly ignored in favor of his documents.

"Hey. Listen kid," she said to Rennick. "You know better what's accurate than all of us put together." She nodded to Eowen. "Am I right?"

"Absolutely," Eowen said. "I've been all over, and you know more about the old world than anyone I've met." Eowen's words put a smile on the little boy's face.

"I know," he said without a trace of self importance. "So Rose should know when she's wrong because otherwise she's spreading false information and there's these wonderful, more accurate designs I can show—"

"Kid, kid, kid," Luu interrupted. "Here's the secret to being a know-it-all; you don't correct anyone. You wait for them to be so wrong they have no choice but to beg you for help, and if you're polite about it, they'll come back again. Trust me, I've been a know-it-all your entire life, haven't I?" Rennick nodded, considered what his mom was saying until a curious look came over his face.

"But I didn't ask you for this advice just now. Aren't you

breaking your own rule?" Eowen shook her head and grinned.

"Doesn't work like that for a mom. Now eat and get out of here, no kids in the house when they got better things to do." She pushed Rennick's plate in front of him and took the scroll out of his hands. The boy dug in, but turned to Eowen.

"Can I ask you some questions, Eowen?" he said between bites.

"Not while you're eating," Luu said. "Eowen, you're with Miles today?"

"Yes, I don't have a funeral to do." Luu's family, with their eclectic talents and skills, had accepted Eowen's work immediately. Luu largely treated Eowen like one of her own kids, keeping track of her activities the way she did theirs. Eowen did not need it, as she'd long since gotten used to organizing her work, but it felt good to be looked after.

Rennick finished his meal, and Rose emerged from the back with Miles. The children followed them out of the house as their mother cleaned up. They made their way across the landscape as Rennick interviewed Eowen about her tribe's culture and customs. He ate up everything she said and recorded it for posterity. It was staggering how much he'd been able to learn about other cultures from the confines of their people's land, but he desperately wanted to travel the new world. Luu had said she'd let him do so once he was seventeen. Eowen had procured one of Ordwell's translation orbs that had made its way into a city's market to give to Rennick. She'd traded a manifested heron with feathers colored red and blue and the disposition of a pet. Rennick loved it, but he already had a staggering talent for languages and insisted upon learning them all anyway. He said that to truly understand people you had to know their language, even with such a wonder as the translation sphere. Thus, he used it as a learning tool rather than a crutch, and even as they walked to Mr. Jit with Rose, Rennick spoke with Eowen in a broken version of her language, asking about the religion of the jungle and savannah people.

"Your gods do not make?"

"No, they can't actually do anything. They live within events, like a wave crashing, or a baby being born. Or did live, or maybe never did. I don't really believe in them anymore."

"They are in when thing happen?" he asked.

"Something like that. They were all connected to each other. The more similar the event that happened, like the wind being similar to a storm, the more in communication they could be. They didn't actually control anything, but they had knowledge. Our leaders learn to listen to them for advice about the future or the past or other things."

"Next, I ask... uh." Rennick switched to his own language. "How did your religious leaders perform the rites of listening to your various deities?" He looked annoyed that he'd had to switch languages, but being slightly annoyed was the default state for Rennick.

"Oh, I don't really know. I never had the talent for it."

"Ok, ok." Rennick scribbled some notes down. Rose was getting attention from Miles as he complimented her art, and she didn't bother Rennick.

They arrived peacefully at the next settlement where Mr. Jit lived. Mr. Jit was waiting outside, an old man with a mustache and no beard, already covered by many tattoos. They dropped Rose off and she got to work right away, discussing the designs with her client and using her dreaming power to make it bloom onto Mr. Jit's skin. It was subtle, painless, and impressively accurate.

Rennick made some last notes and closed the scroll. "I'll see you later." Then he ran off to some new interview. Eowen sidled up next to Miles and looked over Rose's work, impressed by the girl's craft.

"What's next today?" Eowen whispered to Miles, and he shrugged.

"Nothing till Eria-Leck is finished visiting Delilah."

"Why does your mother always send Eria to her? They get along the worst, don't they?"

"Eria hasn't found a purpose yet, or really anything she is good at or wants to do. So she's the errand girl."

"Like how you're the errand boy?" Eowen gestured to Rose.

"That's different. I offered to show the kids around. Besides, no one knows the landscape as well as I. So it seems my vocation is to be a guide, and it's satisfying work."

Eowen could feel this was not entirely true, as there was a restlessness in Miles that he suppressed. His senses and aura of power were well balanced and cultivated, as most who learn the voice of power are. His abilities to manifest were the greatest among his family, but he used them in very small, understated ways. Still, whenever he relaxed his self control, his being seemed to crave the east. Eowen suspected his realm of power was in what he'd spoken of her first night there, the mysteries. Personal, or of the world, or if that was merely a part of it, she did not know, and Miles did not pursue. She had attempted to bring it up with him, but he shrugged off her theories and questions, insisting that there were mysteries aplenty in the landscape Tavo had wrought. He was not entirely wrong about that.

"Come on." Miles started down the path out of town.

"Mom's going to pick up Rose and Rennick. Let's try to find that toad in the south swamp."

In their free time, which was plentiful, Eowen and Miles had taken to scouring the landscape for its secrets and intrigues. They mounted the heron, back to back, and took off into the deep south. There were fewer settlements there, as the land was interspersed by sharp, craggy mountains and fetid swamps. Few could fly, so few explored the swampy and mountainous places, and there were many rumors about them. It was said that strange entities could be seen wandering through them, that unnatural lights and sounds would emanate. Miles found these descriptions funny, since everything in the new world counted as unnatural and otherworldly. But it was intriguing to find a place that within a few weeks had become strange and mysterious enough to warrant such rumors.

Ahn's temple was situated at the border between the gently rolling hills where Luu lived and those harsher places, and the two of them marveled at it as they flew past. Among all the architecture Eowen has encountered in the new world, Ahn's temple was among the most interesting. From a distance, it might seem to be a plain, gray obelisk, rising above the surroundings and ending with a floral abstraction at the top. On approach, the structure took on more detail, revealing colors, shapes, and patterns of immense intricacy. The building would seem to go from gray to blue to red to purple to green, transitioning so smoothly as to make one think it had always been that way. The patterns that emerged upon closer inspection were sculpted and purposeful, the product of a tamed mind and power. You'd find yourself seeing images from deep within your own psyche in the shifting stone, skimmed off the surface of the mind and projected before you. It was simultaneously a hypnotically inviting place and an utterly alien construct. It was clear to Eowen that its creator had some powerful insights into the mind, yet also saw themselves as an other. The building had powerful barriers such that Eowen could not remotely sense what was inside. It also acted as the conduit for Ahn's defenses against the Storm, extending a great bubble of resistance against the corrupting effects for hundreds of thousands of kilometers around. Just the building alone was a wonder of the highest degree, and Eowen could not decide if she very much wanted to meet the being at the center of it or avoid his attention entirely.

"Amazing how Eria-Leck goes in there every few days and is never impressed," Miles said. "Maybe that's her real ability; nothing can impress her! Someone could recreate the old world, revive all the dead, and she'd just say it was about time!"

"You know, I've actually met people who are entirely immune to the powers and creations of others. They're even immune to the Storm. For all we know, being impossible to impress might actually be a power!" Eowen said.

They flew over one of the few settlements that had decided to stay in the swampland and landed down in the fog around it. The heron looked at home here, but Eowen cast barriers to keep their clothes dry. They set to scouring the vast swamp, which ranged out for dozens of kilometers, only interrupted by wicked crags jutting out of the mud. They'd explored it before, noting which plants and surfaces to avoid, as they'd make you think they were set on fire, or force extra limbs to sprout, or cause a giant mouth to float behind you drooling rainbow spit. They covered plenty of ground, but spoke very little; the fog seemed to insulate the place and give life to the slightest sounds. The swamp was an easy place for the imagination to run wild and the mind to play tricks on itself.

After many hours, they found nothing more unusual than they already had, and it was time to pick up Eria-Leck. Miles called through the gloom and, as Eowen approached, pointed over her shoulder.

"You got a friend," he said, and Eowen looked behind her to see a meter-wide pair of pink lips, agape and spilling out beautiful rainbows.

"Oh, I hate those! I thought I was being so careful." Eowen focused her power on the disembodied mouth, jerked at its existence and, like snapping a twig, forced it out of being. They mounted the heron and flew to the temple of Ahn, where Eria-Leck was already waiting outside on the steps.

"Hi," Eria said, though the greeting sounded more like an expression of disgust.

"Didn't have a good time with Delilah?" Miles asked.

"How do you stand her? She's so..." Eria flapped her hands around her head. "Above it all! She thinks she's so much better than everyone! Do you know what she said to me today?"

"No—"

"She was sitting cross-legged like some meditating mountain folk, barely listening while I told her what we've all been up to, like a good sibling. I don't know why mom wants me to keep updating her on our lives, it's not like she cares." Eria paced on the steps. "Finally, after I've been trying to make conversation for hours, she says: 'Why, sister, are you here?'" Eria used a mock lofty tone, and Miles laughed.

"That's her! But you know her duties serving Ahn are important."

"I know that! She can't help but tell everyone all the time. I try to tell her mom sent me, but she just says: 'Mother sent you, didn't she?' I try to tell her how good of an artist Rose is becoming, how Rennick is probably the smartest kid alive, how Eowen is this amazing and powerful guest but she just says: 'All trivial compared to our lord, the great Ahn.' Ohhh I hate her, I hate her!"

"Don't say you hate her," Miles tried, but he still laughed when Eria shook her head violently.

"Nope, nope, hate her! I don't care if she's my sister. Delilah's a pompous piece of shit and I am never going to visit her in her holy temple again. I tried relating to her at all, tried talking about her favorite foods and games and stories. You know what she said to me next? 'I have no time for such childish things anymore...'" Eria-Leck rolled her shoulders, crossed her eyes, and waved her arms around wildly. "'I mUsT bE vIgIlEnT fOr ThE WhOlE oF hIs WiLl Is BeNt To ReSiStInG tHe StOrM!' Gods!" Miles was giggling, and Eowen was trying not to laugh too much. Eria sat on the ground, grumbling. "Just because I don't have a... thing that I do like the rest of you doesn't mean I should have to put up with her. Why don't you have to visit her?" Eria looked at Miles, and he shrugged.

"Who knows, maybe because I'm an adult? Mom did go completely hands off when I turned seventeen. Same with Thermin."

"Ugh, four more years! I can't wait to be an adult!"

They mounted up, the heron somehow always having enough room for them. Before they could leave, Eowen looked up to see a young woman standing in the doorway of the temple wearing similar robes to Herod, the man at the docks. The young woman in the doorway gestured for them to stay.

"What's she doing here now?" Eria muttered. The young woman, save for some fewer curves and wrinkles, looked identical to Luu. She stepped out of the doorway, and a presence touched upon Eowen's mind as soon as she was past the barrier of the temple. It felt like when Eowen had touched the metal and Harod spoke in her thoughts, but heavier and gentler.

"You're the one my sister spoke of, the... 'powerful' dreamer that deals in the dead." Delilah's mind speak emerged in Eowen's thoughts. Delilah's tone was somehow both kind and imperious. It was clear by the feel of her mind that the young woman truly believed her own importance was great enough that to share her presence was a gift.

"I am Eowen Mortician," Eowen spoke back in her mind, and she let her epithet carry some of her power and authority with it.

Delilah's eyes went wide. Something about the interaction was not going as she'd expected. Eowen could feel the Delilah's mind reach further into hers, prodding around. It was not entirely unpleasant, but it was strange and unwelcome. Eowen instinctively hardened, making her thoughts sharp and unfriendly. In response, Delilah took a full step back behind the barrier of the temple, and her mind disappeared. She was breathing heavily, looking somewhere between frightened and offended.

"You can ask me what you like, but don't go digging around in my mind," Eowen said out loud. Miles glanced between them, trying to puzzle out what had transpired, but Eria-Leck burst out laughing.

"You tried to invade Eowen's mind? Wow, that's rude! I should tell your boss you were jumping uninvited into people's heads!" Delilah glared daggers at her sister, but Eria enjoyed the ire. Delilah retreated back inside after giving Eowen one more curious look.

"That was weird," Eowen said.

"That was amazing! Can you come with me next time?" Eria asked.

"Uh..."

"We'll ask mom," Miles supplied, and they took off on the heron for Luu's home. When they landed, everyone was already inside preparing dinner. Eria-Leck ran in, excited to complain about her sister and brag about Eowen's stand off with her. Miles and Eowen stayed outside for a moment, listening to the commotion and activity. "She'll figure things out," Miles said, the fondness in his voice obvious.

"Eria's so different from me," Eowen whispered. *Even though she doesn't know what she wants to do with herself, she doesn't hate herself for it.*

"What was that?" Miles asked.

"Nothing. Come on." She kicked at his ankle and made for the door. Miles followed and they joined the rest of the family for the arguments, stories, games, and affectionate mocking that made their home what it was.

****

[Listen a little longer.]

I ASKED LOVE WHAT THEY COULD OFFER ME IN RETURN FOR SUCH COMMITMENT TO THEM.

****

A few weeks later, Eowen was meeting with a remote group of coastal folk to the south. Their funeral practices required different ceremonies at different times of the year, and though they'd been able to perform the rites for their people who had died in the fall, they could not decide what to do with those that had died after. They debated over their main options, none of which seemed quite right. It was between trying to precisely calculate what time of year it would have been in the old world, or choosing the rite that seemed most appropriate for the deceased based on when they were born. The least popular option was exclusively performing the rite that had been appropriate when the world had ended, as they'd done for those that had died in the fall. Eowen had met with them very early on when pursuing her work in Tavo's land, but that first meeting had only led to more meetings as they debated endlessly. Finally, after weeks, they had decided to make Eowen choose for them.

Normally, Eowen had something of a sense for what would be the appropriate funeral practice, or could intuit what the true desires in the hearts of the mourners were. Here, she had no sense for it. They had put the responsibility in her hands entirely because they were tired of fighting with each other, not because they felt she was the right one to make the decision. Eowen knew for certain that as soon as she declared how, they'd just argue with her. She faced the elders and scholars of the tribe, gritting her teeth and trying to think up some solution that would actually serve the community.

I want to help them. I just wish it wasn't such a pain to figure out how.

Eowen sighed, and opened her hands to the elders seated

in a semi-circle around her. They were in a temple of bronze trimmings and clay tiles with vibrant colors. The metal was polished and shone bright, while the clay mosaics depicted what old world they'd deemed most relevant to depict. Most of them were stories with explicit morals about great calamity from the gods as punishment for the wrongdoing of a few. This was a tribe that believed in collective punishment, and Eowen was glad they were few in number and kept to themselves. She opened her mouth and everyone tensed.

"Are there any more suggestions?" she asked, and the group looked around. No one raised their hand or spoke, so Eowen grumbled and stood up. The collected authorities of the tribe stood with her, expectant. She dusted herself off and addressed them. "I'll take what you've presented to me into consideration and return to you with an... answer in one week's time." There was the beginning of arguments, but Eowen held up her hand for silence. **"I serve not you, but your deceased and the mourners that loved them. You will not question me."**

Her voice of power rendered them silent, but not satisfied. Eowen left them, maintaining her composure until her heron had taken her far out of sight.

"Shit. I could have demanded a month to figure things out. What were they going to do? Say no?"

The heron carried her back to Luu's place, where it was still quiet, as most of the family was away from the house. Eowen felt a vaguely familiar presence inside, which was not entirely unusual. Luu was somewhat reclusive, but had friends in other settlements that visited on occasion. Eowen reached for the door, and the presence touched upon her mind, making it immediately clear who it was. She shooed the mental presence away and entered the home. Luu was sitting at the table with her daughter, Delilah, sipping something hot. Delilah had not touched her cup.

"Greetings, Eowen Mortician," Delilah said. Eowen had not known someone could sound so stiff and inauthentic. She had seen statues more expressive than the young woman.

"Welcome back, kid," Luu said. "How'd the meeting go?"

Delilah frowned at her mother. "I have more important things to discuss with her, mother," Delilah insisted. Eowen pointedly ignored this and sat next to Luu.

"They've gotten even more bothersome. Now they're expecting me to figure everything out for them, not that it's what their mourners really want. It's all... political. Whoever's ideas I support will use that as a power play."

"Eowen, I am here to discuss matters of great importance!" Color was finally getting into Delilah's voice. Eowen gave Luu a look that asked permission. Luu sipped her drink and glanced between them as if to say: 'Go ahead.' "Eowen Mortician, I am here as an emissary of—"

Eowen cut Delilah's voice off, and she flapped her mouth open and closed for a second before realizing what had happened. Delilah reached out with her mind but Eowen blocked that as well.

"You're in your mother's home. You should show her respect," Eowen said very slowly and quietly. "Luu, thank you for asking about my day. Is there anything you'd like to speak with me about before your daughter and I discuss why she is here?" Delilah was fuming, and Luu was quietly enjoying the spectacle.

"No, you kids talk. I'll be out in the garden." Eowen released the barrier, and Delilah tried to reestablish her poise. Luu stood and kissed her daughter on the head. "It's good to see you, Delilah. Try to visit more often, at least to say hi. Let your siblings know you still love them." Then she left. Delilah softened considerably, blushing and looking down until her mother had closed the door.

"I do love them," Delilah muttered. "I have an important purpose, though." She looked at Eowen and squared her shoulders. "I'm sorry for my rudeness, Eowen Mortician. I was sent here at Ahn's request. Our lord wishes to meet you."

Eowen manifested a drink to sip and internally screamed. *Why do all these annoying, pompous people want to bother me right now?* "Do you know why your lord wants to meet with me?"

"He is our lord. And he did not say... to me." Eowen noted Delilah's discomfort.

"He didn't order you to come find me himself?"

"He... speaks to us through the high priest."

"I see." Eowen was curious, but she didn't want to admit that to Deleilah, so she did her best to mimic the young woman's statue-like demeanor. "When did your lord request my presence?"

Delilah glared. "It is not a request, it is a summons! Already, more time has passed than should and OUR lord is not to be kept waiting!"

Eowen was already annoyed by the coastal tribe from earlier, and she'd developed a poor opinion of this 'lord Ahn' since her first hours in his lands. Delilah's attitude was enough to put her in a properly bad mood. Eowen stood and brought up her power all around her. She spent almost all of her time blending so as to avoid unwanted attention until such a time as she needed it. This rarely happened outside of her work, but Eowen decided this was an exception. She brought rivers of blinding starlight and pillars of iron shadow down upon the room. Her heron stood behind her and Eowen's silhouette flowed out and into it, a banner of her authority. Delilah knocked her chair down in her haste to back up, but Eowen's presence was all around her, hemming her in. Eowen wanted to speak with her voice of power and put Delilah in her place, but did not. She remembered that, when she had let go to make Ennik feel small, it had brought no satisfaction in the end, only an empty confirmation that, yes, she could bully those weaker if she wanted.

Besides, no reason to ruin Luu's house over this girl's attitude.

Eowen sighed, pushed her power down, and blended it back between the dreaming auras around her. "Fine, let's get this over with."

She marched outside, climbed on her heron, and took off for the temple. Delilah ran out after her and watched with disbelief as Eowen became a spec in the sky.

"She left without me!" Delilah complained to her mother.

"Shouldn't have been so rude," Luu said.

"She almost destroyed your house!"

"Didn't, though." Luu stood up and wiped some sweat from her brow. She put an arm around her daughter's shoulder. Delilah grimaced at the dirt her mother was getting on her robe. "I love you kid." She kissed Delilah's head again. "Quit being awful. It doesn't suit you."

Within a few minutes, Eowen landed in front of the temple and patted her heron. "It's just a meeting to see what he wants with me, then I'll leave."

She marched into the temple, and the world completely changed. It was like being suddenly submerged in water, but mentally. Waves and layers of thought flowed over her in increasingly disorienting ways. Voices and presences were in and all over the surface of her mind, flinching back and diving in. Eowen slammed the doors of her mind shut, blocking them all out. She was in a wide, empty entrance hall that very quickly filled with people as they rushed to see who the disrupting presence was.

"Hello. I'm Eowen. Ahn asked to see me."

There was a great deal of muttering until a young woman came through and addressed her. "Greetings, my name is Chukoska. I'll take you to Ahn as soon as you allow me into your mind to ensure you are who you claim to be."

"No."

"Excellent, now to lower your barriers you must—"

"You're not going in my mind," Eowen said, which puzzled Chukoska greatly.

"Uh... It is required—"

"Not for me."

The young woman glared and launched her mind at Eowen, a knife of thought that Eowen easily swept aside. Eowen might not have had their mental training, but all their abilities were tied to their power as dreamers, and in that way she outclassed them entirely.

"Hurry up, your lord is waiting."

"I, uh." Chukoska looked around at her fellows, but they were trying very hard to act as if they hadn't noticed anything going on. Chukoska wasn't nearly as stiff as Delilah, and after a moment's deliberation shrugged and gestured for Eowen to follow her. "Come then."

She led Eowen deep into the temple, up stairs and through corridors till they arrived at two massive stone doors on a floor with no other rooms or adornment. She pressed her hand to the door and concentrated.

"I'm calling for High Priest Greivej. No one sees Ahn except through him." Chukoska stepped back, and the door opened to allow an old man to pass through. He was tall, thin, heavily bearded, and had robes of deep blue and gold.

"Hmm. I was expecting Delilah to bring the girl." Chukoska shrugged. He looked between them, and Eowen immediately disliked the man. There was a surgical way in which he observed her, as if he was judging the best way to remove something from her body. His dreaming aura was more well developed than the rest in the tower, rivaling what Nolyi's had been like when Eowen last saw them. He did not seek out her mind like Chukoska did, but seeped into it insidiously, like a leak through the roof. Eowen almost didn't notice his mind within hers until he prodded upon her memories of Delilah. Eowen slammed him out and marched up to him.

"I told your underlings, no one goes in my mind! No! No protocol, no rules, I'm here to see this lord of yours and tell him to leave me alone! Now out of my way."

Eowen shouldered past the old man against his protests and forced herself into the room. There was a barrier around it, and on the other side of it was the great lord, Ahn. The boy was floating naked in the fetal position with his eyes closed above a floor with a flower petal design. He couldn't have been more than four years old. His dreaming aura was immense, extremely dense, and possibly much greater than Eowen's, yet it was utterly gentle and immaculately controlled. Eowen stepped away, reaching for the door to regain balance as the sheer volume of Ahn's presence shook her core.

"Hello, Eowen of the jungle and savannah tribes across what was once the mountains." The voice was in her mind and no barrier of power could have stopped it. This was Ahn's realm of power, a mental speaking that bridged the gap between people, as if speaking with one's thoughts were more natural than with one's mouth.

"You cannot barge in! You must—" Greivej stopped short as Ahn spoke in his mind as well.

"It's alright, grandpa. She's nice."

The old man looked between them, trying to assert some kind of authority, but came up with nothing. His lord and grandchild had spoken. He slunk out of the room, closing the door behind him. Eowen regained her composure as best as she could and met the child's dreaming aura with her own, two continents pressing against each other. Power cracked as their dreaming auras sought for cohesion.

"I like you," Ahn said in her mind.

"Why?" Eowen spoke aloud and in her thoughts.

"I can tell you're good. I saw you in Delilah's mind." Ahn opened his eyes and they locked onto Eowen. They were impossibly bright, radiating a heat she could feel, like the sun. **"You don't feel like the people that take care of me, you feel like..."** A rush passed between them as their dreaming auras began to merge, mingle, and play against each other. They reached beyond any connection Eowen had experienced other than with Ordwell, immersing themselves into each other's minds. Eowen saw in Ahn's memory how he'd developed his powers almost immediately upon entering the new world. He'd linked with thousands of minds at once, only to feel them suffer and die. He'd manifested a mass atmosphere but had endured terrible fear and confusion until his grandfather, borrowing and guiding Ahn's power, had established a room protecting him from the world outside. From then on, only the most serene and disciplined minds, well-trained to be his caretakers, had been allowed access. His grandfather had also borrowed Ahn's power to establish their means to resist the Storm, the very room Ahn was in. It siphoned off his mental powers to maintain it. Ahn had not tried to leave his room since, living comfortably in the calm and serenity of it while largely terrified of the outside world. No one had brought any significant discord to his room till Delilah. From Eowen's mind, Ahn gained access to the life she'd lived, and he bore witness to her memories, emotions, growths, regressions, a flood of experiences the likes of which he'd been shielded from. Ahn had no real idea what the world outside had become like, only that he was both protecting it and kept safe from it in his room. From what he'd sensed in Delilah's mind, Eowen had intrigued him as a person, not frightened by death like he was but working with purpose among it.

Eowen, with her lack of mental training, had no filter of serenity, and the two soon found themselves in a synaptic loop, their power and thoughts thickening, building upon each other with directionless potential. The world in the room churned, warped, and bent upon itself between them. Great silos of their subconscious selves were spilling out, and a part of Eowen opened up, allowing a presence through. The barriers in the boy's room that kept his mind shielded from the world screeched as they were put through enormous strains by the dreamers' combined powers. Yet at the same time the barriers fed by Ahn's latent psychic powers strengthened from the convergence of him and Eowen. Ahn was unaccustomed to having his power swayed by the chaos of the world. At first, he'd welcomed the novelty of Eowen's mind, but soon her fearful memories and tendency towards chaos put him into a panic. He screamed in Eowen's mind.

"I don't know what to do! This has never happened to me before!"

Eowen knew what to do, though. She steeled her mind, settled her spirit, and guided her dreams to calmer waters.

Eowen opened her mind to the boy, showing him how she'd gone through this before, how it had been terrifying, and how sometimes she'd even hurt people. Then, Eowen showed the little boy what came after the chaos, how every time she thought she'd almost lost herself, she'd ended up learning something important. In Eowen's memories, Ahn could see that Eowen had alway emerged from the discord wiser and stronger. Eowen had almost always had someone to help her until she'd learned to regulate the madness that her own dreaming induced in this world. She wrapped her power around Ahn like an embrace, and rode out the turmoil with him. When the little boy collapsed from the strain upon his mind and spirit, Eowen was there to catch him.

After a moment where he composed himself, Ahn looked up at her with his huge eyes, and the light had faded from them. **"It's happened to you, so many times. So much has happened to you, so many times."** His thoughts drifted through her mind.

"It hasn't been so bad," Eowen responded with her thoughts. "It's nice to meet you."

Ahn smiled, and Eowen cradled him, manifesting a blanket to wrap the little boy in. Many minutes passed. Eventually Greivej opened the door and, upon seeing Ahn asleep in Eowen's arms, rushed over to them.

"Unhand him now!" he bellowed, so Eowen put a barrier of silence around them and established a physical one to keep Greivej away. She found she could feel the man's mind even though he wasn't reaching out to hers. The meeting with Ahn had awakened in her the ability to reach for others' thoughts, so she directed herself into Greivej. It was a bit awkward and rough, and she tripped over his thoughts and memories as she sent her voice into his mind.

"Quiet. He's dreaming."

Eowen did not allow anyone near Ahn while she tended to him in his sleep. The attendants left them alone after they found Eowen's barriers impregnable, save for Ahn's grandfather and Delilah, who arrived some hours later. They waited outside the room, worried over the state of their lord. Eowen layered her dreaming aura upon Ahn's, fortifying his exposure to the world with the strength she'd earned in her time moving through it. She could not remove him from the room, since he was the main bulwark against the Storm, but she wanted to give him a taste of the world outside it.

Fortunately, it did not take Ahn long to recover, and he was back with her in a few hours. The little boy opened his eyes, shining as before with the blinding light, and lifted himself from her arms into the air. They shared their minds with each other, comfortably exchanging what thoughts, feelings, and memories they wished. Eowen was still imprecise at the mental exchange, but Ahn was the master of the mental realm and facilitated their interaction.

"**You were alone when the dying happened,**" he thought, and Eowen shared her memories of the days before the mountain folk found her in more detail. It was a strangely nostalgic thing to revisit. Horrible, frightening, and frustrating, but so long ago, the cutting edge of the memory dulled safely. She'd been a different girl then, but hadn't realized how different.

"That's right. Not for too long though." Eowen glanced at Greivej and Delilah, still behind her barriers, and let them down. "I should be going. I'll come back to visit though," she said out loud. Greivej looked like he wanted to complain and Delilah looked sick, but Ahn asserted that she'd be free to visit anytime she wanted in their minds.

Eowen left the temple with everyone's eyes on her, their minds curiously peeking into her own. She found herself accidentally slipping into theirs as well, but without their training it was a disorienting experience. Eowen bumped into a wall more than once, her perspective shifting between her own and a passerby. Once she was outside the temple, Eowen fell onto her heron and urged it to bring her to Luu's home. The bird carried her in gently, and no one was yet home. Eowen entered, exhausted in spirit but restless in body. She paced, picked things up, then put them down, cleaned, prepped for dinner in the ways she knew how. She passed several hours like this, riding on nervous energy.

When the presence of Luu and her children finally approached, Eowen found her mind pulled towards their minds when their dreaming auras touched. She slipped into the thoughts of Nathalie, which was a chaotic mess of six-year-old attentions. Rose's were overly serious, but committed to not seeming so. Rennick's were even more serious than Rose's and entirely committed to being so. Eria-Leck was a bundle of nerves and insecurities, while Thermin seemed to hardly have any thoughts at all that didn't concern her animals. Miles seemed to be awkwardly suppressing one desire after another. Did he want to run away forever, pursue a romance with a friend he loves, join up with the acolytes of The Nagirr'Om, stay with his family forever? Impossible to know, the young man wouldn't even give himself the space to examine his yearnings. Eowen couldn't seem to keep her mind to itself, and the noise was becoming terrible, but when she landed in Luu's thoughts, things became utterly quiet and organized. She breathed a great sigh of relief, and huddled up in Luu's mind as the family piled into the house.

They got back to their usual games and arguments,

teasing and sharing their days. They talked to Eowen but she waved them off, insisting that her day wasn't worth mentioning. Eowen stayed comfortably seated in Luu's mind, ignoring the myriad of personalities that clamored around her. Miles sat next to her and frowned.

"You look sick," he said.

Eowen focused her attention on him for a moment, but immediately flinched away. His mind was like a barbed creature of theories and wonderings that he was almost violently shunting from his consciousness. Eowen was amazed that he could function at all. She dove back into Luu's mind, and this time the woman noticed. Luu's thoughts were like a library. Things were easily found, though it might take some time, and there was a stern expectation for respect. Once Luu felt Eowen cowering within her mind, she physically and mentally approached the girl, waving Miles aside.

"Go break up Rose and Rennick, they're about to have a row."

"Alright then," Miles said, glancing between them. Luu locked eyes with Eowen and put her hands on the girl's head.

"Go ahead, come on in." Eowen let her mind flow fully into Luu's, where it was safe and predictable. She could still see out of her own eyes and move her own body, but it was as if she were perceiving and piloting the thing from another place. "I thought so," Luu said in her mind. "This was like when Delilah first joined up with that temple. She couldn't stand to be at home, said everyone else was too loud. That about right?" Eowen slumped in her seat and wiped sweat from her brow. The relief was immense. "Mmm. Delilah visits more often than the others think, but not when anyone else is around. You gonna be alright now, kid?"

"Yes, I think so," Eowen responded with her thoughts.

"Hmm. I'll make something that'll put everyone to sleep early tonight, how about that?"

Luu put together a meal of heavy, buttery breads and thick stew. She sprinkled herbs that would make her kids sleep, but withheld them from her and Eowen's dinner. By the end of the meal, the smaller children were asleep at the table, and the older ones were teetering. Luu herded the family into their rooms, and even the most chaotic of her children's minds were too far away in dreaming to touch on Eowen's waking consciousness. Eowen lay down on the bed she'd been given in a little guest room with few adornments. Luu entered as she was fighting to stay awake, the exhaustion having a similar effect as the herbs.

"Alright, kid. Tomorrow we're going back to that temple. I don't recommend you join, but they ought to teach you how to deal with this."

"Thank you, Luu," Eowen whispered.

"Nothing to it. I take care of all my kids, even though sometimes they don't think I am. That means you too." Eowen was fast asleep before she could argue that she wasn't one of Luu's children.

****

[Listen a little longer.]

CAN YOU EVEN GUESS WHAT LOVE PROMISED TO ONE SUCH AS I?

****

Luu woke Eowen up early the next day and sent her off to the temple again. "You go back there and demand they teach you how to deal with this! Also, what was that Ahn like after all? Delilah said it's forbidden to give an outsider knowledge or some nonsense."

"Turns out he's just a sweet kid... A very powerful kid, but sweet. I think he wants friends, but he's been stuck in there so long keeping the area safe that he doesn't think he can have them." Eowen grimaced. "Especially since the only people they let him meet are trained to worship him."

"Well, maybe you'll be good for him too." Luu patted Eowen's back. "Be back for dinner."

It was easy for Eowen to reach Ahn. The boy had given explicit orders for her to have free reign of the temple. Eowen marched right in, still jumping around the minds of others and gritting her teeth. The acolytes in the temple had trained their minds to have a certain serenity, but Eowen still found it disorienting. Ahn was floating as before, but when he saw her he lit up with a smile.

"You came back so soon!" he cooed in her mind.

"I did want to see you again, but I also had a favor to ask."

"Of course I'll teach you!" Ahn was practically vibrating with excitement. **"You have to teach me all about the world outside of here."**

Eowen paused. "I'm not sure I'm the best one to fulfill that request."

Ahn looked at her very seriously and said within her mind: **"But you're the only one who can."**

"Why do you say that?"

"Because no one else who has seen so much is allowed in here. I was lucky to get you to visit."

Eowen mulled this over, bothered by it, but gradually

understanding why the rules had been put in place. If untrained, powerful people developed mental powers like Eowen had after just one meeting with Ahn, there was no telling how it would affect them out in the wider world. Eowen had been so disoriented that, without Luu, she might have fled from people entirely, becoming a hermit.

"I understand... It's a bit of luck that we got to meet, isn't it? If Luu hadn't known Tavo and hadn't had a daughter as one of your acolytes, we'd have never met." Ahn nodded, seeing the organization of thoughts in Eowen's mind. "I believe this will be a good exchange. I'll share all I know of the world with you, and you'll train me."

They started by planning for future meetings, and Eowen shared her current schedule with Ahn. He shared his perception of when he met with his acolytes so that they could advance their mental powers by proximity to him and help provide a serene environment for him. It was all to ensure Ahn wasn't all alone in his tower, as his grandfather had noted that a lack of interaction with others caused Ahn to become despondent and his powers to waver. So began their regular visits, with Eowen going to Ahn almost every day and rapidly getting used to the power. Ahn's grandfather had coined a word for it in the coastal people's language: telepathy. Eowen largely didn't use it except to speak secretly in the minds of those she trusted. Otherwise, in her lessons she learned how to avoid slipping into the minds of others and getting overwhelmed by them. In exchange, she allowed Ahn to page through her memories, drinking in as much of the world as he could through it. Luu kept Eowen's activities a secret from the rest of the house, and Eowen was gone often enough performing funerals that no one asked. By the end of a week, Eowen had learned how to 'float' her mind between others. She could pick up little more than she could have already gleaned from body language or tone of voice, yet she could collect all that information at the distance of her dreaming aura from almost any number of people. She had also become skilled enough to keep her mind out of all but the most magnetic thoughts, and could, for the most part, carefully eavesdrop on thoughts without being detected, though she didn't like to do this.

She still made time to explore with Miles, but his mind was becoming increasingly uncomfortable to be around. The young man's dreaming aura yearned to explore the new world and tease out its mysteries, while his mind constantly repressed his own wants and needs. He justified it by insisting that his family still needed him at home. Eowen resolved to help him untangle these issues as soon as she felt she'd received enough of Ahn's training.

The time had come to return to the coastal tribe, as promised, and make a decision for their funeral rites. She'd hardly given it any thought in the interim and had all but forgotten her duties to them. Eowen despaired at having to deal with their pompous elders and scholars, but she was still Eowen Mortician. She would find an answer and fulfill her purpose.

She flew to them and summoned the council into the temple for her judgment. Rather than faces rapt with attention, she was met with a bobbing crowd debating with each other. None gave her the room to speak though a consistent argument was that: 'No, Eowen would never agree with your terrible idea!' They were as annoying as before, constantly vying for authority. Eowen decided to try one of her new tactics and zoned out during the discussion, letting her mind float between theirs.

In their minds, she discovered that very few actually wanted an absolute, definite decision one way or the other. What they wanted was to have someone with the authority to make a decision. Their months of bickering hadn't truly been over what to do, but had been testing whose authority was worth following, even if they disagreed with the choices that authority made. They had tried multiple times, in private, to vote Eowen into that role, but she was not suited for it. Her work necessitated that she eventually leave, and it had always been clear to Eowen that authority over others was not part of her work; her prerogative was in the ceremony itself and the people, dead or alive, that it served. She knew she could not truly fill the group's collective void, but she had not picked up on its full cultural subtext till now.

A few of the gathered council had gone silent, watching her. It seemed they would soon demand an answer, whether she was ready or not. Eowen sighed, kicked herself mentally for not abandoning them in the first place. Even amidst the shallow folk before her, vying for an endowment of authority, Eowen could feel the threads of the families outside the temple that yearned for a ceremony to say goodbye to their loved ones. She dipped ever so slightly into their minds, and found that among them all, the only answer they'd really accept would be if she stayed and made a different decision each time. Otherwise, if she told them to do one thing or another, they'd just fight about it after she left.

Then, a thought occurred to Eowen, and she couldn't help laughing at how absurd, yet possibly effective it would be. Her laugh silenced the group, and several glared at her incredulously, so she fixed her expression and turned her back on them.

I hope I can make this work.

Eowen raised her hands to the altar in their temple depicting a fish-headed deity particular to their people. She spoke with power and made her presence felt among all the people of their tribe. **"There is only one with the authority to decide the fate of your dead. It is—"** she risked dipping far enough into one of the scholar's minds to pull out a more secret name for their deity, **"—Nogad-Ru, the vizier of the deep. His domain, the seas of the old world, are no more, but his wisdom still lives in your hearts. Together, we will give him the life here to answer this need."**

Eowen's voice rang out to all the members of their small tribe, and was heard and understood by them all. She dipped into her dreaming, collecting the power to manifest a trait into the statue while she reached for the dreaming auras of the tribe, pulling from them just a bit so that they would feel and know that they had given to this creation. Then, like a rising wave upon the sea, shadow and light rushed in through the temple like waves, which broke against the statue and soaked into it. When it was done, Eowen turned back to the gathering around her and gestured for a young scholar, the one she'd felt the most sincerity from, to approach. She was short, portly, terribly shy, but knowledgeable enough that even elders called upon her to quote scripture. They referred to her by the nickname Scroll-rack. Eowen had never even heard them call her by name, and decided that continuing her theatrics by lifting it from the young woman's mind would be alright. When Eowen reached into her thoughts, she pulled out more than she'd expected.

"Daeffid. All of your family survived thanks to you. You were too far from Ahn to benefit from the atmosphere he

provided. Only your husband was lost. He did not die in the fall, but perished days after from starvation."

Daeffid nodded and wiped a tear away. "He was far out at sea. I was only able to retrieve his body because the Storm had not grown so oppressive yet."

"Stand before Nogad-Ru. He will answer to this need." The scholar did as she was bidden, and before she could even voice her question, the statue spoke in a voice that was deep and full of inviting currents. It felt like the voice of a god from the bottom of the sea. The god's voice was not precisely like Eowen's voice of power, but was close, and could only be understood by the listener. Daeffid jumped when it addressed her, and all those gathered listened close.

"He answered me! My husband is to be laid to rest by calculating what time of year he died."

Eowen gestured for another to approach, then another, and another. Many answers were the same, but many were not, as the statue had been imbued with the power to lift from their mind the rite they desired and present it to them as divine providence. After the demonstrations, Eowen made clear that the statue had only been imbued with the power to answer the question of proper burial. She explained that while Nogad-Ru, of course, had more powers, Eowen herself could not awaken anything else in the statue of it than what she already had. Then, she took her leave, letting the heron carry her away. She felt a momentary pang of guilt for tricking them instead of coming up with an actual answer.

They likely wouldn't have accepted another reasonable solution.

Eowen laid on her heron's back, gazing up at the clear blue sky that Tavo had left behind.

Sometimes 'good enough' is fine. These people don't need perfection, they just need... something.

* * *

After a full month of Ahn's training, Eowen was as fully proficient in telepathy as any of his followers. Despite this, she still kept her abilities almost entirely to herself. Entering the minds of others felt too intrusive unless the benefits were weighty enough. It was after that month that Luu's family learned of her secret training. Delilah, for once, came to visit of her own accord while the whole family was home, and mentioned it casually. The reactions were an explosion of questions and excitement, mostly from the younger kids, which Luu had to shield Eowen from. Delilah found it hilarious, and though she kept her cool on the outside, in her mind Eowen could see that she was enjoying the small revenge. Eowen had embarrassed her at the temple by barging in, so she took the attention with grace.

Eowen explained how it all happened and assured them that she was not, in fact, reading all their minds all the time. "Remember how we were playing that ball game the other day and Eria-Leck hit me in the back of the head with it? How could that have happened if I'd been watching your minds?"

Eventually, things settled, dinner was had, slower and sleepier activities progressed, and Delilah was still around. Eowen touched on her mind, and the question of Delilah's presence gently breezed into it.

"I missed them, and I did not realize how good their minds felt at times like this," Delilah said in her thoughts. Eowen had learned from Ahn that one could hide their thoughts if they desired, but that lies could not exist in the mind-speak. Belief in the truth or lies in one's words would be evident in the mind.

When the house grew quiet, Eowen and Miles went off to explore more obscure locations, some of which changed in the night. Strange things would emerge and stalk Tavo's lands with dangerous, unknown powers. Luu's family trusted that Eowen would be safe, and her children had permission to travel the night with her. They flew to a hilltop that was far into the center of the landscape, where the borders couldn't be seen. Miles had discovered that, when one stood atop it, they could somehow view places that should be impossible to see. Eowen could feel that Miles was troubled in his mind, but she didn't give it much attention as it was his usual state. They landed and wandered around the flat, stone top of the hill, gazing at distant places and hidden views. Atop the hill, one could even see into buildings and behind barriers if they knew how to look.

"This is so strange. I feel like it's an illusion, but I can see the statue of Tavo from here!" Eowen pointed for Miles to see, but he was standing some distance away, looking at his feet. "Miles? What's wrong? Didn't you want to show me this place?"

"I did..." He paced. "I'm sorry. I don't believe I'm in the mood anymore, can we leave?" Eowen wanted to ask more. Miles had never quite acted like this before, and there was something unnerving about his despondency. Eowen touched on his mind, but even with her training it was like touching a fire.

"Of course, we'll leave right away." They mounted the heron and were back at Luu's home shortly. The children were asleep when they returned, and Miles went inside without another word, leaving Eowen in the garden. After a moment, Luu walked out.

"Excuse me, Luu..."

"We can talk if you help me." Luu gestured to her garden. The woman's mind was an instant relief to Eowen. Eowen wasn't sure she'd ever met someone more certain and honest with themself. Eowen altered her clothes to better suit the task and knelt beside Luu.

"What's on your mind?"

"Miles was acting... different today."

"Since he learned about your meetings with Ahn." Luu clarified.

"Right."

"Nah, this has been a long time coming." Luu sat up and shook her head at the door. "That boy, he takes after his father."

Eowen froze. Luu had never talked about the father of her children, none of the family had. Eowen had never felt a particular thread pulling her to perform a funeral for them, and they never spoke of him. Whatever had happened, Eowen assumed it was better left alone unless someone brought it up.

"What was he like, the father of your children?" Eowen whispered, though there was no one around to hear them.

"Well, Miles's dad died before he was born. Man was named Bolo, impossible to pin down. Must've had a different lover every week, got into brawls, would go from temple to temple challenging philosophers. Imprisoned more than once, and that's how we met." Luu smiled at the memory. Eowen was having a great deal of trouble imagining Miles doing any of the things described. "I was imprisoned for vandalism, stuck in the cell next to him. We got to talking, and he was a terrifyingly attractive man. He knew a trick to removing the bars and got into my cell for the night. We probably conceived Miles that first time we met." Luu hadn't paused her planting but Eowen was stock still staring at her.

"You and Miles's father had sex in prison? Wait, if he died before Miles was born, then how did—"

"The rest of my children? Oh, the two oldest aren't related to the rest. The second oldest, Thermin, was conceived with a Carrulian man named... Honestly, I don't remember. Former slaver, actually. I was captured in one of their raids, but he and I got to talking while I was imprisoned in the ship's cell. He was a guard and fell madly in love with me. Helped me escape, and I suspect we conceived Thermin on the little boat we escaped on. Then we commandeered another slave ship, killed the crew, and sailed it back to the coast. Hmm. I never really loved the man, but he was fun enough for a few months. Nervous wreck though, was certain his commander would come and torture him, so he eventually drowned himself."

"... Oh..." Eowen was struggling to keep up with the deluge of family history that Luu was divulging. The woman had apparently lived a more exciting life before the fall than most did after.

"The rest of the kids were from my first actual husband, Marrone. Real sweet, boring man." Luu looked wistfully up at the sky. "Those were good years, Eowen. Very good. I still got into trouble here and there, but he was always at home with the kids, ready to bail me out. Miles and Thermin were never in doubt that he was their father, in truth if not by blood. Miles though, he was as wild as both his father, Bolo, and I from the start. Marrone might have been the one that loved him, but Bolo and I made him, and you could tell."

Eowen held up a hand to stop Luu. "Wait, we are talking about Miles." She gestured to the door. "That Miles, right?"

Luu smiled sadly and nodded. "Marrone died in the fall, but he'd been sick for years, probably sick all of Nathalie's life. I didn't lie to the kids, they knew he'd be going sooner than later. We tried to prepare them as best we could. Wasn't easy for a long time, but after the fall it was actually a relief in a way. Fresh start for us and all, makes sense?" Luu pointed to a stone some distance away. It was unmarked and had always been there, but as soon as she drew attention to it, the stone suddenly seemed weighty with implication "He rests right under there, and that's about where he'd stand and wait for me to come home, in the old world." Luu put her hand to her cheek, smearing some dirt there. "Miles might have been Bolo's and mine by blood, but he idolized Marrone, and there wasn't a gentler or more rooted man. It's no wonder the kid's all twisted up inside. That boy wants to fight and fuck and fall in love and explore and get on the wrong side of shit-headed people, it's all in his blood. Used to get into some trouble when he was little, but Miles learned to be a man from Marrone. Lotta love and patience from my husband, lotta guilt from Miles for causing him trouble. You see where I'm going with this?"

"I think so," Eowen muttered, and pulled up a root vegetable.

"Now that man's dead, and Miles thinks he needs to take his place in the family." Luu barked out a quick laugh. "As if I can't keep things going on my own. Honestly, the kid's more trouble staying around and being a burden on my mind, but what can you do?" Luu got back to her garden, and Eowen joined her. "Gotta let them figure things out on their own."

****

[Listen a little longer.]

LOVE SWORE TO CALL MY NAME WHEN I WISHED IT TO BE HEARD IN THE VOICE OF ANOTHER.

****

Eowen took to avoiding Miles, and he did the same to her. She wasn't confident that she could keep from bringing up what his mother had said, and Miles seemed to associate her with certain aspects of the discord in his heart. Months went by with little more than a polite greeting between them.

The last time they saw each other was after they'd both taken Rose and Rennick to a distant town, but otherwise had the rest of the day free. They decided to spend some time together, like when they'd first met. They flew all over the landscape looking for something interesting, but could not decide on any particular area to explore. They glided for hours, back to back. They'd chatted about Eowen's past travels, about what the world had once been like, and about what it might become. They spoke about the future, wondering if there would ever be a time without the Storm, or if new threats would continue to crop up. Eventually, in a long stretch of silence, Miles asked Eowen a question he was clearly afraid to hear the answer to:

"Eowen... how exactly do you feel about... me?"

"You? I'm thankful to you and your mother everyday for taking me in. The rest of your family, as well. I'm glad I've been able to become a... friend of your people." It was an automatic reaction of hers, to make sure she set herself aside from those she'd become close to, to make it clear that she didn't expect a familial attachment despite whatever closeness had grown between them. It felt off though, as if this weren't the right answer, or as if she weren't actually answering the question Miles had asked. As always, Miles' mind was no help for clarification.

"I see... That's good," Miles said, sounding like he felt it was anything but. Miles was silent the rest of the day, even with his other siblings. Eowen spent many nights alone, using her power to resist the need for sleep. She'd begun to feel a part of Luu's family, and now she was being reminded of how harsh it was to have such closeness fall apart for reasons she could not fully understand or control.

* * *

Eowen spent more of her free time with Ahn, but there was very little she had left to show him in her mind, and he'd taught her about all she was intent on learning. One thing Ahn had expressed on several occasions was a desire to leave the room. He knew he could not, as the barrier needed him, but an idea occurred to Eowen:

"Why don't you train others to maintain the barrier?"

"No one is powerful enough to. Even you could not, since it uses not the subconscious self, but the power of the waking mind."

"Why does it have to be one person?"

"What?"

"Couldn't more than one person be in the room, maintaining it together?"

Ahn had not considered this, and he soon began formulating plans to present to his grandfather.

"Greivej won't like it."

"Doesn't matter. You're the one in charge, not him."

Ahn wavered, unsure. His grandfather had been loosening how strict he was with his grandson, but he was still attached to the web he'd spun. The authority he'd gained, the safety he provided for many people, and the love he had for his grandchild were all tangled together for him.

"I'll talk to him about it, if you do something too." Ahn loved exchanges. **"I want to meet lots of other people!"**

"I don't know if I can make that happen. No outsiders in here, remember?"

"If I'm in charge, then anyone can enter the temple!"

"How about we start with Delilah's family? I'll bring them next time."

"I knew you'd say yes!"

"Read my mind?"

"Don't have to." Ahn smiled at her, and it was true. He'd hardly been in her mind except to speak for some time, and they could comfortably exchange thoughts as easily as breathing now.

The next day, Eowen brought Luu's whole family, minus Miles. High Priest Greivej was, unsurprisingly, irritated at the disruption to the temple, but Ahn had made it an official edict. Luu's family was to be allowed. They all loved the strange little boy, and he cultivated a comforting psychic environment for them in his room. Eria-Leck mocked Delilah for being such a stick in the mud when her lord was so delightful, but for once, Delilah wasn't bothered. The two had been getting closer since Ahn's doors had opened up. Ahn and Rennick were immediately the best of friends, as Ahn craved knowledge about the outside world while Rennick was a scholar of the old one. When Eowen left Ahn that day, Greivej was waiting for her at the entrance. The members of the temple no longer gawked at her as she'd become a regular visitor, so they were alone.

"Eowen Mortician, can we speak outside?" Eowen gestured for him to follow her out. "You've been causing a great change in my lord... and grandchild." His tone, while not aggressive, wasn't entirely friendly either.

"Don't you think it's a good change?" Eowen asked. Her heron put its head over her shoulder and she scratched it. Greivej squinted at the sky, then turned his gaze down, seeming to encompass all of the world.

"So many died in the fall, Eowen Mortician, yet so many of those people were not suited for this new world, were they? Perhaps they were meant to die, those that couldn't keep themselves alive with their own dreams." Eowen didn't know how to respond to this. She'd never known someone to so blatantly suggest that those who'd died in the fall somehow deserved it, and she flushed with anger till the next words left his mouth. "I don't think I was supposed to survive." The old man kept his eyes down. "But I was next to Ahn, and I did. I thought at first it meant I was chosen, meant for some great purpose through that boy." He leveled his gaze at Eowen, and she could not help being pulled to the mind of the old man as every part of him radiated a heavy, dark sadness. "I was just lucky though, wasn't I?"

The web of his mind was untangling, Eowen could see it happening right before her. He'd built the temple as a safe haven, but he'd also built a haven in his mind to protect from these thoughts.

"I was not meant for this world, but I'm here, and the one

purpose I thought I had is disappearing." He looked at her pleadingly now. "What am I supposed to do?"

Eowen felt that there was probably something wise that could be said to put him at ease and give him direction, but she didn't know what it was. For all the power and authority they both had gained in this new world, at that moment Greivej was little more than a lost old man seeking answers from a lost teenage girl.

"Why do you think I'd have an answer?" Eowen muttered. "Figure things out for yourself. You did before." Eowen climbed on her heron and flew off before she could see what the expression on Greivej's face was.

****

[Listen a little longer.]

LOVE OATHED TO SPEAK WITH ME WHEN I COULD FIND NO OTHERS TO SPEAK WITH.

****

Eowen had been with Luu and her family for over a year when the opportunity finally came to continue her journey to find Tavo. The disk she'd been given by Harod never signaled that a caravan was going west. The Storm had risen again in that area, and Tavo's land was surrounded by fog and thunder. Ahn had begun training people to carry his mantle as protector. Currently, twelve telepaths could maintain the barrier almost indefinitely, and they were organizing and training squads for that. Greivej had faded from his role, living in the background of his grandson's life. Luu's family carried on much as they always had, save for Miles and Eria-Leck. Miles was often gone, wandering the strange wilds of Tavo's land alone. Eria-Leck and Delilah had become closer than any of the siblings, and Eria-Leck seemed unconcerned with finding a purpose.

"As long as they're happy," Luu had said. "They're young, they don't need to be doing anything right now."

With Ahn now able to leave the temple, he often accompanied Eowen or Rennick as they went about their work. "**As soon as Rennick is able to, I'm going to join him and we'll travel the world together!**" Ahn had told her.

Eowen had developed a routine with Luu's family, and though it had changed slightly over time, she always had a place to return to. There were fewer people that needed funerals, and so her work slowed. Often in her last few months, she found herself sitting on her heron while it glided around aimlessly. The bird was, as always, in tune with her subconscious, and though she gave it no clear direction, it always seemed to take her to the western borders, its wing skimming the edge of the Storm. Eowen would stare out into the clouds, impenetrable to all her senses, yet somewhere out there was her cousin, miraculously able to move through it.

Or dead. She forced herself to entertain that thought, as she refused to be caught off guard by the possibility. Still, it did not seem likely to her, for Tavo had survived so much already.

It was on one such day of gliding along the border that Eowen felt a new thread emerge for one needing her work. The person was at the hourglass city Eowen had first arrived in. Her heron picked up on the sensation and changed course.

Eowen had mostly avoided it for being too loud and crowded, and this day was no exception. The port, as always, was filled with the ships and caravans of those brave enough to risk the Storm. The thread Eowen had sensed was at the docks, so she wheeled her way down to land among the new arrivals.

Eowen did not stand out overly much in such a city where all the cultures of the world seemed to be present. There were those that knew the signs of Eowen Mortician; a girl from south of the mountains in yellow garb accompanied by a great heron. Some few even knew about the mountain folk's brand on her chest, which glowed whenever Eowen exerted her authority. It was the strangest contrast to be elbowing her way past those that did not recognize her while waving off the genuflections of those that did.

Eowen approached the source of the pull to find a massive Nemsto man in full armor, save for the helmet under his arm. He was not a totally unique figure here, as companies of Nemsto warriors were still roaming the world, hunting the Storm. They were perhaps the most powerful single force doing so, but were not as widespread or mobile as The Nagirr'Om's acolytes. The warrior was speaking with someone, but Eowen could not see them past the man's broad shoulders. She sidled up next to him and found that he was in conversation with a young mountain folk man. They spared her a brief glance, but did a double take when her heron stalked up behind her.

"You! You're Eowen, aren't you?" the mountain folk man said. The Nemsto man was shocked, and he pivoted to face her. Eowen heard a dull clack as he turned and looked down to see that one of his legs was a prosthesis. "She is," The mountain folk man said with a touch of a Britchen accent.

"You will not remember me, for I was one among many, but I am a healer trained by Aiyano herself. I was in Nolano when you were."

"I see." Eowen looked between them, then focused on the Nemsto man. It was to him the thread of her power was tied. "Shall we find somewhere quiet to talk?"

Eowen followed the pair as they secured lodging in the inverted part of the city. They sat at a table together, while outside the window Tavo's landscape stretched out as though the ground were the sky. Eowen avoided looking, as it disoriented her.

"You both know of me already. What are your names?"

"I'm called Fis," said the Nemsto man. "A former warrior of the Nemsto. I fought with my company all the way to the borders of Nolano, where a serpent of the Storm took my leg." He gestured at the prosthetic. It was mostly covered by trousers, but Eowen could see a wooden foot sticking out the bottom. "Albme here is the only reason I'm alive." He patted the healer's shoulder.

"No, I was insufficient for such a task. Even Aiyano could not close and heal the wound entirely." Albme glanced at his companion's prosthetic. "She and an acolyte of The Nagirr'Om devised this prosthetic that helps, but a healer is needed to constantly repair the wound and hold the blood in. Otherwise, it just keeps flowing."

Eowen made a gesture of respect to them both. "You're both credits to your masters. I have seen the strength of Nemsto warriors, and I have been saved by the powers of Aiyano." Eowen moved aside her robe enough to show the scar from The Nagirr'Om's spear. This also exposed part of the mountain folk's seal branded on her chest. Albme smiled brightly and offered Eowen his hands.

"That mark, you are a sister of my people then?" Eowen smiled back, but more sadly, and offered her hands as well.

"I am a friend of those closest to heaven, and blessed to be considered sister by some of them."

"I knew we were right to seek you out!" Albme patted Fis's arm excitedly.

"Of course, of course," Fis said. "But am I supposed to know what that symbol is?"

"It is the mark of trust and friendship that mountain folk bestow only on those most deserving. Eowen here earned it along with the legendairy Hani of The Stormwake when they and our leader, Genia, summoned the sacred beasts of our people!" Albme was ecstatic. "The mountain folk have been in your debt since. I've made a pilgrimage to see their new settlement, and they tell stories of how you saved five of our own at the beginning of the fall, then trained and befriended Genia."

"That was a long time ago," Eowen said, her voice quiet and shy. "I'm glad to know Genia is well, however I must return us to the reason we are meeting. Did you say you sought me out? I was drawn to you to fulfill my work." Eowen was still speaking in the mountain folk's language, for it had a formality that made it easier for Eowen to steer the discussion to official matters, and Albme seemed to appreciate speaking with someone in his native language. She looked at Fis to pick up the conversation.

"We did come seeking you, though I never expected that you'd find us first." Fis reached into his bag and placed a stone urn of green marble on the table. "This is my father." Eowen and Albme were silent as Fis closed his eyes and recited something under his breath. When Fis looked up again, he was full of fervent pride. "He was a greater warrior and dreamer than I ever was, and the former leader of our company. He led us through dozens of battles even before the fall. His name was Skelad, and he was called the iron teeth of the wolf, for he fought with two daggers and would wrestle his foes to the ground to slay them. He died so that many others could live." Fis closed his eyes again and recited something else. "We were in the outskirts of Nolano when he died and my injuries rendered me lame. Albme saved my life and tended to me day and night." Fis patted his companion, who shook his head.

"No, it was Aiyano that saved you. I merely assisted."

"Then it has been you giving me life since, and I'll take your tongue before I let you deny it!" Albme couldn't have responded as Fis pounded the smaller man's back. Albme bore it with good humor though, a quiet joy glowing through his mind. "Normally, we will create a grave for our dead where they fall," Fis continued. "But it was unanimous that Skelad the iron teeth deserved something greater. We had certainly heard of you before, Eowen of the Dead—" Albme nudged Fis with his elbow. "Ah, Eowen Mortician. During our rest in Nolano, we heard more of your deeds and saw your great works there of trees and hills and valleys. Magic ones that honor the dead in ways that brought peace and inspiration to the people there."

Eowen felt a warm glow in her chest at the compliments. She'd accepted that her reputation wasn't perfect, but had taken a certain satisfaction in knowing that the good she'd done followed her as well. To know that even now, years later, the people of Nolano were still so thankful for her work was about the greatest compliment she could receive.

"My company decided that to honor our leader best would be to find you. So we followed news and rumor, and here we are." Fis gestured to the table. "Yet, we did not even have to ask where to find you, for you found us! Truly, your reputation is deserved."

Eowen gathered some of her power about her. Her brand began to glow and the heron stood above her like a banner. She wanted to present her best self for the men, to live up to their expectations. She spoke slowly, choosing her words with care.

"You honor me, Fis... and are very kind to have come so far for such a purpose. And you, Albme, are indeed brave and impressive to have conveyed Fis safely to this place. It must have been a long and difficult journey, but now it is at its end." Eowen wanted to tap her feet and grin. She thought she was doing quite well. **"Tell me in what way we are to honor this warrior."**

The voice of power shook through them as it always did, bypassing ears to speak directly to the spirit. Eowen let the power fade as she stared into Fis's eyes. The huge Nemsto man was taken aback, and Albme was looking between them as if to say: 'See? I told you!'

"I admit, I'd believed some of the rumors about you were exaggerated. I see now this is not true." Fis scratched his beard thoughtfully. "Originally, I was prepared for us to perform some kind of ceremony wherever we found you. It was not uncommon in the old world for our fallen warriors to be buried where they died, but for those most honored, we would transport them home and bury them beside their families. I was prepared to settle for something in between this, an honorable funeral with one such as you to perform it while still far from home." Fis was turning an idea over in his head. Eowen could feel the thoughts working. "I believe you can give my father the burial he truly deserves, Eowen

Mortician. Will you return him to our home, across the vast and empty starfield that was once the sea?" Eowen didn't hesitate, the answer was out of her before she even knew she'd spoken.

"Fis, it will be done."

* * *

Several hours later, Eowen sat cross legged on her heron as it carried her through the skies of Tavo's landscape. She cradled the urn which, as it turned out, didn't have ashes, but a compressed version of Fis's father that would emerge to full size when opened. It was a wonder of Fis and Albme's combine efforts. After she'd agreed to carry Skelad's body back to the Nemsto island, they'd shared embraces, thanks, and farewells. Fis and Albme had always intended to return to Nemsto to live out their days, but had wanted to do this one thing first. They trusted Eowen to brave the Storms to the west and resist them. Eowen had certainly believed herself capable of doing so when she had agreed to the request. Now, however, far from those she promised her services to, she wasn't sure. The heron flapped its wings, but Eowen didn't feel it at all, so smooth was its flight.

"Did I do the right thing?" Eowen asked the heron, but the bird did not respond. "I was always planning on going that way, but will I have to wait for a caravan like I have been? At this rate, I'm not sure one will ever show up." The heron reached a great height, then tilted and began gliding down at a speed. "They probably think I'm going to fly there myself." She scratched the heron behind the head where it liked. "I know I can resist the Storm when I'm with a mourner and their dead, but this isn't exactly the same thing.

The thread disappeared when he gave me the urn. For Fis, it's all but done with. He might never even find out if I succeed or fail." The heron tilted its wings, changing from a dive into a swoop at an angle. "I'm not going to abandon his faith in me, but I'll have to wait till it's safe, won't I?"

Eowen looked up from the urn to find she was in the midst of thick, heavy clouds. She looked left and right, up and down, but everything around her was the same billowy gray. The only things that were totally clear were her and the heron. The clouds parted around the bird, and its silhouette seemed to smear and flow over Eowen. Winds and rain battered against her, but Eowen didn't feel a thing.

"Oh," Eowen said. She reached out her hand and pressed it to the gloom, which split around her. "I suppose it's time now, isn't it?"

Eowen had expected the moment her journey was meant to continue to be an excited, triumphant one. The disk would signal to her, she'd rush to say her goodbyes, then fly to the caravan waiting at the crescent port of Herod and be on her way amidst cheers. The heron turned, passed through Ahn's barrier, and reentered the land Tavo had wrought. It now seemed wrong to celebrate leaving, but it was time.

I suppose I'll start with the goodbyes.

Eowen nudged the bird with her mind, and it sped towards Luu's house. She arrived after dark, her day having been taken up by the hours of flying across the landscape. Luu and her family were uncharacteristically quiet as Eowen approached, yet it was late enough that they should all have been inside. She could feel their minds moving in discordant currants, save for Luu herself. And Miles, who was not present. Eowen entered and the children looked up with hopeful expressions, save for Luu and Delilah.

"Hello everyone," Eowen said, but did not move from the doorway.

"Don't hover there, get in." Luu waved Eowen to a seat. "What's that you're carrying?" She pointed to the urn.

"It's for a funeral. I'm going to transport the body back to where they're from."

"I see, and where's that?" Luu's question hung in the air as Eowen tried to prepare herself. This was the moment, this was goodbye, and after saying farewell to Luu's family she'd find Ahn and Miles to do the same.

"It is the remains of a Nemsto man. I'm going to fly him home."

Eria-Leck stood up and slammed her hand on the table. "Not you, too!"

"What?" Eowen asked, Delilah put an arm around her sister's shoulder and spoke up.

"Miles is gone, he left to travel east eight days ago."

"I'm the one that told them," Nathalie said. "Miles only told me, and he said to keep it a secret, but Leg-Friend said I should tell everyone now."

Rennick got up from the table and ran to his room, looking close to crying. Thermin went after him. "I've got it," she said.

"Miles told Rennick and Ahn that they'd travel together," Rose informed Eowen. "But he left without keeping his promise, and now you're leaving too!"

"It's a lot of changes at once," Luu said. "But you know this is a good thing, don't you? They're doing what they have to do. We love them for that, don't we?"

"That's not the problem!" Eria-Leck threw off Delilah's arm. "Miles left without saying goodbye! What if he dies out there, and we didn't get a chance to say anything, or tell him that we loved him!" Eria was crying now, so Luu walked over to embrace her.

"How many of us told Miles that we loved him the last time we saw him? I know I didn't," Luu said.

"But the last time I saw him was two weeks ago and we argued over something stupid," Eria said into her mother's shoulder, but Luu laughed at this, which made Eria pull back and glare at her.

"Eria-Leck, you argue more than anyone I've ever met. At this point I'm convinced that it's how you tell people you love them." This made Eria crack a smile, and her mother rubbed her back and cooed.

"He's really gone, then?" Eowen asked Nathalie. The little girl looked mortified and on the verge of tears herself.

"I-I'm sorry!" Nathalie whimpered. Everyone turned to her. "I didn't mean to do anything bad, but Miles asked me to keep it a secret, and you're not supposed to tell secrets, and now Eria and Rennick hate me because I ruined everything for them!" She was in a full meltdown, but before anyone could say or do anything else, Eria-Leck wiped away her own tears, broke from her mother's embrace, and swept the youngest of their family up in her arms, kissing Nathalie's face furiously.

"You are the greatest sister there has ever been, you hear me? You're the best secret-keeper and secret-teller there ever was! Miles is a dumb piss-brained buffoon, and you're the best sister in the world, ok?" She showered Nathalie with more kisses.

"B-but, Rennick—"

"HEY RENNICK!" Eria shouted, and after a moment his door banged open with Thermin close behind.

"What?" He couldn't seem to decide between anger and sadness.

"Nathalie thinks she did something wrong!"

"What!" Rennick decided on anger and launched himself at his sisters, furiously hugging Nathalie. "You're the best sister ever!"

"That's what I said! Come on, we need more arms." She gestured to the rest of the family and they rushed in to pile on the little girl who was equally crying and laughing as they showered her with compliments and kisses. Luu, on the outside, patted Nathalie's head and gestured for Eowen to join.

"Family hugs are for the whole family," Luu said in her mind. Before Eowen could respond, Legs-Friend extended no less than twenty appendages, scooped Eowen in, and wrapped the entire group in a cocoon of affection. They only stayed like that for a few seconds before Nathalie squealed from the center.

"It's too tight now!"

"Then tell your damn pet to let us go!" Eria said.

"Oh yeah, Legs-Friend, off!" The appendages released them and the family fell apart, some laughing, some still on the verge of tears, and some out of wind. Eria-Leck still had Nathalie in her arms. "You can stop hugging!"

"Not until you say you're the best sister ever," Eria-Leck insisted from her position on the floor.

"No, you're the best sister ever!" Nathalie countered. Eria paused and thought about that response.

"That'll work, too." She released Nathalie and the two grinned and giggled breathlessly. The mood was lightened, and the family, despite Miles's absence, felt whole and loved. Luu looked at Eria with such pride, and her mind was so alight with it that Eowen could practically hear the thoughts radiating from her. Delilah noticed as well, and mirrored the expression for her sister. As everyone picked themselves up and took to their seats, Eowen detected a mental conversation passing between Delilah and her mother. She didn't eavesdrop, but mentally prodded them to let them know she was aware and curious. Luu and Delilah locked eyes with Eowen, then each other. Luu clapped her hands loudly for attention.

"I have an announcement to make. We're having another family meeting right now, take your seats." Eowen got up to leave but Luu walked behind her and forced her down by the shoulders. "You've been with us a year, kid. You're family now, whether you like it or not." Eowen tried to protest in Luu's mind, but the older woman did the psychic equivalent of slapping Eowen's hand away. "Now, we all agree that your oldest sibling, Miles, is an inconsiderate, piss-brained, belch-breathed—"

"Butt-faced!" Rose offered her own addition and the youngest kids giggled.

"Yes!" Luu pointed at her daughter. "Butt-faced man! He is all those things and worse, isn't he?" There was a chorus of laughter and yeses. "But we love him, and he loves us. He was bound to go off like this one day. Some of us knew that about him, and some of us had to find out now." The family was quiet this time, but they all nodded. "Miles took care of half of you when you were in diapers, and he kept us together when Daddy was sick and dying. He stayed with us after the fall, even though he wanted to leave to see the new world." Luu looked at Rennick. "Just like you, kid. He waited longer than he needed to, but now he's off, and I love him for it, and I love all of you." Luu hadn't shed a tear. She was as collected and organized as she'd always been. She spoke as if she'd rehearsed this speech, and it was entirely possible she had. "Many of you will leave home, maybe for good, so when it's your time, don't hesitate and don't leave with regrets. Miles held himself back until he could take it no longer and had to disappear. I think he feels guilty for it. I think he knew if he had to look in your faces and say goodbye, he wouldn't be able to leave." Luu's smile was warm, and her confidence uplifted her family. "We all fight and disappoint each other sometimes... Except for Nathalie, you're perfect." There were more cheers for the blushing little girl. "But more often we disappoint ourselves, don't we? Yet each day, I see you all honoring yourselves with the efforts and choices you make. Even butt-face Miles." Nathalie loved the insult and pushed the laughter down with her hands. "Soon enough, it'll be time for more of you to leave, like how it's Eowen's turn to leave." Luu looked at Eowen. "Will you stay the night, so that we can properly send you off in the morning?"

Eowen was taken aback, she'd only planned to stop by, say a quick goodbye and thank them for their hospitality. Now Luu was talking about proper send offs and grouping her with her family.

"I, uh, suppose I can wait till the morning. I wanted to say goodbye to Ahn, and he'll be asleep." Eowen shrugged.

"Then it's settled. Everyone, if you have any last gifts or wishes for Eowen, then prepare them and get to sleep. We're all going to visit Ahn tomorrow!" The family sprang into action, with the youngest children crowding Eowen with hugs and promises before scampering off to bed. Delilah said to her mother that she'd return to the temple to prepare for the whole family to visit. It had become more common to have visitors in it, and even people outside Luu's family were now allowed to stop by. Still, the temple preferred to be alerted before a crowd showed up. Thermin stayed in her seat as Luu corralled the rest into their rooms. The atmosphere of the evening had been completely transformed from despondent to hopeful and excited.

Once all the children were away, Eowen stood in the room shifting from foot to foot. "Luu, can I speak with you? In private?" Eowen looked to Thermin, not wanting to offend, but the eldest daughter shrugged, unbothered.

"Let's take a walk, kid," Luu said.

Out in the night, the landscape Tavo had left behind could sometimes feel eerily like the old world. Despite Eowen's senses, the way the moon shone and the way the wind moved the grasses and leaves felt very nostalgic of the times before the fall. Luu led Eowen down the path and up a grassy hill near the home.

"What did you want to talk about?" In truth, Eowen didn't know where to start. So much was happening so quickly and she suddenly felt out of time to address it all.

"I just wanted to ask you about..." She searched for a topic and landed on the only one close at hand. "Miles." His name was sour in her mouth. Despite his not saying goodbye to anyone, Eowen couldn't help feeling like she'd been personally slighted. She tried to repress or reconstruct her feelings into a more sensible framework, but she couldn't help it. Miles was a presence that burned unfairly in her spirit. Luu was waiting for Eowen to continue, and she sought for something to say about him that would focus on what bothered her. "The last time we spoke, he asked me how I felt about your family, and I think I said the wrong thing!"

"What did you say?"

"I said... that I felt you were all very kind for taking me in. That I would always be grateful, and that I was glad to have made friends of your people." Eowen looked at Luu imploringly. "And I meant it! I absolutely do!"

Luu settled Eowen down with a hand on her shoulder. "You don't need to convince me of anything, Eowen." Luu seemed, for the first time since Eowen had met her, unsure. "Gods below. Why are you always so formal?"

Eowen was taken aback. "It's just proper, I'm a guest in your land and home." Luu shook her head and sat, pulling Eowen down with her.

"I'm honestly astounded at how thick you are sometimes." Luu was so deadpan that Eowen didn't even think to be offended. "There's a lot to address here, and you're leaving soon, so I'll try to cover as much as I can."

"Oh, uh, alright then?" Eowen glanced around and fixed her posture.

"Every one of us, except Miles and Thermin, love you like family, Eowen. I know you don't think of us the same way, and that's fine. I don't know why, but you've got your own reasons. I've respected that."

"Everyone but Thermin and Miles... why them?"

"Thermin doesn't consider anyone family, not even me. It's just convenient living with us." Eowen gave Luu a worried look, but the old woman waved it off. "It's one of her quirks, don't worry about it. Miles, on the other hand... well, he thought he was in love with you." This made Eowen flinch back as an uncomfortable, prickly heat rushed her upper body.

"I didn't know anything about that!"

"Of course you didn't, like I said, you're thick." Luu tapped her head. "For someone with god-like powers and Ahn's telepathy, a lot gets past you, doesn't it?" Eowen's whole upper body felt like it was burning, and she had the energy to feel offended this time.

"I try not to use that power, Luu! Do you know how private people's thoughts are? How poorly they control them?" Eowen stood up and paced angrily in front of the woman. "And how could Miles just... decide that about us? Did he leave all of you behind because he had feelings for me? How was I supposed to know? I don't have feelings for him, we weren't like that!" Eowen rounded on Luu and glared at her. "Is that what everyone thinks? That it's my fault?" Luu was totally calm staring at Eowen with such patience and empathy that the fight went out of her. "I-I didn't know. I... think I love him, I think I love all of you. You're not my family, but you and your children are the closest I've ever come to having one again!"

Luu had never asked what had happened to Eowen's home tribe, and Eowen had actively dodged giving out such information. Luu didn't press the issue now, but gestured for Eowen to sit back down with her.

"I know all that." Luu opened her arms for Eowen and, after a pause, Eowen shook her head and wrapped her arms around herself. "Miles didn't think you were in love with him. He had feelings for you, or thought he did briefly. The kid... he's too restless. His heart was always looking for ways to leave us while his mind was always looking for ways to stay. What I think is that you represented something in between that for him." Luu closed her eyes and sighed. "That kid, somehow I can't help thinking he'll get into more trouble than Bolo or I ever did." She opened her eyes again. "Eowen, no one blames you for Miles leaving, and he never truly fell in love with you. It was just a passing fancy. You two became such fast friends, and he always knew you'd be leaving us. I think you inspired him in that way." Luu smiled, and it was warm and sad and marked with the most weakness Eowen had ever seen her show. "I'm worried about that boy, how can I not be? I'm his mother. But if I'd asked him to stay he'd have never left! I'm sorry. I pushed you two to spend time together hoping you'd learn something from each other. Maybe I was being selfish and only thought about what my son could learn from you." Luu looked down into her bowled hands as if some wisdom were waiting there. "Maybe I've only done more harm than good."

Eowen was caught in a sort of loop of readdressing all of her interactions with Miles, with Luu, with the whole family, and with everyone she'd met since arriving in Tavo's land. Something had been bothering her for some time, the way Luu so comfortably pushed her children to go out and pursue their work, and how easily she let them go. Eowen had rarely ever compared her mother to anyone else, but after a year with Luu, Eowen couldn't help doing so. Monda had always blamed Eowen for her lack of status, and refused to speak of Tavo except to speak of what she'd lost when he had abandoned them. For years before the fall, Eowen had been sent away to make something of herself, and had returned time and again in failure to a mother that beat her for it.

As I deserved.

The thought bloomed in Eowen's mind, but didn't feel right as she weighed Luu against her own mother. It wasn't as though Luu's children didn't fail on occasion. Rennick could offend with his intrusive questioning, Rose had practically disfigured a few people with poorly applied tattoos, and Eria-Leck had still not found a specific purpose for herself. Yet Luu never lost faith in them, never took credit for their achievements, and there was never a moment that Eowen could see where they didn't feel supported and loved.

Then there was Miles, relaxed on the outside, a fire in his

mind, a restless seeker of the unknown, and a committed servant to his family. Yet, he was also the type to carry secret feelings for one who thought of him as one of her closest friends. The type of man to disappear with hardly a word to anyone. Eowen felt like she'd wasted a year with Luu's family, never doing enough for them. Atop that hill, mere hours away from leaving, Eowen only felt a sort of bitterness in her.

"Luu, I don't know what to think. I'm confused and hurt and sad, but I don't think I should be! Or maybe I just don't want to be. I... can't be a part of your family, I can't be!" Eowen was quiet, avoiding Luu's eyes. "I think I want to be though, but it's not—I mean." She pushed at the tears in her eyes and grit her teeth. "I don't want to cry either! I'm not angry, but I feel like I have to be!" Eowen dropped her face into her hands. "Why do I feel like this! What do I do?"

Luu scooted up next to Eowen and stretched out her legs, leaning back on her hands. She nudged Eowen with her elbow and it took a few long seconds, but eventually Eowen looked up, her expression vacillating between a glare and a plea.

"It's startling to see someone going through exactly what you once were, and terribly painful," Luu whispered, then gestured at her head in an inviting way. Eowen, after some hesitation and a moment to psychically balance herself, reached out for Luu's mind. The woman next to her, in that perfectly organized and serene library of a psyche, led Eowen from memory to memory. They weren't concrete images, physical experiences, nor places or times. Just feelings that Luu had gone through, eras of her life defined by certainty, loss, anger, bewilderment, and love. It washed over Eowen, artificially putting her through the states Luu had been in. All of them were familiar, or at least relatable in some way, save for Luu's lustful phases, which had no impact on Eowen at all. Luu finished the tour of her past emotional landscapes and gently ushered Eowen out of her mind. Eowen was confused, but felt better, calmer.

Luu spoke again: "I used to think that life was simple, when I was younger. I did everything on impulse, and sometimes that brought me joy. I found friends, lovers, and a son that way. Other times, I'd do things on impulse and it'd get me tossed in jail, or beat within an inch of my life, or captured by slavers. Later, when I was less young, I thought life was complicated and I had to think everything through ten times over. That didn't always work out either, got me paralyzed between choices and great things slipped through my fingers more than once. That's the problem in thinking things have to be done one way or the other to be done right. There is no doing things right, you just gotta go through them, and things'll end up however they do. The only real answer I've found is to accept how it is, that make sense?"

Eowen nodded. "I think I've heard that before, but I don't remember where."

"So, what are you feeling right now? Something simple and true," Luu whispered.

"I... want to leave, and find my cousin more than anything, and I'm glad my work is going to let me do that. In a way it always has." Luu nodded. "But also, I'm really going to miss you all." Luu offered Eowen another embrace, and this time, Eowen accepted it.

"I'm glad you're leaving, I know how important this is for you, and I'm going miss you too. Terribly so." After a moment, Luu stood up to go back inside. "You coming in, kid?"

"No... I don't think I want to sleep tonight."

Luu planted a last kiss on Eowen's head and left her be. Luu entered her home and sat down heavily into a chair in front of the fire. Thermin was in the other chair next to her, and the young woman reached over to run her fingers through her mother's hair.

"Thank you, Thermin. You're a good daughter."

"I'm a good friend," Thermin corrected, and Luu grinned.

"Right, right. My mistake."

When Luu was out of sight, Eowen mounted her heron and let it take her where it wanted, wheeling around and around Tavo's land for many hours while she let her mind drift. During that quiet night, Eowen let her power flow out unrestrained, gently releasing manifestations into the world as the ocean of her subconscious moved with currents she had long since learned to navigate. She didn't sleep, but she did dream.

****

I'll listen a little longer. I'll listen as long as it takes. For all the confusion you've brought me, whoever or whatever you are, you've also brought me so much peace. You've been there at times to do what I couldn't, and you've always spoken when I've been on the right path. That I am certain of. So please, speak, and I'll gladly listen.

[Just for a little longer.]

LOVE PLEDGED THAT, WHEN ALL I WANTED WAS TO BE LISTENED TO WITHOUT SHAKING THE FRAGILE FRAMES OF GODS TO PIECES, THEY WOULD LISTEN.

****

Eowen arrived at Ahn's temple hours before Luu's family was awake to tell him that she was leaving. "Ahn, I'm leaving today."

"I know. You've been shouting it in your mind for hours."

"Of course." Eowen caught the little boy's hand as he floated by and pulled him to sit on her lap, like when they'd first met. She played with his hair, and he hummed contentedly. The little boy reminded her of Zerinley, the little mountain folk girl she'd left behind. Perhaps it was the easy way they loved, or the natural wisdom they had, or maybe it was just their age.

Eowen felt like she hadn't had enough time with the boy. They were peers in this world. She'd taught things to others before, showed them manifestations to replicate or helped them cultivate a mindset of creation, but with Ahn it was different. He was someone she could share her burden of power with, and in doing so better fortify him against his own. In a small way, Ahn was like her apprentice, and more than anyone she'd left behind, Eowen feared for his development without her.

"You've been ready to leave for a long time. It's good that you can now." Eowen froze. Of course Ahn knew what she was thinking. **"I've almost trained enough people to**

completely replace me and maintain the barrier. I'm not afraid to leave, and I've got Rennick!"

She smiled softly, then lifted Ahn up and pushed him back into the air, sending him spinning slowly away. Ahn floated past Eowen upside down, holding his feet with his hands and smiling. He still preferred not to wear clothes, but he'd taken to wearing a satchel with scrolls in it, like Rennick. Ahn's scrolls all had drawings of things he'd plucked from people's memories of the old world, and Rennick would cross reference them with his research.

Luu's family arrived within an hour, and the three youngest piled onto Eowen. Nathalie told her how much Legs-Friend would miss her, and not for the first time Eowen wondered how much of a mind the strange creature actually had, since neither she nor Ahn could sense it. Luu had a knot of yarn, dyed deep blue, that created a twisting pattern like flower petals.

"I haven't bothered with family iconography for a long time. Didn't think I'd need to since I was disowned at sixteen, but this should let any other coastal tribes-people you come across know that you're a friend. Not as dramatic as a brand on your chest, but it should do."

"Thank you, Luu." Eowen embraced her.

"Come, let's put it on."

"I've got it, where do you want it?" Eria-Leck took the yarn, and Eowen removed her head-wrap for her to affix it. She pinned it on and handed the wrap back to Eowen. It hung down the left side of her head "I don't have any great gift or anything, but I'm really glad we had you around." Eria hugged her, and Eowen felt the touch of Delilah's mind, warm and thankful as well. Thermin hadn't shown up, she had her animals to tend to, and wasn't the sort for such get-togethers. Finally, Rose and Rennick had worked together to prepare something for Eowen. Rose pulled out a scroll with a drawing on it and Rennick explained.

"We've researched into the jungle and savannah tribes and found this design that, according to other sources we spoke to, is a common one among your people. Rose is going to tattoo it on you if you want."

Eowen almost didn't recognize the charcoal drawing of intermingling geometric shapes, but after a brief inspection, realized what it was. It was a common base pattern carved into woodworkings that was meant to symbolize the grasses of the savannah. Eowen hadn't seen it for years, but it was the very same pattern her father carved into his workings. Eowen reached for the parchment and stared at it, awash with memories of the oasis she'd manifested, her former people she'd hurt, her father she'd almost killed and never got to say goodbye to. The tension was palpable, and Ahn was the only one fully aware of why in Eowen's mind. She swallowed down the discomfort and rolled the scroll back up.

"Oh no, you hate it!" Rennick turned on Rose. "I knew you got it wrong."

"I did not, I copied it down exactly like you described! Not my fault you did your research wrong."

"Rose, Rennick, it's perfect," Eowen said, and they looked at each other, confused. "It's... a pattern used by woodcarvers."

"Oh," Rose said. "Is that... bad?" Rennick looked to Ahn, and something passed between them.

"No, it's not bad, it's... my father is a woodworker." She smiled at the children through her tears. "I'd like this, please." Eowen took several deep breaths and settled herself down.

She wiped her tears away to see Rennick blushing and Rose all business.

"Where do you want it?" Rose asked.

It's a symbol placed on the base of a woodworker's creations, so...

"Around my ankles." Eowen removed her sandals and manifested a seat. Rose knelt before her and gathered the light and shadow for the task. Rose wasn't particularly powerful, but she was extremely adept at her craft. The pattern crept into being around Eowen's ankles, like grasses emerging from the soil. Eowen didn't feel a thing on her skin. "Thank you."

After that, food was shared, songs were sung, and games were played, but soon enough Eowen felt it was time to go. She could put it off no longer. They saw her to the entrance of the temple and said their goodbyes. Eowen Mortician mounted her bone heron, and it lifted her away from the land and out west towards the wall of fog. It had grown thicker with the Storm's presence in each passing day, and now the lands protected by Ahn's barrier appeared walled on each side. The new Storm-being must have been of great power, but it had not directly besieged their lands.

Eowen had one more errand to run, and she approached the city of Gonda in the westernmost part of Tavo's land. She alighted upon a long desk, more empty than she'd ever seen it, and withdrew her token from the heron's feathers. Eowen reached out for Harod's mind and found it without touching the metal of the bar.

"Hello again," she said into his thoughts, and he cracked an eye open.

"Well, I'd heard things had changed over at that temple. Good, they needed to for a while."

"That's why you left." Eowen put a questioning feel to her

thoughts and Harod offered up memories of his expulsion. He'd seen how Ahn was cloistered away, and had tried to convince his acolytes to let him leave.

"What brings you back to my humble station?"

"I'm returning this." Eowen put the token onto the counter.

"Finally realized no one is going west in this kind of weather?"

"Not exactly." Eowen mounted back on her heron and it turned to face the Storm. "You should go visit the temple sometime. I'm sure Ahn would be happy to see you, and you'd be happy to see how it's changed."

Harod chewed on the thought for a moment. "I'll consider it." He glanced at the Storm wall, then at Eowen, then spoke out loud. "Are you sure about that, Eowen Mortician?"

"You know my name," Eowen said out loud as well. Harod only shrugged.

"Word gets around, and you've been here a year."

"I'm sure... It's really been over a year, hasn't it?" It was the longest she'd been in one place since Tavo had left, long before the fall. *Mom sent me away to so many different villages that I haven't been in one place for a year since I was ten years old.*

"Safe trip, then," Harod said in her mind, then closed his eyes and settled back into his thick robes. Eowen took off, and a thousand pairs of eyes watched the girl on the bone heron leave in the direction no one else dared to go. Many believed she would die the moment she passed the border, but the clouds pulled aside like great curtains. There was a moment of joy as the Storm was briefly overcome, but then the curtains closed as if swallowing her up. Eowen was gone, deep in the thick of the Storm, fully alone. Eowen let her heron do the work and put herself into a meditative sleep.

"Just let me know if you need anything," she whispered to it before leaving the world behind.

****

[Listen a little longer.]

CAN YOU IMAGINE BEING PROMISED SUCH THINGS?

****

Eowen awoke on the back of her heron several days into the great stretch of empty starfields that had once been a vast ocean of the old world. She looked around her and only saw more churning clouds and forked lightning. The heron was holding up against them, but at times the winds were strong enough to disturb its flight. She scratched the creature's neck, and it snapped its beak. There was no telling where exactly they were in relation to anything else, the only thing Eowen was certain of was that they were still going west. The world's compass kept them on track even in the thick of the Storm.

"Thank you. I'm going back to sleep." She let her dreaming carry her far from reality, trusting the voice in her sleep and the heron to bring her through the dark stretch.

****

[Listen a little longer.]

NO, YOU CANNOT, NOT UNLESS YOU CAN IMAGINE A BEING AS I AM, BEING SO UNREACHABLE SUCH AS I.

****

Eowen awoke, and weeks had passed, though it had felt like but a moment. The clouds were thick enough that she could not see the tips of the heron's wings through them. Darkness was all around, and her smallest attempts at manifestation, whether it be light, food, or comforting jungle air, exploded away from her into serpentine Storm beasts that roared with glee at being released from the prison of nonexistence. The protection of her purpose still held, like a second skin upon her body, spirit, and mind. Despite that, the winds and rain of the Storm clung to her, hungrily trying to drag her down and find a way in. Eowen curled up again and dropped herself back into sleep, away from the cravings of the entity.

****

[Listen a little longer.]

LOVE SAID GOODBYE TO THE SUN, GOODBYE TO THE MOON, GOODBYE TO AH'OM, BUT LOVE COULD NOT BEAR TO SAY GOODBYE TO THEIR DEAREST COMPANION, THE CAVE AT THE BASE OF THE MOUNTAIN.

******

She awoke to check on her progress again, but found herself amidst vast necks of coiling clouds and teeth of lighting. Serpentine beasts of the Storm with trench-like maws and tsunami tongues snapped and writhed. Eowen trusted in her heron and in her power; there were rules that governed the new world. Yet, as jaws filled with fire, ice, and lightning bore down upon her heron, she screwed her eyes shut and covered her ears against the roil. The Storm beasts were gargantuan, dwarfing even those that had coiled around the flayed giant. She clutched the urn to her chest and urged the heron to speed on. The roaring attacks became deafening, and Eowen's barriers of sound could not keep it out. She begged the Storm to leave her be, she uttered phrases of worship to the gods of the jungle and savannah tribes that she had thought lost to memory. The Storm beasts crashed against the heron, causing it to rock and tilt, yet her power still held, cutting through the violent churning of it. Eowen called desperately upon the voice in her dreams to protect her, to comfort her, to give her any sign she was still going the right way and doing the right thing.

It answered, in a way. It called her back into her dreaming again, where the waking world was too far to reach her, and it said what it always did.

******

[Listen a little longer.]

LOVE PROMISED THE CAVE TO MEET ONCE AGAIN, AND THE CAVE PROMISED IT WOULD BE SO. TO MY KNOWLEDGE, THIS WAS THE ONLY LIE THEY EVER TOLD TO ONE ANOTHER, AND THE ONLY LIE LOVE EVER UTTERED.

****

Months passed, deep in her forced hibernation, but she awoke to the burning of the scar in her chest where The Nagirr'Om's spear had pierced her. Eowen opened her eyes to find herself on a small island amidst the starfields and Storms. There was dirt, long orangey grass, and a cozy cabin perched off to the side. A river that emerged from nowhere ran alongside it, partially diverted to feed into the cabin. The island was surrounded by a barrier of silver bamboo, powerful enough to have been from The Nagirr'Om herself. Eowen stood up and stretched her sore limbs, noticing a few creatures wandering about, strange things that Eowen had never seen before. Some were humanoid, one had bat wings, another was cat-like but with a body far too long and with too many legs. Eowen could see at least seven such strange creatures napping, climbing, or wandering about. One, a creature like a man up to the neck and a head like an antelope, approached her with a hand extended. It was robed in black and its hand was chalk-white.

"Is this your home?" she asked the thing, and it only held its hand out. The creatures didn't seem like people twisted by the Storm, yet Eowen was sensing something like dreaming auras from them. She decided to take a chance and clasped the things hand. When she did, the robe pulled aside slightly and she saw that instead of a chest and abdomen there was only a frame of flesh and many small, rodent-like heads watching her. Eowen let go and backpedaled immediately. "What are you!" She scanned around to see that the Storm was still very present, but could not pass the barrier around the tiny island. She was safe. "Where am I? Heron, why did we stop here? This can't be the Nemsto land."

The door of the cabin swung open, and a middle aged woman of mixed mountain folk and valley tribe descent came out. She was wearing an apron and sensible work clothes, and was covered in clay.

"Another one? What do you want?"

Eowen glanced between the heron, the woman, and the strange thing that had offered its hand. "I'm sorry, my bird brought me here, I think. Uh, you're not a Nemsto person."

"No, obviously I'm not." The woman went to the edge of the river and put down a pail. She sunk her hands into the clay there, and scooped out heaps with a sucking noise.

"Wait, I recognize you. You're the woman that makes living things out of clay statues. We caravaned together!"

The woman stopped her digging to turn her head in Eowen's direction. Her eyes moved, but didn't seem to be looking at anything, and Eowen remembered she was blind. "Oh right, the death girl. What in the hells are you doing out here?"

"What am I—what about you? What about these..." Eowen flailed her hands at the strange creatures, "...things!" The woman finished filling her pail and hefted it up.

"I like my privacy, this seemed like a good place to get it. No caravans were going out this way after a while, but I ran into a strange man with a lantern that took me far enough." The woman returned to her cabin. "Well, don't hang around out there, come on in."

Eowen eyed a meter long centipede-thing hanging over the door that looked to be made entirely of glass. The thing's feet made little tinkling noises as it climbed along and flexed its pincers at her. Eowen approached the door, but paused as the centipede-thing faced her and manifested a ball of fluffy gray wool into her hand with a flash of light and shadow.

"Uh!" Eowen said.

"Don't mind them, they don't see people very much, so they're excited," the woman said.

"Are they... people?"

"Not conventionally. Don't stand in the doorway, it's rude." Eowen sidled past the centipede and into the home. "Name's Hori. We probably told each other back in that old caravan, but it's been a while."

"Eowen." She reintroduced herself and looked around as her eyes adjusted to the dimmer cabin. The place was filled with strange forms made of clay, but none of them were complete. There was a massive brick kiln in the back at least a full meter taller and wider than Eowen, with a red glow emanating around an iron door. A huge pile of clay was off to the side in an area only slightly more devoted to the craft than the rest of the cabin. Some of the river's water had been diverted inside where Hori could access. Eowen had many questions and plenty of places to start, but all the strange things that drew her attention had to wait as a door to the side opened and an enormous woman, naked, pregnant, veiled, and glowing with an unearthly silver light, emerged. Eowen's scar burned as if the spear was in it again.

"Eowen Mortician? What are you doing here?"

"The Nagirr'Om," Eowen whispered, her voice hoarse with the pain. "I'm, ugh, wondering the same thing." Eowen dropped to a clay-splattered stool next to a clay-splattered table. The scar was searing all the way through her body, and Eowen's breathing came heavy and strained. The Nagirr'Om sat next to her, and its silver light waned till it was almost all gone. The pain followed the light, and Eowen wiped sweat from her brow.

"That should be better," The Nagirr'Om said, its voice strange without the usual power.

"Thank you." Eowen spoke carefully and eyed the silver being seated next to her. Eowen had not known The Nagirr'Om to do selfless things. It did helpful things, but always for its mission. "Why did you lower your power for my comfort?" Eowen asked.

The veiled woman tilted its head to the side. "Should I have not?"

It unnerved Eowen to hear the actual voice of the entity next to her. The inhuman speech of power suited the strange being far more than the voice of a young woman it now spoke with. The voice was pretty enough, but mechanical and lifeless.

"That depends on the reason. What do you want from me?"

"I... do not want anything from you, Eowen Mortician." The Nagirr'Om had its hands folded in its lap, but they twitched up to the swollen stomach and held the weight of it. "My apologies, I must resume. Brace yourself or **Leave.**" With the last word, the Nagirr'Om's silver light of power surged back, and Eowen had enough time to grit her teeth as the burning resumed.

"Agh! Y-you're not making any sense!"

"I see you two aren't going to let me get anything done today," Hori said as she pushed her project over and wiped clay off her hands. She whistled at the rafters, and a thing like a red bean the size of a fist emerged from the shadows. From no apparent opening, the bean-thing sprouted long furry tentacles with fanged mouths that it gripped the rafters and walls with to climb down into Hori's hand. "May I have some serum, please?" The thing swished one of its mouths around and spat out a glob of saliva, which immediately gathered up into a pearl. "Much appreciated, you can go back into the rafters if you want." The bean-thing opted to hang on Hori's belt from one of its mouths. Hori felt for Eowen's shoulder, knelt next to her with the pearl, and pointed at Eowen's chest. Eowen was confused, but the pain was worse, and she readily pulled aside her robe to reveal the scar. Hori's fingers quickly identified its location and pushed the pearl, solid as it was, into the flesh of the scar, where it sank right in. Eowen felt the matter of the pearl disperse within her, moving through to where there was pain and melding with it. Within seconds the pain had stopped completely. It was as if the flesh through which the spear had pierced didn't exist anymore at all. "There, how's that?"

"I don't feel anything." Eowen pawed at her chest and felt for the scarring on her back. It was still there, but the pain was gone, as if the flesh through which the spear had pierced didn't exist anymore. "How did you do that?"

"I didn't," Hori said. "It's just a thing this little guy does. Now listen, you can both stay here for a bit to rest up or whatever you need, but I want my privacy back. So sort out whatever your issues are and then leave." Hori walked out of the home and left them alone.

Eowen pressed on her scar a bit more, curious about the numbness there, but also avoiding looking at The Nagirr'Om. The thing that looked like a silver woman, for its part, didn't look very comfortable either and was shifting on its seat.

"So, how have you been?" Eowen asked.

"The hunt for the Storm continues."

"Of course, of course." Eowen glanced at The Nagirr'Om, and though its veiled head was looking away from her it gave off the impression that it was looking directly at her. "I've noticed you found lots of people to become acolytes."

"Many appreciate the importance of my work."

"They do, that's true." Eowen nodded while looking around for anything to break the tension. "The things Hori makes are amazing, aren't they? She used to bring clay things to life, in a way, but now they have dreaming auras like people!"

"Hori of Earth To Life is capable, but—" The Nagirr'Om paused. **"There are things she cannot do."**

"What are you referring to?" Eowen asked, but The Nagirr'Om couldn't seem to decide if it wanted to pursue this conversation or not. The Nagirr'Om was acting so strangely that Eowen couldn't help taking a peek into its mind.

When Eowen reached for the thoughts of the thing before her, she found a paradox. The silver woman didn't seem to have a mind at all. There were no thoughts, emotions, or anything that Eowen had come to expect in her telepathic training. There was power though, a dreamer's power present in the physical workings of the woman's brain. The power moved through the brian and body like termites in a tree. The passages of the body had never been designed for such a presence, yet that did not stop them from being navigated with ease.

What is happening?

Eowen's mental question echoed into The Nagirr'Om's mind, revealing her presence there. Silver light flared and Eowen was ejected from the psychic plane. She returned to her own body and mind to find The Nagirr'Om staring through its veil.

"What did you do?"

"What did you do! You're not actually... this person." Eowen gestured to the whole of the silver woman. "You're something else, inside her, moving her around and speaking for her." Eowen tensed for a conflict. The Nagirr'Om had always been a being of action and certainty, but for once it did nothing, only staring intensely at Eowen through its veil.

"Very astute, Eowen Mortician. You've seen through the workings of The Nagirr'Om." The Nagirr'Om reached up to its head and grasped the veil. Very slowly, it lifted the circlet off its head and placed it on the table. Eowen held her breath as she saw the face of The Nagirr'Om. It was the face of a young Britchen woman with a small nose, full lips, thin eyebrows, and dark brown eyes. The thing's face was normal, utterly bereft of the inhuman strangeness that The Nagirr'Om carried themself with. Eowen was disappointed, as she'd been expecting, even hoping for monstrous features with fangs and tusks, or for an empty black hole, or a tangle of worms and fire. Really anything other than a normal woman's face.

"I'm honored that you would expose yourself to me in such a way." Eowen glanced over The Nagirr'Om's entirely naked body as she said this. "I have never heard of you doing such a thing, so I take this as an unusual circumstance. I, uh, am wondering what this is supposed to mean."

The Nagirr'Om was utterly still. It hadn't blinked, or even breathed as far as Eowen could tell. **"Look into my eyes."** Its mouth moved in an unnerving, mechanical way that dipped down to the bottom of the uncanny valley. Shivers ran down Eowen's spine, but she leaned in closer and stared into the thing's eyes. At first, there was nothing unusual other than the unblinking stillness of them, but after a few seconds Eowen realized the eyes weren't actually watching her. They weren't blind, just unseeing, as if they were drawn to nothing in particular, taking in all the information before them but not processing it. Eowen felt watched, but not seen, as though the eyes were sending the images somewhere else.

"What are you really?" Eowen said under her breath.

The Nagirr'Om's head tilted as if on a hinge to face its belly, and it placed its hands upon it. Eowen's eyes went wide, and she stared at the swollen stomach of The Nagirr'Om. Eowen projected her mind again, searching for the mind of its unborn child, and she found it. The baby was there, largely unformed, and with no memories save for the dark warmth it had always known. Yet, as Eowen examined the child for the first time, she found its dreaming aura to be the same as that which possessed the mother, only different, different in the way the sunrise is from midday. The unborn child's power was soft, dim, and incapable of the feats of The Nagirr'Om, while the power within the woman was full and mature.

"How did this happen?" Eowen whispered.

"I can't understand it fully. This body died in the fall. Its child was too powerful a dreamer to perish, yet they could not dream of anything beyond the womb." The Nagirr'Om prodded its dead body. **"Eventually, the child will fully awaken their power, and it will be immense. Strong enough to reach through time itself, strong enough to preserve the vessel that gave it life. Yet it will still be bound by the limits of the mind, body, and spirit it inhabits. It will be a god's mind."** The Nagirr'Om leveled unmoving eyes at Eowen, and through time and space, the future of the child saw her. **"It may even become more powerful than you, Eowen Mortician."** It lifted the veil from the table and placed it back over its face. **"But until the Storm is banished, this child cannot safely emerge. They are more fragile than what they will become, and the Storm would take them for its own to become a terrible thing."**

"That's why you made the tools to fight the Storm, and why you empowered the acolytes to do the same." The Nagirr'Om nodded. "But, if this mind is strong enough to reach through time, does this mean you know the future?" The Nagirr'Om paused, then readjusted itself.

"No. This vessel is too weak, too limited. It can hold only a drop while the power that will be is an ocean." The Nagirr'Om's hands had formed into fists; its silver light was dancing like a flame. **"It is... vexing."**

"She is dead, though," Eowen asked. "The woman that once lived in this body?"

The Nagirr'Om paused before addressing her, settling its shaking hands and placing them back in its lap. **"Of course, you are Eowen Mortician. It is the dead that concerns you most."** There was a hint of annoyance in the voice of power, but Eowen took no offense. **"In the conventional sense it is... dead. It will not rot and the child will survive, the power assures this."**

"I think I understand why you're out here, then. The Storm is growing again in the west." Eowen looked in the direction. "What I don't understand is why you're here, on this island." The Nagirr'Om paused again, shifted in its seat, and, to Eowen, seemed somehow embarrassed.

"Hori of Earth To Life can give true, dreaming lives to formerly inanimate matter. It was within this vessel's hope

that Hori could... **bring the child into this world through a body of her making."**

"Do you really think Hori can do that?"

"It is... uncertain. Yet it seems to be within the bounds of her abilities."

"Why bother, though? Shouldn't you continue fighting the Storm?"

"Despite the guiding power, this vessel must still act upon the structures of its mind."

"What was her name?"

"Whose name?"

"Your mother's."

"Why?"

Eowen fixed her attention upon the body before her and enveloped it in her dreaming aura, making it soft and gentle. She reached for that place where her power and command was, and she spoke to the body itself. **"Because even in death you carry the burden of life, and I will have you acknowledged for it."**

The body shuddered as some part of it understood. Seemingly against the will of the power that commanded it, it leaned forward, whispered a name into Eowen's ear, and recoiled, as if it had touched a fire. It stood up and retreated towards the room it'd emerged from.

"Goodbye, Eowen Mortician." A tear fell from behind the veil, and The Nagirr'Om closed the door.

Eowen let out a pent up breath. "That was weird," she whispered. Eowen wanted the feeling of hot food in her stomach, so she manifested a thick fish chowder with culinary traits amalgamated from a dozen cultures. She wolfed it down and relaxed into the feeling of a warm, full stomach. Then she left the house to check on her heron and

Hori. Her bird was still curled up in the grass, seemingly oblivious to the long cat-thing stalking around it in serpentine waves.

"It'll leave your bird alone. That one only acts like a cat sometimes, it doesn't actually cause trouble," Hori said from the creekside where she was sifting through clay, shaping it.

"Do you ever name them?"

"Na, I'm not their parent. I don't raise them or make them who they are, I just give them a chance to become something all on their own." Hori glared nebulously at the clouds surrounding her island. "Not that they have much of a chance to, stuck here like this. I sure hope that Nagirr'Om lady gets rid of all this nonsense." Hori lifted up an appendage of clay resembling a bear's arm and carried it past Eowen. She began affixing it to a huge, hulking thing of clay, seemingly held together by canvas and rope. "Mind helping me get this into the kiln?" Hori gestured to it.

"I can't lift that, but I might be able to float it in."

"Works for me." Hori stepped aside, and Eowen drew in shadow and star, transmuting them into a lightness that levitated the object. Hori cleared furniture out of the way and opened the kiln door. A wave of heat poured out into the cabin, making Eowen sweat. She guided the statue in, though it barely fit. The thing had many limbs, several heads, and the implication of fur and scales and many many other materials, but was still largely an undetailed, lumpy mass.

"Will it look like that?"

"Not after it's done. Never can predict exactly how they'll turn out though." Hori closed the door and put her hand against it. "I just give them a piece of myself and let them **Be.**" She spoke the word with power, and the kiln shimmered with a different sort of heat. It felt less like the heat of a fire and more like the heat of a life, a heat one could touch and share. The thing in the kiln was becoming alive. Eowen could even feel a new dreaming aura flickering into being behind the door.

"Do you think you can really make a body for the child in The Nagirr'Om?" Eowen asked.

"None of your business. Now how long are you planning on sticking around?" Hori glared with her hands on her hips, but somehow it was good natured, as if she were offering for Eowen to stay.

"I'm ready to go. I think I just needed a rest."

"Hmm. You're on your way to the Nemsto, right?" Hori walked out to Eowen's heron and shooed away the cat-thing.

"That's right, straight west... I hope." Eowen nudged the bird with her sandal, and it opened one eye. She'd never seen the creature look so normal as it did then, tired and grumpy, but it unfolded itself and stood. Eowen mounted up and stared at the wall of clouds, churning with serpentine heads and burning with lightning. Hori's island was well insulated from the sound and the powers of it, but a dull rumble still occasionally pulsed through. "It was nice to see you again, Hori. I hope it's not the last time."

Hori only shrugged and walked back toward her house. "Fine, fine. Get on with it."

Eowen smiled, and her heron rose up in the air. She held the urn in her lap and cloaked her power around them. The bird flew forward and they cut through the Storm as before, untouchable only by the surface of their skin. Eowen steeled herself for another long flight, hibernating in turns and desperately trusting her purpose to protect her. A silver light flashed by, blasting the clouds apart and opening a tunnel westward. Eowen turned back to see The Nagirr'Om standing outside Hori's door with her bow in hand.

"Hurry, Eowen Mortician, before the clouds close." The voice reached her like a whisper on the wind, and Eowen laughed joyfully at the figure.

"Thank you, Nagirr'Om! Come on then," she urged her heron, and it shot forward, almost as fast as the silver light, at the ever lengthening tunnel ahead. Many thousands of kilometers later, the arrow landed. The Nagirr'Om had launched a spear of silver several times the height of the heron almost perfectly west, and it buried itself into the starfield. There was no longer a tunnel for them to follow, only the boiling clouds ahead full of monsters. The world's compass was still clear though, and the heron was well rested. Eowen hoped the way would not be much further. She went into her hibernation as before, and let her mount carry her the rest of the way to the Nemsto land.

****

I'm listening.

THEN AGAIN, IS IT A LIE WHEN THOSE WHO SPEAK IT KNOW IT IS NOT TRUE?

IS IT A LIE WHEN THOSE WHO SPEAK IT BELIEVE IT IS TRUE?

FOR BOTH, I THINK NOT.

****

Back when the world's compass had first split the world into the four directions, it had woken Eowen up, disorienting her with the sudden knowledge of where she was, which, for the entire time she had been in the new world, was the southeast. Eowen was again started awake by the world-setting lines in her mind, and realized that, at some point, the heron had crossed an invisible markation. She was no longer in the southeast of the new world, but the northeast. She wrapped her arms around the heron's neck and pulled herself up. Storm clouds twisted all around her, but they were less violent, no less dangerous but domesticated somehow. Eowen patted the heron and looked to her left, to the south.

"Heron, fly that way for a bit." The bird did as it was bidden and, after a few minutes, Eowen crossed the border between north and south again, putting her in her original hemisphere of the world. "We must be close to the center of the compass," she muttered as the heron crossed back into the northern hemisphere.

Eowen chewed on the inside of her cheek and cast a worried eye to the great anvil clouds that surged around her, but they did not move in violence. The hours wore on, and the clouds became more sparse until she could even see the starfield below. The Storm's presence felt weaker here, and she decided to test it. Eowen raised a great light above her, as massive as the sun that hung above her old oasis. It shined warmly through the haze, cutting some of the heavy dampness away. Random manifestations still curled off of her as they always did, but only in small ways did they become twisted by the Storm.

"It almost feels as if the Storm is afraid to act here."

She urged her heron on, and could see below her that the

starfield was giving way to water. At first it was just a strange push and pull upon the darkness and light below, but within hours the starfield had been entirely replaced with a sea of gem-like green. Waves crested white and the waters stretched out as far as the eyes could see. Soon, the sea below her went as far as her dreaming senses could pick up.

Did Tavo create this too? Or was it some other great dreamer, maybe—people!

Eowen sensed them in the distance, still beyond her sight but within the field of her power. A vast landscape making a horizon where before there had only been clouds and darkness. Her pulse quickened as she felt the presence of dreaming minds at the edge of her own and she stood on the back of the heron, craning her neck to see further. The bird banked around a great bruise of clouds that drifted in front of them, and in a burst of light the civilization was in sight.

"Nemsto!" Eowen whooped and laughed, dancing on the back of her heron and very nearly losing her balance. The bird had to snap her robe with its beak and pull her back down. "Sorry, heron! Oh wow, look at this place!"

The ocean below broke against sheer cliffs, throwing spray upon tough grasses and craggy rocks. A chilly atmosphere cloaked the island, but for once the cold didn't bring Eowen discomfort. As she passed into the airspace of the land, it was not merely air she breathed, but nostalgia layered with the creator's memories. Eowen manipulated her robes to be thicker and warmer, drinking in the comforting concoction of mountainous flowers, mulled wines, crisp ocean spray, and a hint of animal warmth. The place was drenched in power, but it felt like an embrace from someone large, warm, and soft. The Storm was still present here as it domed the land beyond, yet seemed loath to get too close.

The strangest thing was that there didn't appear to be any actual barrier in place. The Storm, both its physical manifestation and its presence within Eowen's mind and spirit, seemed to avoid the place entirely.

Eowen continued her approach, very nearly crossing over the last of the ocean to alight on the land, when a wave of force rocked her and the heron. She staggered in the air, righted herself, and scanned the area with her senses extended. She briefly touched upon the minds of the citizens, but recoiled as static-like shock jolted through her.

"Girl on bird!" A voice like thunder rocked the air, speaking in a broken version of her own language. An immense aura of power was attached to it. She followed it to a man that was heavily armed and armored in the way of the Nemsto warriors she'd seen. His features were hidden, save for thick black braids and a braided beard that spilled out of his helmet. "Down bird!" the man boomed. The Storm clouds around them backed up, but Eowen held her ground, or rather, air.

"How does he know my language this far from the jungle and savannah?"

Eowen commanded her heron to descend slowly while she stood on its back with her hands clasped before her. She stopped just shy of a meter above him and saw how truly massive the man was, easily the tallest person she'd ever met, and the broadest as well. He looked like he could carry a fallen tree on each shoulder. None of his physical prowess was as intimidating as the dreaming aura that radiated off him like steam. Eowen could feel that the land and atmosphere was of his making, and she extended her own power towards him. The forces of their presence played against each other, Eowen's polite and regal, the man's a hearty greeting. The energy was great enough that even the Storms above pulled apart and slammed into each other, jerked about by their metaphysical handshake. The man's intense, somewhat aggressive posture broke and he laughed, gesturing for Eowen to land.

"You interesting, good girl. Come!" He removed his helmet, revealing familiar skin and features. The man was dressed as a Nemsto and spoke with their accent, but he was undoubtedly from her part of the world, either a jungle and savannah tribe's person or a southern islander like Hani. The heron landed next to him in the grass and Eowen got a better look at him. He was grinning, an excitable and infectious spark in his eye. There was a sword at his waist without ornament other than the many nicks from heavy use. His armor was the same, function over form with evidence of countless battles past. He approached, and she flexed her power, settling barriers in place.

"Who are you?" she asked, trying to add a deep and commanding aspect to her voice. "And why do you look like someone from the jungle and savAHNnah tribes?" Eowen flushed at the crack in her voice.

"You speak the tongue of my childhood! Can you understand me?" He spoke in the Nemsto language now. Eowen nodded.

"That's right."

"Impressive, girl! Almost as impressive as all those shields you have about you." His keen eyes roved over the space around her, seeing her defenses. He looked like he wanted to try breaking through them. Eowen's heart hammered, and the air stopped tasting of flowers and grass and took on the tang of blood and steel. Eowen gathered her own strength and it crackled around her. There was no fear or nervousness in her; the man's battle-lust was infectious, but the beating of her heart pushed out the desire for peace. As soon as the man noticed her preparing to fight, he put up his hands innocently and his beard scrunched into a smile. "No, we will not fight I think." As soon as it appeared, the scent of blood and steel was gone, and Eowen reeled from the sudden lack of desire to fight him. There was something increasingly familiar about the tang of his power she could not yet place.

"Do I know you?" she asked.

"I think not, girl."

"But you are from the jungle and savannah tribes?"

"Only by birth." He removed the leather gauntlet from his right hand and offered it to her. "Varik, of the Nemsto by adoption."

"I've heard of you!" Eowen clasped hands with him, though he could have fit four of her fists in his one. His hand was as muscled and calloused as the rest of him, and Eowen felt more like hers was being sandwiched between two stale loaves of bread. "The great leader of the Nemsto warriors, I was saved by a company of them!"

Varik grinned and pumped her hand, practically lifting her off the ground before letting go. "I'm glad to know they are doing good work out in the world!"

"They truly are. I am called Eowen Mortician, I am she who serves the dead and grieving."

"Ah, a much welcome service in this world of ours." He looked her up and down, then scanned her heron. "You are very powerful to have crossed the thunder-wilds to reach this place. Tell me, what has brought you so far from our people?" Varik took a seat upon the grass and gestured for Eowen to join him. The heron curled up behind her and she took her seat, leaning against it.

"There is... much to that question, but to put it simply, I was able to cross the Storm, uh, the thunder-wilds, because I was charged by one of your people with delivering the body of his father and company leader." Eowen held out the urn to Varik, and he cradled it. **"In your hands you hold the remains of Skelad, the iron teeth of the wolf, father of Fis, from whom I was personally commissioned to deliver him to a fitting resting place."** Varik raised a curious eyebrow when Eowen spoke with her voice of power.

"I knew Skelad. He trained many of my peers and was the leader of my first company. The man campaigned valiantly in the old world and the new." Varik held the urn in silence for a moment before handing it back to Eowen. "Nemsto warriors are usually buried where they fell. Why was this not done?" Varik asked, inquisitive, not accusing.

"His company believed that Skelad should be returned home for his exceptional valor while they continued campaigning."

Varik crossed his arms and nodded approvingly. "They are the greatest warriors of any world! Thank you for this service to my people, Eowen Mortician. I will show you to Skelad's family after I have shown you proper hospitality!"

"Thank you, Varik, but I'm afraid I must insist on pursuing this business as soon as possible. I... did not travel so far from the jungle and savannah tribes for this reason only. I have other things that I must attend to." Eowen looked away and hunched her shoulders.Varik cocked his head to the side. "I have been seeking someone; my cousin, a young man named Tavo—"

"Ha ha! You know my good friend Tavo?" Varik slapped his leg and grasped Eowen by the shoulder to give her a friendly shake. She was speechless for a moment, her mouth opening and closing before she could find the words.

"You know him?"

"Yes, yes, we've been friends since before the fall! Your cousin, eh?"

"You know him! You've known him for years?"

"Of course, he was here no more than a month and a half ago!"

"He was here!" Eowen jumped up and paced around her heron, grinning ear to ear, vacillating between crying and laughing. Varik stood as well, greatly enjoying the girl's reaction. "Only a month and a half ago, he really was here. And you know him, you saw him!"

"I did, I did!"

"I've been searching, tracking him for so long, and he was really... he..." Eowen stopped pacing and looked at Varik, worried. "He was here."

"Ah, the lad stopped by then left after a few minutes. Couldn't even be bothered to have a drink with me."

"To find his wife," Eowen said.

"Yes, that Niude girl, Duwiyin. He must be headed to their lands by now." Varik's expression became grim and he looked to the northwest. "Or whatever's left of them." Eowen clasped his hand, bringing his attention back to her.

"Please, you have to tell me what happened! How was he? Do you know the way for me to find him?"

"Eowen—"

"I've been searching since before the fall!" Eowen pushed the plea with her eyes, her dreaming spirit, even upon the surface of his mind. She couldn't stop, not when she was this close. Varik was taken aback by the force of her need, and his expression softened.

"Of course I'll tell you. Come, we'll speak on the way to my home. You'll be an honored guest."

"No, thank you, just point me in the right direction." Varik shook his head though.

"You say you got here through the thunder-wilds because you were carrying Skelad here?"

"Oh. Yes. I have the most power when I am performing my funeral work."

"Then you're not going anywhere yet. He is beyond the thunder wilds, and Skelad's family is here. Come along, we'll see what we can do in time."

Varik started down a worn path in the grass towards a copse of trees. It vexed Eowen to be forced to wait again when she was so close, but Tavo wouldn't be traveling anymore. It seemed clear that once he reached his wife, he'd finally stay put. Eowen sighed. As long as she knew where he'd be waiting, she could still find him. She hurried after Varik as he led her into the trees ahead.

"When that lad arrived, I didn't know it was him at first. He was far to the east when the sky fell, so I'd never tasted his power before." Varik gave Eowen a serious look. "I've still never felt anything like it. Tavo came through the clouds, no armor or barriers or special missions like you. Just the lad on his own."

"I've heard a bit about that, most people need protections to move through the Storm but from everything I've gathered Tavo has another way."

"Indeed." Varik tugged his beard. "I was very excited to see him, I'll tell you that! I saw that young man walking across my sea and called out to him: 'Tavo my boy, it's been too long!' I invited him in, but he said he was in a hurry to reach his wife and make sure she was alright." Varik grimaced. "A reasonable concern. The thunder wilds have been thick in the northwest since the beginning." Varik stared thoughtfully in that direction. "Strangely enough, few monsters emerge from that way though. Seems that all the fighting to be done is in the east. Anyway, that cousin of yours was in a rush. I offered armor and weapons or to scrounge together a company to escort him, though most of our warriors are away."

"You don't have a force defending your land?"

"Oh, we do." Varik grinned and bared his teeth, pointing a thumb as his own chest. The clouds that domed over the Nemsto lands seemed to shiver and back up. "Well, that's the last I saw of him. He didn't even take the time to set foot on the land here, just went on around through the thunder-wilds... I'm sure that lad's alright, but we can't help but worry about his sort, can we? His kind's always looking for trouble and needing my sort to get them out of it. Though with the sort of power he had, I'm not surprised he was so bold." Varik patted Eowen's shoulder. "Your cousin's a force, Eowen Mortician. We shall find a way to reunite you in due time, I swear it." Eowen hadn't stopped staring to the west during Varik's recounting, but when he patted her shoulder she attempted a weak smile.

"Thank you, Varik. I suppose this last stretch isn't much compared to how far I've already gone."

"That's the spirit! I'm impressed you found your way here just by following rumors of the lad."

"Well, it helped to know the general way he was going. Whenever I ran out of rumors, I just kept going north and west."

"Ah! I'm glad the directions I carved into the world have been of use to you."

"Yes, they were very useful." Then she comprehended his words, and her eyes widened. "You made the compass!" Eowen shouted at Varik, and he bellowed with laughter, patting his belly with his free hand. "You? You're the source of it?"

"You're absolutely right, girl! It was I who set the directions of this world to order!"

"Unspeaking gods, I have been wondering about that for so long, everyone has been! Do you have any idea how far away it reaches?"

"Ha ha! My proudest moment, even more so than my wedding and birth of my two sons! Don't tell my wife I said that, though."

Eowen was dumbstruck, unable to decide what to do with this knowledge. *I might be the only non-Nemsto person that knows this!* "Varik, you don't understand." She patted his arm. "You're probably the greatest legend across the whole of the new world, except no one knows it was you!"

He gestured dismissively. "Ah, let them wonder! The world is more interesting with mysteries in it, especially if those mysteries can be solved and the answers are not horrors." His words reminded Eowen of Miles. She hadn't thought of her friend in some time without a sour feeling accompanying it, but Varik made the memory sweet again.

Her guide continued into the wood, whistling a tune and beckoning for Eowen to follow. As they walked, Eowen examined the beauty of Varik's land. It was not so vast and spectacular as Tavo's, but there was a more stalwart quality to it. Its trees were coniferous and tall, standing like spires that held up the sky. Its stones were a hard gray, the undergrowth tough and rooty. Lichen clung to everything, and there was something lovely about the sturdy flora there.

Flowers didn't grow huge and bursting with color and scent as in the jungle, but more like the small, tough ones of the savannah. It cheered her to find even one small similarity to her old home as far as a continent, an ocean, and an apocalypse away. The path through the woods was long and winding with many branches, but Varik knew the way.

"Varik, you said you knew Tavo before the fall. How did you meet?"

"Of course you'd want to know that! How much of Tavo's adventures did he tell you?"

"Uh... none. He disappeared from the jungle and savannah tribes when I was only a child of ten." Eowen was a bit embarrassed to admit how little she knew of her cousin in recent years.

"Did he not reach you before the fall though? I understand he was headed back to gain a blessing. Devout lad."

"No, he never reached us. He was in the Britchen lands, just over some mountains when the fall happened. That's why he was there then, for a blessing for his wife?"

"That's right. I don't know what he's been up to since the fall, but when I first met him, Tavo was running for his life from skeevy rat-bastard bandits from further north. Carrulians!" He spat the word. "Thin footed, thorn pissing, seven fingered bastard slavers, the lot of them!"

"Ah, I've run into some of them. Most were just... people, but there were some turned to monsters by the Storm. One woman I met was even freed by a Carrulian slaver." Varik huffed at this as if he doubted it, but there was a bright joy in his eye.

"You remind me of Tavo, there. Your cousin thought he could make friends with anyone. Bright lad. He was cornered by those Carrulian slavers after hours of being tracked and chased and he still wanted to reason with them! Foolish lad. Brave and kind, but terribly foolish. My company and I slayed the Carrulians, freed those they'd already captured, and took them with us. Imagine my surprise when I found a boy of my own ancestry so far from home. I took him home and he was like a little brother to me. Nemsto see so few people from the jungle and savannah sort that most thought he was my brother even though he was just a string-bean!" Varik patted his huge frame. "Built more like you, eh?"

"Oof!" He had given another hardy pat to Eowen's back that nearly sent her to the ground.

"He tried to help with work in the fields with my boys, but your cousin is made of sticks and skin, just like you! Fast lad, decent with a weapon, but not built for such labor. But you know, that lad knew how to read, write, and speak in a dozen tongues. He could identify metals and gems, plants and crafts from a hundred places I've never heard of." Varik shook his head as if in disbelief, brimming with pride. "That boy's been everywhere; he's met kings, rescued damsels from peril, and befriended the most arcane cults to gain their knowledge." Varik raised an eyebrow at Eowen. "If his stories are true. So, I set him up to educate my boys and the rest of the town, then he went and fell in love with the baker's apprentice!"

"His wife?" Eowen asked.

"Indeed. Duwiyin, sweet girl, traveler like him but from the north and west. She's of the Niude people. The Carrulians have a presence out there, but she'd managed to dodge them a good sight better than your cousin! Not as well read as him, but a good bit more sensible, I'd say," Varik said with a wink. "She ended up in our town to live for just a few months. Your cousin fell madly in love, and they decided to settle back in her home land. Duwiyin knew a family there that'd take them in, since she's an orphan. Tavo was all for it, and wanted to get access to the knowledge of the Niude scholars there. They got some secretive monks in that part of the world, or used to. Legends said they knew special magics and ancient lore about the start of the world." Varik shrugged. "How could he resist?"

"I see..."

"That's right. Not a year after they left, Tavo passed back through here on his way back to the jungle and savannah tribes. Said that he was headed home to get the blessing for their marriage and their child. Turns out she was pregnant with their kid, but her people can't name a kid, or even acknowledge them as a person, unless they get the blessing of some kind of family from both parents. She wasn't that far from her original home village, but our jungle and savannah tribes are a bit further away, so Tavo made the journey alone." Varik patted Eowen's head. "Brave lad, he'd do anything for that girl, and seems he almost made it too. But of course he had to return to make sure they're alright. I dearly hope they are." Varik shook off the worry. "No use getting worked up about things that can't be helped. Besides, now Tavo doesn't have to go all the way back to the tribes for his child to be acknowledged!"

"Oh, did he say he gave up on the tradition when he passed through a month ago?" Eowen asked. Varik laughed and mussed her hair.

"Of course not, he's got family coming to him! He'll be able to fulfill the rite for his wife and child and he doesn't even know it!"

Eowen smiled, a warmth spreading in her. Tavo was close, and after she reached him, her life could begin again. She watched the eyes of the big man guiding her through the woods as ahead of them the trees opened up to reveal rolling hills with houses of stone and wood scattered among them. Thatched roofs and smoking chimneys promised hospitality in each one.

"Varik, how did you end up here?" Eowen asked.

"Oh, I haven't talked about that since I met Tavo." He stopped and pointed back the way Eowen had come. "I was exiled from the tribes when I was but a babe."

Eowen's eyebrows shot up. She hadn't expected Varik to have a similar story to herself.

"Half Britchen by my mother, but dumped on my jungle and savannah tribe father. They were always looking for a way to get rid of me. He found her parents across the mountains, and I got passed around from one extended family member to the next till I ended up with some distant aunt of a distant cousin that happened to be Nemsto. I saw more of the continent across the ocean than most people do in their whole lives, though I was too young to remember most of it."

Eowen was horrified that he'd been put through an exile as a young child. When Varik saw the sad, sympathetic look in Eowen's eye, he patted her head.

"Don't look so down, young girl." The word he used for 'young girl' was in Eowen's language, and despite his poor pronunciation, it brought a wave of bittersweet nostalgia to hear it. "It's only the past. The Nemsto lands have long since been my home."

"I can tell," she said quietly. "This whole place... it feels so familiar." They passed by the village, and Eowen could see Nemsto people going about their business. Many waved and called to Varik, who waved back. The whole of the land

and atmosphere was suffused with the nostalgia Eowen had felt upon first approaching, a strange experience since she'd never seen Nemsto lands before. "Is this very much like the old world?" Eowen asked.

"It feels very much like it sometimes, though it's not exactly like any one place in the old world. The land is the same sort there might have been, but not exactly like any place that actually was." They paused atop another hill with the path leading further into the woods. "I hope one day my children will feel that this is their home."

Eowen patted his arm. "You've done well in manifesting this place, even I feel a great deal of comfort here."

"Hmm? Oh, no I didn't create any of this!" Varik swept his hand out to indicate the whole landscape.

"What? But... I can't sense anyone else powerful enough to have manifested so much." Eowen extended herself into the far reaches of her perception, feeling out for dreaming auras with great potential. She found none, though it was hard to sense much else besides Varik's intense presence.

"I've got no skill for creation myself. My domain is in battle, violence, but even the simplest things slip through my fingers." Varik attempted to manifest something into his hand, and though an enormous volume of shadow and light gathered at his call, they only pushed awkwardly around each other, like oil and water. "No, an old woman named Kamali is our crafter. I only supply her with the power for bigger things."

"I've participated in such works before! I've even seen whole villages collaborating. Did she create some kind barrier to keep the Storm away? I couldn't detect one, yet I've never seen it keep its distance like this." Varik shook his head and looked proudly at the sky.

"No, there's no barrier here. The thunder wilds just know better than to encroach on my lands. They cannot touch me when I choose to fight them, and with my sword I can cleave right through them." He patted the pommel of his weapon, and it seemed to Eowen that the dome of clouds shivered. "Come, we are close to my home. You will stay with my family while I muster a force to escort you to your cousin. I'd escort you myself, and do so better than a thousand of my warriors! But I must stay to protect my lands." They continued walking into the woods that lead up to a very large and wide hill beyond them. Varik seemed deep in thought as something occurred to him. "Hmm, though perhaps I could leave my weapon here, give it to one worthy of wielding it. It is the other part of my power."

"I've seen companies of your warriors clad in armor and weapons with glowing symbols on them. Were they made like your sword?"

"Not quite. This blade is one of the only things I created myself, it emerged from me as a part of me. All the armor and weapons our warriors use are made by Kamali with my aid, but they are linked to this blade and its power, which is linked to me." They followed the path around the hill till the trees parted to reveal a cottage very much like those Eowen had seen before. There were chairs out front, hewn from the kinds of trees they'd passed that surrounded a large oval table. "Cerapha! I'm home! I have a guest with me!" His voice practically shook the thatch.

"A guest? I thought there might have been a fight?" A gruffly melodic voice called out, muffled behind the door. Just before Varik and Eowen reached it, a Nemsto woman pushed it open. She was stout with graying hair that had once been blond, shorter than Varik but still much taller than

Eowen. Her resting expression seemed to find a joke in everything she looked at. She was bouncing a baby on her hip rhythmically, and had some kind of mess on her tunic. "Take her, Varik, I've got to clean off this spit-up." She handed off the child to Varik, who cooed at his daughter and settled her onto his belly as she tried to scale his beard.

"My wife, Cerapha," he said as the woman returned to the house.

"We'll meet properly as soon as I change!" Cerapha called over her shoulder.

"And my daughter, Elshaddai." Varik leaned so that the baby was eye level with Eowen. Eowen smiled and waved. Elshaddai tried to fit her hand in her mouth. Varik took one of the chairs in front of his home and gestured for Eowen to join him. He bounced the baby on his knee and babbled with her till Cerapha returned. "My darling, this is Eowen, Tavo's cousin and a dreamer of great caliber. Yes she is, isn't she?" Varik said the last part in a baby voice while offering his daughter a finger, which she proceeded to gum on. Eowen stood and bowed to Cerapha, offering a coastal tribe gesture of respect. The way Varik looked was expansive, seeing past Eowen, but his wife's gaze was piercing and perceptive, as though Eowen were a tangle of knots she was planning to undo.

"It's a pleasure to meet you," Eowen said as politely as she could, but Cerapha just eyed her, produced a pipe from her shirt, and knocked some ashes out of it. She gestured for Eowen to sit, and took the chair next to Varik. Cerapha pushed something into her pipe and held it out for Eowen.

"Mind giving it a light?" Without even thinking, Eowen made the material inside burn, and Cerapha took an appraising puff. "You do clean work."

Eowen blushed. "With small things," she said quietly.

"She's being modest," Varik said while playing with his daughter, who made gurgling noises and rubbed her eyes. "She's Tavo's cousin, and plenty powerful. Made it here through the Storm by herself on that great bird of hers." Varik gestured to the heron stalking around the yard, poking its beak through the tough flora.

"I was wondering what that creature was doing here." Cereapha looked the heron up and down. "Interesting... Tavo's cousin, eh?" Eowen shifted uncomfortably.

"Um. Yes?" she said, hoping to spark some conversation. Cerapha continued to exhibit no particular power, but seemed to see through Eowen in a way that reminded her of Mein.

"You're a long way from the jungle and savannah tribes, young lady. Did you come looking for your cousin?"

"Yes, I've been tracking him since before the fall." Eowen updated Cerapha on what she'd already told Varik, and more. She spoke about much of her journey, focusing on the noteworthy places and people she'd seen, the heroics of Varik's warriors, and the abilities of other powerful dreamers. Cerapha listened intently while Varik played with their daughter. By the time Eowen had finished speaking, Elshaddai was asleep on his chest. "And Varik has generously offered his forces to escort me to my final destination," Eowen finished. Cerapha puffed out smoke rings while considering what Eowen had told her.

"You've been following him since before the fall?" Cerapha asked.

"Um, yes. That's when I heard the rumor of Tavo being in the Britchen lands. No one in my tribe even knew he was alive before then."

Varik spoke up. "We must know our roots, for that is what we grow from, we must also seek beyond them, for it is in the unknown that we will become more than, uh..." He tugged on his beard thoughtfully. "More than... that. Hmm, your cousin used to say things like that, not that I can remember it properly. He was always quoting from some dead philosopher!"

Eowen laughed. "That sounds like the sorts of things he used to say when we were little, only more poetic! I've missed him for so long, and I know he's not the same as when we were kids, but speaking with Varik has reassured me that some parts of him haven't changed." Eowen looked down into her hands, and her expression vacillated between being shy and eager. "He once took me up to the top of a small mountain called Joramu some miles from my home village. It was dark when we got there, and I was scared and little, but he knew the way even though he was also young. We climbed all the way to the top in the dark, and I was cold and scared, but he found a cave sheltered from the wind and built a fire. I asked him why we were out so late and he said something like what you just said, Varik, something like; 'Because we don't know what it's like away from home. How can we know what home is like if we don't see what's different?'"

The memory had returned so vividly that it gave Eowen pause, and she held her breath a moment. It had been years since Eowen had thought of that day, yet as she thought back on it, her journey had begun on Joramu mountain. She'd even camped in the same cave. Speaking with Varik was opening clear memories that Eowen had forgotten from the fog of childhood. More than the survival lessons Tavo had taught her, she was recalling the juvenile philosophies that he'd wax.

Ultimatums about freedom, knowing oneself, curiosity about the world beyond, and respect for one's origins. "It's so good to speak with someone who really knows him now," Eowen whispered. "He's the only family I've got left."

"You lost the rest of your family in the fall?" Varik asked gently.

"I was banished." Eowen froze as the words left her mouth. She hadn't meant to state it so openly, but it had slipped out. She glanced between them, nervous to see their reactions. Varik had his eyes closed and was nodding slowly. Cerapha was puffing on her pipe in a nonchalant way, still staring at Eowen.

"Banished, eh? For some foolish reason like me, I'd wager," Varik said. Eowen didn't know whether to correct or agree with what Varik had said, so she opted to stay silent. "Doesn't matter either way, you're our guest now and you'll have our aid in reaching your cousin," he asserted, his expression a mix of empathy and camaraderie. "Isn't that right, love?"

"That's right." Cerapha blew some smoke, then tapped out the ashes from her pipe and stowed it back in a pocket. "Well spoken, husband." She looked up at the overcast dome of their land. It had gone from a bright gray to a dark bruise of purple. "It's getting late, I'll start on supper." Cerapha started to stand, but Eowen waved her down.

"Please, I'm your guest, allow me." Eowen closed her eyes and dipped into familiar places in her dreaming, conjuring a spread of her favorite foods from across the cultures she'd visited. Grilled fish from the southern islands, spicy hot-root soup from the valley tribes, Britchen breads, hearty and sweet porridge from the jungle and savannah tribes, and a dozen other delights from across the lands.

"Hmm, nice to have someone around that can actually make things," Cerapha said, nudging her husband.

"Just eat, woman! Thank you Eowen, you honor us."

They feasted, and it grew dark as the sourceless light of the Nemsto land faded. After, Cerapha fed Elshaddai while Eowen answered more of Varik's questions about the world, its dreamers, and the things she'd seen along the way. He wasn't terribly interested in the forms the Storm-warped people had taken, only that they were defeatable. What Varik did enjoy hearing about were the other powerful dreamers and their abilities. Eowen told him of The Nagirr'Om, Hani and his crew, Aiyano and Nolyi, and some of the stranger beings, such as the lantern bearer she'd traveled with for a time.

"The variety in this new world is invigorating!" Varik crowed. "Our scouts can't go far and the companies of warriors we've sent have not returned, so we have heard little of the world."

"Were you worried your warriors were all dead?" Eowen asked.

"Not at all, I can feel them drawing from my power through the sword." Varik looked to the east. "Some have died, but they are strong and, in force, unbeatable. I'm glad you've come all this way, Eowen. You've probably seen more of this new world than anyone other than your cousin, or maybe that Hani person and his crew."

"We receive very little news here," Cerapha said. "We used to get some from the west before the thunder-wilds got worse." Cerapha didn't smile, but a subtle, warm joy was present in her features. "The world is still peopled, and they still make things, sing songs, dance, and tell stories. So many of our people feared we were the only ones left in this empty world, but it is not empty. It is full and filling up, who knows what the new generations here will bring." Cerapha sighed and settled more comfortably into her chair. Elshaddai was asleep at her breast and Cerapha kept the tiny girl swaying gently in her arms.

"Your daughter... She was born after the fall," Eowen realized, and though it was an obvious thing by the girl's age, there was still a certain gravity to the observation. Cerapha kissed Elshaddai's head, and Varik gazed at them with such love and tenderness.

"You didn't see many babies born after the fall in your travels, did you?" Cerapha asked, and Eowen shook her head. "So many loved ones lost and so much to fear, it makes sense that we would not see much new life in the world. Elshaddai, she is the first of the Nemsto born after the fall. She is a symbol of hope to our people that, despite the loss of our world, we will have a future." Cerapha sat, rocking her child and closed her eyes. "We've got to seize hope wherever we can, don't we?"

Varik leaned over to kiss his wife on the forehead. "You're awfully dramatic this evening, my love."

Cerapha pushed him away but was smiling. She closed her eyes and sighed. "Go show Eowen to a bed, you fool."

Varik stood, and Eowen dismissed the remains of their dinner from the table. "Of course, come along."

"Thank you again for your hospitality," Eowen said.

"Tavo is family to us, young lady, that means you're family too." Cerapha waved them off. Varik led Eowen inside the cottage to a loft with a mattress full of feathers. It had a curtain for privacy and smelled of pine and straw.

"Tomorrow, I'll take you to Skelad's family and begin mustering my forces," Varik said. "Sleep well."

He left her alone, and she put barriers of sound around herself so she could have complete silence. The heron came in a moment later, stalking along on its stilt legs and snaking its head back and forth. It found Eowen in the loft and nudged her with its beak so that she could make room for it.

"Ok, one moment." Eowen lifted herself to scoot over, but stopped. She ran a hand up and down the heron's smooth spear of a beak, then gently pushed it away. "I'd like to be by myself while I sleep this time." The heron backed up, shrugged its wings, and left her be. Eowen snuggled into the mattress with the blanket over her, and fell into her deepest dreaming.

****

I'm here, I'm listening... Please, tell me more about Love and the Giant, it's how I've always known I'm going the right way. Why are you silent now?

****

Eowen awoke bitter, confused, as though a friend had badgered her into a game of hide-and-seek but had left her hiding without ever seeking. She descended from the loft, grumbling, and came across a young man that was the spitting image of Varik if he was a teenager, lighter skinned, and less muscled. He had shorter braids and not much beard to speak of, but his similarity to the older warrior was still jarring.

"So you're Tavo's cousin," he said, looking her up and

down. Cerapha emerged from a room in the back of the cottage with Elshaddai in her arms. She flicked the young man's ear. "Ow!"

"Introduce yourself properly. Good morning, Eowen."

"Morning, Cerapha." Eowen got fully down from the ladder.

"My apologies for my rudeness," the young man said with a flourish, looking mischievously at his mother. "I am Branlyn, son of Varik and Cerapha." He and Eowen clasped hands.

"My name is—"

"Eowen!" he interrupted. "Cousin of Tavo, as I said, and also from the tribe where Father was born. I hear you've been across the whole world!" He pumped her hand excitedly.

"Not the whole world." Eowen disengaged.

"And that you work with the dead, and that you're very powerful, but not in the way my father is, so in what way are you?" Cerapha sighed and opened the front door.

"Varik, your son is menacing Eowen!"

Branlyn rolled his eyes and dashed out the back door. "We'll talk later!" He bumped into his father, who was already in the doorway. Varik steered his son out the door and around the house.

"Come on lad, we're off to see what kind of force we can muster."

"Let's spar later!" Branlyn called through the door. Cerapha shook her head after them.

"He pretends he's more of a fool than even his father was at that age, but the truth is he's more a thinker than a fighter. Let's get ready, I'm taking you to Skelad's family."

After a quick meal, Eowen, Cerapha, and baby Elshaddai were through the woods and back to the village Eowen had seen with Varik. The heron followed behind and attracted plenty of attention. Cerapha didn't know Skelad's extended family personally and had to ask around, but it didn't take long. One village over, to the south of where Eowen had arrived, they found the home of Skelad's mother, Gwenhwyfar. Cerapha approached the door, but Eowen stopped her by the sleeve.

"She's not home," Eowen said.

"That so?" Cerapha glanced at the door then at Eowen. "I suppose we can always come back later."

"No need." Eowen was scanning the village, looking for something. "I know your people are buried with their families, excluding when they must be laid to rest on the battlefield." Eowen turned to Cerapha. "Where do you honor the dead here?"

Cerapha led Eowen through the misty woods around the village till they reached a fence of black iron. As they approached the gate, Eowen's eyes were fixed on a hunched form at the back. The gate squealed when Eowen opened it, a shy noise that seemed to fit the place. The woman didn't seem to notice.

"I'll go ask if that's her," Cerapha offered, but Eowen felt certain it was, not through a thread of power leading her on, but from some subtler place in her spirit that told her this was the place to be.

"No need, I'm certain she is Gwenhwyfar. Thank you for guiding me, Cerapha, I will proceed from here."

"Are you sure you don't want an introduction? After all, you're a stranger here." Eowen made a polite gesture of dismissal. Her power was about her now, the shadows and light slowly gathered in a gentle aura around her that layered the world in a haze of her presence.

"Wherever I have gone, I've always arrived as a stranger, but we all have this in common." Eowen swept her hand to encompass the cemetery, met Cerapha's eyes, and let her see the tight knot of pain she carried in her chest. Eowen was seeing through Cerapha to the grief the older woman had already passed through. "See, we've only just met and already we know one another."

Eowen approached the hunched figure wrapped in a thick cloak. The woman was older than Eowen would have thought, her hair long since white, her skin as layered and wrinkled as her clothes. Cerapha waited at their periphery to see what would happen.

"Gwenhwyfar, mother of Skelad?" Eowen whispered.

"Who're you?" The old woman looked Eowen over till she noticed the heron. "That's a great big thing you've got with you. You look a bit like that lad, Varik."

"My name is Eowen."

"You've not speaking Nemsto, how can I understand you?"

"I knew a man who could create things that let people understand each other." Eowen tapped her lips, and Gwenhwyfar huffed.

"Not the strangest thing I've seen, I suppose." She returned to contemplating the graves.

"Who were they?" Eowen said, gesturing to the three markers before them.

"Hmm. My youngest son, my daughter, and my granddaughter. You're too young to have children, so you wouldn't know that no parent should have to bury their children."

"Let alone their grandchildren," Eowen whispered. To Cerapha's surprise the old woman smiled at Eowen, and Eowen smiled back. "You've honored them well though."

"As much as I could, I suppose, but not so much as I'd like." The old woman responded with a breath of a laugh. "How'd you know my name anyway, Eowen-girl?" Eowen turned to the heron and reached into its feathers to retrieve the urn. "What's that you got there?"

"I have been looking for you, Gwenhwyfar, Mother of Skelad, the iron teeth of the wolf. I am here on behalf of your grandson, Fis, whom I met far from here."

"Fis? Wasn't he off with his father?"

"He was," Eowen whispered. "Fis no longer fights. He was injured beyond his ability to do so, but he has found love and a place for himself in the world, though it is far from here."

"That so? For the best it is, that lad wasn't suited for warring. You didn't come all this way just to tell me that, though." Gwenhwyfar glanced at Eowen, a hint of the old woman's sharp mind glinting through her eye, though age had done much to dull it.

"I'm here to deliver the body of your son, Skelad, who died in battle." Eowen spoke simply; her voice was quiet enough that it seemed to be swallowed up by the earth and the fog and the graves, but Gwenhwyfar heard her.

"Oh..." she said when Eowen handed her the urn. "His body's in here then?" Gwenhwyfar stroked the urn with her knobby fingers. "This all that's left of him? A hand or a foot?" The old woman stared at the urn looking very tired. Eowen shook her head and reached for the lid, popping it off. Tendrils of light and shadow leaked out in slow, graceful ribbons that coalesced upon the earth before them. First, the ribbons formed an oblong shape, then they took on a human shape, and soon the remains of Skelad, the iron teeth of the wolf, lay before them. Fis had cleaned and dressed his father's body, though his body and armor still bore the damage from his final battle. Skelad was not as tall as Eowen had thought he'd be, but was quite broad. He had white hair that was braided, lines from a lifetime of frowning rather than smiling, and even in death did not look at peace. He had his mother's pointed nose, different eyebrows, and a certain wildness that continued to permeate through his still features.

"Such useful magic, fitting bodies in little pots to take dead boys home to their mothers." Bitterness entered Gwenhwyfar's tone, and tears wet her eyes. "Such clever magic you've used to bring me my son's corpse. I suppose you didn't have enough clever magic to save him, hmm?" Eowen stared into the old woman's eyes and did not flinch.

"No Gwenhwyfar, I did not have enough power to save your noble son, only to bring him to you." The old woman was shaking, her lips set in a grimace. For a moment, her features perfectly matched the battle-set ones of her son, but in the next moment the fight left Gwenhwyfar. She didn't have the energy to keep it up.

"Fine, fine, that's how it is then, isn't it?" Gwenhwyfar eyed an empty plot next to the other three. "I've buried three children already, what's one more?" Eowen felt the thread spring into being between them. The brand over her heart from the mountain folk glowed and the heron stood over her, no longer a mere creature, but a herald.

"Have courage, Gwenhwyfar. I will be your hands in this." The old woman took Skelad's hand and stroked his face while Eowen dug the grave in the space next to the others. She lifted Skelad's body and set it in. Gwenhwyfar gave Eowen instructions for manifesting the stone, and in less than an hour the iron teeth of the wolf was laid to rest beside his family. Eowen and Gwenhwyfar sat together staring at the stone, but the thread had not fully dissipated. Eowen did not push the old woman though. Gwenhwyfar would speak in her own time. During the process, Cerapha watched and waited and paced, but did not approach, for even the thought of doing so prompted the heron to turn and fix an eye upon her. Cerapha did not want to interrupt the proceedings, but feared that Eowen, unaware of their culture, would misstep somehow. The artificial light of the Nemsto land moved from midday to afternoon, and Gwenhwyfar, who'd been lightly dozing for some time jolted back awake as her head bobbed down. She looked at Eowen curiously.

"What are you still doing here?"

"I'm not sure, I only know we're not quite finished yet, are we?" Eowen scanned the graves. "Have we missed some kind of ceremony?"

"No, no, nothing like that," Gwenhwyfar said. "We've done the best we can."

"What do you mean? Is there something missing?"

"Hmm, not in the way you're thinking, Eowen-girl." Gwenhwyfar shrugged off the question, but Eowen was staring at her intently. "This is plenty good enough, thank you."

"But?"

"Hmm, but... there is a flower that grows, or rather, grew a long time ago. We'd plant them on graves in the old world. I've tried to make them myself." The old woman reached out with a trembling hand and manifested a flower into the earth of the grave. It had thorns, a straight stalk, purplish petals that dipped into a bell shape, and saw-edged green leaves. It was a woefully incomplete creation, more illusion than anything. "It was called elstith, the silent bell. I've no skill for that creation that people do, so this is the best I can manage."

"I see." Eowen reached into the woman's mind as carefully as she could, so as not to be detected, and found memories of the flower. Eowen saw what it was supposed to look like, but also what it represented to the old woman; the thorns warded fell spirits away, the purple petals were valor, the leaves collected the tears of other spirits as dew, and the stalk grew as tall as the life that had been lost. The Nemsto believed it was shaped as a bell that would ring only for spirits to wake them from their bodies so that they could go on to the afterlife. It had been grown upon graves since ages past, longer than any record or memory. **"There is always worth in the effort,"** Eowen told the old woman, **"but let us do this right for him, for all of them, yes?"**

Eowen took the woman's hand and placed it palm down on the mossy grave. When their fingers met, the dark earth beneath the green Eowen reached down into the waters of her dreaming. Shadow and light flowed and a flower bloomed upon the grave, but it did not stop there. Together, their power danced through the cemetery, and on each plot elstith bloomed. Soon, there was an entire field of silent bells swaying in the breeze, ringing out their choir that was only for the dead. Eowen stood and helped Gwenhwyfar up.

"Thank you," the old woman said. "This will do." The thread was gone, and Eowen's power faded to its normal presence. "Who are you, really?" Gwenhwyfar asked. Eowen turned away and stroked her heron's neck.

"Just someone passing through." Eowen left her there and rejoined Cerapha. "Thank you for your guidance. My work is finished."

"So that's what your work is like." Cerapha scanned the

cemetery appraisingly. "Should we see her home?" She gestured to Gwenhwyfar.

"No, I think she'll be here a bit longer," Eowen said as they watched Gwenhwyfar pace through the cemetery, gazing at the flowers with a curious, distant look on her face.

"Come, we'll take the long way." They started down a path in the opposite direction they'd come from. It was a foggy, winding one that took them through many woods and past other villages. They were back at Cerapha and Varik's home just before dark.

"Hello ladies, how did you fare?" Varik's booming voice greeted them as they entered. He was with his son and another man as they pored over scrolls on a desk in the corner.

"Eowen found her right away and planted elstith on every grave in the cemetery." Cerapha said, handing her daughter off to Branlyn. "It was very impressive."

"A bunch of flowers? Impressive?" Cerapha's son scoffed. "That's nothing! Now, my father's compass was impressive."

"You'll show respect for our guest, you brat!" Cerapha flicked at her son's ear but he dodged out of the way, dancing with his little sister in his arms. "Besides, your father's compass is crooked."

"It is?" Eowen looked to Varik, who was suddenly very invested in the lists before him.

"It absolutely is!" Branlyn crowed. "Come outside, I'll show you." He shouldered out the back door with his giggling sister, and Eowen followed him to a training field. Embedded in the ground in the middle of the space were two intersecting lines. When Eowen stood over the X the lines made, she felt that she was indeed in the center of the world's compass.

"It *is* crooked! Southeast and northwest are smaller than the other two directions! How did that happen?"

"My father, for all his power and skill, is not the most precise person," Branlyn said, though he was glowing with pride. "With two swings he set directions of the world, but did not take the greatest care in ensuring they were angled correctly. But he's noble and strong, and one day I'll be powerful enough to travel the new world like my brother and carry out his will."

"What's your brother like?" Eowen asked, and Branlyn began dancing around the field, flourishing an imaginary sword with one hand while he pretended Elshaddai was a shield with the other.

"I'll tell you about his first campaign against the Carrulian slavers, turned by the thunder-wilds into monsters!" Branlyn went on, telling stories of his father and his brother's bravery while, in the cottage, Varik continued pouring over the scrolls with the other man.

"You just have to point that out everytime, don't you my love?" Varik said.

"Can't have people thinking you're perfect." Cerapha kissed him on the cheek. Varik smiled under his beard and stepped back from the desk, rubbing his eyes. "Thank you, Ugin. We'll continue tomorrow," he said to the Nemsto man.

"We do not have many warriors suitable for a campaign into the western thunder-wilds," Ugin said as he collected his scrolls. "Are you sure it's worth the effort and risk? We could always wait for some of our warriors to return."

Varik took a seat and rested his hand on the pommel of his sword, which hummed under his touch. "Maybe, maybe not. Either way, we cannot trust that our warriors will return at all. We should prepare for that possibility."

Ugin scratched his chin and glanced at his scrolls. "Tomorrow, then." He made a gesture of respect and left. Cerapha sat beside her husband and took his hand.

"You're thinking of sending Bran with Eowen," she said.

"How'd you know?" Varik asked.

"You can't hide your thoughts from me, love. You're as clear as water."

Varik sighed. "He's the most capable warrior left in our lands. Which, unfortunately, isn't saying much." A long pause passed between them.

"Varik, I love our son, but he isn't... You."

"I know." Varik and Cerapha stared at the back door, through which they could hear the muffled sounds of Eowen, Bran, and Elshaddai laughing and playing. "So, she made flowers?"

Cerapha stroked her husband's arm and let him change the subject. "They were... special somehow, more than they appeared to be." Cerapha shrugged. "It's hard to explain, but it was impressive. You should go see them tomorrow."

"I've got to meet with Ugin again, figure out who to send. Then I need to get armor and weapons made for them and get them trained up, which will take a long time. Especially to forge the equipment." Varik pinched the bridge of his nose and let out an exasperated breath.

"Let me take some of that burden off you, you're no good at such things anyway." Cerapha pinched his cheek and Varik laughed.

"You're right about that, my love. What did you have in mind?"

"You get to forging with Kamali. I'll get Branlyn trained up and pick out the rest of the company." Varik eyed his wife suspiciously.

"I thought we agreed he wasn't much suited for the warrior's life?"

"And have I ever failed to prepare someone for war?" A wild look came into Cerapha's eyes, a reflection of the battle-lust that Varik had shown Eowen upon her arrival. Hers was sharper than her husbands, colder and more cunning. If Varik's battle-lust was an infectious, raging fire, Cerapha's was an insidious frost in one's bones.

Varik shivered, then laughed. "Poor Bran might not love you after you're through with him." Cerapha shrugged.

"He'll love me again when he doesn't die in the maw of some monster out there. He'll be cleaving through a great and terrible beast shouting: 'Thank you, Mother!'" Varik laughed and kissed his wife's head, then stood and walked to the back door.

"I'm certain you're right, as always." He pushed open the door. "Enough playing, it's time for supper!"

****

Where have you gone? Did I do something to drive you away? Or do you not want me to listen anymore? I still don't know why I had to listen before, I still don't understand. Will I ever understand?

****

Eowen spent weeks with Varik's family in the Nemsto lands. There was little work for her to do, as most had already made their peace with those that had died from the fall and could not mourn the warriors that were dead far afield. So Eowen spent most of her time wandering the lands and seeing its beauty. Between that, she meditated or accompanied the family on errands or to visit their friends. She learned a great deal about the Nemsto; how in the old world they had worshiped only one god, but recognized a rotating pantheon with the current head-god decided by the stars. They adored dishes with pickled and fermented fish, which Eowen found disgusting and subtly changed in her mouth to taste like other food. They had a complex writing system that, unlike most Eowen had encountered, had a different symbol for almost every word, though apparently more often than not most of their scholars couldn't agree on which variant was correct. Eowen also told her hosts more of the world to the east, describing her adventures, Tavo's creations, and the wonders of the world.

The Nemsto land contained many types of stone and earth with a richer variety of colors than Eowen had heard of anywhere else, and their art often involved layering sand and carving into the stone. Their designs were terribly dull compared to what Eowen had grown up with, but apparently the point wasn't to make them pleasing. They'd pick the toughest stone and prove their skill by the clarity of the design they could produce in such unforgiving material. She learned that the Nemsto had always been a culture of warriors, but hadn't been a militant one till about seventy years before the fall. A king rose to power by unifying the disparate people to end the threat of Carrulian slavers. The Nemsto had once been scattered tribes of dangerous, wild people, too risky for Carrulians to antagonize. They used to have their own slaves as well, and the king that unified them did so on a platform of creating an organized slave-trade.

Eventually, new leadership suggested capturing the slaves of other cultures, primarily Carrulians, and giving them places in the Nemsto military to exact revenge. By campaigning, the former slaves could earn plots of Nemsto land or safe passage home.

By Varik and Cerapha's time, the Nemsto and Carrulians had become the two dominant feuding forces in their part of the world, jerking the neighboring peoples around in their conflicts. After the fall, the Carrulians had doubled down on capturing others, exposing themselves to the Storm, while Varik, the immensely powerful dreamer that he was, directed his people toward the fortification against and the hunting of the Storm. The Nemsto had simultaneously become one of the most impactful and most secluded peoples of the new world, which they all seemed to take great pride in.

Sometimes, Varik would ask about he and Eowen's former tribe, and, on occasion, she'd be willing to answer. Eowen tended to focus on simple things like food or songs or celebrations. Other times, Varik or Cerapha would ask about Eowen's family, and those were questions Eowen was less willing to answer. 'What was your father's craft? Your mother's? What were they like? Did you have siblings, cousins, aunts, uncles, grandparents? What was Tavo like as a child?' After three weeks with Varik's family, Eowen was more open to answering such questions, though she still deflected most that didn't have to do with her cousin.

"Tavo was... the best of us," she answered one night after dinner. "He was a natural leader, even as a little kid. All the other children followed him, though sometimes we got into danger as a result. He wasn't afraid of any of the animals that maybe he should have been. Have you seen a scar on his back from here to here?" Eowen drew a line from the back of her left hip up to the middle of her spine.

"I asked him about that, he said it happened while fighting a monitor-bear," Varik said while he and his son gathered some practice equipment to train with out back. "Those beasts are massive and got eight limbs on them! I doubted it, but he's never lied to me about anything else."

"Ha! It was a baby, he was just lucky the mother wasn't hungry and dragged it off without killing him. He didn't cry in front of the village when his friends brought him back. Tavo always tried to act tough in front of adults. I think that and how the other kids followed him is how he got picked to be the apprentice to the ranger."

"And he was like a sibling to you?" Cerapha said.

"His parents died before I was born, so we took him in. Even when I was a baby, he'd take me everywhere with his band of friends. When he was apprenticed to our ranger he'd teach me what he learned. It wasn't much, but I'd never had trouble traveling alone in the jungle or savannah because of him." Eowen let out a small laugh devoid of mirth. "I was getting sent to other villages every few months from the age of ten, often without an escort. Who knows, I might not have survived without what he taught me."

"Why were you sent to other villages?" Cerapha asked.

"My mother—" Eowen hissed and cut herself off. She'd sounded so harsh saying that word, it had given her pause. Varik and Bran weren't paying close attention, having wandered off outside, but Cerapha was watching Eowen very closely. "M-my... family was hoping I would find work that suited me." Cerapha was silent for a time, and Eowen avoided her eyes by playing with Elshaddai.

"They must be proud of who you became after the fall,

then." Cerapha spoke slowly and carefully. "You've clearly become an impressive young woman, and you have found a worthy calling." Eowen glanced up and saw the look Cerapha had about her, the one where the older woman seemed to see right through her.

"That wasn't till after I left." Eowen tried to indicate that the conversation was over with her tone. Cerapha shrugged and let it go. At times, Eowen wondered what Cerapha and Varik would think if she told them everything, how she'd been a disappointment to her mother all her life, how she'd abandoned her people to look for Tavo and that her mother was dead because of it. How she had been banished for nearly killing her own father with her former lack of control.

It's the past, it's not who I am now. I have found my work and I have grown beyond my mistakes, but would they still help me if they knew? Would they still trust me, or like me, or feel like... Tavo's family.

Eowen didn't let conversation move back in that direction if she could help it, and a month after she'd arrived, Branlyn and the other recruits' training began in earnest. They were all around Eowen's age, none with the stature or experience of other Nemsto warriors she'd seen, but she trusted Varik and his wife make them capable. For all of Varik's dreaming power, his skill as a fighter was incomparable to Cerapha's. When armed, she moved in a deadly blur of strikes for which there seemed no defense or counter. Even without a weapon she was terrifying, and could disarm and down any of the students, or several at once. When Varik wasn't out forging equipment with Kamali, he was Cerapha's practice dummy. Her recruits ran, swam, climbed, and fought in full armor for hours each day, and Cerapha trained right alongside them while still making time to nurse Elshaddai.

Branlyn was indeed the most capable of the students, but was still miles behind his mother and father. After two weeks of her brutal training, Cerapha deemed them capable enough to survive in the thunder-wilds, but not strong enough to escort someone into the west. She gave them a week to rest and recover before the next phase of their training would begin. There were plenty of bruises, broken bones, and concussions to shake off. Branlyn didn't grow cold towards his mother as Varik had joked, but bore the strains with silence and steel. His parents were surprised to see such a hardened side to him, and it became clear that he had his mother's penchant for strategy and technique. Varik, on the other hand, was a rage fighter through and through and had never properly learned much technique. Not that he'd needed it, for he could enter into a state of madness and achieve feats of violence paralleled by few. It was not an uncommon thing for Nemsto warriors to use madness to fight, but they historically had achieved it with herbs that induced the state. Varik was one of the rare few that did so without such supplements, and this state of mind seemed to partially source his dreaming power as well.

After their week of rest, Varik was ready to take Cerapha's recruits to train in the wilderness. All they needed at this point was to become tougher and more experienced. No one was more suited to putting the feel of a real battle into a heart than Varik. He would teach them as best he could to dream like he did, with a rage and battle-lust that could resist the Storm or even repel it. He'd hunt them through the woods, make them know desperation, and force them to face unequal odds valiantly. Cerapha and Eowen watched them depart, then they returned to the cottage. Eowen prepared tea and bread with honey, while Cerapha sank into a chair.

"Gods, I've gotten old and soft," she said.

"Doesn't seem that way to me," Eowen said, picking up Elshaddai from her crib to bounce on her hip. She floated the refreshments over to her host, and Cerapha made a gesture of thanks. "I didn't see all the training, but you were..." Eowen searched for a word that wouldn't offend.

"Oh they're terrified of me, I made sure of that." Cerapha downed a mug, and Eowen filled it back up. "But I'm still out of practice. I used to lead armies in the old world, trained them too." Cerapha held out her arms for Elshaddai and Eowen handed over the squirming baby. "I settled down when my oldest was born, I'm out of shape." Cerapha gestured to indicate her whole body, but what little skin Eowen could see was all steely muscle and battle scars.

"Right."

"Not many know that, before the fall, Varik wasn't considered much of a hero." Elshaddai was squirming too much, so Cerapha put her on the floor to crawl about.

"He wasn't a... bad person, was he?" Eowen asked, taking a seat next to Cerapha.

"Oh, Varik used to be brutal." Cerapha lit her pipe and blew out some smoke. "He was so full of anger and hate in his youth. When I found him, he was more beast than person." Eowen had trouble thinking of the big gentle man full of joy and love in such a way. She knew he could fight like a wild animal, but he wasn't that way day-to-day.

"That rage warrior trait," Eowen said. "Is that what you mean?"

"That's a part of it. Why do you think Varik was passed around from one distant family member to the next in his youth all across the continent? It wasn't because they wanted a better life for him, I'll tell you that." Cerapha's eyes were far away in memory. "That man grew fast, and he grew strong. His guardians would try to discipline him with violence out of fear, and he'd savagely fight back. Got himself kicked out of every village and family there was by the time he was fourteen. I don't think he was in one place long enough to learn much of their language. Eventually, a Nemsto raiding party found him in a village they'd tracked Carrulian slavers to." Cerepha met Eowen's eyes. "He'd already killed every last slaver and a number of villagers. The family he'd been with claimed he had a distant family in the Nemsto lands and begged them to take him. I doubt he was ever related to a Nemsto, no matter how distant, but they took him anyway. Wanted him because of his ability to kill. For years, that man was treated like a beast, kept chained up till one of our raiding parties let him loose on their enemies. He killed a few of his handlers, but they let it slide."

Eowen's palms were sweaty when she remembered her first meeting with Varik, and she now realized how close she'd come to death at his hands. Had she pushed to exert her power against him, he might have cloven right through her. Yet the man Cerapha was describing couldn't possibly be the same that cuddled with his daughter and treated his wife and son with such love.

"How'd he become the way he is now?" Eowen asked as Elshaddai gummed on her robe from the floor. Cerapha's lips curved into a prideful, self-congratulating smile.

"That was all my doing, dear. When reports of a squad killing so many Carrulians by themselves in such a short amount of time came in, I was dispatched to assess why and possibly invite them to be honored by the court. I expected to find a most elite force, but instead I met with a pathetic crew full of cowards that had been sending one feral man to do their bidding for years. I ordered Varik to be taken from them and brought to my training grounds." Cerapha massaged her hands and blew out a long stream of smoke. "Those were some of the hardest years of my life. I told the court that the success of the squad had been the work of one man, but that he was untrained and could become even greater." Cerapha looked terribly sad then, her age showing more than Eowen had seen before. "It took months just to get him to stop trying to kill me." Cerapha pulled aside her clothes to show scars in her shoulder, chest, and ribs that looked less like they'd been from weapons and more like the scar Tavo had from the monitor-bear. "He was all hate and pain, Eowen. I don't think he'd ever known much love in his life at all. I tried everything I knew to establish communication. I brought in translators who knew foreign languages, offered food, comforts. I tried beating it out of him, and I certainly left more scars on him than he did on me."

"You... civilized him, though?" Eowen said. "Eventually?"

"Hmm, I wonder if it counts as being civilized if the beast is still in there? All I know is that one day, about a week after my mother died, he stopped fighting me." Eowen froze and held her breath while Cerapha paused. "I came to his cage and he was sitting there, calmer than I'd ever seen him. He knew enough Nemsto to speak with me, and for the first time he did. He said I seemed happier now." Cerapha breathed out a small laugh. "I was. I hated my mother. She was scum who drank and beat my siblings and me. I had to pretend I loved her, otherwise people would think there was something wrong with me. It's why I ran away to become a warrior, but Varik... he understood my hate, the kind one has for the people that are supposed to love you but don't. I laughed about her death with him and showed the scars she'd left on me. He showed me the scars his guardians had left on him. Eowen, you've no idea how strange it was to find out that Varik had been hurt more by his guardians than the dozens he'd fought in campaigns. It's an incredible feeling, knowing the cruel people that were supposed to protect you are dead."

Cerapha grew quiet and looked at Eowen, smiling warmly. Eowen was still stiff, nervous, curious to hear the rest of the story but uncomfortable with where her thoughts now wanted to go. Cerapha reached out to take Eowen's hand. The young woman flinched, but after a breath she let the older woman give it a squeeze.

"So... You bonded over... hating? Your family?" Eowen asked in a whisper, as though it were dangerous to say out loud.

"Not really, we didn't bond, we just... stopped fighting each other. If anything, we bonded over our love of battle. He'd been fighting so long he didn't know how to do much else. Sometimes it seems like that's still all he's good for. He never asked me why he was brought to a battlefield, or what we wanted from him. Varik isn't a stupid man, but he is a simple one. I suppose, in my own way, I'd also been doing nothing but fighting all my life. Early on I thought I was better than him because he was feral, but that same beast is in me, too. Mainly, he let me speak with him, and I learned that he understood everything going on. He didn't care about much; women, comfort, drink; so long as he had someone to fight. I promised him the opportunity if he'd follow my command, and it was as simple as that. I led squads and armies of the most skilled warriors for years. Varik was among them, but I didn't use him as a crutch." Cerapha looked triumphant. "My warriors have always been the best, and Varik learned to master himself, though many were still afraid of him. We fell in love in those days, ranging far and wide, fighting many battles. He mentioned his first squad leader was Skelad? That man was under my command as well! He didn't act out anymore and even let other warriors train him in the arts of war at times. More as a way to show he was on our side than to actually learn anything. Varik is a man who needs no instruction in the art of killing." Cerapha thought for a moment. "It was a terrifying thing, to love someone again after so long."

"How..." Eowen's mouth was dry and she tried to wet it. "Are you saying it was hard to love again because of your mother and how she treated you?" Eowen asked. Cerapha nodded.

"How can you trust yourself to love when you hated the people you were supposed to love? How could I love a husband or children if I hated my own mother, if I laughed when she was dead? It's hard to find a new family when you're still afraid of your old one, even long after they're gone."

Cerapha was watching Eowen closely again, and Eowen didn't need to look into the woman's mind to see what she was doing. *She's trying to talk about me, but I know who my family still is, that's why I'm looking for him. And I'm not a fighter, I don't hate my —*

Eowen slammed her thoughts shut and smoothed her expression out. "I'm going out."

She dislodged Elshaddai then moved to the door. Cerapha didn't stop her. Once out of sight Eowen put up barriers of sight and sound so she'd be imperceivable to most. Then, she approached her heron that was curled up in the grass, napping.

"Let's go," Eowen said, but the bird didn't respond. "Get up, I want to fly!" The heron opened one eye to look at her, then closed it. "Wake up!" Eowen kicked the heron.

The world froze, the creature's power somehow solidifying the world around her like ice. She was held like that, immobile and helpless for only a few seconds as the bird made her helpless, then let her go. Eowen stumbled back, unfrozen. It wasn't a hard kick, Eowen was not strong, it wasn't even a very accurate one as it glanced off the heron's side. The bird didn't flinch or even register that it had been struck, but Eowen had never tried to hurt it before. The heron was eerily still, eyes still closed, but somehow she felt like it was watching her.

"I-I'm sorry, I don't know why I..." Eowen backed up, hot tears welling up, a furious burning in her stomach growing along with a coldness in her hands. She turned and ran. When she'd run out of sight, she launched herself into the air, flying without the heron, and when she'd flown for hours over the Nemsto lands and reached the southern border, she stopped. Eowen's tears fell and she gasped for breath. She beat her fists against her legs, and the twisted knot in her chest burned worse than the being pierced by The Nagirr'Om's spear.

I hurt her! Me, not the other way around, it was me! I was a useless disappointment, I couldn't do anything right and she's dead because of me! Cerapha... doesn't understand.

Eowen stayed there, curled up and floating with her tears and frustration for hours until she fell asleep. The bone heron arrived, swooping under the floating form of Eowen, her eyes crusted with salt and her face twisted up. The bird moved so that Eowen was on its back, and it gently nipped at her robe, tucking it around her like a blanket. Then, it flew

Eowen back to Cerapha's cabin and deposited her outside the front door. Eowen cracked an eye open and met the heron's.

"I'm sorry," she whispered. "I shouldn't have kicked you." The heron nipped her ear. "Ah! Stop, I said I was sorry!" The heron continued nipping at her till she got up and stood before the door. "Fine, thank you for bringing me back." Eowen took a deep breath and entered the cabin. Cerapha was asleep in her chair with Elshaddai on her lap, playing with a wooden toy. The baby squealed when she saw Eowen and tried to crawl off her mother's lap.

"Woah, there." Cerapha caught her daughter and glanced up at Eowen. "Feeling better kid?" Eowen shrugged.

"A bit."

"Want to talk about it?"

"No." There was a stiff, woody silence between them broken up by Elshaddai's baby babble.

"Take her, I'm going to make us something to drink." Cerapha handed her daughter over before Eowen could respond. Eowen didn't mind. She liked taking care of the little girl. Cerapha prepared a sweet, thick drink made from tree sap with water strained through dried mushroom powder. She handed Eowen a cup and they went out back to sit in the yard behind. Eowen manifested a cloth to dip in her drink so that Elshaddai could have some and would stop trying to grab at her cup. It half worked. Cerapha was looking up at the sky, overcast as always by the dome of the Storm. In the distance, Eowen could feel Varik's dreaming aura as he trained the recruits.

"I don't want to talk about me..." Eowen began.

"Understood."

"But you never finished telling me how you and Varik did

it. How you moved past your fear of love." Eowen pulled up some grass and handed it to Elshaddai, who flung it away.

"You're holding the reason," Cerapha whispered as the baby pooped in her diaper. Eowen handed her over when the smell spread, and Cerapha was laughing. "Good timing, kid!" Cerapha tickled her daughter's belly with her nose and set to changing her.

"So it didn't happen till she was born? But that was after the fall, and you've had two sons for years before that."

"Ah, well, I didn't literally mean Elshaddai, I meant when we had children together. We had a lot of sex on our campaigns, and soon I was pregnant with my oldest, Yets. Varik and I have always been rough with one another when sparring or making love, which was fine with me. He didn't know how to be gentle, I think, or he found it convenient that I was someone he didn't need to hold back with. As soon as we knew I was carrying a child, he changed completely." Cerapha shook her head. "You can't really know or understand, Eowen, how completely he changed. You've only known the Varik of now, but before he was so terribly powerful and so uncaring of the harm he caused. It was fine with me, that made our sex more exciting and our sparring more effective. I told him I was pregnant, fully prepared for him to abandon responsibility, abandon me." Cerapha was beaming, her joy apparent. "I thought he would, I was ready to accept that and give the child to some family better suited to raise it, but for a week straight he did not leave my side once, not even to shit!"

"What! Why?"

"He didn't trust anyone with my and the baby's safety! Not even me." Cerapha poked her daughter's belly and Elshaddai swatted her away. "Eowen, he was by my side at all times. He learned how Nemsto marry and proposed. He built the home we lived in before the fall." She gestured around them. "It was just like this. I was still terrified. How could I trust a man with such a history of violence with my child after only nine months of gentle care? How could I trust myself? But... He insisted we try, and all my worries disappeared when he held Yets. That kid fit in the palm of his hand, but Varik curled his whole body around to hold him." Cerapha laughed. "The way Varik held his child, a tree could have fallen on him and Yets would've been fine." Cerapha sighed. "How could I be afraid with a man like that by my side?"

A long silence spread between them, but it was comfortable. A breeze rustled the leaves outside, a distant voice rang out from the closest town, Elshaddai yawned and squirmed into a comfortable position.

"I am afraid," Eowen whispered, and Cerapha had the grace not to say: 'I know.' "Why did your mother beat you and your siblings?" Eowen asked.

"I don't know. My eldest brother killed her himself." Cerapha's voice was clinical, her expression neutral, but Eowen could sense in the woman's mind and dreaming aura the rage that these memories once had. Time had disarmed them though, and they'd cooled into stale sadness. "I think she saw us as a burden, or a curse thrust on her."

"A burden... Cerapha, I don't know if I'm the same as you, but when my mother died I was—" Eowen took a deep breath that hurt, "—happy!"

Cerapha wanted to reach out to the girl, but something stopped her, a sense that she needed to let whatever was happening happen.

"I was so, so relieved! I felt so light and free, and I hate myself for feeling that way. I miss her, but I also hate that I miss her, and I hate myself for that too and it all hurts so much that I don't know what to do or think or feel!" Eowen pressed her fists to her chest and gritted her teeth. "And I'm not allowed to feel this way because if I'd just made something of myself it would've all been ok, but I didn't and I ran away, and then the fall happened and she died because I wasn't there!" Eowen coughed out a sob. Cerapha waited patiently. Elshaddai slept soundly in Eowen's lap. "She died because I wasn't there to save her, and I should feel so terrible for that, and I do, but I'm also so happy I wasn't because if she was still alive I'd still be... there." Eowen slumped over, and Cerapha gently moved Elshaddai to her lap. Then, the older woman put an arm around Eowen and pulled her close, leaning their heads against each other, side by side.

"Sounds rough," Cerapha whispered, and Eowen nodded weakly. She felt there was more to say, more context to give or more thoughts to work through, but her spirit was so terribly weary she had nothing left to give to the moment. "How about I be your mother?"

"What?" She gave Cerapha an incredulous look.

"Why not? I'm good at it." The older woman stroked Elshaddai's hair, a wry smile on her face. "Much better than either of our mothers, I'd say." Eowen couldn't help letting out an exasperated laugh.

"Wouldn't that make Varik my father? No thank you!"

"Fair enough!" Cerapha patted Eowen's back and laughed quietly to herself.

"How'd you get me talking about this?" Eowen asked. "I don't talk about it, I don't think about it at all if I can help it." Eowen pressed the tips of her fingers to her chest. "There's no answers, just more confusion and hurt."

"I know."

"What do I do? You fell in love and had babies, then suddenly your life was all better, wasn't it?" A bitter edge was in Eowen's voice, but Cerapha didn't take offense. "Is that what I'm supposed to do?"

"It really was better after Yets, and after each kid it kept getting better." The older woman gazed at her daughter. "The old fears always came back, but year after year it always got better because of that man, our boys, and now this little one. I don't think that's for you though, is it?"

"No, it's not," Eowen answered immediately. It was one of the few things she was entirely certain of.

"I don't know, Eowen." Cerapha stood up with Elshaddai and yawned. "I'd wager no one really knows what to do with this kind of mess inside you. But there's me, and plenty of others that'll stick by you while you figure it out." Cerapha started rocking her baby and singing softly. "To the west he came, the king of stars, with skin of silver and eyes of golden—"

"Cerapha!" Eowen called to her and she turned. "Thank you." Eowen tapped her chest with her finger tips. "It did help, just a bit." Cerapha bobbed her head, then left to walk out alone into the yard.

Eowen lay on her back and stared up into the Storm, too full of thoughts and feelings to parse them apart in her exhausted state. The heron entered her field of vision, its spear-like beak splitting the sky, and when Eowen saw it, things felt much simpler.

"Hey, come here," she said to the bird, which dipped its beak down to her. She stroked the beak and scratched the feathers on the back of its head. "I think I love you. It's easy to, you're always with me and you always support me, even though you're just a bird. Do you love me, too?" The heron nudged her with its foot, then squawked, opened its wings, and drifted off to land on the roof of Cerapha's cottage. "I'm going to take that as a yes."

****

I'm still listening. I'll be patient.

****

In the following days that Eowen spent with Cerapha, neither encroached on the subject of old families. They were content to appreciate the quiet and peaceful time they had now. The Storm that domed their lands was an ever-present reminder that such peace could always break, but it had not yet and they took advantage of it. They traveled across the Nemsto lands and met with Cerapha's friends. Young folk that looked to be around Eowen's age invited her to games and asked her questions. Elshaddai spoke her first word, which was 'no,' and used it as a surrogate for a full vocabulary at every opportunity. It seemed the peaceful respite in Eowen's life would be maintained until Varik returned with his recruits. He'd taken them to the far western edge of their lands where it was almost entirely wilderness. Varik didn't have to worry too much about the damage he could cause there, but occasionally Eowen would feel his aura of power cleaving through the world dozens of kilometers away.

Eowen was awoken one night, feeling reverberations

through her far-reaching senses from a powerful presence. At first she was annoyed, thinking it was Varik causing a ruckus, but it couldn't be, because the presence was coming from the east, and Eowen could feel Varik to her west. She rolled upright from where she'd been dozing in the grass and ran for the cottage.

"Cerapha!" Eowen shouted as she slammed the door open. Elshaddai woke up wailing and Cerapha burst from her room a moment later, groggy and wild-eyed.

"What's happening?"

"Something is coming." Eowen pointed east as, with each passing moment, the approaching presence revealed itself to be more and more powerful. "I don't know what it is, the Storm's making it hard to identify, but it's big." The presence of more entities encroached on the edges of her aura, and Eowen's hands began to shake. She reached out with her mind for Varik's and found it.

It's Eowen, I've sensed something powerful approaching. I'll go to meet it, back me up when you can.

Varik was startled, but there wasn't time to acclimate him. Eowen put the message into his mind, then turned her full attention to the east.

"We need to find Varik," Cerapha said.

"I've already contacted him," Eowen said, and rushed back out the door before Cerapha could ask how. "Stay in the house. Heron—to me!" Eowen took a running leap and her bird swooped under her, taking off. Eowen laid the most powerful barriers she could over the cottage, drawing in huge, crashing waves of light and shadow that knit into an invisible wall. She hadn't drawn on so much power outside of a funeral in some time, and the atmosphere around the cottage popped with scents and sounds and unintended manifestations. Eowen ignored it; she didn't have time to carefully reign in her dreaming, the entities were approaching too fast. The heron bolted for the cliff-edged border of the Nemsto lands and within seconds landed where Eowen had first arrived. She let out a mirthless laugh as thick shadows from above and harsh starlight from below twisted about her, craving form. *Not long ago it was Varik greeting me like this.*

The entities were close now, moving through the thunder-wilds at a clipped pace. Eowen rose into the air, bolts of abeyant dark and quiescent light burning in her fists. Pools of water from which sprang birds of crystal, orange songs, drips of burning honey, and a thousand other strangenesses curled off of her as she sailed into her dreaming and gathered her power about her. Eowen could still sense the presence of the Storm at the edges of her spirit, but the threat of Varik kept it at bay.

The mass of powerful presences, heralded by one particularly massive one, cut through the Storm-wall on a huge ship that loomed over her. Eowen had never seen such a vessel. It was easily a hundred and fifty meters long, with its tallest mast half that in height. Most of the passengers' auras of power deflated when Eowen pushed her presence down upon them, but one, the largest, met her with a wall of its own. A sliver of worry entered her as she pushed against the being, and it pushed right back, all but matching her. The force of the two played against each other like continents and the dome of the Storm around them shook under the forces.

I should say something... what would Hani say?

Eowen floated out over the waters and spoke to the beings on the vessel with an enhanced voice. "You approach the new world lands of the Nemsto, which are under the protection of the greatest warrior of the new world, Varik, and **Eowen Mortician. Submit and make your business known.**"

Among all the responses Eowen had expected or hoped for, joyous laughter from a somewhat familiar voice was not it. She glared down at the deck, looking for the source among the crowd. One of the crew, a young man with long, twisted hair, skin darker than her own, and a bright smile leapt into the air and flew directly at her. He was the source of the great power, and he was pushing right through the force of her presence.

"Stay back!" Eowen launched an arc of destruction at him, but it curved around him and dissipated, as if her subconscious itself had rejected the attack. The young man came to a stop, floating about a meter from her. His dreaming aura dancing with hers in a familiar way, as if they'd both been waiting to do so. In seconds, they merged into a vortex of unbound potential. The young man grinned, and waves of familiarity washed over Eowen as the ocean in the depths of her spirit met the mountains in the depths of his. "Hani?" Eowen whispered.

"Finally, I found you!" He was taller, longer haired, and more defined in face and body. The last of his baby fat had been shed, and the beginning of a beard and mustache were forming. Despite the changes, the smile was unmistakable, and his eyes still shone with a thirst for adventure. He held out his hand for Eowen to take but she launched herself at him and they went tumbling through the air laughing. The crew of the ship watched as their captain and the powerful stranger cannoned into the sea. "Woo!" Hani cried as he burst from the water holding Eowen's hand and dancing her through the sky as manifestations saturated with joy shot off them like fireworks. Eowen wrapped her arms around the young man and tackled them both to the grass on the cliff edge.

"Hani! What are you doing here? You look so different, your ship is so different, you have so many crew members now!"

"Ha! Eowen, you look the same, but..." Hani's dreaming aura washed over and through her own, so different yet familiar. "You've changed, too." A wide wooden ramp appeared on the edge of the cliff, and the members of Hani's crew stepped onto the Nemsto lands single-file. "I felt a pull here, like a thread," Hani said. "You might have heard, but I'm the patron of all those who quest! I feel a pull when someone is close to their goal but needs my help." Eowen's eyes went wide and her expression took on an aspect of wonder which Hani matched, seeming to glow with excitement. "That must mean you've almost found Tavo!" Before Eowen could confirm, she saw another familiar face among Tavo's crew, an old Britchen man with kind eyes.

"Ordwell!" Eowen rushed to the man and embraced him.

"Oof! Gently, I'm not as young as I used to be. It's been some time, my friend." Eowen could feel his quiet laughter as he hugged her back. Eowen felt the touch of a mind upon hers and recognized it immediately.

"Ahn?" she said with her mind-speak.

"Eowen! Your friend Hani visited Tavo's land and everyone except Luu said Rennick and I should go with him! So we snuck aboard." The little boy shared a disorienting reel of memories from the time Eowen left to the present.

"Too much, kid! Show it all to me later," Eowen said in her mind, and Ahn laughed.

"I'm going to stay in my room on the ship, but I'll send

Rennick up to visit you." Eowen pulled back from Ordwell, and Hani slung an arm over her shoulder.

"I'll introduce you to the rest of the crew!" They turned in a circle with Hani rattling off names and stories that Eowen immediately forgot. She met them all with grace and friendship, greeting as many as she could with their own languages, cultures, words, and gestures. Hani seemed to have achieved all his dreams of amassing a crew of powerful and amazing people from almost every corner of the new world. Even the first few he'd left with from Nolano almost three years ago were still with him. He had three new acolytes of The Nagirr'Om, and Eowen recognized a Nemsto warrior, the man named Nifroht she'd heard was traveling with Hani. Even Strife made themselves just perceivable enough to say hello before disappearing again.

"Greetings, Eowen Mortician. I am pleased to meet with you again."

"Nice to see you're still around as well, Strife," Eowen whispered.

"Alright, enough introductions! Nifroht and Yets have assured us of the hospitality of their people, and we've been stuck on the ship for far too long! Let's celebrate!" The crew cheered and Nifroht led them to the path Varik had taken Eowen through.

"Wait!" Eowen called. "Did you say there was someone named Yets?" A man in his early twenties responded to the name and turned to face Eowen.

"You called for me, Eowen Mortician?"

"I can't believe I didn't recognize you, you're the spitting image of your father," Eowen said, approaching the mountain of a man and offering her hand. He was as tall and broad as Varik, darker skinned than his siblings, but with a certain Nemsto beauty that was all from his mother. "Yets, it is an honor to meet you. Your family took me in, just as they did my cousin Tavo in the old world." Yets took her hand, and the way it closed around her own was just like Varik's.

"I've heard much about you, but not all of that. You're from the same tribe as Father, correct?" Eowen nodded. "Eowen Mortician, you are the first of Hani's crew, cousin to my best friend Tavo, and already beloved by the rest of my family!" Yets pulled Eowen in for a crushing hug and laughed loudly. "Then you are already my sister!"

"Oh! That's nice! Too tight!" Eowen squeaked out, and Yets set her down on her feet.

"Son!" Varik's voice burst out across the field. His sword had been drawn, but the moment he met his son's eyes it fell from his hand.

"Hello, Father!" The two warriors barreled across the field and slammed into each other, pounding each other's backs and shouting merrily.

"Eowen! This is my eldest!" Varik shouted and pointed at the young man as if he weren't almost a clone. "Come, everyone! Whoever you are and whatever your reasons for being here, so long as you are in the company of my son, you are our most honored guests!" A cheer went up and the crew paraded through the woods to the rhythm of Varik and Yets's laughter. Eowen and Hani held back as Rennick ran up the ramp and jumped into Eowen's arms.

"Hello, kid!" Eowen used the word that Luu did for her children. "You've gotten taller!"

"Did Ahn tell you we left without telling mom?" Rennick's eyes were shining. "She's going to be so mad!"

"When did you get a rebellious streak?" Eowen mussed his hair. "Come on, we've got a lot of catching up to do!" She met Hani's eyes and held them, each moment with her old friend awash with the strange interply of the familiar and not. Yet despite all that had happened, both could still feel what they had upon first meeting: That in all this new world, they were each other's greatest equals, true peers amidst gods and horrors alike. Eowen pulled Rennick by one hand and clapped her other on Hani's shoulder, pulling them into the heart of the Nesmto lands.

Not only Hani's crew and Varik's family, but the entire village they passed through on the way there got caught up in the festivities. For all that Eowen had learned of Nemsto culture, she'd never seen them celebrate, but in that they were professionals. Before the parade had even reached the village, barrels of wine, mead, spirits, and alcohol made from fermented livestock milk were rolling into the streets. Cookfire pits as long as small ships were dug and burning merrily as children ran around being menaces. Bright clothes were donned, ancient dances drunkenly reenacted, and songs were forcefully metered to the stamping of feet that shook the ground. Hani's two Nemsto crew members had apparently introduced the rest of the crew to some of their classic traditions, and within minutes the entire mass of them had acclimated to the revelry. Hani and Eowen lagged behind with Rennick covering his ears. Eowen manifested a barrier to deaden the sound so that only someone standing next to them could be heard, the rest were muffled.

"That better?"

"You must show me how to do that." Rennick rubbed his ears then laughed at something out of nowhere. "Ahn is excited to see what drunk minds are like! Greivej wouldn't let people get inebriated." Ahn did the mental equivalent of an innocent shrug, and Eowen laughed and patted Rennick's head. "Oh, did you ever find out why Tavo was traveling so far before the fall?" Rennick asked.

"I actually did," Eowen said. "He was following some Niude tradition from his wife where their marriage must be sanctified by the family of both for their child to be named, I think." Eowen shrugged. "It's something like that."

"I've heard of that before..." Rennick was deep in thought now, poring through his library of a mind. "It's called giving your toti, or otuary, or... I can't remember the term! I'll check my records and get back to you later."

"Still obsessed, I see." Eowen squeezed Rennick's hand. "I'll take you somewhere quieter that I know you'll like." She led them to the home of Kamali, where the old woman had put power into her cottage that acted much like Eowen's barriers. She could keep out light, sound, and the presence of those she didn't want to bother with. Eowen knocked on the door, and it opened just enough for a suspicious eye to peek out.

"Leave me out of all that nonsense! I don't care whose birthday, wedding, or death it is!"

"Kamali, let me introduce you to Rennick, the greatest scholar of the cultures of the old world." Rennick blushed and looked down at his feet.

"Who, this lad?" Kamali glared and scanned Hani up and down. "He's too handsome to have had his nose stuck in scrolls. Makes you wince, gives you wrinkles and a bent back." Eowen shook her head and nudged Rennick forward.

"Rennick, let me introduce you to Kamali, the foremost expert in Nemsto runes and culture."

"That kid? Puh!" Kamali took on an imperious tone, but opened her door a crack wider. The boy had gotten over his embarrassment and was looking over the runes he could see on Kamli's door with great interest.

"You combine the far east under-shade runes with the standard set here," Rennick muttered, fumbling for parchment he always kept in his pocket. "I know the grammar of both, but I can't make out the meaning here. Are you invoking... wooden feet and... the frozen net of Ikol?" Eowen had never seen Kamali impressed by anything, but the old woman's prickly manner flicked to immediate warmth.

"Close! There's a third, less common set with a separate grammar mixed in called the West-Moss Kufk after Hwrang Kufk who—"

"Who was the third Nemsto to put their oral tradition into writing!" Rennick was bouncing up and down, and for the first time Eowen saw Kamali smile.

"What a delightful child! Come in, come in, I've got some cookies and recreated manuscripts I know you'll appreciate."

"So did runes have power in the old world?" Rennick asked.

"Some think so, but that was never true. I use them because they help me focus my dreaming power, but otherwise they're just random shapes." The old woman ushered Rennick in amidst scholarly discussion and slammed the door in Eowen and Hani's face. Hani caught Eowen's eye and she shrugged.

"Well, he'll be fine for the next week," Eowen said. Hani laughed and gestured for Eowen to follow him back to the revelry. The whole village and crew were parading their way to Varik's residence. Eowen met with Cerapha to explain that everything was alright, then she and Hani found a semi-quiet seat atop Varik's house to catch up. As the mass celebration got drunker, rowdier, and more mirthful by the second, night descended. The favorite game was walking in a circle around Varik's compass and exclaiming that it was crooked. Varik's recruits had returned to enjoy an evening of celebration before returning to their suffering in the woods. Eowen and Hani had some mead of their own, introducing their friends and acquaintances from a distance. Hours passed, and as things wound down the conversation turned to Eowen's search for Tavo, how she'd followed his rumors all the way to Luu's family, and had been stuck there for a year. She told him about Tavo's history with Varik, and where her cousin was now. Hani listened, drinking up every detail and adding it to what he'd heard in his own travels.

"So, he can really move through the Storm without any kind of escort," Hani said. "I wonder what his aspect is that lets him do that?"

"Maybe it's landscapes, or biomes? Like the one he made near Luu's family."

"Wouldn't he have to stop moving for that to work?"

"Maybe." Eowen shrugged. "Maybe it's as simple as the atmosphere around him."

"We'll find out soon." Hani snapped his fingers, letting loose streamers of manifestation that twirled through the air in ribbons of citrus and crawls of bats. "I'll get you to him, don't you dare doubt that."

"How could I?" Eowen said. "You're the famous Hani, through whom any quest or journey can be done. You're famous!"

"As if there's not plenty of rumors about you! Some of them hard to believe." Hani gave Eowen a strange searching look. "Eowen of the Dead, cowing people into honoring the deceased. She faces off against cults and the Storm alike, changing the landscape of the new world by confronting death with an iron will, an open heart, and sometimes a mountain of corpses."

"So some still call me that, do they?" Eowen muttered into her drink, and Hani laughed.

"Quite a lot of people are afraid of you!" He nudged her with his elbow.

"Sometimes I have to be scary." Eowen shrugged. "But sometimes... it was the Storm." Hani closed his eyes and nodded. It was a fate he'd seen many fall to.

"Most do call you Eowen Mortician, or some equivalent in their language." He looked to the west, nostalgia radiating off him. "Did you know that some people worship you now?"

"Excuse me? I think Ordwell's translator wasn't working there," she said, though they were speaking the same language.

"It's true! There are statues and even shrines to you in some of the Britchen lands and beyond. Though that's not totally uncommon, there's little cults to a lot of powerful folk. Old habits from the old world." Looking at Hani now, the way he moved and spoke, Eowen could believe that a religion would emerge in his wake. Her friend wasn't a child anymore, and in many of the ways Eowen had imagined the heroes of old stories to look and carry themselves, Hani seemed to embody them.

"If it's rumors then, there's quite a lot more circulating about you," Eowen said as they left the town and joined the procession through the woods to Variks home. "You and Stormwake have done more to fight the Storm and bring people together than even The Nagirr'Om." Hani shrugged, nonchalant, but Eowen wouldn't let it go. "Hani, I couldn't have made it here without you." She held up a hand to block his rebuttal. "We only traveled together a few months, but I still look back at that time as when everything changed for me. I couldn't have gotten through the new world without the hundreds of ships modeled after yours or manifested by you personally. You've made it possible to move through this world, but... for me you made it possible long before then." Eowen paused and they let the cool night, the smell of food, and the fading revelry wash over them. "Even after we parted ways, you kept me going," Eowen whispered.

"That's... uh." He squirmed, embarrassed and stifling a smile. "What about your cousin?"

"Well, of course, but until I find him my search for Tavo is... abstract." Eowen frowned. What she'd said felt true, but it also felt strange to phrase it that way, as if it diminished Tavo or her search for him.

"What are you going to do after you find your cousin?" Hani asked.

"Well... I've thought a bit about that." Eowen chewed on the inside of her cheek, trying to summon up details from erstwhile daydreams. Hani waited patiently. "He and I could live together of course..."

"Of course."

"He does have a wife and kid, so I'd have to give them space."

"Makes sense to me."

"His kid would be like my nephew!"

"What about your work?"

"My work..." Eowen hadn't thought about that. "I suppose... I'd still travel at times, following the need for Eowen Mortician." She gestured to Hani. "I sometimes thought it would be nice to rejoin your crew. Before I found out about Tavo's wife and child, I'd thought he could too."

Eowen looked down into her hands. "Of course that probably won't happen. I don't know, I haven't given it that much thought, I assumed it would all work out somehow." Hani looked like he'd expected that answer.

"You've performed a lot of funerals, haven't you?" Hani said.

"I suppose."

"I've been beside many on their quests, as well. Most are just seeking loved ones that they were separated from, but many were seeking answers about this world, or the old one. Some were seeking love, or revenge, or power." A strange look came over Hani, eager but also pained and tense. "Sometimes all someone wants is something from the old world again, a song or a flower, or a recipe their mother used to make. The stories don't tell you about those moments. You'll hear about Captain Hani and his crew fending off a Storm-monster that looks like a giant fish, but you won't hear about Tula, who only wanted to remember a single verse from a poem her father used to recite." Hani breathed a small laugh. "That took a year and half, sailing across the world, looking for someone who knew that damn poem! We did it though." He waved a hand dismissively. "What I'm getting at is, I've seen a lot of people get exactly what they wanted, but it wasn't always what they needed. More often than not it left them adrift with no real sense of what to do with their life next." Hani threaded his hands together into a bowl and stared into them. "I'm going to get you to Tavo, I swear it, but... don't let that happen to you, please. There will always be those that need you, and you'll always be the first member of my crew."

Eowen put an arm around Hani's shoulders and swayed back and forth with him for a moment till she felt him get less tense. "You're a little drunk, aren't you?" she whispered.

"No!" He pushed Eowen off, and she started laughing. "I'm being sincere because I... well. I am a bit drunk, but I care about you!"

"Ha! When did the Hani I remember become so serious?"

"You're a fool!" he shouted, but couldn't keep up his grim countenance any longer. "I get it, you'll be fine, the great Eowen Mortician of the Dead need never fear the pitfalls of the rest of us mortals!" Eowen laughed, choking on her denials and the two flopped around on the roof; their drinks had gotten to them both.

"No, no, no!" Eowen got out. "I never had to worry about what I'd do next because I could always join back up with you, even if Tavo wasn't with me." It took Eowen a moment to realize how true that statement was, but she couldn't pin down when she'd started to feel that way.

"Well, I'm flattered, but what if that wasn't an option?" Hani asked as he twirled a hand in the air.

"What do you mean?"

"Suppose I didn't want you back in the crew?" he said, and Eowen snorted.

"Impossible, I was your first member."

"Hmm." Hani paused to think about it. "Suppose I was dead?"

"How would that even happen?"

"I don't know, from the Storm or a fight with someone more powerful. The how isn't important, just indulge me."

"Well, then I'd probably go back and live with Luu." The words left Eowen's mouth before she'd had time to think, and they surprised her. She didn't know if it was the drinks or Hani's sudden presence or the spirit of the party below loosening her up. Either way, thoughts and declarations were flowing freely. It was occurring to her just how many lives she'd touched and how many would take her in. "And if I can't go back and live with Luu, I can come back here. I'm like Elshaddai's aunt; that's Varik's baby daughter. If that doesn't work, I can go live with Gran in Nolano, or with Genia and the mountain folk." Eowen's voice drifted off and she found herself staring into the distance, heat in her cheeks and pleasant tingling in her hands. "I've got... people everywhere," she whispered, and in the silence that followed a thought occurred to her. "What about your quest? Did you ever find your father?"

Hani froze with his cup at his lips. He turned away so that Eowen could not see his face. "What, is something wrong?" Hani shook his head but didn't speak, so Eowen reached out with her senses, her mind, and her dreaming, already tangled up with Hani's, searching for what his reaction meant. There was nothing there though, nothing at all in his mind or spirit to back up his reaction. It was as if the part of Hani that she was looking for simply did not exist. He gave her a hearty pat on the back and stood up.

"It's a long story, we'll get into it another time." His expression was back to one of excitement and joy, but Eowen could sense nothing from him, not even a shroud.

I suppose he's not hiding something. Even if I didn't know what it was, I'd sense a barrier.

Hani walked to the edge of the roof and whooped loud enough to get the attention of his crew. "Tomorrow, we sail into the heart of the Storm! The Storm started in the west; it is the origin of our world's madness. We do so in search of the legend; Tavo of the jungle and savannah!" The crew's response shook the cottage. Eowen tugged on her friend's sleeve.

"Hani, no. Varik has been training his recruits to escort me into the Storm. We should wait till they're ready as well."

"Oh, I see." Hani cleared his throat. "Maybe not tomorrow, but when Varik's warriors are ready!" Another round of cheering went up, and Varik stood as soon as it had quieted enough for him to speak. He pulled his son, Branlyn, up by the wrist with him.

"I testify that they are ready to take up my mantle, tomorrow you sail!" The gathering exploded with cheers, and the singing, dancing, and drinking began with even greater vigor than before. Hani pulled Eowen by the hand off the roof to join them. They drifted down, and soon her worries were swallowed up by dance, song, and the whirl of unbound dreamers filling the air with drunken joy.

* * *

Eowen awoke with her head resting on her heron in the center of the compass, surrounded by resting Nemsto and Hani's crew. They'd all managed to find soft grass, warm beds, or boulders to sleep on. Eowen groaned, forced herself up, and gathered the power to heal her hangover. Hani stirred behind her where he'd passed out on the other side of her heron. The grass next to him shifted strangely, and Eowen realized that Strife was beside him, barely perceivable.

"Welcome back to the world of the living." Eowen turned to see Varik sitting nearby looking worse for the wear.

"Hungover?" Eowen asked.

"I doubt any will not be."

"Here." Eowen extended her healing to Varik, and he perked up as soothing waves pushed the pain out of him. "Picked up a bit from a healer I knew. Her apprentices were better than this, but it does the trick."

"You all are so capable of using the power this world

affords us in such spectacular ways that it never ceases to amaze me." Varik looked at his hands, enormous, scarred and calloused. "There is only one thing I can do." He looked up, a curious expression on him. "Wake that lad." Varik pointed at Hani. "Bring him inside." With that, the big warrior made for the cottage, pushing aside unconscious folk as needed.

Why's he acting so strange? Eowen thought, but she followed his instructions and shook Hani by the shoulder. "Wake up, Varik wants to talk to us about something." She applied a healing power over him as well, but he still looked terrible for a minute.

"Uh, I think I might vomit," Hani muttered.

"Just hold still, this'll help soon." After a moment the two of them were feeling better, and they headed into the cottage. Varik, his sons, and Cerapha were already seated around their round table, waiting. Eowen and Hani took two open seats.

"Greetings," Cerapha said to Hani. "We met briefly yesterday, but you have already been a dear companion of my son for some time. He speaks highly of your quality as a captain." Yets nodded to confirm what his mother had said. "Thank you for looking after him."

"I guarantee you, it was the other way around," Hani said. "He's gotten us out of plenty of scrapes."

"And I'll get you out of plenty more!" Yets clapped Hani on the back. Cerapha gestured for them to settle down and squared her shoulders. She was not being a mother at the moment, but the commander of armies as she'd once been known.

"As you may have heard, Hani, Yets, before your arrival we were training a company to escort Eowen into the Storm."

Everyone but Varik nodded. "Varik and I said as much, but it was a lie."

Branlyn looked at his mother in disbelief. "Do you mean we won't be helping Eowen to reunite with Tavo? What did we train for then?" Varik put a hand to his son's shoulder and shook his head. Bran was breathing heavily, anger and shame evident on his face, but he retreated and was silent.

"Eowen will still receive an escort from the Nemsto, but it will not be you and your company, Bran."

"Ah, of course, it'll be me!" Yets said. "No offense little brother, you've definitely gotten bigger and stronger since I last saw you, but there's no substitute for experience." Bran stewed but kept his silence.

"No, Yets, you'll be staying behind as well," Cerapha said.

"What? Then who's going on the quest?" Yets looked around the table, and Varik stood up.

"Bran, rise," Varik said, his voice deep as stone. Bran did as he was bidden. "We lied, Cerapha and I, to you and your company. Only two things safeguard our home from the Storm; myself, and my blade." Varik drew his sword from its scabbard and held it flat across his hands. Its simple scarred iron hummed with such power as to rival all the dreamers in the room. Silver runes glowing on the blade were the only other trait it seemed to possess. "This sword carries my spirit, son. It connects, links, and empowers all the weapons and armor our people wield in this new world. Even if I were to fall, it will give strength to our people for generations. It cannot leave our lands, do you understand?"

Branlyn looked as though he didn't understand anything that was happening, but nodded anyway.

"You and your company have made us proud, and you are as worthy as any Nemsto warrior in history to campaign against our enemies... but you are not fit to face the danger in the west." Varik turned to Yets. "Nor are you, son. Nor are any of our people a match for those thunder-wilds... Except for me." Varik whispered the last part. There was no brashness in his declaration. He was not putting down his sons or extolling his greatness, but plainly stating the truth of the matter. Cerapha bobbed baby Elshaddai on her knee, the only one unable to grasp the gravity of the moment. Varik moved to stand before Branlyn and handed the young man his sword, and the moment he did it was as though a page had turned in the world. The atmosphere shuddered, Bran stood straighter, and Eowen could feel the Storm watching them.

"Me?" Bran whispered.

"Yes."

"Him?" Yets gestured incredulously.

"Show respect." Cerapha flicked her son's ear. "There stands your captain." Yets opened and closed his mouth, looking around as if expecting someone to tell him it was all a joke, but the room was silent, the tension in it thick.

"You, Branlyn, have proven yourself to be loved and trusted among your fellows. You've proven yourself skilled and clever enough to lead like your mother. You are strong enough to bear this responsibility." Varik met Yets's eyes. "I predict that in five years time Bran will have no equal among our people save me, but for now he still needs you to support him, Yets. For now, you are stronger and more experienced, but together, you, my sons, will keep our lands safe." Varik put his hands on Branlyn's shoulders, and fixed him with the animal eyes of the warrior he kept under control, always. "Do not doubt yourself. Your mother and I are not wrong in our judgment."

He let go of Bran, and the young man sank down to his seat, staring at the sword as if he couldn't believe it was there. Yets stared at his brother, deep in thought but no longer arguing. Varik took his seat again, and Cerapha cleared her throat.

"It is Eowen's campaign though, and she will approve all decisions." All eyes turned to her and she glanced around the table, very much uncomfortable with being given such authority.

"I... uh, defer to your wisdom." Cerapha broke from her serious countenance for just a moment to give Eowen an encouraging look. "I mean, I approve this."

"Then it is settled. And with the arrival of Hani and his crew, our path becomes ever clearer. Hani, you have arrived with a large and impressive group, but not all of them are suited for such battle, are they?"

"No, they're not. We've sometimes left the more vulnerable members of my crew under the protection of local settlements when we needed to face significant danger. I had intended to request such hospitality from your people." Hani made a gesture of respect.

"Granted. Your people are free to create their own dwellings on unoccupied land. Or make more land if able." Cerapha met the eyes of those gathered until she stopped at Eowen. "The only matter left is for you to determine when to embark."

Eowen put up a hand and immediately deflected. "Oh, you should probably ask Hani, it's his ship and crew after all."

"I can be ready tomorrow," Hani said.

"Uh, but what about Varik?" Eowen gestured to the big man.

"I've been stuck here without any action since soon after the fall!" Varik tugged his beard with a look of craving about him. The gathering turned back to Eowen and waited.

"Tomorrow then," she said, almost too quiet to hear. "We set out tomorrow."

Hani stood up, and the air about him shifted, becoming denser and more textured. A wind that touched no other seemed to be at his back and light bent around to shine upon him. His outfit was loose, and through it Eowen could see the same mountain folk brand over his heart that she bore. It was glowing anew, as if freshly set.

"**Tomorrow, a journey that began before the fall of our world will see its final steps taken.**" Hani faced Eowen, and in his eyes she beheld a spirit as vast as the sky and timeless as the stars. "**I am Hani of the Path, and this will be done.**" Hani took Eowen's hand, and the greater spirit within him filled her own with his sense of certainty. She found herself thirsting as never before for the deck of a ship upon rolling waves with the wind at her back. After a moment, Hani closed his eyes and let go of Eowen's hand. The brand on his chest faded along with his greater spirit, and when he opened he looked again it was the look of her old friend. There was still a spark of the divine within his expression, able to be called upon. "Ready now?" he asked.

"I think so." Eowen nodded, and after that things happened very quickly. Varik and his sons went to meet with the other warriors and explain the situation. Hani was delighted to stir his crew into action, but Eowen stayed in the cottage with Cerapha and Elshaddai.

"Funny lad," Cerapha said. "So eager to rush into danger." Her voice lilted strangely.

"He's always been that way," Eowen said.

"Not that my husband's any better, seems like all those men want is to go to war. Foolishness." Eowen noticed how Cerapha's unruffled countenance had been rapidly deteriorating. Her leg had a nervous bounce and her jawline was tense. Eowen took a small peek at her mind, and couldn't help but laugh. "Did I miss something?" Cerapha asked.

"You want to come along too, don't you?" Cerapha rolled her eyes but Eowen pressed her. "You're more thirsty for battle than your husband!"

"Kid, you..." Cerapha cut herself off and chewed on the thought. "... Are absolutely right. I can't, though." She kissed Elshaddai's head. "I'm not powerful like the rest of you. I can't fight the Storm. Besides, how could I risk making this little one an orphan?" Elshaddai stared up at her mother and, without any preamble, spit up on her. Eowen stifled a laugh as Cerapha sighed and got up to wash the baby off and change her clothes. "You're making it tempting, little one," Cerapha said to her daughter. Eowen manifested a shallow tub of warm water and took Elshaddai from her mother to bathe.

"I suppose you're right," Eowen said. "Still, I'd feel safer with you around, general Cerapha of the Nemsto." Eowen looked up to see the older woman hide a smile.

"Get out of here, you've got your own preparations to make don't you?" Eowen took the hint and left Cerapha alone with Elshaddai. She hopped on her heron and let it glide around the Nemsto land, which was awash with activity. Varik and the recruits were going over the particulars, Hani's crew were carrying their possessions off the ship and setting up camp. Eowen could feel Ahn's mind reach out to hers, lightly linking her with the chosen members of the campaign.

"Hello again!"

"Hello Ahn."

"I'm very excited to be on this trip with you. Rennick is sad he has to be left behind, though."

"It's for the best, he'd be too vulnerable." Ahn didn't respond to that.

"I've already linked us so that we're accustomed to it, but Ordwell will manage how we actually feel each other's thoughts and experiences. He's very good at balancing such things."

"He is."

"Some people are even calling us The Bridges, like how people call you Eowen Mortician."

"It suits you." Waves of Ahn's joy and excitement flowed into her mind, but they were interrupted by another's thoughts intruding.

"Keep the link quiet for now, there's too much going on!" Hani's thoughts rang out clumsily across the link, carrying psychic fodder from a hundred other minds. Ahn closed the link to a barest thread, but sent some last thoughts to Eowen.

"I've been teaching the others, but they're not picking it up as quickly as you." Eowen breathed out a small laugh and Ahn did the psychic equivalent of a wink before going silent. Eowen sat atop her heron, taking deep breaths and letting it carry her where it would. Within a few hours it had arrived at the far western border of the Nemsto lands. Here, the Storm writhed, watching and waiting. Eowen did not sleep as night fell, but skimmed along the wall of clouds for many hours, watching the flicker of lightning and the currents of wind.

* * *

When light touched the Nemsto lands again, the night had seemed to pass in but a moment. "I am afraid of you," Eowen whispered to the roil before her. "And that is why I won't underestimate you." Eowen patted the heron's neck and it wheeled away.

The chosen members were gathered at the edge of the cliff. Hani, Varik, Ordwell, the ship's three acolytes of The Nagirr'Om, and even Ahn, were gathered to be seen off. The audience were of Hani's crew and the local Nemsto with Varik's sons at the front, though Cerapha and Rennick were nowhere in sight. They had all been outfitted in light, leather Nemsto armor, save for Varik, who wore his heavier, iron stuff.

"You kept us waiting!" Hani called to her as she landed.

"Just needed some time." Ahn flew into Eowen's arms and snuggled his head into her chest. "Good to see you too," she said in her mind.

"Greetings," Ahn said out loud in the Britchen language, and Eowen's eyebrows went up. His pronunciation was terrible and the word came out awkwardly. **"Rennick has been teaching me, he says it'll help me make friends."**

"You don't need help with that, kid." Eowen let Ahn go and he hovered next to her. "Where is he anyway?" she said out loud.

"He was too upset at being left behind to see us off," Ordwell said.

Hani approached with a set of leather armor and held it out for Eowen. "They prepared some for you too."

Eowen took the pieces and turned them over in her hands. Then she dipped into her dreaming, lifting the armor with great hands of light and shadow. She molds the pieces like clay into her yellow robes. When she was finished, the robes had changed from their comfortable, loosely flowing form to tightly wrapped cloth with leather padding throughout. The runes that glowed upon the armor were distributed across her entire outfit. Hani raised an eyebrow and clapped his hands.

"That'll work," Hani said, and looked around at the gathering. "We're ready, cast off!"

He turned and made for the ramp to the ship, but a stirring in the crowd got his attention. The audience parted as Cerapha strode through them in full armor, with a sword at her waist and a shield on her back. Varik met her halfway, and the gathering waited with baited breath. Elshaddai was sleeping in her arms.

"We agreed, one of us has to stay for her," Varik whispered, though he couldn't conceal the joy on his face.

"We did, but this journey is Eowen's, and yesterday she requested my presence." Cerapha caught the eye of a friend and handed Elshaddai off. "Besides, Tavo is like a son to us, you think I'm going to leave finding him in your clumsy hands?" Varik laughed and clapped his wife on the back, staggering her.

"As always, you're right my love!" He swept her in his arms and kissed her deeply, to her initial protest. The crowd cheered and Varik marched toward the ship with Cerapha at his side. "Captain Hani, permission for one more!"

Hani put his hands up helplessly. "Eowen?" he asked, and she nodded enthusiastically. "Then it's done, now board already!"

The Stormwake set off, cutting through the starfield faster than its original version ever had. They rounded the eastern, then northern sides of the Nemsto lands, and within the hour were headed fully west. The wall of the thunder-wilds were before them, but Varik and The Nagirr'Om's acolytes stood upon the prow, rejecting it. Hani assured them that the ship itself was enough to resist the Storm, but with Varik present the clouds were slammed back by the force of his will.

"Cerapha, how long does it usually take to reach the Niude lands?" Hani asked.

"There were no sea routes in the old world, so it would take over a month by foot, less by mount. Am I wrong in assuming that this vessel is swifter than those of the old world?"

"Much faster, the wind is always in our sails and the starfield parts more smoothly than any water. We crossed the stretch that was once the vast ocean between your lands and the coastal tribes there in less than a week!" Hani patted the side of his ship. "We'll reach the Niude lands in less than a full day!"

Hani might have been right if the winds were always in his sails, but as hours passed the cold fog closed in tighter and tighter. Varik held it back as best he could, but by half a day it was clear he couldn't resist it so well without his sword. Distant thunder shook the ship, and things moved within the starfield. Conversation died and the crew huddled together around Hani at the helm. Ahn and Ordwell kept them linked, but even on the mental plane there was a cloying fog. They all knew it was the working of the Storm and that it was watching them, but what twisted beings would emerge from it they did not know.

"Varik, Cerapha, what kinds of things have you seen emerge from the west?" Hani asked in a hushed tone.

"What do you mean?" Varik asked.

"I think he means those monsters that were people," Cerapha said. "Horrible things have come out of the thunder-wilds before, but not for many months has anything come from the far west." Hani nodded, thinking.

"Yet, the power here never diminished, did it?" Hani muttered, and Cerapha shook her head. "Almost as if it's been waiting."

"A trap, then?" Varik squeezed the pommel of his sword.

"It wouldn't be the first time."

Strife's voice passed through them.

"You're right," Hani muttered. One of the acolytes yawned and rubbed their eye and, as if that were the trigger, Eowen felt a wave of exhaustion. "We've seen a trap like this before." Hani's words appeared in their minds through the link. "Ordwell, Ahn, share the memories of the Storm entity we faced five months ago. It was among the southern peninsula tribes."

There was a shifting in their minds, a blur like when one moves their head too quickly, leaving streaks of light. Then the memory bloomed: An insidious sleeping myst that made them vulnerable to invasion, a being in the form of a great pillar of stone that fossilized you in its likeness as you slept. The answer was not to stay awake either, for the longer you did the weaker you became. They'd only won by rapidly overpowering the entity and destroying it.

"Cerapha, strategy?" Hani asked when the memory had played out.

"Half sleeps while the other half keeps watch over their bodies. At the signs of possession, wake them," she responded.

"Good, Strife is unaffected and does not need sleep, they'll keep constant watch." Hani said, then turned to an empty space next to him. "If you would," he said out loud. Strife made themself visible enough for all to see them nod. Ahn floated toward the stairs below deck but Hani called him back. "No, we all stay together. We're too small a group to split up with this kind of attack."

"I'll be safer in my cabin." Ahn was hiding something in his mind, but only Eowen seemed to notice.

"Ahn, what's in your cabin?" Eowen asked, and immediately sent her senses down to it. Ahn made to block her with barriers, but she was faster and stronger than him. There were thin barriers for privacy around all the cabins, but she burst through it and her mind alighted upon Rennick hiding in Ahn's room. "You brought him?" she shouted out loud. Hani felt it too, and rushed below deck.

"What happened, who did he bring?" Varik asked. Ahn was too embarrassed and frightened by Eowen's outburst to form a coherent response, but Ordwell stepped in.

"What's done is done, we can only turn back and drop him off." Eowen was seething though, her power was about her in rage, tinged by the Storm.

"You think I'll just let it go! I never had to perform a funeral for Luu before, I'm not going to start with her youngest son!" Eowen's aura crackled, and it was joined by Hani's as he emerged from below, dragging a frightened Rennick. Eowen's mind felt like it was on fire, her spirit pulsing. She advanced on Ahn, raised her hand to slap him, but Varik caught her by the wrist. She turned on him to attack, but he headbutted her, sending a crack of power that shook all the aggression out of her and left her forehead bleeding.

"Settle, lass," Varik growled. "The beast was in you."

Eowen gasped as the blood trickled down her face. The

Storm had gotten in her, even with all their safeguards. She'd thought it was putting her to sleep, but it had also alighted on the rage it had inspired in her before. She looked over at Hani to see Strife holding him by the temples, whispering something to him. Ahn and Rennick were huddled next to Ordwell.

"I'm sorry," Eowen whispered to Ahn. "I didn't mean to..."

"We know," Cerapha said. She cleaned the blood from Eowen's face. Varik was glaring westward as the thunder in the clouds seemed to laugh at them.

"I'm alright now." Hani pushed Strife aside. "We still need to take Rennick back, though." He approached the wheel and spun it so that the ship leaned and started a gradual turn. Eowen sat beside Ahn and Rennick and hugged them close.

"I didn't want to be left behind, and Ahn showed me how safe it always was on Captain Hani's ship. I thought it would be fun."

"Maybe it was safe those other times, but this is already different," Eowen whispered to them. The exhaustion was already setting back it, but when Eowen tried to resist it she could feel hot, electric rage close at hand as the Storm pulled her between the feelings. Eowen could sense the others struggling as well, a pendulum in their spirits ticking from sleep to some other failing. Fear in Rennick, indignation from Hani, self doubt in Cerapha, everyone was teetering. All base emotions they'd never normally give in to.

Hani finished the half rotation of the ship, but all could sense that something was wrong. "Why aren't we heading east?" Cerapha pointed to the prow, her finger aligning almost perfectly west. Hani glared, and spun the wheel the other way, held it, then spun it right and held it again for a time.

"There is no east. The other compass directions are gone," he said between clenched teeth. "Everywhere leads west."

There was nothing to say to that. The crew huddled around the helm and hunkered down to take their rest and watches. Time moved like molasses with Strife walking between them, shaking the crew awake when they showed any sign of possession. Things coiled through the fog, snaked in the starfields below, occasionally butting up against the ship, yet it was terribly quiet. Varik paced, desperate to fight something, but nothing in the thunder-wilds drew close enough for him to strike. They were surrounded, yet had no enemy to face, only a direction to follow that led, no doubt, into a trap. Eventually it was Eowen's turn to sleep, so she lay against her heron and shivered, for its warmth was insufficient against the chill, cloying mist.

****

There's nothing more to listen to, is there? The story of Love and the giant has ended, and you've truly left me. I'm not alone though. And togeth—

****

Eowen slammed onto the deck. All was in chaos as the ship keeled and its passengers cast about for handholds. Eowen pushed herself up just as a maw opened above her, intent on swallowing the ship into a vortex of fire and ice.

Varik roared and swung his blade at the great beast, severing its head from its neck. Blood like lightning poured out onto the ship, sending shrapnel everywhere. A piece as large as Eowen's arm slammed into the leather armor on her chest, knocking the wind out of her and bruising ribs. She gasped for air as someone hauled her to her feet.

"Well made, that," Cerapha said into her ear. "Get to the acolytes, they've got a barrier up." Cerapha threw Eowen towards the rest of the crew that were huddled around the helm, where silver bamboo was stuck in the deck. Hani and Ordwell were wrestling with the wheel, but the ship could not stay upright. A beast struck it from below, and the whole vessel lifted into the air and paused for a breath before slamming back down into the starfield. The crew fell about like dropped marbles and scrambled for the barrier. Varik and his wife were the only ones outside it, the warriors burning like the sun through the gloom. Cerapha was at Varik's back, shouting instructions as the huge man clove the sky apart, fending off the serpents. But he couldn't stop them all, and he couldn't strike at the ones below. Eowen called for her heron and pulled the children into her arms as it swooped in and wrapped its wings around them. The ship lifted up again as a beast cut through the starfield below, and slammed back down. Ordwell was thrown off the wheel and his head cracked against the deck. Hani was valiantly holding on. The children were screaming, Varik roared, but Eowen could barely hear them through the scythes of wind that cut their voices and spirits away. Something smashed into the tiller, ripping it from the ship, and the wheel was wrenched from Hani's grasp, snapping his wrist.

"Hani, no!" Eowen scrambled from the safety of her heron to his side. She put her power into his wrist, forcing it to heal and not caring how the Storm nipped at her manifestations and warped them into chaos around her. His bones and tissue latched back into place with none of the finesse of a true healer. "Ah! There, now get back to safety!" Eowen shouted.

Hani met Eowen's eyes and gritted his teeth. "**No, there is no power that will drive my ship off course!**" Hani stood, and the winds and rains of the Storm cracked back. He caught the wildly spinning wheel with one hand and the ship centered immediately despite the lack of a tiller. Varik's booming laugh echoed out from where he was fighting, and he cut through another beast of water and wind, clearing the way ahead. Hani threw the wheel to the left, angling the ship for the opening. Eowen secured the children in the heron's wings as Hani summoned his uncorrupted winds to drag them forward. The Storm beasts were in retreat with Varik slashing after them, and the ship was sailing on smooth stars once again.

"Ha! We're unstoppable!" Varik shouted, and the rest of the crew cheered and laughed out of pure relief. Then, the ship struck something, stopping it dead. The crew went flying off and into the roil. Eowen flailed in the air, powers failing her, and landed on the starfield below. The clouds rushed in, coiled around her, and drank in her power and desperation, squeezing out mind and life. She stood, blind in the gray, and staggered about with her hands held out.

"Hani! Varik! Anyone!" She could feel something ahead, and stumbled towards it till a hand grabbed her by the back of the neck and slammed her face into the stars below. "Get off me!"

"Follow the stars!"

Strife commanded. Eowen strained against them, but no

power could resist Strife, and they pressed Eowen's face down till she breathed in the clean air filtering up from the starfield below. Her mind cleared some, and she reached around to pat Strife's hand on her neck.

"I'm ok." Strife's grip lessened, but didn't release her. "I am, let me up." They did, but Eowen stayed close to the starfield, drinking up her clean atmosphere of air. Her companions were all around her, keeping close to the stars as well. Hani still burned with his power against the Storm and had the wheel of his now wrecked ship still in his hand. He walked with Ordwell under his protection and added Eowen to it when they drew close. Ahn and Rennick were on the heron, Varik and Cerpaha were holding hands, and the acolytes were together. "We're ok," Eowen whispered.

"I promised you that nothing would divert us while under my protection," Hani said, and as if listening, the wall of clouds opened, and the party found themselves in the eye of the Storm. Two figures approached from far away, walking calmly across the starfield towards them. Three great and terrible coils of smoke leaked from their faces, obscuring features and converging into the weather that encircled them.

"Tavo," Varik whispered. "And Duwiyin."

No!

The warrior hefted his blade and stood between the two approaching and the group. "So you are lost."

No!

Eowen tried to run for them, but Hani held her back. "I'm sorry Eowen. They're lost," Hani whispered as hot, furious tears ran down her face. She beat at his arm, but he kept her there.

"They're not! Tavo could move through the Storm! He—"

"Never set foot on our lands," Cerapha said, facing the

couple with her husband. "He never approached where Varik's power was, just like the rest of the thunder-wilds."

"No, Tavo it's me, Eowen!" She pushed against Hani, her power striking against Hani's equal defenses as Strife moved in to block her as well. In the eye of the Storm, their minds were clear: the Storm beasts kept their distance, watching and presiding over the moment, their forms occasionally emerging from the wall of clouds around them. "He can't be!" Eowen sobbed and tried to see her cousin's face, certain it would be clear eyed and welcoming if only she could see it, but everyone was in her way. The two approaching people were close now, meters away. Varik moved forward, bore down upon them, and raised his weapon, shoulders shaking. "Varik, stop!" The warrior roared, his arms and shoulder twisted, and the weapon struck with a power that could render the world asunder.

Eowen held her breath, waiting for the bodies to fall, but nothing happened. Varik grunted, and drew his blade back to strike again. There was no blood on it. The second strike never came. Varik collapsed as a bolt of lightning punched a hole through his armor. Varik wheezed as the wound pooled out blood and he collapsed to the starfield below. Cerapha rushed to his side and pushed all the healing power she had into the wound. Tavo and his wife stepped over the struggling couple and continued their approach, as if it had never happened. They halted just past Varik, who was holding Tavo by the ankle.

"Not another step!" he growled.

Eowen's vision was blurred from tears, but she watched as the acolytes, Varik, and Cerapha sprang into action. Tavo reached out his hand to strike Varik down, but Cerapha put up her shield in time. A blast of elemental violence spewed out, smashing the shield and cracking Cerapha's arm in half. She cried out but held her ground, deflecting another attack with her blade as Varik burned in his battle-rage, pinning Tavo in place. The acolytes sprouted, cut, and shot their bamboo arrows, but Duwiyin deflected them with gusts of wind. Varik managed to get back on his feet, healing his wound as best he could with sheer force of will. He joined his wife, hacking and parrying blasts, but between their wounds they couldn't keep it up. Tavo opened his mouth and another bolt of lighting shrieked out. Cerapha blocked, but the force of it sent her weapon flying and the deflected attack carved a burning chunk of flesh out of Varik's leg. He fell, his battle-rage broken.

Ahn and Ordwell reached out to link them, but the group's minds and spirits were severed apart effortlessly. The acolytes fought bravely but were knocked aside like twigs, tossed away with broken bones and leaking wounds. The rest of the crew could only watch as the warriors were downed and the eye of the Storm closed around them. The possessed forms of Tavo and Duwiyin approached Hani, Strife, and Eowen next. Tavo extended his hand and pointed it at Eowen's chest. Duwiyin cradled a bundle to her chest.

"Tavo, it's me, I came all this way to find you!" Eowen cried. Hani and Strife were shouting but she could not hear them. They cast about for something to do or somewhere to run, but were trapped in the den of the beast.

Eowen wiped her tears away and beheld her cousin and his wife clearly, though smoke still seeped from their faces. Tavo was taller than she'd thought he would be, his hair long and twisted past his shoulders and his beard braided in the style of the Nemsto. His wife was caramel skinned and freckled, with curly hair that formed a mane around her.

Eowen reached out to them with her mind and spirit, a desperate smile on her face, but her power slipped through them as though they weren't there. It was like she was trying to grasp the wind. Only fragments of their minds remained in the husks of their bodies, points of singular purpose and desire that the Storm had latched onto and fed upon. Eowen locked onto those points as well, desperate to find even the barest crumb of personhood left in her cousin, and saw what had driven him across the world and what had been his downfall. A simple, terribly common wish: To know his family was safe, and for his child to be acknowledged.

Something else met Eowen inside the place where their spirits should have been. It was something terribly familiar, lurking in another body and puppeting the other two. Eowen pulled her gaze from the vacant eyes of her cousin and his wife to the bundle in Duwiyin's arms. A shift of blanket and a tiny face peered out at her with eyes that saw through Eowen and into the ocean of her dreaming with an unearthly, violent craving. The truest host of the Storm, a dreamer born so powerful that, even when possessed, the beast hadn't twisted its form into a monstrosity. The alien entity that had besieged their new world boiled under the child's skin, and it drew Eowen in with eyes like wells into the deep dark places between stars. She reached out to touch the child, and a tiny hand emerged to meet her. Strife and Hani pulled at her body, trying to shake the power that possessed Eowen, but they were no match. Her quest was over, her family sycophant to the Storm. Soon, it would finally have its teeth in Eowen as well, and she couldn't care less.

It was all for nothing.

Eowen's mind clouded over and her spirit dissolved into the roil within.

A searing fire crashed through Eowen and the Storm-possessed child screeched in pain. A silver spear of bamboo had burst through Eowen's chest and another slammed through Tavo's hand, pinning it to the starfield below.

"Eowen Mortician!" The voice of The Nagirr'Om rang out like a bell, clearing their minds. Her great mount wheeled around as Storm-beasts snapped their jaws at it, enraged for interrupting. **"You will not fall here!"**

The thing in Duwiyin's arms that had once been a child pushed itself up and unhinged its jaw, screeching at the Nagirr'Om and shaking the world around them. Thick smoke and lightning poured from its face, boiling up into the most massive Storm serpent any of them had seen. Its eyes were like suns, its teeth mountains of lightning, and it's maw enough to swallow the sky. Eowen coughed blood. The spear had pierced her perfectly through the scar from before, but she was stronger this time and kept her life going like Aiyano had. She gripped it with both hands and pushed against it, trying to dislodge herself. Hani and Strife grasped her shoulders and pulled, freeing her from the spear with a sucking noise of flesh on bamboo.

"Eowen, we have to leave! The Nagirr'Om can hold it off while we escape!" Hani shouted as her senses returned, The Nagirr'Om's power keeping the Storm at bay by the spear in her hand. Ahn and Ordwell's link between them lit up, and her mind was awash with orders for escape.

"No," Eowen said, her voice rumbling through them. A new thread appeared in her spirit, binding her to a mourner, but she didn't have to follow it far. The thread was wrapped around her own heart. Eowen wrenched the bamboo spear from the starfield below, snapped it in two, and handed half to Strife. Then she locked eyes with Varik, and sent a thought into his mind. He nodded to confirm he understood her orders.

With The Nagirr'Om firing its arrows into the Storm to keep its attention, Eowen strode forth, tears catching fire as they fell from her eyes. She reached out and grasped the smoke that was pouring out of the baby's mouth. The brand on her chest burned brighter than ever before, the tattoos around her ankles rooted her to the starfield below like savannah grass, and the heron stood behind her, wings spread wide. The Storm writhed in her grasp like a worm in the beak of a bird.

"You foolish thing. You took my family from me, and in doing so gave me the means by which to destroy you!"

Varik pressed his weapon into Cerapha's hands and said something to her. A flow of his spirit, like when the silhouette of the heron first emerged from Eowen, flowed into Cerapha. She burned with Varik's battle-rage, hefted his blade, and charged for Tavo's back. At the same time, Strife plunged their half of the spear into Duwiyin's chest. They pressed the weapons in, but the husks fought desperately against them as the Storm fed off what vestiges of their minds and wills remained. The bindings between the parents and their child were too strong to break, the Storm within them empowered by their final wish. Eowen was barely holding onto the smoke coming out of the child's face. They needed a weakness.

What could ever get through to what remains of their minds? All they want is to protect their child, which we threaten. Protect... and for their child to be acknowledged.

"Varik, Cerapha!" Eowen shouted into their minds through the link. **"The tradition of acknowledgement for their child! The reason Tavo returned to the jungle and savannah tribes, what is it called?"** They didn't know, their confusion bouncing through the link, but Rennick's mind called out through the din:

"The Tha-Eno! It is called giving your Tha-Eno!"

"Tavo, Duwiyin!" Eowen called out to them in the voice of power that could not be ignored. **"I give your child my Tha-Eno! They are acknowledged!"**

A shudder passed through the husks. Their faces, devoid of all humanity, sparked with it again. It was only for a moment, the barest second, but it was enough. Varik's and The Nagirr'Om's power burned through the bodies, severing them from the entity that possessed them in a shower of lightning and fire. The only one left was the child, which Eowen pulled into her arms, still spewing out black smoke and violence. It launched itself at her, tiny arms flailing with the power of a god, but it all glanced off. Eowen wept over the struggling monster in the body of the child, one hand still viced around the smoke of the Storm beast within it. She pointed her half of the spear at its chest and the beast squealed and squirmed. She paused.

"Does it have to happen this way? Can't I save even you?"

Hani stood beside her and took hold of the spear as well. **"It must, but you will not face this alone."**

Eowen wept hot, bitter tears, and set her mouth in a thin line. They knitted their power as one and, together, pushed the spear into the child's body, piercing the entity that possessed it. It let out a shriek that pulsed through the world and all the lands the Storm had blanketed. Fire spewed from the place where the spear had entered, blistering their skin and filling their lungs. The strain drained them of will and strength, but they held on, all but fused to the spear. Hani looked Eowen in the eyes through the roil, then looked over her shoulder and spoke words she could not hear to the heron behind her.

{You can end this, can't you? She can't, but you can.}

[Only if you let go.]

"Who are you talking to? What did you say?" Eowen shouted, but Hani was slipping away from her. His mind and spirit were retreating. His hands were loosening their grip on the spear. He found Eowen's eyes in the madness once more, smiled his joyful, excited smile, and let go. Yet, his power did not. It launched her, the power of quests, of journeys, of destined conclusions to be reached. Not to be reached by Hani, but by those he had carried to that final step. Eowen didn't have time to process what had happened before she was overtaken by the rush of her and the Storm's power, and fell into darkness.

****

We lost.

[Not yet.]

You're back.

[I never left.]

Will you help me?

[Yes.]

How?

[You must come with me.]

Where are we going?

[To where Love and the giant met,
the mountain known as Ah'Om.]

I don't know the way.

[You know. You have gone the way before,
in dreams, in the company of the giant.]

North of here, west of there, ten paces forward, and three
looks back.

[Yes.]

Why do I need to go there?

[To become yourself.]

****

The bone heron swooped in, became light, shadow, and
silhouette once more. It wrapped itself around Eowen and
melded into her till they were one thing, as they'd always
been. The combined form stood like the girl, but was as tall

and as thin as the heron. It held the Storm-possessed infant and the spear with human arms, yet great wings spread out on its back. A human-like head with a spear beak rested upon a long, snaked neck. Feathers grew off it like a sweeping robe of the heron's greyish blue and black and Eowen's soft yellow.

The being turned and faced north, then turned and faced West. It took ten paces forward, and looked back three times.

The first look was at Tavo.

The second had its beak pointed perfectly at the oasis Eowen had wrought so long ago.

When the bird looked back a third time, it saw across the world to the body of Monda of the jungle and savannah tribes.

****

To become [myself.]

****

On a mountain called Ah'Om, a being that was not a bird nor a young woman, not a metaphor nor a mortician, but somehow both and more, arrived. It was Eowen, and she took a form more fitting for the place where she would direct this funeral. Something else arrived, a thing too massive to know. The thing looked upon Eowen, and made the hairs she did not have on a neck that did not exist stand up.

THANK YOU FOR COMING.

The thing deposited a body at the base of the mountain, at the mouth of a very old cave. Eowen went there and found the body of Love, a normal mortal being by all accounts. She took the body into the cave at the base of the mountain, and placed it deep within the depths. The sun and the moon followed to bear witness, and the giant watched from outside. Eowen gave the sun, the moon, and the cave time to speak of Love. They did not have much to say, and the cave could not speak, for they were inconsolable.

[Giant, it is your turn.]

And the giant spoke.

TO LOVE, WHO I WILL MISS MORE THAN I KNEW I COULD. LOVE NEVER RETURNED TO AH'OM UNTIL NOW. THEY WERE TAKEN BY ME TO FAR-FLUNG PLACES FULL OF ANSWERS AND QUESTIONS. THEY SPOKE WITH ME AND CALLED MY NAME OFTEN, SUCH THAT I NEVER HAD TO REQUEST THAT THEY DO SO. THEY LISTENED AND HEARD ME, AS SO FEW CAN AND EVEN FEWER ARE WILLING TO.

IN LOVE'S JOURNEY, MANY GREAT BEINGS OFFERED THEMSELVES, PROMISING LIFE ETERNAL AND POWER UNRIVALED. LOVE ALWAYS TURNED THEM DOWN, FOR THEY WISHED TO LIVE ONLY AS THEMSELVES, AND SO THEY DID. TO MY KNOWLEDGE, THEY ARE THE ONLY BEING THAT EVER HAS. PERHAPS THEY ARE THE ONLY BEING THAT EVER WILL.

LOVE DIED, FOR DESPITE ALL THE IMPOSSIBILITIES THEY PERFORMED, THEY WERE A

NORMAL, MORTAL BEING, WHOSE PASSING WAS INEVITABLE. THE SPAN OF THEIR LIFE WAS SO MEAGER, SO IMPOSSIBLY SMALL TO ONE SUCH AS I, THAT IT CANNOT BE COMPREHENDED. ONE SO SMALL AS THEY, SO BRIEF AND SO WEAK, SHOULD NOT MATTER. YET THEY DID MATTER, AND I MATTERED TO THEM. BUT THEY ARE NO LONGER HERE TO FEEL THAT WAY FOR ME, AND THIS HAS LEFT A HOLE THAT WILL NEVER FILL, A HOLE THAT WILL EVER GROW WITHIN ME. THE HOLE WILL SURELY BECOME BIGGER THAN MYSELF, FOR LOVE WAS BORN WHEN THE WORLD COULD NO LONGER BEAR TO BE WITHOUT THEM, AND NOW I KNOW THAT I CANNOT BEAR IT EITHER.

[Life is a burden, forever beyond the strength of those who must carry it. This little one's burden is gone, but you, giant, must go on.]

SO I MUST, SO MUST YOU, SO MUST WE ALL WHO HAVE YET TO MEET OUR ENDS. WE WILL, BECAUSE WE MUST. WE MUST BECAUSE WE CAN. WE CAN, UNTIL WE CANNOT.

The giant left Ah'Om and carried Eowen back to her world: three looks forward, ten paces back, east of here and south of there. She saw how the Storm was still there, writhing around at the edges of her fallen world as it poked and prodded for a new way in. The child of Tavo and Duwuyin had been such a perfect host; a dreaming mind unparalleled, even greater than her own, as some already had been; protected by its parents, such that it had been able to grow as a host. Circumstances aligning just right. The perfect Storm. Fate carved of chance.

[I see, Nagirr'Om. This is what would have become of your child.]

The baby had truly been a perfect host. Yet, when the Storm took it, the child's dreaming mind had never been able to grow, as Eowen's and so many others did. She saw that the Storm was just a thing, like so many others, seeking a way to become more than it was and had been.

[Do what you must, but not in my world.]

She reached out and plucked it, the small thing that it was in her world, and shooed it away, it a mouse and Eowen the cat. It watched her, larger in its wholeness than her but too small where they were now, and left. Eowen looked down upon her world and understood that she could know it all, from its farthest and still expanding reaches, to the form she'd taken with the bone heron that still faced the direction of her mother—

* * *

Eowen awoke to a terrible pain in her chest like a knot twisting tight. The Storm was gone from their world. All could feel it. It had been as though a giant pair of fingers had plucked it out and tossed it away. Eowen found herself on her knees with the child cradled in her arms and the bone heron curled up beside her. The Nagirr'Om landed beside them, dismounted from her great beast, and ran to Eowen.

"Finally! It has ended! Eowen—"

[Leave now.]

The voice brooked no quarter. Eowen pulled the spear from the child and dropped it, wet with the blood of many, with the blood of an infant at The Nagirr'Om's feet.

[This is now a place for mourners.]

The Nagirr'Om bowed their veiled head and backed away, her silver light flaring away as if a flame being pushed by the wind. Eowen carried the child to where Tavo lay, his head on Cerapha's lap. She had taken the sword out and closed his eyes. Eowen gestured to Strife, who removed their half of the bamboo spear and carried the body of Duwiyin to Tavo. Once they were side by side, Eowen set the baby between them. All the strength that had been in Eowen faded out and she dropped to her knees, empty save for the hurt. She reached out and stroked Tavo's face and held it for a long time. The person she'd crossed the world and fought horrors to find, the person who, despite all her power, all her knowledge, all she'd gone through, she could never save.

But we've got that in common, don't we, Tavo? We both traveled across the whole world to reach the people we loved, only to find them dead.

"I-I-I..." Eowen opened her mouth to speak, but only stuttering, coughing sobs emerged. She took a deep breath and tried again. "I-I am E-Eowen, of the jungle and s-savannah tribes, and I give my T-tha-Eno." She felt the touch of Ahn in her mind, linking her with Rennick as the boy fed her the words to say, words from an old world. "I am cousin by blood, and sister by spirit to Tavo. In the name of our people, I sanction this marriage, and testify that this child is one of our own." Eowen placed Tavo and Duwiyin's hands together over the body of their baby. She searched their dead minds for memories, anything that would let her know what name they would have given their child, but there was nothing left. It was all too late. "I don't know what it was, but I have to believe they gave you a name," Eowen whispered to the body of the child. "And I know you were loved." She put her face in her hands and wept till the world was gone.

****

**[And now, I must do for myself
what I have done for so many others.]**

****

When Eowen awoke, it was in the ship cabin that Hani had made for her back in Nolano before they'd parted ways. It smelled like rain in the jungle and dust in the savannah. Hani was sitting in a chair beside her bed. He noticed she was awake and breathed a sigh of relief.

"I'm glad you're ok," he whispered. "When I let go... It seemed like the right thing to do at the time." He ran a hand through his hair. "But I can't remember why. What happened back there?" Eowen didn't answer right away. She couldn't quite figure out how to explain, it was beginning to feel like a dream. "You stopped it, I know that... but how?" Eowen reached for Hani's hand and held it tight.

"It was just a Storm," Eowen whispered. "It came and it passed." She lifted herself from the bed to Hani's protest.

"You shouldn't move so soon! You've been asleep for—"

"A month," Eowen cut in.

"Yes... so you should take it slow." His voice trailed off.

[He's still in the dream, and... something is missing from him. Something even I cannot see.]

"Nothing's missing," Hani said, though his brow furrowed and he glanced around nervously. "Sorry, I thought I heard you say something."

Eowen patted Hani's hand, then stood. "Thank you for watching over me, but I've been asleep long enough. Now, I have work to do."

Hani followed Eowen out of The Stormwake, up the ramp, and back to the Nemsto lands. She passed through the village, drawing eyes and whispers, their minds sparking with thoughts that Eowen could follow clearly. The hero who'd vanquished the Storm was awake. Eowen made her way to Varik's residence as word spread across the Nemsto lands. She sensed that Ahn and Rennick were with Kamali, and when word reached her of Eowen awake, she sent them out to follow. Rennick ran up and took Eowen's hand and Ahn floated over to perch on Hani's shoulder.

"I'm glad you're awake!" Rennick whispered. "And I'm sorry I stowed away."

"Thank you," Eowen whispered back. "I'm glad you did. We wouldn't have succeeded without you." They approached the cottage beyond the woods to see Varik seated outside, asleep with his daughter on his lap while his wife blew smoke rings next to them.

"Welcome back," Cerapha said. She and her husband sported new scars, but were fully healed.

"Baa, ba!" Elshaddai woke Varik with her babbling.

"About time," he muttered, his expression one of bittersweet affection. "Come with me." He handed Elshaddai off to his wife and walked around to the back of the cottage. Eowen followed, leaving the others behind to wait out front.

In the back of the cottage, past the training ground and nestled at the edge of the woods, was a stone crypt. It was twice as wide as Varik and four times as long. It glowed with Lokah's runes, and Eowen could feel how they preserved the space inside, keeping it cool and unspoilable by time. A thick metal door had been set into the crypt, and Varik pulled it open to admit her. Eowen stepped through, raised a small light, and looked over the inside. It was a simple stone room without adornment, save for the three shelves at the back with three blanket-wrapped bundles resting upon them, one much smaller than the other two. Varik came up behind Eowen and put a hand on her shoulder. She could feel the great man shaking and hear the sound of his suppressed sobs. Eowen stayed facing the bodies but put her hand on his.

"I'm sorry," he croaked. "I-I thought I was ready for this." Eowen didn't respond, and stayed like that with Varik till he stopped shaking. "So... how are we going to do this?" Varik whispered.

[I need somewhere to plant a tree.]

At the far eastern edge of the Nemsto lands, on the cliff where Eowen and Varik had first met, a great union of shadow and light took place. From the ocean of Eowen's dreams emerged a bone tree and bone heron. Hundreds were in attendance, from Hani's crew to every Nemsto that had met or heard of Tavo and Duwiyin. When Eowen finished with the tree, she turned to Varik and Cerapha, who held the adult bodies in their arms. Eowen held the nameless child in hers. They laid the three bodies at the base of the tree and unwrapped them. Eowen stared at the face of her cousin for a moment that stretched out in silence. It wasn't him though. It was just the vessel he'd left behind for her to honor.

Eowen didn't move for a long time. There was a bowstring sort of tension within her between who she'd become, and who she still was; the legend of Eowen Mortician, worshiped across the new world as a god of the funeral; Eowen, disgraced exile who'd had failed the ones she loved time and again, and would never make it right. She waited for the tension in her to snap, for some sign to tell her that it was time, that she was good enough, that the pathetic girl she'd been was gone for good and now only the god remained. It never came, and deep in her heart she knew it never really would.

[Still, there is work to be done, and it is mine to do.]

The heron stood beside her, and from its feathers Eowen drew forth the knife she'd created in Nolano almost three years ago. Her hands shook, everyone could see, but when she touched Tavo's cold body and put blade to skin, the shaking stopped. She cut through Tavo, separating his skeleton from his flesh, as had been done for her people since time immemorial. She laid the bones at the base of the tree and buried the flesh in the earth under its roots.

Then it was Duwiyin's turn. Eowen had learned from Rennick how the Niude treated their dead. They had kept their bodies till the middle of winter, where they were left out to become as solid as ice. The frozen bodies were then crushed into fine, icy powder and the powder boiled till all the moisture was gone, and only solids remained. The solids were mixed with their strongest alcohol and drunk, for it was believed that this method was the only way to completely eradicate the curse of a death upon their people. Eowen did all this for Duwiyin, sharing the drink with Cerapha and Varik.

Then, it was time for the child. Eowen removed the skeleton, in accordance with her people, and froze the flesh in accordance with the Niude's. She laid the bones at the base of the tree with Tavo's, and drank the potion on her own.

An old woman shuffled forward through the crowd with something cupped in her hands. It was Gwenhwyfar, the mother of Skelad, bearing an elstith flower from the Nemsto cemetery. She offered it to Eowen, who cradled the thing, so freshly dug that its roots still had loamy soil on them. Eowen planted the elstith flower at the base of the bone tree, then stood and turned to face the gathered people. No one but the party that had braved the Storm alongside her knew that Tavo and Duwiyin's child had been the host, no one knew that they'd had to battle and kill them. This was to be a secret kept to preserve the honor of who Tavo and Duwiyin had once been. Eowen bowed to Varik and Cerapha, to Hani and his crew, to the Nemsto people that had come to pay their respects. Some were weeping, some looked on with stony faces, and some who hadn't known the deceased well enough to mourn were looking to those that did with empathy.

[All of you came because there is love in you, but do not carry this loss any longer.]

Eowen's lips never moved, yet her voice was in everyone.

[Their burdens are gone, but we must go on with ours. Let not the dead be one of them.]

She folded her hands in the wide sleeves of her robes, and mounted her heron. The bird took off, bringing Eowen high above the Nemsto lands, past their atmosphere, past the reach of Varik's power and Ahn's telepathy and even Hani's powerful senses. There, alone in the dark, empty void that was her world's firmament, Eowen collapsed onto the heron's back and wept as the weight of the dead crushed down upon her.

* * *

A week later, Hani and his crew were ready to set out once again to explore the new world. They were partying throughout the town, but the group that had sailed into the Storm to find Tavo were at Varik's cottage. It was night, and they were gathered around a great bonfire set upon the center of the compass. Varik's sons were wrestling with their father, Ordwell was already asleep, Ahn and Rennick were with Kamali, and the musician boy Lokah, who'd been with Hani since Nolano, was playing a tune to wind things down. Eowen sat with Cerapha and Elshaddai while Hani seemed to be sitting alone, but one could notice an outline beside him if they looked carefully.

"You going with him, kid?" Cerapha asked.

"I don't know," Eowen said.

"You're always free to stay here, with us." The older

woman put an arm around Eowen's shoulders and pulled her close.

"I know, Cerapha, but I can feel this isn't where I'm meant to be."

"Thought that might be the case. You might as well go with that lad for a while. He's bound for places."

"I will..."

"But?"

[But there is still something in him hidden from me. I could see all the world if I looked, so what could it be that is in him that I cannot?]

Eowen felt a prickle on her neck from someone watching her and looked up. It was Strife, visible for only a moment before flickering out of Eowen's perception.

"Excuse me, Cerapha." Eowen rose and approached the log where Hani was sitting.

"Eowen, take a seat." He patted the log next to her.

"Actually, I was hoping to have a word with Strife," Eowen said, looking at where she believed them to be.

"Oh, uh... if that's alright with you?" Hani looked at the empty space as well. His hand moved, then Strife appeared next to Eowen.

"Do you wish to speak with me in private, Eowen Mortician?"

"Please." Eowen started towards the forest and gave Hani a small wave. "We'll be right back." After a moment, they'd passed out of the bonfire's light and into the darkness of the Nemsto woods.

"What business do you have with me?"

Strife was keeping themself unseen and unheard again.

"I was considering rejoining Hani's crew again, but something has been bothering me." Eowen left space open for Strife to respond, but they remained silent. "What has been bothering me is that there is something about Hani that I cannot sense, something I feel is important."

"You feel you have the right to know all his secrets?"

Strife's voice normally held little inflection, but there was the hint of an accusation in it now.

"Everyone has a right to keep their secrets, but whatever this one is, I do not think he is the one keeping it."

Strife was silent, invisible save for a vague silhouette, but even something about the silhouette seemed annoyed.

"You have always been very perceptive, Eowen Mortician. You are correct, Hani has requested that I hide something from you. Understand this: There is no other I care for, and I will not betray Hani's trust for your sake."

"Fine." Eowen put her hands up. "But would you do it for his sake?" There was a long pause where the silhouette of Strife seemed to be mulling it over.

"How do you know it would be?"

"I don't, I trust you to know," Eowen said. There was a long pause, then Strife disappeared completely, taking whatever barrier they'd put between Hani and Eowen with them.

The change was immediate. A mourner's string in Hani calling desperately for Eowen burst through her spirit like a dam breaking.

Strife's been hiding this from—

[Me? How?]

Eowen extended her senses back through the woods to her friend, laughing and singing with the others as a deep aching in him called out to her. She returned to the celebration and took her seat beside Cerapha again.

"I've made my decision. I'll be leaving with the crew."

"You don't sound happy about it," Cerapha said, and Eowen shook her head.

"It will be nice, but I won't be staying with them for long, just until we reach a certain place." Eowen could feel where the thread between her and Hani wanted to take them, someplace to the far south of the Nemsto lands that held some significance to Hani. A part of her could have looked further into Hani and into the world, but Eowen was content to learn what awaited her in time. Cerapha kissed Eowen's forehead.

"So, tomorrow you're gone?"

"I'll be back someday," Eowen promised.

"Course you will."

The old woman stayed up with Eowen the rest of the night. They spoke of small matters; Elshaddai growing up, what people might visit the Nemsto lands now that the world was open, what her foolish husband and sons would do with themselves now the Storm was gone. The next morning,

Cerapha and Varik's family saw them off at the cliff where the Stormwake was still anchored and the new bone-tree stood like a pillar to the sky. Eowen hugged dozens of Nemsto and shook many hands. Varik picked her up like she weighed nothing and wept incessantly. Cerapha held Eowen's head between her hands and kissed it, then whispered prayers from the old world to gods she no longer believed in.

"And... just be safe," Cerapha finished.

The crew boarded, sailing off and into the east with Hani at the helm, beaming as the people of his ship danced, sang, and drank to a rowdy Nemsto song that Lokah was playing. Eowen was beside him as her heron flew circles around the mast.

"Where to next?" Hani asked her.

"Letting me decide, just like that?"

"Almost everyone on the crew had a turn plotting our course." He winked roguishly, playing up the pirate persona. "Newest member usually gets the next pick."

This'll make it easier.

"Move aside." She elbowed him out of the way and took the wheel, throwing it till the ship was pointed at the place she sensed that Hani's mourning was called to, the place he'd been avoiding. It was far to the south, and even at the great speeds the Stormwake could achieve, it would normally take a few days.

[That won't do.]

Eowen's power folded through the starfield below, more than she'd ever held and perfectly in control.

"So where are we going?" Hani asked.

"I don't know yet." Eowen kept her tone neutral.

"An adventure into the unknown! About time you got a feel for that!" Hani jumped down onto the deck to dance and sing with his crew.

In hours, they could see a settlement approaching, and the crew cheered. Hani celebrated with them, but as they drew closer the place became more and more familiar to him. When they were close enough to see a grand city of coral in the distance, Hani's face fell. Other members of his crew were glad to be home, or giddy to see a place they'd enjoyed visiting in the past. Hani approached the helm as Eowen steered straight for it.

"Eowen, why did you bring us here?"

"Should I not have?" She avoided his eyes.

"Ye—I mean, no, it's just that." He gestured vaguely, then looked around as if trying to find someone. "Have you seen Strife?" he asked.

"They don't show themself to anyone as much as you." Eowen guided the ship alongside the city, and the crew leapt off to meet old friends and show new ones around. Hani stayed aboard though. He looked sick and was backing away from Eowen.

"No—I'm not going in there."

Eowen approached, but he ran to his private quarters. Eowen followed him to a locked door with powerful barriers in it.

[Not powerful to me, though.]

She undid the barriers and entered to see a panicked and distraught Hani. "H-how did you do that?"

"Hani, it's alright." Eowen stepped forward to take his hands, but he pushed her away.

"Why would you bring me here! You told her, didn't you?" He whipped around looking for Strife, but they were nowhere to be found. His mind was on fire and he backed into the corner away from Eowen. "I told them not to let you see, I told them!" Eowen didn't have to ask what he'd been wanting to hide. It was shining bright in his mind.

"You found your father," Eowen whispered, and suddenly the world was like marble. Hani's power was everywhere, suffusing the atmosphere with a density that would have suffocated someone lesser than Eowen. She pushed through it and approached him as if he were a wounded animal. "Hani, what happened?" She knew what happened, she could see it in his mind, but he needed to tell her himself. Hani's breathing slowed down, he swallowed the lump in his throat and plastered a smile on his face.

"Nothing happened! He didn't get taken by the Storm, if that's what you mean." Hani looked dead.

"Hani, come here." Eowen pulled him into her arms, but for once he didn't embrace her back.

"What? Why so dramatic? I expected this. If anything I'm surprised, he survived as long as he did!" Hani's voice broke at the end and his fake joy shook.

"It's ok, you're ok. I'm here."

"I know I'm ok. I am ok!"

"What happened, Hani? Please, talk to me."

"What's there to say? He died in the fall, that's it. Plenty of people did, turns out he wasn't the dreamer I'd thought he was, but that's alright."

Eowen held him tighter. He was shaking. "You never said goodbye to him," Eowen whispered.

"How could I!" Hani balled his hands into fists, pressed them into Eowen's back, pushed his face into her shoulder, and wet it with tears. "I knew what his men were doing, they were pirates who raped and they pillaged and they killed people, but I thought... He wasn't a part of it, I thought he was trying to do good with bad men, but h-h-he was a part of it all! He did all th-th-those things-s too." Hani shuddered in Eowen's arms, clutching at her as a strangled sort of wail twisted out of him. They stayed like that for minutes that felt much longer than they were. Hani whimpered, repressed his sobs, pushed Eowen away, then clung to her as if his life depended on it. Eventually, he tapped her shoulder and she shuffled back. "I'm ok now." He sounded anything but.

"Come, let's stand up." Eowen rose and pulled Hani to his feet. He stood over a head taller than her now but at that moment he seemed the smallest, most fragile thing.

"What do you want?" Hani asked, avoiding her eyes. "To do a funeral for my father? He was a monster, he doesn't deserve to be honored and mourned!"

Eowen reached out and took his hand. "Oh, Hani. We do not mourn for the dead themselves, they are beyond our reach. We mourn for what we, the living, have lost." She started out of the room, pulling him along. "And you lost someone not just in death, but in memories tainted by the truth of the life he lived." Hani followed her, though he kept his eyes down, staring in an unseeing way.

"It doesn't matter, I don't know where the body is. Strife hid it for me." Eowen noticed a shimmer in the air beside Hani, and Strife slipped their hand into his. He looked at his hand and glared, though he lacked the strength to put venom into it. "You told her after you promised."

"Despite my efforts, Eowen Mortician noticed something on her own. It would not have lasted."

Strife made themselves more visible than they ever had for Eowen, and looked at her in a dissecting sort of way.

"I could feel this thing eating at you, always. Every moment I kept you shielded, it ate at me as well."

"I-I'm sorry. I didn't know." Hani let go of Eowen and took Strife's hand in both of his. "I never would have asked if I'd known you'd suffer with me." He looked between the two of them, wheels turning in his head. A mirthless look came over him. "This has to happen, doesn't it?"

"Nothing has to happen, Hani." Eowen clasped her hands together and met his eyes. "But maybe it is something that should happen."

"I'm not ready, though."

"Of course not, how could you ever be?" Eowen moved aside. "Since when has that ever stopped you?"

Strife pulled Hani along. They left the ship and circled around the outskirts of the city to an old camp someone had manifested upon first arriving in the new world. It was full of scraps of what could barely be considered food, poor attempts at clothes, a desolate reminder of what it had been like in the first days after the fall.

"What are we doing here?" Hani asked. "This is just where we found him, where'd you hide him?" Strife pointed to the center of the camp and undid a shroud of theirs, revealing the body of a man laying there. Hani wouldn't budge. He stared at the body, eyes wide and teeth clenched. Strife still held one of his hands as they looked to Eowen for a cue, so Eowen took his other hand and pulled him forward.

"It'll be alright, I promise. Come on."

"I'm not ready." His mouth sounded dry, but Eowen and Strife continued to guide him to the man's side. Eowen's first thought was that Hani didn't look much like his father. Captain Asobrab had squarer features, longer ears, a different complexion, but there were some similarities. Hani had his hair and his eyes, despite how time and death had changed them. Eowen could imagine the man's eyes shining like Hani's did with a thirst for adventure. *But that was long ago.*

Hani let go of their hands, inched forward, dropped to his knees, and stayed there looking over the man for a long time. Strife knelt next to him, but Eowen stood back.

"So, Strife. This is my father. Father, this is Eowen and Strife, my closest friends, and you're lucky I've got them around, because otherwise I'd have never come back here." Hani ground his teeth, looking for some words to say. "You— before I knew who you became, you were my inspiration. Everything I've done and become was because of you, because of what I thought you were. But you ruined so many lives!" Hani's free hand curled into a shaking fist. "You ruined yourself!" His power started to gather around in harsh, heavy currents. He glared at the corpse, and for a moment Eowen thought Hani might attack it, but Strife wrapped their arms around him, and the violence faded from his spirit. "Thank you," Hani whispered to Strife, then faced his father again. "You didn't ruin me though... Eowen."

"I'm here."

"You'll do whatever I want, right? To the body."

"Whatever you need."

"What if I need it to be gone?" He turned to face her, a harsh, burning rage filtering through tears.

"You need only say when."

"Now!"

The starfield beneath the body of Captain Asobrab of the southern islands erupted in a flash of light, and the corpse was gone, so completely unmade that no trace of it remained. Hani closed his eyes and took deep breaths through his nose.

"Strife, is it gone?"

"Yes."

"Good." He met Strife's eyes, though they were invisible to Eowen. "I want to leave now."

* * *

Hani stayed in his cabin for a day, but when he emerged the captain of The Stormwake was his usual, jovial self. He sang with the crew, danced with Strife, and was beloved by them all. Few noticed much of a change in him; the redness in his eyes, his voice being more hoarse than usual. Only those that had known him the longest could feel the real change, the new intermingling of sorrow and lightness in his spirit.

At the end of the day, Eowen gathered Hani, Ahn, and Rennick. "This is goodbye, for now," Eowen said. "I hope we'll meet again, but if our paths don't cross, I want you to know that I love you all." Ahn had known her intentions for some time, and was at peace with it. He'd told Rennick as much, but the boy still ran into Eowen's arms and cried out that he'd miss her. She bid the children farewell, then faced Hani.

"You were right, I needed to face him," he said.

"I understand," Eowen replied.

"I feel like... I understand something now, about myself or something greater. I don't know if there are words to describe it but—"

"It feels like you're waking up."

"Yes."

[For now, you're still in the dream.]

"The Nagirr'Om called it the godmind," Eowen said. Hani felt the presence meet with him. It was like Eowen's dreaming aura but immense and alien, yet still loving and familiar. He smiled.

"Godmind, that sounds right." He pulled her into an embrace. "Till next time, savannah girl. You're still the first member of the great Captain Hani's crew, don't forget it!" He squeezed her tighter. "I'll always keep that cabin open for you." Eowen laughed and pulled back.

"You'd better, I'll find you all again and claim it." She took her seat on the bone heron and it rose into the air. "Goodbye."

A few beats of its great wings and the bird was a spec in the darkness. Eowen watched over her shoulder till The Stormwake and its crew disappeared from sight. A part of her could still sense them, the part that was a godmind and existed almost purely in power.

[But it is a part that does not ache at farewells.]

The other parts of her felt lonely and terrified of what she would find in the oasis, which even her godmind shied away from. Both those parts ached terribly.

[It is my turn now.]

The heron flew east and north till it passed over the land that Tavo had left behind, where Luu and her family lived.

Eowen extended her senses over it and understood, as she had never before, the madness that had created it and the way the twisting corruption of the Storm had puppeted Tavo. It had called to him through the love for his child, yet she could now feel in the land how long her cousin resisted falling to it.

"Could anyone else have done as well?" she mused.

Eowen spied on Luu's family from above, feeling how they were. Eowen saw that they were prospering: Eria-Leck and Deliah were getting along better than ever, and were making plans for a school. Thermin was still working with her animals, manifesting new ones and caring for the ones she'd already created. Rose had plenty of clients for her tattoos, and Nathalie still had the strange creature Legs-Friend hanging about her. Finally, Eowen peered down at Luu and lurked around the woman's mind and spirit. Eowen put a hand to her chest, overwhelmed as the woman's simple joy and love seemed to pour out of her into Eowen. Eowen didn't think she'd ever known a parent as proud of their children as Luu. The woman was even happy that Rennick had run away from home.

Eowen hadn't planned to stop for a visit, but she couldn't help the pull she felt towards Luu. The woman was out in her garden, as usual, so Eowen directed the heron to glide down beside her. Luu looked up from her work, squinted, then made a gesture of approval and got back to her work.

"Welcome back, kid." Her tone and mannerisms were casual, but her mind and spirit were alight, warming Eowen's like the sun.

"Hello, Luu." Eowen sidled up next to her. "I ran into your son out west."

"Miles?"

"No, actually it was Rennick with Ahn."

"Never thought he'd be the next one to go a-wandering," Luu said, ripping up something with red roots and orange flowers.

"He's doing well. We got into some danger, but Rennick was actually the one that got us out of it." Eowen crouched next to Luu. "He's a brave kid. You should be very proud."

"Hmph, as if I need you to tell me to be proud of my kids." Luu stopped working and faced Eowen. "What are you doing here anyway? Don't you need to be off finding that cousin of yours?"

"I... did, actually."

"Oh, I see. Come here kid." Luu was covered in dirt, but Eowen didn't care and hugged her. Luu pulled back and examined Eowen at arm's length. "Look at you though, all bloomed up."

"Really?" Eowen looked over herself. She didn't think she looked any different, and still hadn't physically aged since the fall. "What's changed?"

Luu caught Eowen's eyes and stared deep into them, then let out an approving huff of air and kissed Eowen on the forehead.

"You never answered my question, what's got you back here?"

"I'm... going back home. To the jungle and savannah tribes."

"That so? You take it slow when you get there, you've been gone a long time. An awful lot can change, but an awful lot can stay the same, too. In my experience, most people aren't ready for either."

Eowen leaned over and kissed Luu on her dirt-smeared cheek. "I'll keep that in mind." Luu waved her off.

"Go on then, I'll be here." The heron stalked over and knelt for Eowen to mount up again.

"Goodbye, Luu." Eowen and the heron took off again, flying east over the lands she'd crossed after her departure from Nolano. She passed by temples full of monks, hidden valleys, grand cities, small villages, even the water-walled settlement she'd attacked. There were caravans and ships everywhere, landscapes manifested, and companies of Nemsto warriors going home.

After hours of flying, Eowen found herself at the outskirts of Nolano. She circled the city and was soon joined by the bone heron she'd left there. It caught her eye, recognizing her and her mount in its animal way, then wheeled back down to the bone tree. Eowen sensed Gran there, snoring under the bone tree. Aiyano and Nolyi were away from Nolano, helping to establish another Britchen settlement.

Eowen urged her own bird on, and they passed over the old city of Port Disoke and on to the stretch she and Hani had first traveled through together. She passed over each small island they'd manifested to rest at, tasting the air they'd created to remind them of their homes in the old world. To Eowen, the air felt stale and fake, not nearly so accurate as she remembered.

Is it that because we weren't powerful enough to make it more accurate back then, or have I truly forgotten what the old world smelled like?

She moved on, flying towards the settlements of the mountain folk. Part of Eowen's senses knew what to expect when she arrived there.

[They have all gone, moved to other lands in a great caravan. Genia leads them well with the others at her side.

Yawin is healthy, Ne is her right hand, Hale has grown strong, and Zerinley is mastering herself. They are well.]

"One day, I will find them again."

Eowen wheeled around the empty place, directing her heron to alight on the border of the impromptu cemetery where she, Genia, and Hani had manifested the great eagle and wildcat. She looked around, but it seemed that even the divine beasts had gone as well. The buildings were left, but the culture had moved on. Eowen drank in the stony silence of the place, avoiding the last short flight she had left, but her heron was having none of it. It leapt into the air, almost dismounting Eowen, and rushed south.

"Woah! What's gotten into you?" She pulled herself back into position by the feathers on the neck and held on tight as it put on another burst of speed.

They reached the border of Eowen's lands in minutes, meeting with the barrier she had unconsciously set so long ago. It had seemed so indomitable at the time, but when the heron stopped before it and Eowen placed her hand to the bubble of power, she found it to be the thinnest and weakest sort of thing. Three years had given even the lesser dreamers of the new world the ability to manifest such a thing. With barely a thought, she undid it, but the heron hesitated, not pushing forward.

"What, are you shy now?" Eowen asked, but the bird only snaked its neck around and locked its eye on her. "Fine, I'm the shy one... Please, take me home, heron." The bird dipped its neck, almost seeming to bow, and glided in.

As they passed into the lands, Eowen could feel herself shrinking away, collapsing, her divine self pulling back into the tiny, pathetic vessel that had caged it for so long. She put up what barriers she could to pass invisibly and silently, too nervous to face a direct reception. It turned out not to be necessary for, just as Luu had promised, everything had changed.

Grand structures laced the land with kilometer high aqueducts, hanging gardens, fountains, mosaics, squares, and beautiful towers trimmed in blues and golds. Her people meandered and played, sang and manifested freely, expressing their art and joy in every manner. There was a constant buzz of excitement across the lands, as it was filled with constant activity. They were dressed richly, and had spread out far. Eowen kept herself hidden, though. Her heart was hammering and her gut twisting up, still too nervous and too filled with anticipation to accept that nothing would go wrong.

Then she saw it, at the center of all the lands. The oasis still stood, seemingly untouched by the progress. The only difference was a temple that had been erected upon the pool of water in the center. Eowen dismounted in the shade of the jungle and moved forward to see that the pool was still serving its original purpose. Her people drank from it, bathed in it, and washed their possessions in water that stayed miraculously clean. All around her, the trees still hung with fruit that would fulfill all the body's needs. Above, Eowen's mini sun floated over the land, bathing it in the golden light of the jungle and savannah lands. Eowen soaked in its rays, let out a small laugh and wiped a shallow welling of tears from her eyes. She basked in these first wonders of hers, so simple, juvenile, and poorly controlled, yet wonderous all the same.

I know there is no way to know for sure, but if ever the sun in the old world felt like anything, I am certain it was like this.

Eowen stepped into the pool and felt cleaner than she had in years, despite her power automatically keeping all filth off her for months. She swam through the temple's open archway, the only entrance. A set of stairs emerged from the water, and she took them up to a raised platform. Eowen passed groups of her people meeting in the place for meditation, discussion, or just each other's company. It felt surreal to hear her language for the first time in so long all around her. She'd relied on Ordwell's translator for years, and that she no longer needed it was strange and disorienting.

Eowen moved through a wide, pillared corridor and into a central sanctum of the temple. In the sanctum was a crowd of people facing a statue at the far end of the room and one person seated in front of the statue. Eowen's eyes locked on the statue. She put a hand to her mouth, choked on her sobs, and fell to her knees. It was a statue of her, carved simply and out of the ghostly wood of the bone tree. She knew immediately that the statue had been wrought by her father's hands. There was no power in it, no trace of it having been created through dreaming other than what had been done to create the tree it had been carved from. She'd seen many statues in her travels, grand ones of bronze and stone that towered into the firmament, depictions of gods and legends from the old world, and sometimes even shrines of worship to the powerful dreamers of the new world. Of all the art she'd seen, none were like this, for though it was a statue of her, it did not depict the great Eowen Mortician. In the wood, Eowen saw only herself as her father always had. It was Eowen, daughter of Di and Monda. It didn't depict her nervous expression, with a crooked smile, nor her shame, nor anger, or pleading, or repentance. There was no expression linked to Eowen's failures upon the carved face before her. What her father had rendered, roughly, simply, and unmistakably, was her wonder.

Eowen approached the statue, weaving through her people, and saw that someone was giving a sermon of sorts to the crowd gathered there. Eowen peeked around a body and saw that the speaker was Mein, sitting cross legged on the cushion in front of the statue. Eowen sat down behind the listeners and joined them.

"—she spilled it all over me! I smelled like versumath for a month and there was none left for the ceremonies. As your elders will know, in the old world it needed to be harvested and dried properly for a quarter year! We couldn't perform the rites of fire reading without it, so I had to burn my robes caked in the sacred powder!" Children giggled as Mein pretended to tear her clothes up and feed it to a fire, while the elders confirmed to them that her claim was true. Eowen laughed with the children but cringed at the memory of that day. As with most of her mistakes, it had resulted in a beating. "That girl, always trouble I tell you... and we... we never treated her right." Mein looked at the congregation very seriously now. "Listen well, because I will tell you stories every day about the fool Eowen made of herself in the old world. But I tell them so you may understand that it is we who made a fool of her." Mein met all the eyes, nodding seriously. "We... I put her down time and again, such that she felt the need to leave us even before the sky had fallen. And then... despite that, Eowen came back, and she saved us." Mein gestured at the oasis around them. "She could have left us behind, or chosen revenge and killed us all. There would have been nothing we could have done to stop her. I would have you meditate upon that, upon the depth of kindness a person must have to endure such treatment and—" Mein stopped short, noticing the young woman in yellow sobbing silently at the back of the congregation.

Mein cast a barrier of invisibility over the young woman, a sound barrier as well, just to be sure. She stood up, walked through the congregation and knelt beside the invisible person. She continued speaking, but made sure to seem as though she were addressing the crowd. "There are stories that reach us of a young woman who is of our people that matches the description of Eowen. They call her Eowen Mortician, Eowen of the Dead, Eowen who lays to rest. They describe a girl who gives aid, who fought the Storm in Nolano, and who mingles with other legends. Regardless, all the stories have one thing in common; she gives of herself to others. That is who we drove off, a young woman so resplendent with power that though she could have made this entire world her own, she used it for kindness. We drove her off twice!" Mein held up two fingers. "And yet, she had the heart to give us life before she left. Understand this. Know in your heart what kind of spirit such a person must have." Mein couldn't hold back anymore. She looked right at the invisible Eowen, to a somewhat confused congregation, and she broke down, her words shaking through sobs. "There are no words, no apologies sufficient, for what I wish to say to her now!" Mein covered her eyes and waved off an approaching man who had his arms out to comfort. "No, no, thank you. I'm sorry everyone, that's it for today." With thanks and bows, the congregation exited. Mein received them with a bob of her head and a smile till the last one left. Then, she released the barriers around Eowen and put one up over the entry to give them privacy. "Welcome back, girl."

Eowen crashed into her arms and Mein held her, shaking

from laughs to cries and back again, running her nails through Eowen's hair.

"I love you, Mein! I missed you, I missed everyone! I'm sorry! I'm so sorry!"

"Shh, shh, girl, calm down, shh. We got along just fine without you, we did. You left us alright girl, because you showed us how to get by. We had all we needed thanks to you." Mein put her hands on either side of Eowen's face and looked her in the eye. "And eventually we learned to get our heads out of our asses!" The old priestess pulled Eowen in, holding her as tight as she could. "Took too damn long, but we did, all because of you. It was all you, girl, all you!" They held each, whispered till their voices cracked from sobbing how they loved and missed each other, and eventually Eowen lay with her head on Mein's lap. Mein stroked the girl's hair feeling a weight come off her that had been piling on since before the fall. "Welcome home." Eowen squeezed the old priestesses hand.

"I'm so glad to be back, that things have changed like this... I can hardly believe it, I..." Eowen closed her mouth.

"What is it, girl?"

"I want to see my dad." Eowen's voice cracked and she sat up. "I need to see him!" Mein nodded and sighed.

"He's right where you left him, in that little hut you two shared. He rebuilt it all himself. And your mother..." Mein wiped away a tear and smiled sweetly. "He never prepared her even though everyone else did. We made a bone tree and heron, and we performed the rites for all the dead, but your father didn't do it. He's waited all this time, he really believed you'd come back." Mein laughed. "More than any of us, I'll tell you that!"

Eowen got to her feet and helped Mein up. "Thank you. I'll be back to see you, I promise!"

She ran out of the temple, passing right through its walls. The heron was waiting where she came out, ready for her to hop on its back. Once above the canopy she spotted the roof of her and her father's hut as if drawn to like a magnet. She laughed. Of course he'd forsaken all the grand new comforts and manifestations for something familiar, just like he'd choose to carve her likeness by hand. Eowen jumped off the bone heron into a run and nearly slammed into the wall. She hesitated and wondered if she should knock. After all, it used to be her home as well, but it had been so long.

But I suppose it hasn't been my home for a long time. What if I scare him, what if Mein was wrong, and he hasn't been missing me? What if he's actually been harboring a grudge this whole time, and the moment he sees me—

[I see. I wasn't ready after all.]

Eowen left her body down at the hut, in her father's arms. Her consciousness had retreated into the godmind, as far away as far can be. She was too afraid to look at her father through mortal eyes, too afraid to feel his touch through mortal skin, to hear his cries of joy, and relief. After all she'd been through, the wonderful and horrible, this turned out to be too much. She was afraid, because there was too much to feel, too much for one person to feel. She knew that if she dropped back into her body, she'd break somehow. She would break open, and somehow all of her would come spilling out. So Eowen decided to stay up in the godmind, where the moment could be so far away that it was barely real. Where a second could be stretched into infinity. Where she didn't have to be afraid anymore.

[The fear will never really disappear, for there is no amount of power that can separate you from love and its consequences.]

Something in Eowen did break, something that had been hiding inside a tight knot in her chest for longer than she could remember. She lost her legs, lost her arms, and it was all she could do to lean into her father and keep breathing. He squeezed her till all that was left was a girl who had lost her mother, run from home in search of a dream, and gotten tough enough to survive without this: The greatest feeling in the entire world. She was scared again, because she was all soft and weak again for the first in a very long time. Eowen knew, somehow, that the moment he let go, it would kill her. It didn't matter if she was a dreamer, or a god, or a giant. Eowen knew that the moment he let go of her, she'd die on the spot, because there wasn't enough guilt, or pride, or power, or joy, or sadness, or self actualization to make up for what she'd lose the moment he did. But eventually, she did let go, and it didn't kill her. Di sat Eowen down on a mat on the floor, exactly like the one from their old home, and he hugged her again, and let go again, and somehow she was still alive. Eowen stared at her father without the words for her feelings, and he stared back the same way. She didn't break, even though all the hard things inside her had just been crushed. Eowen laughed and her father laughed back.

"Welcome home," he finally managed to say, and the sound of his voice broke her daughter down and built her back up all over again tenfold.

"Hi Dad," she managed to say, and she laughed again, and so did he. "Can I see Mom?"

Di's smile faded and his face wrinkled up in pain and

empathy. He nodded and helped his daughter to her feet. They went through to a back room that hadn't been a feature of their home in the old world. On a mat, covered in a blanket, was Monda, and when Di uncovered her Eowen saw that she had not rotted.

"Hi Mom," Eowen whispered, and placed a hand on her cheek. Things bubbled up inside her, things she needed to say even with her father present. Eowen couldn't stop it. It had to come out now. "I was really happy when you died. Things were hard in the beginning here, in the new world, but they would have been so much harder with you around. I don't think I could have become the person I am now if you were alive." Eowen trailed off, and her tears started to fall onto her mother's chest. "But I also couldn't have done it without you! Without who, you made me to be before it all ended, and I don't know who I could have been if you'd lived through it, or if you'd died even earlier. But everything I was, everything, from the day I left home was because of you and because of Dad. I still think it's better you died, I do, because I don't know if I could have ever left a second time if you were here. I think you would have taken it all from me, all my hopes and inspiration and eventually my dreams. But, but Mom... I still wish you were here, right now, because I don't think there's any way you couldn't be proud of me now! And I don't know if that's something I need, or needed, or want, but—" Eowen looked at her father for an answer, but Di put a hand on his daughter's shoulder and nodded at her.

"Keep going."

"Ok... ok." Eowen took a few deep breaths. "I don't know if, even now, I need you to be proud of me, or if I needed it before, but... I think you needed that, and for so long I thought that all I needed was to make you proud your way. I know that's not true now, but still—" Eowen's voice cracked hard and she choked on cries, but finished. "I wish I could have given that to you!"

She lay down on her mother's chest, crying as her father held her, and though he whispered that he was proud of her, it wasn't enough, it was a hole that would never be filled. But as she laid there, the knot in her chest unwound, and was no more.

* * *

Eventually, she and her father ran out of tears and could only sit, eat, and just be together. They remained in silence for hours, holding each other, dozing, waking up, and reaching out just to feel that the other was really there. When the moon above the oasis transitioned back into the sun, Eowen and Di felt that there was no putting it off any longer. Together, they carried the body of Monda of the jungle and savannah tribes to the base of the bone tree. With Eowen's knife they removed and cleaned her skeleton to lay against the tree and they buried her flesh beneath the roots. Then, the bone heron came, Eowen's bone heron. It stalked over to the tree and locked its eye on Eowen. They stared at one another till Eowen looked closely enough to see herself reflected. Then, gingerly, it started picking up the bones, and flying them to the top of the tree.

For the first time since returning among her people, Eowen let her full godself flow out. It reached to the far edges of the ever-expanding world, it touched all the people she'd known and all those she didn't. It told them that she was here, and that she would lay the dead to rest.

Then Eowen reached out with her power into her father, and she found the part in him that she had long come to know in herself, the part that is in all people who love each other and carry the burdens that the dead no longer do. His silhouette flowed out of him, taking on a great bipedal shape, and it solidified into a bone heron. Di gazed at the creature in wonder, stroked its beak, and watched as it chose a bone from among his wife's and flew off to build its own nest. It was done, and together they went to the cleaning pool of their people and washed the gore of Monda off them.

Chapter 3

The mortal part of Eowen that slept in her and Di's home awoke.

[It is here.]

One moment, Eowen was laying down, the next she materialized outside the hut to stand before a silver glowing woman.

"Eowen Mortician."

[Nagirr'Om.]

The Nagirr'Om stood, unveiled and divested of its tools, though it held something new in its arms. A baby was cradled there, the umbilical cord still tethering the child to the dead body of its mother. The mess of birth had been cleaned from them, and the child glowed with a silver light. Eowen could feel an untrained but already budding godmind from the baby. It would have been an even more horrifying host of the Storm than Tavo and Duwiyin's child had been.

"Once we are cloven, all that has kept me as I am will cease."

[I know.]

"The child will not know me, and so cannot mourn me.

You must know that is not why I am here." Eowen gestured for The Nagirr'Om to continue. "**They will have the greatest godmind, and will be of the greatest power. They may even surpass you.**"

[They will.]

"**I would have you take them, Eowen Mortician, greatest of all in this new world.**"

Eowen stepped forward, took the child into the crook of her arm, and lifted the umbilical cord with that same hand. Then, she summoned her mortician's knife in her other hand. The child slept soundly, deep in its dreams. Eowen looked into the dead eyes of The Nagirr'Om, finding what spark of the woman it had once been still there. When she and the spark met, The Nagirr'Om nodded, and Eowen severed the link between her and the child.

The child didn't seem to notice as The Nagirr'Om collapsed, its silver light gone. The body did not stay down, though. Eowen looked at it, and a new power moved into the empty vessel, one greater than the Storm, more present than a future godmind, and more suited to corpses than any other.

[Rise, Nagirr'Om.]

The body twitched, jerked, and picked itself up as Eowen Mortician's power roused it to life and action. "**Why? What has happened? I am no longer bound to the child, it's future self cannot reach me, so how is this possible?**"

[I can reach you here and now. The child may never truly

know you as you lived, but I know you as you died. I mourn you, Nagirr'Om, and you are under my power. You are not a person, but a vessel that has carried this child and protected it. There is no better way to honor this vessel than for it to continue the work it most desired in its final moments of life.]

The Nagirr'Om took back the baby from the dreamer and cradled it as before. "**Is this what is best for the child? To be raised by a corpse?**" Eowen nodded.

[**This way they will know how great the love of their mother was. This is where that bond, which allowed you to become The Nagirr'Om, came from.**]

The Nagirr'Om looked down at the baby, and it opened its eyes. They glowed with a silver light and power, but did not know the face before them. In time they would.

"**I see.**" The Nagirr'Om bowed to Eowen. "**Thank you, and goodbye, Eowen Moritian.**"

[**Goodbye.**]

The word was not spoken only for The Nagirr'Om, but to the whole of the new world. A part of Eowen would always be there, living with her father, traveling with Hani, visiting old friends and loved ones. A part of her would always perform funerals for those who needed her most.

[**But another part of me, even greater than that part, has already grown beyond this place and will keep growing. It will reach past the places where giants tread, and to some**

beyond it cannot yet know. Still, a part will always be here as well.]

Eowen of the jungle and savannah tribes returned to her home and laid down next to her father. "I think that part is my favorite," she whispered, and fell back to sleep.

About the Author

Brian Reiss was born May 19th 1995 at 11:59 pm and he graduated from Sewanee with a BA in theatre. Brian spent his childhood obsessively absorbing all manner of fantastical books, games, shows, and movies. This trend has largely continued into his adulthood such that he's now hyperfixated with Magic The Gathering, Elden Ring, Avatar the Last Airbender, and more. Brian has also been a fencer since the age of eight. He now lives a mostly nomadic life while writing, indulging in hobbies, and seeking new friends and experiences. His narratives, more often than not, touch upon themes of love and its many forms, family as a choice, and what it means to leave a place. He tells his stories to encounter personal truths but hopes his readers will find value of their own between his words.

ABOOKS

ALIVE Book Publishing and ALIVE Publishing Group
are imprints of Advanced Publishing LLC,
3200 A Danville Blvd., Suite 204, Alamo, California 94507

Telephone: 925.837.7303
alivebookpublishing.com